JOHNNY REB

AND

BILLY YANK

JOHNNY REB
AND
BILLY YANK

BY

ALEXANDER HUNTER

SMITHMARK

This edition published in 1996 by SMITHMARK Publishers,
a division of U.S. Media Holdings, Inc., 16 East 32nd Street,
New York, NY 10016.

SMITHMARK books are available for bulk purchase for
sale promotion and premium use. For details write or call the
manager of special sales, SMITHMARK Publishers,
16 East 32nd Street, New York, NY 10016; (212) 532-6600.

This edition published by special arrangement with
W. S. Konecky Associates, Inc.

ISBN: 0-8317-5622-5

Printed in the United States of America

10 9 8 7 6 5 4 3 2 1

To

"JOHNNY REB"

that tattered son of fortune and the nursling
of many a dark and stormy hour, this book
is affectionately dedicated by the

AUTHOR

CONTENTS

PART I

PREFACE

There were thousands of soldiers on both sides during the Civil War, who, at the beginning, started to keep a diary of daily events, but those who kept a record from start to finish can be counted on the fingers of one hand. I was so fortunate as to save most of my notes made during the four years of conflict, and in 1865, having no fixed pursuit in life, I spent most of the time in arranging and writing up these incidents of camp life while fresh in my memory.

I have given in these pages veracious account of the life of a soldier in Lee's army.

The public have been surfeited with war literature. There is hardly a prominent officer North or South who has not rushed into print at every available opportunity; yet no officer high in rank dared write the exact truth, for the reason he has the feelings, the self-love and the reputations of those who served under him to consider.

A private in the ranks, who has learned something of the art of war through tough experience in two branches of the service, should be able to write understandingly of that internecine conflict which rocked America like an earthquake.

At least he can afford to tell the truth as to what he saw, heard and thought without fear or favor. And above all, a private in the ranks, having no grievance, can be fair and just.

In those days "Johnny Reb" and "Billy Yank" were good comrades when off duty. They had a profound respect for each other, and, as Bulwer says, "It is astonishing how much we like a man after fighting him."

A. H.

Washington, D. C., November, 1904.

PART I

CHAPTER I.

THE RISING OF THE CURTAIN.

Few people have any conception of the fearful ordeal through which the private in the ranks was called upon to pass during the four years of our great civil contest. It shall be my task to portray the soldier's life both in sunshine and in shadow, from the gathering of the storm-clouds which burst upon the wide plains of Manassas, to the hour in which the blood-red banner went down at Appomattox.

It was my good fortune to serve in two branches of the service: infantry and cavalry—two years in each. This necessarily widened my experience and furnished scope for observation.

The terms "Yankees" and "Rebels," as idioms of the camp, have been used without offense meant to either side. It has been my earnest endeavor to present a faithful and non-partisan statement of what passed under my own observation, so far as the life of the private was concerned. Of the facts of war upon which history is founded, I have not hesitated to make use of the most accepted authority on either side, having ever felt that profound respect for a brave foe which every veteran cherishes for another.

Pope says: "There are two events in a man's life that he never forgets: the first, when he discarded small clothes and put on his primal breeches, and again when he transferred those small clothes to another, and that other his wife." Yet there are days more strongly impressed on my mind than these—days whose memory is as ineffaceable as if wrought in bronze. The 20th of December, 1860, was one of these.

Under the peaceful shadow of a Virginia college, its assembled students, from a conscientious regard for duty, had resolved to pay no heed to the mutterings of approaching war that came to them borne on the wings of every wind, and to consider the marching of squadrons, the tramp of hurrying battalions, the rumbling of artillery as naught but a phantasy of the brain or a winter night's reverie.

But in vain! As day after day passed the air grew heavy with signs of coming tempests, and as the excitement continued to increase, study and routine became impossible. Books were thrown aside and daily papers only furnished food for thought and discussion.

Among so many, there were enthusiasts who urged an immediate break-up, but the majority decided to remain until further developments.

The end came soon. On the 20th of December, 1860, startling news reached the college that South Carolina, taking the initiative, had seceded. That much was certain. Besides this there were a thousand rumors; among others that Gov. Letcher would bring about the secession of Virginia by a *coup d' etat,* and was preparing to attack Fortress Monroe immediately, and to that end had secretly organized a volunteer force who were to storm the fort before reinforcements could be thrown in. It was confidently asserted that there would be no resistance, inasmuch as the majority of the garrison were in sympathy with the South and would throw down their arms.

This was read by one of the students from a letter from his brother, who strongly asserted the truth of his information, stating also that he had become a volunteer and calling upon his associates to leave books and take up arms in the glorious cause.

As may well be imagined, such words were as a match to tinder.

That night the pupils held a meeting and after an exciting discussion decided, by almost unanimous vote, to leave for their homes on the morrow, after which they dispersed to their rooms, but not to sleep.

As for myself, imagination ran riot and rose-hued visions passed through my brain. Ah! does not youth always so dream, and are not the siren songs of hope ever sweet? What scenes of glorious excitement opened before the boy's enraptured gaze, who does not know what his fate should be! Has he not read "Charles O'Malley, the Irish Dragoon"? Where is the soldier who has not had the easy, rollicking, glorious time that he enjoyed—He and his "Mickey Free"?

War! It is "a little fighting every now and then, just to keep his hand in," leading a forlorn hope at intervals, meeting with adventures at every picket post, making love at every camp, living on deviled kidneys and grilled bones washed down by the best of sherry, and marrying an heiress at last. Yes! and Napoleon told his men that "every one of them carried a marshal's baton in his knapsack."

What glory it might be to show the world another Massena—

another Ney, *"cet homme le brave des braves."* Abercrombie, Wolfe, Caesar, Pompey, Hannibal, Cyrus,—names great to all times. How the boy's very soul longs to emulate their example, to win their glory, honor and everlasting fame.

Ay! so I too dreamed and so I too believed in the soldier's life, its ease and happiness, as devoutly as a boy holds his faith in his Robinson Crusoe, the child in his Santa Claus, and Mohammedan in his Mecca.

But the night wore away, the day came at last and the dream was ended.

CHAPTER II.

THE PROMPTER'S BELL.

No parting ever seems really sadder than that of college mates. The feelings are then so fresh, the intuitions so unbiased, the imagination so vigorous and the flush of youth so vivid in its joys and sorrow. The world is a beautiful unknown land, and standing on the threshold of life not even Prince Fermoraz of the "Arabian Nights" had brighter visions.

Sorrows then, no matter how they may dwarf into insignificance in after years, have a bitterness peculiarly their own; there exists no room for cynicism, doubt or distrust in that golden age when every woman is an angel; every eye that looks into ours seems honest and every man's word his bond; and so, many faces that morning were turned aside to conceal the trembling lip—to hide the tear ready to fall.

Those young faces! they return oftentimes to memory as I knew them in the old happy, careless time—hopeful, ardent, aglow with youth's enthusiasm, joyous with spring-tide anticipations, reflecting faithfully every sudden impulse of the heart. How the life faded from them on battle-fields and in hospitals.

Alexandria is an old, we may even call it an ancient, town on the northern border of Virginia, but six miles from the National Capital. To a stranger it has all the quiet sleepiness, the deep repose of some old cathedral town in Europe. Named for the family of Alexanders, owners of its land full three-quarters of a century before General Washington was born; its streets laid out and named in its old English royal style the while that worthy gentleman walked there a mere stripling. We may yield it the attributes of honorable old age, pregnant with memories, and say it has earned the right to rest. Its proximity to the Capital of the United States, whose incessant stir and pulsing life might have infused something of activity into its sluggish veins, has only served to lull it into deeper repose. It stands aloof with the exclusiveness of the old regime and virtually says to the new-comer, "Keep to your side of the river and I will keep to mine."

At the breaking out of the war, though the heart of loyalty beat so near, Alexandria was decidedly Southern. Washington organs spoke of it as "a hot-bed of treason," hence it woke into sudden life and prepared for strife with an impetuosity defying restraint.

Political questions of the hour seethed and bubbled in a very maelstrom of excitement; the streets became in appearance those of a fortified city. Nearly every man wore a uniform; the rattle of the drum, the scream of the fife was heard day and night. Soldiers everywhere were in squads, companies and battalions, drilling, marching, counter-marching and parading. Hotels were crowded. In the lobbies people were discussing in ever shifting groups the latest news. The glitter of the bayonets, the thousand rumors flying from mouth to mouth, the inflammatory appeals of the newspapers, all conspired to keep up the abnormal enthusiasm to the highest tension. At night huge bon-fires blazed, casting a lurid glare upon the assemblage of human faces flushing with excitement or paling with emotion as rival orators, on hastily constructed platforms, with vehement gestures and loud voices, descanted on the merits of union or disunion. No one could remain calm, even little children caught the infection and discussed "Secession."

Business was in a great measure suspended, all were on the qui vive for the latest news. Crowds hung around the newspaper and telegraph offices all day. The "Reliable Man" was in his glory, and could be encountered at every corner, leaning generally against a lamp post and surrounded by an eager audience. He always knew more than any one else, and could tell to the minute just what was going to happen. A wonderful fellow is our "Reliable Man."

Alexandria was at first a conservative city, and at the commencement sent a delegate to the convention instructed to vote against secession. Party feeling ran high, while each side stood firm to his convictions. Young men in general were in favor of seceding. The older and more cautious espoused as earnestly adherence to the Union. The women and preachers, it is needless to say, were all disunionists.

As each day went by one party grew stronger, and it was not long before the advocates of secession had everything their own way. Those opposed were taunted as "submissionists, cowards and traitors"—epithets which induced many to join the now ever-increasing throng bent on overt measures.

The *Alexandria Gazette* espoused the cause of the Union, and under its worthy editor, Mr. Edgar Snowden, Sr., counseled moderation.

2

The secession organ was the *Sentinel,* edited by Mr. Smith, a forcible writer and an able manager. This paper was admirably suited to stir up and keep alive popular sentiment. It was described as "red hot." Its sensational telegrams and reports were read twenty hours out of the twenty-four by a surging, struggling crowd around the bulletin board. The *Sentinel* performed its duty well, its printing presses ran day and night. Fresh dispatches were posted up on the board every half hour and heralded with large capitals, such as: "The work goes gloriously on. Fort Pickens to be attacked to-night. Thirty Thousand Stands of Arms Captured at Montgomery," &c., &c., &c. Inflammatory appeals calculated to arouse men to frenzy were also blazoned on this board.

"Arm, Virginians. The Crisis is upon you. There is no Union but the Union of the North against the Union of the South. Which will you choose? Arm! Arm!! Arm!!! The Long Bridge will be crossed to-morrow and Virginia's sacred soil invaded by the enemy. Virginians, defend your homes against the hirelings of Lincoln." Even the ignorant street Arabs and little gutter snipes went about the streets singing:

> "A red cockade, and a rusty gun,
> Makes them Yankees run like fun."

Hot, eager eyes scanned these utterances; swift and ready tongues repeated them, while embellishments were not wanting to fan the rising flame. Madness? Yes! It seems as if nothing short of insanity could so inflame the people. It was like the wildest kind of emotional insanity, too universal to make it seem strange. No one stopped to reason and no one suggested failure. It is no wonder then that the work of volunteering rushed forward. All were accepted, sick or well, half blind, deaf or crippled— it mattered not, they were enrolled at once, enlisting for one year. Toil-worn farmers and school boys, gray-haired merchants who had spent their lives behind their desks, and their dapper young clerks, pale-faced students and brawny blacksmiths, the gentleman of means and elegant leisure, and the hard-working mechanic, all stood shoulder to shoulder in the ranks, forming a contrast that might have caused a smile if every one had been in less deadly earnest.

Five full infantry companies, one cavalry and one artillery, were organized in a short time in this small city. The latter was commanded by Del Kemper, a born artilleryman. In his company were found principally roughs and fancy men, in all as desperate and reckless a set of fellows as one would care to meet. It was Kemper who delayed until night the Federal advance in their first attempt on Manassas, thus gaining two hours when every second was precious. It was Kemper who brought the German General Schenck to untimely grief when he made his virginal scout in a train of cars, an original move in tactics, to say the least.

The infantry formed the nucleus of the Seventeenth Virginia Regiment. Its first company was the Alexandria Riflemen, an organization dating back many years, and the pride of the city. It was composed of the elite of the place, and commanded by Captain Morton Marye, a natural military genius, albeit a martinet by nature, under whose efficient instructions the company became, with probably the single exception of the Richmond Grays, the best drilled and most proficient in the State. Not only were its men taught in the evolutions of the line, but also in skirmish drill. This command was armed with the Mississippi rifle.

The second company composing the Seventeenth was the "Old Dominion Rifles," a hundred strong; made up chiefly of clerks and young merchants with a sprinkling here and there of well-to-do shopkeepers. This was commanded by Captain Arthur Herbert, a fine disciplinarian and a splendid type of the Southern soldier. He had an able second in Lieut. William H. Fowle, who a year later commanded the company all through the war, and led his command in many a hard-fought battle. Captain Fowle was nicknamed "The Game-cock," and well he deserved the title.

The Mount Vernon Guards was composed mainly of elderly men, small tradesmen and mechanics, and commanded by a certain Devaugn.

The material of the two remaining companies were Irishmen. Later the regiment was filled up with companies from the country, the plains and the mountains.

To sum up all within the ranks of this same Seventeenth, we find the city-bred; farmers, used to handling arms from childhood; men from the mountains; country gentlemen, proud of race and lineage, and the sons of old Erin.

We may not wonder then, that this Seventeenth with such material gained laurels all its own, winning and wearing proudly its hardly-earned guerdon.

CHAPTER III.

LIFE IN THE BARRACKS.

The battalion now being organized, the pride of the soldiers was complete. There was no hard work at first, only a triumphal march up and down King Street, with all the people cheering the troops to the echo.

A popular fallacy existed: that a warrior's fitness was measured by his size. A brawny six-footer was the pride of the ladies, the admiration of the street gamins and the envy of his smaller companions. As he marched at the head of his company, his head towering above the others, his hat cocked in a defiant way, his features set in martial frown, he looked not unlike Mars leading mortals to battle.

In the bar-room the big man was always surrounded by a group of admirers, who listened to him with open-mouthed wonder; the big man knew what war was and he knew what he was going to do; he did not want ammunition, his weapon was the bayonet or bowie-knife—give him that! And here the big man looked so terribly blood-thirsty that the timid ones shuddered with absolute terror.

It was amusing to see the big man pat the young, slender boy on the shoulder and tell him to cheer up, that a year or so in camp would spread him out and then he could hope to be a fighter too; then the big man would roll up his sleeve and let us measure his arm and strike him in the breast.

The boys and little men were laughed at, they did not brag; a warlike sentiment from anything under five feet eight was derisively laughed down, and so they sensibly held their tongues. What availed a quiet voice where the hoarse tones from the big man completely drowned it? If the boy or small fellow spoke, he was squelched. "Wonder what he will do when we close with them Yankees with bayonets and bowie-knives, where will he be then?" At that the big man would give his mustache a ferocious pull, and walk off, leaving the smaller soldier utterly extinguished.

That this was, and probably (now that the war is over) is, a popular error will be shown further on. It was a natural mistake. Size and strength are thought to go hand in hand with courage. Every boy who has read the "Iliad" infers that prodigious stature, a strident voice and thews of iron are necessary to make an Achilles or an Ajax. Ulysses and Æneas were men of doughty mould, the three guardsmen of Dumas were athletes; Mad Anthony Wayne, Sergeant Jasper and Moll Pitcher, heroes and heroines of the Revolution, were all big people. What chance or place is there for little people?

So for a time the giants had their day, ours was to come after while.

On the seventeenth of April events reached a climax, news was flashed over the wires that the State Convention assembled in Richmond immediately upon tidings of Lincoln's proclamation calling upon the governors of all States for seventy-five thousand men to coerce the South, had passed the ordinance of Secession. The long agony was over at last and the North confronted the South. Whose the better chance of success?

The South was overweighted from the start. Our adversary was of the same race, equally brainy, and of greater persistence. But the North's great superiority lay in the fact that the Slave States were not united. The five richest States in men and money, Maryland, Delaware, West Virginia, Kentucky and Missouri were divided in sentiment, and instead of presenting a solid front, gave to the Union Army over a quarter of a million men. Missouri gave 169,111, Kentucky 79,025, Maryland 50,316, West Virginia 32,068, and the State of Delaware 13,670, a total of 344,190, while the recruits from the loyal States in the Confederate Army, not counting deserters, could be counted on the fingers of one hand.

In summing up the chances between the two factions, the South, to an impartial observer, did not seem to have the ghost of a chance.

The North was one of the richest established governments on the face of the earth and better equipped to wage a long and costly war than any nation in Europe. They had no national debt and they had a sound currency on a solid basis. Their cities were rich and populous and filled with shops, mills, factories, foundries, vast store-houses and arsenals. The North had also the finest agricultural region in the world, full of diversified agricultural products, which could be transported at will by her extensive railroads and inland waterways. One incalculable advantage the North possessed was her immense merchant marine and an efficient navy; and in addition to these they had unlimited credit, and could command all the outside globe to aid them with munitions and men.

The wealth of the South was in her raw cotton, which had to reach the market in driblets in order to realize. With the exception of Richmond, there was not in the South a mill or foundry that had the machinery necessary to construct a decent fire-arm. There was not a store-house within her realm and only the ruins of an armory. A few poorly equipped railroads, with poorer rolling stock, was her only means of transportation. In all manufactures the South had ever been the bond-servant of the North, and now at the beginning of the struggle she had absolutely no manufactures and no credit. In a word, the South had to create and use make-shifts all the way along.

The strength of the South lay in her immense territory, traversed by vast watercourses; and mountains which would prove a refuge to her troops in case of defeat.

Another element of supremacy the South had was her docile slave population, who tilled the fields and raised grain and meat for her armies in the field. Another thing was in her favor: her people along the Atlantic coast-line were as one. As for men, the North could place in the field three soldiers to the South's one, and what was more, the Northern soldiers would be thoroughly armed and equipped; but to off-set this numerical difference the Southern men were of Anglo-Saxon lineage, with heart and soul enlisted in their cause, and fighting for their hearthstones, while the Northern man was often an alien born, and almost always the invader.

The personnel of the Southern army was excellent; it was superior to that of the North. The Southerners were inured to arms from infancy and all good shots, and the sons of the men of the Revolution or the Indian wars stood like their sires, ready to fight or die for what they considered their sacred rights.

The Southern people were full of hope, the battle was not always to the swift and strong. They remembered that history was full of examples of successful rebellions: The victories of Thebia at Thrasynemus and Cannae, gained by Hannibal over disciplined forces. The great conquest of the Rebel Arminius over the consular legions of Varrus forced back the boundaries of the Roman Empire to the Rhine, where they remained forever afterwards. Scotland for centuries resisted the power of England and never was conquered; and the barefooted rebels of Valley Forge were victors in the end.

When Thursday morning, the 21st of April, 1861, dawned, the city seemed to have changed entirely. All classes settled down to hard work, the fiat had gone forth and nothing remained but to prepare the soldiers for the field. There had been a wonderful change in public opinion; but yesterday, there were hundreds of Union men in Alexandria; the day after Lincoln's proclamation, if any remained in Virginia they were hard to find. It was but a question now of espousing the cause of the South and casting lots with State, friends, family, or taking up arms against all that was nearest and dearest. It was no longer "Union or Disunion," it was home, kindred and country. There was no middle course, no convenient fence upon which a man could climb to drop later on either side—the tide of feeling ran too strongly for that. Party lines that hitherto had divided Unionists from Secessionists were now impassable barriers that separated friend from foe; to maintain the cause of the North at this juncture would have been to render one's self a social pariah, to cast aside all that was most precious to the heart of man, to earn and wear, for years at least, the name of traitor.

The whole city was a vast workshop, and here it was that women (*Dieu les garde*) stepped in. Recognizing the momentous issues of the hour, ignoring class distinctions, rich and poor, cultured and untutored, young and old threw themselves into the breach, and side by side labored with full heart and soul for the cause that from the first had owned their entire allegiance. All day long and far into the night, even on Sunday, the click of the sewing machine was heard, and every Southern woman in that city, stopping midway in her fashionable life or in her daily round of duties, devoted every moment to making clothes for those so soon to take the field.

Having no stable government, the troops were obliged to rely on voluntary contributions. And these were ample; company after company was equipped and their knapsacks filled, and still the work went on. Certainly no tribute can be too great for those noble women. They clothed us, fed us, not only in the first flush of a new excitement, but through all the long, weary years of war; gave up sons, brothers, husbands—never stopping to count the cost or weigh the sacrifice. They nursed the sick and wounded with such unfaltering patience, such tenderness, that only the pen of the "Recording Angel" can ever do them justice.

We were ordered into barracks on the 18th of April, 1861, and settled down into a quiet but hard-working routine. Guards were posted, pickets set, and in short, everything was brought down to war footing.   Volunteers now fully realized that this was to be no child's play, but war in grim, hard earnest.   There was no longer marching along thronged streets behind a big brass band, with a gorgeously-attired drum-major leading the way and a hurrying crowd to follow the showy pageant with admiring shouts.   There was no longer the nightly feast at the "City Hotel," where mirth and wine held high revelry and unnumbered toasts were drunk in glasses of "Mad Cliquot" or "Mons. Roederer."   Alas! No quail on toast, no champagne, no wine and olives to welcome the close of the day; instead, a piece of bread, a cup of coffee, a thin blanket and hard floor.   The contrast was disappointing, to say the least.

Then arrived an old army officer, Major George Hunter Terrett, a West Pointer, to train these untried soldiers into more military bearing.   He at once treated the dilettante volunteers as regulars, and ordered that the private salute the officer; he placed guards at the door of the barracks and permitted none to leave for an hour without a pass countersigned by himself.   One drill was hardly over before another was called; no fancy drilling, but hard work in fatigue uniform.   The fine holiday of the past month was over, and it was arduous labor, harder than grubbing, stump-pulling, or cracking rocks on a turnpike; and to render matters worse, soldiers by that time had become too common to render this petted company (The Riflemen) of any special notice.

The new volunteers who flocked to the armory every day to be enrolled were drilled apart in the first rudiments of forming in line, marking time, &c., and were known as the "goose squad." Some of them were very green and had never handled a weapon before, and could have as easily jumped through a hoop or per-- formed the great bare-back act in a circus as to load their muskets properly.   It must have been men like these that Artemus Ward put the questions to:

"Do you know a masked battery from a hunk of gingerbread?

"If I trust you with a gun, how many men of your own company do you think you can manage to kill during the war?"

Every morning at 5 o'clock the drum beat the reveille, and up would jump a set of poor fellows huddling on their clothes, half asleep, trying frantically to shove a number six foot up the arm of a jacket and getting an arm in a breeches leg.   Then would be formed a line of miserable, sleepy-looking wretches, who would stand yawning and gaping until roll call and the order given "break ranks," after which there would be a rush back to bed again.   Jupiter! what a change from soft feather beds or a tender hair mattress to something so hard that no rest was found. Nothing but continual tossing all night long, as uneasy as the Sybarite who found a rose leaf under his pillow.   Hearken to the undertone of complaint rising and falling like the minor wail of the wind amongst the trees on some wintry night, now loud, now sinking into silence:

"What in the name of the Old Scratch is the use of being waked up at this unearthly hour, with two hours yet before breakfast?"

"Who can get to sleep again after being roused up in this fashion?   Major Terrett must have cramp or a bad fit of something and wants to take it out on us."

Heaven rest his soul, he has enough to answer for.

After breakfast one hour was given for recreation, and if grumbling was recreation, every man had plenty of it.

This was the routine:

Nine o'clock, and the "old confounded sheepskin" was heard again and the sergeant was wont to put his carrotty head in at the door and yell out:

"Fall in, men, for squad drill!"   And for one long blessed hour there was nothing but tramp, tramp, tramping on the commons, until there was not a square inch in all its limits that had not felt the tread of each man's foot.

At eleven, guard mount!   ("As if the guard could not mount itself without the rest of the company.")

Dinner at twelve.   ("Nice time for men to dine!")

Battalion drill at two P. M.   ("The old hour for napping.")

Then no sooner had the men, half-dead, come limping back than they were ordered to re-form and practice "Company drill." Any reasonable person would have imagined this would wind up work for one day, but no! after crawling back there yet remained "Dress parade."   (Oh! the mockery of that name to one who in happy days gone by "had known a claw-hammer coat and white kids.")

About dusk a weary, wretched lot would wriggle back to the barracks and be given supper at seven.

At eight, "Roll call."   ("Evidently for the purpose of seeing how many had been used up during that day.")

At nine the drum sounded the "Tattoo," and "All lights out!" ordered and obeyed.   *They* went out, Alack! not we, and then in utter darkness mutterings and murmurings began again, and warm discussions.

"I'd have won that game!"

"Not you, I had a full hand, so I want that dollar."

"You'll play no such game as that on me!"

"Say, Bob, going to drill to-morrow?"

"No! I've a sore foot!"

"So have I!" from a dozen throats in a chorus, so loud and full that the sergeant cries out through the half-open door:

"Silence there!" and silence reigns.

The surgeon was called in to examine those feet and announced that the disease was called "Shamming."

After all, there is ever some sunshine intermingled with the shadow, and even under those circumstances pleasure was extracted. There was music in plenty: fiddles, banjos and flutes. What if the neighbors did complain of the uproar, especially one irate old fellow, who said in his wrath, "I will sue the barracks as a nuisance!" He had no soul for music, the said barracks had, and so melody floated in the prisoned air about one-half of the time.

On one occasion, with the permission of the captain, a serenade was planned for Major Terrett; but those artistic, well-meant efforts were treated ungratefully—scornfully, in fact, and sad to relate, the amateur band was confined to the guard-house the next day. It happened thus:

After permission had been granted for this pre-supposed treat to the commandant, the few lucky performers were excused from evening drill that they might practice and furbish up old tunes. To aid the memory, a nip of brandy came between each tune. As night drew on every single man of them, having imbibed so much, was in that blissful state where he felt he was a band unto himself.

The performers started out with their instruments, accompanied by a quartette, whose sole instruments were a flask of brandy to each, merely as a matter of throat medicine. They reached the commandant's residence quite late. That worthy man, all unconscious of the treat in store, had long since retired. After a discussion, which came near ending in a fight, as to whether the vocal or the instrumental should open the serenade, it was decided that the quartette most merited the honor. So clearing their throats by a long pull at their melody-inspirer they opened up with "Come where my love lies dreaming," but in spite of the tenderness of the refrain the window remained closed. This was rather discouraging, so the band struck an attitude; the flutist leaning against the lamp post, the cornet propped alongside a tree trunk, the small fiddle sitting comfortably on an ash-barrel, the bass viol squatting on the doorstep, while the banjoist found himself most satisfactorily lodged on the pavement. As for the quartette, they were almost anywhere; one lying on the cellar door, sound asleep, from whence he was, at the close of the performance, carried home in a wheelbarrow. The other three had voluntarily commenced in stentorian tones, "Look into my eyes, love."

In the meantime the instrumental was doing its best. The bass viol grunted, the fiddle shrieked, the cornet tried to blow the roof off the house, the banjo thumped away on its own individual merits, the flute was black in the face and out of wind, when the window was raised at last, the Major's head protruded, and he thundered out: "What the devil is all that noise about? What is the meaning of this?"

"Meaning," replied one of the quartette in a hiccough; "we've come to serenade you, ole boy. Come and take a drink, won't you?"

"Take yourselves off," shouted the voice, thick with passion, "or I'll court-martial every mother's son of you in the morning."

A dead silence then followed the sound of the gurgling liquor as it flowed down every throat. The cornet suddenly revived and shouted back:

"You be d—d; we've come to serenade you, I say, and we are going to keep on; ain't we, boys?"

A chorus of assent responded, and the music struck up where it had left off.

While this was going on the commandant slipped down-stairs and dispatched his orderly for a guard. Soon the sound of tramping feet was heard. In a voice of thunder the Major ordered them to arrest his serenaders, and the guard closed round. Then ensued about as pretty a fight as ever was witnessed. However, the quartette was soon secured, especially the one who was asleep; but the performers, using their instruments in a manner never intended by their manufacturers, made most vigorous resistance. Forgetting that they had ceased to be free American citizens, at present devoted to the muses, they knocked and banged and struck out valorously, while the guard, not willing to use their weapons, closed in on the musical fighters, and after a fierce struggle and with many bruises, mastered them one by one. The cornet flattened his weapon on the corporal's occiput, raising a bump unnamed in phrenology; the fiddle was smashed to atoms over some other skull, while the banjo came down squarely, or rather roundly, on the top of a guard's head; he wore it as a necklace, the handle sticking out behind like a gigantic queue. The flute, just about the size of a police officer's club, might have been a dangerous weapon, only being hollow it shivered to pieces at the first blow, its sound and fury signifying nothing. The bass viol performed prodigious antics, describing a huge parabolic curve, and striking with fearful force the cranium of yet another guard; there was a confused jangling of the strings and down went the guard prone on the ground; a second blow and one more guard fell, while a third man was happy enough to catch the blow on the butt of his musket. This finished the irate old "big fiddle," but with the head-piece the serenader laid about with such vigor that victory might have perched thereon, only, seeing the odds, the valorous warrior broke out of the surroundings and took to his heels; in short, the whole party were lugged to the guard-house, where they remained all the next day. As for the bass viol, he was found in the morning sound asleep on a pile of planks in Smoot's lumber yard, with the head-piece firmly clutched in his hand. It is safe to add no more permissions were granted serenading parties.

And yet another incident:

One evening a party was given in the city, to which several of the company were invited. Not one of them but thought he would give a year of his life to be present. They sought the captain's consent, and laid before him in moving terms the necessity of going; but this he did not quite see. The truth was this—Captain Marye was in an awful humor, which, by the way, was his normal condition; at any rate he refused those heart-rending appeals, leaving no alternative but to go without permission; but how, that was the question?

Believing that in a multitude of counselors there was much wisdom, they put their heads together to devise some plan. Each suggestion was discussed and discarded in turn; the guards had been played upon so often that they understood every trick, they would not be bribed, they could not be fooled, to get out by the door was impossible, escape by way of the window had been tried so many times that it was useless even to think of—what could be done?

In this dilemma it was finally determined to consult the Mephistopheles of the company, Tom Douglas. He was waited upon in

a body and the grievance solemnly laid before him and his assistance earnestly invoked.

"Boys," said he, puffing slowly at his pipe, "go out and let
me think; come back in a half-hour and I will see if I cannot help
you, and say! if it is convenient, one of you step down to Appich's
and get me a couple of bottles of ale or porter; for nothing,"
added Tom sententiously, "aids the imagination like malt
liquors."

The desired articles were duly forwarded and Tom was left to
his supine cogitations. It was noticed at the end of the allotted
time, when his clients returned, that both bottles were empty;
but there was a light in Tom's eyes that shone as a beacon of
hope, and proved that the appeal to the friends of his imagination
had not been made in vain.

"Now, boys," said Tom, "always come to me when you want to
get into a scrape or out of one. Have I ever failed you yet?"

A chorus of negatives followed this question.

"Well," continued Tom, "I am tired of working for nothing;
you all know that I have no invitation to this party and have to
stay here; but if I arrange a plan for you I must be paid for it, in
other words, you must promise me three things if you can, otherwise just help yourselves, that's all!"

"Not to lend you money, Tom?" anxiously inquired one of the
party.

"Who said anything about borrowing?" gruffly interrupted
Tom, whose credit was none of the best. "No, it is this: If I
get you out safely—safely, mind, I shall exact three things:
Firstly, whenever any of you receive a box of anything to eat I
shall share it; ditto as regards drinks, malt or spirituous. Second-
ly, I shall not be wakened in the morning for roll call; some one
of you must answer to my name; that to be arranged among you
to suit yourselves. Thirdly, if I shall ever be placed on extra duties one of your number will take my place; that also to be arranged among yourselves."

"By Jupiter, Tom! that's asking altogether too much," said one
of the audience in indignant remonstrance.

"Do you expect these things to go on all during the war?" broke
in another.

"No," answered Tom with a grin, "only while we are here in
barracks."

"Agreed," said all.

Then Douglas unfolded his plan and gave his directions:

"To-night when you are marched to supper one of you slip into the kitchen and bribe the cook,—that black rascal would sell his soul for a dollar,—bribe him to send up to my room two or three large baskets, and mind the baskets must be filled with tin pans, kettles, bread trough, rolling pins and three or four old ragged coats, it doesn't make much difference about the pants; another of you hurry down the street before tattoo and buy two pounds of cork, and have everything ready at half-past seven."

The drum beat the supper call. When the coast was clear Tom opened the window, which was on the second floor, and gave a shrill whistle; the signal was answered by a like one, and in a few seconds a small specimen of humanity known as the "street Arab" appeared below. Tom wrote a few words on a piece of paper, directed it and threw it to the boy, with the injunction to fly. The boy disappeared in the gathering gloom.

All were assembled in Tom's room, and in a few moments were as black and tan as any horse-opera troupe. A whistle was heard outside; it was Tom's Puck, who had girdled the city in less than forty minutes. Tom let down from the window a small line, which on being drawn up brought with it a large bag containing several suits of female attire of the roughest kind. Several of the party-goers soon got inside of them, and then the conspirators were ready for the denouement.

"Keep your nerves steady, boys," whispered Tom; "don't over-act your part, and don't speak unless you are obliged to! Now if you are ready, follow me down into the kitchen."

Under instructions, one seized a fiddle and played, the rest of us commenced, as ordered, such an uproar that speedily the entire barracks were aroused; then Tom went to Captain Marye, with his coat off, his head bound up, and looking for all the world as if suffering from an attack of illness.

"Captain," said he in a faltering voice, "I don't like to complain, but the truth is, I am sick, and it is impossible to stand that fuss any longer; do you hear that noise?"

"Hear it," said the Captain, "it is enough to waken the dead; why, the house will be shaken down next! Who in the devil is kicking up all that rumpus?"

"It's Mills and Hunter," said Tom solemnly.

"That noise must be stopped anyhow," interrupted the Captain angrily. "Any old officer coming here would imagine he had made a mistake and gotten into a free and easy concert saloon!

Listen to that!" he continued, working himself into a passion, as howls and screams rose above the sound of the music.

"Just listen to that! I think my company is composed of the wildest set of rips in the world! I would rather be the keeper of a menagerie or an under doctor in bedlam! What in Heaven's name is the matter? Mills surely cannot be making all that noise!"

"No," answered Tom sadly and unwillingly. "Don't tell the boys I told you. I wouldn't if I were not so very sick, but Mills and Hunter have those infernal fiddles of theirs and are scratching away for some niggers to dance." Here Tom put his hand touchingly to his head and his agony was for the time most intense. The Captain had turned white; for a moment he was speechless, then came the tempest.

"What! WHAT!! Niggers in my barracks! Niggers dancing! Niggers dancing in MY barracks!!!! What would Major Terrett say? Get a guard at once and turn the whole lot out into the street and tell those black, impudent rascals if I ever catch them here again I'll cut their ears close off, which I have a mind to do anyhow. Stay! Tell those boys to send their fiddles home, they are a confounded nuisance anyway! Turn those darkies out at once and allow me to thank you for your information, I will remember it."

Tom received these acknowledgements meekly—nay, modestly, and hurried off with alacrity, considering his previous illness, to get a guard.

The whole tribe were incontinently marched out at the point of the bayonet and set adrift, feeling very much like Aesop's old hare, who begged when caught to have any punishment rather than be turned out on a frosty morning. They shook hands all round ecstatically, and an hour after were keeping rhythmic time to a divine waltz with a diviner waltzer; it was the last for many long days—many weary months.

Why dwell on these trifles? Merely because they describe the little simple pleasures of barrack life, present the private in his best light, that of a careless, happy being (at least it seemed so afterwards), and marked the transition between the raw volunteer and the trained soldier.

The temptation to linger tenderly over each bright, happy episode of that time is only the greater since there were rapidly approaching the days of gloom, of sickness, sorrow, blood-shed, and death.

CHAPTER IV.

PUBLIC OPINION ON BOTH SIDES.

It is with something like amusement that we look back upon the fallacies entertained at that time by both North and South.

That an intelligent people should, at the commencement of this war, have permitted themselves to be so duped passes all belief. Southern editors characterized their foe as "Yankee riff-raff," "Hessians, whom in fair encounter we could conquer three to one." The good marksmen, the fine riders, the daring and dash were pre-eminently their own, so that if ever arrayed in solid phalanx, their troops so distinguished might laugh to scorn anything like failure.

Many formed their opinions of the coming contest from the Mexican war, where Southern volunteers were largely in the majority, and imagined that in military qualifications the Northern army could not in anywise be more advanced than that of Mexico. As Taylor and Scott invariably routed forces vastly superior in numbers, it was deduced that the South would be equally successful in any actual encounter.

That the war would be of any duration never entered the mind of any one; some were pleased to extend the time to six months, but it was generally imagined that the first battle, then rapidly approaching, would end the conflict. Men, women and children were thoroughly sanguine of victory, while to doubt success was treason to the cause. A mental blindness pervaded the land.

It is not surprising that the rank and file held such opinions, inasmuch as press and public speakers instilled them in their minds.

A prominent speaker, an ex-Governor of Virginia, in denouncing Helper's book on "The Impending Crisis," said that nothing could conquer his hatred and prejudice against New England.

"Why!" continued he, becoming excited, "What is the reason of all these musterings, these warlike preparations? The Southern army needs neither cannon nor rifle to beat back the hordes coming to desecrate this sacred soil.

"No! Give the Southern army but their slave whips, and they will send the Yankee hirelings flying back from whence they came."

The press asserted that the Southern soldiery would prove irresistible; and argued that if a Baltimore mob could put to flight trained troops from Massachusetts, our volunteers, thoroughly armed and equipped, might defy any force. "Have no fear," said a Richmond daily, "Bob Toombs's prediction will yet prove true. Ere another year rolls round he can, if he chooses, call the roll of his slaves in Faneuil Hall." Hence, the volunteer, discussing in his barracks the future, expressed the honestly felt desire to meet the foe in combat; a foe he had come to despise; a foe he felt certain would never stand long enough to look him in the face.

Imaginative battles were rather of the "Iliad" order—a few rounds, then a rush of cold steel, and all was over.

It was agreed that Company A should go into action with each man carrying a revolver in his belt and a bowie-knife in his boot-leg; it would look decidedly war-like and unique, we thought, to see the handle protruding from the leggins. The pistols were intended for close quarters, and when each chamber should have done its deadly work, the bowie, conveniently carried between the teeth, would be expected to step in and carve up the foe.

Thus we sat in earnest conclave, day after day, fighting our coming battles. We mapped out our program to suit our untutored fancy. The most harmless fellow amongst us, who would have hesitated to kill a fly, talked by the hour of bayonet charges, until the blood in our veins ran cold.

There was one little fellow, a private named Hunter, who grew meditative as the discussions waxed more thrilling, and spent many a sleepless night communing with himself. This bowie-knife business might be a very good thing, he thought, for immense fellows like Raymond Fairfax, or for one of those big Irishmen, but for a sixteen-year-old soldier of ninety-seven pounds fighting weight, it might not prove so very amusing after all. In a tight place, when cold steel was letting out blood, might it not be advisable, after having stood up to the fight like a man, to drop down on the ground for a little while and pretend to be dead? The big "Bowie-knife" would hardly stop to stab such a little corpse. A boy in battle, he continued to reason, could discharge firearms with the biggest, and do damage enough; having this advantage besides, there would be so little of him to hit; but as for an advance,—who would be hurt, the big blue? Not he! And making up his mind that until he had grown bigger, the question of cowardice would not be involved; and his anticipations of the future assumed a brighter aspect.

3

One morning Mills, a son of Clark Mills, the sculptor, and myself determined to run the blockade to Washington City. We kept our intention a profound secret, as discovery would have resulted in confinement in the guard-room for merely entertaining such an idea.

Across the Potomac extended a rickety structure known as the Long Bridge, guarded at either end by pickets, the one Southern and the other Northern. Travel across this thoroughfare had ceased and visiting Washington by this route was not to be thought of.

The steamers that plied between the two cities had discontinued their trips; not only that, but a strict watch was kept up in Alexandria along the wharves, even sail and row boats having been interdicted.

But where there's a will there's a way. We donned citizen's dress and went to a certain farm three or four miles above Alexandria (of which I was the prospective owner), where a row boat was kept, and bribed the gardener, old Uncle Sandy, to row us to Washington, reaching there about noon.

Then commenced our tour. How thick the blue-coats were! How many officers there were in the city! How elegant their uniforms!

A general passed, his epaulets, buttons and sword flashing in the sunshine, followed by a brilliant staff with orderlies in the rear. How many gaudily dressed women were on the avenue! What splendid bands! What soul-inspiring music! How martial looked the troops as they marched along the streets! As we watched them we noted their soldierly appearance, their perfect step, their fine drill, and the illusions of the hour faded away and the thought that flashed through both our minds was, that it would take more than "one Rebel to whip three" of these Yankees, and Mills exclaimed: "Good Lord! Let's hide!"

We wended our way to Willard's Hotel; the lobby was filled with an excited crowd; in the bar-room the discussions were fiery.

"I'll tell you, gentlemen," said an officer to a group around him, "that in two months from the word go we will march from the Potomac to the Rio Grande and drown the last d—n Rebel in the Gulf!" "Yes," said another, "we want a bloody war, and if I had my way I would raise the black flag and hang every Rebel caught with arms in his hands!" "How long will it be," inquired a citizen, "before the Long Bridge is crossed?" "In a few days at the furthest," responded an officer in zouave uniform.

So the talk drifted on, and proved that they had no higher opinion of their foes than said foe had of them.

We bought some Northern newspapers and found the same tone pervading their columns; the same contempt for the easy task laid out; the same appeals to the passions of the hour as that which marked the journals of the South; they alluded to us sneeringly as "Chivalry;" called us "slave drivers and pampered minions;" declared they wanted a sharp, sudden, bloody war; endorsed Seward's prediction that "the rebellion would be put down within ninety days." In one paper was a speech made in Chicago by some public man, in which he said: "My fellow-citizens, I do not indorse President Lincoln's call for seventy-five thousand men. He should have called on Illinois alone; this is an Illinois war. Let the President recall his troops, and let this State fight the slave-holders' rebellion, and I'll stake my life and all that is dear to me that Illinois alone and unaided can conquer the South before the year is out."

If the South had run mad, the North was demented; neither side considering the overwhelming proportions, the fearful, far-reaching consequences of the impending struggle. In such wise both parties boasted and raved before closing in deadly combat.

CHAPTER V.

THE FIRST RETREAT.

April had passed; May had come and gone and still the busy hum of war continued. Soldiering had ceased to be a novelty. Our volunteers were rapidly settling down to barracks life and were becoming contented. As our muscles had grown stronger, fatigue was felt less; besides, drilling was not looked upon with such disfavor, inasmuch as the nearer approach to perfection in manual the shorter became the drills. It was not long before Major Terrett had a battalion which even he or any other West Pointer might look upon with pride.

Virginia was by this time practically out of the Union; for the Confederate flag—"the Rebel rag," its enemies called it—waved over the public buildings. Jackson, the proprietor of the Marshall House, had published his own anti-Union sentiments by affixing over the roof of his hotel the insignia of rebellion. Against this he had been warned, as in case of an advance, his house being public, was endangered, involving perhaps the safety and property of his guests as well as that of his own. To all such counsel he turned a deaf ear, quietly remarking that as the house was his own he would defend it with his iife, and that whoever should attempt to lower that flag would do so at their peril.

His threat was made good, for it was at this spot that the first blood was spilled; it was there that Ellsworth was shot and Jackson also lost his life.

The morning of the 23rd of May dawned upon our world. It was a bright, sunny day, with one of those languid noons that rendered it an enjoyment just to live, move and have our being. We had only had two drills, both hurried through, and then the men lounged and slept and the usually busy barracks were silent as the grave.

Toward evening life began to stir throughout the building; the drummer, rubbing his eyes, seized his sticks and beat the rataplan, the men reached out for their weapons, the officer girded his sword, and as in Tennyson's Enchanted Castle, the Prince kissed the sleeping princess and broke the spell.

At six o'clock, dress parade. There in the softness of the evening lay the beautiful Potomac, its water gliding placidly by without a murmur, its surface undisturbed by a ripple, reflecting in its beauty the golden sheen of the setting sun and the gorgeous coloring of the sky; all nature seemed at rest, lapsing into the deep serenity of night, but on the river floated an unsightly blur that marred the otherwise peaceful scene. It was the U. S. Sloop of War *Pawnee,* riding lazily at anchor not a hundred yards from the wharf; she had arrived that morning and taken position, amid much speculation and wonderment of the good people of the place.

There she lay, dark and forbidding, revealing the grim muzzles of her twenty-four pounders. Suddenly in the twilight a gun was run out and immediately a long, bright flash poured out of the muzzle, succeeded by a thundering report that rattled windows in their casements and startled the town; an interval of a few seconds and the signal was answered from the Navy Yard at Washington; then the silence of night came on, and nothing further startled or jarred the gathering shadows.

Nine o'clock, the tattoo beat and the barracks were in Cimmerian darkness. Sleep weighed down our eyelids, and only the guard's solemn tramp broke the quiet. Midnight came, and the cry of the sentry was "All's well." The town clock chimed "one," and still the city slept on; the streets, deserted by every living thing save perhaps some houseless dog, had sunk into a quiet as unbroken as that of the wilderness.

Three o'clock, and yet no sound other than the measured strokes of the old town clock, albeit the faint light of coming day had begun to streak the east.

Four o'clock. The quick, sharp beat of a horse's hoofs on the stones reverberated upon the air and its rider, at full gallop, dashed up to the barracks. It was Major Territt's courier.

"Halt," said the guard. "Who comes there?"

"A friend."

"Give the countersign."

"Oh, d—n the countersign! I come from Major Terrett, and must see Captain Marye at once."

The Captain was awake in an instant. The commandant's dispatch was short.

"Wake the drummer, and beat the long roll," ordered the Captain. Then came the rattling of the drum.

As though by instinct the men were in line before they were fairly awake. In hurried tones the Captain told them that the town would shortly be in possession of Yankee infantry, who were even then in the suburbs, and he added, "I will give you ten minutes to get ready, not one second more. Pack your knapsacks and have your accoutrements and be prepared to march when the order is given; whoever is not ready will be left behind."

Instantly everything was in confusion.

At last a dim glare was thrown over the scene and rendered it visible as well as laughable. The men, all unused to night alarms, were panic-stricken, and huddled on the first clothes they could get their hands on; rammed everything in their knapsacks, taking what they would not want and of course leaving what they did, complaining bitterly of the very short time allowed.

The idea of time is purely relative. Ten minutes with a dentist hacking away at a nerve is an age, ten minutes with one's sweetheart on a moonlight night is simply nothing, but those ten minutes!—There, they were gone!

The drum beat, the clear tones of Captain Marye's voice rang out the order, "Fall in; steady, men!"

The sergeants distributed sixty rounds of cartridges to each man, a proceeding which sent the blood away from many a cheek, especially as the march of the enemy's troops began to be distinctly heard, while at intervals the sound of cheering that came to our ears showed how rapidly the danger was approaching.

Nearer and yet nearer! We had often prayed to meet the enemy, but not so early in the morning, and certainly not with so little ceremony. We had thought, too, of marching out of town, but it was to have been in broad day, with banners flying and bayonets gleaming, the band playing "Dixie," while the entire population, hanging around, would wipe their weeping but admiring eyes. This hurrying away like a thief in the night had not much glory attached, but yet it was with infinite relief that we heard the next order: "By the right flank, by the left, march!" And not a minute too soon, for as we marched out of the town the enemy's column, by a parallel street, marched in. A collision seemed imminent, but the discipline of the company was here evinced.

We marched as regularly as when on parade. One square, two squares were passed, when just in front was seen a body of infantry crossing a square farther on and at right angles to us, going at double quick. It looked as if our first battle had really begun. Then came the order, "Company! Shoulder arms! By the right into line! Forward, march! Right shoulder, shift arms!

Double quick; March!" And then we started to break and force our way out. A square farther on, and in the uncertain light of dawning day we could see troops standing a hundred yards distant, but whether friend or foe could not be distinguished. The company was halted and ordered to load, the line was dressed, and extending from sidewalk to sidewalk, we continued on our way, expecting a volley to be poured into us every minute. Just at the final moment we discovered that we were mistaking friends for foes. It was Company H, who, in their turn, were laboring under the same delusion. It is needless to say that no blood was spilt that morning.

In a brief space other companies came up, keeping on in a solid column to the railroad. All the infantry escaped, but the cavalry company of Captain Ball was captured to a man.

The battalion was not halted until some three miles outside of town, where we boarded a long train of cattle cars. The whistle sounded slowly at first, then faster, and the cars started; the crowd broke into that favorite song, "We'll be gay and happy still." Middle-aged and elderly citizens who heard the alarm rushed out and joined the singing throng. Had the advance of the enemy been delayed but a few hours, not an Alexandrian, from a budding youth to palsied age, would have remained.

A moralist would have found much food for thought in that miscellaneous party. There were men of ripe wisdom and wide experience, long headed, cautious business men, who were leaving their ware-houses full of garnered goods, shop-keepers deserting their stores which a life time of frugality had built, planters abandoning their estates, and farmers with their granaries full, their barns stuffed, stables filled with blooded stock, and cattle grazing on the hills, and the simple negro slaves without a guide—and, worse than all, men left their families all unprotected. It was passing strange.

It is a curious fact that when a community of men labor under an intense mental strain for a length of time, their reasoning faculties become numbed.

These people (and Alexandria was but typical of the entire South) had talked of war, dreamed of war, and had simply become war mad. No domestic or business thoughts could find lodgment in their brain; the cold, calm-eyed "Goddess of Reason" had fled from the land, and wild-eyed, shrieking "Ate" reigned supreme. There was no retrospection, no future, only the thrilling present. In those perilous times men's very natures were changed; when the stirring notes of "Dixie" or "Maryland, my Maryland," filled their ears, the softer strains of "Home, Sweet Home," found no responsive chord. It was madness, it is true, but yet a transcendent madness, in which greed, envy and malice had no part, and so these elderly fellows,—deacons, vestrymen and communicants,—sat in the crowded flats, and as their homes, their families, and their fortunes were left behind, they joined in the jubilant chorus, "We'll be gay and happy still."

Take for instance the case of my own family. We lived on a splendid estate of 650 acres, lying on the Potomac, between Alexandria and Washington.* I doubt whether in the whole Southland there existed a finer country seat; the house was built solidly, as if to defy time itself, with its beautiful trees, fine orchards, its terraced lawns, graveled walks leading to the river a quarter of a mile away; the spacious barns, the stables with fine horses (for which my father, a retired naval officer, had a special fondness), the servants' quarters, where dwelt the old family retainers and their offspring, some fifty or more.

In addition to this stately place, my father owned a second

Between Washington and Alexandria, on the banks of the Potomac, is one of the oldest and finest estates in Virginia. It was the family seat of the Alexanders and Hunters, and has been in the family for nearly three centuries. The family is descended from the powerful clan of MacDonald of Scotland, from Alexander, son of John, Lord of the Isles, by Lady Margaret his wife, who was the daughter of Robert the second King of Scotland. John IV, son of the Earl of Sterling, emigrated to Virginia in 1659 and had all the land from Georgetown to Hunting Creek, by letters patent. When he died in 1677 his will bequeathed to his son John all the land from Four Mile Run to Hunting Creek, so that the historic home referred to became the home of the Alexanders. The mansion is still standing and is most solidly constructed. The beams and rafters are of solid oak, two feet in diameter, and strong enough, as was proven, to bear the weight of two centuries.

Descendant after descendant inherited the estate, until it, together with Arlington, fell into the hands of Girard Alexander. Girard sold Abingdon to General George Washington, who bought it for his step-son, John Parke Custis. Here he and his wife lived several years, and his four children were born at this home, except G. W. Parke Custis, who was born at Mount Airy.

Abingdon passed away from the Custis family; it had been paid for in Continental money by General Washington and the heirs of Girard Alexander brought suit to recover the money. After many years of tedious litigation the sale was set aside and Abingdon passed once more to the Alexanders.

It was sold to one of the Wises, who kept it for some time, and resold it to General Alexander Hunter, a member of the original family. General Hunter was a famous soldier in the British invasion when General Ross burned the Capitol in Washington; and he was Marshal of the District for twenty years. He willed Abingdon to his nephew, Alexander Hunter; but before his majority Abingdon was confiscated in 1864, while he was in the Black Horse Cavalry, in the Confederate Army. (Lockwood's Historic Homes of Washington, page 202.)

plantation called Brookdale, but a few miles away, and adjoining Arlington, General Lee's estate.

It was the custom of our family to spend the summer months at Brookdale, so as to escape the ague and fever that attacked every one who lived on the banks of the Potomac. In April my father removed his family to the city of Alexandria and abandoned these two places, with all of their goods, chattels, servants, stock,—in fact everything except the clothes we wore, not even employing a care-taker, for overseer we had none.

The land was there after the war, but that was all.

In the National Capital my father owned a fine mansion of forty rooms, and spacious grounds, corner of C and Third Streets, N. W., besides a dozen or so of smaller houses, and many lots.

Mr. Lincoln sent him word that he would not be called upon to draw his sword against his native State, and asked him to let his name remain on the retired list, pledging him that all of his property would be strictly guarded. My father refused the President's courteous request, and infected by the rabid contagion that swept through the South, lost all reason, and he left all his great business interests to go to the dogs, without one precaution whereby he might protect his rights.

CHAPTER VI.

BREAKING IN THE VOLUNTEERS.

The cars stopped at Manassas, a station on the Orange & Alexandria Railroad, a small, insignificant-looking place, but destined before long to become a household word in America. The landscape was either a dead level or gently rolling and heavily wooded.

The battalion on its arrival found everything in a disorganized state, and only a few independent companies. The First South Carolina Regiment was in camp. Our coming, however, was altogether unlooked for, and Governor Letcher, having made no provisions for our nine hundred men, we found ourselves in that lone spot without rations, cooking utensils, tents, or any of the necessities of a soldier's life, simple as they were. Possibly at this period the Confederate Commissariat had not been organized. We went immediately into bivouac, which consisted in laying down our knapsacks and taking off our accoutrements; that done, we looked into each other's faces and wanted something to eat; but wanting was one thing and getting was another.

For a while all discipline was relaxed; some favored of fortune at once engaged board at a small tavern, while others, with never a cent in their pockets, prowled like lost dogs around the camp of the Carolinians, thankful for a bone or a crust. For three days some of us were literally on the verge of starvation.

There were no drills now; only roll call in the morning and evening. We slept under the trees in our blankets, those who could sleep, for if the barrack mattresses were hard, the ground was still harder.

Money was tight in the market in those days—a very Rothschild in the ranks could not have borrowed a dollar, and those who were too proud to beg nearly starved.

In my diary are these entries:

"First day, 25th May. Tried to sleep but could not; the ground hurt my body. Am so hungry!"

"May 26th. A soldier gave me a cracker and a piece of cheese. Hung around the camp of the South Carolinians, but nobody asked me to have anything. If this is war I won't last long.

Slept a little better last night, but dreamed all the while of eating; waked up every now and then and rubbed my stomach to ease the pain. So hungry!"

"May 27th. All day not a morsel has passed my lips. Spent most of the day in the woods, almost crying with hunger. I can't beg—nobody ever offers me anything—am starving. I have dreadful pains in my back and stomach. This evening as I wandered in the fields, wondering what I must do, I saw a dog go by; a lean, starved cur, the meanest, dirtiest, ugliest, boniest, bow-legged creature imaginable; shot at him and missed; put out after him. 'Old dog,' said I, 'you will make a first-rate stew, even if the sun does shine through your ribs, and I'll have you if I can get you.' Ran my best, and the dog, who loved life as well as I did, ran his best; nearly reached him once where two snake fences met, but he squeezed through just as I jabbed at him with my bayonet; ran him about a mile farther, but my breath gave out, gave up the chase; last I saw of him was a yellow streak disappearing over the hill. Lost my dinner."

In retrospection one cannot help pitying the innocence and ignorance of men starving in the midst of plenty. A hundred yards or more away there were farm houses where it would have been only necessary to ask to receive. The Rebel soldier was, in the eyes of the people, one for whom too many sacrifices could not be made, and it was with pleasure and willingness that they administered to his wants. To the soldier of the Army of Northern Virginia every house was home and he soon learned the fact, but in the first year of the war he had not acquired the art of foraging and was content to cook his camp rations without the aid of farm produce or the delicacies of the good wife's dairy and store-room. Later on he felt no hesitancy in asking, believing that as he bore the hardships and did the fighting, it was the duty of the citizens to provide the food and keep him from starvation; all were in the same boat, doomed to sink or swim together.

As people waxed poorer and provisions scarcer it became impossible to supply the wants of each soldier as they would be made known to every farm house in the vicinity of the camp, and hundreds would be turned away, not unkindly but of necessity. A lady once counted such applications at her door in one day, and they numbered over two hundred, and these did not include the many with whom she had hospitably shared her own frugal meal. Fortunately the army was not stationary, and such extraordinary demands were not of long duration; but it is only just to bear grateful testimony to the unselfish devotion, the ready generosity of the people whose fair fields were made a battle-ground for four weary years; so long as they had anything to give, they gave cheerfully; the burdens laid upon them were borne uncomplainingly, their self-sacrifice was heroic.

Some soldiers felt great repugnance toward going up to a stranger's door and making a plain request, but they were strong on hints. The Georgians, the best foragers in the army, were of this ilk. A group of them would halt at the gate and choose the thinnest, saddest-faced, hungriest-looking one of their lot; he would meekly knock at the back door, wait until his errand was asked, and then humbly: "Please, Mam, give me a drink of water. I hain't had a single bite for the last three days, and hain't slept on a bed for a week."

Johnny Reb's eloquence, especially when he was hungry, generally prevailed and obtained him all he wanted.

Happily our commissary embarrassments were but temporary, and supplies began to arrive from Richmond. The season of want was over for a time at least, and as if to make amends for our fasting, the finest kind of rations in the greatest profusion were used; not only this, but large plank barracks were erected for our company, of which we took quiet possession.

Then hard life commenced, so we thought. We missed our noble women, their acts of kindness, their words of cheer; and remembering our grumbling in the old home town, would gladly have returned to take up the thread of existence there just where it had broken off. But as Goethe says, "We never float again on the same stream."

The company was divided into three or four different messes, each mess having two cooks, chosen by regular rotation, turn and turn about. The cooking at first was simply awful; not one of the detailed chef de cuisines could tell the difference between a frying-pan and a skillet, hence the horrible stuff they were wont to serve would have given dyspepsia to an ostrich; but slowly yet surely these amateurs learned the art, becoming so thoroughly competent that they could make a palatable stew or fricassee out of a lot of old bones and a handful of flour.

Affairs by this time had begun to assume a warlike turn; train after train crowded with soldiers was arriving every day. The troops hailed from every Southern State, proving that Manassas was considered a point of great strategic importance; the hitherto quiet station now resembled a fortified camp. General Bonham, of South Carolina, was post commandant. He was very lenient with the men, rarely refusing them any request, and consequently a great favorite; his office was alike open to the private and the staff and he affected no style whatever.

About the first of June, 1861, General Beauregard arrived and assumed command of the post; then a decided change took place. Our cool, roomy, comfortable barracks were exchanged for tents, which as every veteran knows, on a warm summer day are about two degrees less hot than a Dutch oven; and we had four drills a day in the hot sun. A change indeed! As David Garrick once said on going from London to Cheltenham, "It was like stepping from Elysium into Hell." At night sleep was possible, but in the day, with the fierce fervid rays of the orb of day beating down upon us, intensified by the white glare of the cotton sheeting, the heat became almost unbearable. The tents proved also first-rate breeding places for flies, which almost amounted to a plague.

The different companies were formed, ten of them into a regiment; the crack Rifles losing their proud individuality and sinking into plain "Company A, Seventeenth Regiment, Virginia Volunteers." This regiment was placed in a brigade, which it completed, and was known as the "First Brigade of the Army of Northern Virginia," commanded by General Longstreet. The brigade was composed of Virginians; the First from Richmond, the Seventh from Piedmont section, the Eleventh was from Lynchburg.

The regiment was ordered to leave its pleasant quarters in the woods and camp with the rest of the brigade in a vast field, without so much as a huckleberry bush on its surface; then we had to give up our large tents and take miserable little "belltents" with four men in each; they were so short that when a long-legged man stretched out at length he found his feet outside.

On bright days we would take refuge in the woods and lie around in the shade; but behold us in a long, wet, rainy spell; a fine spray showers down upon the inmates, the breathing of four people in a contracted space fills the interior with a dense fog; everybody is steaming, and the only simile is a kitchen on washing day; the one is about as pleasant and comfortable as the other.

General Beauregard had reduced everything to a "system."

We rose at dawn, answered roll call, ate our meals by the tap of the drum, drilled, went for water, retired to rest and fell asleep by the same rolling notes.

O ye innocent sheep! Ye fleeced and slaughtered. Meekness personified! Why did not nature give you a thicker skin or none at all? Why of all animals in the world was your blameless hide chosen to be beaten, thumped and rolled, to the discomfort and unhappiness of man? Surely your meekness is revenged on the human race for all your wrongs!

One grievance more. A failure to be present at drill, and we booked ourselves for police duty—an innovation with a vengeance, for "police duty" was but a polite name for the work of the man we call "scavenger" in the city.

Every morning squads detailed for that purpose, armed with brushes, brooms and shovels, roamed all over camp, cleaning and clearing up generally; the men considering it degrading, disliked this duty more than any other, and many were placed in the guard-house for refusing to work in such capacity.

The regimental camp was surrounded by a perfect cordon of guards, who were instructed to allow no one to pass save field officers; neither the officers under that grade, much less the rank and file, could leave camp without a written pass signed by his own regimental officer and countersigned by the general commanding, hence we were as strictly guarded as prisoners of war.

But there was no suffering for want of exercise on account of these circumscribed limits; eight hours were spent in drilling on a large level plain in a double-quick running through the different evolutions, until every one of us felt like lying down and giving up the ghost.

Woe to weak legs! For like the wicked, they had no peace; neither were the hands allowed to fold themselves at rest. What with cooking, police duty, and digging entrenchments, the soldiers soon found that Beauregard, and not the Devil, had work enough for idle hands to do; he piled "Pelion upon Ossa, and Ossa upon Pelion," in the shape of labor; from penitentiary convicts farmed out under the contract system, more could not have been exacted. He had details—a certain number chosen from each company—chosen to erect breastworks and elaborate fortifications after Vauban. They were marched to the designated spot, picks and spades placed in their hands, and the order given to fall to.

It was ever an incongruous assembly of workmen. Pat was in

his element, holding between his teeth a pipe of that curtailed description which all Irishmen love, and making the dirt fly as he plied his pick with the measured strokes of a machine. This muscular, brawny son of Erin seemed never to know the meaning of fatigue, but for the delicate man at his side, with soft muscles and weak sinews all unused to manual labor, and exposed to the sun, it was too hard a task; sooner or later he would break down and be sent under guard back to his regiment.

Those poor, proud fellows! Manfully enough would they strive to accomplish the allotted task, too great for their strength, and labor desperately on in the morning glare of the sun, contracting, all unknowingly, those deadly typhus germs, and digging but too often their own graves.

Our life during the month of June was destitute of any incident of note or excitement. It was the daily round of the galley slave; the same systematic duties day after day. Of course the fatigue and monotony of camp life superadded to the constant exposure to the sun caused much sickness; besides this, the water around Manassas was hardly drinkable, being almost stagnant.

As the summer advanced sickness broke out among the troops, and destitute of the proper medical attendance, the mortality became frightful; the wailing tones of the "Dead March" sounded in our ears and almost every hour could be seen bodies of troops marching with reversed arms, followed in a short while by the volley fired over their dead comrade; it began to have a very depressing effect on the army.

The commander-in-chief became alarmed at the condition of affairs. The mortality was increasing so rapidly that energetic steps were taken; huge water tanks were constructed on flat cars which were filled with pure water from the Blue Ridge mountains, brought down to the junction and distributed among the soldiers.

When the whistle of the engine sounded, the cry of "the water cars are coming!" was on every lip and thousands of men could be seen racing to the depot, carrying in their hands every imaginable kind of utensil, canteens, coffee pots, buckets, tin-pails, kettles and anything that would hold water. The scene at the tank baffled description—a confused mass of men struggling, each trying to fill his bucket first, the guards trying to preserve order, the whole resembling pandemonium by sunlight rather than anything else, and not until the last drop of that heaven-sent, life-giving fluid, fresh from the cool, pure mountain stream, had been scooped up did the place resume its quiet.

About the middle of July, drills in the heat of the day were discontinued, but notwithstanding these sanitary measures the hospitals continued to be crowded to excess and the death-roll in the army, especially among the troops from the far South, was startling. The Eighth Louisiana regiment lost by typhus fevers, dysentery, scurvy and measles the awful number of two-hundred men out of a total force of nine hundred strong; nearly one-fourth, or two for every nine.

Those troops from the extreme South suffered far more from the heat, strange as it may appear, than either Virginians or North Carolinians, and succumbed more quickly to disease when once attacked.

The days passed slowly, as they must always do for the weary watcher of the night, the captive in his dungeon and for the tired soldier, who, fettered by an iron system, could only sigh for change and stirring action instead of wearisome, dull routine.

June had gone and July was on the wane before anything occurred, when one sweet morning, the seventeenth of July, 1861, the long roll sounded and our camp life was broken.

CHAPTER VII.

BULL RUN.

The beating of the long roll!

Did you ever saunter down the quiet streets of a city on a windy night when the rattling of a passing vehicle was almost drowned in the whistling of a norther, a night when one loves to bask in the cheering warmth of a glowing fire and a large arm-chair, a night when none were abroad unless tempted out by anticipated pleasure or pressing business, and when hurrying along the deserted thoroughfare, have you ever heard the sudden clang of fire-bells,—"the Iron Bells," Poe calls them,—heard the answering cry from scores of throats that dread shout of "Fire!" that, echoing fast from square to square, brings the lover from his mistress, the artisan from his sleep, the printer from his task,—all to mingle in a common throng and fill the hitherto quiet street with an eager, hurrying crowd?

If you have, you can form some idea of the effect of "long roll" beaten on a quiet summer day.

Where there had heretofore been an apparently deserted camp, with but a cordon of sentinels around, now swarmed thousands of excited, hurrying soldiers. The fire-bell in the city is the alarm drum of the camp.

The officers had but little trouble in preparing for a move, servants attending to their traps and a headquarters wagon carrying them, so they generally bustled around and hurried up the privates. "Fall in, men! Fall in!"

What a time those same privates had trying to make a knapsack answer the purpose of a wheelbarrow!

By the way, those small trunks, peculiarly the soldier's own, hold about as much as one can stuff in the bandana handkerchief such as the emigrant bears hanging onto his stick when he lands at Castle Garden.

It is always the fault of new soldiers to load themselves down with extra baggage; give the veteran his blanket, a full cartridge box, a full haversack, and he is content; as for perfumed soap, books, extra suits, bowie-knives, revolvers, &c., when it became a matter of transporting them on his back, such vanities lost all attractions and were relegated to his "salad days."

4

The Army Regulations wisely abstained from prescribing the number of pounds each man should carry, knowing that before long, experience would teach them wisdom; in the meantime, if any soldier chose to make a pack-horse of himself, the commanding general made no objection.

In about an hour the regiment stood in marching order and sixty rounds of ammunition were distributed to each man; then the word "Forward!" was given, and we turned our faces northward.

One could scarcely recognize that dashing regiment, springing along with elastic steps, as the dull, jaded-looking men who a few hours ago were undergoing, with enforced resignation, the daily drill.

Barrack life may suit regular troops inured to such existence, and who look for no change throughout the year, but volunteers are of different mold; keep them unemployed or in camp, cooking, cleaning, drilling, and it breaks their spirits, deadens their ambition, they droop, pine and lose vitality; give them action, stirring action, and you may starve them, overmarch them, overwork them, and they will rise to the emergency and come out of the ordeal stronger than before; no matter if in rags, shoeless, hatless, hungry, let them be ever on the go, and they will, without grumbling, be always willing to advance anywhere, even through cold, sleet or rain, shivering all night beneath their blankets, keeping solitary vigils on picket-posts, trotting along in the forced march—they will sit at night beside their fires and be content; they will cheerfully advance *anywhere*, only let there be constant change, constant excitement, for Johnny Reb, like "Little Joe" in "Bleak House," must be kept "moving on."

The march to Bull Run, a small river near Manassas, was under a blazing sun, but there was no straggling. As yet no one knew their destination. As we looked back and saw the long line of infantry stretching out as far as the eye could reach, it became clear to even the most unobserving that some great military movement was taking place, but beyond this everything was conjecture.

Our rapid marching soon brought us to the creek called Bull Run, and the regiment was placed right along its edge, directly opposite Blackburn's Ford, and there halted; guns were stacked, ranks broken, and then, as it was late in the evening, the men were soon busy preparing their frugal supper.

Around the various camp-fires groups were gathered, frying

meat and boiling coffee, while the laughter on their lips and the light in their eyes showed what little thought they were giving to the morrow.

That night, for the first time, the men were compelled to sleep on the ground without blankets, the wagons from some cause having failed to appear; it was no hardship though, for it was a warm, sultry night, and the soldiers, breaking off the branches of the trees, made a fragrant, soft couch of leaves, and lying down with their clothes on and their arms beside them, were soon lost in slumber; nothing stirred except the phantom-like pickets, who slowly paced in and out among the shadows of the trees; a whip-poorwill sounded from out of the depths of the woods his sad, plaintive notes, and an occasional frog from a neighboring marsh prolonged his dismal croak—all else was silent; the camp-fires glimmered here and there before dying out; the prostrate forms were motionless in their sleep.

The night before a battle! the first battle of a long, disastrous war! What a scene for a painter! What a theme for all who choose to think upon it! By the side of the narrow stream, with its silvery waters, pure as yet as the clouds from which they came, and under heaven's own dome, "studded with a golden fire," lay thousands of one country, met there for murderous work; harmless, voiceless, mute as the stars above them were the men who wore the gray. "Sleep that knits up the raveled sleeve of care" was softening each bronzed face and making it tender, perhaps with some gentle dream of home or with some memory of mother, wife or child, for those who could not sleep.

The deep, fierce passions that in a few hours would let loose the dogs of war, were all as stilled as the lead waiting to stop the beating of some foeman's heart, waiting to do its after-work; for the bullet—the shell that tears its way into a soldier's form—is sure to glance aside to rend the hearts that love him, and not till then is its ghastly mission done. Imagination falters awe-stricken at the scene that the constellations watch in their next vigil; the blood! the wounds! the agony! the dead! God! was there no angel to stay the uplifted sword, as Abraham's hand was stayed; for all the prayers that went up that night from the whole wide land for those sleeping armies, could not one mighty hand have interposed?

The early dawn of day found the regiment lying dressed—"dressed" in camp parlance. Toilets that morning, so far from being elaborate, consisted of a soldier's dry wash, which meant rubbing the face on a jacket sleeve.

Our breakfast likewise was no studied affair; a cracker or two, a slice of uncooked pork washed down by a mouthful of "Bull Run" water, was all; but we were too well satisfied to get that, for in view of the day's work before us there was no disposition to be fastidious.

The rays of the rising sun that bright Thursday morning, the 18th of July, fell in checkered beams upon the ranks of gray infantry that lay along the banks of the stream in line of battle. On the side banks where our position was held were flat, low-lands; a heavy fringe of trees ran along on the enemy's side, the banks rising abruptly and forming a high bluff. We did not know enough of military affairs to be aware of our untenable position, the enemy above us being masked by a dense thicket; but a kind of dawning intelligence broke upon us that we were in a trap if the enemy should choose to attack us.

The Seventeenth rested along the south bank of Bull Run, directly at Blackburn's Ford, and on the extreme right of the Confederate line of battle; our left reaching several miles away and covering the stone bridge at Sudley's Ford, where the Warrenton and Alexandria turnpike intersected.

General Longstreet kept with us at the ford, sitting at ease on his horse, chatting gaily with the officers and men and waiting to hear an advance of the enemy from his scouts or to receive orders from General Beauregard. The commanding general expected Blackburn's Ford to be the battle-field, and the information went from man to man that the left wing would bear the brunt of the day's fighting.

Our men in long line lying flat upon the ground were doubtless wishing themselves moles so that they could burrow down out of harm's way. It was our first battle, our first waiting; always a dread ordeal for raw soldiers.

As we crouched together in a long, serried front, our hands nervously toying with the hammers of our muskets, each one felt that his final departure was near at hand and busily repented him of his sins. Some were silently praying, others were reading their Bibles, all were serious.

The soldier's first battle-field is marked by a variety of sensations; trembling fear, curiosity, and an insane desire to get up and leave, a half-feeling of awe, a strange nervousness, doubt as to his fate, all mingle together, making his heart beat fast and his pulse thrill with nameless horror; his breathing becomes thick and his face deadly pale; no matter what may be the temperament of the man, the first battle causes him more agony of mind than all other conflicts combined. Henry the Fifth said: "Every soldier in the war should do as does every sick man in his bed, wash every mote out of his conscience." Such was the universal endeavor that morning; the sins of a misspent youth never weighed so heavily as when the repenting soldier, all eyes, watched the dark woods on the other side.

Some time after, in speaking of that day's experience, one man declared that he repeated the Lord's prayer over and over about seventy-five times, having in his head the idea that the oftener he said the prayer the better he would become, and the less chance there would be of the Devil getting him in case a Yankee bullet should knock him cold. He would begin slowly, he said, and with much fervor, but always ended rapidly; then, commencing over again, would rattle through at a tremendous rate and dove-tail "Our Father" with "Amen." He threw away a pack of cards and made an oath never again to utter a profane word so long as he might be allowed to live; vowed that if by chance he should come out of the battle safe and sound he would be a moral, as well as a model, warrior; determined to crush down his hasty temper, and carry all the canteens to the spring; to give the first sop of the skillet to his surviving comrades; to do his share thereafter of police duty without so much as a grumble; to black the captain's boots if he should order it, in a meek and lowly spirit; resolved to imitate the noble Christian soldier of the Crimean war—the brave Havelock—and follow faithfully in his footsteps; forgave all his enemies—no! when he came to think of it, all except that scoundrel who stole his canteen the fight before, and about whom he made a mental reservation; thought he would go to church and give up his pipe, and if he got through safely would become a minister and preach the gospel. I know all this too well, for I was that guileless, innocent youth. So the morning dragged by, with the men stretched out at length, watching, hoping, praying, resolving, fearing.

The sun, tired of playing hide-and-seek behind the trees, boldly rose above their tops and gazed glaringly and steadily down. It was now late in the morning, and fortunately, as men's nerves cannot always be kept at full tension, strained expectancy gave way to listless ease; gradually the color came back to our faces, and measured beats to our hearts, while many began to amuse themselves, some reading, some writing, while others, that fair Thursday morning—to their blushes be it spoken—started a game of cards. Among the latter was the young man whose penitence and vows at dawn of day had been so lively. Then light, but subdued laughter, was heard, and the line began to ripple with fun.

"Who's afraid! The Yankees have backed out," said one.

"Never thought they would come to the scratch anyway," said another. Then up spoke an old veteran of the Florida war, "Boys, you are damn fools; you will get your fill of fighting, with plenty over to spare. You won't have to wait long either."

Prophetic words! Wise old Cassandra in breeches!

Eleven o'clock by somebody's old silver watch! Whew! How hot it was! We strained our ears, but not a sound. It was so warm that we wished we could take to the water like frogs, or better still, change into tadpoles. One man went so far as to wish that he were a woman; another a baby, "and a gal baby at that!"

Noon, high noon; and a white ball of fire overhead. The cartridge-boxes that in the morning had been slipped around in front, with the cover buttoned up, ready for immediate use, were now unfastened and laid on the grass. Jackets were cast aside, and the line, so well dressed before, was now about as straight as a corkscrew. The men scattered about in the shade of the trees, lounged and kicked their heels in the air. Scouts were just returning from a hasty and frightened reconnaissance, reporting everything quiet. Consequently, even the most timid felt satisfied there would be no fighting done that day—except with the flies, which had become so devotedly and persistently attached to us that they followed us in swarms.

One o'clock. Half of the men were fast asleep and the other half were dozing. The lookouts were no longer lookouts. Standing, or rather, lazily leaning, against their muskets, with thoughts far away, they heard but the droning of the beetles and the drowsy hum of the blue-bottle fly, while the faint cawing of the vagrant crow, as he winged his flight high up in the air, came dreamily to their ears. Across the stream there was nothing like life to be seen save, indeed, an old patient king-fisher that rested on a high limb, rolling his goggle eyes and nodding his head at the strange people below.

How many *boys* we noticed lying under the shade of the trees! —boys in their teens. Glancing hastily around at the recumbent forms, one would imagine them more in place in the school-room or college grounds, playing foot-ball, knuckle-down or bandy, rather than waiting there to be made food for powder.

A little past one o'clock, then with a sudden, frightful distinctness two guns went off less than twenty yards from us. Our two volunteer pickets, Colonel Terry, of Texas, and another, splashed across the ford to our side. Instantly every man was on his feet, gun in hand. "Fall in, men; fall in! Right dress!" came in quick succession from the colonel, and in a few seconds the line was formed and dressed. Now burst on our untried ears a rattling, stunning volley of musketry. Beginning down the stream some hundreds of yards and rolling toward us, the iron hail approached and hustled in our midst. The volley caused an icy shiver amongst us. The screaming hiss of the Minie-ball was frightful enough of itself to make the heart stand still, but the thud of the stroke against the body of some comrade, the sight of falling men, wounded and killed, was more terrible than any words can describe; it froze the blood in our veins.

How we wanted to run! Many a man of us could have discounted the fabled winged Mercury in a fair-field race.

Gracious Lord! They were shooting at us with artillery! Whir! Whir! Sh!—sh!—sh!—bang!! bang!! Too high! The shells cut the top branches of the trees and they fell showering down upon us.

It was useless to attempt any order now, for every man imagined he was about to be killed. The volley from the muskets had frightened us, but the bursting of those infernal shells was demoralizing. Every one acted for himself, and as the majority, by a process of rapid reasoning, concluded that the farther they were away from the enemy the safer they would be, they gradually, of their own free will and fleetness, lengthened the distance between the foe and themselves.

Every time a bullet whizzed near a man he would wince. Some would half drop down, and some very nervous fellow would give a howl as if he was actually struck.

"There's more honor in a long shot," cries poor Bob Acres, when brought face to face with Captain Jack Absolute on the field; "there's more honor in a long shot! Sir Lucius, if you love me, let me take a long shot!" Some of our men were equally as desirous of long shots—miles long. Discretion was evidently the better part of valor.

But others stood their ground, firing back at an unseen foe, never flinching; others again, who had at first retreated, shamed by such brave example, rallied and advanced, until the flower of the Seventeenth stood game in their tracks and searched the woods on the other side with their leaden messengers.

The firing across the banks at pistol range increased in intensity and violence. It was no longer a rattling volley rolling along the banks of the stream, but a continuous sound like the crackling noise of a forest on fire. For a second it would lessen, and the sound of the martial hurrah, mingling with the bursting of the shells, could be heard; but again would the firing swell into a steady volume, as thousands of muskets were discharged.

The enemy had every advantage; they had a lofty bluff; we, an even plain. They had a dense cover to mask and protect them; we, on the contrary, stood on the bare sward, targets for every marksman. And yet the situation beautifully illustrated one of Jomini's pet axioms on the art of war: "A fire up a declivity," he says, "is necessarily more close and fatal than one delivered down hill, for in shooting down hill the volleys are always too high; in firing up hill, on the contrary, the aim is almost certain to be low rather than high, and, of course, more deadly."

Had the fire of the enemy been lower, victory would have been theirs. As it was, the vast majority of the missiles struck amid the tree tops, and played havoc with the monarchs of the forest a hundred yards or so in our rear, sparing in a great measure flesh and blood, and familiarizing soldiers with the sound. This could not last, for secure in their covert, the enemy made the bank rutilant with rays of luminous fire, and each moment corrected their aim. Bullets now struck the solid tree trunks with a dull thud, instead of whistling through the leaves of the top branches, and many had their billets that day. Men began to fall. Our front line, fighting without order, was borne back to the edge of the trees a hundred yards distant from the run, and it seemed as if defeat were inevitable.

Many of the rank were running in every direction, the officers trying in vain to form them in line. Half a dozen would obey the commands, but when the shrill whing of the bullet was heard or the dull zip of the missile as it buried itself in a tree trunk, and the fearful noise of the whizzing shrapnel, each man would break for shelter. The measured hurrahs of the enemy were not sounds, either, that were calculated to calm the line that kept up the fight.

Captain Pressman fell, wounded in efforts to steady his men. Captain Dulaney dropped; Lieutenant Jarvins was struck; while among the rank and file the loss was proportionately heavy. A very storm of bullets was sweeping overhead, sounding like a swarm of bees above the men, who were lying prone on the earth, loading and firing point-blank into the woody covert where the unseen enemy lay.

In the regiment was a very portly soldier; indeed, it is no exaggeration to say he had fully four inches of fat on his ribs and weighed at least three hundred pounds. How he contrived to gain sufficient nourishment out of our camp to keep up to the top notch of the scales was a question of wonderment and many a learned and solemn discussion. Be that as it may, a rosier, fresher or fleshier Rebel never "larded the earth" on a day's march. There was a little fellow about my size, the very smallest in the lot, who watched this big soldier during the conflict, if not with pride, certainly with interest out of all proportion to the difference in their size. Wherever he went this youngster followed. When he advanced, the other was close behind him. When he stood firm, his little "Duplex" loaded and fired valiantly over his shoulder. More constant than a brother, truer than his shadow, more faithful than Ruth to Naomi, not even death could have separated them. Had this Hercules charged singled handed and alone the whole opposing army, little David would have brought up the rear. Had he hung back, his double-acting, patent attachment would have stayed with him. Had he died, his weeping mourner would have buried himself beside his ample remains. As before stated, the one was the very biggest, and the other the very smallest. The waist of the one measured five feet around, that of the other twenty-two inches. The shoulders of the one spread out like the fabled Antaeus of old,—the other's were close together and all bone. The one stood six feet in his stockings, the other five feet two. Thus protected by this mountain of fat, this citadel of flesh, the little soldier felt bullet-proof and quite safe. With this movable entrement he laughed at musketry volleys, scorned and turned up his nose at hustling shells, kept close to his love and fired all around him, but never knew certainly whether he ever hit anything or not.

There is nothing like getting warmed up to work! Loading and firing sent the blood rushing through the veins. Instead of retiring, many of the men began to advance; and no longer firing wildly at the sun, and pulling trigger at the sky, they became cool and composed and discharged their muskets at the flash of the enemy's guns. It was earnest work; the bulldog instinct of humanity all aroused. No longer were needed the officers' commands. The whole line reformed itself, and standing stubbornly on the fringe of the woods delivered rattling volleys across the stream.

Just here in the very zenith and heat of the conflict, when everything seemed going against us, an incident occurred so extremely ridiculous that even with death hovering near, many gave way to uncontrollable laughter, which, occurring at this terrible time, must have been heard by others, just as Faust listened to the mad merriment of the elfin goblins in the unhallowed rites of the Walpurgis Night.

On the left of the ford there was a large tree. It was about ten yards from the water's edge, a great big sycamore, whose trunk was fully five feet in diameter, and whose spreading branches rose some fifty feet in the air. The flying bullets and hurrying shells had played the mischief with its top boughs, and the ground was covered with leaves and twigs cut off by the leaden and iron shower. On the safe side of the broad, knotty trunk some of the most timid had taken refuge, one behind the other. They had cast away their guns and they hugged each file leader close, forming a string of about forty men. The shells had frightened them, evidently preventing their departure to the rear. It was the screaming, shrieking, bursting shrapnel shot that kept them glued together.

A shell from the enemy's battery on the left would hiss by them, and the whole string would gravitate toward the right, so as to get the sturdy trunk between them and the shot. All at once another battery on the right opened up on our lines, the balls sailing through the empty space, then the men, almost delirious with terror, would hang close and swing around on the opposite side, but only for a second. Here would come a shell from the left, and away would go the line like a pendulum, back through the half arc of the circle, and hardly a moment for breathing time before a half hundred weight of iron would rush by the tree with a demoniac yell, and the long, agonized queue described another parabolic curve. And so the band of brothers were kept shifting to and fro; the fortunate ones next to the tree having nothing to do comparatively, while those who composed the end of the string were kept on the swing all the time. It was well enough, as long as they knew exactly upon which side to expect the shells, but what if both batteries had serenaded at the same time? What then? Laugh! Take it all in all, it would have made the solemn-est old veteran grin.

The violence of the fire was redoubled on our left, as if the enemy were preparing for a charge farther up the stream; Minie-balls swept in showers over our heads.

The men wavered; the officers, hoarse with shouting, stood sullenly leaning on their swords; the dribbling of the men to the rear commenced,—the most potent sign of disaster,—and it seemed as if defeat and retreat were now but questions of a very short time. Just at the critical moment, General Longstreet, with the divination of the born soldier, rode up and ordered a charge across the run.

The men obeyed the summons and made a rush for the ford. They were not formed into line, but streamed across like a pack of hounds after a buck. Once in the woods most of the men scat-tered instead of forming in a skirmish line. They, like a lot of school boys, roamed at will, all eyes. As soldiers we were as green as the budding grass; had our adversaries been veteran troops they could have picked us off one by one with as much ease as a sportsman would bag a flushed covey of quail.

Fortunately, our friends, the enemy, were as a babe to a callow youth. They too were strolling around admiring the scenery, and it only needed a dinner horn and a petticoat to make these adolescent Billies and Johnnies go to the branch, wash their faces and eat their meal together. Remember, we then had had no baptism of fire, except the frenzied shooting across the stream, in which we saw nothing of the foe. We had no wrongs to avenge, and the calm after the storm, the cool, quiet woods was so peace-ful that a reaction came. And the irony of it—Virginia and Mas-sachusetts! The two old Commonwealths were pitted against each other in one of the first engagements of the war; and strange to say the men of the First Massachusetts Infantry were dressed in gray—real rebel gray, only their jackets were ornamented with frogs and gilt buttons, and their caps all had in brass letters, "1st Mass."

I saw several men in gray—and I did not fire my musket; and those I met had no murder in their souls, probably because they could not tell friend from foe, so we did nothing but stare.

I was sitting on a log when two of the foe, beardless youths, came up to me and said they were lost and did not know what to do. I told them that I would show them the way, and we walked back to the ford, and they were very much surprised when they saw our men in solid line of battle, across the stream.

I carried them about a half mile to the rear and they told me that they were from Boston, and that they were glad after all that they were prisoners; that the war would only last a few months and they wanted to see the inner life of the Rebels so that they would have lots to tell their folks at home.

So that's how I captured two prisoners. I am free to confess that had they ordered me to follow them when in the woods, I certainly would have obeyed.

Around the camp-fire that night rather big yarns were told, and most tremendous bragging done. Some went so far as to show notches on the stocks of their rifles for every man they had killed. Others narrated narrow escapes and displayed, by way of illustration, the hole torn in cap or jacket, the only damage done; but more were silent, willing, it is supposed, to let some future record speak their praises. The fat man who acted as rampart in the engagement across the run was pleased to come to a personal encounter with a plucky Northerner, and when seen was lying at the foot of the hill, prone on his back and on top of him his tough little adversary, making him "see stars."

In the meantime, the love of the Union and hatred for traitors (this big old one in particular), animated the Bostonian till his arms worked like a windmill, and every stroke brought a groan. Reinforcements arrived, to whom the stricken one exclaimed: "Thank Heaven, you've come!" and clasping his small foe in his arms in a loving embrace, panted out, "Stick the rascal with your bayonet, but for God's sake don't stick too deep!" The moral was obvious.

The enemy, after finding our position, had leisurely fallen back to the field on the left, where stood a house surrounded by a picket fence. Here they halted and threw a volley into the woods, which sent our forces down the hill and across the stream.

The firing ceased, the crest of the hill having been swept clear of the enemy. Our regiment was reformed and the roll called. Our loss was found to be one man killed and ten wounded, including three officers. The brigade lost one hundred men, killed and wounded. The Seventeenth was relieved by the reserve, and retired a hundred yards or so to the rear. Ammunition was served out, rations distributed, and the order given to "break ranks." Soon the tired men were lying about in groups, talking over their adventures and munching their crackers in the most contented enjoyment.

The repose was soon broken by the sound of a signal gun, and hastily rising we became witnesses of the finest artillery duel that took place during the war. Our position was such that we could see the whole practice, being only about fifty yards away, and it seemed like some grand review in which was all the "pride, pomp and circumstances of glorious war, with none of its horrors."

On our right, in the center of the big field, some seventy-five yards from the run, was posted a battalion of the Washington Artillery from Louisiana, whose guns were formed in the shape of a crescent with the hollow toward the run. The enemy occupied an open space on the opposite shore, hidden from view by the abrupt bank and dense shrubbery. The guns were of heavier metal than ours, as could be told by the report of the pieces.

The Yankee batteries opened the salute first, gun by gun. The rebel pieces slowly replied, increasing in intensity and rapidity, until each gun was fired as fast as it could be loaded, and the detonations swelled into one prolonged roar. At first the enemy's shell flew too high, but that was soon corrected, and then the missiles fell thick and fast among the Louisianians, who would thereupon move their guns forward by hand to get them out of range. After a while a dense smoke hovered over and hid both battalions from view; but through it the flashes of the guns could be seen as they darted out their tongues of flame. Soon the firing slackened; the guns, one by one, ceased; the smoke drifted away, disclosing the blackened meadow. The earth had been ridged in great holes where the shells had exploded, and one or two ammunition wagons had been shattered, but there were no dead bodies left upon the field to add a crowning terror to the scene.

The next day we lay in line of battle, but heard no war-like sounds except an occasional picket-shot across the run.

Another sun rose and set with everything still serene.

By this time many of us were beginning to think the war was over, fancying the little affair at Blackburn's Ford, wherein the enemy had lost a hundred men, had demonstrated the uselessness of any attempt to subjugate the South, and that with enlightened minds they had marched back to Washington, soon to sue for

peace on the basis of the Southern Confederacy.   Heaven bless
our innocent souls!

Company A was ordered early in the morning of the twenty-
first to cross the run on a reconnaissance.   As we reached the
opposite side in carrying out this order, our nerves were shocked
by the frightful appearance of the enemy's dead, which had now
been lying in the hot, broiling sun for nearly three days.   It was
the first time we had been brought face to face with the ghastly
terrors of war, and the sight made us sick in body, as well as at
heart.   The heat of summer had started rank corruption to its
work.   Faces and figures were bloated and swollen to such a
degree that there remained no traces of sweet humanity, and
those who loved them best would never have recognized the
blackened features, the sightless, staring eyes.   It was horrible
and hideous beyond words to describe.

A detail of men was made for the purpose of burying these
dead, but they soon came back with pale faces, declaring that it
could not be done; that the sickening effluvia prevented even an
approach to the bodies.   But another detail of older and more
hardened men was appointed, who executed their task by throwing spades full of earth over the dead just as they lay, and so their
ambitious hopes and aspirations ended in lonely unknown graves
in the depth of the woods —mere heaped mounds raised by foeman's hands.

Leaving one company as scouts, the rest of the regiment
retraced their steps and took up their old position in the trenches.

It was a bright, clear, dewy morning; the birds were singing
blithely in the tree tops, and it only needed the distant chimes
of the church bells to make the unities of the scene perfect.

All at once, without preliminary warning, the enemy's cannon
opened with an infernal salute.   The stirring tones of the officers
were heard, and the clicking of the gun-locks told that the line was
ready for the expected charge.   But the firing ceased as suddenly
as it had commenced, and we were left in peace.   Probably this
was a feint to feel our position, and nothing more.

But away on the left, booming reports of cannon had been
heard at intervals throughout the morning.   Now, however, the
cannonading assumed an angry tone that showed that it was no
longer simply shelling, but a serious give-and-take affair.

Faster came the bellowing thunder, until the reports ran into
each other so continuously they could not be counted.   A heavy

battle was going on evidently; our regiment knew they were to take no part in it, for our duty being to defend the right flank, we were to remain stationary in the old position.

So the engagement went on, and the persistent pounding of the cannon never ceased; sometimes, rising above this, could be heard the crash of musketry, that told our excited imagination how close and deadly was the conflict. Yet no intelligence—not even a rumor reached us—of how the battle of Bull Run was going; no thrilling news of victory; no dread tidings of disaster; while the men sat in serious silence listening to the sound of the fierce fight, or conversing in low tones, speculating upon the result—knowing not that Stonewall Jackson's star had risen on the world.

About three o'clock, however, the excitement became intense, for the tremendous fire of musketry and the terrific noise of the artillery had merged into one, sounding close and clear, keeping up in one continuous volume, with no abatement for nearly half an hour; then there was a sudden lull and the reports ceased to be other than spasmodic.

How had the battle gone? None knew, not even when a courier dashed up, his horse covered with foam, and delivering some order put spurs to his steed and went off down the line like a shot.

"Fall in, men! Right flank! Forward, march!" And we marched across the run, and headed for Centerville pike.

A march for a mile carried us through the woods into a large field, where the splendid brigade halted for a short time, and where the news was communicated to the men that a great battle had been fought and won; that the enemy, panic-stricken, was flying in the wildest confusion toward Washington; and that our brigade was to pursue them even to the banks of the Potomac.

Such excitement ensued as beggared description. The enthusiasm passed all bounds; it approached madness. Cheer after cheer, hurrahs from thousands of throats rent the air; thousands of arms gesticulated; thousands of caps were flung in the air, but only one wild, delirious cry went up, and that was "Forward!"

The order to advance was given and the brigade, wrought up to uncontrollable excitement, increased their gait to a double-quick in the direction of the retreating foe, the officers in vain trying to check their ardor. And so advancing at a run down the pike toward the sound of the random firing,—a half mile or so,—

they came to a breastwork built directly across the road, where batteries and heavy infantry reserves had been stationed.

As we "right obliqued" to avoid it, we had tangible evidence of the hurried retreat. The road was strewn with papers, official orders, letters with seals, some unbroken. The tents of the officers were left standing, with their clothing and trunks untouched; the suppers they were preparing were set out, the camp kettles of coffee actually boiling on the fire, the rations of bread and meat lay ready to be eaten. Guns, bayonets, boxes, ammunition, knapsacks, camp equipage, uniforms, clothing of all kinds, even officers' swords and crimson sashes were among the spoils, to say nothing of the dainties of every description, and the baskets of champagne, upon which the flying enemy had purposed to feast in Richmond.

Never was there a worse rout. Indeed, only raw troops could have become so utterly demoralized. Evidently they had not left five minutes before our arrival, and finding us so close, they must in an instant have lost all organization and were changed by utter panic into this flying, frenzied mob.

Still our soldiers kept on and showed no disposition to stop, even to pick up the valuable plunder within their reach, except that each man stooped and made a grab for the letters lying around, which he thrust by the handful in his haversack for future reading.

The more scared we found the enemy to be, the more brave we became, until the men were in a very fever-heat to catch up with the foe. Exulting expressions burst forth, "We've got them now!" "We will be in Washington by daybreak!" "Forward, there in front!" "Step out!" "Don't stop!"

Every man put his best foot foremost, and even our fat Jack panted on, wiping the dust and perspiration from his face.

But the end came in a way we little dreamed of. A courier rode up and delivered an order to General Longstreet, and his reply was heard by the whole regiment, for he was riding in front of the Seventeenth, which led the column.

"Retreat!" he thundered. "Hell! the Federal army has broken to pieces."

The amazing order was given to halt, and the men stood in their tracks. But when the command was understood, "Right about face," and we started to retrace our steps, there came curses loud and deep. Some emotional natures, so brought down from extreme, thrilling excitement and high, bounding hopes, absolutely burst into tears, while disgusted, depressed and hungry, the whole brigade dragged itself back to the old position on the banks of the run.

So ended our bright dreams of an early peace and a Southern independence. The Goddess "Opportunity" offered her face to us and proffered her flowing locks. The South had but to grasp it and the history of the New World might have been changed.

Like Jerusalem, "She knows not the things that belonged to her own peace;" "she knew not the time of her visitation."

5

CHAPTER VIII.

Not speaking from a partisan standpoint, nor yet straining the truth, in the Longstreet's first brigade there were three thousand one hundred and fifty men who could have marched to Alexandria that night. This brigade had been lying in the trenches for three days, with abundant rations, and had not walked a hundred yards nor fired a gun at the enemy in all that time.

What an irretrievable blunder was committed in not following up the retreat, an impartial history will decide.

Generals Johnston and Beauregard affirm that an advance to Washington would have been unwise; declaring they had no fresh troops to throw against the fast-fleeing enemy. And yet by the official reports of the Battle of Bull Run, both of those commanders state that there were fresh troops which might have been used with such fatal effect. General Johnston says: "The apparent firmness of the United States troops at Centerville, who had not been engaged, which checked our pursuit; the strong forces occupying the works near Georgetown, Washington and Alexandria; the certainty too that General Patterson, if needed, would reach Washington with his army of 30,000 men sooner than we could, and the condition and inadequate means of the army, in ammunition, provisions and transportation, prevented any serious thought of advancing against the Capital." General Beauregard says: "It is proper and doubtless expected that my countrymen should be made acquainted with some of the sufficient causes that prevented the advance of our forces and prolonged, vigorous pursuit of the enemy to and beyond the Potomac. An army which had fought as ours did on that day, against the uncommon odds under a July sun, most of the time without water, and without food, except a hastily-snatched scanty meal at dawn, was not in a condition for the toil of an eager, effective pursuit of an enemy immediately after the battle. And the want of a cavalry force made the pursuit a military impossibility."

In the same report from which the above extract is quoted we learned the number of men who were "fresh"—not so much as having fired a gun on the day of battle, and whose sole duty it had been to guard the fords, wings and communications of the army—all spick and span, and filled with fiery enthusiasm for the advance.

As for the General's assertion that it is a military impossibility for a victorious army to follow up a panic-stricken, flying enemy without the aid of cavalry, it is simply an insult to any soldier's common sense. But if the statement of one so high in authority carries with it the weight of rank and experience, then with all due respect therefor, it may not be amiss to remember that Napoleon did not think so at Jena. Richmond was not of that opinion at Bosworth fields; nor yet Gates, when he followed up and forced the surrender of Burgoyne's army. And to go back to the days of Joshua, that mighty man of war who subdued and smote the countries around about him, it is only necessary to recall the fact that cavalry was forbidden the children of Israel, to be quite sure the overtaking, the pursuing, the slaughtering of those neighboring nations was done by men on foot.

The following is a list of the regiments that took no active part whatever in the day's fighting, merely lying in position, protecting the wings, guarding the fords and watching the enemy.

General Beauregard is again quoted: "As before stated, two regiments of Bonham's brigade, the Second and Eighth regiments of South Carolina Volunteers and Kemper's battery, took a distinguished part in the battle. The remainder, Third (William's), Seventh (Bacon's) S. C. Volunteers, Eleventh (Kirkland's) North Carolina regiments, six companies of the Eighth Louisiana Volunteers, Shields's battery, and one section of Walton's battery under Lieutenant Garnelle, whether in holding their posts or taking up the pursuit, officers and men discharged their duty with credit and promise."

All these troops were idle all the day of the 21st.

General Beauregard goes on to say:

"Longstreet's brigade, pursuant to orders, prescribing his part of the operations of the center and right wing, was thrown across Bull Run early in the morning, and under a severe fire of artillery, was skilfully disposed for the assault of the enemy's batteries in that quarter, but were withdrawn subsequently in consequence of the change of plan already mentioned and explained. The troops of this brigade were the First Virginia (Major Skinner), Eleventh Virginia (Garland's), Twenty-fourth Virginia (Lieutenant Colonel Houston), Fourth North Carolina (Colonel Jones), and Whitehead's company of Virginia cavalry. Throughout the day these troops evinced the most soldierly spirit. Brigadier General Holmes, left with his brigade as a support to the same position in the original line of battle, had also been called to the left, whither he marched with the utmost speed; BUT NOT IN TIME TO JOIN ACTIVELY IN BATTLE.

"Walker's rifle guns of the brigade, however, came up in time to be fired with precision and execution at the retreating enemy."

Now adding the number of troops so shown to have been inactive, and we have:

Longstreet's brigade, then full, not one of its companies having less than sixty men on the rolls; but at least, say:

First Virginia Regiment, 500 men; Twenty-fourth Virginia Regiment, 500 men; Seventeenth Virginia Regiment, 865 men; Twenty-fourth Virginia Regiment, 500 men; Fifth North Carolina Regiment, 500 men; two companies cavalry, 150 men. Total, 3,015 men.

Part of Bonham's brigade: Third Regiment North Carolina Volunteers, 600 men; Seventh Regiment North Carolina Volunteers, 500 men; Eleventh Regiment Louisiana Volunteers, 500 men; six companies Eighth Louisiana Volunteers, 400 men. Total, 2,000 men.

Ewell's brigade stationed at Union Mills: Hill's Thirteenth Virginia Volunteers, 550 men; Holmes's brigade, 2,050 men. Grand total, 7,615 men.

It is here shown that there were 7,615 infantry who were not engaged in battle and ready to continue the pursuit—wild to advance. There were four batteries of artillery which had not fired a gun that bloody day, and who stood harnessed and ready at the word "Go!" in all, eight thousand troops, according to Beauregard's own showing, who had been held in leash all that stirring time.

Besides these, there were at least five thousand more who arrived on the field just as the battle closed, and could therefore have pressed the retreat, viz.: Eighteenth Virginia Infantry, Barksdale's Mississippi Regiment, Cocke's brigade, Early's First Maryland Volunteers, and others which were comparatively but little used and who reached the field only to participate in the glory and not the stubborn contest.

And so with twelve thousand fresh troops at command, Johnston and Beauregard made the greatest military blunder on record; for with that force hotly, fiercely pressing the retreat, none but a fugitive enemy would have reached the defenses in Washington.

How history repeats itself. Here in the New World was a battle fought, the conditions, forces, the very ground nearly identical with the one that decided the destiny of Europe, and as Tallerand remarked, "Set back the march of civilization a hundred years." The English under Wellington, the Old Iron Duke, occupied precisely our position, acting like us on the defensive, and repulsing with an inferior force, attack after attack, charge after charge; standing as a rock against the dashing, rushing billows, waiting for and hoping for night or reinforcements; striking back, giving blow for blow, and hanging to his ground with bulldog tenacity. At last Blucher came to the one, as Johnston came to the other. Wellington advanced; Beauregard stopped his serried ranks and went quietly into bivouac, allowing weeks and even months for the enemy to recruit its demoralized army, while there was not a moment's peace given to the flying French by the vengeful, pursuing Prussians, until they reached the defenses of Paris.

Stuart had a hot argument with Beauregard when he issued orders to recall his cavalry. He often said afterwards, that he wanted to flank Centerville and push on to Alexandria with his cavalry, but received peremptory orders to stop pursuit.

CHAPTER IX.

CAMP "NO CAMP."

Two days after the battle, on the 23d of July, the brigade was formed into line and again crossed Bull Run, keeping on until it reached Centerville. The men manifested no enthusiasm, knowing that the advance meant only a camp at some point near Washington. The whole command was in a sullen humor and received with the utmost disfavor the prospect of spending the summer and fall in the same inane, uneventful, pipe-claying, ever-dulling style that had characterized its former camp life.

We arrived at Centerville and there bivouacked after a leisurely day's marching. The next morning the camp was measured out in an open field a mile from the village, and we went to work like beavers, pitching tents, digging trenches, and doing many little things to make ourselves as comfortable as our limited means would admit.

The cantonment was christened "No Camp," and soon enough we were following the old routine, only enjoying far greater liberty now that we had received our initiation by fire. Having but little to do and the discipline relaxed, the days passed pleasantly enough.

The winning of the battle of Bull Run was in reality a great disaster to the South. It aroused the mighty, puissant North, which, like a lion, shook its mane as it awoke from its fitful slumber. It made a peaceful settlement and separation impossible, and it stilled the South to a fanciful security. Better—better by far—that our forces had met crushing defeat, which would have opened the eyes of the people and caused them to "gird up their loins" for a desperate resistance, or to make terms with the enemy.

The *Richmond Examiner,* of date of July 26th, 1862, stated: "We have assumed all along that the Battle of Manassas determined the fate of the war, and secured our independence. Not only has that battle disorganized and demoralized the Yankee Army (which has returned home, as its time of service expires much faster than the raw and worthless recruits can come in their places), but it has also divided and demoralized the Cabinet, Congress, the Press and the people of the North."

This opinion gained ground. It was so easy to believe, and it pleased the pride of all vain-glorious Southerners.

A fatal lethargy was the result; and it affected all the people south of Mason and Dixon's line.

About a month after we had settled down into our new quarters the paymaster arrived. We were formed in a long line, and as each name was called the owner was made the happy recipient of a bundle of bank notes new and crisp, amounting to forty-four dollars for four months' service to the country. We younger ones were so agitated that we could hardly sign our names to the roll; it was the first money some of us had ever earned in our lives, and we strutted about as proud as a dog with a new brass collar.

Then for the first time we saw and made the acquaintance of that irrepressible character ycleped the sutler. One of them was very much insulted at being called a peddler by a soldier who had not been informed of the wide reputation of the profession; at any rate they soon opened their stock, and as we had been out of funds for months, and debarred of old-time comforts and luxuries, we made the currency fly. A dollar then in Confederate money was as good as gold. These obliging tradesmen, however, made from one to five hundred per cent. on our purchases; and as we bought freely our hard-earned money soon disappeared.

In about two weeks our licensed highwaymen, having sold their wares, consisting of stale pies, mouldy cakes, vinegar cider, canned fruits, fly-blown molasses and other useless articles, cleaned us out completely and "silently stole away," as they had been doing from the first.

It might have saved useless formalities had the authorities at Richmond the next pay-day collected the money in a bale and sent it by express with the address: "Soldiers' Pay, to Regimental Sutler, Care of Quartermaster."

The chief delight of the company was to serve on picket post at Falls Church, and the anticipation of it was like that of Christmas holidays to boys—enjoyed weeks beforehand.

This little village was distant from Centerville about fourteen miles, and as many from Washington. Half a mile on the other side of Falls Church was Taylor's tavern, our most advanced picket post. Two companies from the different regiments were alternately on this duty, and would start out like civilians on a picnic. Novels, papers and cards became in great demand, as away from camp there was nothing of which we were so prodigal as time. Starting early in the morning we would soon accomplish the distance; then selecting some deserted house as barracks, spend the sweet, soft summer days in the most delightful, lazy enjoyments. No drills on the dusty roads or barren fields; no inspection of arms; and—every saint in the calendar be praised!—no police duty. That after all was the soft corn on our military foot. Poor Hugh Hite, one of the F. F. V.'s, as we called them in Virginia, was wont to say in his wrath: "I volunteered to defend the sacred soil with the last drop of my blood; but confound it all, if I joined the army to become—this!"

Send a soldier on picket duty and give him sufficiency of food if you wish to make him happy. The fact that he is close to an enemy exhilarates his spirits, and the danger of sudden attack keeps him in good humor. It has all the charm of novelty to be isolated, as it were, from the thousands who form the army. To be only with chosen comrades and boon companions—this is of itself enough to change the dull, mechanical soldier into a bright, sentient, hopeful being.

While about fifteen men at a time would be on active duty, the rest enjoyed the careless do-nothing-as-fancy-might-devise. Some would be lying under the trees in idle dreaming or in deeper slumber; others reading, writing, with here and there a group absorbed in the mysteries of Old Sledge. But over every head drifted the soft, curling cloud of smoke from the valued briar-roots, reminding one of a cosy lot of chimneys in a small village.

Night would bring the cheering camp-fire, and with it the light jest, the echoing laughter, the roaring camp song, for we boasted a fine chorus in the company, and two musical artists, so that those old rafters of Taylor's often rang with the unwonted sounds of morceaux from Rossini or gems from Mozart. Besides, we had a violin and banjo, in consequence of which stag-dances became the rage, breaking out upon the slightest provocation, and keeping time to those battered instruments with emphasis.

Then the night picket on the outer post was not without its charm, though a half-frightened tremulous feeling ran throughout its experience, as a woof in the weaving. The moonlight made such weird shadows; such uncanny shapes appeared to glide along the edge of the woods; such boding, suspicious noises were heard, that instinctively one would grasp the shining rifle barrel, and stand rigid with expectation. The croak of a frog, the hoot of an owl would thrill him with sudden apprehension, while his fervid imagination would picture creeping figures of the foe stealthily drawing nearer. But dawn would come at last; the haunting moonlight would give place to the lightness of day; distorted objects would regain their wonted shapes, and the picket would smile at the terrors of his watch.

As the summer slowly ended, and the sensitive leaves of the maple first showed by their changing color that the fall of the year was asserting its sway, our existence in camp was pleasant beyond all a soldier could wish. After a simple inspection and dress parade, no duty to be performed, we roamed at will through the shady woods, and bathed in the cool, limpid streams that abounded in that section. And this, too, in the loveliest, divinest season of the whole year.

Our fare was very good, for by exchanging with the farmers our surplus of beef and salt pork, for vegetables, butter and eggs, we made a most beneficial mutual arrangement.

The Confederate Commissariat was in an affluent condition then as compared with its after poverty. No man drew his pound of flour or crackers, his half pound of meat daily, for there was absolutely no drawing of rations. Whatever any of the various messes wanted could be procured from the store tent, which was pitched next to that of the captain, where were piled barrels of flour, meat, mess-pork, peas, beans, &c., all in the greatest profusion. Every morning a freshly-killed beef was brought and laid at the store tent, with the understanding that each soldier was at liberty to cut off the quantity or quality that might best suit his taste.

The country people flocked to the camp with every kind of produce that could be traded or bought, and on very reasonable terms, too. The table of each mess was supplied with roast beef, beef-steak, soup, vegetables, butter, milk, with pastry, fritters and molasses for desert, winding up with coffee. No marvel that the men grew plump and lazy, and even shrank from picket duty.

A few having nothing else to do entered into a system of experimental cookery that almost rivaled the unapproachable Soyer himself. Our crack cooks understood as many ways of dressing and preparing beef for the table as any French chef from Delmonico's. Indeed, many dishes were placed proudly upon the table by the gastronomic discoverers, that no one could tell of what they were composed—the true test of that art. At one time the interest in that subject was so keen, and the rivalry so great, that officers and men alike tried their hands at inventing new dishes for the mess.

Very often the result was rather dubious, and the dinner would have to be thrown to the camp dogs that came, no one knew when or from where; they belonged to no masters, and stood ready to catch any morsel thrown at them, or sneak off with whatsoever bones were within reach; rogues, every one of them, with not an honest dog in the lot.

Dinner was the great event of the day—the one occurrence that broke the monotony of camp.

Below is a bill of fare copied verbatim from my diary:

CAMP NO CAMP.

September 18th, 1861.

SOUP

Beef, Virginia Style　　Mutton, a la Francais

Chicken　　Beets　　Mutton　　Beef　　Mess Pork

ROASTS

Beef, a la Mode

Shoat, Stuffed with Vegetables

Mouton (French Style)

ENTREES

Beans　　Potatoes　　Cauliflower　　Egg Plant

Tomatoes　　Peas

WINES, LIQUORS, &c.

Whiskey (Stone-Fence)　　Brandy (Red-Eye)

Cider (Fairfax Best)

DESSERT

Cakes　　Rice Pudding　　Monkey Pudding　　Apple Dumplings

FRUIT

Apples　　Pears　　Peaches

Coffee　　Pies

The table was not set with snowy cloth, china and cut glass; neither were there waiters to change the plates. No! The private was his own waiter and his own cook, and it was this distinguished detailed chef and his assistants who served things by merely transferring pots and pans to an adjacent shady place. Notice being given that dinner was ready, a hungry crowd would soon gather, and each person taking a tin plate on his lap, help himself without grabbing—for there was plenty.

Good humor and contentment reigned. The soldier learned to go back to his school-boy sports—marbles, "follow my leader," football, &c., and seemed to enjoy them as much as in the days of his youth.

Five men out of six played cards, and some gambled day and night; draw-poker of course being the game. Those who had money staked it, but those who had none played for credit or "O. P.'s," which meant "Order on Paymaster."

Some unfortunates actually lost their four years' pay in advance, never drawing a cent during the entire time of the war; but they afterwards had the grim satisfaction of knowing they had not lost much. To such an extent was this gambling carried on that men played for the clothes they wore, and discounted every earthly thing they possessed. Indeed there were some inveterate old sports in the First Brigade who would have played with the "Old Scratch" himself, and paid the forfeit with their own souls.

The abandon, the dream of the soldier's life were all ours now. But sometimes, when there was a grand review of the whole army, there were but too many to deplore the inaction of that splendid body of men who marched and counter-marched in solid column across the level plain; they deplored that such troops, with their high discipline, their wondrous enthusiasm and "esprit de corps," were not forcing an offensive campaign instead of leading the lazy, enervating life, which, while it was good for health, was yet almost destructive to morals and training.

Just at this time occurred the famous conference at Centerville, when Mr. Jefferson Davis commenced the role of "Military Dictator." Bred as a soldier at West Point, and afterwards serving with distinction in the Mexican War in a subordinate capacity, his brief experience in one short campaign seemed to have convinced him that he was one of the foremost soldiers of the age, and the great military genius of the New World. Time proved that his strategy was faulty, his decisions ill-considered, his mind prejudiced, his nature obstinate, and his head far from clear—he lacked, more than anything else, poise and calm judgment. He often differed from the conclusions of the generals in the field;

and to his blindness and obstinacy the Army of Northern Virginia were indebted at this time to their rusting inactivity.

On the 6th of September Gen. J. E. Johnston wrote to the Secretary of War urging that President Davis should visit the headquarters of the army and have a council of war to decide upon the question whether or not the army should commence an offensive campaign on October the first.   In compliance with this request the President came to Centerville, where General Beauregard's headquarters were located, and met the officers as designed.   There were present Generals G. W. Smith, J. E. Johnston, and G. T. Beauregard.   An account of this interview was drawn up and published in the *Richmond Examiner* shortly after, the document being subscribed to by all three of the officers referred to.

Gen. Smith submitted the propositions:

1st. That the Army of Northern Virginia was at its highest point of efficiency, both as regards morals and numbers, and if kept inactive it must retrograde in every respect during the coming winter.

2nd. The Federal Army was daily growing in numbers and discipline.

3rd. That the best chance of ending the war was to strike a sudden and deadly blow.

These deductions being unanimously agreed upon, General Smith then addressed the President:

"Is it not possible, Sir, to increase the effective strength of this army, and put it in a condition to cross the Potomac and carry the war into the enemy's own country?   Can you not by diminishing the forces at other points as they will bear, and even risking defeat at other places, put us in a condition to move forward? Success here gains all."   In explanation and illustration of this plan, the three generals gave their unqualified opinion, that if for want of adequate strength on our part in Kentucky, the Federal forces should take possession of that entire State, and even enter and occupy a portion of Tennessee, that a victory gained by this army beyond the Potomac would, by threatening the heart of the Northern States, compel their armies to fall back, free Kentucky and give us the line of the Ohio River within ten days thereafter.

On the other hand, should our forces in Tennessee and southern Kentucky be strengthened so as to enable us to take and hold the Ohio River as a boundary, a disastrous defeat of this army would at once be followed by an overwhelming raid of Northern invaders that would sweep through Kentucky and Tennessee, extending to the northern part of the Cotton States, if not to New Orleans. Similar views were expressed in regard to the ultimate results in northwestern Virginia being dependent upon the success in this army, and various other illustrations were offered, showing that a triumph here was triumph everywhere; defeat here, was defeat everywhere, and that this was the point where all the available forces of the Confederacy should be concentrated.

It was conceded by all that the Army of Northern Virginia was not sufficient in numbers to assume the offensive beyond the Potomac.

The President asked General Smith what number was necessary, in his opinion, to warrant an aggressive campaign; to cross the Potomac, cut off the communication of the enemy with their fortified Capital, and carry the war into their country. Gen. Smith replied: "Fifty-thousand effective men—sound soldiers—and they can be drawn from the Peninsula, Norfolk and West Virginia." Generals Johnston and Beauregard said that a force of sixty thousand and more men would be necessary.

This force would require large additional transportation and munitions of war. In this connection there was some discussion of the difficulties to be overcome, and the probabilities of success, but *no one doubted the disastrous results of remaining inactive* throughout the fall and winter. Notwithstanding the belief that many soldiers in the Northern army were opposed on principle to invading the Southern States, and would fight better in defending their own homes than in attacking ours, it was concurred in, that the best if not the only plan to insure success was to unite our forces and attack the enemy in their own country.

The President gave no definite answer as to what number of troops he deemed sufficient, and no one present considered this question to be decided upon by any other person than the Commander-in-Chief.

Finally the President delivered his ultimatum:

That *at this time no reinforcements of the kind wanted could be furnished the army.* He ended by stating that the whole country was demanding protection at his hands, and praying for arms and troops for defense. He had been expecting arms from abroad, but was disappointed. Want of arms was the great difficulty. He expressed regret, and that was all.

When the President had thus clearly and positively given his opinion, it was felt that it might be better to run the risk of almost certain destruction fighting upon the other side of the Potomac, rather than see the gradual dying out and declension of the army during the winter, at the end of which the terms of enlistment of half of the troops would expire. The prospect of a campaign commenced under such discouraging circumstances was rendered more gloomy by the daily increasing strength of the enemy, already much superior in numbers.

The answer of the President was deemed final, and there was no other course left open but to follow the same masterly inactivity. If the enemy did not advance, we had but *to await* the coming winter and its results.

During the conference, or council, which lasted about two hours, all was earnest, serious and deliberate. Gen. Smith said afterwards, in referring to it:

"The impression made upon me was deep and lasting, and the foregoing statement is correct, and as far as it goes, gives a fair idea of all that occurred at that time, in regard to the question of crossing the Potomac."

The report was signed in triplicate at Centerville, Va., January 31, 1861.*

The whole brigade during the autumn went on picket at Falls Church once in a while, and we usually kept northward until we reached Munson's Hill, a few miles from Washington. This high elevation was our farthest post, though not regularly picketed by either army, but each in turn occupying it. If we held the hill and our enemy advanced to take possession, we were too polite not to yield the point; and when we felt like indulging in a survey from its lofty summit, including the church spires of Washington, not to be outdone in gallantry, the politest of foes marched cheerfully down as we marched up.

From the crest of Munson's Hill a magnificent scene did indeed stretch out before the eye; the cities, the fields, the broad Potomac all spread out like a panorama at our feet. No grander spot could have been selected by the Moses of either side to "view the landscape o'er," of a land he yearned to enter, the while for very strong reasons he could not. Strong? Well, the huge forts spanning and dotting each rise of ground were very sugges-

---

*For full report of the famous conference, see De Bow's Commercial Review, Vol. 8, p. 758.

tive hints in their way, that our company was not desired in the National Capital while Bull Run still lay between Richmond and our See-saw Hill.

In those autumn marches the buoyant feeling of the men found expression in song. One voice would start a favorite camp refrain, either "My Maryland," or "Gay and Happy we Will Be," the soldier next would take it up; another would join in, another, and yet another; then the company, the regiment—until the whole brigade would swell the chorus, and with thousands of voices rising and falling in measured cadence, the effect would be indescribably grand, the music irresistibly inspiring.

Brigade drill was a heavy affair, very tiresome, and an infliction to be endured while it lasted. It is ever a difficult manoeuvre to throw a brigade into a hollow square, especially if the commanders of the companies are not well versed in "Hardee;" the wrong movement of one company will delay or throw out the formation of the whole square. When this would occur, our colonel, genial and sociable off the field, and a martinet on, as all officers should be, would fume and fret, until the luckless captain, losing what little self-possession he had, blundered more and more and generally ended by tying up his company in a hard knot.

Question. If it took so many minutes to form a square on parade ground, how long a time would be consumed if the enemy's cavalry were charging and the solid shot plunging through the line?

Even such a wearisome proceeding as drilling was not without its humorous side. Sometimes in making the soldiers charge bayonet in line, they would increase their speed and keep on, and never stop until they reached their camp, when the whole force would disappear, as if the ground had been the whale and they were Jonahs.

Very often in manoeuvring in the field an old hare would jump up, shake his white tail by way of challenge and bound off. In that case good-by to all discipline. Regardless of officers' commands, the soldiers with one shout would start after him. True, some crack companies would keep firm so long as the rabbit did not run close to them, but not a minute longer; for catching the contagion, they too would start yelling and screaming on the chase. A strange characteristic of this Southern army was their insane desire to run a hare. Regiments that stood immovable under the severest fire, that never flinched while a charge of cavalry dashed themselves in vain against them, would go all to pieces at the mere sight of a "Molly Cotton-tail." Nay, the cry of "Old hare! old hare!" would set a camp in a blaze, and soldiers would drop everything to join in the pursuit. Away they would go like so many hounds after a fox, filling the air with their shouts—just so many thousand men after one poor little animal.

On the 12th of October the brigade to which our regiment was attached drilled for the last time under the command of General Longstreet, who had been appointed general of a division. In severing old ties, he addressed a very complimentary order to the First Brigade. Sorry enough were we to lose him. He had won and held the entire confidence of rank and file, who would have followed him blindly anywhere; and this is more than they would have done for many who commanded them afterwards. It was a subject for congratulation that the brigade was incorporated in his new division.

The late fall of '61 was cold and rainy, and the men kept closely in their tents. The regiment was ordered on picket duty, when there came an alarm of the enemy's approach, and we started on a run, not stopping until we reached our reserves some ten miles back; then we advanced in heavy style, only to find that some little Yankee drummer, beating his sheepskin for his own private delectation, had started some two thousand Rebels at full speed for the rear.

It was abominable weather and the woods and fields at Falls Church were like Mr. Dick Swiveller's description of the marble floor of the Marchioness's, decidedly "sloppy."

After a day's march we had camped in the woods and built huge fires, before whose glowing warmth we were fast drying our wet clothes when the drum beat the long roll. "What is the meaning of that racket?" was the universal query, expressed or unexpressed. The officers, forming the line, soon showed what was in the wind; and the grumbling was fearful. Each man seemed to consider it a personal insult to himself, and had almost to be dragged into the ranks. Wet boots were savagely jerked and pulled on to undried feet, damp garments were drawn over shivering limbs, sobby, dripping hats were put on aching heads, and the "miserables" started to march back to Centerville, the very place from whence they had just come.

The slanting rain soon wet everything; the road became a quagmire; and the sleepy, weary soldiers tramped mechanically on. Though the rain continued to pour, and the road had become but a bed of liquid mud, sleep fought and conquered us, and the soldiers actually slept as they marched in ranks.

No greater torture falls to the lot of man than to feel an irresistible desire to sleep and yet be obliged to combat it. Truly the members of the old Venetian "Council of Ten" were devilishly wise when they banished sleep from the eyes of its victims.

For a hundred yards on a smooth road we could march perfectly unconscious, animated by a force independent of mind or will. The feet could take the same step, while the soul was far away in realms of dreamland. But should the ground become uneven, or a ditch or stream run across the highway to break the level, a bad stumble or pitching fall was sure to result. Then with restored consciousness we trudged along, fighting with Nature, the power that claimed us. Another level, easy stretch of ground and again somnambulism ensued, followed by the same inevitable gymnastics; and so on through the long night. The intense effort to keep the mind clear, the wide-open straining of the eye, the feeling that the brain is succumbing to an overmastering influence beyond the will, is simply horrible; and many of us would have dropped out of ranks and laid down anywhere along the road, but for the report that the enemy was close behind. So we staggered along, asleep and awake, and reached the village at last.

In Sir John Moore's withdrawal of his army in Spain we read of the same thing; and we know how common it was for Napoleon's wearied soldiers to slumber in those long marches during the retreat from Moscow. The physical endurance of man is simply wonderful, and his power to adapt himself to surroundings none the less strange. Veterans have lain down by a six-gun battery, whose throats were belching flame and smoke and earth-shaking thunder, and become as sweetly locked in sleep as if the iron storm were the mildest south wind sighing a lullaby among the trees.

We had once a remarkable opportunity for noting the automatic power of the muscles while the senses were locked in deepest sleep. It happened in this wise:

Not long before this night march a party had been given near Fairfax Court House to a soldier and his bride, wherein the fair women of the country turned out in force to do them honor. We danced to the music of a fiddle, played by an old negro, and played well too; for to use his own expression, he "could knock a fiddle

6

cold." About two o'clock in the morning this ancient Orpheus began literally to play out; his arms grew weak, his fingers were cramped, and he laid aside the instrument, exclaiming:

"Fo' de Lord, gen'lemen, de ball must come to an end, for de music can't feel de fingers on his hand, an' dis makes three nights I's been up."

We plied the old fellow well with liquor, and after a promise of double fee he agreed to make another effort to play the "Old Virginia Reel," as a winding up. It was about three o'clock and the two lines formed across the floor as the fiddler struck up the tune.

The dancers went at it with a will; faster and faster the music; quicker the answering feet kept time, until the old house shook and quivered again. While each was doing his level best, deep in the mystery of "making his steps," it was noticed that the music was not always keeping time; "Sally come up" was being repeated over and over again without variation. Calling in vain for another tune just for the sake of variety, the ancient African was found to be sound asleep. His head had sunk on his shoulder, his breathing was regular, while from his nose was issuing an orthodox, unmistakable snore. The violin was held in the usual way, except it was not resting under the chin, but on the breast. He played well the half tune, only at times the bow would glide on the wrong side of the bridge and produce a scratching sound. As he reclined there, sawing away in most profound oblivion, we stopped and watched the strange phenomenon, our host remarking that old Dan, the fiddler who now lay sleeping before us, was noted for combining the power of Orpheus with that of Morpheus; that while the latter held him, the former used him.

CHAPTER X.

THE GHOST OF CHANTILLY.

A large ball was to be given near Fairfax Court House. A very high-toned affair, with the brigade band to furnish music. All the generals were to be there, with now and then a colonel; but nothing except a star on the collar passed muster, with the exception of a few who could be counted on the fingers. I was well acquainted with the lady of the house, a dashing, brilliant brunette, reminding one of Di Vernon. She had no respect for buttons just because they were buttons, and would leave a general of a division any time to take a moonlight stroll with a gray jacket if she liked the wearer better. Yes! It was to be a grand party, and the soldiers, from the highest to the lowest, discussed the great event around the camp-fire and envied the invited ones.

When the day arrived, by judicious borrowing I had succeeded in getting up a very respectable costume. A white shirt was loaned me by one of my comrades, whose name I was asked to conceal for fear the whole company would bear it in mind and try to borrow it on some future occasion, it being the only one in the company. An officer, a friend of mine, supplied me with new military trowsers with a gold stripe down the sides; I found a handkerchief lying around, not very white it is true, and I had a diamond ring on my finger; so I intended, under all this nimbus, to hold up my head with the highest general in the lot.

As I sat in my tent busily rubbing and polishing my buttons, letting anticipation have full sway, I was awakened from my dream by the sergeant of the guard, who put his head inside, saying, "Hunter, report at once for guard duty!"

"You must mean somebody else," I answered; "do you know there is to be a party to-night, and that I am invited to it?"

"I have nothing to do with your party; you are on the regular detail to report at the guard-house at once," replied the sergeant gruffly, as he pulled his hat over his eyes and walked off, leaving me numbed with despair.

I went to the captain with the sad story; but something had gone wrong and he was cross, or rather sarcastically kind; asked whether guard mounting should be stopped because there happened to be a party in the neighborhood, and whether a wedding would not have to be preceded by a flag of truce? I appealed to the colonel, but he was not invited, and being an old bachelor, wanted to go; hence he took savage pleasure in denying my request. I sought the brigadier, who laughed at me; so, with a heart filled with the keenest disappointment, I reported to the guard-tent, where I was told I would not be posted till evening. I wandered off by myself with grief too profound for words—too poignant for consolation. Never did city belle, with her new dress ready for the ball which she was compelled to forego, feel more keenly the defeat of her hopes than I did mine; relinquishing them, too, only to walk up and down a beat and cry "All's well" to the moon.

Evening came and brought no joy to me. I smoked all the tobacco I had, for comfort, and then answered to my name at roll call. It was six o'clock, when instead of donning brave attire I followed the sergeant and struck out from camp.

"Where are you going, Sergeant? I thought I was to be placed on a beat in camp!"

"No," he said, "you are detailed by the officer of the day to guard Chantilly."

"Oh!" I replied, "I am glad." And then I began to recall all I had heard of this famous ancestral place.

Chantilly, the home of the old Stuarts, was one of the handsomest country seats for miles around. In the olden days of Virginia it was kept up in baronial style, and was the center of profuse and lordly hospitality.

Many were the gatherings within its walls of the sporting gentry who assembled to celebrate the annual meet from far and near. Imagination can picture the gay throng, just as tradition and old letters delight to hand them down.

Let us see! There was my Lord Fairfax from Greenway Court, mounted on a splendid Arabian, followed by his faithful body servant Scipio, a recluse whom they called "the Cameron," but he was ever ready for the hunt. Then young Byrd of Westover, owner of a celebrated plantation on the James, which the Marquis de Chastelux, on a visit in 1770, pronounced the most beautiful estate in Virginia. Byrd was a zealous sportsman and had the finest hounds in the Colony. We must not leave out, either, Major Bullet, who knew and was known by everybody; for a roaring blade was the Major, who loved the wine cup, the chase and the sound of the rattling dice; he was tall and slender, with soft brown eyes and a gentle voice—the mildest-mannered man that ever scuttled ship or cut a throat, so 'tis said. Not a desperate-looking fellow by any means, though the Major was in the Colonial Army, and was noted for cool bravery and determined nerve. He was nothing of a bully,—not even quarrelsome,—but his temper was rather quick and fiery; and a more devout believer in the Code never lived; indeed, he had the reputation of being the most famous duelist in Virginia. A crack shot and accomplished swordsman, it made little difference to him on the field whether the saw handle or the slender rapier was the weapon chosen.

And there was Mann Page, the richest man in the Old Dominion; with his plantation of eight thousand acres in Frederick County, called "Pageland;" ten thousand acres in Prince William—"Pagewood;" four thousand more in Spottsylvania—"Glenpage," by name; and one thousand in King William—"Pompadike;" two thousand in Hanover; two thousand in James City; and a score of other farms of a thousand or so apiece, while his slaves were numbered by hundreds.

Among the horsemen I see another character, and a most marked one of those times; one who gives us a blessing when we come into the world and who throws the earth on us when we leave; who by a few words changes the whole tenor of our lives, and makes Van Winkles and Mr. Caudles of the wisest of us— who is loved by women and hated by men. I mean the Parson, as he was commonly called at that time. The preacher was a jovial fellow in those days, not much given to praying; who kept up with the gentry in the maddest of their sports. If the truth were told, he preached on Sunday, rode on Monday, got drunk on Tuesday, and so on through the nursery song. Yes! We can imagine them all—men with the historic names, which are as well known to us as household words handed down and worn by so many of our best and bravest. Selden, the handsomest man in the Colony. McCarthy, "Fighting Randolph Carter," Washington, and hosts of others too numerous to mention.

If the meet was striking, what must have been the glory of Chantilly in the Christmas time, when hosts of relations, friends and even strangers gathered around the immense yule log. Even around our camp-fires we had heard of old memories handed down from sires to sons, of those splendid entertainments; the table groaning under the weight of its feast; the rare old china; the massive family plate; the smoking haunch of venison; "old Virginia cured" hams, sweet as sugar; wild fowl from the Chesapeake; fish from Hog Island; rare old wines from famous cellars; and the silver punch bowl filled with that most delicious of festive brews.

We had heard too of those gay old balls where the proudest, the fairest and best of the Colonists met, where satin rustled, velvets trailed, and brocade swept over the polished floor; where jewels rich flashed in the soft, becoming light of numberless wax candles. And the dress of the cavaliers! Why, the homeliest man would shine "a thing of beauty" in such arrayal, brought in big strong chests from across the sea—velvet coats with gold buttons; elaborately embroidered satin vests worked in delicate designs; dainty ruffs of fine old lace; shorts that reached to the knee and tied with a garter; stockings of finest silk, and long, pointed shoes with jewelled buckles. Decked in these, with an embossed belt hung over the right shoulder, to which was attached a slender rapier in bright steel scabbard, and a three-cornered cocked hat, and you have the outfit complete in which shone the cavalier colonist in all his glory. A decided contrast to the stiff, ugly, conventional black of our present day, in which a man hardly can tell himself from his own waiter. Call to mind the stately gallantry, the elegant courtesy that makes the very mention of their names and their son's names, and their son's sons (generations all passed away) synonym of all that is refined and polished, of all that is courteous and chivalrous to women, and we once more people Chantilly with the men who trod its now deserted boards, and woke the slumbering echoes with dance and song and jest.

Well, I confess the theme has ever had strange fascination for me, and many is the day-reverie in which they have been as present to my mind, in fancy, as if I had seen them with my own eyes; and before we leave the brave old chevaliers, with names that shone, some of them in Revolutionary annals, let us linger with them a moment at their banquets, then relegate them to the shadows from which we brought them—and peace be to their souls. See! The dining hall is all ablaze with waxen lights in silver candlesticks. The glare from the huge hickory logs, burning and snapping in the deep old fire-place, is touching and playing upon the burnished heavy plate. There are no ladies present— all the better, perhaps, if there had been, for these cocked-hat gentry imbibed like fish in those days, and got drunk on principle.

Lucullus held as a maxim that women should be excluded from the feast, and Epicurus made it a practice to so banish them because dinner was considered too serious a thing to be trifled with. They both held that a man owed too sacred a duty to his digestion to risk it, since life becomes a burden without its perfect condition. The fullest enjoyment was not to be secured, they said,—the heathens!—with women present. A man could scarce hope to enjoy his wines, his soup and his roasts, and at the same time play the agreeable *aux dames*. There was a time for everything; and the time to eat was to attend to one's gastric juices in undisturbed repose.

The courteous host is doing the honors with a graciousness his wife could scarcely rival. George Mason is in the crowd, the very prince of good fellows. Lord Fairfax, representing many miles of Virginia land, is here to-night, bending from his stern dignity and helping to swel! the wassail, and by his side is his young friend, George Washington, trying to forget his dismissal by Mistress Cary, as he drains a bumper from the huge punch bowl. But why attempt to name them all! Look how they rise and clink their glasses to that telling toast. How pleasantly it sounds, the roaring fire, the ringing of glasses, popping of corks, and the confused mingling of voices. You may be quite certain that the flowing bowl is circling round without stop or stay, and they are drinking without flinching to their host, each other, the chase and their sweetheart's eyes.

Not till the cloth is removed is the revelry fairly at its height. With no fears of waiting wives or stern old governors, the men and youths are drinking deeply. Faces are already flushing to a deeper hue and voices are raised in tone. Steady old goers are speaking of dashing runs and desperate exploits of the chase; the statesman is forgetting his caution and revealing the secrets of his heart; the planter is discussing his crops; the parson, with rubicund nose all aflame, is arguing in thick tones the relative styles of beauty with that rake, Major Bullet, and—but my dream is ended; the conjured picture vanishes into thin air as did my reverie, of which this is but a shadow, when the sergeant's lips, which had been in solemn communing hitherto with his pipe, gathered voice to say:

"Here we are!" I started, collected my wandering senses, and looked up. Before me was Chantilly, a stately old place, with spacious porch and a passage running from end to end, so broad that a four-horse wagon might have driven throught it. A wide stairway led up to the apartments above.

The house was built of brick brought over from England, but

the various wings, added at intervals, were of solid oak. Around the house was a splendid park of full-grown chestnut trees that shadowed and adorned the fine old mansion.

No one inhabited the house when the enemy made the first advance to Bull Run, its owner having collected previously all his negroes, "lares and penates," and started for Richmond. The said enemy had carried off all that was portable, but had had no time to gut and sack the house. To protect it from further plunder by our own soldiers, a guard was placed over it, with orders to allow no one to trespass upon the premises, and so it fell out that instead of tripping the light fantastic toe, I was doomed to guard old Chantilly that night.

It was a beautiful, soft, balmy Indian summer night, and both grounds and mansion looked lovely. After sauntering some time along the porch I entered, and commenced a tour of inspection. On the right a door opened into the parlor, a long, handsome apartment extending the whole length of the house. There was no furniture left except an ancient spindle-legged piano of German make, whose keys were yellow with age. I struck a few chords. It gave out a jingling sound, but appeared to be in passable tune. The instrument was at the front end of the parlor, between the door and the long window that opened into the porch. I am particular in describing its position. Across the room and directly opposite the piano there hung two portraits, the one of a woman, but so blurred with age as to be nearly indistinguishable; the other a man's, judging from his attire; the features had faded with time, all except the eyes, which shone out with startling distinctness from the shadowy face, with an expression of intense surprise, as if questioning my presence there.

Leaving this room I went up the broad, handsome stairway leading into a long gallery, from which a suite of rooms opened, looking to the front of the building. In nearly all of these apartments there was furniture, rather cracked and antique specimens, which no one but a curiosity seeker would care for. Evidently all articles of value had been removed and only these few old relics of a century past left as lone sentries at their post. Oh, sad! This dismantled home, with its rich association of years, endeared to its owners by all the refinements of cultured life, left to a ruthless and reckless soldiery! The old King Lear of a house, turned adrift in its old age to bear the raging tempest. Nothing but the body of the old house left—the soul, the life, all gone!

I explored the building all over, its every nook and corner, its lofty rooms; it seemed as if a whole regiment might have found shelter within its spaciousness. Descending, I went out upon the porch, paced up and down, and watched the camp-fires breaking out one by one, like sentinel stars in the sky. Through the branches of the grove the night wind murmured a gentle plaint.

It was dusk, and

> "Darker and darker
> The black shadows fall;"

the neighboring forest became one with the night, and the house was indistinguishable in the gloom. The reveille from camp had sounded eight o'clock; it was time the relief was coming. I went on at six and had been two hours at my post. Four hours off for me, and then I was to go on again at midnight. Eight o'clock and dark as pitch! I was getting nervous, I could swear that I heard a door slam. But, thank Heaven! there came the sound of the advancing relief. Their steady footfalls, the clink of their accoutrements was sweetest music to my longing ears.

They advanced up the gravelled walk.

"Halt! Grand relief! Friends with the countersign."

"Advance, one with the countersign!"

The guard came up to the porch and gave the password "Potomac." I yielded him my place, and repeated instructions, which were to let no one enter the house, and should it be attempted, to halt three times and then if necessary fire. I joined the relief, marched back to camp, and turning in the guard-tent was asleep in a moment.

The quick, stern cry of "Guards, turn out!" brought us to our feet at once. Sergeants and men were talking in an excited tone and for a few moments no one could tell what was the matter. But the officer of the day came, and in the silence that then fell, the cause was soon understood. One of the relief was brought in the tent by two guards, and if ever there was a man literally frightened out of his senses, that man was before us then. His hat was gone, his hair hanging over his face, half hiding his wide, protruding eyes; his features were deadly pale, huge beads of perspiration were dropping down upon his jacket and he trembled like an aspen leaf. But he could answer no questions, and only begged that we would spare him the details of that which he had seen. Even after we had given him a heavy drink, and his pulse had assumed its wonted beat, and the color had returned slowly to his face—even then he said he could not put in words

the terror of the past two hours. He had been detailed to guard
Chantilly, and it was there at his post that he had heard and seen
what he would never forget. And this was all we could learn—
or ever learned.

Again the trembling seized his limbs, again we noticed the
deadly paleness of his face, when even the officer was moved to
pity, and instead of having him handcuffed and tried in the near
future for one of the most serious infractions of military law a
soldier can commit,—that of leaving an outpost without permission,—was so much struck with the man's abject condition that he
only ordered him back to his post.

But with this command the soldier positively refused to comply. He said without equivocation, he would be shot first, and
that nothing earthly could induce him to go into that house again,
or even near it after dark. He said too he knew it was now his
business to try and put some people out of the world, but once
out, he considered he had no further use for any of them; and
that he was willing to stand a court martial any day, but that he
was *not* willing to stand up against ghosts.

"Ghosts," said the officer contemptuously; "ghosts! Why,
are you a baby? Some old woman's tales have been frightening
you!"

"May be they have and may be they haven't; but I am not
going into that house again. You know yourself, Lieutenant, I
don't sing second to any soldier on the battle-field."

"Yes, that is so," cordially assented the officer, "and that is
why I had thought better things of you; but go in the guard-tent
and consider yourself under arrest."

Then turning to me he continued, "Hunter, get your musket
and take his post; and, Sergeant, go and place this man on duty."

I stood speechless and almost petrified. What! When a full-
grown man, and one of the most daring soldiers in the regiment,
had been scared almost to death at Chantilly, that I, a mere boy,
should be sent in to that ghost-haunted place! Me! Ordered
to go! Me!

I could not believe anything so cruel, and I found words to
protest.

"Lieutenant, for God's sake don't send me to Chantilly!"

"That's your post, sir; go and take it."

"But, Lieutenant, let some soldier go with me."

"No, sir! Here you came to me this morning to be let off that
you might attend a ball at the Court House, and now because

this man has listened to some old grandmother's yarn, and frightened himself half to death, raised himself a shadow to run from, you must needs follow his example. Don't be a coward!"

That word stung me and settled the matter so far as I was concerned. I would have gone inside a tomb and lain down, as Romeo says, "amid dead men's bones, reeky shanks and yellow, chapless skulls" in a charnel house, much less Chantilly. So I made but one request, to be allowed to take a light with me, which was granted, and then with my long tallow dip in hand, amid the good-bys of my comrades and their parting salutations and advice, I started with the sergeant for Chantilly.

It was a moonless night, though the sky was brilliant with stars as we entered the dense grove. Passing through the gloom strange figures seemed to glide in and out among the tree trunks; spectral arms reached out toward us; the breeze, which had sprung up since night-fall, sounded like boding voices from the grave. I began to quiver with long, low, creeping shivers, that curdled the blood like a congestive chill. I thought

"Of shapes that walk at dead of night,
And clank their chains and wave the torch of Hell around the murderer's bed."

I clung close to the sergeant, who was under the influence too, and was leaning over toward me; and in such affectionate manner we passed from under the trees and went stoutly up the walk to the house standing dark and grim in the background.

I lit my candle, and unscrewing the bayonet from the gun, made use of it for a candlestick, and stuck it in the open piano.

Ugh! How chilly the cold air felt inside the room; and how the old villain's eye glared from the portrait, to see me there again. I glared back, while the dip flared ominously, as if it meant to leave me in utter darkness.

"Don't leave me, Sergeant!" I pleaded huskily. "Stay with me! I swear I would rather go into heavy battle than stay here for ten minutes by myself."

"I would do so, old fellow, but I have all the guard-mounts to attend to. Keep a stiff upper lip! Two hours will soon pass by, and if I possibly can, I will be here before that time; besides, you won't be in the dark," he added as he turned to go.

"Do you think that candle will last two hours?" I inquired anxiously.

"Oh, yes. Good-by, and don't allow your imagination to run

away with you." And so saying the sergeant struck a match, lighted his pipe and left me.

I looked at my borrowed watch; it was just twelve—the mystic hour when spirits most do walk abroad; and here behold me in the old haunted house alone!

Alone! It meant more than at first appeared, when even the company of a dog would have been invaluable.

I tried walking on the porch, but I had an insane desire to go inside; so stepping across the sill, I entered the parlor. The candle was flaring and wasting away in the draught; the old cavalier never ceased to look at me with those fierce, questioning eyes, as if bent on draining every secret of my soul. I struck some chords on the piano and the reverberations came back, it seemed, from every chamber in the house. I began to feel uncomfortable. The candle did not fully light the great room with the little ghostly glare it shed, and in the distant corners, lying in shadow, mystical spirits seemed to congregate, pointing and gibbering at me.

> "Black spirits and white,
> Blue spirits and gray."

I grew so fancifully nervous that I went out in the open porch once more; and there I heard singular muffled voices up-stairs— voices as of women talking, it seemed to me. I turned cold, and back into the house I wandered in my restlessness, only to feel an added thrill as the eyes gleamed threateningly at me from the canvas. Again those sounds from the upper rooms, screams of laughter and—I could stand it no longer. Forming a desperate resolution, I grasped the candle in one hand, the musket in the other, and marched up the stairs. Each step woke a separate echo, and it seemed as if feet long since moldering in the grave were walking along the floors and ascending the back stairway and all the stairways at once, up into the gallery, while the high old clock stood like a spectre on the landing—I could swear that it was ticking. Nothing there. Through the front rooms—farther up, and I was appalled by a furious noise somewhere. I started to run, but knowing if I once took to flight I would never stop this side of camp, I retreated slowly. I saw nothing—not even a shadow. I turned to descend, and as I did so, I became conscious that something was following me. I could not hear it nor could I feel it or touch it; but my sixth sense told me the shape was there, dogging me close behind.

For the life of me I could not look around, so I kept on increasing my speed until I burst into the parlor with a rush, and then I turned and stood at bay. Nothing was there! Absolutely nothing; and though I felt sick I tried to laugh it off but could not. Once more placing the bayonet candlestick in the piano top, I sought the open air of the porch and then lighted my pipe.

O sweet and noble comforter, what a friend thou art in need! for as the smoke curled up from my lips it left in its wake sweetest and purest comfort. The bounding heart-beat became quiet and shaken nerves firmer, and I began to smile at the vivid imagination which made my ear take note of sounds that never smote the air. So I seated myself on the steps and watched the camp-fires which were fast smouldering out, leaving only one here and there to tell where a great army lay. And then I commenced to sing in a low voice our favorite air:

"All quiet along the Potomac to-night,
Where the soldiers lie peacefully dreaming."

"Hark! What sound was that! The piano—yes! the piano, as I live! There goes a running scale, and now a full crash!"

I could scarcely get my breath and my heart thumped like a trip-hammer. I rose to my feet and stood like one turned to stone, and then by a strong effort of will I went across to the window and looked in. Everything was just as I had left it, only the candle was nearly burned up, and there remained but a death wick hanging down to chronicle departed time. The old fellow on the wall was scowling menacingly, and thrilled me with horror. I went back to my place again on the steps, again relit my pipe and sought to restore my shattered equilibrium.

But my thoughts were far beyond my control and refused to be soothed by tobacco. They dwelt defiantly on every ghost story I had every heard. "Banquo" shook his gory locks at me with eyes that had no speculation in them, and I remember how Macbeth said: "It was a bold man that dare look on that which might appal the Devil." Old Mr. Hamlet, Sr., walked abroad with his slugged-up ear, rattling his "canonized bones hearsed in death." Clarence sat heavy on my soul; and all his fellow shadows struck as much terror to my heart as ever they did to Richard's. I hardly know whose ghost the Witch of Endor brought up, or whether somebody brought up hers, but I am pretty certain she was at her worst and favored me with her company.

I recalled lines that I was not conscious had ever lingered in my mind, nor do I remember now where I have ever met with them.

"We have no title-deeds to house or lands.
Owners and occupants of earlier dates
From graves forgotten stretch their dusty hands
And hold in mortmain still their old estates."

Shades of Erebus! How many of those hapless landlords of Chantilly might take it into their heads to stalk abroad to-night.

Here I was brought to my feet more quickly than if a whole salvo of artillery had been fired in the yard, for the crashing tones of the piano came again startlingly clear to my ear. There was no ground for a mistake now. I felt as if an icy hand encircled my heart; my head spun so I could not see. My brain teemed with horrid, hideous images, and skeleton hands seemed to grasp my throat. Rising to my feet with a spasmodic step like a sleep-walker, I turned toward the point from whence the sound proceeded. Yes! Yes! Clear and loud the piano keys were being touched by ghostly fingers! My eyes seemed to fill with blood; and then like a felon walking from the cell door to the steps of the gallows, I moved to the window and looked in.

I saw, or fancied I saw, a brilliant company in gorgeous array—but, oh horrors! Instead of smiling, beautiful faces, there grinned each skull with awful cavities where eyes and nose should have been, and every toothless mouth was gaping wide.

A dozen skeleton fingers suddenly pointed to me, and a burst of hideous laughter followed. By the expiring flicker of the candle wick it looked to me like a scene from the Inferno.

Unless I could break the spell I felt I should go mad; so with a last convulsive movement I raised my gun, levelled it and pulled the trigger. A burst of light—a stunning report—and darkness! A shriek! A long, loud shriek! I turned and fled!

How I reached camp I never knew. I suppose I ran myself clear out of breath. I reached camp without hat, gun, or cartridge-box, and speechless.

I told my tale by degrees to a believing audience—none doubted me.

That night the lieutenant went with a guard and examined the premises. In the garret they found half a dozen swallows that had just tumbled down the chimney, and so those mysterious noises that had frightened my brave predecessor and myself were explained. So far so good. And now must I spoil my ghost story —they generally all end as did mine, so I had better add a few words more before we turn in for the night.

In the parlor were found the remains of the candle, and on the keys lay a huge rat which my bullet had struck before it had embedded itself in the solid wood. The explanation now is easy.

Frightened when I started, I became wrought up to such a state of nervous excitement by the noises up-stairs and my own vivid imagination, that when the old rat sounded the keys of the piano by jumping on them, I believed that beings of another world were present in bodily shape. Nay, I actually saw them, for superstitious terror had made me as mad as any patient in Bedlam, and with my own voice ringing in my ears, I broke away from the scene.

You will say it was because I was a mere boy, but that had nothing to do with it—a boy can be as brave as a man. And every man is a coward in the dark.

"Sergeant," -said the colonel next day, "did you give a canteen of whiskey to Private Hunter yesterday?" No, sir—the canteen was only half full, and he was so scared."

Thereafter the doughtiest warrior would not stand guard at Chantilly, and it was left to be pillaged. The bad name it received remained with it.

In 1862, just after the Second Battle of Manassas, the fine old house was burned to the ground; and in a short while the forest was laid low by soldiers; and so faded from earth even the slightest trace of its site. The place that knew it knows it now no more—*Sic transit.*

How curious are the tricks of fate. There was one man of high rank in the Union Army, who in the days of Homer would have been the very incarnation of War. He was the Ajax of his legions, and led them in battle always where the harvest of death was thickest.

Knightly as Bayard himself and as brave as Ney, he was the ideal American soldier of the nineteenth century.

Reared and educated in America, after leaving his good right arm at Chapultepec in the far-away mountains of Mexico, he spent years in Europe, where he was the pride and delight of the Salon and the ornament of the courts of royalty. Coming back to his native land at the commencement of the Civil War, he at once assumed high command, and on the evening of September

1st, 1862, Gen. Phil. Kearny, charging through the oaks of "Old Chantilly," far in advance of his line of battle, with sword in hand and his bridle in his teeth, fell headlong, with a bullet through his heart, but a few steps from the historic mansion. I gazed long that gloomy evening upon his dead face, and wondered at the strange destiny that had brought him to die at the home of the Stuarts.

CHAPTER XI.

WINTER QUARTERS.

It was now the latter part of October, and though the days were bright, warm and sunny, the nights commenced to be very cold.

The troops began to build their winter quarters at Centerville, consisting mostly of double wall tents, well trenched on the outside. The inner arrangements were a fire-place or kitchen stove bought, begged or borrowed, and on each side of it were two bunks for sleeping, while the cooking utensils, which formed no unimportant part of our economy, were placed anywhere and everywhere, hanging on nails, pitched on the ground, or chucked under the beds. None but a woman can keep a kitchen clean, and we did not even try.

Our bread trough served us for two good purposes—used in the morning as a basin, then later for kneading the dough or beating up batter. The camp kettle was, however, the most important culinary implement and was put to a variety of uses. It stewed our hash, it boiled our coffee, it made the soup at noon and cooked our hominy, while on Saturday we boiled our clothes in it.

This was a most convenient arrangement and worked to our entire satisfaction. We were saved the trouble of rubbing and scrubbing our garments, and soon found that boiling would make them clean.

Washing gave us more trouble than all the rest of our vexations combined. It was far more distasteful to a soldier than even police duty; and when we could not get the task done for hire, we would be too often tempted to wear our underclothing until it fairly dropped off, and then apply to the quartermaster. One man could in this way use up enough apparel for a dozen. The waste was most lamentable and that at a time when we had need of the greatest economy, for it incurred a vast and useless outlay to the Government. In the European armies all these details are noticed and directed by the officers, and every soldier is required to take as much care of his clothes as of his musket and accoutrements.

The winter in camp was simply one of dreary monotony, yet our rations were abundant and there was no complaint—only a little grumbling at the listless existence. But men will grumble

7

anywhere outside of Paradise. The weather was very inclement and drills were entirely dispensed with. The men rarely left their tents; lying huddled up in their bunks like pigs in a hole of a hay stack.

The quietude of the camp was sometimes broken by a "free fight" between the two Irish companies. Whenever there chanced to be any contraband whiskey it was sure to show itself by warlike demonstrations in the men of companies I and G. Liquor, be it noticed, has different effects on different men. It induces a Frenchman to talk, and he shines out, the very embodiment of the graces. A German becomes gloomy and morose; an Englishman grows affectionate; four fingers of stone-fence whiskey will set an Irishman fighting as surely as St. Patrick was a gentleman.

At first the colonel would summon an armed guard to arrest the belligerents, and the whole brigade would be in an uproar. But he found it made bad blood between the contestants; and as the Irishmen never used deadly weapons, but fought in their own loved manner with sticks and fists fairly, he thought it best to allow them to settle their little family quarrels in the usual way. After the melee, wherein had been showered hard knocks on harder skulls,—for they followed the time-honored custom of Old Erin, and in a riot when they saw a head would always hit it,— the most pleasant and friendly relations would be resumed.

Wounds were washed, cuts bound up, bruises bathed, heads bandaged, and the late foes were better friends than ever and ready for another loving tiff. But the hero of them all was Jerry F——, of Company G, who was not unlike Spartacus the gladiator. No two could stand the weight of his puissant arm; no head was proof against that huge shillalah. As the hero of Ballenawhack was "cock of the walk" of Kinsale, so was he among his confreres.

> "He'd a blunderbuss too, of horse pistols a pair,
> But his favorite weapon was always a flail.
> I wish you could see how he'd empty a fair,
> For he handled it neatly, did Larry McHale."

Pick out of any thronged thoroughfare ten Irishmen, and you will find at least six honest men. They are the bone and sinew of our land. They rear our stately structures, build our great industrial works, develop our mines, and join heart and soul in our battles. What a happy, devil-me-care, laughter-loving fellow he is withal! In all the troops of the Confederates, there were none truer or braver.

CHAPTER XII.

THE RETREAT.

The winter of '61-'62 passed with nothing of note except that the Seventeenth enlisted for ninety-nine years, or for the war. We were now practiced in division drill, Longstreet being the only general who drilled by division. His crack command numbered fifteen thousand muskets and were all in splendid condition.

One day was so like another to us that we had to be told when Sunday came, for on that day there were no church-calling bells —no tolling chimes to mark the period of rest.

Occasionally a furlough would be granted to some exceptionally favored soldier fortunate enough to get up any kind of sickness, and we would see him start on his journey with a joy in his eyes and an envy in our hearts which strong words only could describe. One man actually fished for leave of absence by begging from Wash Milburn, the doctor's clerk, a package of ipecac, and had the nerve to take dose after dose. He fell off—grew white, looked indeed as if death had marked him for his own. He passed a rapid examination by the medical board, was granted a furlough, and sent on his way rejoicing.

Cold, blustering March was now at hand, and signalled his approach by blowing down nearly all the tents of the army, thereby becoming responsible for a frightful amount of profanity.

On the ninth of March, 1862, the whole army began its evacuation of Centerville. We had received orders to pack and be prepared to start at a moment's notice, while the news came that the enemy were moving against Centerville and Manassas in heavy force. An earnest hope was expressed by the troops that they yet might be ordered to remain and defend the breastworks upon which they had spent so much time and labor; but the packing kept on and soon every knapsack was filled to bursting. The various articles of comfort the soldiers had collected in camp were doomed to be left behind, for everything that the private in the ranks carried must be on his back.

The army had been paid off in the winter, and as there were a goodly number of sutlers in Centerville, the men purchased anything that happened to strike their fancy, finding that when

the winter was over their money was gone and their tents were
filled with any quantity of useless impedimenta.

Each soldier, though, loaded himself down, hating to leave anything behind to the enemy, and such a set of heavily-weighted
men were never seen before; they looked for all the world like
an army of porters, or rather buccaneers, who, having sacked some
town, were returning laden with booty. Some had immense
knapsacks bulging out ready to burst; others carried carpet-bags,
old valises and even camp kettles, filled with every imaginable
article that could be of no use, and lugged for many a weary mile
only to be thrown aside at last. One infantryman was seen with
a pack greater than ever peddler carried, and heavy enough for a
dray. A huge knapsack was on his back, his musket rested on his
right shoulder; his belt with cartridge-box and scabbard was
buckled around his waist, a frying pan, coffee pot and tin cup
were suspended by the straps of his knapsack, his haversack, with
three day's rations, hung over the right shoulder; a large writing-
desk was under his left arm, a dressed turkey was transfixed by
his bayonet and waved aloft in the air, while an enormous grain
bag, filled with everything he did not want, was dragged along as
a horse drags his cart, and so, snail fashion, he carried his house
on his body.

As the march proceeded, the heavy-laden began to unload.
First one thing after another was discarded, and as mile after
mile was traversed and heavier grew the burden, the more reckless they became, fairly strewing the route with clothes, cooking
utensils and provisions. But these household goods were not
lost, for the country people in the vicinity reaped a rich harvest and
laid in a large supply for future use.

The troops now, for the first time, discovered what marching
really meant, as day after day they kept up the long winding road
leading southward, with a steady, ceaseless action that soon broke
many down. The weather too was of the real March kind. It
seemed as if it snowed the first hour, rained the second, was
sunny the third, clouded up the fourth, hailed the fifth, rained
again the sixth, sleeted the seventh, cleared up beautifully the
eighth, and a hurricane the ninth, and froze everything solid the
tenth, thawed the eleventh, with clear starlight the twelfth.

The highways were in a woeful condition. Huge ruts seamed
the road where the artillery had passed; while the long train of
heavily-loaded wagons had made the way a mire through which

the soldiers toiled painfully in sullen silence—or muttered anathemas against the weather and mud.

At night, tired and stiff, we camped in some convenient woods, and using the axe remorselessly we soon had immense campfires blazing with a vigor and snap that sent warmth and joy to the marrow in our bones. A camp-fire is the delight of a soldier's life; it is the one soft place in his heart; and the larger it is, the happier is he. When its flames mount upward and entwine in loving embrace the very overhanging branches, when the coals lie hot and ruddy beneath, there is nothing he thinks he cannot dare of high emprise and valorous undertaking; but let them fade into dullness under an old green log, and he feels at once life is not worth a continental cent.

Given: some vast monarch of the forest lying prone on the ground, with a fence near by whose rails are dry enough to burn, and in a short while our soldier will furnish you a picture of contentment as he lies on his blanket for hours placidly smoking his pipe, gazing into the burning embers and ascending flames, and building goodness only knows how many castles in the air.

Our week's tramp brought us to Orange Court House, where the whole army camped until the sixth of April, when the march was again resumed, and this time toward Richmond.

Mud! Mud! Mud! Everywhere and on everything—real sticky Louisa County mud, which is dark red loam, as hard to get rid of as if it had been tar and turpentine. It was no fun, either, to trudge along with three inches of the sacred soil clinging to each foot.

The information that Yorktown had been attacked and the first assault upon Dam No. 1 had been repulsed with loss of the enemy, put new life into the army, so that it accomplished the distance in a very short time.

Richmond was thronged with soldiers, for every man would leave camp just as it pleased him, and the citizens, full of patriotism then, would go out to their highways and compel them—it did not require much force either—to come into their homes and partake of such food as did not often fall in their way. Those army men were a well-behaved set; and the city was as quiet and orderly as in its most peaceful days. The provost guard was not needed. A drunken soldier or two would be gathered in here and there, and no harm done, for those visiting were obliged to leave their arms in camp. Indeed, they had in the main the instincts of gentlemen, and were ever found more ready to protect and be polite to men and women, especially the latter, than to cause disturbance anywhere. The courtesy of the rank and file was ever a theme of strongest commendation; and looking back upon the peace and quiet of Richmond during those four years of war, it is a matter of no little comment that the inhabitants of a city always thronged with soldiers, at times surrounded by the whole army, should at a time of such intense excitement have retired to rest night after night feeling as safe as a child in its mother's arms.

House-breaking and robbing were unheard of; acts of violence were unknown; while the ladies felt as safe to walk the streets after dark, without fear of even a rude word spoken, as they did in the old days of peace.

The private's cap was raised as courteously from his head at a woman's greeting as was the greatest general's—and any word of kindness or sympathy met immediate response. It is only to compare this state of things with any large city of Europe—to show how remarkable it was; for the strong and well-trained police force of that restless, surging tide of human life cannot succeed in keeping down the acts of violence and murder that fill columns of its daily journals and throng its police courts and jails. To account for it fully, we must bear in mind that the rank and file of the Southern army contained a majority of the best and wealthiest in the land; men in most instances who stood socially higher than some of the officers who commanded them; and this had its effect—leavened the lump, as it were.

I have heard many ladies of Richmond, who gave much of their time to nursing the sick and wounded, say that in the hospitals, where men of every state, age and rank lay side by side, suffering, delirious and dying, they never heard or saw the slightest word or look that made them hesitate to minister to their wants.

Every soldier in the army owes a personal debt of gratitude to the women of Virginia, for sooner or later they were ministered to with the tenderest care when sick or wounded. In all the four years of the war no one ever heard of a woman being insulted in the streets of Virginia's Capital.

CHAPTER XIII.

IN THE TRENCHES AT YORKTOWN.

In March the brigade received orders to pass through Richmond en route to Yorktown. The men, already tired of the quarters, gladly fell into ranks. It was a scene never to be forgotten by any old Johnny who had cleaned his musket, washed his shirt and mended his rags to show off before les grandes dames of that city. It was one of those rare, lovely spring days, a relic of the summer, cut short by the waning fall, that, seeing its chance, edged in among the blustering days of March and beamed proudly in its sunny splendor.

The whole city was on the *qui vive;* for nearly all the Army of Northern Virginia were to file for the first time through its thoroughfares. Every one was astir—as if a herald had gone to each house, as they did in Rome during Caesar's triumph, and cried out:

"Come hither to see what none of you have ever seen before or ever will see again."

The windows, balconies and porticoes of Main Street were filled with the beauty and fashion of Richmond, and Richmond had the loveliest women in the world then. The side-walks were jammed with a vast enthusiastic crowd of old men, boys and girls, with here and there a hobbling wounded soldier, but no able-bodied civilians were among them.

Oh! but it was a gallant showing—invincible, we thought—as they marched in solid column down the roadway, a full brass band to each brigade, and a drum and fife to each regiment. On they came, Longstreet's corps in advance, stepping jauntily to the air of "The girl I left behind me."

As the Seventeenth reached the foot of Main Street near Rockets, to turn and look back was to have such a sight meet the gaze as the "Old Dominion" city never saw before.

As far as the eye could reach, for nearly a mile, came the Confederate Army of Northern Virginia in all its martial array.

The steady tramp of marching thousands to the measured beat of soul-stirring music, scintillating sun-gleams on burnished guns and glittering bayonets, the floating of banners, the waving of hats to the shouts of the multitude wrought into irrepressible ardor by the splendid pageantry, was a spectacle that photographed itself upon the memory of every bystander and all soldiers who witnessed it or were in the ranks that day.

We made a quick march to Williamsburg. "Magruder is in danger," flew from lip to lip and spurred the soldier on. We reached the old colonial town late in the night, and camped a few miles distant. A brief rest and then we took position in the trenches of Yorktown.

A more desolate, dreary, abominable place to camp and picket it would have been impossible to find in Virginia. Our duty was to guard the outer line of the trenches near Dam No. 1. The trenches ran along a low, swampy region of wet, sickly, yellow-clay soil, which held water as a sponge and stuck like a mustard plaster. The breastworks, thank Heaven! we did not have to build. That infliction at least was spared us, for Magruder's men had thrown them up, perfect in execution and design. They were fully six and eight feet high, and solid in construction.

The Seventeenth took position just on the left of Dam No. 1. Across the way, not three hundred yards distant, were the enemy's picket lines, and farther back were the heavy batteries of columbiads and mortars, regular mounted siege guns, whose thunderous roar could be heard for miles, and the scream of whose shells as they flew through the air was like the savage shriek of a demon ready to seize his prey. The guns gave us no rest by day, and startled us at night with spasmodic shots.

After sunset we expected an attack and were not allowed to drop out of ranks.

The first night it commenced to rain; not a rushing, driving rain, but a ceaseless, persistent, business-like rain, that gave no promise of letting up. In a few moments everything was wet through, and a shivering set of wretches stood in line with chattering teeth and cramped limbs, hugging their guns. It was pitch dark; not a gleam of light anywhere—and to make matters worse, the trenches soon became the bed of a torrent. Oil-cloths, overcoats and blankets were but sodden things, that soaked in the water only to let it distill into our chilled bodies beneath. No place to lie down, no fire to warm the well-nigh torpid form, no comfort in the dark but one's own thoughts; no hope but for the day to break. Like the weary watchers on a wrecked vessel, our only cry was, "Will the morning never come?" It seemed as if the light had left the earth forever, and those laggard hours, when we stood the whole night through without sleep, are now recalled as a frightful nightmare. Forced to stand all night on tired limbs, up to the knees in running water, and wet to the skin, proves how strangely wonderful is man's physical endurance.

Day broke at last, but the pitiless rain came down with the same resolute, dogged, never-stop style, as if intent on drowning both armies. Three solitary crackers apiece, washed down by a mouthful of dirty water, constituted our rations for breakfast. The rain kept on. The heavens above us seemed to frown with a leaden, angry countenance, as if we were responsible for this turmoil on earth and it was retaliating. Night came again, and we rose stiffened, cramped and trembling from our muddy holes. Three crackers again were given us, and then the relentless order, "Back into the trenches, men!" After that, another night of agonizing endurance and unutterable wretchedness.

Some smoked their pipes, others talked in low tones, and others still, in hideous mockery, tried to sing—sing, did I say? Those songs were like the hurrahs of the trembling boarders of "Dotheboy's Hall" over Mr. Squeer's coming back home—shuddering sighs with the chill on. All those voices ceased at last from sheer hopelessness. Every now and then would be heard a splash as some tired fellow's legs would give way under him and he would drop into the muddy water. Ever and anon would sound the warning notes of the look-out sentinels who were watching and peering into the inky darkness; for we had every reason to believe that another attack on Dam No. 1 would be repeated. The officers certainly looked for it every moment.

Once and only once was the situation varied.

A little after midnight a gun went off by accident, and half asleep, the whole line sprang to the parapet and blazed away in air. For half an hour a tremendous fusilade followed; every one loading and firing like mad, expecting the enemy would soon be swarming over the walls. But it was a false alarm. The pitchy blackness took the valor out of some, and frightened many half out of their senses.

In the day time an advance could be seen and was rather liked; but this firing alone in darkness, without being able to see friends, and worse still—enemies, had a quelling effect. However, each man loaded and fired as best he could, and when his musket would not go off, stood to set it a good example and went off himself. Certainly, had the enemy attacked, he might have carried the line easily, as not one musket in five would fire—the barrel being full of water.

Silence at last, and the color came back to cheeks that had paled, while all drew a long breath.

Blessings on the man who invented tobacco! Who can speak of its delights, its joys, its consolations like the soldier in the ranks! Who but he can know how the weary march is shortened; how hunger and cold are forgotten; how with a panoramic fidelity old scenes and old faces are reproduced by that great genie and magician, the little briar-wood pipe! Would I could immortalize you, O guide, counsellor and friend! in glowing verse and song, for you were the truest ally that ragged, tattered Johnny Reb could ever claim. Quartermasters might fail him, commissaries disappoint him, sutlers forsake him—but tried companion and faithful comforter, *you* were never, never missing to cheer and solace him.

We took those cherished pipes from our jacket-pockets—bosom friends they were—filled them with "The Soldier's Joy," a celebrated brand at that time, begged a light from a comrade if we had none ourselves, and then, like a touch of Prospero's wand, the scene would change.

"Look! How bright the lights! How beautiful the passing women! And that strain of music, how dreamily it flows into the slow, gliding waltz! How smoothly the couples float over the polished floor in rhythmic movement to the measured cadence! A glass of champagne! Here's to wives and sweethearts; and success to our Confederacy—another glass, old friend! And now excuse me!—for there she passes! Flowers in her hair, gleaming neck and arms! A glance, a smile—a happy flush upon her cheek. A stroll into the dimly lighted room, fragrant with exotics. How beautiful the face! How blue her eyes! How tender the lips! Gentle are the words of welcome, but—the pipe is out; the vision is gone, and you are nothing but a poor private, and the rain is pouring down and your teeth are chattering like castanets."

I said few slept, none restfully, but there was one exception. His eyes closed as peacefully, he slept as dreamlessly as if on a bed of down. In the Seventeenth was as gallant a son of "Old Erin" as ever fought the battles of other lands—Jerry, of Company G; of stalwart frame, and with a heart big enough for ten men, as gentle as a woman's and as tender as the one that beat in Bayard's bosom.

On many a march he would carry for miles the musket of a little fellow of Company A, whose willingness was greater than his strength.

That night in the Yorktown trenches, when the rain had made
a deluge of the place, he hunted up his little friend, leaned against
the parapet, opened his heavy overcoat, buttoned the cape close
around the chilled and shivering figure, and pillowed the tired
head on his breast; then throwing one arm across the boy he lit
and smoked his blackened pipe, while his charge, in the new-found
warmth and shelter, slept the whole night through.

Stiffened and almost numbed, hardly daring to move lest he
should rouse the sleeper in his arms, morning at last released
him from his vigil.

The clods of the valley were soon to rest upon that kindly
heart instead of human touch, and the sands of life were running
swiftly out; but ere then, in all the great round earth, no nobler,
tenderer deed was done.   Saints might stop to witness it—Recording Angels write it down: In the thousand and one incidents that my diary recalls of the Civil War there is none that
so touched me as the loving care that Jerry ever took of me, in
shadow and storm.   If his last resting place could be found and a
stone were planted to mark the spot, it should proclaim but one
inscription:

"The merciful obtain mercy."

As light routed darkness and established its sway, the scene
was not enlivening, and a bluer, more disgusted-looking tribe
could not have been found outside the Seventeenth Regiment.
They were too forlorn even to curse their untoward luck; and
could only wonder in a torpid, stupid way, wherein consisted the
glory of a soldier's life.

That morning we were relieved from duty; and returning into
the woods in the rear we built huge fires and disposed of the full
rations that were issued.   The sun even came out with his cheering beams, and the regiment, like a bedraggled game-cock after
a thunder-storm, dried its feathers, dressed its plumage, and with
crest erect once more, walked about in its own usual complacency.
Again the jovial song, light-hearted laughter and ringing voices
resounded in the ranks, and the heavy rations of spirits that were
distributed had no little tendency to bring this sudden forgetfulness to their minds.

I well remember that drink—it was the only one the Southern
Confederacy ever issued, to our company at least.

No attack was made at all; and only the siege guns kept up

their ceaseless firing; and as their range was entirely too high, we soon became accustomed to their noise.

It was a great mistake that McClellan made in not moving to assault Magruder as soon as he had his army, which consisted of 112,392 men, fit for duty. (Report on Conduct of the War, Part 1, p. 18.)

President Lincoln, with his usual clear-headedness, wrote to McClellan April 9th, 1862:

"I think it is the special time for you to strike a blow. By delay the enemy will gain steadily on you; that is, he will gain faster on you by fortifications and reinforcements than you can by reinforcements alone." (Ibid, p. 18.)

So with 112,000 men McClellan proceeded to build forts, sap and mine in his endeavor to drive 14,000 of Magruder's men.

McClellan, on the 5th of May, when he was ready to open his guns, found the place empty.

"The number of men comprising the Army of the Potomac on May 1st, 1862.

Gen. Staff, Engineer Brigade, Escort to Headquarters and Provost Guard	16,657
Second Corps, General Sumner	22,002
Third Corps, General Heintzelman	39,710
Fourth Corps, General Keyes,	39,561
Franklin's Division	12,448
Fifth Corps, General Porter	26,561
Army Corps, General Division	11,025
General McCall's Division	12,263
Total	179,999

"I hereby certify that the preceding statement was accurately compiled on June 20th, 1862.

"E. D. TOWNSEND,
"*Act. Adj. Gen.*"*

*Report on the Conduct of the War, Part 1, pp. 323-337.

CHAPTER XIV.

SHARPSHOOTERS AND SHARPSHOOTERS.

As the day was bright and sunny, myself and two companions, with Captain Herald at our head, started on a sharpshooting expedition. Our breastworks had been thrown up on the outer side of the woods; but about two-hundred yards in front stretched open fields for nearly half a mile, and then came a fringe of woods. Running just back of those trees were the enemy's breastworks; and in our front, about a hundred yards distant, was a solitary, isolated fort that we held with a four-gun battery.

Passing the outer row of rifle-pits, and disregarding the advice of the officer who commanded it, we commenced to creep on hands and knees through the swampy woods, keeping a sharp lookout. Suddenly we heard several faint reports; whing! whing! zip! the angry bullets flew over us. Sinking down at full length on the ground, and peering out with beating hearts for a sight of the hidden enemy, we could detect nothing; not so much as the rustling of a leaf.

"Shall we advance or go back?" whispered one of the party to the Captain.

"We will try once more; keep close to the ground and don't make any noise," he answered.

We crawled along some fifty yards farther, amid deathly silence, and then stopped to consider. We were now far beyond our last picket post, with no knowledge of the country, and no idea as to where the enemy's videttes might be. "It is foolish to go on," said the Captain, the most prudent of the number.

We felt the truth of his remark, still the situation had its charms. It was a strange feeling, half fear, half bravado, mixed with a good deal of curiosity, that restrained while it urged us on.

"Go back," said Common Sense, "you are doing no good, while running a heavy risk."

"Keep on," said Recklessness, "and see what will happen; 'nothing venture, nothing gain;' besides, what will your comrades say if you return without having fired a shot?"

So the Captain was overruled against his better judgment. Once more was heard the report of a rifle not far off, and Walter Addison, of Company A, called out quickly: "Get behind that log and look at the top of those trees," at the same time falling flat and peeping over the trunk in the direction of his extended finger. It needed no keen sense of sight to see what he was pointing out, for bright flashes of fire, followed by puffs of smoke, were issuing from the tops of the trees, not seventy-five yards distant. We all took careful aim and pulled trigger. Instantly the fire from them increased; bullets hummed around us like a raging swarm of bees; we started to load, when two or three balls, searching the covert about us, knocked the bark and splinters from the very log behind which we were lying.

"It is time to be getting away from here," sang out Captain Herald. "It's too d—— hot for me, and now every man for himself!"

Then, like rabbits that had been jumped by the hounds, we broke away and ran. If anything is calculated to increase a man's speed it is to hear solid lead tearing its way after him when he is on a home run. As we raced in to our own breastworks, one or two guns discharged therefrom threw us into mortal terror lest we should be shot by our own men. We could not cry out, for breath was gone; so it happened, when we reached the top of the parapet, we found our own soldiers kneeling with cocked guns on a ready. As we threw ourselves down, all exhausted and speechless, the officer said that with the noise we made in running to covert, the crack of the rifles, the whizzing of the cannon-shot, he felt sure that a storming party was about to attack our lines; furthermore, that in his front were the enemy's videttes, the celebrated "Berdan Sharpshooters," considered the finest shots in their army.

During the Peninsular Campaign, when we were in the trenches, this same organization kept us close within our works, hardly daring to lift our heads above the parapets. They were a full regiment, commanded by the colonel of that name, and composed of men picked from the Army of the Potomac for skill in handling the rifle. The North went into ecstasies over them, and the fugitive copies of *Harper's Weekly* which sometimes reached us abounded in complimentary wood-cuts of their achievements and prowess in the trenches before Yorktown—representing them, for instance, crowding us close to our works, and picking off Rebels with as much nonchalance and coolness as a farmer boy would blackbirds and mud-larks. Their arms were beautiful and costly pieces of heavy calibre; each rifle had its handsome leathern cover.

The men of the "Berdan Sharpshooters" received thirty dollars per month, and had no picketing to do; neither were they sent into actual engagements, nor yet subjected to any of the hardships which the infantrymen are obliged to undergo; their only duty being the extreme advance.

Some of these sharpshooters had holes dug in the ground close to our trenches, within which they had every comfort, while they kept a close and constant watch over us. We used to place a hat on a stick and lift it above the embankment just to see them put a bullet in it.

We lost in the Seventeenth, by these sharpshooters during our occupancy of the trenches, a sergeant killed, one private killed, and two wounded.

While at Yorktown the reorganization of the army was held by the privates electing their officers in accordance with an act of the Confederate Congress passed in 1861. It would have been better for the country could all those legislators who voted for the resolution have been blown high in air by some Confederate "Guy Fawkes." For this was the "Iliad of all our woes."

Before, we had good officers, proud of their position and zealous in the discharge of their duty—officers who laboriously drilled the men, knowing the value of good discipline. They had exacted implicit obedience, and of course were looked upon as martinets. When this reorganization act was carried out it was found—as might have been expected—only a source of demoralization; and all uncalled for as it was, set every lazy or ambitious musket-carrier to lobbying, begging and electioneering for the position of officer. By specious promises, infinite lying and servile mendicancy, some of the most worthless men in the army were placed in authority, sworn to let the soldiers have an easy time, and pledged, in other words, to relax all discipline, thereby destroying the efficiency of the volunteers. Many splendid officers were relegated to the ranks by this reorganization—demoralization—scheme, for, too proud to beg for votes, too true to their own sense of right, they stood aloof and watched how spurs could be won by a despicable play on the worst passions of men, rather than by bravery and military accomplishments. On such occasions, it has ever been the experience of the world, the unworthy are most apt to rise and ride into power.

Had the Confederate Congress but passed an act making valor and skill on the battle-field the sole and only medium of promotion, the Army of Northern Virginia would have been twice as efficient—but more of this anon.

This election foisted upon the Seventeenth several worthless officers whose names afterwards became bywords of reproach, ridicule and scorn.

CHAPTER XV.

THE FAT AND LEAN OF A SOLDIER'S LIFE.

Once more the regiment was ordered back into the trenches, and no sooner did we leave the works than the clouds gathered, the air grew dark and murky and it began to rain. It seemed as if the sky was one vast mill-pond with the sluice gate opened. The trenches, as before, became creeks and rivers, and our past experience was repeated. The same old fortitude had to be summoned; the same suffering borne.

At least one-fourth of the regiment succumbed; many caught violent colds, neuralgia and rheumatism, and were sent to the hospital tents. These, fortunate in escaping the trenches, if unfortunate in suffering pain and illness, were packed in an ambulance and carried some two miles to the rear, where a number of large hospital tents were pitched.

In one of these some four of us were placed on beds consisting of blankets spread upon the bare ground, with no extra covering and no pillows. We had much to be thankful for; we were not extremely ill as some were, lying tossing with fever, or shivering with chills as they rested upon the earth; while above all, the ground inside the tent was dry; and it was happiness to feel ourselves once more outside of a puddle of water. So the sick quartette lay curled up in their tent three whole days, under the care of the M. D. of the Seventeenth, Doctor M. M. Lewis, as grand a specimen of mankind as ever lived; a glorious man in every way; with a skill in his profession that ranked second to none, and withal, the handsomest man in the division.

The fourth day, when the Doctor visited on the rounds, he brought with him a gentleman whom he introduced to me as my uncle, and who was living only a few miles from Yorktown. The said relative was a bachelor of long standing, the possessor of a large plantation on the James, with scores of darkies at his command; and never was the sight of the "long lost father's" face more welcome to a son than was his to me.

I blessed my grandfather's memory for having such a son.

"Are you well enough to go?" asked the Doctor.

For answer, the erstwhile sick man jumped up and cut a pigeon-wing, which rather surprised that disciple of Esculapius, who had found me so weak a few minutes before that it was necessary to raise my head to administer medicine.

"Can I take my comrades?" I asked of my new-found relative. Well, he "reckoned so"—a whole company if I wanted, there was room enough, and rations for all. Whereupon three figures sprang from the blankets and had a private stag-dance all to themselves.

"A most wonderful cure," said the Doctor. "I must send you all back to the trenches!"

Four figures sank back simultaneously on the blanket, with a groan; four faces twisted themselves in contortions of intense suffering; four voices made themselves heard in tones of weak, yet bitter complainings.

Said one resignedly: "Well, I might as well die in the trenches as linger on here."

"Just my luck," groaned the second. "I never expected to go anywhere except into battle that something didn't turn up to prevent. No use trying to get to heaven, that I can see; I'd be sure to go the other way!"

"I was born unlucky," moaned the third. "If it rained mush it would find me without a spoon."

Meanwhile I just rolled over and over in anguish of soul.

"Well, boys, I hardly think that Yorktown will be surrendered if I let you go," said the Doctor; "however, let me feel your pulses!"

Four dirty paws, that had not felt water for three days, were pushed toward him, and four pairs of strong lungs stoutly held their breath in order to make each beat as slow and weak as possible. "Here—hum," he reflected. "Castor oil for number one." (Something like "dam" was heard to issue from the lips of number one.) "Blue mass to bring up the bile from number two's stomach." (A muttered exclamation from said number, to the effect that he had not had anything in that locality for a week past!) This caused my old uncle to grin and remark confidentially that he would soon fill it up. "Quinine to be taken regularly by No. 3." The alacrity with which the faithful promiser gave himself away to the Doctor was suspicious to any one who knew him intimately. "Strict diet for No. 4." A smothered exclamation, with the information that that had been the trouble with him all along, running off into a right good chuckle, was exhilarating in its influence on the whole party.

And so, with their prescriptions and sick furloughs, and hearts brimful of happiness, we jumped cheerfully into a light **wagon** and rattled along to our destination.

8

The plantation, situated on Swift Creek, turned out in honor of young "Massa" and his confreres, and they held a levee, from the head-waiter to the lowest field-hand, for the servants on old Virginia homesteads were wont to be more clannish than the family itself, and the return of any member "to the old place" was regarded as a special compliment to themselves, which they were in honor bound to reciprocate to the best of their ability. And only let the child of some "young missus" or "young massa" come on a visit, and the satisfaction in their beaming faces knows no bounds.

"Lor', now, you don't say this is Miss Mary's chile!" in tones of varied exclamations of surprise and wonderment from the older servants, while the young ones gazed wrapt. "Favors her now, don't he?" "Bless my soul, honey, I knowed yer ma! Haven't I tole you, nigger, what a pretty young lady she was?" The rest yielded glad assent, for the most valued traditions handed down around the cabin fires are of the family, of whom they are ever proud. Indeed, they consider their own standing in dusky society more or less impregnable, as they were owned by masters of long lineage and purses, while they refused association with those less favored.

However, money was of less importance in their eyes than family. To say, "I am one of Mass. ———'s servants," filling the blank with the name of the owner of some well-known plantation, with a descent from irreproachable ancestors, was for them equivalent to a coat-of-arms.

If one of the daughters of the house was anything of a belle, the smallest darky on the place, who stoned the cows, chased the geese, or jumped at a cent, could tell the name of the discarded lovers who had ridden hopelessly away; and discuss the favored suitor. A wedding was a most momentous incident in their lives, the memories of the grandeur of which was handed down to the third and fourth generation. The children of the family were always borne in mind, and the retainers were as faithful chroniclers of collateral relations and connections as the big family Bible.

Richmond society smiled amusedly in old ante-bellum days when it was told how a genteel-looking old darky had refused to occupy a pew with others of his color, because, as he said, he belonged to Chief Justice Marshall, and he was not going to demean himself by "sitting in the pew with any nigger whatsoever." But this jealousy of grade went farther down, and had a wheel within a wheel. On the plantation, for instance, there were as many stratas of society as ever existed in a city or the Queen's drawing-room.

First, there was the very *haut ton* of plantation aristocracy— the butler, who was ever a pompous old fellow, with nothing to do but serve the meals and wait on the table and act as his master's confidential valet; he was always well-dressed, inheriting the master's clothes, and he was ever most observant of ceremonious etiquette. Under him were various lackeys who received instructions and awaited his orders, regarding their course as quite collegiate. Then there was the head nurse, "Mammy," as she was always called—an elderly, important, bustling individual, who raised her mistress, and mistress's children, and from this high standpoint she was mistress of society.

The children she had nursed with such faithful devotion loved her next to their own mother; went to her in all their perplexities and joys, and poured into her listening ear all their youthful confidences; she called them *her* babies, *her* children, and they were hardly second in her heart to her own. She petted them, sympathized with them and scolded them by turns. The family treated her with deference, trusted her implicitly, and consulted her judgment, while her own race regarded her as some great prime minister.

Only second to her was the cook, generally as black as the ace of spades; always rotund, and supremely dictatorial. In her realm she was as absolute as Pluto, and had a tribe of assistants to do her bidding. She could be seen in front of the kitchen door in a huge splint-bottomed chair, on a warm, sunny day, with a flaming red bandana handkerchief coiled like a serpent around her head, giving directions to her scullions; or perchance deep in consultation with her mistress about the coming dinner. One peculiarity about the cook was that she never had a husband; like the imperial sultana, she had her connubial fancies, only they did not last long; so acknowledging no lord or master, she governed her kingdom in her own way. One other peculiarity she had—she permitted no children in her domain, and were they ever brave enough to enter its precincts, the dish-cloth they would afterwards find pinned to their clothes, by way of deep disgrace, served to remind the world in general that they had been out of their proper sphere and in forbidden quarters.

Still there would come propitiatory offerings in the way of horse-cakes, and cakes in the shape of many animals whose anatomy would puzzle the brain of Agassiz himself, thus proving the existence of a soft spot under the layers of culinary adipose, which it were otherwise hard to find; only let no one presume on such favors.

The coachman must not be forgotten by any means! He held his head high, you may be sure, and scorned to do manual labor. His horses were his delight and pride; the stable his kingdom; and sitting in state, clothed in all the majesty of livery, behind a pair of thoroughbreds, he was an object of unapproachable and reverential awe to every darky on the place, especially to the little fellows who coveted the coming honor, and whose very dreams, if they ever had any, were tinctured by the hope of it. These officials, high in office, with their wives and children, moved in the upper tendom. Their language was most pretentious, and they treated each other with exaggerated politeness; being especially fond of using long words, and never uttering a short one if they could find another of more extended syllables; and on the principle that familiarity bred contempt, the less they knew of its meaning the more respect they had for it.

The house-servants formed a second grade, visiting and associating among themselves; occasional intercourse with *la creme de la creme,*—not enough to make them too proud, however,—advancing them considerably in their own estimation. The dining-room servant and under-waiters, the seamstress, the chambermaids and young assistants, the vice-nurses under mammy belonged to this most genteel set. The footman, gardeners and the laundresses were still another layer in the strata; while all looked down with extreme disdain upon the "common niggers," as they termed the field hands, who, with their cottages away off from the house, never rotated outside of their own especial orbit. Any advances from these ranks were as strange as the bestowal of the baton on the private, the title on the commoner, for such things usually went by right of heredity.

Changed—all changed! The freedman has absorbed every element of those old Southern slaves, and if advanced to the dignity of voter and citizenship—our legislators and rulers withal—they yet have lost all their light-heartedness, the happy-go-lucky carelessness that made of them the jolliest race in the world. The old masters, as if a heavy responsibility were taken from them, would not reshackle a single wrist; rather do they make each sable brow welcome to its furrows of care, its anxious lines that come with the new existence. But for all that, it is with tender memories of those olden days that we linger over the past, just

because it is so completely dead, perhaps. Four generations of
these sons and daughters of Ham have lived since the war, and
but a remnant of the old plantation race is left; but it speaks well
for former masters, hardly-judged as they were, that in a moral
point of view the negro has seriously deteriorated; few understanding the meaning of honesty, much less its practice—nor the
value of an oath, while the marriage bond is a rarity, comparatively speaking; and above all, the former tie that bound the two
races in such affectionate relationship has weakened into self-
interest, suspicion and enmity. Yes! The old type exists no
longer; they fill the unmarked graves in the plantation-burial
ground; and take them all in all, we ne'er shall see their like again.

The plantation we were visiting was a large one and worked
nearly three hundred slaves. It looked like a village, with its
barns, granaries, stables, corn-houses, tobacco-houses, wheel-
wright and blacksmith shops, cotton-houses, store-houses, spin-
ning- and weaving-houses, mansion, outbuildings and long rows of
cabins, each with its small garden in front.

The house was filled with servants who did nothing but get into
each other's way, bask in the sunshine, or huddle around the fire
if it were cold. When asked about their separate duties, one
said: "I combs Massa's head;" another, "I rubs Massa's feet at
night"—and so on through. One had no need to pick up a handkerchief, for a half dozen pair of hands stood ready to perform
that service.

What a change from the watching and waiting in the trenches
to the freedom of a bachelor-home. Four privates no longer;
they lived and moved, gentlemen; nay, barons, princes, for they
were ready to over-rate themselves, reveling in new dignity. How
they kept the darkies flying on errands! What roaring fires they
had in those wide chimneys, which held nearly a cart-load of
wood! What dinners they ordered—"Help yourself to everything in the house," the most philosophic of relatives had said.
"Command anything the place affords, for if you do not, the
Yankees will in a short time."

And so we did our very best, and made valiant efforts to crowd
a bushel of food into a peck-measure stomach. Old hams, sweet
as sugar, oysters, chickens, fish, wine,—Ah well! Words are so
weak. We considered it only a duty to quaff the cup of pleasure,
for as the gentle Anacreon has said:

"Death may come with brow unpleasant,
May come when least we wish him present,
And beckon to the sable shore,
And gravely bid us—drink no more."

A week passed by; a week filled with such pleasant memories that often, months afterwards, when rations were scarce and the commissary absent, we would go over the old bills of fare and try to forget hunger in a Barmecidean feast.

A week—one short week—and then came news of a contemplated retreat the next morning. A courier galloped up from the colonel with orders to join our companies on the retreat, if well enough. So with sad hearts we packed off into bed that night, thinking with Mickey Free, "what a cruel thing it is to tear ourselves away from the best of living, with the run of the house in eating and drinking."

The dawn had hardly broken when our host and kinsman came in with a lighted candle and roused us in a hurry. He was one of those nervous, fidgety men who never knew how to meet an emergency, but always lost presence of mind and ran from it.

He had determined to retreat, and as no argument or expostulations nor reasonings could move him, retreat he did. On seeing how fully bent he was upon his course—leaving an estate with all its adjuncts, well stocked with cattle of all kinds, utterly uncared for, he by reason of his age a non-combatant, his departing guests determined to help him and retreat with him.

Nothing so delights the soul of a private as tearing down and pulling up. "Ate," the destroying goddess, should have been his divinity. He follows in her train most naturally and devotedly.

After breakfast, three four-horse wagons, one cart, one two-horse carriage and two saddle-horses were brought around to the door; then, as the keys were missing, drawers were broken open, trunks knocked in and the contents turned upside down on a fast gathering pile; wardrobe-doors were broken, beds tumbled up, pictures unswung and leaned against the wall, books taken from shelves, while from the attic, where stood a large linen-chest, counterpanes, sheets, pillow cases, all the cherished hoardings of long years, articles of attire worn by generations now passed away, barrels of old letters and old family Bibles, all helped to make a heterogeneous heap that was a marvel to behold. Lastly came the wine closet, formed by the sloping eaves of the Dutch-built house, close under the roof. Bursting open the door, the cobwebs were brushed away and the precious liquor carried down into the porch. This proved a veritable bonanza of its kind. There was a barrel of old cognac, a barrel of peach of old vintage of 1800, a barrel of apple-brandy, any number of bottles of sherry, hundreds, it seemed; several flat stone jugs of Holland gin, a half dozen or so demijohns of whiskey, and several kegs of home-made wine—the latter, however, were absolutely scorned.

"By George!" said one of the number, surveying the collection, "I wouldn't change places with the commander-in-chief!" And so he continued, drawing up a pitcher of old brandy, "Here's to a safe fight through the war, a rich wife at the end of it, and a long life to enjoy her money."

"No trouble about that," answered another, sipping his cognac with the air of a connoisseur; "after the war is over so few men will be left alive we will be able to pick and choose as we please."

But these pleasant speculations suddenly came to an end as our host entered, with an aspect of perfect dismay and profound despair.

"The darkies have all run away," said he, "and are hiding in the woods!"

"Impossible!" was the rejoinder, in various tones of exclamation and surprise.

We went out and surveyed the scene. They could be seen dodging in the bushes, and when called would not answer.

In their cabins the fires were still burning, but men, women and children were nowhere visible.

Doubtless they would never have left the old plantation if undisturbed, but the thought came in their untutored minds that they were to be carried away down South and sold, and so they determined to stick to their homes. To be sold to work cotton down the Mississippi was their idea of all that was hateful in life.

So we offered our services and soon had everything taut. There was enough to fill the wagons to the top and leave something over—kitchen utensils, feather beds, pictures, books, barrels of flour, bags of meat, jars of pickles, dried beef, barrels of cider and vinegar, two hundred hams, corn, oats, household linen, trunks, lard, boxes of pork,—anything and everything!

The cart carried most of the liquor; the balance being smuggled in the different vehicles; none of this was left behind, not so much as a drop.

At this juncture two negro men and one woman put in an appearance and volunteered to go with the expedition; and of course they were accepted.

Everything being ready for departure, we soldiers held council of war to decide whether it were more expedient to return to the regiment or accompany the wagons; and in solemn conclave it was deemed advisable under the circumstances to keep on a little way and join the command when its whereabouts were found. Other decision than this would have required more virtue and patriotism than any private possessed, hence we mounted the wagons, found soft places, gave a "hurrah" that caused many a dusky head to be pushed through the bushes, and the cavalcade started.

An imposing train—the carriage leading the way, the wagons piled high, we perched on the topmost peaks; the cart following, the led horses hitched thereto and bringing up the rear.

Yes, the start was imposing! Like Massena, we were obliged to retreat, but like him, too, we were hauling off with flying colors, munitions of war and all the baggage and commissary stores.

The commander was somewhat proud of his caravan and his military tactics, and little suspected—good, easy man—the trials, temptations and dangers of traveling two hundred miles (the retreat was to another plantation on the other side of Richmond) and through an army with such tempting freight as that wagon-train contained. But it was decidedly imposing, for all that.

Reverse the picture twelve days later, and witness the arrival. Two thin horses that could hardly drag their limbs along, pulling at a two-horse wagon, only because there was nothing in it to pull except a feather bed that had in some unaccountable manner escaped the general wreck. Teamsters, negroes, soldiers, all had left when the brandy gave out; the latter departing within three days, never having tasted water in all that time. As we made it a point to treat every Confederate soldier we met, the barrels, casks, demijohns, and bottles were soon empty, then—not before —we joined our regiment.

As for my uncle, considerably poorer than when he started, and deserted by his command, he sold the remaining stock for a mere song, and so reached the end of his journey.

The family group were drawn up to receive him, and exclaimed, as the truth burst upon them—in sorrow, not in anger:

"What, all! This all! Negroes! Stock! Furniture! Liquors! Everything! All gone!"

Yes, too true! One rickety team and one feather bed were all that was left of the household effects of one of the finest plantations in Virginia.

CHAPTER XVI.

"RUNNING THE BLOCK."

It was now May, with all the budding loveliness and delicate beauty of this sweetest month of the twelve. The season was, however, far advanced this year, and had rather the warmth and maturity of June.

The army lay encamped around Richmond, recovering from the fatigue of the toiling march from the Peninsula. They were in the best of spirits, too, for the affair at Williamsburg had a cheering effect upon the troops, and their morale was never better.

The First Brigade, with rare good luck, had pitched their tents in a pleasant grove, at whose foot ran a clear stream of water, while lower down was a large branch affording ample means for bathing, the greatest of all luxuries to a soldier, and indispensable from a sanitary point of view.

Here for two weeks we remained in a state of positive happiness; rations were abundant and of good quality, a half pound of meat, hard-tack, coffee, sugar and beans; and there were no drills except dress parade, and an occasional practice by the company in skirmishing. The days were spent in perfect abandon, lying on our backs in the shade under the trees, and whistling for want of thought. Then again new uniforms had just been issued to us—good, serviceable gray pants and jackets, with metal buttons, also coarse gray shirts and drawers, yarn socks and brogans.

We had long past ceased caring for dress, and that man was brave indeed who would essay a white shirt and collar in camp. Questioned in every conceivable manner, ridiculed, jeered at by every one he met, made the butt of a thousand witticisms, in sheer desperation he would be forced to remove the obnoxious garments and return to the primitive gray and check. The laughter-loving, fun-loving army, like all institutions, had strong opinions of its own, and a code of fashion which was as unalterable as the Medes and Persians. Any gray of the ranks who in camp aspired to cast his chrysalis and bloom into a butterfly might as easily have stormed a fort alone as defied those mighty weapons of raillery and ridicule. Such a simple thing as a tall beaver hat once came near throwing the brigade into fits; such an article as an umbrella would have raised a regular cyclone of wrath and doomed its unfortunate possessor to an early grave, provided banter and satire could have killed him. And we all remember —oh, how tenderly, as we cherish all such memories of Stonewall Jackson!—how when he once donned a showy new uniform which had been presented to him, brave with stars and gilt, and gone outside his tent, his men opened upon him with such shouts and exclamations of amazement and wonder that he who never flinched under the deadliest fire, who would have led the forlornest hope without a tremor, flushed, pulled his hat over his eyes, reentered his quarters, and when next seen wore the old rusty, faded gray, with its missing buttons and its gilt tarnished almost black by sun, rain and storms.

This spirit was not confined to the army by any means; citizens were sometimes as freely criticized as soldiers in their camps. No matter how hard it rained or snowed or hailed, any man who effeminately ventured out under an umbrella was invited by every little boy and every soldier to "come out of it," asked anxiously about his health, or how long it took for water to dissolve him.

A shining new overcoat, showing by its length its recent make, for such was the new style of cut, was ever greeted with "Mister, I see your feet!" While a gaily colored necktie, a conspicuously displayed handkerchief, or any article of attire calculated to attract attention, invariably paid the penalty. Citizens were the soldier's own *piece de resistance,* his to jeer, to laugh at, to comment upon whenever he passed his little jokes around, and be sure he never hesitated to say behind their back what he greatly preferred to say to their faces. Next in order was the quartermaster, or boom-proof, department, upon which was launched volleys of running fire; and woe to any one—citizen, quartermaster, commissary or cavalryman—who took offense thereat; it was all that was needed to fill the adversary's cup of happiness to the brim; then, for the nonce, better for the poor soul had he ne'er been born.

Of course, when visiting Richmond, the soldiers made their toilets as carefully as the Simple Simon dons his Sunday suit to go to meeting with his Mary Jane; cleaning and furbishing, polishing and beautifying generally, but not the slightest display of vanity or fashion was ventured upon.

While in camp we witnessed for the first time a "drumming-out." Two soldiers who had deserted were caught, tried and sentenced to be "drummed-out" of their regiment. The brigade to which they belonged was drawn up in line, as if upon dress parade, the ranks being in open order. The adjutant advanced along the line until reaching the center. He faced to the front, stepped forward several paces, halted, saluted the colonel, then, turning to the regiment, took a paper from his sash and proceeded to read the charges and specifications against the accused; after which came the findings of the court martial. Sheathing his sword he retired; and from the left of the line the two prisoners were marched twice up and down the extended ranks, a guard on either side, with a drummer and a fifer in front playing "The Rogue's March."

One of them, a young fellow, seemed to feel the shame of it keenly. He hung his head and the hot flush and deadly paleness alternated on his face. The other brazened it out, and proved himself of such hardened fibre that disgrace, if he felt it, made no outward impression.

The heads of both were closely shaven, and though their appearance was ludicrous in the extreme, not a smile was seen along the entire ranks. It seemed worse than a funeral and more solemn, for it meant the burial of manhood and self-respect. After they had been marched up and down twice they were brought back to the center, halted, and, branded in their souls as it were, carrying each his stigma, were permitted to go their way.

This proved the first and last instance of "drumming-out" that ever occurred in our army, for such kind of punishment met with so little favor from officers and men that it was universally condemned. This unexampled public degradation, they reasoned, would kill all self-respect, and in nine cases out of ten ruin a man's future entirely. No gallant conduct or desperate bravery in the field could ever restore the honor that was lost. Dead to all incentive, utterly paralyzed to all exertion, the man would be sent adrift in the world, about as well ticketed to moral destruction as he could well be; for when you break a man's spirit and take all hope away, you do your very worst for him, both in this world and the next. It is all over with him.

Then, again, men were too scarce to be turned out of the army to make citizens, perhaps criminals, or both—or worse yet, deserters to the enemy, thereby increasing their strength just in proportion as ours was weakened.

The bullet and barrel shirt were substituted.

Orders now came to move the brigade nearer to Richmond, and with many a regretful sigh we left the pleasant grove, and after a few hours' march, pitched our tents in an open field about two miles from the "Seven-hilled" city.

The old routine of camp existence was only varied by running the blockade into the city. This was no easy task, as the cordon of guards enveloped the place and picketed every road, with strict orders to stop every soldier without a pass and send him back to his regiment. There, in the enforced solitude of a guard-tent, which on a warm summer's day was only a little less hot than the furnace-room of a steamboat, he could spend days bemoaning his sins, or rather his bad luck, for the former implies contrition, and in this case the offender only wanted the chance to try again. The truth is, it required sharpness, good fortune and address all combined, to avoid detection, and even after a soldier had reached the city, it was a jump—as the old saying is—"from the frying pan into the fire." The provost guard patrolled the streets, and woe to any poor soul who fell into their clutches; he was ignominiously hurled into Castle Thunder for the day, and afterwards forwarded to his company; there his arrival was signaled by derisive cheers from his comrades, who, having once been caught in the same trap, were delighted to have others in like predicament.

The soldiers sometimes wrote their own passes and countersigned them with the name of the colonel and generals. But that ruse failed to be effectual, for officers well versed in all the wiles of soldiers' strategy, as well as detectives who could tell at a glance whether or not the countersigns were genuine, scrutinized each pass with as much care as an expert does the signature of witnesses in a disputed will case.

On one occasion two of Company A (myself and comrade), with anything but tender consciences, lay awake at night trying to devise some plan that would obtain free ingress to the city, keep us unmolested while there, and bring us safely out. The result was, that after so many hours spent in sifting the pros and cons, it settled down to a single, plain, stubborn fact, that unless we could get the bona-fide signatures of the general commanding, all efforts would be in vain. That was a bright idea, surely, as bright indeed as the young rodent in the fable, who moved in a congress of rats, "that the cat should be belled." So with us it was who was to "bell the cat," and how?

We drew straws for the unlucky one of the two, and Walter Addison drew the short straw, and was thereafter left to his own devices; and from the depths of down-reaching ruminations, which he feared would unsettle his brain, evolved the following letter:

"My Dear Aunt:

"As requested, I hereby send you the autograph of our Commander-in-chief, General Johnston."

Then, going boldly to his tent, he asked the orderly for admittance, for with General Johnston the private could often obtain an audience when officers high in rank were kept in waiting. The soldier handed the General his letter, who with one quick glance at his petitioner, seized his pen and wrote his name at the bottom. To salute and get out of the tent was the work of a second; and then the young rascal ran as fast as his legs could carry him to his confrere in camp. Together in banded iniquity, we rubbed out the words in pencil and inscribed others, so that the paper read:

"Pass in and out of Richmond, at will, the bearer and friend for two weeks.
                                    "J. E. JOHNSTON,
                                 "General Commanding."

On that pass we went in and out, and out and in, till the very stones in the road knew us; so virtue is ever its own reward.

However, emboldened by success, we overdid the matter, and remaining in the city on a regular visit of several days, were confined in the guard-house for nearly a week. But we kept our secret and our precious piece of paper.

Our rations for the month still continued good and wholesome; a pound of flour, half a pound of bacon, a quarter of a pound of rice, sugar and coffee, with now and then an allowance of beans and onions.

The health of the men was excellent, the discipline of the troops perfect; and the army had a profound confidence in General Johnston. No private soldier in the ranks feared for the result in the impending struggle which all knew was close at hand.

CHAPTER XVII.

THE BATTLE OF SEVEN PINES.

Toward the last of this month (May, 1862), a bolt like that hurled from Jupiter's hand burst so suddenly and unexpectedly that it startled, as with an electric shock, the people of both sections, and filled the graveyards and hospitals with dead and dying.

To give the reader an idea of the mighty events that had shaped themselves in this dangerous fashion, I will present a brief outline of the events that had happened up to this time.

After the affair at Williamsburg between McClellan's advance and Longstreet's rear-guard, the Yankee army followed Johnston in a leisurely manner toward Richmond until it reached the Chickahominy River, when McClellan divided his legions; a step which nearly involved its destruction. The right wing swung around toward the north, striking the Chickahominy at New Bridge, directly in front of Richmond. The left, keeping to the south, reached the river at Bottom Bridge, thirteen miles below, and camped in that vicinity on May the twentieth, 1862.

The bulk of the Rebels were at Mechanicsville, a little village about five miles from Richmond, and were easily driven back by a simple shelling. On the 21st a Yankee division crossed the Chickahominy, occupied the high ground, and made two reconnaissances, one reaching below the Seven Pines to within four miles of Richmond. The rebels were nowhere found in force, and no traces of defensive works were discovered.

The two corps of Keyes and Heintzelman were sent across the river to take up their position near Seven Pines.

Johnston in his retreat had neglected to tear up the railroad from Richmond to Pamunkey. He had indeed partially destroyed the bridge by which it crossed the Chickahominy, but by the 26th of May the road was in operation to the river, and the bridge was nearly reconstructed. There was no military reason why McClellan should not have crossed the Chickahominy and united his forces and fallen upon Richmond with his whole strength, but with his superb army of over 100,000 he greatly over-rated the number opposed to him.

The entire Confederate force only showed 54,000 men all told. He let the opportunity to take the rebel Capital slip.

On May 28th the army of McClellan was thus posted; the corps of Heintzelman and Keyes were on the west side of the Chickahominy, massed checker-wise for the distance of six miles along Williamsburg road.

The stronger corps of Sumner, Franklin and Porter, forming the right wing, were stretched some eighteen miles along the east bank of the river. The two wings formed an acute-angle triangle of unequal sides, the apex being at Bottom Bridge. The distance from center to center of the wings was barely five miles, but between them there was the Chickahominy, across which there was then no practical passage except the Bottom Bridge. If the left wing of the Northern army was assailed in force, the right wing could only come to its aid by a march of over twenty miles, which, in the condition of the roads in the springtime, could not be made with artillery, and certainly not under two days. (See General Johnston's Report; General McClellan's Report.)

For a hostile commander with anything like an equal force, two courses were open. He might throw himself upon the weaker left, with hope of annihilating it before assistance could be obtained from the other wing, or he could assail the extremity of the right wing, threatening its weakly guarded line of communication with West Point.

General Johnston, at the end of May, tried the first and most obvious plan, and failed in his design by mere accident.

General Lee, a month later, essayed the second plan and succeeded.

On May 30th General Johnston learned the military position of the enemy. He made the great mistake of supposing that one corps instead of two was across the river, and supposed that he had but twenty thousand to deal with, whereas the actual number was something over thirty thousand men.

The attack was to be made with the four divisions of Huger, Smith, Longstreet, and D. H. Hill, numbering about fifty thousand.

During the afternoon and night a violent storm swept over that region. The channel of the Chickahominy was already full to the brim, and the stream, swollen by the rain, would have prevented any aid being sent from the right wing to the left.

The attack was to be made by the four divisions simultaneously at day-break on the 31st of May. The storm delayed the movement of the troops, but by eight o'clock Longstreet was in position waiting for Huger to come up, but he did not make his appearance. Soon after noon Hill began his attack. Casey's division of Keyes's corps was three-quarters of a mile in advance of the Seven Pines; its pickets being thrown a third of a mile farther up toward the edge of a wood.

The Confederates burst through the screen, forced back the pickets to the entrenchments, where a short stand was made, but Longstreet was now pressing upon the Northern center and left; and Rodes's Alabama Brigade charged. After an hour and a half of stubborn resistance, the Seven Pines was abandoned with all Casey's division camp. The Yankees fell back to a belt of woods, where Heintzelman succeeded in rallying most of the men of the two divisions, who formed a firm front and poured in a fire so deadly that the assault was checked.

Night was now coming on and the Federals fell back a mile to their entrenched camp, unmolested.

Meanwhile the battle was going on with desperate fury a mile away, and McClellan, on the opposite side, directed Sumner to cross over on the two pontoon bridges he had just constructed, and take part in the fight. The river had begun to rise and the bridges were almost impassable, many of the timbers being already floating. After several hours of hard work, Sedgwick's division succeeded in crossing over the shaking bridge, and dragging his artillery by hand through the swamp, he arrived just in time to save the left wing from utter rout. He made a vigorous charge late in the evening and arrested the Southern advance. General Johnston being wounded about this time, all offensive movements were summarily stopped.

After Johnston was disabled he was succeeded by General R. E. Lee.

Huger's failure to come up lost the day.*

On the 30th of May, early in the morning, Addison and myself were detailed to go to Richmond, with strict orders to return that night. About noon it commenced to rain—a regular pour, filling the streets and rendering the crossings nearly impassable. We waited patiently for some rift in the clouds, until the lamps were lit, shining dimly through the blinding rain; and then, seeing how

---

*The Official Records state McClellan's loss as 800 killed, 3,627 wounded, 1,222 missing; in all, 5,739 men.

There was no official loss on the other side published. Longstreet reports the casualties in his command near 3,000; Smith says his division suffered 1,233; Hill probably lost 2,000—which would make Johnston's fully 6,000.

useless was the hope of any cessation, we started upon our journey campward; but hardly had we gone several squares before the storm became so violent that we were obliged to seek the Monumental Hotel for shelter. There we waited until after ten o'clock.

A large crowd of officers were sitting around the big table in the center of the room, criticising and discussing the conduct of the war, as every man, woman and child thought it their first special province in life to do. If babies could only have talked about that time, they would have deemed themselves fully up to the occasion.

While each had his own pet idea on the subject, all agreed that the present rain would effectually put a stop to military operations for days to come; for it would flood the streams, render the roads impassable for artillery, wet the ammunition, and prevent the moving of trains. All this sounded just as pleasant to the poor fellows who cherished an antipathy to having their heads blown off by a shell as a reprieve to a gallows-bird. So we were in a pleasant frame for listening, when an old officer, with a flowing white beard, came up to the party and gave his views upon the subject—views which impressed his listeners all the more, because they were recognized as the result of accurate information and solid judgment.

"The Chickahominy," he said, "rises in the swampy uplands about twenty miles northwest of Richmond, and flows about fifty miles parallel to, and nearly midway between, the James and York. The operations of McClellan embrace that portion of the stream from Bottom Bridge on the south, where it crosses the Williamsburg turnpike, to Malon Bridge, fifteen miles farther, at which point it is traversed by the Fredericksburg Railroad. Richmond lies nearly in the center, and about six miles distant from the stream. At this section the river flows through a wooded swamp a few hundred feet below the level of the surrounding country. In dry weather the stream is a mere rivulet, but a moderate shower fills the channel, which is about a dozen yards wide and some four feet deep; while a continuous rain floods the swamp and overflows the adjacent low-lands. These bottoms are intersected and seamed with deep ditches, and even when not overflowed, are so soft as to be impassable for cavalry and artillery. The stream could only be crossed on bridges, with here and there fords passable only in dry weather."

9

"Then we hardly need fear an immediate attack, think you, Colonel?" asked one of the group.

"Oh, no. It would be an impossibility at present," replied the officer; "for this spring of 1862 has been unusually rainy, and the channel is not only full to the brim, but the swamp and bottoms are all flooded,—any shower can do that now. Infantry might possibly pick their way through the swamp, but horses would sink to their girths and artillery trains to their axles."

"Could not bridges be put up?" queried some one.

"Not readily," was the answer, "for it would be necessary to build them above the level of the highest floods, and provide them with long approaches through the swamps; hence we can easily understand that this narrow Chickahominy is a greater obstacle, with its bordering swamps and mirey lowlands, than a broad river might be, across which forces could be carried in boats, or over which a pontoon bridge could be thrown in a few hours.

"And so, gentlemen," added the speaker, as he slowly lighted his pipe and was about to walk away, "we may surely make our minds easy on that score, for a while at least."

We eagerly listened to every word, and discovering the lateness of the hour, now rose to go. The tempest was at its height, but further dalliance was impossible; so buttoning our overcoats tightly, we set off for camp. It was as dark as pitch, but traveling along a broad turnpike one could not well be lost. We, however, plunged in mire up to our knees, with a big lump of mud on each foot and a stream of water pouring from each hat rim straight down the backbone beneath it. It was not a pleasant walk,—we had known better,—but after all, is there not a kind of enjoyment in breasting the elements? An indescribable exhilaration, which lingers in our natures as a faint trace of savage ancestry,—the wild man, not the monkey. Perhaps so; at any rate the suggestion can go for what it is worth.

About midnight we reached camp and by instinct, for we had no other guide, found our tents. Wrapping up in a blanket, we lay down on the muddy ground, with the last sweet thought that the deluge would put a stop to drills, parades and battles, and permit us to sleep the next day in peace.

But it seemed as if our eyes had scarcely closed in slumber before the camp was rudely awakened by the light of swinging lanterns and the voice of the sergeant crying out: "Get up! Get up! Put on your accoutrements, pack up your knapsacks and fall in right away!" From without came the warning drum, beating the long roll. We had no light, and groped about as best we could; but in five minutes we had packed up, and were feeling for our places in the forming line. By this time the driving rain had sobered down into a gentle drizzle.

Soon the ranks were established and dressed; and the ordnance sergeant, coming along, distributed by the light of his lantern sixty rounds of cartridges to each man; forty to go in his cartridge-box, which was all that they could hold, and the remaining twenty to be placed in his haversack. This looked like business. Following in his footsteps came the commissary sergeant, putting in each soldier's haversack three days' rations.

Yes, we were in for it now! That, every soldier knew.

Our work was all cut out and there was nothing left for us to do but face the music.

Thus with the knowledge came the thought into every soldier's mind, "Will I be alive this time to-morrow night, or will I be lying stark and stiff, with my sightless eyes blindly staring toward heaven? If I should come out, will it be unhurt; or with a slight wound, enough to give me a furlough and send me away rejoicing? Or"—dreadful thought—"will the leaden missile shatter my bones, tear through my yielding flesh, take from me a limb and send me maimed through life, or lay me on a bed suffering, there slowly to linger unto death?" It was an interesting problem which he was mentally computing, and it took all the man's philosophy to enable him to wait for the answer. And it was not altogether a selfish one, either; the deepest sting ofttimes is in the thought that others suffer in his misfortune or his death— others whose happiness is dearer to him than his own.

It is only by lying amid danger, being in battles again and again, passing through a score of skirmishes, scouting,—a vidette in an unknown land, when

> "Death rides in every passing breeze
> And lurks in every flower,"—

that the soldier becomes utterly fearless and holds his "taking off" in indifference, if not in disdain. We had not yet reached that point, and so when the brigade, in obedience to the order, swung itself to the right and struck the Williamsburg road, there was no reckless sound of voices or laughter, but a solemn, thoughtful silence. The marching was awful; several small streams that crossed the road, now swollen by the torrent into rushing creeks, we had to ford; some of them were breast-high, and we held our cartridge-boxes and haversacks way above our heads to preserve them from the water. But we did not mind it, neither did we complain, for hot work was waiting for us, that would soon dry the wringing garments or make us heedless of them.

About five miles from Richmond the brigade came to a halt; it was now broad day, but a gentle drizzle obscured everything in a mist; the men sat on both sides of the road, each exercising his inventive genius in improving a seat of a stone, fence-rail, or an old log,—anything to keep out of the wet.

After moving down another hundred yards or so the regiment was again halted, and orders were given to get breakfast, by hook or crook. Some few fires were started, but it required infinite patience to kindle a flame, with everything streaming with dampness; however, by persistent blowing and careful nursing enough smoke was encouraged to boil the coffee and fry the bacon, then over our pipes we discussed the situation, for up to this time we had not heard a single gun. Devoutly we hoped it might be a false alarm, though reason told us what a vain hope this was. I have heard of soldiers whose "bowels yearned" for a fight, but such "bowels" were not inside of my anatomy. In an hour or two the rolling of the drums brought the soldiers into line, and continuing our march, we halted two miles farther on and lay at rest.

It was now high noon by the town clock in our old home, if we could have heard it striking; the rain had ceased, the fog had lifted, and only the clouds still hung low their somber curtains, hiding the heavens' clear blue and making the scene dark and dismal.

"What did this mean?" we asked ourselves! Had some plan of the enemy's miscarried so that they failed to attack? None dreamed that we were to storm the works of the enemy, believing the while our role was strictly on the defensive. But we were on the wrong track it seemed.

At last it came! A little after twelve o'clock a gun sounded on our left, followed directly after by a peal of artillery. Hardly had the roar died away when was heard the rattling of small-arms. Now battery after battery joined in the chorus, as if the World and Satan had concluded to join in the battle and fight it out. Was ever greater noise made anywhere, not excepting Pandemonium? What grand and awful discord, as musketry and cannon's roar blent together! See! The smoke—dark purple, rising like mist from the ground and spreading upward, and those little puffs of white, which the bursting shells leave in the sky to dissolve slowly in the gray ether!

We moved forward and bore to the right; evidently destined to be held in the reserve. At four o'clock the pounding was going on as heavily as ever. Still no sign of action on our part, so we began to hope that there were too many men on our side to need us, when just as this juncture an aide-de-camp came up in a wild gallop, his clothes spattered with mud from head to foot. He hardly stopped to utter some words to the commanding officer ere he was off like a flash.

"Fall in, men!" cried the colonel. "Forward by the left flank! March! Double-quick!" And for a mile we went with a rush. As we approached the scene of action, the crash of musketry was appalling. Long streams of wounded made their appearance on their way to the rear, in every species of mutilation; some borne on stretchers, others swung in blankets, from whose folds blood and gore dropped in horrible exudations, staining the ground and crimsoning the budding grass. Still others were carried in their comrades' arms. Many more were slightly wounded and could walk, their hands pressed to their wounds, or hobble slowly along with a musket for a crutch; but their faces bore a contented look, feeling sure that a leave of absence stood ready waiting for them, and because they had escaped so well when matters might have gone so much against them. It was a sickening sight on the whole, and tried the nerves of the men to the utmost.

As we approached more closely to the scene of conflict, with its many terrors increasing at every step, the shells bursting in our midst, we beheld a sight that proved there was but "one step from the sublime to the ridiculous;" and even in this field of horrors, with the curtain rolled up (for we were all hurrying to play our parts in the bloody drama), such was the farce enacted before our eyes that the regiment burst into a peal of hearty, unrestrained laughter, that must have sounded as much out of place as tones of merriment in the torture chamber of the Holy Inquisition.

The object of our mirth was a soldier slightly wounded in the arm—the skin scratched off, perhaps; but he had kind, sympathizing friends, who said unto him, "where thou goest, I will go," and that was out of the reach of murderous shells. Two supported him tenderly, one on each side, and two more, equally kind and sympathizing, followed after, the one lovingly sustaining the wounded man's hat and the other affectionately bearing his musket. The countenance of the sufferer was twisted into a look of supreme anguish; while the assiduity and devotion of the four comrades was something beautiful to behold; sooth, they were ready to fight for the honor of helping him—and, if it must be said, for nothing else. Ah! It was a most touching sight, and to a man the regiment responded to the emotions of the hour.

"He who fights and runs away—"

Such was the philosophy of our heroes; but they broke and ran as the jibes and hearty laughter from the whole line reached them, relegating themselves to safe arcades. Later on in the war, all such poltroons were seized and placed in front of the advancing line.

The brigade, by order, bore obliquely to the right, and then, without stopping to form,—Kemper commanding the brigade,—charged across the field, with a battery enfilading the line. Men dropped at every step we took, but nothing stopped the momentum and we crossed the field at a run.

After we had reached the vicinity of the wood-pile, where stood a big barn and several outworks that had been thrown up by the enemy and recently captured by our forces, we could see the camp of Casey's division, not a hundred yards from us. The shelling had now become terrific. We double-quicked it across the field in plain view of the foe, who had trained upon us several batteries located on the edge of the camp; and shell, shrapnel, round shot and grape screamed about and around us.

Now was the time to form in a line! Instead, we kept on without changing formation—"not but the soldiers knew some one had blundered." *In fours* we advanced, or in other words, we pushed toward the enemy like a lance, instead of spreading out in a line. Company A of the Seventeenth was in advance, the lance-head of the column. As we approached the wood-pile, the musketry joined the artillery, and to go into that fire-swept camp seemed like entering the jaws of hell itself—

"A looming bastion, fringed with fire."

"Why do we not form a line of battle?" the rank and file cried as the men began to drop. In column as we were, none could fire their muskets! What did it mean? Who was responsible for so lamentable an error? But the onward gait was kept up by the column. "Forward! Forward!" cried the officers, wildly waving their swords above their heads. "Don't stop, men! Charge right into the camp!" And right into the camp we *did* charge—burst in the midst of it, with the Rebel cheer ringing high above the uproar of the guns. As we dashed in between the wood-pile and redoubts we passed a Rebel four-gun battery deserted, every single horse killed, and the living remnant of men forced to seek shelter elsewhere from the terrible concentrated fire that swept through the camp like an iron and leaden rain; all save one little boy, "the powder monkey," as they called his genus, who cowered behind the wheel of one of the guns, with eyes protruding, hands clasped, teeth clenched, and face wearing a look of horrified fright,—face so white, so startling in its terror, that it haunted me for days after.

As we passed the barn and got in among the tents, the tempest of war was undeniably frightful, its severity beyond belief. Every deadly projectile which could take away human life and maim and disfigure lusty manhood was showered upon us. The air was alive with their coming, and shrill and shrieking with their passing.

> "The mailed Mars did on his altar sit,
> Up to the ears in blood."

We saw no enemy, but the whole of Casey's division, some eight thousand strong, had formed around their camp in the shape of a half moon, and poured a converging fire at the attacking Rebels.

It is sickening to the heart to recall what followed. A result that could not have been otherwise.

Mixed up, mingled, crowded as we were amid the breastworks, barns and wood-pile, the brigade bunched in a mass, unable to fire a gun, its organization became a mob. Our splendid brigade of three thousand muskets, that stretched out fully five hundred yards in line of battle, could have carried the camp by storm or retreated with comparatively little loss; but owing to the incompetency and criminal ignorance of our commanding officer, it was thrown into a contracted space, without order and without form, with never a chance to fire a shot, and there butchered like cattle!

It was shameful!

While from the half circle on the other side the enemy were raining a *feu d'enfer* upon the struggling mass, our men fell in groups. The noise of bullets ripping through the canvas of the tents added to the horrors of the day. Men screamed as the balls struck them down. The officers shouted out unmeaning cries. The flag went down. Morrill, the color-bearer, the tallest man in the regiment, sank to the earth. Capt. Fairfax caught him as he fell, in his left arm, and with his right hand took the colors, waved them a moment, and handed them to Corporal Digges, who dropped prone on the ground. A private grasped them, raised the staff, and in a second he sank face downward, a bullet through his heart. Another gallant private, Harper, lifted the flag and bore it through the day.

In five minutes seventy-four officers and men out of the Seventeenth Regiment fell. A blind rush was made for shelter, and the soldiers scrambled over the breastworks or hurried behind the wood-pile. The rifle-pits, built by the enemy to protect their camp, proved a blessed refuge—nay, our very salvation; for to have attempted running the gauntlet across that open field in our rear would have been to rattle dice with death. Few would have lived to tell the tale.

Not many of us could recall distinctly all the combined horrors of that useless massacre. The chief incident, and the one fully distinct, was that on rushing back to the protection of the redoubt I stopped to help the color-bearer, Morrill, and had raised him half way up, when two more balls struck him and passed through his body with a sudden thud, and he sank back with a deep groan. He had been married only a few days before, at the bedside of a dying sister, and had left both bride and sister, immediately after the ceremony, to take part in the battle.

Safe behind good shelter, there was time to look around and collect our scattered senses—time to breathe freely and hold ourselves in readiness for what was yet to come, that is, if the day was fated to hold further horrors. We learned that Rodes's Alabama brigade, earlier in the evening, had stormed Casey's division camp, and with such vim, and so sudden a dash, that the enemy were driven from their tents on a run. Casey, however, reformed his men on the outer edge behind an abattis, which with wise precaution he had constructed for just such an emergency, and from thence he rained a torrent of fire upon every force that undertook an attack. He could not reoccupy his camp, but he could keep us from holding it; consequently, when Kemper's brigade came rushing on in column crowded into so small a space, he converged his whole fire upon it and caught it in a death trap.

The Fourth Alabama, of Rodes's brigade, had been forced to retire from the charge and seek shelter behind the works. They had witnessed our useless rush and vain sacrifice, and had we charged in line as many as were in the vicinity would have rallied and advanced with us.

We had listened to some heavy firing in our day, had heard the music of many a missile singing through the air, but never before had there been anything that could compare with that of Seven Pines. There was such a ceaseless pour of shot and shell that at least twenty men were struck while climbing over the breastworks. The bullets hissed like snakes around us, and that without a moment's intermission. Every second they hit the works and buried themselves in the damp earth; or striking higher would scrape the top and send the mud spattering over us. The soldiers of the different regiments and brigades were cowering beneath the parapet; but few had the curiosity or daring to lift their heads over the works and take aim at the running line of fire that showed where the foe lay concealed. Indeed, it was a dangerous experiment. Two men, an Alexandrian and an Alabamian, glanced over the parapet for a second and both fell back dead. I was looking at the former, Higdon, of Co. H, as he lifted up his head to look, and saw the red spot come on his forehead.

The very sky seemed alive with little fiery devils, who sang their songs, each in its own tone, as they flew over the works. The canister sounded more direful than any; and when *they* struck the earthworks the bravest would cower more closely to the ground. A life insurance agent could have taken out any number of policies just then, though whether his business would have been a money-making one is open to discussion.

For fully an hour did this metal rain keep up; for fully an hour did we lie there and listen to the flying projectiles striking the earthworks; for fully an hour did we congratulate ourselves upon being able to hide behind such friendly shelter; for fully an hour did we thank our stars that we were alive at all. A soldier's first thought at the close of a battle is always a selfish feeling of thankfulness at his own escape; after that other emotions can find place.

Behind the works where we were, ooze and mire were so deep that it reached to our waist-belts. Many of the enemy had been killed just here, by Rodes's men, and had found graves without burial, for their corpses had sunk beneath the surface. We could feel that we were standing on bodies, but the danger all were in prevented any remarks and excited no feeling whatsoever.

Around the barn and breastworks the water lay in pools, into which some of our wounded had fallen and were drowned. The body of one of our comrades was examined; it showed no mortal wound, but having dropped face downward in the water, he had suffocated—his mouth and throat were filled with liquid mud.

Late in the evening, when the enemy's fire had at first slackened, then died away, Colonel Corse jumped to the open space and sung out for the Seventeenth to form. No regiment in the army ever furnished more substantial proof of splendid discipline than did his when we responded with alacrity to the order. After such a terrible shock and fearful loss of life, it yet retained its morale. Its men came running from behind their different places of concealment, none lingering, and in ten minutes were formed into line. I got hold of a drum left by the enemy, intending to beat a *pas de charge,* but the sticks were missing and I threw the useless instrument away. I might as well say here that this was the first and only drum I ever saw left on a battle-field, though in every war picture a shattered drum always occupies a prominent position, along with the overturned caisson and dead horse. Then the order was given to guide by the colors, and we advanced again through the camp—no longer a mob, but a crack organization, free to return the enemy's fire. The regiment went at a double-quick time, aiming to reach the shelter of the abattis; and there we arrived, panting and breathless, while not a hostile shot had greeted us. Breaking our way through the fallen trees of this obstruction we kept on some distance in the woods beyond, but saw no vestige of the enemy, who had retreated, carrying off their wounded. As Rodes had had it all his own way at first, there must have been many hurt.

We could easily see where the line had stood that fought us so relentlessly, for torn cartridges and useless muskets lay scattered around. Doubtless it was fine fun to stand and shoot us, crowding between the forts and wood-piles. The war did not offer many such chances, and not a man of them in after years had need to regret that he did not improve *this* shining hour.

As it was nearly dark we were halted just on the verge of the camp, in the low ground, and of course half under water. Here we remained for fully an hour, up to our knees in the black mire, suffering, be it said, the peculiar trials of Tantalus. After all the loss of life, and the hardships we had borne in the attempt to secure and capture this camp and to hold it, we were not allowed any of the spoils of war which we considered legitimately our due. Here we were, just on its edge, half buried in the mud, with nothing to do, the enemy safely miles away across the Chickahominy, standing hungry, thirsty and wet and passive, while new troops, who had never fired a gun, were brought in under our very eyes and turned loose to help themselves at will! Was it not enough to make a saint swear? We fairly ached to enter that camp, and could have rapped the heads of those marauding Rebels over yonder, with a will.

It seems that the Yankees were at dinner when the Third Alabama crowded in upon them as uninvited guests.

A member of the Seventeenth, Hector Eaches, disappeared that evening most mysteriously and never made an appearance until next morning. With that instinct that marks the true soldier—with that intuition which is born in some men, he had spent the night in Casey's camp, and conscientiously looked after the booty and the spoils. He reappeared, loaded down—provisions, clothes, swords, pistols, and some fine old Otard brandy! His report, while it showed us what we had missed, was interesting too. "Barrels of flour," he said, "bags of fruit, boxes of meat, hogsheads of sugar, rice and mess-beef, piles of clothes, were scattered around in profusion, while the sutler's tent was filled with luxuries. In the headquarter's tent, a fine dinner, with dainty surroundings, had been left untouched, the bottles of wine, with which it was flanked, standing on the table with corks undrawn. Everything went to show the bountiful system of the Yankee commissariat."

And another incident he related of the night's experience, that exemplified how closely Death ever hovers over the soldier, ready at the most unexpected moment to stretch out his bony hand and clutch his helpless victim.

In a large tent, belonging evidently to the staff, he saw in the dim light a Federal officer reclining in a chair; his head rested on the table before him and his whole attitude was one of perfect rest. Startled at the presence of such a person, he levelled his musket upon the officer and ordered him to surrender; no reply being made, he reiterated the command in a louder tone, and still the figure did not stir; with a strange feeling he advanced and laid his hand upon the shoulder—no movement! he touched the face, it was quite cold. He left the tent hurriedly, and calling some soldiers passing by, narrated what he had seen. They procured a light and together went back to the tent, and found the corpse and raised him up. His jaw had fallen; in his right hand was a dinner knife, grasped tightly by the cold fingers, while on the plate before him was a piece of meat; the table lay spread with a repast half eaten, and he evidently had been in the very act of carving when the bullet, fired by some skirmisher beginning the attack, winged its way and struck him in the temple, killing him instantly.

All that night the lucky troops who were camped in the captured quarters luxuriated in the spoils, and could be heard singing and carousing around their huge fires.

After waiting until it was dark the regiment marched back into the pine woods a mile or two to the rear. Without waiting to build fires—wet, hungry, and sad at heart for those we should miss from our ranks forevermore, and utterly broken down—we threw ourselves on the muddy ground and slept.

Colonel Corse, commanding our regiment, says: "At 4 P. M. I moved the Seventeenth by the left flank in double-quick time for one and one-half miles down the Williamsburg road, passing for 500 yards under a heavy artillery and infantry fire to a wood-pile to the left of the Barker house, when we halted for a few moments to permit the men to recover breath; we there filed to the right in front of a redoubt and into the enemy's camp, encountering a galling infantry fire from the enemy stationed in the edge of the wood. After advancing some distance I received an order to fall back and reform behind the trenches, which was done in *tolerable* good order, which position we held until near night-fall, and holding the enemy in check until they were driven from their position.

"In the advance into Casey's division camp, Color Corporal Morrill was struck down, wounded in three places, and rose on his elbows to cheer the men forward. The colors were caught by Captain Raymond Fairfax, who was struck. Color Corporal Digges next seized them and fell wounded. They were taken by Private Harper, Co. D, who retained them until the close of the day.

"Sergeant Major Francis fell mortally wounded some distance in advance of the regiment; with him was Sergeant Bayse, of Company F, who fell dead. Lieutenant Gray was killed; his conduct was always remarkable for heroism. Captain Knox, Co. G, Captain Fowle, Co. H, and Captain Burke were all badly wounded when leading their companies. Lieutenant Fitzhugh was badly wounded, Major Arthur Herbert was also wounded." (Rebellion Records, Vol. 11, p. 580.)

Colonel John B. Gordon, commanding the Sixth Alabama, of Rodes's brigade, which captured the redoubt, says: "The right wing formed a line on the left of the Fourth Virginia Battalion, and was ordered by General Rodes in person to charge the redoubt; the whole command went over the ditch and embankment into the redoubt, where we captured a stand of colors and six pieces of artillery. The enemy retreated to the abattis and delivered a heavy fire; under this fire some of my best officers and men fell. Two field officers had fallen, three companies had not an officer spared, four others had but one, and more than half had fallen, when under orders they retired." (Rebellion Records, Vol. 11, p. 980.)

The Twelfth Alabama, of Rodes's brigade, which assisted in the rush through the camp, carried in action 408 officers and men, and had 59 killed and 156 wounded, losing more than half.

Now just see the misleading character of the official reports, written two days after the battle, when all the facts had been sifted and the grains of truth supposed to be winnowed from the bushels of chaff.

General James Longstreet, under date of June 10, 1862, gives his official report of the battle:

"The severest part of the work was done by Major General D. H. Hill's division, but the attack of the two brigades under General R. H. Anderson and Brigadier James L. Kemper was made with such spirit and regularity as to have driven back the most determined foe. This decided the day in our favor." (Rebellion Records, Vol. 11, p. 940.)

Now read what General Hill reports a few days later in his official report:

"The magnificent brigade of General Rodes moved over the ground to assault the Yankees in their works. He met a galling fire after capturing the camp, and his advance was checked. Kemper's brigade was now sent me by General Longstreet, and directed by me to move directly to the support of Rodes. This brigade, however, did not engage the Yankees, and Rodes's men were badly cut up." (Hill's report, O. R., Vol. 40, p. 944.)

In the official reports, General J. E. Johnston, the commander-in-chief, says: "Had Huger been in position and ready for action when Smith, Longstreet and Hill moved, I am satisfied that

Keyes's Federal corps would have been destroyed instead of being merely defeated."* (O. R., Vol. 11, p. 935.)

Longstreet states in his official report that had Huger been in position within eight hours of the time he was ordered to attack, the battle would have been a complete success.

Now let us see what the Union soldiers say about the battle.

General Casey in his report says: "I occupied with my division the advance position in the army, and parties were employed up to the 31st of May in throwing up rifle-pits and a redoubt, and also constructed an abattis and earthworks in rear of my camp. About 11 or 12 o'clock I was led to believe that a serious attack was contemplated and immediately ordered my division under arms. My force consisted of four brigades of thirteen regiments and five batteries of artillery, composing the Pennsylvania and New York troops. I placed one battery under Lieutenant Hart in the redoubt. The Eighty-fifth New York occupied the rifle-pits; Captain Regan's battery in the rear and to the right of the rifle-pits—and this battery was supported by the Eighty-fifth Pennsylvania. The One Hundred and Third Pennsylvania were ordered in the front to support the redoubts. About fifteen minutes after these dispositions were made the Rebels advanced, and the One Hundred and Third Pennsylvania came down the road in some confusion, having suffered a considerable loss from the fire of the Rebel advance.

"The enemy now attacked me in the center in large force, and a heavy demonstration on both wings; my artillery in the meantime throwing canister in the ranks with great effect. Perceiv-

---

*After the war I saw a good deal of General Huger. He bought a plantation in Fauquier County, Virginia, and I was often a guest at his house. As a host, raconteur and a man of the world he was without a peer, but he had no military genius; he was essentially and entirely a parlor soldier. His staff was more showy than the commander-in-chief's and he loved the pomp and pageantry of war, but he was not made of the stuff that, like the stormy petrel, "revels in the tempest," nor like the mountain eagle, who "mocks the thunder and defies the storm."

Like General Pemberton, his after life was made unhappy by the criticisms of Southern people. He was very gloomy at times, and always *thought he had been unjustly* condemned.

NOTE.—History of the Seventeenth Virginia, George Wise, page 71, as follows: "During the Battle of Seven Pines, in the redoubt, Watkins of Company H, and Alex. Hunter of Company A, were particularly conspicuous in the heat of the first day's fight, for bravery and unerring aim. Guns were loaded by the boys around them, and the two, standing upon the embankment, fired as rapidly as they could take the guns; the colors of a regiment in front were cut down three times in succession."

ing at length that the enemy were threatening with both wings, for want of reinforcements that had been repeatedly asked for, I then, in order to save my artillery, ordered a charge of bayonets by the four supporting regiments at the center, which was executed in the most gallant and successful manner, the enemy being driven back when the charge had ceased, but not until the charge had reached the edge of the woods, when the most terrible fire of musketry commenced that I ever heard. The Rebels again advanced in force, and my flanks being threatened, a retreat to the works became necessary.

"To be brief, the works were retained until they were most enveloped by the enemy, the troops with some exceptions fighting with spirit and gallantry. The troops retreated to the second line in possession of General Couch's division. On my arrival at the second line I succeeded in rallying a small portion of my division, and with the assistance of General Kearny, who had just arrived with one of his brigades, attempted to regain possession of my camp, but it was found to be impracticable. The troops of General Couch were driven back, though reinforced by the corps of General Heintzelman. I cannot forbear to mention the loss of my Chief of Artillery, Colonel G. D. Bailey, who fell in an attempt to spike the guns in the redoubt. If a portion of my division did not behave as well as could have been wished, it must be remembered what a terrible ordeal they were subjected to." (Rebellion Records, Vol. 40, p. 909-910.)

That fatal redoubt and the narrow passage between it and the wood-pile, the only entrance to the camp, was a death-trap to the foe, as it was to ours. Colonel Henry Briggs, of the Tenth Massachusetts, states: "I was ordered by General Keyes to proceed with my command to the road, and form a line near a large wood-pile near the works. I proceeded at once to execute this order. At this point on the left of the road there was a small oblong open space about thirty yards wide, and long enough to form five companies in line fronting the enemy. All at once a severe fire opened from the woods and underbrush on my left flank, not more than fifty paces distant. It was so severe that the lines were broken, and the narrowness of the open space made it impossible to change front. I gave the order to retreat. Colonel Day was killed here in a fight almost hand-to-hand with the enemy. This position amounted to an ambuscade, and I believe no troops could stand the overwhelming fire they were subjected to. I myself was struck by two musket balls and carried to the rear; my loss was one hundred and twenty-one killed and wounded." (O. R., Vol. 11, p. 910-912.)

The foe that our brigade met face to face was the brigade of Naglee, and the Seventeenth's immediate opponent was the Fifty-sixth and Eleventh Maine. General Naglee, commanding, says: "At 4 o'clock I ordered the Fifty-sixth New York to save the guns [meaning some of Casey's]. The regiment moved toward the Williamsburg road at double-quick and held its position some distance in front for over an hour. Both regiments again charged but were compelled to retire with loss. These regiments formed in line behind the abattis and they held their line for a half an hour, doing great execution, and repulsed the Rebel advance." (Rebellion Records, Vol. 11, p. 896.)

Further on General Naglee, of Casey's division, says: "Returning rapidly to my Fifty-sixth New York and Eleventh Maine, I found the enemy had been successful in turning my right flank, and had opened a most destructive fire from the redoubt, and this state of affairs could no longer be endured and they were withdrawn, and marched down the Nine-mile road and placed in position in rear of this road, and this position they held for a time.

"Fully confirming the statement of my officers, I saw no running and no panic."

"Yesterday, 31 May, '62, at 1 P. M., the enemy, taking advantage of a terrible storm which flooded the valley of the Chickahominy, attacked our troops on the right bank of that river. Casey's division, which was on the first line, gave way unaccountably and discreditably. (General McClellan's Report, Rebellion Records, Vol. 11, p. 751.)

General N. H. Davis, Assistant Inspector Army of the Potomac, says: "Casey's division at the recent battle of Seven Pines was not surprised, but defective disposition and insufficiency of officers, together with bad discipline, accounts for its conduct in the battle."

It was the common talk around our camp-fires that but for the stubborn defense made by Casey we would have captured every Yankee south of the Chickahominy River. The Confederate attack was like a thunderbolt, and though Casey's troops had to relinquish their camp, yet they rallied and poured such a deadly fire on us that the two crack brigades of Rodes and Kemper went to pieces for a time, and this deadly fusilade was kept up until near dark and effectually kept the Rebels from forming in line and advancing. It is always the case that the defeated gen--

eral must find some scapegrace, and Casey was the one picked out, and he had to bear the whole blame of the defeat, which was owing to McClellan's faulty disposition of his troops.

General Casey must have suffered the keenest pangs that the human heart can feel, when knowing as he did that he had saved the Army of the Potomac from a deadly stroke, yet had all the unsuccessful generals turning on him like a pack of wolves.

Listen to the praise of the enemy. General Hill says in his report: "The gallant charge of my division demoralized the force, and our reinforcements were hotly engaged, the succor brought to Casey *not fighting as well as his own men*. This accounts for the fact that more than half of my entire loss fell upon my division.

"Kemper's brigade halted—Rodes's brigade cut up, losing 801 men killed and wounded, stopped the impetus of the charge and saved McClellan's army from irretrievable disaster, and yet Casey was forced to resign for alleged incompetence."

10

CHAPTER XVIII.

THE NEXT DAY.

The preparation of breakfast was an event of great enjoyment to us. Our meal was of the primitive order, but we dallied and lingered over cooking it, enjoying the odor of the meat and coffee as it came steaming in grateful, fragrant clouds of incense from the fire; anticipation filling up the full measure of the pleasure. And in this wise did our foot cavalry proceed to cook it—each man alike, though there were no regulations on the subject; such knowledge being ever evolved from the innate genius and lofty inspiration of the occasion.

Opening his haversack wherein the rations were carried—an uninviting bag of a store-room, which was by long use grimed with dirt, blackened by smoke, and greased with fat of bacon that came oozing through the canvas—Johnny Reb would extract a chunk of fat wrapped up in a piece of rag and cut therefrom some slices, then from the bottom of the haversack he would exhume his hardtack, as he called the crackers, and prop them up before the blazing fire to toast; next, drawing the ramrod from the rifle, he would run it through the slice of meat and hold it in the flames; when it had caught fire, as he intended it should, he would suspend it over the crackers, which had been toasted brown, and permit the grease to fall drop by drop upon them; and then he filled the old battered tin cup with water and adjusted it nicely upon the coals. This required some art and strict attention, as a tilt was ever dangerous, and chunks were generally very slippery and very treacherous. As soon as the water bubbled, he placed therein a handful of roasted rye or parched corn; and when this boiled some ten minutes longer the coffee was made, and breakfast, dinner and supper, just as you might name it by the clock, (it was all the same to him) was served.

Except when he captured coffee, or exchanged tobacco on picket duty with Billy Yank, Johnny never tasted it pure; and as for sugar, it was rarely issued to him now, so we used sorghum molasses instead, to sweeten our concoction, and because sorghum was of Southern manufacture, one of its chief merits was its abundance. The mixture of rye and sorghum was enough to produce deadly illness in any one who swallowed it, not excepting a

Rebel soldier. But we learned to love it. True, we would tire of the rye sometimes when it became very monotonous; but then we had sassafras tea to fall back upon, "for the sake of a little pleasant diversion," as Handy Andy expresses it; and altogether we did not complain.

It was quantity rather than quality with the soldier; he could pardon the first if the latter suited him; and doubtless Johnny enjoyed his humble meal more than many a guest his sumptuous dinner; indeed, muddy water, and crushed corn and molasses were sweeter to his taste than the rarest wines to the sated palate of the millionaire; the burnt slice of fat bacon consumed with keener relish than was the canvas-back, the mountain mutton, the ham boiled in champagne of the bon vivant—for after all, hunger is the best sauce, and robust health the best stimulant, while there is nothing like a battle for an appetizer! Try it if you are inclined to be skeptical.

Was there ever citizen in the world, think you, who extracted quite the amount of perfect content and pleasant reveries from his fifty-cent Havana, as the private by the camp-fire from his old briar-root pipe? Every soldier smoked; it was a necessity of his being; and then he had the blessing of pure tobacco, carried in a bag hung from the button-hole of his jacket. Most of these bags were beautifully embroidered, for Southern women always gave their sweethearts and husbands two things, and kept them well supplied besides; tobacco bags and Bibles. A soldier, popular with the fair sex, and who never burned the incense of devotion to one—but dozens—had usually enough Bibles given him to supply the whole company.

After a battle the men were ever in a complacent mood, and having escaped destruction and mutilation, they loved to sit and recall each incident. So around the fires after the fray, for the weather was damp and cool, the whole campaign was discussed from first to last; and as we continued to gain information from various sources, the rationale of the attack became clear, the different parts of the puzzle fitted together into a harmonious whole; and that which had been so hard to understand, grew intelligible in the broad light of facts and reason. What was wanting even then, time, which sifts all things, supplied; and so the history of the battle gained its whole completeness.

Our brigade commander came in for a heavy share of censure, and could he have assumed the magic cap of the fairy which rendered the wearer invisible, and strolled along in the vicinity of the different watch-fires any night just about that time, and listened to the expressed sentiments of the rank and file,—heard the un-measured terms in which they denounced his fatal blunder of sending them into a battle four deep, pell-mell, to be shot down with never a chance to retaliate, he would have resigned next day.

General Kemper denied having so blundered, and said he wished to make a display of his force, to prevent the enemy from advancing and re-taking his camp. This may be so; but for all that, the soldiers blamed him and him alone for their mad rush and useless waste of life.

About seven o'clock the morning after the battle, the brigade fell in line and halted on the spot where it had fought the day before. Its dead lay thick around, just as they had fallen. The regiment then took position in a redoubt, where was placed a four-gun battery of Stuart's horse artillery but a little distance away. Colonel Corse made a short speech to his regiment, in-forming the men that in all probability the enemy would attack us in heavy force to try and re-take his captured camp, and that the regiment must hold the fort and protect the battery at all hazards.

In for it again, we thought; but then we would be fighting behind breastworks, and the enemy would do the storming; so with the metaphorical boot on the other foot, the men answered by a cheer that had the genuine ring in it.

The ranks of the regiment were quite full by this time, and the stragglers had all returned. In every organization there were always many such, who slipped out when going into battle and as surely returned the next day with wondrous stories of what they had seen and heard and done—stories, indeed, which imposed on no one, not even themselves.

Of course a good many in the company became separated from it in the charge through the camp; these returned, and so it turned out that several who had been deemed killed were re-ceived safe and sound, to the great joy of their comrades; and welcoming them not exactly as repenting prodigals, but as one "alive from the dead," the regiment was only too sorry it had no fatted calf to kill.

And now after we had been placed in position and sharp-shooters told off, the Colonel issued orders that we should pay the last sad duties to some Alexandrians. Most of the dead had been already buried. A shallow grave was dug in the redoubt and

Lieut. Gray and three others, privates Higdon and Marray, Co. H, Lunt, Co. A, were laid on one blanket side by side, and covered with another; a prayer was read and then the dirt thrown upon them. One of the four had been a great traveler; had passed through many lands and crossed many waters; had walked along the Corso at Rome, sauntered through the Prado of Berlin, ridden through the great Arabian desert, had seen the rush of gold seekers to the El Dorado of the New World; here at last to sleep in death, side by side with those whose lives had been so unconsciously linked with his; unknown one to another, these men, day by day and year after year, had woven out the woof of their separate lives; the Fates who weave the thread of life had drawn these strands together and woven them into one; but yesterday Atropos cut the cord; and now one grave.

A more lonesome, forbidding spot than the place where we had charged the evening before can scarcely be imagined. The camp had been plundered of everything of value; not a pound of coffee nor a pint of liquor or a piece of meat was left. The ground all along the scene of conflict had been trampled into a perfect quagmire and looked like a barn-yard on a rainy day; here and there lay the body of some Rebel or Yankee soldier, half submerged in the mud, the mire around now tinged to a reddish hue by the life-blood that poured through some bleeding wound; often on dragging out the corpse and washing off the muck and mire they would find some comrade whom they thought had escaped or was missing.

It was only on going to the barn just in front, where the colors of the Seventeenth went down three times, that the tremendous severity of the enemy's fire could be realized.

The whole side fronting them was shattered and torn by the missiles; there was not a space as large as the human hand that had not been struck by either shot, shell or ball. Talk of a building being riddled, one might not understand the meaning of the term who had not looked on such a sight as this. With such tangible proof before the eyes, of how thick and fast the bullets flew, to say nothing of the grape and shell, it was a source of wonder how, in the face of such a fire, any man had come out alive.

It was nearly nine o'clock when the sound of distant guns was heard, and in a few moments the regiment was formed into a line inside the works.

"The Yankees will be along soon," our captain was heard to remark. The four guns were placed and sighted, the ammunition piled in heaps beside each gun; the rammers threw off their jackets and bared their arms to the elbow, and officers and men bent forward, shading their eyes with their hands to catch a first glimpse of the foe.   But the pine woods effectually concealed all that was going on.   Evidently there was fighting progressing somewhere on the left.

 . All at once the noise of a stirring hurrah was heard, and from the woods about three hundred yards on our left there came a long line in blue advancing against the brigade on our left, commanded by Generals Mahone and Prior.   It was a thrilling sight and we held our breath in intensity of excitement.   The charge was made with all the regularity of a parade, but encountering a heavy fire from the brigades, retired in confusion.   There was further fighting on the extreme left, but none of the men in blue favored *us* with their especial compliments, and the hours passed quietly by.   After a while some of our slightly wounded wended their way to the rear, and being interrogated, told the same tale that ninety-nine out of a hundred ever tell,—tales of fighting against fearful odds and of dreadful slaughter amounting almost to annihilation.   In every battle the exaggeration is invariable. Perhaps this class of soldier, feeling himself for the once safe and lucky too, takes a malicious delight in heightening the effect for the benefit of others going into action; perhaps his fears had actually magnified the state of affairs, and out of the abundance of his terrors he spoke what to him seemed truth; perhaps, having been terrorized, he wanted misery to keep him company; however it may be, the same chorus was ever kept up in the rear of the battle; and at first it had the effect of exciting the reserve to run, at the bursting of the introductory shell; but the boys soon became used to the recital and took it thereafter as a matter of course.

While waiting in this state of suspense for the enemy's advance, an officer, seemingly about thirty-five, splendidly mounted and high in command, rode up, and slapping Col. Corse familiarly on the shoulder made some jocular remark; his was a striking figure and he sat in his saddle like Hotspur himself, who "witched the world with his noble horsemanship;" his face was bronzed, his eyes, the most noticeable feature, were of a light blue, of that kind that keeps deep in their depths changing lights and shadows, but whose prevailing expression was mirth and laughter; a huge beard, full and flowing as the Norseman's of old, covered his face; his uniform was rich, even foppish; the sleeves of his coat slashed with gold braid in the form of a Hungarian knot that extended nearly to the shoulder; his pants, light blue with silver cord, were met at the knee by a pair of embroidered cavalry boots, at the heels of which were attached large silver Mexican spurs that jingled with every motion of his impatient horse; on his head he wore a wide-brimmed slouch hat with a golden cord around the crown, one side looped up with a gilt star, while a large plume fell from the brim nearly to his shoulder; his voice was rich and vibrating and his laughter was music to the ear—so full, so joyous, that once heard it lingered in the memory.

As he reined up his horse at the entrance of the redoubt, sitting there with the surroundings of glittering bayonets and unmuzzled cannon with a back-ground of battle-smoke drifting through the air, he made a picture that would have inspired an artist.

One could imagine just such a princely form in those stirring scenes which Froissart describes; or picture him in the Holy Land surrounded by the Douglas, as he threw the heart of Bruce, encased in the jeweled locket, straight in the midst of the Saracens, plunging and forcing his way among the countless infidels and dying at last beside his Scottish Prince.

Imagine just such a man leading the Imperial Guard of the Grand Army as it struck the Austrian center at Wagram. At all times the born dragoon, the fearless soldier; or best of all, see him as the Prince of Cavalrymen, one of the bravest spirits that ever fought for the Confederate cause—one of the noblest that ever unsheathed a sword; one of the truest that ever offered up on a country's altar a stainless life; one of the knightliest that ever graced the page of history.

> "As full of valor as of kindness,
> Primely in both."

General Jeb Stuart! Commander-in-Chief of the Cavalry.

The enemy on our front and left began in a desultory way to shell our troops on the Williamsburg road, though doing no special damage. A Rebel regiment, just fresh from camp and newly organized, was marching not two hundred yards from us across the field, when suddenly two or three shells from the enemy's battery burst high above their heads; instantly every man, from the colonel down to the drummer-boy, dropped flat on all fours with a promptitude and in a perfection of time that was wonderful to behold. In a short time officers and men arose and kept on in the line of march. Again the little puffs of blue smoke appeared in the sky, followed by the peculiar noise made by a shell in bursting, and again the whole command sought the embrace of Mother Earth. While in this ridiculous situation, floundering on the ground, a mounted officer—probably a general—rode up, and from his earnest gesticulations we could see that he was not mincing words or flattering the hearers. After a while they proceeded on their way without practicing manoeuvres—manoeuvres not laid down in Hardee's Tactics. Evidently from this, they had been under fire in more ways than one.

This weak-kneed regiment was afterwards placed in the First Brigade, and a braver set of men never shouldered muskets; proving that all men are timid in encountering for the first time an unknown danger. A year afterwards, and a whole battery might have played upon them and not so much as have broken their dressed lines.

The day passed; the musketry died away and the guns only fired at intervals; most of the soldiers lay around the redoubt and dozed. After sundown the regiment was formed and commenced the march back in the direction of the old camping ground. The roads were badly cut up by the artillery that had passed and repassed during the twenty-four hours; full of holes and ruts, into which, amid the utter darkness that surrounded them like a pall, the soldiers were falling and wallowing every step of the way.

After a most exhausting wade the brigade halted in a swamp and went into bivouac. There was not a soldier in the command who had not been spattered from head to foot with mud. The prospect of a night spent in this spot was not cheering. Some of us found two fence rails apiece, which we laid parallel to each other about six inches apart and slanting from an old stump to the ground, upon which we lay down with our oil cloths for covering and slept the dreamless sleep of utter weariness. How the rest fared who were not so comfortably provided with beds, no one asked and no one cared; a short campaigning renders men selfish enough. Many were heard grumbling next morning and cursing their superior officers for making them pass the night in a noisome, miry swamp.

In an hour or two we reached the old camp; and so ended the battle of Seven Pines; it was a splendidly conceived movement, and but for the wounding of General Johnston and the incompetency of General Huger, as well as the miscarriage of the General's orders, it would have put an entire new face upon the state of affairs; indeed, after General Johnston was wounded there seemed to be no fixed plan nor concerted action. In no case did any of our attacking force have the proper reserves, and thereby we failed utterly to accomplish anything except at an enormous cost of life, to drive the enemy from his camps and hold them. General Johnston, when he determined to attack on the 31st, and had informed himself of the position of the enemy, made the mistake, as I said before, of supposing that only one corps instead of two were across the river.

Seven Pines was called by the South a battle of blunders.

Believing that one-third of the Yankee force was cut off by an impassable stream and swamp, he intended hurling his whole force upon that third before it could be reinforced. Through the wonderful industry of the foe the Chickahominy was bridged by pontoons, impossible as we thought it would be, in an inconceivably short time, and reinforcements were hurried on by thousands, but—the history of the war for us is full of "ifs" and "buts"! The head that conceived, the hand that pointed the way was stricken down by a bullet and then chaos came. Brigadiers and major-generals blundered; desultory attacks were made; and instead of driving the enemy into the swamps of the Chickahominy, they reformed their line and drove us back, holding their position until dark and then retreated to their reserves. It is true we held Casey's division camp, but it was a barren honor; and the dreadful loss of life it entailed upon the two brigades of Kemper and Rodes did not begin to pay for its capture.

The New York papers gave highly-colored accounts of this great military wrestling match. The description of the first day's battle was partisan, of course, but rather fair, for they acknowledged the loss of Casey's division camp with all its munitions and stores; but they averred on the next day, June 1st, by a magnificent bayonet charge in which they had fought an overwhelming force, they swept away the Rebel divisions and recovered the camp which had been lost the day before; the Rebel loss being estimated at thousands.

How with such enterprising correspondents, such a plain, unvarnished falsehood should have remained uncontradicted and allowed to go down to posterity as history, is inexplicable, for Mr. Swinton, the fairest and most impartial historian on either side, in his book, "The Army of the Potomac," is misled by these grape-vine reports, and states that "General Sumner advanced on

.June 1st and re-took much of the ground lost on the previous day."

Longstreet held the redoubts and occupied Casey's division camp all that day, awaiting an attack; none came; the fight we witnessed having been only a heavy skirmish that could not under any circumstances have been designated as a battle.

The truth of the whole matter was that both sides claimed too much; and there was just a little too much bragging all around. The conclusion that must be deduced after weighing the merits of both sides and their losses, was that it stood a drawn battle.

In this great game of military chess there was no checkmate; the enemy lost their castle; we our knight; and the vast contest remained still to be played. The Northern papers spoke, however, of their churches having celebrated the great victory by "Te Deums." There was no exulting for us, no rejoicing—only a great nerving of the people for deadlier encounters; only a tighter strain upon the muscles for this life-or-death tug.

As for our crack brigade between three and four thousand strong, we have seen how it was handled; how it was placed in action; had this been managed skilfully—who can tell? Seven Pines might have been a proud name to Southern ears; as it was, the brigade lost between three and four hundred killed and wounded and in return killed hardly a half-dozen of the enemy; for probably not twenty-five of the whole command fired off a single gun.

From that time—from the battle of Seven Pines, whether justly or unjustly—the privates of the brigade lost confidence in their commanding officer, and ascribed all the useless bloodshed to his incompetency.

This was but one instance in many, of bloody blunders that were constantly happening in our army, made by men of no military training and who possessed no soldierly qualities. They were not only *not* court-martialed, but every effort was made to hush up the untoward affair and they were allowed to keep in command and concoct fresh butcheries. What mattered it? In this case of storming a camp in a column of fours, only a hundred homes were made desolate, and twice that number of stalwart men crippled for life. Between the upper and nether millstone the private in the ranks had a dangerous time of it.

CHAPTER XIX.

RICHMOND AFTER THE BATTLE.

The brigade moved into its former quarters, and but for the missing of old familiar faces Seven Pines would have seemed but a dream. Our camp was just as we had left it, the tents never having been taken down nor anything disturbed. For guard, the colonel had left various teamsters, convalescents, and others who always managed to get sick on the eve of any aggressive movement; and these had kept so faithfully to their posts in time of danger, we had no occasion to complain that our camp equipage had not been well protected.

In the city, busy, bustling and sad enough scenes were being enacted on every side. New regiments from the far South had just arrived and were marching through the streets, cheering and waving their hats as they passed; batteries of artillery were defiling along the thoroughfares, the drivers cracking their whips and urging their horses into a trot, all going toward the front, down Main and Broad streets into the Williamsburg road. Long lines of ambulances coming from the opposite way toiled slowly along, filled with the wounded from the battle-field, who were being carried to the various city hospitals—the long, torturing way marked by the trail of blood that oozed drop by drop from the human veins within, or else might be seen a wagon-load of dead piled one upon another, their stiffened, rigid feet exposed to view, showing to the horrified spectator that for just so many the cares and sorrows of this life, its pain and misery, were passed forever.

Every vehicle from the battle-field was crowded to its utmost capacity. The more slightly wounded were made to walk, and long lines of them could be seen hobbling along the street, their wounds bound up in bloody rags. The citizens turned out in full force and did all in their power to alleviate this suffering; there was scarcely a house in Richmond wherein some wounded were not taken to be nursed with tenderest care; indeed, in some instances parlors and passages as well as chambers were converted into temporary hospitals, and everything done that unwearied nursing and gentlest attention could devise, and that for the roughest soldiers in the ranks as readily as for the highest general who wore his stars. Ladies stood in front of their homes with waiters of food and drink, luxuries and wine, which they dealt out unsparingly to wounded soldiers that passed them.

The Capitol square was filled with officers, privates and citizens; it had ever been a kind of news mart and a general rendezvous for the soldiers, while the ladies always loved to frequent its shady walks or rest on the seats beneath its trees, but the morning after the battle it was crowded. Many who were in doubt as to the fate of some loved one turned their steps to this battle park as the surest and easiest way of gaining information; comrades met and congratulated each other on escape; citizens listened to recitals of the battle; dirty, mud-covered soldiers, looking as if they had been dug out of a clay bank, were met and hugged by the whitest of arms and kissed by the sweetest of rose-bud lips; handsomely dressed and beautiful women, with tears streaming down their fair cheeks, greeted husbands, brothers and lovers. Many of those soft-eyed, soft-voiced women had dauntless souls, and when sobbing in agony at their parting they yet could murmur with pallid lips, like the Roman wives when handing their shields to their husbands and sons, "Return with them—or upon them."

It had been a time of terrible anxiety to the people of Richmond. The first battle to occur near them, they had listened all day to the thunder of the cannon with agonizing feelings, with nerves strained to the highest tension, awaiting the result. Not only did they have their own near and dear to think of, but from all the South had poured in letters from friends and relatives charging them to watch over kindred and take charge of them if wounded. Then from all quarters of the Confederacy wives had followed their husbands to the scene of action, filling with other refugees every available boarding-house, public and private, in the city. To these strangers in a strange land it had been a trial of no light moment to listen to those death-dealing monsters and know *one* life was at stake. Ah, yes, this battle had thrilled the city to its depths!

Such an extraordinary call for hospital accommodations had found the Richmond authorities entirely unprepared; buildings were hastily fitted up with the barest of comforts; medical stores on hand were entirely inadequate for the demand. The city doctors were employed day and night, and as for nurses—if the women of the place, young and old, had not volunteered their services, matters would have been very much worse than they were.

Soups and delicacies were sent from private houses, and so the suffering was in a measure mitigated. After some time, and throughout the war, the hospitals of Richmond were organized and better conducted, with their efficient surgeons, skilled nurses, and admirable routine; but at that time chaos reigned supreme, and many precious lives were lost from want of ordinary attention, that otherwise might have been saved.

For days and nights wagons and ambulances never ceased to empty their wretched loads before the door of each of these hastily improvised hospitals, never ceasing until the building overflowed with maimed humanity and could accommodate no more. In some instances empty stores were taken, and pallets of straw placed on the floors and counters. At the handling of wounds,—rough it must have seemed, in spite of every effort to make it gentle,— the racking of quivering nerves passing all bounds of patient endurance, screams of agony would sometimes break out upon the air with startling emphasis. Here was some poor fellow being taken from an ambulance with an arm shot so nearly off that it needed only one stroke of the knife to quite finish the work; another with a mangled leg—yes! it were better to look away from such a piteous spectacle; a boy with his face so torn by a shell that his mother would not have recognized him—and a dying soldier, his countenance already pallid in the fast-coming chill of death; and—"Here one is dead, died on the way," they say as they lift a corpse from the wagon, while the passer-by, grown rapidly familiar with such fearful sights, glances hastily and passes on.

And so passed the long procession of wounded, nearly five thousand, young, middle-aged and white-haired; from the private to the highest ranks,—hurt in every conceivable manner, suffering in every way, parched, feverish, and agonized, wearing a look of mute agony no words may describe, or else lapsed in an almost fortunate unconsciousness,—men from every State, pouring out blood like water and offering up lives of sacrifice for the cause they had espoused. No city in the world was sadder than Richmond in those days; all the misery and woe of Seven Pines had been emptied into her fair streets and homes, and she had "no language but a cry"—an exceedingly bitter cry, that rose in the night to God on High, if the heavens were not brass.

It was sad enough to walk the streets, that is, if one were in the least observant. Ten to one you would see some scene enacted that would make the heart ache in sympathy. The dreaded ambulance might draw up before some residence whose doors would open to receive a burden borne in tenderly—father, brother, son or husband; there might gather hastily on the steps members of the family to receive him, dead or hurt,—some wife, sister, mother,—whose words of tenderest meaning or bitterest weeping you might hear ere you passed quite out of the sound of voices. Or (for women take such matters differently), it might be you would only catch a look of mute despair, as if a face had turned to stone. Crape waved its sad signal from the door of house after house; and it was no unusual sight to see three or four funeral processions on their way to the city of the dead at the same time.

The people realized with a sudden shock the actualities of an internecine strife and it was brought to their very doors. Before, they had seen only its pride and pomp, and a martial showing; they had heard only the rattling of artillery over the stony streets, and the tread of passing columns; but all at once, with the sound of hostile guns, gaunt, grim-visaged war touched their hearts, and sickened their souls with horror.

It rendered them more determined, more earnest, more serious; it made them feel it was time to perform their part in the great tragedy and not waste the hours in light comedy, vain regrets, or childish longings.

In one day Richmond was changed from a mirth-loving, pleasure-seeking city into a city resolute and nerved to make any sacrifice for the cause she loved.

One day—Paris; the next—Sarragossa.

CHAPTER XX.

A BREATHING SPELL.

After a week had passed we changed our position, for what reason none could guess; but it was not for the better, so far as our comfort was concerned, the new camp being pitched on the slope of the hill, without the vestige of a shade tree near; about a hundred yards off was a small fringe of pines, sufficient to furnish necessary fuel for cooking purposes; the food issued was of good quality and fairly abundant.

As we had been paid off and Richmond was so near, we made our hard-earned money fly; the most economical man in the regiment saw no use of hoarding paper in times so prodigal of human life; a pocket full of notes, we thought, would not turn away a bullet; and it was as well to die poor as rich, consequently no sailor from a three years' cruise made greater haste to spend his long earnings; every cent went for the stomach, none for the back or general adornment; it was literally, "Let us eat, drink and be merry, for to-morrow we may die."

Blockade whiskey abounded; strict orders had been given to keep it out of camp, but where money is, there also is found liquor; and no law, human or divine, though backed by the bayonets of all the military, could guide its flow or gauge its overflow; it would be carried on drill in musket barrels, with a cork drummed tightly in the muzzle and a close cap on the nipple; and made to go through sundry evolutions, which in some remarkable manner always improved the flavor. Soldiers going to the spring to fill canteens would, strange to say, come staggering back, leaving upon the minds of the beholder the impression that the stream ran brandy or some other fluid whose "shallow draught intoxicates the brain." It seemed too as if the Fairies of the Midsummer Night were at work upon the magic decoction, for just as sure as you hung a canteen on the branches of a pine tree some moonlight night, not forgetting to put a dollar around the cork, just as certainly as you chanced to pass that way next day you would find that same canteen filled with stone-fence whiskey—and the dollar mysteriously gone. Humble-looking old negro men, who only wanted the chance to talk religion by the hour when they brought baskets of fruit or fowls around, always had a bottle somewhere.

Simple Moses, from the country, meek as his namesake's proverbial lamb, generally carried concealed under his belt half a dozen flasks; the old black pie-woman was famous for her jug, which in some manner, known only to her feminine devices, she smuggled in upon her person; the very newsboys knew by intuition where a demijohn lay buried in the swamp; in consequence everybody was drinking camp juleps and smashes (and every soldier knows what they are), while on divers occasions it was seen that some of the dress parade failed to exhibit that regularity of line upon which the old brigade was wont to pride itself.

The regimental sutlers reaped a rich harvest on this one item alone, ours of the Seventeenth once stating that he had cleared as much as six thousand dollars in one day; and then Confederate currency was comparatively good—about fifty per cent. in value.

The middle of June was now upon us, and so hot had it become that we found it simply impossible to remain in tents. During the early part of the day and until the late noon, the heat inside was worse than that of the blazing sun without; the canvas seemed only to draw the rays to a focus and keep them there in one white blaze.

And to add to the discomfort, swarms of flies infested the tents and could never be induced on any account to leave them; they seemed to think exposure to the outer air not at all conducive to their health, while anything like a walk abroad would be positively fatal.

Sometimes we fancied one of Egypt's plagues had been spread out again upon the land; or else that the North had sent good, loyal, flag-loving flies over the lines to harass the enemy and eat up his substance. Talk of a mule's persistence—obstinacy—how it fades into insignificance and dwindles into nothingness when you compare it to a fly's! You might take a mule's whole "cussedness," all that stands out in his ears, tail and legs, and fills his body besides, so that when he takes it into his head to stop you have need to build a fire under him to make him go—take that, I say, and condense it to fit a fly; expand this last to the mule himself, and there is enough of power in it to blow him up like dynamite. No! for consistent, double-acting, perpetual motion, aggravating obstinacy—commend me to a fly! For instance: feel the day to be unusually oppressive; take up a book or linger on the nearest verge of dreamland ready to fall into placid unconsciousness—then let one big old fellow of the swarm fix you with his eye, let him turn his bulging, calculating old orbs on your nose with intentions of his own; let him roll those same eyeballs around once or twice in their sockets while he selects a particularly delectable spot for his own future edification and arranges his plans with a view thereto; let him scratch his confounded old head several minutes with his fore feet to help along the idea; let him sharpen his teeth and whet his tongue; let him polish his claws and give himself a final rub all over; then fix his gaze steadily on the coveted morsel of a spot and make for it! Well! You might fight that fly for an hour, you may strike out with your soul in every blow, you may shock his delicacy by every big, bad word known to the English language—and back he comes with the persistent regularity of a pendulum; spite of threats and battling and profanity, back he comes! ! and comes ! ! ! into that identical spot he comes, and nothing but Death himself will turn him from it!

Death! you cannot kill him; he bears a charmed life. So at last, with your temper gone, your strength exhausted, your face reddened, you take refuge in flight ignominious, with a last recurring jab at your nose and a farewell defiant buzz ringing in your ears.

Anyhow, it was impossible to eat our meals in any comfort whatsoever; and on a rainy day we were driven as nearly fly-crazy as men can conveniently run. Our dinner generally wound up with a favorite dessert of toasted bread and molasses stewed in the camp-kettles; we thought it the very best thing to end off with, and so too thought the flies; in perfect unison of taste and opinion, they prepared to contend for every morsel and opened their whole flying artillery upon us; they assailed us with all their forces, front, rear and on both flanks. We fought with one hand and carried with sudden jerks the food to our mouths with the other. Indeed, one man of the regiment, glorious Hector Eaches, known as the best-tempered fellow in the world—a perfect Mark Tapley, who always "came out strong" in adversity and under fire, had it recorded against him in the book of chronicles—memory's great volume—that so beset, aggravated, tormented, distressed, devoured, and so tortured was he by the swarming multitudes (each one beset by forty devils), that, having lost all patience, he on one occasion was seen to seize his canteen and plate and lay about him in a perfect paroxysm of rage, cursing worse than any of the Army of Flanders.

11

In the middle of the day, after morning drill and roll call, some of us would beg, borrow or steal for the time, papers and novels and repair to the creek about a mile away from camp, then, undressing, we would lie in some shallow place in the water under the umbrageous foliage and so spend hours. It was a rather singular scene at first, to witness these heads with books before them rising above the water's level, with no other intimation of men anywhere about; the features dimly seen through the smoke that curled up from apparently the bottom of the water. One could almost imagine that the trunkless heads of the Forty Thieves had floated to the surface from below, and were exhaling a little of their sulphurous breath.

At least it had the good effect of keeping us clean, cool and in cheerful spirits, while but few of the regiment had the camp-fever that was filling the hospitals.

The camp-fever was like the old typhoid, only the surgeons pronounced it somewhat different. Many, very many were stricken down with it, and the regimental ambulances were too often employed in carrying patients to the hospitals. Dysentery and diarrhea sent many an enlisted man to his long home, though the sickness was confined to the raw levies of the Southern troops, the veterans of a year suffering but little. Causes were easily traceable to the heat of the tents and their impure air more than anything else, and exposure to the sun, bad water and unripe fruit. With several men sleeping in each tent, and the curtain down, there was absolutely no ventilation; and every pair of lungs breathed over and over vitiated air that became with each exhalation only more poisonous. One sick man not caring to complain at the first symptom of approaching illness, would remain in his tent and infect half a dozen more; then it would be discovered how very ill they were, and the doctors would forward them to Richmond.

Only two from Company A were sent away for this cause; but neither returned—the fever was fatal to them both. The truth is, the Seventeenth, in the person of Dr. Lewis, was blessed with the finest surgeon, the most skilful physician, the truest friend, the most compassionate man in the army, and the good he did, the lives he saved, and the misery he averted can never be told in this world; it would take other than an earthly pen to write what the recording Peri has entered upon her tablets.

It was a strange fact, and one that furnished subject for much conversation at the time, that the largest, stoutest and apparently the most healthy were the first to be suddenly attacked; the big, strong, bearded men were the ones to lie tossing and moaning with fever in the tents, while the delicate—those who seemed as if they could stand no fatigue and would be the first to succumb—were the fortunate ones who escaped.

The dread fever, so fatal in many cases, did not confine itself to the camp, but spread its devastating infection in the country round about. Women and children fell victims to all its long days and nights of tossing wretchedness, and helped to swell at last, and but too often, the fearful list of mortality.

The medical staff of the army learned by actual experience the unhealthiness of tents; and whether through poverty or design, they were no longer issued to the troops, who ever afterwards tabernacled in the woods in summer and built log huts in winter.

The soldier does not need them, except indeed the little shelter tents that button together, and when spread, open at both ends; these serve to keep off rain and dew and that is all he cares about. As for the regulation Sibley tent, they must become, from natural causes, the prolific source of disease and death.

When the news of Stuart's dashing raid around McClellan first reached the troops it contributed no little to raise that branch of the service higher in their estimation. The infantry and artillery had ever expressed a most sovereign contempt for the cavalry, bestowing on them nicknames that were anything but complimentary; let a squad of them pass through camp, on the principle that "listeners hear no good of themselves," their ears were regaled with such epithets as "Bomb proof," "Grub scout," "Kitchen ranger," "Buttermilk spies" and "Loons." They ran the gauntlet of ridicule and banter.

In truth, the cavalry had been having rather a good time for the past eighteen months, and because they had enjoyed such an easy, careless, roaming life, they were depreciated by soldiers who had to do their own walking, and up to this time all the fighting; then, too, there was a good deal of envy at the bottom of it all, if the whole truth must be confessed. But this brilliant achievement of Stuart's brought his men prominently to the front and gained the thorough respect of the infantry. Certainly every dragoon engaged in it was a hero for days afterwards.

The days of leafy June in all her beauty queened it right royally. About us the trees wore their fullest and deepest robes of green, the meadows bloomed with the brightest of field flowers, as if shot and shell were not soon destined to tear the one and stain the other with crimson. But then it seemed as if the month would pass in perfect peace and serenest rest.

To us who watched each coming day as one likely to usher in the impending conflict, this quiet inaction was altogether inexplicable. However, as time slipped by and nothing was heard to awaken expectation, we ceased to addle our brains as to the whys and wherefores, and revelled in whatsoever pleasures our four months' pay might buy us.

From the Northern papers that always managed to reach us by the grape-vine route, we gained a pretty clear idea of the existing state of affairs in the United States, and especially of their National Capital. Probably no contrast was ever greater than between the cities of Washington and Richmond—each the glittering prize that rival armies eyed longingly and set their hearts upon possessing.

In the former, money that poured from an open Treasury—and recklessness that knew no curb, were holding high carnival. Wealth had come suddenly to the vast army of contractors and speculators. Men unknown a short while past drew large salaries as Government officials. Lavish expenditures blazoned the way of *"les nouve aux riches,"* and gilded the residences of those who but as yesterday were hewers of wood and drawers of water. Shoddy reigned supreme and lorded it grandly. The people were fiddling and dancing, attending and giving balls, receptions, matinees and soirees; the while their wounded soldiers filled the hospitals and their army stood in long, serried lines, grimly waiting the word of advance, and the carnage to commence. Gaiety, feasting and revelry were in full blast, while events of great pith and moment were slowly unfolding, and the denouement close at hand.

In Richmond there had been no upheaval of society, bringing a lower strata suddenly to the surface, with such a longing for display, such a greed for new-found honors, such zest in the novelty of them as made their sudden possession entirely heartless for the time. The war was no gala spectacle for poor Richmond— Capital of a country against whom were closed the ports of all the world, with never a hand extended to her as she stood defiant and alone, battling for existence, rich in nothing but the blood that was being poured out so profusely and freely; no! it must have been a brave person indeed who would have dared to violate public opinion, and court its censure by giving or attending public entertainments in the Confederate Capital just then; they had not gone through the hardening process; this was not the time, they said, for gaiety, at least when sons and brothers stood with sabre and musket in hand, waiting for the onset of a brave, determined foe flushed with hopes of conquest and proud in the might of overwhelming numbers. Besides, her new-made sabre-hewn graves were still too fresh. As soon expect poor Rachel to stop weeping for her children, and no longer refusing to be comforted, array herself in ball attire and step out to the tune of the "Devil's Dream."

But Venus and Mars could not circle in each other's orbit and not mingle their rays, even if there was "blood on the moon." So much valor on one side and so much wit and beauty on the other could not meet without their own quiet enjoyment. Every house was a center of hospitality; every soldier who could get from camp, by fair means or foul, might be sure of his welcome. And so porches and balconies those warm summer nights generally held their quota of military visitors.

The Army of Northern Virginia was in splendid condition; its men were in the best possible spirits, and confident of victory. We had been furnished with new uniforms, officers shining forth especially resplendent; every day brought new regiments of infantry and batteries of artillery, which, marching through the streets, added to the feeling of confidence pervading soldier and citizen alike. Indeed, so sanguine were the Richmond merchants of a successful and speedy ending of the war, so different was the hopefulness from the despair of a month ago, that they sold the troops all they wanted at cost prices. Gold fell and the fortunes of the Confederacy never looked brighter, or promised more. Its star, waning, obscured at times, now gleamed with dazzling brilliancy, when on that memorable month of June, Lee with his army of some 80,000 men confronted McClellan, who had under him 103,000, and stood prepared to try conclusions with his foe.

It was so calm, there was so little news to tell, that even thousand-tongued Rumor took a rest. Jackson's Valley Campaign had during this month been of most absorbing interest to us; the army's pride and faith in him knew no bounds after the glories of his recent achievements. Banks, Shields, McDowell, Fremont and Milroy were all in pursuit; all baffled, never hemming in nor conquering that erratic warrior and his fleet foot-cavalry. "Oh! if we only had him with us," we say, "what an army Lee would have!" never dreaming in our wildest imaginings such a thing within the scope of possibilities.

CHAPTER XXI.

HOT TIMES AROUND RICHMOND.

The twenty-fifth of June, and the curtain was about to rise on our theatre in Virginia, with the whole civilized world for audience; the play is a tragedy it seems, and now the shrill whistle of the prompter is heard; there is that indefinable murmur as people settle themselves down in their seats, and then the silence of breathless expectancy.

The forenoon had passed and dinner had already been prepared and eaten; the men were lying without their tents smoking post-prandial pipes, when their meditations, sweet or otherwise, were rudely broken upon by the rat-a-tap tap of the drum beating the long roll, and each soldier started to his feet as if touched by the wire of an electric battery.

It meant much, this tap, how much we dared not stop to divine! only the stars above us might guess for how many it was sounding the summons that comes to each of us but once.

Yes, the time had come, the play was to begin, the curtain rises. Ladies and gentlemen of the world, the armies of the North and South are making their best bow to you!

"Get your accoutrements, men," said the sergeant, "and fall in! leave clothes and knapsacks behind!"

In ten minutes, in light marching order, the brigade turned by the right flank and went into a swinging gait in the direction of Mechanicsville. The whole army was in motion; regiments, brigades and divisions passing and re-passing en route; long trains of artillery went by us on a trot, couriers and staff officers were galloping about like mad, making all the noise and dust possible; ordnance wagons and ambulances were hitching up—types of the doctor and the undertaker who always hunt in couples.

We marched along the suburbs of the city, and late in the evening reached a large earthworks about three miles from Richmond on the Mechanicsville pike; therein the regiment filed, and received orders to bivouac for the night. We managed to pick up enough sticks to make a fire to boil our coffee, and then we sat about the parapet in the moonlight discussing the coming campaign and the relative merits of "Old Peter" (Longstreet's *nom de guerre*) and Stonewall Jackson.

Thursday was the 26th of June and we remained inactive in the breastworks all day; and it was hot in the fort surely, but the soldier is an ingenious animal, and with the aid of his bayonet and blanket secured a good shade, while a breeze was kept up by means of a tin plate used as a fan.

About four in the afternoon a signal gun boomed through the stirless air, and we lined the parapet to see what was to follow; another gun answered ere the echo had died away and then all noise ceased, and the grim barking of the war dogs was heard no more. Tired of waiting, we had slipped down to our blankets and were sleeping or dozing through the sultry heat of the evening. Suddenly the battle opened, and the tremendous pounding of the cannon showed that a hard struggle was going on within two or three miles; the furious discharges of the musketry could plainly be heard, and evidently there was hot work in front. A silence fell upon us as we sat all unconscious of the setting sun's glare and listened to the sounds of a struggle upon which hung such momentous issues. The firing never faltered until the sun sank beneath the horizon and twilight made each object misty and indistinct. Even when the stars came out, the sullen guns boomed upon the night, as if loath to leave their inhuman work. Once or twice the cannonading swelled into a volume, brightening the edge of the sky by its glare like the faint flashing of lightning after a storm. The shells were beautiful as they exploded against the dark background of the sky, seeming as if a Titan's hand with his giant brush had illuminated the vast opaque with a sudden crimson streak. It was nine o'clock before the firing died entirely away.

Friday is an unlucky day, they tell us; sailors say so, and doubtless the young Napoleon thought it, for it was for him a day fruitful of disasters; be that as it may, every private was of that opinion before another sun set in the heavens.

Hours before the morning dawned the First Brigade was in motion, and marching by way of the pike toward the battle-field. The men were yawning pretty generally, yet the excitement kept them thoroughly awake; the stars shone out with all their radiance from an unclouded sky; as we moved along the road, we saw some score or more of our soldiers lying asleep, with their blankets well drawn up over their heads, not at all disturbed by the moving troops. One of our number, in a spirit of mischief, fell out of the ranks and went up to the sleeping figures; four or five lay under one blanket, and this he selected as the fittest one for his purpose. He seized it by a corner and gave a jerk; though it flew off, not one that it had covered roused up or changed his posture. Wondering at the stillness, instead of the wrath for which he was prepared, he struck a match, held it over a face; it was the sleep that knows no waking; killed in last evening's battle, they had been brought and laid together by loving comrades, for identification and private burial. It was not a pleasant memory to carry into action!—not a happy augury one would think, and perhaps the saddened group who gathered around thought so. After marching about an hour, we were halted in the road—or rather causeway—that crossed the Chickahominy, the swamp being on either side. It was yet dark, and the order was given to "break ranks," so the soldiers spread their blankets upon each side of the narrow road, and in less time than it takes to tell it, were lying unconscious. Suddenly there came a cry of "Cavalry!" In a second the whole line went over like a set of water rats, right into the swamp, and reappeared, some hundreds of them, with a handsome coating of Chickahominy mud, that remained with them through the whole campaign. It was a false alarm; and as the men crawled back into the road, out of the black pools, the cursing on the eve of battle was not edifying. Well! The swamp *was* rather damp and foggy and we shivered and waited for His Majesty, the sun, who never hurries himself by so much as a second. At last he sent his slanting beams across the road, as much as to say: "Here I am; you would have me, but you may be sick enough of me before I go to rest across the way!"

Roll call soon after showed full ranks and no stragglers; and then after having performed the dainty duties of the toilet by scraping the mud off with a pocket-knife, we were prepared for breakfast, which consisted of a cracker, a piece of raw bacon and swamp-water. Strict orders had been issued to build no fires, and from this we knew our blue neighbors were not far away.

A signal gun went off! "Beginning early," the soldiers said; and the line was formed, the ranks dressed. As we stood at ease, a horseman, followed by a single aide, rode slowly by, touching his hat to the ranks; it was the man with the iron-gray beard and the slouch hat, General Robert E. Lee.

The sun that rose at Austerlitz was no brighter than the one now circling full in sight; nor was the army of Italy more devoted to their little Corporal than were these troops destined to be to him.

"Right dress! Right face! Forward, march!" The order was quick and decisive as it came from the colonel's lips, and the head of the column soon neared Mechanicsville. When we reached the village it needed no tongue to tell us that it was here a battle had been fought the evening before. Awful evidences of the conflict lay scattered everywhere; the dead and dying were stretched out all around; horses torn to pieces by bursting shells, overturned wagons, empty ammunition boxes, bayonet scabbards, hats, tin cups, playing cards and all the debris that helped to mark the footprints of dread Mars; wounded men lay moaning on the ground, others were sitting bandaging their own hurts and waiting for the relief; ambulances moved about the field and surgeons gave direction and helped to fill each vehicle with its pale, wan burden; even hacks and barouches from Richmond were there, with groups of citizens moving about, doing what good they could, and removing in their kindness a wounded man here and there to be taken back to their own homes. Through all these sights, so eloquent of the misery of war, we passed, seeing all around us the dead in every attitude in which death can lay the human form. Many of our soldiers were killed by grape and canister, as they charged up the hill-side upon the enemy's batteries; and so torn and mangled were they by the iron projectiles, that the women who loved them best would scarce have recognized them, poor, shapeless masses of crushed bones, scattered flesh and lacerated limbs that they were!

Into the fort which had been stormed and taken by our men with such fearful sacrifice, our brigade was halted for an hour or more. Soon many of us, filling canteens from the branch that ran near by, went among the wounded who (blue and gray) lay mixed together, and tried to alleviate, as far as we could, the world of agony around us. Uniforms made no difference in such an hour; common suffering reduced all to an equal; common anguish humanized the bitterest partisan.

Our route then lay along a succession of sloping hills interspersed here and there with groupings of trees. The sound of cannon borne by the breeze gave token that our advance was pressing the enemy's rear-guard, and we caught sight of their blue uniforms on a lofty hill some two miles off. Our march was now becoming exciting, for like fox-hunters on the trail, we had warmed up to the work and were following with the quarry in full view. Our way was through the enemy's camp, which they had abandoned. Great piles of hard-tack, coffee, bacon and other stores lay roasting and burning and charring; and as far as the eye could reach, the hills seemed a mass of flames. Such immense amounts of commissary stores surely never greeted a Rebel's gaze before! There were piles of pure ground coffee—hundreds of bushels, stacked fully twelve feet high—that, consuming slowly, made the whole atmosphere everywhere redolent with the rich aroma. Barrels and hogsheads of new pork were piled and built upon each other, roaring in very ecstasy of flames, and contending with the fumes of coffee every inch of the way as to which should yield the most appetizing of odors.

Our very path was lit with flame! O, the fire had a good jolly old feast of its own, and it crackled and snapped in its unshackled mirth, as if to say: "Who can stop me?" It mocked, taunted and fairly roared as it curled up in defiant wreaths of fragrant smoke.

A blind man, consulting his nose, might have sworn that both armies had laid down arms and gone to cooking (and we know they might have been worse employed); as it was, we who looked upon the waste could do nothing but step from ranks and pause long enough to load our haversacks with choice rations, then with a slow, long, lingering, loving sniff march sadly on.

The First Brigade was in the advance, and we kept close to the heels of the blue coats. Right ahead of us was our battery of artillery, and every time the enemy made a show of halting, the guns would be unlimbered and the shells sent screaming toward them, by way of gentle reminder to hurry up. Of course they would fire back, but only to gain time when too closely pressed. After a few compliments of the sort, both would limber up and keep on the way.

In the afternoon, when we had halted and were eating our bacon and crackers, we heard the sound of a gun far away in the enemy's rear; not only one, but two, three, four—and then they came so fast we could not count them! What could it mean? We did not know; we could not guess. At last, as the sound of the reports kept gathering in intensity, an aid passed us who stopped long enough to give an answer.

"Stonewall Jackson has arrived from the Valley and effected a junction with Lee."

Could it be true? A deafening shout burst from our men; thousands of throats took it up and rent the very air; it died away only to be repeated in greater emphasis and volume. The news ran along the lines like an electric flash, to other regiments, and the whole brigade, now fairly ablaze, put its whole soul in a shout that expressed the wild enthusiasm of the hour. Stonewall Jackson here! the genius of our Southern cause—its very soul—what could *he* know of failure? Every soldier in the ranks felt safe; the magic of that name, the prestige of his corps, was such that the most doubting Thomas had no longer any fears, but gave himself over with a sigh of relief to perfect faith and peaceful assurance.

We halted early in the evening, and kept position while other brigades continued the pursuit. McClellan having been defeated on his extreme right, and knowing Jackson was in his rear, drew in his wing and massed his army about a mile from us at Gaines' Mill, six miles from Mechanicsville, awaiting our onset.

The First Brigade, located in a strip of woods, could not see what was going on around, could only hear the tramp of the troops and the clatter of artillery. Where the enemy were or what they were doing was only a matter of conjecture; in fact every one in the brigade thought the fighting over for the day.

It was about six o'clock in the evening and the fiery rays of the sun had become more tempered as he sank slowly in the west. The men had obtained permission to make a fire and prepare some coffee—the first in two days. A heavy picket firing had sprung up some six hundred yards away, but it attracted no attention. The men had stacked arms and were sitting around the fires that were nearly hidden by the regiments of tin cups in which the coffee had slowly begun to boil; just at this time, when each one was watching his cup, or searching in his haversack for a cracker, or cutting off a slice of meat preparatory to a supper, they were thrilled through the depths of their pulsating hearts to the very ends of their fingers by an awful tempest of musketry which burst not half a mile away. It opened like a hail storm, and the firing came in showers; so close were we that the bullets hit among the trees.

The ranks were formed in a second, our rations, our bubbling coffee was left on the fire; hunger and thirst alike forgotten. Who could eat when probably it might prove the last meal ever taken on this earth? Heavens! What furious musketry! like the rattling of trains of a dozen cars commingled, so loud and close, so deafening that one had need to raise his voice to a loud pitch in order to be heard.

The fearful work was going on in the field over yonder; and men must have fallen by hundreds before that death-dealing hurricane of lead and iron. No living man would care to face such destruction unless he wearied of his life, yet each felt he would have to enter it; and reserves always had hotter times than the advance. And so the men stood pale and still, but with clenched jaws, waiting for the command to march. None came; but the bullets began to hit among us and the whole line lay flat down, while the balls and solid shells ricochetted through the woods. It was the one hard thing that veterans had to stand, that of remaining motionless under fire; not a man moved in the line.

The green of the forest was aglow with one last gleam of sunlight when the order was given to form ranks. In a double-quick we neared the scene of action. The brigade was forced to reduce its speed to a slow walk, for the road was filled with long streams of wounded men making their way to a place of safety. One of the wounded wore a major's star on his collar, and he sat his horse as easily and gracefully as if indulging in a pleasant evening's ride, though his arm just below the shoulder had been cut clean off by a solid shell and was kept from dropping only by a fragment of his coat sleeve; the severed arm swung dangling and turning round with every motion of his horse, yet he gave no moan. The man, whoever he was, was a hero—*grand* in his suffering. No hackneyed tale of mischance and reverse came from his lips, but dropping the rein upon his horse's neck, and saluting the advancing reserve, he cried out in clear, unfaltering tones:

"Forward, boys! we are driving them, and the Virginians are in front!"

A hero? The man was sublime!

A ringing cheer answered him, for the soldier's superb courage inspired the heart and soul of every man who saw and heard him. A few steps brought us to the old grinding meal and flour edifice, known as Gaines' Mill, where the road takes an abrupt turn. It was just here that the fighting began, and the mill, in consequence, looked like a sieve, ready to fall any second at a breath. Splinters, planks, bricks lay tumbled in heaps, while the huge fissures and rents made in its walls evidenced the severity of the fire.

The ground all around was absolutely covered with dead. Keeping on and picking our steps so as not to tread on the fallen, the brigade marched up the hill on the right, where were situated those breastworks of the enemy which Hood's Texans had stormed and carried a short time ago. Reaching the crest, we halted behind our artillery, which vomited forth a stream of fire upon the plain below. Nothing could be seen, the thick smoke nearly choking and blinding the men. The guns were served with a will and the very ground appeared to tremble with the force of the concussion. The gunners were so blackened and begrimed by the sulphurous vapor, that they looked like blackest chimney sweeps.

The fighting was indeed heavy in the pleateau below, and the Rebel yell and the Yankee hurrah clearly distinguishable. The batteries ceased their fire so as to allow us to advance. Darkness was near at hand. The line was formed, and the order given to "Charge bayonets!" Then the speed changed into a double-quick and the rush was made. The line reached the contestants; one volley, and all was over! An officer rode along the front, slightly wounded. "Boys," he exclaimed, "you came too late; we drove them without the reserves."

And such was the fact; they had carried by assault the enemy's works—strong positions, strongly fortified—without reserves. No wonder Stonewall Jackson, when he viewed that hill, said to the officers with him:

"The men who stormed those forts were soldiers indeed!"

The stars were in the sky by this time, and the brigade was marched to the woods about a hundred yards away, and orders given to bivouac for the night. Many started over the field to pick up such spoil as they could find; others, not quite so fond of plunder, and worn out with the excitement of the day, threw themselves on the ground and slumbered.

Capt. Smith called my name. I was sent for water, and carried fully a dozen canteens to be filled from the stream that ran through the battle-field at the bottom of the hill. Scrambling down as best I could in the dark, I filled the canteens from the running brook and took a long, steady drink; the taste was somewhat brackish, but then I was not fastidious—so what mattered it? Carrying the water, I distributed to the owners each his canteen. No sooner did the obliged and grateful party proceed to drink out their thirst than they, with one accord, spit out the fluid, and asked, "Where in the name of all creation did it come from?" The water-bearer was not by nature a patient man, while black ingratitude is ever distasteful to the generous soul— therefore he answered rather curtly, and in the worst of humors, that he never knew a branch to run with but one thing and that was water—they were at liberty to drink it or not as suited them.

"Water!" exclaimed one faithful soul, while another, of a quietly investigating turn of mind, had gone to the camp-fire and poured

the liquid in a cup. It was of a deep crimson hue; he smelled it
and pronounced it blood!

And blood it was.

Hundreds, in their mad craving for water, had crawled down to
this stream to drink and bathe their wounds in its cool running
current, which accounted for the blood.

But their Ganymeade had suddenly collapsed; his spirit was
quite broken for a day or two; his words were few—indeed he
said, when affectionately questioned of the cause, that he was ill;
then dropped the subject most mysteriously, and no after inquiries gained an answer. From this time on he examined with a
private microscope every drop of water that passed his lips.

One hour before day we formed ranks and leisurely took up
the line of march, bearing toward the right about a mile away,
where as stubborn a defense and as determined a storming had
been made as we had witnessed at the Old Mills. About ten
in the forenoon the brigade halted at a hastily thrown up breastworks which had been a part of the Yankee defenses, and from
which they had been driven with much loss. These rifle-pits were
constructed, not at the top, but at the foot of a steep hill. Directly
in front of this work and running its entire length was a deep
chasm or natural ditch that had been formed by the flow of water
when heavy rains had swollen the streams to a high mark. This
fosse of Nature's own making was about twenty feet wide and
nearly twelve feet deep, imposing a most formidable barrier to
any Rebel assault. The enemy's right was defended by thick woods
a hundred yards deep, and made secure by rifle-pits on its edge.
It will be seen that their position had been strongly chosen, for
all in their front was open ground, half a mile across which the
Rebel advance would have to be made. Yet it was a bad place for
the Federals in case of retreat; to cross a level meadow of a mile
in extent and obtain the shelter of the woods away back would
have been equivalent to running amuck.

These works were heavily garrisoned, and an attack as confidently expected. To Pickett's Virginia Brigade was given this
task of storming and capturing the line. Pickett did not charge
it in front—well for him he did not, for the situation was simply impregnable, and any attempt to take it by direct assault would have
eventually ended in a bloody repulse—but formed his line behind the brow of the hill, marched left oblique and carried the
woods on the right in a run; then swung his line by right wheel,
and struck the enemy in reverse and rear. A heavy fight occurred

here and the Virginians lost many men; but when the enemy broke, and instead of surrendering undertook to escape by running through this meadow, as level as a billiard table, and in which were no trees nor anything to serve for protection save a ditch through its center, the loss was simply frightful, and the men were picked off by hundreds. Some of the Seventeenth went over the field afterwards and counted between six and seven hundred dead on the ground. Most of the wounded had all been taken by our ambulances, in the night and early morning, and sent to the hospitals in Richmond. The battle of Gaines' Mill, though ending in our favor and practically relieving Richmond by sending McClellan back to the shelter of his gunboats, cost us heavily. Our loss exceeded that of the enemy, for in the whole battle we had been the attacking force; our opponents fighting behind their breastworks. Their loss was killed and wounded six thousand five hundred men; prisoners, two thousand five hundred; making a total of nine thousand. They lost by capture two guns, besides thousands of small-arms and munitions of war. The Rebel loss was nine thousand five hundred men killed and wounded. The moral effect of the battle was great; on one side it had demoralized an over-confident enemy, causing him to retreat and burn his stores; while on the other it had inspired exultation, and had given us the prestige of having defeated the enemy and compelled his withdrawal from the field.

The brigade spent all day in these works, very pleasantly engaged, many of them reading the letters which were to be had by the thousands for the mere picking up. They were of every style under the sun, for human nature is much the same all over the world. But the love letters, the tender effusions, interested us most, especially those love-lorn Rebs who had none of their own.

The plunder left by our friend Billy Yank was calculated to gladden the heart of every poverty-stricken Johnny, and of such abundance as satisfied even the rapacity of the professional camp follower. The ground in the vicinity was plentifully strewn with knapsacks; all around in the greatest profusion lay new Minie and Enfield rifles, which our soldiers gladly exchanged for their old Springfield smooth-bore muskets, altered from the ancient flint-lock to the percussion-cap style. Nearly every man in the brigade furnished himself with these new arms of approved pattern, together with the accoutrements, and there was hardly a soldier in Longstreet's division who did not obtain a complete outfit of clothes, besides knapsacks, haversacks, blankets, oilcloths, and all those munitions which add to a soldier's efficiency and comfort, and which now lay on the ground just ready for the men to help themselves.

And they surely did.

The Yankee knapsacks were a revelation to our impecunious Confederates, whose entire outfit was nothing to draw forth a single brag from the army itself. Each Federal had a good blanket, oilcloth, and overcoat rolled up and carried across his shoulder; strapped on the top of his knapsack outside, he had an extra suit of blue clothes for dress parade, two suits of under-clothing, an extra hat, and a case containing needles, thread, but-tons, &c. Then there were razors in nearly every knapsack (there was hardly one in our Seventeenth!), besides soap, brushes, comb, portfolio containing writing paper, stamps, flash novels, pens, song books, while several daguerreotypes generally com-pleted the inventory. Many canteens were filled with whiskey, which was confiscated in the most satisfactory manner without loss of time. Haversacks held sugar, pork, dried beef, rice and beans, with hard-tack of course.

The brigade that occupied the works proved to be from the Empire State; the regiment in the breastworks immediately in the front opposite the ditch was the Forty-fourth New York. Its men made a gallant fight, but must have lost nearly one-third their number.

There are men in every regiment totally callous and brutal, who go over the battle-field and search the pockets of the fallen for money and watches; nearly every one of the dead had his pockets turned inside out. They lay, stricken by every kind of wound. Some rested as calmly and serenely as if asleep; others had their bodies twisted, and fingers clutched and sunk in the blood-stained ground, showing the agony of their dying. Many lay with eyes wide open to the sky, their feet to the foe, and jaws clenched tightly with desperate determination. Here was an old man with his arm extended at full length above his head, ramming the cart-ridge home when the bullet made that ugly hole in his forehead. Not a rod away was a little drummer-boy who had fallen on his face; a ball had struck him in the side and he had died a hard death, evidently having lived hours after he was wounded, for the ground showed where he had tried to crawl toward his lines, leav-ing a bloody trail. Death might well have spared him.

Another body, that of a young Union soldier, was calculated to interest and touch the hardest heart. He had been shot while endeavoring to reach the shelter of the woods beyond, the flying ball having overtaken the fleeing form, and struck him in the small of the back, going clear through the body. It had not been an immediately fatal wound, for the earth bore evidence of his death-struggles; his last effort had been to pray, for he had gotten on his knees, and his hands were clasped when nature yielded up the strife; he had evidently died with a prayer on his lips. Out of his breast-pocket protruded a photograph, which proved to be that of a lady, so obscured by his life-blood, and so torn by the passing bullet that the features were obliterated; some woman "watching and waiting for him—loving and praying for him," we said; and gently put it back upon the blood-stained breast, just where she would have had it stay.

Then again there lay a pale, slender boy, who could scarcely have numbered sixteen years. The azure veins beat no longer beneath the skin that had all the fairness of a maiden's; light hair was curling upon the brow in short, crisp, wavy ringlets; the eyes that gazed so blankly upward seemed as if heaven's own blue was mirrored in them; the face was infantile in its grace and touching in its rare beauty and sweetness of expression—no sign of pain, but a smile instead, lingering on the lips! The hands and feet were well shaped and small, the form almost dainty in its symmetry. A grape-shot had done the fell work, and he had simply bled to death. But tender hands—either of friend or foe —what matters it, had performed some last kindly office; a blanket had been spread over him, while another formed a pillow beneath the head; a canteen half filled with water lay beside him, and some hasty efforts had been made to bind the gaping wound.

Vindictive feelings toward a foe pass away at sight of the battle-field. None with a human breast can see the agony, the pools of gore, the dead without being profoundly stirred—without stopping to ponder over the hearts that are riven; the hopes that are crushed; the firesides made desolate, North and South.

Many a bullet after it has done its deadly work has stricken friends as well as foe; many a ball that sped from Southern ranks has rebounded into Southern homes; many a Northern missile has found its after-mark in Northern hearts. A mother had a son who wore the blue and another who wore the gray. Father and son have fought on either side. The dearest ties of blood and friendship stand suddenly separated and arraigned in deadliest enmity, and yet Nature will assert her sway at last; and

12

should Death intervene to lay one low, as passionate, tender tears are shed as if the war had been a dream.

Strange, in a land whose people name themselves for Christ the Merciful, this should be so! The commandment from the Mount, "love one's enemy," finds strange translation in bursting shells and tearing shot, and screaming bullets and gaping wounds, and holocausts of precious lives, and bleeding hearts, and broken homes and fiercest hatred. However, to the end of time "there shall be wars and rumors of war!"

But in all the range of Creation, from the shore of the world's beginning until the Angel with one foot on sea and one foot on the land shall proclaim time's ending, has there ever existed, or ever shall exist, aught so ruthlessly, utterly, hopelessly cruel as civil and internecine war?

CHAPTER XXII.

THE BATTLE OF FRAZIER'S FARM.

On the morning of the 29th of June the brigade started on the back track for Richmond, following the same road and repassing the same one it had traversed two or three days previously. Not a trace remained of the abandoned munitions or of the vast stores left by the enemy. Quartermasters and commissaries had taken the lion's share, while the camp-followers, country people, and the ubiquitous darkies, acting the part of jackals, had swept away the last vestige of everything that could be put to any use. Not a tin cup, a battered canteen, a useless musket, nor even an old torn rag had been overlooked; indeed, it seemed as if a vast army of chiffoniers and gutter-snipes had passed over the field, like so many Egyptian locusts, and made a clean gathering of pickings and sweepings in general. The only thing they had not carried away was Virginia's soil.

That the movements of the army may be better understood, a brief outline of the campaign is given.

In the first place it may be well to state just here, that when General Lee assumed command of the army he had, all told, Smith's division, Longstreet's, Magruder's and D. H. Hill's, one cavalry brigade, and one regiment of reserve artillery; in all an effective force of 53,688 men. Just before the Seven Days' Battles he had been reinforced by Ripley's brigade, numbering twenty-three hundred and sixty-six men; Holmes's command, ten thousand strong; Lawton's Georgia Brigade of thirty-four hundred, and Jackson's two divisions, eight thousand two hundred and eighty-four; making a total of reinforcements received, twenty-four thousand one hundred and fifty altogether. Eighty thousand seven hundred and sixty men as the effective force of General Lee.

Opposed to this force, we have from the Official Returns of the Army of the Potomac, as given by Mr. Swinton in his History of that Army—that on the 20th of June, 1862, General McClellan had present for duty one hundred and fifty thousand men.

At this time Lee had driven McClellan in two battles from his strongest positions, and the prestige of a great victory rested with the Southern army. But Lee had placed himself in a perilous position. Nearly two-thirds of his original force of less than fifty-four thousand men were east of the Chickahominy, while the remaining third were on its west, of which latter number 7,000 were across the James. Between them lay McClellan with his 115,000, a third of which could easily have guarded the river, for the nature of the ground rendered any attack upon him extremely difficult; while with the remainder of his forces, say some seventy-six thousand strong, he might have marched into Richmond in a few hours. We had then but few troops in the city, and it is only a question whether they could have held the defenses sufficiently long to have enabled Lee to throw in reinforcements. The citizens of Richmond, at least those who appreciated the dangers of the situation, were terribly alarmed at this juncture, fearing just such a result; and breathed freer when all possibility of an attack had passed. McClellan, for the strongest reasons, of which he no doubt was the best judge, determined on retreating to the James.

The movement called "the change of base" means in reality a retreat. It was a very simple thing to accomplish on this occasion, however, and merely involved a march of fifteen miles with no enemy in front; but with one, supposed to be superior, on one flank and possibly in the rear.

White Oak Creek falls into the Chickahominy rather south of the Federal left, in their position at Seven Pines. It is bordered by White Oak Swamp, which near Richmond is many yards wide, and slopes up into a wooded tract extending to the James. The main roads, the Charles City, Darbytown, and New Market, starting from near Richmond diverge southward toward the Chickahominy, skirting the swamp on its southern side. The whole region near is intersected by obscure cross-roads, upon which was here and there a clearing. The roads were ankle deep with dust, which rose in clouds in the air as it was stirred up by the movement of troops.

Lee's plan of action was simple. Magruder and Huger, with their divisions, were ordered to move down the Charles City and New Market roads, to take part in the flank attack. They were to be assisted by Holmes's and Wise's brigades from Fort Darling. In this attack, intended to cut McClellan off from retreating to the James and so surround him, the entire Southern Army was to take part.

Early on the morning of the 29th the divisions of A. P. Hill and Longstreet crossed the Chickahominy by the new bridge, which had only been partially destroyed on the 26th, passed through the deserted Union lines almost to Richmond; turned eastward, and heading for the White Oak Swamp, moved down the Darbytown road, and at nightfall encamped not far from the center of McClellan's retreating army. The Northern line was eight miles long, one end almost touching Malvern Hill while the other rested at the crossing of White Oak Creek.

The bridges over the Chickahominy were down in front of Jackson, and he was unable to repair them until the morning of the 30th, having no organized Sapper and Mining Corps; and to this fact, more than all others combined, we attributed the miscarriage of Lee's plans, and the failure of his device to envelope the Federal army in his toils. This inability of Jackson to cross in time was the hole in the web that was being spun around the hornet. Had it been woven intact, whether the hornet could have broken through is a problem that will never be solved. As it was, Jackson, finding the bridges down, had to sit on the opposite side of the river all that afternoon and listen to the heavy battle taking place not two miles distant from him, in which he was expected to have been chief actor, and which his corps could in all probability have decided in our favor.

Holmes and Wise had come in sight of the head of McClellan's column, upon whom they had opened a distant fire; but a few rounds from the gunboats and heavy fire from the enemy's batteries scattered their force of raw levies, and they took no further part in the operations that ensued.

Longstreet and A. P. Hill resumed their march down the Darbytown road, and at noon came in sight of the Union line drawn up at Frazier's Farm near a point where a road leading from the James crosses those from Richmond.

Huger was supposed to be moving by the Charles City road to the same point; *but he mistook the way*, so he said, and did not make his appearance all that day; and for this weak and unsoldierlike ignorance—to use no harsher term—he was removed from command by General Lee within twenty-four hours, and relegated to an obscure post where his proven incapacity could work no further harm.

The enemy's line invited an attack, for it was so long, owing to the retreat and the topography of the country, of which they were ignorant, that its continuation was broken into great gaps. The Federal forces were placed: McCall, with his Pennsylvania division, at Frazier's Farm; on his right was Hooker's division, on his left Kearny's, while on Kearny's left was a strong force. Sumner's corps was held back in the center behind McCall, as reserves. Keyes's and Porter's corps were nearly within reach of Malvern Hill. Franklin's corps was in the rear at White Oak Creek.

At four o'clock the attack was begun by Kemper's brigade upon McCall's division. It was driven back with a loss of two hundred and fifty killed and two hundred prisoners—one-fourth of the whole number. Other divisions were sent in, and forced McCall to retire; but reserves from Sumner's coming up, the contest was prolonged until night put a stop to the conflict. The enemy's loss was five hundred and sixty killed and four hundred and fifty wounded, and several hundred prisoners.

On the morning of July 1st the Union army was strongly posted on Malvern Hill, an elevated plateau a mile and a half long and half as broad. Its flanks were well covered by woods, and the front protected by a gully, rendering any hostile approach difficult, except by the roads that crossed them. At the crest of the hill seven siege guns were placed in position, and the artillery so posted that the fire of sixty guns could be concentrated on any point that might chance to be assailed. Of course such a position could easily be held against any triple force brought to bear against it.

Clearly all along the force of the foe, as seen in the light of history, was vastly underrated in this whole campaign. When General Lee crossed the Chickahominy on the 26th he supposed the greater force of the enemy to be on the east side, but at Gaines' Mill, he, having a preponderance of numbers, fairly assumed that the Yankees were weak on the other side, otherwise they would have brought more men upon the field. At Frazier's Farm the two divisions of Hill and Longstreet were inferior to the force opposed to them; and the dispositions made by Lee in the attack clearly evidenced that he did not suppose himself to have been confronted by an effective force of more than fifty thousand men.

At nine in the morning Jackson received orders to attack. Including D. H. Hill's division he had, after deducting all losses, about thirty thousand men. Hill being on the Confederate right was opposed to the Union left where Hooker was posted. The attack was commenced, but Jackson found the heights so strongly fortified as to make the attempt one of sheer madness, consequently the assault was suspended; but he was ordered to make the trial and of course was beaten back. Magruder, with his splendid division, next advanced, and met the same inevitable result; nevertheless, these mad, hopeless charges were kept up until sundown brought the sanguinary scene to a close. In this battle every advantage remained with the enemy, for every attack upon him had been defeated with great slaughter. Our loss was nine hundred killed and three thousand five hundred wounded, against three hundred and seventy-five killed and fifteen hundred wounded on their side, a proportion of nearly three to one against us.

The result of the week's battles, taken as a whole, were very gratifying, for Lee in one week had raised the siege of Richmond. The whole Confederate loss was some 9,500 men; that of the Union army 6,500, besides 2,500 prisoners, 22 cannon and a vast quantity of small-arms.

After this synopsis of military events the thread of the narrative is resumed just where the brigade on the morning of the 29th had taken up the line of march.

After a short halt the column was put in motion following hard on the heels of the foe; then the brigade bore to the right and crossed the Chickahominy by the pontoons known as New Bridge, which the enemy had built and only half burned. It was the first thing of the kind our troops had ever seen, and it excited our admiration by the simple yet effectual manner in which a deep, sluggish stream, and an apparently impassable morass could be crossed by long lines of soldiery—crossed without even so much as the wetting of a shoe. We had here before our eyes another proof of a hurried retreat, in the shape of a long brass forty-eight pounder, half submerged in the slime of the swamp, which had slipped from the bridge and been there abandoned.

"Lie there, old broadside," we thought; "better there than shuffling off our mortal coils. Would that the rest of your Yankee fraternity were sleeping peacefully by your side!"

After we had crossed the pontoons, reached the highlands and defiled into a meadow beyond, a sight met our eyes that caused the boldest to shrink back. About half a mile away was a perfectly-constructed chain of breastworks, redoubts, and rifle-pits; and in the embrasure of the former we could see the dull muzzles of the cannon pointing in our direction, while from the latter the bristling bayonets gave proof that the fortifications were filled with men. The brigade was formed in line of battle in the center of the meadow, and then came a halt, while several officers rode away to reconnoitre. The men's faces were decidedly blank, and some hundred Testaments and Bibles were openly taken from pockets and conned with the same zeal that a school-boy crams for the holiday commencement.

"They are not going to make us charge those works!" remarked one of the men.

"We will be wiped out clean!" responded another.

"Not a man left alive!" ejaculated a third, sadly shaking his head in all the solemnity of prophecy.

"I am going to take a last chew of tobacco," said Ad. Saunders, of Co. A, close by—a long, slab-sided fellow, made so by attack of camp fever.

"Pass that plug around, then!" answered Connie Johnson. "You'll have no more need of it!"

"No I'll be d—— if I do," Ad. replied, returning the plug to his pocket decidedly. "I might get wounded; I might be taken prisoner; I might—— Anyway, it is a handy thing to have around."

"You need not be afraid," remarked Mark Price, another of the crowd—a short, broad, thick-set boy. "You just turn yourself sideways and no Yankee can see you to take aim at you. The only danger is that the wind of a cannon ball might blow you away; you're about as fat as a match, anyhow. As for me," he continued, "they might as well try to miss a barn as not hit me."

"Boys," said Walter Addison, of the same rank and file, in most solemn accents, "I am not going to set the example, but the first man I see running, I hope I may die if I don't follow him!"

"Well," soliloquized John Zimmerman, of a philosophical turn, "a man can't die but once; and we are all bound to get killed before this war's ended, so what's the odds!"

Just then I saw a fine rifle, of the latest pattern, lying near, so I slipped out of the ranks to exchange it for an old Springfield musket; and it so happened that precisely at that moment our colonel came riding by. Seeing a man out of his place his wrath knew no bounds, and he shouted out in such stentorian tones that the whole regiment heard him.

"Fire and brimstone! What are you doing out of ranks? Fall in there instantly, do you hear? And, Alex Hunter, if I catch you at it again I will send you straight back home!"

"I hope you will, Colonel," I responded; "I hope you will, for though I never want to be drummed out of the army—there's no place like home now, I'm thinking."

A roar of laughter followed this remark; for there was not a man present who did not feel at this hour that home had never before held such charms—such allurements.

Soon the officers returned and reported that they were our men and not Yankees who were garrisoning the works. A smile illuminated each face, that broadened into a full broadside of a grin. The playing cards so repentantly thrown aside were carefully and painstakingly gathered up; Bibles sought their wonted retreats, and a most genial feeling of relief was felt. As we approached the works abandoned by the foe, now manned by our own men, cheers greeted us instead of shot and shell.

We kept up a steady tramp, and as the day advanced the rays of the sun became more and more ardent, while the marching was beginning to tell upon the men. No halt at all was allowed, not even to give us time to eat or drink. Toward the afternoon the gait became almost a run, and with scattered ranks we went at a sling trot, almost blinded with the dust, which lay nearly ten inches deep, and had been so trodden and ground down by the wheels of the artillery and the feet of thousands that it was ready now to fly out at the slightest breath of air. Like the patient worm it turned under the foot that crushed it, rose aloft in wrath, filled our eyes, noses and mouths with an impalpable powder, and whitened our clothes as much as the meal dust does the miller's. It was simply impossible to keep in close ranks; that would have resulted in nothing short of suffocation. Every now and then the men spread out like an opened fan into a field to get fresh, unburdened air.

To add to our troubles we were tortured with thirst. Water was very scarce, not a full canteen in the whole brigade, and when we passed a house that had a well, hundreds of soldiers would rush toward it, and such a scene would then ensue as made the good people of the domicile hold up their hands in holy horror. A frenzied crowd, struggling, pushing, fighting, cursing, trying in mad efforts to reach the brink; and when the bucket was drawn up, fifty hands holding fifty tin cups extended, and in their eagerness spilling half the precious water! Fortunately we passed a running stream, and in a moment a line extended for half a mile up and down its banks, many throwing themselves down at full length and, like animals, lapping the grateful, cooling liquid; but not one soldier in a dozen got a mouthful; I know I did not, and I almost went mad. I thought with Sheridan, "All that I have, all that I am, all that I hope for; my property here, my interest in heaven—all would I give for a full drink of water." What queer, yet most painful, tantalizing pictures flit through the brain of a man who hungers or is athirst. I thought of the enticing pictures of the "Gardens of the Faithful," as told in the Koran, and of the fountains running with frozen sherbet; I recalled that exquisite ode from Horace wherein Naera, with "ruddy, glowing arm," holds out the earthen cup of freezing, snowy goat milk, while on the other hand Lydia extends with a Circean smile a silver flagon "filled to the brim" with old Falerian wine chilled with snow.

All that afternoon our speed was not relaxed, and we kept on at the same rate, the officers urging the men forward. It proved too great a task for many; the clouds of dust, the difficulty of walking, the impeded breath, the extreme heat began to tell; many, completely exhausted, began to fall out of ranks. The thermometer was over 90 in the shade. Satan only knows what it was in the open air. Some staggered and fell with sunstroke, and were laid out on the road-side and left with the doctors.

About four o'clock scores of men lined the highway, while some had even fallen dead. Later on in the evening there were hundreds reclining under the shadow of friendly trees, utterly prostrated and unable to move a foot farther.

It was not that the men were shirking or straggling,—there was very little of that,—but they had simply given out and nature had rebelled against the inexorable task.

The sun set, blazing defiance as it did so; and the sultriness did not seem to decrease. Darkness came on, but still the cry was "Forward!" The men who had not so far succumbed, with jackets off, wet with perspiration, their waists girded tightly, did their best, and dog-trotted at the rate of six miles an hour. They had reached a state of sulkiness, and each man determined to keep up if it should kill him; but nearly a third fell from exhaustion, and the rest of the soldiers staggered down the road like drunken men, before the order to halt was heard; but at last, about eleven o'clock that night, the welcome cry was given. Foot-sore and with chafed limbs, the soldiers, too tired to eat, fell in their tracks, lying on both sides of the road for a mile or more, motionless as if they had been slain in battle. No sound came from that inert mass except the panting,—like hounds broken down, with the scent cold and the quarry lost.

We were up at the earliest dawn, and after eating our crackers and a slice of raw meat, prepared to move. It was a lovely morning, that thirtieth of June, 1862, and a day to be remembered by all.

We kept our onward march very leisurely now, frequently halting. The scene was enlivening; long columns of infantry, in the vicinity of Frazier's Farm, could be seen wending their way to take up their positions; batteries of artillery went by at a gallop, the horses white with foam; stragglers were beginning to drop into line and the ranks were pretty full; this was optional with them, for then we had no provost guard to hurry the men up from the rear; the troops were in good spirits. It is astonishing what magic power for recuperation there is in a good sleep and a humble breakfast. No one would have recognized these serried, solid lines of infantry as the same hurrying, jaded-looking stream of men that seemed last night more like fugitives than anything else.

On the road which we were so leisurely pursuing were many cherry and mulberry trees in full bearing. Against the most stringent orders, the soldiers would break ranks and fill the branches with a struggling, clamorous crowd, cramming the fruit by the handfuls into their mouths, breaking the boughs and pitching them down to comrades below, for whom there was no room above, while they made the welkin ring with their shouts of laughter. And the trees! one moment vigorous with growing life, rich in shade-giving leaves and brilliant in their red-hued fruit, the next,—a stump with a few stick twigs extending therefrom, and a leaf only here and there, that rather displayed its poverty than served to cover its nakedness.

About three o'clock we halted on the verge of a large swamp and lay on our arms; we failed to hear the echo of a distant gun, whose music had so filled our ears for the past week that we had come to miss it when it stopped. All Nature seemed asleep, and many of the soldiers had followed her illustrious example. Nature and soldiers both suddenly awoke, and stayed awake, it is needless to say, for the rest of that day.

Cannonading had begun on our left, and increased with every moment; battery after battery along our line, to the right and to the left, merged and intermingled, until not one seemed' wanting in the chorus, as in one of Sebastian Bach's fugues, where the first violin leads off alone, and then one by one each instrument joins in until there comes the grand crash of the whole orchestra.

We had had no idea that the enemy was so close to us until they began to compliment us in such wise, saluting us with messages of cannon whose shells sang joyful sounds to the far off as they sailed through the air. Now there is something honest, rough and straightforward about solid shot—it goes straight to the mark and scorns anything crooked; there is nothing mean about it, it is open and blunt, and turns neither to the right nor left for anything; if it hits you it does so squarely, after a timely warning of the wrath in store, and then only because you get into its way; it likes a clear, rich, full, parabolic sweep; all its methods are lofty in scope and big in execution. So too with a Minie-bullet; it follows the solid on general principles, and is as independent as the Fourth of July, and as cool as an iceberg; it has the most killing ways about it.

There is something rascally low and mean about a shell—it never goes straight, it is never reliable; it always starts so high and ends so low; and then again it is a born spy. If there chances to be a dark wood a half mile away, a shell is sent there to try to find out whether or not anybody is lurking within. If a half dozen scared, harmless men are running to the rear, what is it but a cowardly shell which flies after them and fairly bursts itself to stop them. If there be an ambulance skulking along the road, the shell must go across to see what it is doing there; it has a sardonic way of screaming as it approaches you, the bully that it is, to frighten the heart into your mouth and induce you to run, for it has no notion of letting you up if it can help it, any more than a cat with a mouse; it loves to strike a man who is down, and it will not prove a good stroke either; not straight from the shoulder, but piecemeal. It will tear the body from the soul and lacerate the flesh and mangle the bones; like a fiend possessed, it will not only aim for *you* but for your friends also; in fine, it is sneaking, tyrannical and cruel, and if there is any dirty work to be performed, the shell is ready for the task.

On our left the musketry began to play, and soon the battle raged. The shells flew and burst around, and then followed an hour of torturing suspense. The same scene that we passed through at Gaines' Mill, was reenacted here. At last, a little after four o'clock, the whole brigade, in line of battle, swept forward; it passed through a narrow swamp, nearly dry from the excessive drought, and entered on a broad meadow beyond. The men advanced on a run, one straight, unbroken line, with the guns before them at a charge, the bayonets like lances projecting forward and fencing off the rays of the sun, the colors waving proudly, while thousands of feet beat the earth in rhythmical time, the officers well in front with their unsheathed swords in hand.

It was indeed a gallant array for the moment, and many eyes brightened at the glorious spectacle. Across the fields, with ranks as perfectly dressed as in a review, the brigade was double-quicking, and not a shot was fired upon it. Across the field, into the dark, gloomy recesses of the swamp, the line entered. The trees were not close, but the vegetation was rank; the trailing vines were thick and barred the view. We could only see a few paces distant; we lost sight of our proud line and struggled to keep in dressed order, but it was impossible. A fence broke the formation as we climbed over it zig-zag, and then in somewhat loose fashion the Seventeenth reached the other side of the swamp, and entered into a border of thick wood. Here a full volley of musketry came in our faces.

"Too high, Messieurs!" The balls skimmed the branches and perforated the leaves, but not a man fell; not a gun answered from our ranks, the officers shouting to us to hold our fire. Reducing our pace we straightened the line instinctively as each shoulder touched that of his next comrade.

"Guide center to the colors" was always understood in battle.

We crossed the woods, not fifty feet wide, and entered into an apparently impassable swamp overshadowed by lofty oak and gum trees, whose tops so interlaced as to shut out the light. The ground was seamed with ditches and gulleys, and miry to the feet, the black ooze in some places permitting us to sink to the knees. It was right in front of the enemy, and well did they choose their position, for no troops could charge in any order across that stretch of brambles, trees and mire.

The regiment kept as even ranks as was possible under such untoward circumstances, but some of the men would tumble into the ditches and climb out, while others would sink into the mud. Many dashing, reckless soldiers surged ahead in spite of all order, for the bullets were now striking in our midst and doing execution, consequently the line was rendered most uneven and irregular.

After struggling along in this manner we came to a fence; across this each man swung himself and then stopped a moment to reform. That line was destined to dress by neither the center nor the right for some time afterwards, for no sooner were we across than a column of fire opened upon us; a battery of six guns vomited its grape and canister into our midst at pistol-shot distance, and the noise of the balls cutting their way through all obstacles was incessant and most fearful. The men fell on their knees and held their muskets at "ready." We could not see ten yards before us, but the enemy had our range and were making the situation unusually hot.

"Fire! Aim low, men!" and at the command, flames streamed from the musket-barrels. Then we stood, and it was give and take for about a quarter of an hour.

The officers gave but one order—one single one: "Aim low, men; aim low!"

We were outnumbered, we saw that, but none knew how great the odds were; had we possessed the knowledge which we gained afterwards, our soldiers at this juncture would have struck for the rear without pulling trigger; but the heavy, rolling volleys from their line, and the light rattling ones from ours by way of simple contrast, were not long in disclosing to the most ignorant the unvarnished, unpalatable truth. Our salvation was only due to the elevation of their fire. Most of us were either crouching down and firing, or were protected by the trees; fortunately, also, our line occupied a slight dip in the ground about a foot or two deep, and this saved many from the stream of iron and lead coming vengefully toward us; besides, it became such hard work, firing and loading, that we had but little time to look around or think upon the odds.

The Yankees had been reinforced. A heavy musket fire then opened, while their aim became truer and more dangerous. Evidently the flash of our guns had shown clearly our position, for the opposing lines were not over seventy-five yards apart. Men began to drop fast; some remaining where they had fallen, others limping or hopping away to the rear. Just as we were fighting and dying our gamest and best, we heard the Yankee hurrah on both our flanks, their fire enfilading us from three quarters of the compass. But firing from the front was just as much as our patience could be induced to stand, inasmuch as we had but one pair of hands in front, no side arms, and so the game was up. The order came "Retreat," and to those who heard it, it was *sauve qui peut*.

Regimental officers and men broke and scattered. Some sought the rear, others rushed about, too excited to know exactly what course to follow. The fire of the enemy was now at its height and our soldiers were dropping by fives and tens; a few still kept up the contest; concealing themselves in the fissures and chasms, they would load, rise, deliver their fire and dis-appear again into their hidden security.

No man could take note of the movements of the regiment about this time, for each individual was acting under his own orders—general, colonel, captain and private all combined in his own consciousness. The timid were striking for the rear, the cautious were snugly ensconced in the ditches awaiting developments; the reckless and the bulldogs ramming home their cartridges with unrelenting ardor and aiming carefully along the lay of the land before they pulled their triggers, for no enemy was visible.

The finale was near at hand.

In a very short time, a few moments it seemed, a Yankee line of battle in close order came trailing through the woods. Four of us—Boyer, Ballenger, Hector Eaches and myself—threw our muskets into the ditches and tumbled in after them just in time to have the blue-coats spring over our heads.

Then, rising in the rear of their line of battle and perceiving a great group of Yankees not ten feet off, we scrambled out and halloed:

"Billy Yank, we surrender!"

"All right, Johnny, come along." And we trotted after them contentedly.

"Are you badly hurt?" one of them inquired of me.

I looked and found my trowsers covered with blood. Thereupon I proceeded to find out, pulled up my breeches, rolled up my drawers and—"No, not a scratch," I answered.

In truth, it was the blood of some unfortunate, splashed over me; whose, I did not remember nor would I ever know, nor did I waste much time in thinking over it; I felt that the battle was over and I was not dead, neither was I in heaven, nor yet—the other place.

CHAPTER XXIII.

SIGHTS AND SCENES IN PRISON.

With two guards apiece we made our way to the rear, seeing at a glance what madness it had been to send a brigade against such a force as this—a six-gun battery in our front, one on each flank, with McCall's whole Pennsylvania Division in the advance, backed by a heavy reserve; another mistake, with a heavy slaughter, of course, for us.

It was an exciting time. This wide road was filled with marching soldiers, batteries of artillery dashed by, hardly discernible in the huge clouds of dust which they raised. Brigade after brigade was taking position, going in a double-quick, as if they had no time to spare. How martial and soldier-like they looked, too! How distinguished in their uniforms! Used as we had been to the varying variegated shades of homespun and butternut, which were as ugly as unpretending, the spectacle of those blue-coats, their gleaming arms, together with their bold, warlike appearance, their high discipline, struck us with admiration, a little mixed with wonder.

The struggle was at its height; a vast volume of firing swelled up in a grand refrain. The field was filled with stragglers, and the slightly wounded were coming out of the fight by hundreds.

A brigade passed us on a run to the front, each man with a spade strapped to his left hip. At that time we did not know the exact use of those implements so carried, unless it was to bury their dead; it never occurred to our minds that they were used to throw up rifle-pits in case of need.

After a retreat of about a mile our conductors halted where there were some prisoners seated on the ground, surrounded by a heavy guard. We were turned in amongst the throng and to our delight found others, ten or twelve of the Seventeenth Regiment.

Misery certainly does love company; no one can deny that sentiment in the unregenerate heart of man. To our eager questionings, they could make no reply, having been, like ourselves, scattered from the main body, and gathered up singly or in groups of two or three, by the enemy, who took them in just as a crack sportsman would pick up the dispersed partridges after the covey had been flushed.

The uproar was by this time fairly deafening, while the mingled clouds of smoke and dust hung like a pall over where the blue and gray had locked horns. It was a great fight that was raging, and momentous issues were at stake, so we sat there most absorbingly interested. We did all that our individual efforts could do; all now that remained of duty was to take matters as quietly as possible. It soon becomes a soldier's philosophy to waste no time in vain longing or fruitless regrets, so we watched the denouement.

An hour had passed and still the firing had not lessened. It appeared to be a dogged, persistent, face-to-face, foot-to-foot, stand up conflict.

"Would their reserves never give out?" we asked each other as brigades and divisions flowed onward to the woods; and "Can we ever face such a force as they have massed in column?"

The answer came sooner than had been expected, for in one supreme moment the noise of the artillery and musketry reached such an infernal clamor that it seemed that the last day on earth had come and the sleepers were to be awakened from their graves. Every face was pale, both of prisoners and guards. A thousand stragglers were rushing frantically to the rear, and the battle's thunder came closer. The blue-coats were falling back —no one could doubt that, but there was nothing of a rout in those serried lines, only a giving of the ground, inch by inch.

More closely yet sounded the roaring of the guns, and a stream of wounded now broke through the solid ranks, some without their knapsacks and bare-headed, some panic-stricken; but there was nothing in that—even veterans would tremble as they entered into or retired from the mouth of such a fire-smitten hell.

We were forced to make still another retrograde movement of several hundred yards, for the Rebel shells were bursting uncomfortably close, and the Yankee batteries were taking position immediately in front of us. The dust was blinding, it settled over everything; it covered horses and men with a dry coating, it stung our faces like so many gnats; we breathed it, we swallowed it, it lined our throats and inflamed our lungs, it made our eyes blood-shot, it parched our tongues, it was impalpable, ubiquitous, and almost maddening; withal there was no water to be had.

Just as the sun was sinking behind the woods, quiet settled over the front of the battle-ground; even the skirmishers had stopped their firing, when a brigadier general with his staff rode up to our squad and opened conversation:

13

"What brigade do you belong to?" he asked.

"Kemper's," some one answered.

"Where is Jackson's force?"

"In your rear, I reckon."

"Is Longstreet commanding in our front in person?"

"Reckon so, haven't seen him."

"Is it true that General Lee is killed?"

"No, it's a damn lie."

Just as he was about to ride off, one of his aides—a spruce young fellow in a natty uniform—said to me:

"What are you Rebels fighting for, anyway?"

The question struck me there and then as supremely ludicrous. Here were we Virginians standing on our own soil, fighting on our native heath against an invading army, defending what every man holds dear—his home and fireside. As well ask a game-cock why he crows and bares his spurs on his own dung-hill. So I replied:

"We are fighting to protect our mint-beds."

There was an Irishman on the staff, and he nearly fell off his saddle; he spurred his horse forward and slapped me on the shoulder and said:

"True for ye, me boy, there's not a lad in ould Ireland that wouldn't do the same for his poteen."

Even the brigadier smiled, and said that he had heard often of a Virginia julep but never had tasted one, and the group clattered away, laughing.

Again, for the last time, the approaching storm of battle forced both guards and prisoners back. It was dusk when this occurred, and the sounds of the battle died away with remarkable suddenness, only one rattling volley, then silence.

"The same story over again," we thought. "A desperate struggle, blood flowing like water, and nothing decisive."

The night was lovely; a full moon slowly rose from the horizon, and its resplendent light made the scene almost as bright as day; the soft rays covered the earth with a mantle of charity, hiding what was rough and unseemly, and bringing out in greater beauty all that was fair and lovely before. They "made a fairyland of fallow fields," they touched the woods with mellow radiance; they entered the soldier's heart and softened it with thoughts of home; they breathed upon the air, so lately rent with the mad sounds of vengeful strife, a holy "peace, be still;" they calmed the fierce passions of contending armies into a lull that had the solemn quiet of cathedral aisles fragrant with the incense of ascending prayer; they rested as softly and solemnly on the faces of the dead as would some farewell kiss, dedicating them to their future rest, lovingly, like the benediction of God.

The prisoners could not sleep, but sat in a circle and talked over the events of the day. The Yankees around us had claimed a victory, but we knew better than that; at the very best for them, it could have been only a drawn battle. Our sole anxiety, therefore, was for our regiment and brigade. We knew the loss must have been heavy, charging with a single line such a heavy force in front; so we waited and watched anxiously for news. Prisoners, singly and in squads, were being brought in every few minutes now.

Here we had conclusive evidence before our eyes that the accounts of the demoralization of the Yankees, which had been told and believed by our troops, had not the slightest truth or the barest foundation. These soldiers around us were full of enthusiasm, they actually claimed every engagement that had taken place within the last few days. When asked why McClellan was retreating and burning his stores behind him, they replied that he was merely consolidating his forces with the intention of taking Richmond in the rear; that it was, in other words, only a voluntary change of base. Never was an army in better plight than the Army of the Potomac on that evening of the thirtieth of June, 1862.

A murmuring sound way off in the distance attracted our attention; it came nearer, rising louder every minute, until it swelled into a mighty shout as thousands upon thousands of voices rang out their enthusiastic cheers. Asking the meaning of this demonstration, a soldier, in answer, pointed out a group of passing horsemen, which he said were "Little Mac" and his staff. It was not quite light enough to distinguish the features of the commanding general, nor was he sufficiently near, but we could see that he held his hat above his head in acknowledgment of the tribute his soldiers paid him.

At last, overcome by fatigue, we lay down in the middle of the road in the dust, for we had neither blankets nor overcoats, and like a litter of pigs, nestled closely for comfort. Hardly had we fallen asleep before the cry of "Here comes the cavalry!" scattered guards and prisoners right and left. It was a false alarm, but it was some time before everything was serene again.

How easy to have escaped during that stampede, especially as the dust had made it hard to distinguish between friend and foe. None of us thought of it till afterwards, except one, a member of the Seventeenth, who had quietly stolen away.

Coolness and self-possession are not always inherent; they are faculties that need training well and long in the rough school of experience ere they stand one in good stead.

About ten o'clock the prisoners were formed into line for a long march. The officer in command told us that we should observe perfect silence en route; that our lives depended on a strict obedience to this order as the guard would bayonet any prisoner who might venture to offend by so much as a word. It is needless to say that the most talkative man in the squad soon became remarkably mute. Our faces were then turned toward the James River and we commenced our silent march. Not a syllable was even whispered, nor did we stop at all, except to let troops pass and repass every now and then, which they did without so much as the rasping of a gun or the jingle of a canteen against a bayonet resting within the scabbard. It was a weird scene! the moving of that noiseless host through the shadows which the pine trees cast beneath the moon. Almost as if the disembodied souls from the Seven Days' Battles had taken form again, and were marching phantom-like to the sound of spirit music through the woods, joining forces and moving in one vast procession into the unseen world.

We could easily see that this road was the open line of their retreat, which they were fearful might be closed; hence all this secrecy and silence. This looked more as if the Yankees were escaping from a trap set by the Rebels than a victorious army taking a new position.

The march became wearisome after a while, and both guards and prisoners had hard work to keep their eyes open. A few of us started to escape several times, but wanted the nerve. It looked so easy to jump by the weary, unsuspecting guards into the dark recesses of the woods before they could fire. Indeed it is not certain whether, under the circumstances, they would have fired. Every prisoner there could have gotten away that night had he only made a rush.

The small procession was halted about one o'clock, in a small field on the edge of the swamp, and were asleep, all of them, before they could have been introduced to that ambiguous Mr. Jack Robinson had he come along for that special honor; but a dozen times were we aroused from our rest and made to fall into line and then drop down overcome, only to be aroused again and tortured until we prayed for the light—destruction—anything, rather than the darkness and disturbance.

The dawn came at last, faintly tinging the fog, and resting on the swamp like a dark veil, heavy, opaque and damp. The mists seemed determined to contest the advance of the day-god, but when the sun rose above the tree-tops it swept away its phantom foe with a few glancing beams, and soon set the earth simmering in a sickly heat.

Falling in line, hungry, unwashed and unrested, still keeping the road, we soon overtook another squad of prisoners belonging to the Seventeenth. Hector Eaches was limping painfully along with them, a buck-shot having lodged in his knee-pan.

After about three hours' march our captors came in sight of the James River and there halted for a time. The sun's beams poured down; the river shone like burnished silver; before us lay broad, sloping meadows, reaching away for miles, with not so much as a grove to intercept the view. On this immense plateau were two corps of McClellan's army, looking as fresh as if they had never fired a gun or marched a mile. One of our number said that he tried to count the regiments by the flags, and had reached as high as twenty-five when he lost the tally. There could not have been less than twenty thousand men.

Keeping on we soon reached Harrison's Landing, and to our surprise and universal satisfaction saw sitting under the trees about seventy of the Seventeenth Regiment, with Colonel Marye at their head. There were three captains, nearly a dozen lieutenants and the balance rank and file; they were busily engaged in some discussion, and when we perceived each familiar face a mutual shout went up and handshakings were liberally indulged in all around.

Now for the first time we learned all about the battle and the extent of our loss. Nearly five hundred men were killed, captured and wounded in the brigade, fully one-fourth of the whole number. The Seventeenth had lost one-third of its fighting strength. Company A suffered severely; four killed outright, nine wounded badly, thirteen prisoners. Conrad Johnson was seen lying at the foot of a tree, dead. A staunch friend, and as fearless as any soldier who ever sighted musket! Brave, true heart!

That band of captives resolved themselves into an indignation meeting, in which the blame of the present disaster to the brigade was laid at the door of the brigadier; a second time had that crack organization been rushed into the jaws of destruction through his gross mismanagement; it seemed he had ordered his command to advance into an unfamiliar, interminable swamp for the purpose of capturing a battery on the other side. How many supports that battery had or just where the battery was, he had not the slightest conception, nor did he send skirmishers before attacking; instead, he formed the line, with no reserves, no supports in the rear. With what results? Just what might have been anticipated: the brigade dashed like incoming waves upon a rock, in the form of McCall's division with its heavy reserve force, and in place of a single battery (as it had been assumed they would attack and capture), they found—a whole battalion of artillery. When we charged in such poor strength, the reserve division flanked our limited line, and took the troop by flank and front; the other regiments made their escape, but only by running the gauntlet and incurring heavy loss.

Comment was not wanting, and conjectures upon the—well, say mistake if you will, were severe among the rank and file. Good God! to think of one thousand of the very flower of the Old Dominion sacrificed by the incompetence of a man who surely should have known better, caused the privates of the Seventeenth to use language strong, indignant and to the point.

The color-bearers of the command had gotten out safely with their flags, which was all the consolation we could manage to extract from such an accumulation of woes.

We remained in this cool, shady grove all day, for which we were duly thankful. We had rations issued; crackers, coffee, sugar and meat of good quality and fair quantity. The rumbling of artillery in the vicinity of Richmond became more frequent as twilight drew toward night, and as we lay stretched at ease, enjoying the glories of that exquisite summer evening, we could not help but remember that the contest of the Titans was being now enacted, and that yonder setting sun was sinking behind a sea of blood.

The next morning it commenced raining and we were ordered into ranks and marched one or two miles, only stopping when we had reached the marshiest bottom possible to find. There a square was marked out on the ground, around the edges of which the sentinels were posted; and we learned for the first time the meaning of a dead-line.

It was simply a line drawn upon the ground, a step beyond which was death.

All that day we had literally to "stand it," for the ground was too wet to sit upon, and the rainfall which always follows a great battle now came down in a continuous stream, just as if Nature had many ugly stains to wash away from earth or else was weeping for her children, for their wrath, their wounds, their dead, with great splashes of tears which knew no stint or comfort.

The space in which we were confined was very limited, indeed not larger that a moderate-sized sheepfold, and the mud trodden by many feet was soon a mire. It was tiresome rather, standing first on one foot then on another, like an old rooster. The hours dragged by and then came the evening, but with no diminution of the rain nor of our misery; our faces were well washed by this time. The hope of being removed to some place of shelter, a hope which we had fondly cherished, was doomed to disappointment, for the painful truth forced itself upon the mind that we were to spend the night in this worse than hog pen. Our officers, field and staff, fared better, having been put, as a signal mark of favor, in a corn-house near by.

The Federal rank and file of the Army of the Potomac were not held in the estimation of their officers as in the Army of Northern Virginia. It was a rare thing for men of great wealth or high social standing to be found carrying a musket or swinging a sabre. At the beginning of the war, when brimming over with patriotism, all classes rushed to volunteer, but when war became a business, any man with any degree of prestige or influence sought and obtained shoulder straps. In our army it was different; there was not a company, in the Virginia forces at least, where the privates were not the social equal of their officers. When the son of the Commander-in-Chief, Robert E. Lee, served as a private he made an example that all were proud to follow. The women of the South made it a point to honor the private in the ranks above all others.

Dark! yes, pitch dark, the essence of blackness and a flood coming down at the same time. The question we ruefully asked each other was, "Where are we to sleep?" "What are we going to do?" As we stood shivering, with water above our army brogans, the situation was deplorable; not one of us had a blanket, much less an overcoat; nothing but our simple jackets, which had become thoroughly soaked during the first five minutes of rain. We shouted to the sentinels, we appealed to the officer of the day when he came to relieve guard, but a rough answer was all he vouchsafed. Huddled close together like cattle, some stood in sullen silence, others cursed and swore, a few in a desperate effort chanted a social glee, while Hartley, the best singer in the regiment, and like poor Yorick, "a fellow of infinite jest," caused a spasmodic grin to pass over the faces of the most miserable as he sang the sea song, "I'm afloat," then he ended by ringing out, as it seemed in mockery, that gay camp song, "A soldier's the life for me, boys."

Some of the "Billy Yanks" showed us most disinterested kindness by sharing with us their hot coffee and doing all in their power to alleviate our woes, but they were not at liberty to carry us to shelter nor to give us blankets; however, we thanked them in our hearts for what they had done and would have done.

It was very chilly and our teeth were chattering so we could scarcely eat our crackers, for we knew the rain would saturate them in the thin haversacks, and a soldier eats by instinct. How stiff, aching and numbed were our poor legs.

The voices so lately chanting their songs now sank to a dismal howl, then to a savage muttering, and soon even that was stilled.

In this manner we passed the greater part of the night, and when at last fatigue had made us insensible to the mud, the water, and the rain, we crept close together, and lying down with caps drawn over our faces, forgot our misery in the oblivion of sleep.

The drum beating for guard-mounting awoke the prisoners to a scene which was not enlivening. It was still raining and the men were numbed and stiffened by the exposure of sleeping on the ground, their features wearing a look of dumb misery.

"The rain it reigneth every day;" it came down when it was time that any reasonable pour would have held up; but the leaden-hued sky did not show a rift in the clouds. The men were not allowed to move out of the narrow limits, not even to get water to drink; what they used was obtained from the little holes or miniature wells which they hollowed out with their hands in the mire; it was so muddy, brackish and filthy, that nothing but the sternest necessity compelled them to drink it. Imagine water out of the puddles in a barnyard, and some idea may be gained of what this form of suffering was—of what we had to endure.

We now beheld the strict discipline that prevailed in the ranks of the Regular Army of the United States, and in what low consideration the soldiers were held by the shoulder-strapped officers.

On one occasion during the guard-mounting of the regiment,

which was the Eighth United States Regulars, as the officer of the day was going through the routine of inspecting muskets of the men detailed for guard duty, he came across one weapon which was slightly rusty; taking it out of the bearer's hands he deliberately drew back and drove the butt end of the musket full in the soldier's face, knocking him backward and mangling his features terribly.

No notice was taken of the cowardly act and the brute kept on down the line. Had one of the officers so treated a private in the Confederate Army he would have been bayoneted on the spot; had the overseer on a Virginia plantation so punished a slave, the master, had he been a gentleman, would have shot him in an instant.

Our pen was now changed from mud into a liquid slime. It was impossible for the men to become any muddier, dirtier, or more thoroughly soaked, so they lay down in the filth that even a hog might reject. But where was the remedy? The Yankee guard and soldiers cried shame at our treatment, and noble fellows that they were, did the only thing that was in their power to mitigate the wretchedness, shared their hot coffee; but the officers took no notice of our complaints.

Toward evening the prisoners became reckless and desperate, for they saw it was impossible to spend another night in that quagmire already up to the knees, and in which none could have lain down without sinking beneath the surface. We shouted so long and loud for our colonel, that he came to us under guard, and when he saw our condition—so dirty, muddy and swinish indeed, that it hardly needed the touch of Circe's wand to convert us into hogs, a more angry man it would have been hard to find in the two armies.

He had to swallow his wrath, but he went to the officer in command and painted our woeful condition in such strong colors that it had a beneficial effect, inasmuch as in an hour or two a large squad of men came, bringing arms full of hay, which they distributed lavishly to the prisoners; then they brought rails and sticks of wood, which served as foundations for the beds. Though it rained hard all night, we managed to sleep through it comfortably.

The faint beams of the sun striving to dispel the mists showed us the worst was now passed; under his warm rays we dried our clothes and the blood was sent circulating through the erstwhile numbed limbs.

In the afternoon we were formed in rank, and leaving our "wallow," though we carried away plenty of mud by way of mementos, we were marched up the river and bivouacked for the night in a grove of trees. It was not until late in the evening of the next day that we stepped on the wharf at Harrison's Landing prepared to take passage on the steamboat, en route for a most compulsory visit North. Marching single file across the gangway plank, then to the upper deck, we scattered in groups; the whistle blew, the ropes were cast off, the paddles revolved slowly, and the boat sluggishly turning prow in the direction of Old Point, steamed swiftly down the river.

Each man now received a blanket, also full rations, and as the shades of night fell on the scene, the songs of the Seventeenth's Glee Club, or what was left of it, floated through the air, and they sang as men only can who have light hearts and full stomachs.

Well! soldiers are but children at best; for them the past was gone, the future was hidden, the present only was theirs.

The foe in our immediate front in this battle was the Sixteenth Massachusetts and Second New York, the latter capturing our battle-flag, on which was inscribed "Williamsburg and Seven Pines," and the Seventeenth charged in their ignorance the First Brigade of Hooker's division. General Grover, commanding, says in his official report:

"About 3 o'clock P. M. the enemy moved upon General McCall's lines in our front, and having broken them, came down in great force upon our position. The Sixteenth Massachusetts Volunteers being in position and on the immediate left of the road along which the advance was made, received and repulsed the heaviest and most persistent attempts of the enemy to break the lines. The Twenty-sixth Pennsylvania Volunteers, on the left of the Sixteenth, were not hard pressed, and had not an opportunity to deliver its whole fire upon the enemy.

"The Eleventh Massachusetts was thrown upon the extreme left of our division lines, in anticipation of an attempt to turn our flank. As no such attempt, however, was made in force, this regiment did not become engaged during the day. The First Massachusetts and Second New Hampshire occupied a line in rear of the Sixteenth Massachusetts and the Twenty-sixth Pennsylvania Volunteers, but the steadiness and determination with which the first line met the enemy, not only checking his advance, but causing him to withdraw from his position on the field, rendered

any assistance at this time unnecessary from the second line."
(Reb. Records, Vol. 11, p. 123.)

Colonel Kirk, of the Tenth Pennsylvania, also had a hand in our
defeat. He says (Reb. Records, Vol. 10, p. 425): "The enemy
charged boldly upon the breastworks occupied by the Twelfth
Pennsylvania, when I charged successfully upon their flanks, completely routing the enemy, killing many and capturing about 60
prisoners. The Seventeenth Virginia, by their extreme losses in
killed, wounded and prisoners, were almost wholly annihilated."

The official loss of the Seventeenth Virginia was 18 killed, 23
wounded and 73 taken prisoners; as in Seven Pines, the Seventeenth lost more in killed than all the rest of the brigade put
together.

Now just read what our brigade commander says about this
fight:

"About 5 P. M. an order was received from General Longstreet to advance by line. Advance continued to be conducted in
good order until very soon, coming upon the pickets of the
enemy, the men seemed to be possessed of the idea that they were
upon the enemy's main line. The whole brigade charged forward
in double-quick time and with loud cheers; nothing could have
been more chivalrously done and nothing could have been more
unfortunate, as the cheering of the men only served to direct the
fire of the enemy's batteries, and the movement in double-quick
time through dense woods, over rough ground encumbered with
matted undergrowth and crossed by a swamp, had the effect of
producing more or less confusion and breaking the continuity of
the line, which, however, was preserved as well as it possibly could
have been under the circumstances. But a single idea seemed to
control the minds of the men, which was to reach the enemy's
line by the directest route and in the shortest time; and no earthly
power could have availed to arrest or restrain the impetuosity
with which they rushed toward them, for my orders, previously
given with great care and emphasis to assembled officers of the
brigade, forbade any movement in double-quick time over such
ground when the enemy were not in view. The obstructions were
such as to make it impossible for any officer to see more than a
few files of his men at one view, and it was apparent that any
effort to halt and reform the entire brigade would be futile, and
would only serve to produce increased confusion. But whatever
the error of the men advancing too rapidly in disregard of pre-

vious orders to the contrary, it was an error upon the side of bravery.

"After advancing in this way probably 1,000 or 1,200 yards, crossing two bodies of woods and a small intermediate field, the lines suddenly emerged into another field, facing a battery of the enemy, consisting of not less than eight pieces, distant but a few hundred yards, while the enemy's infantry were found protected by an imperfect and hastily-constructed breastwork and a house near by. At the same time it became apparent that another battery of the enemy was posted a considerable distance to our left. These two batteries and the enemy's infantry poured an incessant fire of shell, grape, canister and lead upon our line, and did much execution; still there was no perceptible faltering in the advance of these brave men, who rushed across the open field, pouring a well-directed fire into the enemy, driving him from his breastworks and the battery in our front. The guns of the battery were abandoned to us for the time being, and my command was virtually in possession of the chosen position of the enemy. A more impetuous and desperate charge was never made than that of my small command against the sheltered and greatly superior forces of the enemy. The ground which they gained from the enemy is marked by the graves of some of my veterans who were buried where they fell; and those graves marked with the names of the occupants, situated at and near the position of the enemy, show the points at which they dashed against the strongholds of the retreating foe."

The idea of this brigade rushing blindly forward was preposterous. A mob might have done so—but this command was splendidly drilled, was commanded by educated officers, and the discipline was perfect, and when General Kemper writes that these veteran soldiers broke into a wild fool-rush over hill and dale, ignoring their officers' commands, and he too being present in person, he simply states a fact that military men cannot credit. Some officers lose their nerve, their brains refuse to act, their judgment becomes numbed in times of great peril. It is not a question of bravery—it is simply a matter of temperament.

CHAPTER XXIV.

PRISON LIFE AT FORT WARREN.

The "Glorious Fourth" was clear and warm; no one ever saw a wet or cool Independence Day; it is always the sultriest, dirtiest day of the whole year. In old ante-bellum anniversaries it was a time full of loyal excitement; a time of fire crackers and of noise; a day of patriotic speeches wherein the American Eagle flapped his wings and crowed like a rooster, and the orator took drinks between whiles to cool his burning patriotism, and wiped the perspiration from his glowing brow.

For ourselves we did not hail the dawn with many loyal thoughts whose eloquence might find no tongue; nor did any of us try a speech or apostrophize the American flag, except Hartley, who stood on a stool and commenced:

> " 'When Freedom from her mountain height
> Unfurled her banner to the air
> She—' "

a voice here interrupted—

> "She took a julep and got tight."

The orator was somewhat daunted by the irreverence of his audience and lost the cue of his peroration; however, he began again:

> " 'The Glorious Eagle soared in pride
> Far up o'er reach of mountain peak—' "

"He caught old Freedom in his beak," suggested another.

"She gave one piercing, yelling shriek," exclaimed a third, with violent gesticulations.

"He picked her bones and so she died," pathetically put in a fourth—when

"Say there, Johnny Reb," said one of the guards, "you just shut up; if you don't, I'll make you!"

"I always like to oblige a gentleman," responded Hartley, bowing politely; and so, baffled at every point, the only poetical inspiration of the occasion came to a sudden halt.

About nine in the morning we arrived in sight of Fortress

Monroe. The water shone beneath the sun like gold, and broke into diamond sparkles at his touch, while its burnished surface gently rose and fell with long, quiet, lazy swells that scarcely rippled the water. Hundreds of vessels, from the stately man-of-war down to the little fishing smacks, lay at anchor, every one of which was decorated with streamers, flags and bunting in honor of the day.

Our steamer rounded the point swiftly, her prow seeming scarcely to cut the clear blue water. We passed the line-of-battleship *Cumberland,* where it had been sunk by the *Merrimac* not many months before, its lofty masts appearing above the water, a splendid monument of American valor, whose crew went to the bottom sighting the guns. The monitor *Ericsson,* that gained a world-wide celebrity in her contest with the iron-clad, was anchored not far off, an object of great interest. We were disappointed in the half-sunken canal-boat-of-a-looking craft with a turret in the center, having had an idea that she was an immense structure. It was difficult to believe that this insignificant little vessel before us had fought to a standstill the mighty *Merrimac.*

The steamer was made fast to the wharf and the prisoners marched into the fort. To us it was a splendid pageantry, the waving flags, the mounted guns, the fine, showily dressed garrison, the officers in full uniform, the bands playing and the booming cannons firing salutes.

Our squad was halted at the barracks, and for the first time in many days we had the eating of a good dinner, to which we did full justice. As we were about reforming, a Yankee lieutenant, who had been drinking heavily, came out with a canteen of whiskey.

"Boys," said he, "I will give you a pull if you will drink success to the Union."

A silence fell upon us; we wanted a drink, but could we indulge in a toast whose sentiments were so repugnant to our feelings? And yet we were so thirsty! so very thirsty! not a drop of old rye had we touched for many a long day; it smelled delightfully fragrant and it kept on smelling, and—and—

Well, Esau was not such a wretch after all!

We blush to recall it; as many as could grasp that tin cup took the liquor and repeated the toast.

"Success to the Union."

A doctor was called to see an Irishman whose native drink was whiskey. Water was prescribed as the only cure; Pat demurred, he said he never could drink it; then milk was sent for and Pat promised to get well on that; the doctor was soon summoned again. Near the bed where the sick man lay was a table on which rested a large bowl of milk strongly flavored with whiskey.

"What have you there?" inquired the doctor.

"Milk, Doctor, just what you ordered."

"But there's whiskey in it, I smell it."

"Well, Doctor," sighed the patient, "there may be whiskey in it, but milk's my object."

A parallel case was ours—Union was in the drink, but whiskey was our object. Some of our officers began to jibe and taunt us, but they were soon silenced with the reminder that they had been sleeping in a corn-house while we had paddled in a puddle.

The warning of the steam whistle hurried us to the wharf, and instead of our steamboat, there was a large steamship, called the *Ocean Queen*, which was to carry us to New York. Just as the sun went down the steamer started, and soon the last glimpse of Old Virginia faded from our view. The steamship carried no passengers except "dead-heads;" for with the exception of the crew, prisoners and guards, there were none others on board. Our quarters were good, yet men will rarely ever consent to let well enough alone, for within six hours of the time of starting a plot had been started by one of the officers, Lieutenant Slaughter, of Company K, to overpower the guard, seize the steamer, turn her prow toward Virginia, then beach the vessel on shore and make our way to Richmond.

It would have been a comparatively easy task, fraught with but little danger. The guards were not many, and scattered all about the boat, each one generally surrounded by a group of prisoners conversing on the theme of war or kindred subjects. Really no attempt had been made to show us that we were under surveillance, for each man could roam at will all over the vessel, even climb the shrouds and up the main mast if he chose. The prisoners numbered some seventy-five or eighty; the guards all told were sixteen, under charge of one officer.

The privates, with three exceptions, anxious for any excitement, eagerly joined the conspiracy and faithfully promised to obey all orders and run all risks; and they would have done it. The plan only needed the sanction of our colonel to be put in instant execution.

The plot was laid before Colonel Marye, who after careful consideration vetoed the whole scheme for the following reasons:

"In the first place," he said, "there is no engineer or pilot on board who can take charge of the boat in case the present crew shall refuse to serve. Then the supply of coal is limited, while the gravest obstacle lays in the fact that it will be impossible to get beyond Fortress Monroe, either to go up the James or the Potomac. The steamer will be required by the gunboats to show her papers, and success will be almost impossible.

"It is true," he continued, "that the prisoners can probably escape by going to New York and overpowering the guard as the boat steams up the harbor; but then no one has any money, and the risk will be too great. Besides," the Colonel reasoned, "we will soon be exchanged, and so what will be the use of taking all this trouble, incurring all this risk, without a particle of necessity for such a step. We will get back home very soon in the natural course of events." In concluding he added: "If I were not very sure in my own mind that we would be exchanged without delay, I would head the movement myself."

These words, so full of sound sense, put the matter in a new light. Some reckless, hotheaded fellows wanted to go ahead notwithstanding; but the men held back, having confidence in Colonel Marye, well knowing how fearless and gallant he was.

Just here Billy Harmon, of Company A, one of the most popular soldiers in the regiment, came forward with a new plan:

"Why can't we take the steamer to the North Carolina coast and beach her? Then we can make our way to our lines without any trouble."

A majority of the men agreed to this, and started for the door, with Billy at their head.

Up sprang Colonel Marye and commenced talking at the rate of one hundred and fifty words a minute, and at last persuaded them to have a ballot taken. A poll was then taken and it was found that a majority of one was in favor of standing by their head officer, and so the matter ended; but it was as Hartley expressed it:

"A d——d close shave."

A view of the sun rising from old Ocean was a spectacle that many of the squad had never before witnessed, and great was the wonder thereat. We were on the Atlantic, with not the slightest trace of land. A school of porpoises sported around the vessel and introduced themselves to landsmen, but Mother Carey's chickens were objects of greater interest; indeed, everything we saw served to amuse and fill the hours with a pleasant excitement.

The breeze began to freshen up a little, for Neptune had no idea of letting us go by without giving him the customary tribute. Every prisoner had eaten a hearty breakfast, but two-thirds of these Rebels had no appetite for dinner. Their cheeks began to turn white, their noses cold, and then one by one they would disappear. A roar of laughter followed each receding figure as a slight token of sympathy. They were all to be seen in the evening, however, lying around the deck or in the saloon in a state of hopeless woe. The guards were in as bad a plight as the prisoners, there being scarcely two of them out of the whole number who could hold their heads up.

Some of the healthy ones played cruel jokes on their languishing sea-sick comrades thus wise: they took a piece of rancid pork and tied it to the end of a string attached to a pole. Much as if intent on a fishing expedition, the angler would steal up to his victim—some limp, almost lifeless form—and suspend the rank, strong-smelling meat right under his nose. A shudder of disgust would thrill the sufferer, his eyes would unclose, and the whole inner man, revolting against the procedure, would yield to fresh spasms of misery that knew no stint nor mercy.

It was mean, it was heathenish, but we thought it irresistibly funny; at least it served to illustrate the saying of Rochefoucauld, that "the greatest enjoyment a man can feel is in witnessing the suffering of others."

In the evening, when the stars had jeweled the sky, those few of the Seventeenth who were well enough assembled on deck and passed hours in singing strains, now martial and now sentimental. That chorus of well-trained voices sounding on the steamer's deck and floating away over the wide expanse of water, with no roof above it but the dome of heaven, seemed to us the sweetest music that ever fell on our listening ears. We could not break the charm by so much as a word, and hence were silent as the holy calm around us, while song after song rose and died away upon the air.

The morning of the second day the boat passed Sandy Hook and made her way up the harbor amid a forest of shipping, steering her path toward Governor's Island. The steamship stopped at the wharf and the prisoners were marched ashore, where the garrison under arms received us. We were the first Rebel pris-

14

oners to land there, and such was our appearance that it failed to make a favorable impression on our Northern friends. In truth, we were a cross between a scare-crow and a chimney-sweep.

After standing several hours in the sun, going through roll call and arranging preliminaries until our patience was threadbare, we were marched by the demi-castle which stands on the edge of the island, to a large row of tents that were pitched alongside of the beach. Rations were then distributed, consisting of crackers, coffee, rice, meat and potatoes; better indeed than we had ever received at home. Then the dead-line having been marked and a guard stationed, we were left to our own devices.

That evening we enjoyed a surf bath, and for the first time had a chance to wash off the Chickahominy mud, that had stuck to us through all adventures and travel "closer than a brother." We were sadly in need of underclothing; not one of us having had a change for nearly three weeks. Those we wore were grimy and black, but we washed them that evening after a fashion, and at night some fifty men could have been seen hovering over the camp-fire, their backs shining in the glare, while each pair of hands held up before the blaze the wet, streaming articles of wearing apparel.

Lights were out at nine, and then followed the first perfectly restful slumber that had visited us since the twenty-fourth of the past month.

Our stay at Governor's Island only lasted two or three days, during which we were in a high state of enjoyment; with as much rest, exercise, bathing and good rations as were consistent with our position. The only thing of which we had reason to complain was the brutality of our guards, militia of course. Veteran soldiers never illtreated their prisoners, such was the experience on both sides. It was only those "dressed in a little brief authority," only those whose sole acquaintance with war was gathered from the daily papers, who carried on the only warfare they knew anything about and at the same time gratified their malice by insulting defenseless men under their charge. You see it was so safe! Some men of the Seventeenth were knocked down by musket stocks in these valiant hands.

On the evening of the ninth of July our squad, composed of the Seventeenth Virginia, was started again on the tramp. A small steam tug carried us over to New York, from whence we were transferred to the deck of one of the superb steamers that ply between the Empire City and Fall River, Massachusetts.

"Where the mischief are you going to carry us?" asked one of our captains of the officer of the guard. "Turn us loose in Canada, or send us to some watering-place to improve our health?"

"You fellows ought to be very glad that you are going where you are," he answered, "instead of being sent to Fort Delaware. I have orders to carry you all to Fort Warren in Boston Harbor, and a fine place it is."

"Do you think we will be well treated there?" one of us asked.

"Yes, for there are no prisoners except political ones."

The steamer was filled with a gay company going to Saratoga, Canada and Niagara Falls.

"Not much secesh in them," remarked one of the guards to us confidentially; "see how spiteful they look."

So they did. Their pretty noses went up and their red lips curled disdainfully as they passed our ranks on the way to the saloon. At this point one of the fair ones dropped her handkerchief and I, who loved the sex to a weakness, was only too willing to pick up the dainty article and restore it to the owner, which I did with a sweeping, Sir Charles Grandison bow. The gentle dame received the handkerchief, but a fixed, stony stare rewarded the bow, and chilled it to the bone, while her escort, a little, slim-waisted, dainty-looking fellow, perfumed and yellow-kidded, scowled like the humpedback Richard when he ordered the princely Buckingham off to execution.

We had left the island in such a hurry that the commissary either forgot or neglected to issue the rations; at any rate, we did not receive them; and after the steamer had gotten under way we awoke to the fact that we were ravenously hungry. It happened that we were placed in an upper saloon with steps leading down in the front and rear, or rather in the bow and stern. In the center of the saloon was an open oval space some twenty feet long, around which ran a railing, and which, being directly over the dining-room, commanded a most complete view of all that passed therein. An appetizing odor, the clattering of knives and forks, brought us to our feet, and looking down all sleep was banished from our famished eyes while the pangs of hunger became intolerable. We reminded ourselves of poor Dives looking up from his place of torment "upon Lazarus, who was being comforted."

It was a long, luxuriously furnished apartment; in the center the long table was laid with snowy damask, glittering with cut glass and plate, and decorated with brilliant-hued flowers.

Why attempt to particularize the viands, the fish, the fruits and all the dainties which passed before our eyes like the distempered visions of a dream. Bowls of crimson strawberries, piles of luscious raspberries, whose rich coloring grew more intense contrasted with the powdered sugar, the rich cream and sparkling, crystal ice; Malaga grapes, whose looks suggested a cool touch to the parched tongue; jellies, ices, cakes, salmon, mutton, ham, fried chicken, deviled crabs, salads, vegetables, a hundred dishes, it seemed, we did not know, but whose combined odor filled our souls with longing unspeakable.

We heard the popping of champagne corks; we recognized the long, slender bottles of Chambertin, the St. Julien, the Medoc, while the steaming coffee rose as incense; we watched each mouthful that passed between blessed lips; we grudged every dish —nay, we could have fought over every cooling drop.

It was a sight to awaken appetite in the satiated epicure, to make the eyes of the bon-vivant brighten; then imagine what pangs it caused the rationless, empty crowd above, whose eyes were burning down upon it yet whose clutching hands were all impotent to grasp a single glass or touch a single dish. Poor Johnnies! we sat there for two mortal hours, our jaws working spasmodically as we fathomed the very depth of a punishment which only Dante could have conceived for the souls of his "Inferno."

The scene had its fascinations though, and chained us to the spot. There were beautiful women whose eyes outshone the diamonds which sparkled on their hands. Sitting near the center of the table was (so a negro waiter informed us) a bridal couple, whom we watched; the groom, an old fellow with the love-light in his ancient eyes, and well gotten up, she fair as a lily and young enough to be his grandchild. The same old story, so many charms for so much money in Vanity Fair! You need not shrink, my lady, from those obtrusive attentions, you were fairly bought! Bargain and sale!

Another bridal couple not far off, going to Niagara, where all the newly married go; both were young, both bashful, both radiantly happy; indeed they were too ecstatic to eat. He, however, poured wine glass after wine glass of champagne down his throat, but love and champagne go together.

There sat a wounded officer with his arm in a sling; nobody seemed to take much notice of him; indeed, one of the servants cut up his food and attended him. "Ah, old fellow," we thought, "if you only wore the gray and were in the South, every woman at that table would deem it an honor to wait upon you."

At the head of the board was a general, of what especial rank and name we could not learn. He was exclusive, and it showed how great people gravitate toward each other, when the portly butler stood by him and paid him the most distinguished consideration.

The butler—we must not pass him over, for though last, he was by no means least—was a venerable gentleman of color, so stuffed and bloated by rich living and good liquor and a sense of his own importance he could only waddle slowly across the floor. He never condescended to do any service except to pour out a glass of wine for some individual as high in the world as himself. He was evidently what we would call down South "an aristocratic nigger." Attending in full dress, broadcloth and white vest, his big hands encased in white gloves, with marvelous studs and massive gold chain hanging from his neck, he felt as great as mighty Caesar. With a lofty wave of the hand he signalized his pleasure to a sable servitor, who flew to do his bidding. Indeed, surrounded by his crowd of satellites, he was a very sun of a system, and the air with which he gave them brief directions proved him to be a Prince of Deportment.

But even watching these different types of humanity failed to stifle the gnawing pangs of hunger which were growing every moment more intense; so several of us held a council of war and resolved to get something to eat by hook or crook. We counted funds; all told they amounted to twenty-six dollars, a goodly sum enough, but woe the day—it was Confederate money, worth just about as much here as the old Continental. One of the Rebels, tall, gaunt Jack Ballenger, took the money, determined to try anyhow, and slipped down two flights of steps to the diningroom; there, calling a waiter, he offered him the amount if he would manage to provide a supper for six. He seemed undecided; said he would go and see. Approaching the old fat, bloated butler, he asked his consent, but that mass of flesh hated a Rebel with every pound of his swelled carcass, and gave the waiter such overwhelming, withering rebuke that he slunk away and never came near us again.

However, one or two hands on the boat took compassion on us and brought us a dish of cold tripe and bread. Ah, that tripe! it hung as heavy on our souls as Meg Merrilies's curse. It was true Union tripe, and refused to give any aid or comfort to the enemy whatsoever; instead, many pains and many qualms. It is probable that not a man in that lot has ever eaten tripe since.

Early in the morning the steamer reached Fall River, where, leaving the boat, we were marched to the depot and took the train, a whole car having been allotted to us alone. Had we wished to escape, the guards allowed every opportunity. We were at liberty to stand on the platform of the cars by obtaining permission of the officer of the day, who was disposed to be very friendly toward us. Passing through a long tunnel, where the train went very slowly, it was debated among a few of us whether or not it were better to slip off; but we thought that in our gray uniforms and without a cent in our pockets and in the midst of bitter enemies it would be only avoiding Charybdis to fall into Scylla, and so the idea was dismissed.

Boston and its suburbs, with its villas, stylish country seats and neat farm houses, was a revelation to our Southern eyes. The houses and grounds seemed spick, span and new, so different from the let-things-go-and-take-it-easy style to which we had been accustomed.

To be sure there was nothing of age to be met with anywhere, not even as much as of the hundred years to which as a new country we are entitled; but on the other hand there were no hanging gates, no tumble-down porches; no veteran pumps; nothing but what showed promptness of repair and energy, opposed to our put-off, lazy plantation principle. The Southerner takes pride in his old house and will keep it intact as in the days of his grandfather or great-grandfather; the same old portraits hanging on the wall, the same old furniture; he may add wings to the building and a porch here and there, but the old parental roof remains like a hen with her brood around her. The spirit of decay is not kept down on his grounds and rolling acres. He is in no hurry to improve things; he will tie and prop up where a nail should go; paint he does not hanker after; his very equipage is often wheezy, and so a flavor of age tinges his home as it does the hair on his head and his wine.

"What was good enough for my father before me is good enough for me" becomes a maxim on his lips to be handed down to his son after him.

The Northern spirit is essentially progressive, if not reverential. When the patrimonial mansion descends to a younger generation and increasing coffers are the reward of thrift he says, "I will pull down my house and my barns and build greater;"

and on the site of the old foundation-stones arises a structure
whose elegance and comfort is only limited by the length of purse.
Where money is no consideration, palatial residences are built
fit for the nobles of the old world. Everything is modern, the
more modern the better. His carriages are all glaze and shine,
his furniture changes with the fashion, his grounds are laid out
with mathematical exactness, the very trees are grown to shape,
the hedges are cut according to pattern, the lawns are sown and
rolled to velvet precision, and Nature is made to step back and
yield to the aesthetic as it may be apprehended at the time. The
Northern characteristic, however, is essentially that of cleanliness;
he is obtrusively neat; he hates dust and dirt more than anything
else, snakes and sin not excepted; in soap and scrubbing is his
national faith. If he had his mother-in-law cremated and the
sacred dust were by accident to escape from the precious urn, a
servant with soap and mop would wipe her up.

Early in the forenoon we left the cars and found ourselves in
the spacious depot in the ultra-Union city of Boston, the first
Rebels that ever pressed with sacrilegious feet its loyal streets;
the first Rebels who walked under the shadow of Faneuil Hall.
No! now that we think of it, a large gang of them passed its doors
about a hundred years or so ago on their way to burn some British tea that a loyal tax had been placed upon. It was rebellion,
of course, but all New England gloried in the name Rebel then.

Boston, that city of furores, the Athens of America, the Hub
of the Universe, the city of many titles, rarely enjoyed in those
war-times a greater sensation than was caused by the appearance
of a hundred live, genuine Rebels, captured on the battle-fields.
The great sea serpent, taken off the coast; the walking giant,
nay, even a grand circus parade of wild animals, with a hippopot-
amus and a giraffe heading up the thoroughfare, would not have
collected a larger crowd in a shorter time. Had Bunker Hill
Monument stepped down from its stately perch and walked away
on feet, decorously wrapped in the American flag, bowing right
and left to the multitude, they could hardly have excited more
curiosity than did that line of simple gray-jackets.

A mob followed us up the street, a good-natured mob though,
that only used its eyes. After having passed a square or two, the
crowd became so dense, the pressure upon us so great that further progress became impossible. The guards could not keep off
the throng that hemmed them in; so we were halted while a
heavy detachment of police formed an outer cordon and another

squad in front opened the way; then we slowly made our progress through the streets. The pavements, the balconies, the very housetops were filled with an inquisitive, gazing multitude, while the little street Arabs swung like monkeys from the trees. Shops were suddenly emptied of clerks and purchasers; windows sprung open, shutters flew wide, heads were thrust out and eyes stared us in the face whichever way we looked. The newsboys neglected to call their papers; the hackman pulled up on one side of the street, forgetting for a moment to lash his bony, lean horses; carriages came to a sudden halt; in fact, all business was as effectually suspended as on that day when Jack Cade rode through London, announcing the arrival of the Millenium, ordering all work to cease and promising that quartern bread should be half penny a loaf, and that conduits should run wine. Old men peered at us through spectacles; women stopped to watch us; boys gazed; and the children, bless their innocent hearts! there is no knowing what tales those infant Bostonians had heard about the Rebels that brought that look of fright into their young eyes. It was the same expression with which they gaze upon the man-eating lion in the menagerie, and they clung to their mothers and nurses as if they had been brought face to face with just so many monsters.

What the citizens thought of us we had no means of finding out; yet it must have been rather a disappointment. Each one of us, to accord with the popular idea, should have been at least seven feet high, with a villainous countenance overshadowed by a wide-brimmed hat. We should have had a shock of unkempt, flowing hair, and a beard like that of the giant in the fairy tale, who wore seven-leagued boots and ate a child at every meal. Bowie-knives should have been our chief personal adornment, and scowling our pastime.

As it was we were rather too commonplace, though our procession was quite imposing. First the police at our head; next followed our officers, with our colonel leading, and a handsomer, more distinguished-looking man to serve for our frontispiece would have been hard to find North or South. Last came the privates strung out in twos, with the guards on each side, the police escorting. Altogether the train stretched out for fully a whole square.

A more reckless, dare-devil set of boys, for nearly all those privates were no more than boys, were never before brought together by the fortunes of war. It may be safely surmised that they kept no decorous silence as befitted *"les miserables"* on the way to prison. They scattered greetings right and left, they bowed to every pretty girl, they complimented every handsome woman in the same manner. So we went, making slow but steady progress. Not one rudeness nor insult was offered us during the whole route, which spoke well for the charity, the refinement and good taste of the Bostonians.

Many onlookers tried to get inside the line to talk, but were repulsed by the police, the soldiers not caring one way or the other. Only the newspaper men joined our ranks—they can get anywhere. As they talked with us they asked question after question, and it must be feared the papers next morning recorded strangely contradictory stories and some right hard tales, that required much faith for digesting, inasmuch as none of the privates so interviewed had any serious fears of the fate of Ananias, or rather they were not disposed to talk as if they had, and though from the same State as the youthful Washington, living almost under the shadow of his tomb—well, they would not have compromised that good little hatchet as he did.

It was an hour before we reached the wharf where a steam tug lay in waiting. Going aboard and bidding our police escort a polite farewell, the little boat picked her way down the river, reaching Fort Warren, at the mouth of the Bay, after a pleasant ride.

This fortification was an elaborate and massive work, commanding all of the approaches to the city. From the upper tiers of guns a plunging fire of forty-five degrees could have sunk any vessel, iron-clad or otherwise. Fort Warren, well garrisoned, was to our eyes simply impregnable.

After we landed a guard took us in charge, our former sentinels returning in the boat. We were led within the parade grounds, where we remained until arrangements were made for our comfort. We were soon surrounded by the political prisoners, who were of influence and had been incarcerated for their outspoken Southern sentiments or for some acts considered by the authorities as disloyal, but whether justly or unjustly so, remained to be proven. There were also some of our officers high in rank, Generals Buckner and Tilghman, captured at Fort Donaldson; Commodore Barron, of the Confederate Navy; Marshall Kane, and Doctor Magill, of Maryland, and some other citizens of less note. There were none of the rank and file other than ourselves, and we blessed our stars that we had fallen into such a soft place.

The political prisoners had a splendid dinner ready for us, such a dinner as the Confederacy in all its length and breadth could not have given us; a dinner that we had dreamed of in our days of short rations. It is needless to say that our onslaught was a heavy one; indeed the amount of food that we consumed and the bottles of wine which we emptied in that one meal would seem incredible to any one not informed as to the expansive power of the Rebel soldier's digestive apparatus. The donors watched our efforts with the keenest delight.

After a good smoke the prisoners were assigned their quarters, consisting of two long casemated apartments, one for sleeping, the other the mess-room. In the former, bunks were built one above the other like berths in a ship. A blanket per man was issued, while the political prisoners presented each of us with a suit of underclothing. No rations were given, but instead the store-room was open, to the contents of which the messes could help themselves as it might please them. Certainly no prisoners of war had ever been treated so luxuriously before, nor were they ever afterwards. Breakfast consisted of coffee,—*real,* not ground rye or corn,—fresh loaf bread, mess-beef, hominy, broiled ham and eggs *ad libitum.* Dinner was proportionately good. The mess-room was a large vaulted apartment, cool even in the hottest part of the day, the casements allowing a refreshing ocean breeze to pass through. A large cooking-stove was at one end, around which were hanging all the necessary utensils, and on one side was the temporary store-room with barrels of hard bread, flour, mess-pork, beef and groceries of various kinds.

Later in the day a few of us visited the Maryland prisoners. Their quarters were luxuriously fitted up with Brussels carpets on the floors, mahogany furniture and a fine library; at the same time they had their own servants in attendance. The officers and citizens, with one exception, were not prisoners except in name, inasmuch as they had no guard placed over them. They had the freedom of the Fort and were on terms of cordial intimacy with the family of the commandant. With such a pleasant mess, theirs must have been a regular club-house life, very enjoyable to look back upon in after years.

The authorities in Washington evidently entertained against our officer in rank, General Buckner, some bitter feeling, for by the explicit and positive orders of Mr. Stanton, Secretary of War, he was kept in close and solitary confinement, the parole extended to all of his comrades in arms having been denied him, with the exception of a short walk every evening which he took for exercise between two armed sentries.

The commander of the fort was not responsible for this, for a kinder and truer gentleman, a more gallant or chivalrous officer never lived than Colonel Dimmock. He was an old army officer and had commanded at Old Point several years before, when that place was a fashionable pleasure resort. Some of us having met him in those happier days, found no difficulty in recalling the erect, soldierly figure, the benevolent-looking face and the kindly voice. In that large heart of his no bitterness, no malice, no sectional hate could find an abiding place. There was not a prisoner under his charge who did not learn to respect and love him before a week had rolled over their heads. While doing his duty as a soldier he did not sacrifice his humanity as a man.

It was the brave Archduke Charles who once said: "The flattery of friends I think nothing of; but the praise of the foe I value indeed."

Most of the first day our men spent in writing home to relations and friends who lived within the Union lines. In their letters they were confined to business and family affairs, all political and war themes having been strictly forbidden. These communications were read by the garrison officers, and if there were found in them the slightest allusion to those subjects, the effusion was destroyed or handed back to the writer with an admonition to be more careful in the future.

A good many men were taken sick a day or two after reaching the Fort; several nearly shuffled off their mortal coil. Too much indulgence in rich food was the cause of it, though there were some who traced the primary cause back to "that tripe" eaten on the Fall River boat. Nothing but skill and unremitting watchfulness of one of the political prisoners, Doctor Magill, of Hagerstown, saved the lives of those who were so very ill that it was but a touch-and-go with them.

What a noble specimen of humanity that man was! Of Herculean stature, outspoken and fearless as a lion, yet with a heart and touch for the sick as gentle as he was brave. Generally speaking a private's life was considered by the outside world as comparatively nothing; only valued as so much finger power to pull a trigger or as good for powder. This good man sat up with these gray-jackets through the long hours of the night, watched the flickering pulse and nursed the wavering powers with just the same fidelity and untiring devotion as if those poor soldiers had more than thanks with which to repay him.

A few days after our arrival innumerable baskets, barrels, boxes, and packages of all sizes came pouring in for the prisoners, filled with clothes of all kinds, books, luxuries, indeed everything that could be worn or eaten by man. Most of the freight was from Alexandria, Virginia, where the majority of the Seventeenth had lived, though Baltimore, New York and even Boston added a quota. We were overwhelmed with presents and were made the recipients of clothes sufficient to supply a brigade. All the fine citizen suits and underclothing left by the volunteers when they made their hasty exit from Alexandria were boxed up and forwarded promptly to Fort Warren. Several Dutchmen who had been taken prisoners found themselves apparelled in broadcloth and fine linen such as they had never worn before. In fact there was so much the men could not use that they gave the garrison guards a good deal of clothing.

Not only clothes, but money was sent; and some of us found our pockets full for the first time in many a long day.

The better class of prisoners who had funds formed a mess, and as there was a sutler at the Fort we lived like fighting-cocks.

The consequence was soon seen, as thin faces commenced to round out, stout figures began to change into fat ones; and in three weeks the difference between the hungry, gaunt crowd which made its way over the drawbridge and the well-dressed, lazy men sauntering about the fort was as marked as that between Pharaoh's seven lean kine and his "well-favored and fat-fleshed cattle that fed in a meadow."

We find tares in all wheat; nothing is quite perfect in this world, and so in the Union-loving, Hail Columbia, super-loyal city of Boston there were actually Rebel sympathizers. They came on the steamer to visit us, but as such a procedure would have been contrary to military discipline, which permitted no visitors to enter the Fort, their kind wishes took a more practical form in presenting each prisoner with a handsome gray uniform.

Those were halcyon days, those days of July, 1862; light spots in a generally dark life. Our soldier prisoners, so inured to hardship, want and suffering, had now not a care on their minds, not a trouble in their hearts; they drew in long breaths of content and could only sigh sometimes at the thought of the dark future which was doomed to hold so marked a contrast to that perfect

rest and satisfaction. It was too good to last long, that life of
ours.

Roll call in the morning at seven; breakfast at eight; cards,
chess, conversation or reading until dinner, just as fancy listed;
dinner at three; coffee and cigars at four; then came the post-
prandial nap; at six an hour's stroll around the ramparts "en
parole," or if preferred a bath in the briny deep; supper at eight;
music until ten, then "taps." Such had been the order of our
lives for three weeks, when the command was given to prepare
to leave the next morning for Virginia.

Well, of course we were glad to go, and yet sorry. Two dry
crackers a day, washed down with parched-corn coffee, did not
present quite an enlivening prospect; then, too, everybody seemed
to regret our departure. Our citizen-prisoners would miss us
dreadfully, for we stirred up the monotony of their quiet lives.
The garrison guards would feel our absence, for many were the
flasks of whiskey we had given them, and clothes; the sutler
who absorbed our money would gaze wistfully after our receding
pockets, "all that was left of them," while the Dutch girls employed by the garrison to do our washing and mending would
cry their blue eyes out we feared; they came to see us once more,
poor Gretchens, and told us, in broken English, they would think
of us when we were across the rivers in that "strange, dreadful
country of Virginia." We swore that just as soon as the cruel
war was over we would "return and marry every one of them,—
make them mistresses of a hundred slaves to do their bidding,"
and so they smiled through their tears.

Then the idea arose to celebrate the last night by giving those
girls a dance. Colonel Dimmock's consent was good humoredly
accorded, with the proviso that the frolic should end at twelve. The
mess-room was selected for the scene of action. Word was sent
to the Dutch maidens to come at eight exactly. The men were
placed upon various committees; some to see the sutler and arrange about the supper, others to take down the stove and clear
up the room, while others attended to the music. All worked
with a will and promptly at the minute the fun began.

It was the famous "Lannigan's ball" over again.

At ten, supper was served, and in half an hour the dancing was
resumed and kept up with a vim. Whiskey flowed like water, and
the Dutch and English language became so entwined thereby
that it was an impossibility to distinguish one from the other;
every one talked enough and to spare, but no one understood

any one else. As the fated hour approached the revelry was at its height; the fiddlers played as only drunken fiddlers can, the dancers shouted and swung each other, the onlookers in excited tones urging them to renewed vigor, while the uproar made the rafters of the vaulted chamber fairly ring again.

Then the drum beat; "Lights out!" shouted the guard. The Cinderellas of the evening had touched the magic hour, the Prince's ball was over, not a moment's delay. Sad, tearful and hurried partings and protestations were sworn to in English and whispered in Dutch, when presto! more quickly than the change of scene in a pantomime the hall so brilliant in lights, so animated with moving figures, so resonant with music and joyous voices, was still, dark and empty; the banquet-hall deserted.

Next day came the leave-takings. The "Quartette Club" serenaded by sunlight Colonel Dimmock and his family in that sweet farewell song of Schiller's; and afterwards every man of the Rebel line went up to the Colonel, and out of a full heart and with dewy eyes thanked him for his undeviating kindness and generous consideration. He was touched by this sense of gratitude and showed that he felt it. His sleep that night was none the less sweet, doubtless, that so many Southern hearts held him in kindliest remembrance, and had never the memory of one harsh act to bring against him in this world or the next.

Soon the farewell words were spoken and we went aboard the *Osceola,* a fine ocean steamship. The last we saw of the Fort, the daughters of Dutchland, like so many black-eyed Susans, were still standing on the ramparts waving their handkerchiefs. Gradually their figures faded away in the distance and became invisible; and as the powerful strokes of the engine sent the boat surging ahead through the blue waters, Fort Warren looked like a speck in the horizon and then faded utterly away.

CHAPTER XXV.

BACK IN OLD VIRGINIA.

The voyage to Virginia was pleasant but uneventful. After arriving at Old Point the prisoners were transferred to a steamboat, which carried its human freight to Aiken's Landing on the James. This place we reached in the early morning; then the steamer anchored in the middle of the river, where it swung in the current all day.

It was emphatically a hot morning, hotter noon and hottest evening, with not a breath of air stirring through the long hours. The sultriness inside the boat became almost insupportable, while the memory of the cool casemates of Fort Warren and the refreshing breezes of old Ocean were quite too recent to permit the change to salamander heat to be other than absolute suffering. So it happened that several of the guard who had come from the cool ramparts of Fort Warren were utterly prostrated and would have died but for the energetic efforts of a surgeon who chanced to be aboard.

Three other steamboats were anchored near us, crammed to excess with prisoners from Fort Delaware. If the torrid night was made bearable to us who were comparatively few in numbers, and who could lie on deck and go to sleep counting the stars, what must it have been to them—packed in the saloons, upper and lower decks like sardines in a box, with only room to lie in rows?

Yet another blazing day was passed on board while the Commissioners of Exchange were arranging tedious details. Several more of our guards became ill, and we nursed them carefully and tendered all the comfort and attention it was in our power to bestow. So, good actions are not lost in this world; the bread cast upon the waters returns. The kindness they had meted out to us was not wanting when nothing but the careful attendance of Rebel soldiers and the prescriptions of a Rebel surgeon saved their lives. Like us, they were very grateful.

As the day advanced and the glowing sun rose higher in the unsullied blue arch, the impatience and anxiety of the men were intensified. It looked so cool under the shadow of the trees which lined the river banks; the grass was so inviting in its vel-

vety greenness that our officers had to assert all their authority
to prevent the prisoners from jumping overboard and swimming
ashore.

On board the other steamers the suffering had become terrible.
The men were standing huddled together in a close, contracted
space, like chickens in a coop, gasping for breath; and to make it
worse, the water had given out entirely, the men drinking the
almost hot river water, which so far from alleviating, only intensified their thirst.

Night had come and yet the tantalization was kept up. The
men were beginning to swear rather roundly that under any circumstances they would go ashore the next day. That the guards
might have something to say on that subject never entered into
their calculations, for these worthies had never so much as tried
to keep us together, but sat on the deck in the lightest possible
costumes, their clothes thrown one way and their arms and accoutrements another.

"If this is a specimen of a Virginia summer," they said, "we
have had enough of it; never will we come South again of our
own free wills!"

After breakfast the longed-for order was given:

"Prepare to go ashore!"

The steamer jarred heavily against the wooden pier, and without waiting for the gang-plank to be put in position and despite
the orders of the officers, the expostulations of the guards, the
prisoners jumped on the rails, and springing on shore touched
Old Virginia soil once more, prisoners no longer.

Some of our simple-minded ones, fearing from the difficulty
they had in landing that they might even then be carried back
to prison and to a much worse captivity than it had been their
good fortune to know, took to their heels and struck manfully
for the woods.

Our boat having discharged its cargo, backed down the stream,
while first one and then the other of the waiting steamers came to
the wharf. Those prisoners that trooped slowly over the gang-
plank, looking like the van-guard of the Resurrection, were from
Fort Delaware. Scores seemed to be ill; many were suffering
from the scurvy, while all bore marks of severe treatment in their
thin faces and wasted forms. They were in the dirtiest, filthiest
condition imaginable, not a face there looked as if it had been
washed for weeks. Their clothes were torn and ragged; in fact
some had not enough tatters to cover their nakedness. Take it

all in all, it was the saddest sight that our eyes had ever looked upon and made the heart ache to witness it.

Some of the men were now being carried ashore on stretchers, so enfeebled by illness that they could not walk. Several died a few hours after they had landed. There were brought off, also, the bodies of those few who had died on the voyage.

A large portion of these men had been languishing in the gloomy Fort Delaware for over a year. It was curious to watch their delight as they touched Southern soil again. They would throw their caps in the air and dance about in an excitement of feeling that seemed impossible to control. Strong men, whose nerves were all unstrung by their long confinement and harrowing trials, burst into tears. A few, a very few, took matters coolly, and sauntered quietly away or stood meditatively looking upon the scene with feelings, perhaps, that were only deeper in that they found no expression.

Scores of ambulances, wagons, hacks, carriages and buggies stood waiting at the landing, their drivers anticipating a rich reward in greenbacks (which commanded a high premium), for carrying the returned prisoners to Richmond. Nor were such speculations vain. No man of the whole crowd but was anxious to reach the city to secure passports and have his furlough made out to visit home.

In a single rush every vehicle was jammed as close as a street car, with not even room for "one more." Not one-half were accommodated; many started to walk, hoping to reach Richmond, fifteen miles distant, by night. Others again preferred to sleep at Aikens, and next morning ride back in the carriages, which were expected to return.

One of the Seventeenth, Hector Eaches, who had been separated from us on account of his wound and sent to Governor's Island, had been removed to Fort Delaware. One boat still remained in the stream, whose prisoners would be landed in the night. I waited, hoping to find him in the last cargo.

Lying on the shore on a bed of fragrant clover I waited for my true and tried friend and mess-mate. After all, it was sweet to be free again, sweeter still to be at home. No sentinel in blue standing guard, no prison bars! Even though captivity be of the most pleasant kind, it is captivity after all. On the faces of those so lately prisoners, but who were now lying on the grass

15

smoking their pipes in an abandon of liberty, there rested expressions of unmixed satisfaction, which were but the index of a grateful feeling within.

Close by lay the bodies of four soldiers who had died on the boat from Fort Delaware, whose last wishes, "that they might be buried in the land they loved so well," were to be gratified. On their faces, too, marble white in death as they were, rested a look of deeper rest, a rest no earth-troubles would ever break. The hand which released them from their suffering and set their souls at liberty could have been no unfriendly one, albeit Death's.

My comrade joined me that night; his residence in Fort Delaware had sadly changed him; for gone was the rich color of his once round face, now thin and attenuated and pale to ghastliness; his eyes stared strangely and were sunken, two crutches enabled him to hobble along; his voice, formerly so ringing in its sweetness (he had the sweetest voice in conversation and in song one ever listened to), was weak and faltering. I never again heard the laugh that once was ever ready to break from his lips. In short, a month's residence in Fort Delaware had changed him from the very picture of health and strength, of robust manhood, into a lame, halting invalid, whose body and mind seemed to have received some great shock.

By his actions, feeble as they were, and by his words he expressed most extravagant joy at getting back alive. I made him as comfortable as I could and soon both were dreaming.

Next morning he related all the horrors of his prison experience at Fort Delaware, to which his appearance, made all the sadder-looking by bright sunlight, gave full emphasis. He told a plain, unvarnished tale, in which nothing was exaggerated and naught set down in malice; a recital that every man who had crossed that gangway the day before would corroborate, for they all had but one story to tell, a summary of facts to which those rigid forms lying yonder bore silent and eloquent witness. With the smoke of our pipes curling about our heads in concentric circles we heard him tell his experience; and it is one I do not care to repeat, for what was Fort Delaware to us or we to Fort Delaware? The Federal Government had treated us royally. Why the seventy-five men of the Seventeenth Virginia had been chosen above all others to be sent to Fort Warren we never could tell; our officers said that it was admiration of our reckless bravery in so small a force charging, all unsupported, the center of McClellan's army. If so, the Federals did not know the facts;

it was the very last thing we wanted to do, and there would have been many stragglers in our ranks if the regiment had known what work was cut out for us to do. Certainly never during the war was such an instance ever known. It stands solitary and alone. Later on it would have been impossible; but the passions, the sectional hate of the people North and South had not been fully aroused in the summer of 1862. In truth, our captivity was but a summer jaunt North, an ocean voyage and several weeks at a watering-place, where we were treated more as honored guests than as prisoners of war. The difference between Fort Warren, Elmira, Point Lookout and Camp Chase was that of Paradise and Purgatory.

CHAPTER XXVI.

THE ADVANCE.

After a furlough of two weeks the exchanged prisoners who had arrived at Aiken's Landing were ordered to report to their regiments immediately. The seventy-five men of the Seventeenth, then enjoying those warm summer days in cool, shady country homes, were to repair at once to Gordonsville, and there join the First Brigade.

We were loath to break the charm of ease and comfort which the past six weeks had thrown around us, but "needs must when the Devil drives," as the old saying has it, and military orders are not like either pie-crust or a politician's promises—made to be broken; so with full haversacks, if not with full satisfaction, we started for our destination.

A passing outline of the state of the armies during the past month, and a rapid horoscope of the future, will enable the reader to understand more clearly the movements of the troops at that time, and the grand climax to which they were tending, viz., the Second Battle of Manassas.

After McClellan's change of base from the front of Richmond to the banks of the James River, both armies, like two gladiators in the arena, took a long breathing time preparatory to closing in mortal combat once more.

About the first of August the military authorities in Washington had begun to make preparations for the campaign they knew must soon commence, to guard the National Capital against a sudden flank attack by Jackson, whose name had now become a household word and synonymous with rear attacks, flank approaches, and all sorts of unexpected advances. The War Department had gathered, as Mr. Swinton characterized it, all the fag ends of armies in Northern Virginia, lately under McDowell, Banks and Fremont, and consolidated them into the Army of Virginia.

The command of this force was entrusted to Major-General John Pope, whose appointment had been made out as far back as the twenty-sixth of June, the day before the battle of Gaines' Mill, but was not delivered until a month after.

General Pope now found himself in command of three corps:

McDowell, commanding the Third Infantry Corps.....	18,575
Cavalry	8,738
Banks, commanding the Second Infantry Corps and Artillery	14,567
Sigel, commanding the First Infantry Corps and Artillery	11,498
Total	53,378

These figures are from the official returns of the Army of Virginia, July thirty-first, 1862, General Pope's Report.

General Halleck had been recalled from the West and appointed by the War Department in Washington, general-in-chief of all the armies in the field.

Pope assumed command of his army in fine spirits. He evidently had perfect confidence in his own powers, and from the certainty and strength of his convictions impressed others with a like assurance. He was the typical new broom which the Department had secured to sweep clean, and he proposed not only to sweep the Confederacy out of existence, but the very "cobwebs from the sky." We all remember the nursery song.

His method of conducting the campaign was certainly simple in design and according to strict mathematical rule. A straight line being the shortest distance between two points, that line he proposed taking. Though his first duty was to protect Washington, his avowed intention was to capture the Rebel Capital by the untried way of an overland advance in this straight line. By aid of his eloquence he convinced the United States Committee on the Conduct of the War that this route would be the safest and best of all others.

"Give me," he said, "such an army as McClellan had and I will march straight to New Orleans."*

When Pope assumed command he issued a proclamation to his troops which will stand alone for its amazing grandiloquence, charming simplicity, and its sententious bombast through all the tides of time.

Caesar had his *Veni, vidi, vici.* Napoleon reminded his soldiers that "Forty centuries were looking down upon them," but General Pope wrote this:

---

* "Question: Suppose you had an army that was here on the first day of March (1862), do you suppose you would find any obstacle to prevent your marching to New Orleans?
General Pope: *"Should suppose not."*
Report on the Conduct of the War, Vol. 1, page 282.

"Soldiers:

"I have come to you from the West, where we have always seen the backs of our enemies, from an army whose business it is to seek the enemy and beat him wherever found, whose policy has been attack and not defense.

"Disaster and shame lurk in the rear.

"JOHN POPE,
"Major-General Commanding."

Prophetic words! Wonderful seer!

How the grim old veterans of McClellan's splendid army, who had come back from the jaws of death, must have smiled, sardonically smiled, when that order was read.

It might have seemed easy enough to Pope to whip the Rebel army, but to them it had been so far rather a tough job. Pope evidently looked upon it much in the same light as the Irishman did the playing of the fiddle. When asked if he could play, "I never played before," quoth Pat, "but it has the looks of baing aisy, and by me sowl I thinks I kin do it if I thried."

In the meanwhile, McClellan, the best organizer in America, had gotten his army in good condition, despite the sickness prevailing in his ranks. Every day the skies in the North were brightening, and every day the clouds in the South were darkening.

General Lee, resting with his forces around Richmond, perceived that without some steps taken on his part the combination being formed against him meant ruin and disaster. There was McClellan near to the Southern Capital in an unassailable position, able with ease and celerity to transfer his army across James River and operate on the south side, threatening the city in reverse and rear, and compelling the Rebel general to remain where he was, locking him up, as it were, in his own fortifications. At the same time another Federal army of over fifty thousand were preparing to launch themselves directly in his front, hence unless some steps looking to extrication were soon taken, General Lee knew that the game would be ended and checkmate given.

When contemplating any great undertaking or a vast strategic combination, General Lee had an abstracted manner that was altogether unlike his usual one. He would seek some level sward and pace mechanically up and down with the regularity of a sentinel on his beat; his head would be bent as if in deep meditation while his left hand unconsciously stroked his thick iron-gray beard. In such a manner did his brain evolve and shape the plans upon which hung the lives and destinies of thousands, the weal or woe of a people. This was the man quietly pacing up and down, upon whom rested the responsibility of baffling these two invading armies of a vast nation; a nation rich in treasure, rich in resources, fertile in expedients, and with the world at large from which to fill its overflowing ranks.

When General Lee was in one of these "moods," his staff and orderlies, aware of the momentous results depending on these deliberations, never approached him themselves nor allowed any one else to interrupt him. Like General Jackson's old darky, "by these signs, they felt a battle in their bones."

> "For whenever de masta's wakeful
> And whenever he prays and groans,
> Why dem dat lies by his camp-fire
> Feel battle in dere bones."

Jackson! Stonewall Jackson! What a magnetism there is in that name even now. Bravest warrior! Truest Christian! Knightliest soul! His was the one strong arm upon which Lee in all his trials and difficulties could always count. His was the mailed hand to strike the stunning blow; his was the ripest counsel that advised and knew just when to strike and where. "My right hand" Lee called him. So in this emergency Jackson was summoned and came; sitting under the shadow of a tree in the cool of the evening, Lee unfolded to his lieutenant his plans, which were as follows:

Jackson with his corps would proceed northward to engage General Pope, while Lee stood ready to strike McClellan should he advance on Richmond, or join Jackson by a forced march should General McClellan see fit to combine his forces with Pope.

It was General Lee's great hope that McClellan might evacuate his base at Harrison's Landing, and transfer the war to Piedmont, Virginia, for Lee well knew that his opponent across the James threatened the most vulnerable point in his defenses, and that it was there that true military policy dictated the base of an advancing army. He knew also that an attack on his communications was what McClellan most dreaded, and that he therefore would very likely decide upon the route, as affording the greatest safety and facility in that respect. Hence, he trusted that the alarm awakened at Washington by Jackson's advance against Pope would cause a withdrawal of McClellan's army and a change in his whole plan of campaign.

General Halleck, commander-in-chief of the Federal Army, fell into that trap, and urged the retiring of McClellan's army. Therefore, on the third of August the young Napoleon commenced his retreat from the Peninsula to Aquia Creek, there to make a junction with Pope.

When Lee saw this false movement of the enemy he must have been greatly relieved, for it gave him the chance of neutralizing numbers by strategical combinations on a broad area.

About the fifteenth of July Jackson started for Gordonsville, which he reached on the nineteenth. There he halted, hearing of the large force under Pope, and sent to Lee for reinforcements. A. P. Hill's division, in response, was forwarded to him, reaching Gordonsville on the second of August. At this time Pope's army was along the turnpike extending from Culpeper to Sperryville, while his cavalry did picket duty on the Rapidan.

On the eighteenth of August Jackson began to start things in earnest. Breaking camp with his troops in light marching order he moved down the road to Culpeper Court House. Eight miles south of the Court House he ran into Banks's corps, which had taken position on Cedar Mountain. A hard-fought action occurred, which, though indecisive in its immediate results, yet caused Jackson to establish his base at Gordonsville, and created in the minds of the authorities at Washington the liveliest apprehension for the safety of the National Capital.

Halleck sent urgent telegrams to McClellan to hasten and join Pope, as the danger was imminent.

McClellan was doing his best, but it required time and infinite labor to change one base for another, and to transfer a large army across several rivers or carry them by steam to the desired point. He had marched his army from Harrison's Landing on the James River to Fortress Monroe, and by transports and steamers forwarded his troops by instalments to Aquia Creek.

Watching with a cool and critical eye these different movements unfold themselves, Lee now determined on his course of action. It was so simple, so plain that every private soldier in his ranks could understand its workings. Relieved from the menacing presence of McClellan, he intended moving his entire army northward to join Jackson, and together destroy Pope before McClellan could reinforce him.

On the twelfth of August Lee broke camp around Richmond and put his columns in motion. On the fifteenth the van of his army, Longstreet's division and Stuart's cavalry, united with Jackson's forces at Gordonsville.

As soon as Pope discovered that this dangerous bolt had been forged to hurl upon him, he drew his army back behind the Rappahannock and shouted lustily for help. This retreat was in good sense, but Pope did not lie off the flanks of the Rebel army as he had promised the War Department to do, but decided upon the more sensible thing of concentrating his army in a compact space where it could be easily handled.

Lee now determined on acting on one of his bold conceptions— to send Jackson around in Pope's rear and cut him off from Washington, while he would attack in front. Such a step was rash and fraught with many dangers, for Pope, by turning his whole army on Jackson, might overwhelm him before Lee could assist. It was a game full of nice calculations as well as chances; and if the Rebel general had not entertained a rather poor opinion of his adversary's military talent, he would hardly have dared to divide his army into two parts with a chain of mountains between in which there were but few gaps. At all events a great deal of danger was incurred, not to speak of the difficulty and doubt of reaching his lieutenant in time had an emergency arisen calling for a junction of forces.

However, he decided; and Jackson, with 17,300 rank and file, set off on the morning of the twenty-fifth of August and moved up the western side of the Bull Run Mountains, lying between him and the Yankee posts. (See Jackson's Official Report.) A forced march of twenty miles brought him to Thoroughfare Gap, by marching through which he would gain the Union rear. This pass, which by the commonest instinct of military prudence should have been guarded by General Pope, was left open to his enemy. Early in the morning of the twenty-seventh, Jackson slipped through, and that night struck Bristow Station on the Orange and Alexandria Railroad, from which depot Pope drew a large portion of his supplies. Of course Jackson's men filled their haversacks and themselves, and around their camp-fires that night feasted on potted game and canned preserves washed down with Rhine wine and champagne.

On the morning of the twenty-eighth Jackson's foot-cavalry reached Manassas Junction, where there was a town such as one sees in the mining camps on the Pacific slope. The sutlers had brought along liberal supplies, and judging from the neat frame buildings erected by them, they had come to stay. Here it was that Pope's quartermasters had collected a vast depot of supplies for the army. In about fifteen minutes the sutler stores were sacked. Then as the drum beat for falling in the match was applied and soon the flames from these buildings were mingling with those that shot toward the sky from the burning camp supplies. In a couple of hours the town of canvas and pines was a smouldering waste.

Lee had remained in front of Pope, but on the other side of the Bull Run Mountains. On the twenty-sixth Longstreet's division set out to reinforce Jackson. Pope, suspecting the intent of this movement, began to fall back toward Manassas, where half of Jackson's troops were standing upon their arms. Ewell's division was still at Bristow Station, at which place they were attacked on the morning of the twenty-seventh by Hooker, who did not, however, press the advance.

This slight engagement convinced Jackson that he was in danger of being himself surrounded by the enemy, who were even then closing upon him. His only chance was to fall back to Thoroughfare Gap and effect a junction with Longstreet, who was hastening to his relief. As a feint to this movement, he moved off toward Centerville, then turned abruptly to the west, crossed Bull Run and took position about a mile northwest of last year's battle-fields. The position was selected with great care and judgment; the abandoned cutting and the embankments of the railroad forming the best kind of rifle-pits.

Pope was close behind and now felt that the great opportunity of his life had arrived. On the morning of the twenty-ninth he commenced to throw his whole army against Jackson, purposing to crush him before Longstreet could come with succor. Sigel and McDowell hurled their separate corps against the Rebel line and were driven back with great loss. Jackson by hard work held his own and late in the evening received the welcome news that Longstreet would join him in the morning, the van of the approaching division being seen filing through the gap as the sun went down.

At nightfall Jackson's extreme left was considerably drawn in toward the left-center, a movement which had the aspect of a retreat.

On the morning of the thirtieth neither party, it seems, was anxious to begin the fray; but at noon Pope, thinking that Jackson was in full retreat, ordered his whole line to advance. Never was a greater mistake. Longstreet's corps had now arrived and were taking position. Lee massed his forces in the form of an irregular L, Jackson's command forming the longer line and about half of Longstreet's the shorter; the balance being held in reserve.

So, stripped to the waist, both parties commenced the fight, eager for the fray.

On the morning of the thirtieth of August, the decisive day, after deducting the losses in the engagements of the twenty-seventh, twenty-eighth and twenty-ninth, General Pope reports his effective strength (including reinforcements) as follows:

McDowell's Corps, including Reynolds's Division, ... 12,000
Sigel's Corps, ... 7,000
Reno's Corps, ... 7,000
Heintzelman's Corps, ... 7,000
Porter's Corps, ... 12,000
Banks's Corps, ... 5,000

Total, ... 50,000

(General Pope's Report, page 156.)

In addition to these troops there were in reserve the divisions of Sturgis and Cox and the corps of Sumner and Franklin. These two corps together, numbering thirty thousand men, were only a day's march distant from Pope, but did not join him until after his retreat to Centerville.

Sturgis's division was ten thousand strong, and Cox's seven thousand, so that from first to last there were assembled in front of Washington, as shown by official reports, not less than one hundred and twenty thousand men, though not half were brought into action. Pope put his strength the day after the battle at sixty-three thousand men.

Lee's fighting force all told, comprising both Jackson's and Longstreet's corps, amounted to forty-nine thousand and seventy-seven men. (Adjutant-General Walter Taylor's Report in his book, "Four Years With General Lee," page 62.)

Pope having made the fatal military blunder of advancing his forces before he knew to a certainty Longstreet's position and at what time and place to expect him, paid dearly for his folly. The corps of Reno and Heintzelman, making the attack, were driven back with much loss. Fitz John Porter's corps, which up to this time had taken no part in the events of the campaign, was ordered to move upon Jackson's right, their line of march, all unknown to them, passing by Longstreet's division, which thus lay upon its flanks.

Porter's assault was so vigorous and determined that Jackson called for aid, but Longstreet, perceiving his advantage, instead of reinforcing Jackson, opened by order of Lee all his batteries upon Porter, and in a few moments advanced his infantry. Porter, outnumbered, was hurled back straight across the plateau toward Bull Run. Jackson now received a courier from Lee and simultaneously advanced his line, pressing back Heintzelman and McDowell. The angle between the Rebel wings gradually lessened and the sides seemed to enclose Pope's army like a vise.

The Yankee retreat threatened to become a general rout, more disastrous than that on the same battle-ground a little over a year before. The man to save the Grand Army of the Potomac was on the spot, Colonel Warren, who was then commanding a small brigade.

He, seeing the threatened disintegration of the Federal host, with one of those happy inspirations born of the occasion, threw his brigade, without waiting for orders, upon an eminence west of the Henry House called Bald Hill, and held it until surrounded on three sides, for just that space of time keeping the Rebels in check. His men fought unyieldingly and with the savage tenacity of bulldogs. Never was bravery more signally acknowledged, for it saved the army. Out of one thousand and ninety men with whom Warren maintained this position, he lost in about fifteen minutes four hundred killed and wounded.

This check enabled Porter's corps to retire across Bull Run by the stone bridge, and forced the Rebels to halt and reform their lines. It was nearly dark by that time, but Longstreet's corps carried Bald Hill by an impetuous attack, and the battle was ended. Under cover of the night the wearied, beaten Federal army retired to Centerville and took position on its heights. Owing to the darkness and the uncertainty of the fords of Bull Run, General Lee attempted no pursuit.

At Centerville Pope united with the corps of Sumner and Franklin, there remaining during the whole of the thirty-first.

Lee had not given up the pursuit; for leaving Longstreet leisurely advancing northward, he sent Jackson by a detour on Pope's right to strike the Little River turnpike, and by that route to intercept if possible Pope's retreat to Washington. Jackson did strike Pope's right at Ox Hill near Germantown, and close to Chantilly engaged the enemy with Ewell's and Hill's divisions, beating them back.

Pope had his troops massed. Jackson, seeing no chance of succeeding in his task, halted and awaited orders from Lee.

So ended the great "Second Battle of Manassas," which came near being the Federal Waterloo, through the military blunderer and vain pretender, General John A. Pope.

There is no account of the losses in this bloody battle, but they must have been terrible. Lee's general reports put the Rebel loss at one thousand and ninety killed and six thousand five hundred and fourteen wounded; total, seven thousand six hundred and four. Only partial reports of the Federal loss were given and these indicated a loss of eleven thousand killed and wounded and seven thousand five hundred taken prisoners; in all nearly twenty thousand men.

General Pope, who hitherto "had only seen the backs of his enemies," whose business it had been to "seek the enemy and beat him wherever found," whose policy had been attack and not defense, fell back to Washington and resigned his command.

"Disaster and shame had lurked in the rear."

CHAPTER XXVII.

THE SECOND MANASSAS.

Having outlined the main events of the present campaign in the preceding chapter, we return again to the Seventeenth, which we unceremoniously left at Gordonsville cleaning muskets and cooking three days' rations preparatory to the march.

Saturday night, August sixteenth, the brigade camped at Orange Court House. On Sunday the drum beat the long roll and the men fell into line. The troops were all in light marching order; a blanket or oilcloth, a single shirt, a pair of drawers and a pair of socks rolled tightly therein was swung on the right shoulder while the haversack hung on the left. These, with a cartridge-box suspended from the belt, and a musket carried at will, made up Johnny Reb's entire equipment. As for uniforms, there were not two men clothed alike in the whole regiment, brigade or division; some had caps, some wore hats of every imaginable shape and in every stage of dilapidation, varied in tint by the different shades of hair which protruded through the holes and stuck out like quills upon the fretful porcupine; the jackets were also of different shades, ranging from light gray with gilt buttons, to black with wooden ones; the pants were for the most part of that nondescript hue which time and all weathers give to ruins, or if with the eye of an artist you still sought to name the color, you would be apt to find it, with a strange fatality, like that of the soil; white shirts there were none, shirts of darker shade were scarce, owing to the stringency of the market; some of the men wore boots, others the army brogans; but many were bare-footed; all were dusty and dirty, for no clothes had been issued since the commencement of the early spring campaign. This accounted for the rags and tatters, though the cones and pins of white pine must be held responsible for some of the holes. Human looks did not count for much in this crowd, with whom, though everything else were dull, eyes and gun-barrels yet flashed brightly; neither had the hopes which loomed in their breasts become dimmed, and all else was subservient.

In marching, the troops had learned how to get over the ground without raising such clouds of dust and choking themselves with the flying particles. The ranks of fours would split, one-half to the right and the other to the left, and then choosing untrod ground they would proceed with infinitely less trouble and annoyance than in the old way of marching in solid column. Of course the ubiquitous camp darky, with cooking utensils piled high on his back, brought up the rear of each company.

Our rations were doled out in sparing quantities; three crackers per man and a half pound of fat pork was the daily allowance. The cravings of hunger were hardly satisfied by the dole, but soon we were to get nothing from the commissary.

Every soldier in the army knew by these measures that they were on the way to meet our old enemy who had left the vicinity of Richmond only to appear somewhere in our front between the Rappahannock and the Potomac. The men were becoming veteran soldiers rapidly, and began to understand their work; they were no longer found burdening themselves with useless articles; they ceased to brood over the possible or probable results of the war, its length and its hardships; they had acquired the habit of implicit obedience to superior officers; they had learned how to make a pound of meat and bread go a long way by eating at stated times; they had become adepts in the art of foraging and they knew how to practice self-denial as a virtue when it had become in fact a necessity; they had learned too a hundred little ways of adding to their comfort; for instance, taking off their shoes on a level stretch of sandy road, of bathing their feet in every running brook, of carrying leaves in their hats as protection against the sun, or lying stretched out at full length at every halt instead of sitting down; indeed, the devices to make the best of each opportunity filled every spare crack and crevice of the soldier's brain, and were too numerous to record. They were little things, it is true, but in the aggregate they amounted to much and were such as marked the difference in a personal combat between the strong unskilled man and the trained athlete.

When a soldier had learned how to take care of himself in this manner he rarely broke down, never grumbled, never straggled unless he had a positive cause, and with enough to eat was bound to answer to his name at the evening tattoo.

In this march the Sibley tents—those abominations, those breeders of disease—were forever discarded, and the troops either bivouacked in the woods or strung themselves out along the road, anywhere in fact where there was a rail fence and water. Many of us carried a little thin cotton tent, sufficient to shelter four men from rain, miniature affairs about the size of a sheet, that only weighed about two pounds, and buttoning together answered every purpose. This was a Yankee invention, our Government not issuing them, but nearly every soldier had one, confiscated from our obliging friends across the way, upon whose patent we infringed without the slightest compunction.

For over a week the column tramped steadily along, passing Kelly's Ford, where the old familiar scream of the Yankee shells greeted our ears. It was only a retiring battery, which limbered up before any reply could be dispatched. A whole day's rest was vouchsafed us at Stevensburg, which place in commerce and population consisted of only one house. On the twenty-third the division halted at Brandy Station, and marched to the edge of Rappahannock Run, across which could be seen the long line of Yankee infantry marching off, while their artillery crowned the hills ready to pour a rain of iron upon any who should attempt to advance.

In the evening, as the brigade was resting on the ground, there came one of those sudden violent thunder-storms so common during a hot mid-summer term. The sky grew dark, the air became heavy, the wind died away and then the tornado burst in all its fury.

The men were strongly averse to getting their clothes wet, and wishing at the same time to take a shower-bath fresh from the sky itself, they disrobed speedily. Placing their clothes under oilcloths, they sat or danced around with as much glee as if the storm had been gotten up for their benefit, and much in the same way that Adam must have done. It was rather an amusing spectacle, and if our well-dressed enemy had burst among us with a sudden flank attack, they would probably have run in very amazement, thinking a world of bedlamites had broken loose, or that the storm had rained down beings from another world who were performing weird and mystic rites. The clouds emptied themselves at the right time, for it had been weeks since the men had bathed, and this great shower-bath of Nature's was therefore as kindly in its offices as it was refreshing.

After the rain had washed men and earth, had bathed the trees and grass until they glistened, had started a hundred rivulets flowing on a long journey ocean-ward, had laid and exorcised for a time the demon Dust, had revived and furbished up all Nature, the clouds rolled back, the sun came out and dried the bodies of our dripping warriors, and that night the division bivouacked at Waterloo.

On the twenty-fifth of August, 1862, to the sound of random cannon shots the soldiers stepped out briskly, crossing the Rappahannock River by a ford at Waterloo. Just before noon, when we were on the opposite side, the brigade witnessed the destruction by the enemy of Warrenton Springs, whose two splendid hotels were burned to the ground. The large and lofty ball-room, wide passages and spacious corridors with lofty columns were soon crumbling masses of ruins.

On the twenty-seventh the division reached Salem late at night, after a forced march of many miles which broke down a good many of the men. The little village was occupied by the Yankees, but they suddenly concluded to leave as Longstreet's van-guard filed in. Wearied and prostrated by the heat, and fatigued as were our troops, they were called into ranks again after a short rest, and did not stop until they had reached the Plains, a little hamlet close to Thoroughfare Gap. It was long after midnight when about one-fourth of the original force limped into a field and stacked their arms. The balance were strung out along the road, but they soon began to come in by twos and threes, and before sunrise nearly every absentee was in ranks.

In the morning no hurry was manifested by the leaders to advance, though the booming of the cannon came at intervals from across the mountains. A squad from the regiment, a few choice spirits who could never let well enough alone, who if they could not find trouble or danger ready at hand always went out of their way to seek them, obtained permission from our colonel to proceed in the advance and await the arrival of the brigade at the Gap. So Walter Addison, Harmon and myself started on ahead, leaving the division resting in a large field right at the base of the up-rearing mountain. We were soon at the Gap, which was found to be strongly guarded by the enemy.

Here was "a go," as Joe would say, "a precious go," for our picket refused to let us approach any closer. An hour or two passed, when suddenly there was a commotion at the Gap. A rattling volley came from the rear, and the enemy broke and ran, leaving behind some fifty killed and wounded. One of our brigades had crossed the mountain higher up at Hopewell's Gap and stormed the enemy in the rear, while our troops menaced the front. Of course the foe had to strike for his home and his country, especially the former.

The van of Longstreet was now passing through the Gap and Jackson was safe.

16

Keeping along the railroad track, and impelled by that spirit of adventure which urges an advance in a strange country, not knowing what to expect, we continued our way. About a mile farther a picket on our side halted us, saying he was the last vidette and that the enemy held possession only a few hundred yards up the track. Turning to retrace our steps, we heard the sound of rapid cannon firing on our left, and proceeded in that direction until the scene of action was nearly reached. Close enough for those who were not obliged to go into battle, for the shells were hitting around rather carelessly and the purplish rim of smoke demonstrated that the musketry, not a half mile away, was engaged in its deadly work. We halted and held a council of war wherein all had equal voice, for all were "High Privates," whether 'twere better—but just here a noise was heard up the road, and two batteries of the Washington Artillery went by at a gallop, half hidden by the cloud of dust that was raised. The men were hanging on as best they could, or were keeping alongside at the top of their speed, while the drivers were lashing their horses unmercifully.

"Where are you bound?" shouted one of the party to an officer who reined up to let the caissons pass.

"To the front!" was the reply; "the Yankees are pressing us hard."

This settled the rising discussion, and the council quickly passed a unanimous resolution to see the fun out. We kept on in the rear of the artillery until it took position on a high crest; there we seceded and started in the direction of the musketry firing, passing on the way Pickett's Virginians lying on the ground drawn up in line of battle in a strip of woods. Most of the men were asleep, though the artillery was thundering and the volume of musketry was growing greater every minute. They had become used to these sounds, and as the turning wheels in the mill is to the miller, as the lullaby of the nurse to the fretful child, so was the music of cannonading to these veterans, only lulling them to a deeper sleep.

Not far in the advance we came upon a group of general officers who, mounted on their horses, were intently studying the field through glasses. Seeing us wandering aimlessly about, one of the number ordered us back to our regiments, and so we had to retrace our steps. Every man of us had come out to see something at any price, consequently we flanked the officers and bore to the left, where there was a hill covered with trees. Selecting the tallest we climbed it, though as the shells went by from the enemy's batteries, not two thousand yards distant, one of us slid down in a hurry.

From the top of a tree a glorious view unfolded itself, a panorama of hill and vale far off in the distance. Right in a valley, a little over a mile away, were the combatants nearly hidden by the opaque curtain of smoke that had fallen upon the scene like a heavy fog upon a river. Through the slate-colored vapor the vivid flashing of the guns and blaze of musketry would burst as lightning from a cloudy sky; then the smoke would lift from one part of the field, and give a passing glimpse of irregular lines advancing or retreating, of men falling, of glittering arms, and then dense volumes of smoke from the cannon would roll over the scene once more and hide it from our gaze. For hours we kept on our perches, entranced by the spectacle of a great battle raging before our eyes, and did not move until night put an end to the conflict.

I thought then that if it were possible to build lofty seats where we were, with tickets placed on sale, what an enormous price they would bring. What were the combats of the gladiators in the Coliseum of Rome in the days of Nero to the grand spectacle of two of the bravest armies in the world contending for mastery, where, in the space of a mile, forty thousand men in plain view were engaged. There was not a charge upon Jackson's position that was not plainly in view. There was not a battery vomiting their death missiles that was not distinct. Individual suffering none could see, but the glorious panoply of war was all there. Yes, the box-office receipts would have been immense, and there was not an emperor, a king, or sultan that would not have graced the occasion by his presence. When years afterwards I gazed on scenes of mimic warfare I always thought of that spectacle, the like of which but few eyes ever beheld.

Collecting some fagots, we broiled our meat, discussed the chances of to-morrow's battle over our pipes, and solaced ourselves with the hope, fortified by a strong determination, that if our lives were spared, by this time the next night we would each have a Yankee haversack lined with a little bag of pure coffee; ditto, one of sugar.

The twenty-ninth of August was a sultry, hot day, and we expected every moment to hear a renewal of the battle just where it had left off the night before. Everything, on the contrary, was most serene; and as our scout returned with the information that the Seventeenth had not yet filed through the Gap, we determined to visit the battle-field of yesterday.

Burial parties had been at work at the earliest dawn, and long trenches were seen, which marked the place where scores of brave men were lying coffinless side by side. The wounded had all been removed in the night; hence there were but few shocking scenes to revolt the mind; only an overturned caisson, a few mangled horses, the blackened grass, bloody rags, and that was all.

A large number of Rebel and Yankee wounded lay together, cheek by jowl, in blankets under the shade of the trees. They were treated impartially, no difference of any kind being made. Many of the wounded were only slightly hurt, and the blue and the gray jackets mixed with one another with the utmost fraternity, joked, sang songs, bantered each other upon the length of the war, told camp stories, while some were drinking coffee from the same cup; men at whose hearts each had aimed the deadly rifle only a few hours before.

How the Yankees did enjoy smoking the Rebel tobacco! At the North they sold the soldiers a vile compound made of chickory, cabbage and sumac leaves ground together and christened tobacco. It burned the tongue, parched the throat, and almost salivated the consumer.

It was a subject for meditation to a politician of the extreme type to watch Johnny Reb and Billy Yank smoke the pipe of temporary peace. The privates of both armies never personally disliked one another; they were the best friends in the world as soon as they met on neutral ground.

The rapid pounding of the artillery caused us to hurry through the morning meal, almost before the sun rose above the hill, and we pushed for Thoroughfare Gap to rejoin the regiment. We knew by instinct that there would be a battle that day; for there was blood upon the moon. We fancied we could perceive, with another sense, the marshalling in mid-air of cohorts from the unseen world, preparing to take their part in the coming struggle, guiding a bullet home here, interposing to save a life there, taking charge of disembodied souls after the mortal had put on sudden immortality and stood shivering on the borders of the Unknown Shore. The air was coming from the mountains, every breath so pure and fresh, odorous with the scent of ripening fruit and clover blossoms; clean, sweet air, so soon to be tainted with corruption and putrescence. The mountains were looking down upon the plains with patience infinite it seemed, not stolidly as the Pyramids watched the French squares and the Mameluke cavalry arrange themselves for war, but as sad, pitying witnesses of a coming scene their holy presence would fain have calmed. Never had life seemed more worth living than on a morning such as this; never existence sweeter; never Death so loath the dying.

Long streams of soldiers were wending their way to the front. The troops seemed everywhere; they filled the railroad track as far as the eye could reach; they emerged from the narrow gap in the mountain, and spread out over the fields and meadows; they wound along the base of the hills, and marched in a steady tramp over the dusty highways; following a dozen different routes, but each face turned directly or obliquely northward. Ordnance wagons were being pushed rapidly ahead; batteries were taking position, staff officers were riding at a gallop, as if seconds and minutes were golden. In short, all fighting material was pushing to the van and all the peacefully inclined were valiantly seeking the rear. By a law as fixed as that which bound the Stoics, as unalterable as those which govern the affinities of the chemical world, this separation of the two types ever occurred on the eve of battle. An instant sifting of wheat from the tares took place quietly but surely in every company, and the mass of men so lately mingled became as incapable of mixture as oil and water.

The great receding tide at full ebb sank back toward the Gap; the mighty army of the backsliders whom naught could hinder, non-combatants, camp darkies, shirking soldiers playing possum, and camp followers. Warm work was expected and all this genus, like war-horses, "sniffed danger from afar."

Some were on foot, carrying arms full of muskets which the ordnance officer was sending to the rear; others were loaded with accoutrements and blankets which they were transferring to a secure place, watched and guarded by a sentry; for this riff-raff of the army was not noted for its honesty. A few were the possessors, for the time, of a broken-down horse or spavined mule and were urging these poor animals to their fastest speed.

It was this crowd belonging to the wagon-train or detailed for work such as blacksmithing, using every artifice to avoid the marching and the fighting, which hung on the army like barnacles on a staunch ship's bottom, impeding its course and weighting it down. It was the impedimenta that flocked to the battle-field as soon as the shot and shell ceased firing, and despoiled and stripped friend and foe alike, dead or wounded, it mattered not, though they never killed or illtreated the injured or maimed.

Reaching the Gap we found that the brigade had passed through. Following hard upon the track, our little squad after an hour's march caught up and took its place in rank.

The men were in a fearful humor, grumbling at their luck and cursing the commissary. They had ample cause; not a single ration had been issued to the troops for several days and the soldiers were savage from hunger.

The brigade halted in line of battle about half a mile this side of the famous Chinn House, on the outskirts of a large corn-field. There it was that the lines were broken, and the brigade dispersed in a second. The officers, tired of shouting themselves hoarse, joined the men in the rush for roasting ears, which were now in full ripeness, and never was a field gleaned so completely and in such a short time. Three thousand men made onslaught. There was a confused noise of breaking stalks; the tops and waving tassels of the whole field were shaken violently as if a sudden tornado had passed over them, and each soldier returned lugging in his arms a pile of succulent, juicy corn. No fires were allowed to be built, so the ears were devoured raw. We secured more than our share, for the other brigade commanders sent details with wagons all over the county, taking all the corn they could lay their hands on, and issuing daily rations to the troops of three ears of corn to a man, and nothing more. It is a solemn fact that Longstreet's corps had received no rations for four days, and lived on daily allowances of green corn, fighting and winning a great battle on empty stomachs.

The forenoon had passed and the sound of hostile cannon was breaking the silence in our front while a battle was being fought on our left. At this dread hour, when the human mind becomes alive to the awful problem of its final abiding place, and hope, fear and wonder pass through the preternaturally excited brain, then it is that the devout soldiers look resigned, the thoughtless grave, and the scoffers solemnly silent. The Christian soldier's Bible is in brisk demand, and as that type of manhood was now rare in the old brigade, the "Good Book" was very popular and a score of famishing Rebs were waiting to read a chapter before the signal to commence the fight was given. It would have been pathetic to watch the erstwhile laughing, reckless, jeering infantryman waiting his turn to cram several chapters of the Bible so as to increase his chance of salvation, had it not been so humerous to hear the exclamations of the impatient throng.

"Hurry up there, Ned, we'll all get killed before you get through," one remarked earnestly.

A second soldier on the outside of the circle chimed in,

"What does Ned care if we all are damned, so he is saved?"

"That's Ned all over," responded Walter Addison, his bosom friend.

"Make haste there, Ned Sangster, they're firing like hell over yonder!" and so on, until a vast cloud of dust began to ascend toward the sky, evidence that great bodies of men were in motion.

"Fall in!" the officers shouted, and the men sprang to their feet, the line was dressed, and the brigade headed to the front to take position. On the way we were halted, and every soldier was compelled to strip for the fight by discarding his blanket,—if he had one, which was not often—oilcloth or overcoat. All these were deposited in a large pile, and guards set over them, looking very much as if we did not intend to retreat. Cartridge-boxes were filled with forty rounds, and in our haversacks we carried twenty more, making sixty rounds per man.

Soon the crack of the skirmisher's rifles were heard, then the artillery opened, and the purple-colored smoke drifted like mist from lowland marshes, across the valley.

"Forward! Guide to the colors! March!"

Across that level plateau the First Brigade moved, the flower of Virginia in its ranks, the warm blood rushing in its veins as it did in warrior ancestors centuries ago. It was a glorious and magnificent display, the line keeping perfect time, the colors showing red against the azure sky. There was no cheering, only the rattling of the equipments and the steady footfalls of the men who trod the earth with regular beat. As the brigade swept across the plain it was stopped by a high Virginia snake fence; hundreds of willing hands caught the rails, tossed them aside, and then instinctively touching each other's elbows, the ranks were dressed as if by magic.

The first shell now shrieked over us. Another burst not ten feet from the ground directly over the heads of our forces. The long chain kept intact, though close to the spot where the explosion occurred; the links vibrated and oscillated for a moment, then grew firm again and pressed onward.

How the shells rained upon us now; a Yankee six-gun battery, on a hill about half a mile off, turned its undivided attention upon us and essayed to shatter the advancing line. It did knock a gap here and there, but the break was mended almost as soon as broken, and the living wall kept on. Shells were bursting everywhere, until it seemed as if we were walking on torpedoes. They crackled, split and exploded all around, throwing dirt and ejecting little spirts of smoke that for a moment dimmed the sky.

Colonel Marye dismounted, drew his sword from the scabbard, and looking the beau ideal of a splendid soldier, placed himself at the head of his men. He stopped for a moment and pointed his sword with an eloquent and vivid gesture toward the battery on the hill. A cheer answered him, and the line instinctively quickened its pace. Though the shells were tearing through the ranks, the men did not falter. One man's resonant voice was sounding above the din, exercising a magical influence; one man's figure strode on in front and where he led, his men kept close behind. We followed unwaveringly our colonel over the hill, down the declivity, up the slope, straight across the plain toward the battery, with even ranks, though the balls were tearing a way through flesh and blood. The brigade stretched out for several hundred yards, forming, as they marched, a bow with concave toward the enemy. The Seventeenth was on the right of the line, and the other regiments dressed by our colors as we bore right oblique toward the battery, which was now hidden by a volleying fume that settled upon the crest.

Still the advance was not stayed nor the ranks broken. We neared the Chinn House, when suddenly a long line of the enemy rose from behind an old stone wall and poured straight in our breasts a withering volley at point-blank distance. It was so unexpected, this attack, that it struck the long line of men like an electric shock. Many were falling killed or wounded, and but for the intrepid coolness of its colonel, the Seventeenth would have retired from the field in disorder. His clear, ringing voice was heard, and the wavering line reformed. A rattling volley answered the foe, and for a minute or two the contest was fiercely waged. Then the colonel fell with his knee frightfully shattered by a Minie-ball. Once down, the calm, reassuring tones heard no longer, the line broke. Now individual bravery made up for the disaster. The officers surged ahead with their swords waving in the air, cheering on the men, who kept close to their heels, loading and firing as they ran. The line of blue was not fifty yards distant and every man took a sure, close aim before his finger pressed the trigger. It was a decisive fight of about ten minutes, and both sides stood up gamely to their work. Our foes were a Western regiment from Ohio, who gave and received and asked no odds. The left of our brigade having struck the enemy's right and doubled it up, now sent one volley into their flank.

In a moment the blue line quivered and then went to pieces. Officers and men broke for the rear, one regimental colors captured by Jim Coleman, of the Seventeenth. In a few moments there were none left except the dead and wounded.

There was hardly a breathing spell, only time indeed to take a full draught from the canteen, transfer the cartridges from the haversacks to the cartridge-box, and the enemy was upon us with a fresh line.

We were now loading and firing at the swiftly approaching enemy, who were about two hundred yards distant, advancing straight toward us and shouting with their steady hurrah, so different from the Rebel yell. It was a trying moment and proved the metal of the individual man. Some ran, or white with fear cowered behind the Chinn House, while others hid in a long gulley near by; others yet stood in an irregular form and loaded and fired, unmindful of the dust and noise of the hurtling shell and screaming shot.

On what small trifles hang a man's life in battle! Not a soldier in the army but can recall some incident, some trivial event that kept the vital spark within his frame. A stumble, a step to the right or left, a mere turn of the head, the raising of a musket, a book in the pocket, a handkerchief, a button, such slight things save hundreds of lives, and what is harder to contemplate, lose them. A half inch here or there, the tenth part of an inch it may be, and lo! the result is as widely different from what it might have been as time is from eternity. No wonder that so many soldiers are fatalists.

I was capping my gun in desperate haste to fire, when Frank Ballenger, gallant soldier he ever was, jumped directly in front of me and fired. At that very instant, before his finger could have left the trigger, a Yankee bullet, speeding invisibly through the air, bent on its deadly purpose of passing through my body, struck him, and he fell back into my arms nerveless and almost pulseless. I heard him cry out, and then came from his throat the horrible sound of the death rattle, which smote my ear for the first time. I placed my canteen to his lips. He tried to swallow, and then his glazing eyes showed that he was dead. Tearing open his jacket in frantic haste, I found that the bullet had struck him below the heart, passing clear through—the bullet meant for me.

There was no time to indulge in feelings there; it is only around the camp-fire that we can afford to do that.

The brigade was scattered everywhere now. For an hour they had fired as fast as the cartridges could be rammed home. When the Union troops came up to retake the Chinn House, our men began to give ground. On came the Yankees in splendid style, with the Stars and Stripes waving and their line capitally dressed. It was a perfect advance, and some of us forgot to fire our muskets while watching them. In their front was a little drummer beating a *pas de charge,* the only time we ever heard the inspiriting sound on the battle-field. The dauntless little fellow was handling his sticks lustily, too, for the roll of the drum was heard above the noise of the guns.

It was high time to be leaving, we thought, and now our men were turning to fire one good shot before heeling it to the rear, when right behind us there came with a rush and a vim a fresh Rebel brigade aiming straight for the Yankees. They ran over us and we joined their lines. Not a shot was fired by them in response to the fusilade of musketry that was raining lead all around. Every man with his head bent sideways and down, like people breasting a hailstorm, for soldiers always charge so, and the Gray and the Blue met with a mighty shock. A tremendous sheet of flame burst from our line; the weaker side went to the ground in a flash, and with a wild yell the Gray swept on toward the six-gun battery that had been sending forth a stream of death for the past hour. We could only see the flashes of light through the dense smoke.

The line stopped a moment at the foot of the hill to allow itself to catch up. It was late in the evening and the battle was raging in all its deadliest fury. On our right, on our left, in the front, in the rear, from all directions came the warring sound of cannon and musketry. We could see nothing but smoke, breathe nothing except the fumes of burning powder, feel nothing save the earth jarred by the concussion of the guns, hear nothing but the dire, tremendous clamor and blare of sound swelling up into a vast volume of fire. How hot it was! The clothes damp with perspiration, the canteens empty, throats parched with thirst, faces blackened by powder, the men mad with excitement.

The left of the line came up and then some one asked:

"Whose brigade is this?"

"Hood's," was the answer.

Then burst a ringing cry, "Forward, Texans!"

The line sprang like a tightly-bent bow suddenly loosened, and rushed up the hill in a wild, eager dash—a frenzied, maddening onset up the hill through the smoke, nearer and nearer to the guns.

When about a hundred yards from them the dense veil lifted, floated upward and softly aside, and discovered to us that the battery had ceased firing. We could see the muzzles of the guns, their sullen black mouths pointing at us, and behind them the gunners, while from the center of the battery was a flag that lay drooping upon its staff. It was for a second only, like the rising of the curtain for a moment on a hideous tableau, only to be dropped as the eye took in the scene in all its horrors, yet it impressed itself, that vivid picture, brief as it was, upon mind, heart and brain.

At once came a noise like a thunder shock, that seemed as if an earthquake had riven the place. The ground trembled with the concussion. The appalling sound was heard of iron grape-shot tearing its way through space and through bodies of bone, flesh and blood.

Mercifully for us, but not intended by our foes, the guns were elevated too high, or it would have been simply annihilation; for when those six guns poured their volley into the charging lines they were loaded to the muzzle with grape, and the distance was only about pistol shot. Of course the execution was fearful, and for a second the line was stupefied and nearly senseless from the blow. The ground was covered with victims and the screams of the wounded rose high above the din and were awful to hear.

The advance was not stayed long.

"Forward, boys! Don't stop now! Forward, Texans!" and with a cry from every throat the Southerners kept on, officers and men together without form or order, the swiftest runners ahead, the slowest behind, 'tis true, but struggling desperately to better their time. Up! Still up! until we reached the crest! As the Yankees pulled the lanyards of the loaded pieces our men were among them. A terrific shock. A lane of dead in front. Those standing before the muzzles were blown to pieces like captured Sepoy rebels. I had my hand on the wheel of one cannon just as it was fired, and I fell like one dead, from the concussion. There was a frenzied struggle in the semi-darkness around the guns, so violent and tempestuous, so mad and brain-reeling that to recall it is like fixing the memory of a horrible, blood-curdling dream. Every one was wild with uncontrollable delirium.

Then the mists dissolved and the panting, gasping soldiers could see the picture as it was. The battery had been captured by the Texans, and every man at the pieces taken prisoner. Many were killed by a volley that we had poured into them when only a few paces distant, and a large proportion wounded. The few who escaped unhurt stood in a group, so blackened with powder that they ceased to look like white men. These soldiers had nobly worked their guns and had nothing to be ashamed of. All that men could do they had done.

The voices of the officers now called the men to rally. The grass was blackened, indeed the very ground beneath our feet was burnt to a cinder and still smoking. From the top of the hill we could see dark masses of the enemy about a mile off, rushing to the front, while on the right and left the reek and fog of the field hid the combatants from view.

Not a dozen of the Seventeenth could be seen in one place. They were scattered everywhere, mixed up and absorbed for the time in the reserves which ran over them. As for myself, I had the fight taken out of me by a bullet through the arm. It was but a flesh wound, but it hurt and prevented me from firing.

In the valley below the Chinn House, where the dust was dense and blinding, the smoke heavy and stifling, it was hard for the brigade and the division to keep intact, and so the different organizations were all mingled, but maintained no less a heavy and deadly fire on that account. Occasional glimpses of the enemy were discernible, and as the evening wore on it was discovered that they were giving ground. This yielding was only temporary, for about a half an hour before the sun went down their reserves were brought up, and then the fire increased in volume until the detonations were something to make one shudder.

In the line with which we were, the men lay flat on their breasts, firing more accurately and coolly than could have been done standing, delivering their pieces without calculation or aim.

Just as the day was drawing to a close a mighty yell arose, a cry from twice ten thousand throats, as the Rebel reserves, fresh from the rear, rushed resistlessly to the front. Never did mortal eyes behold a grander sight; not even when McDonald put his columns in motion at Wagram or Ney charged the Russian center at Borodino.

It was an extended line, reaching as far as the eye could see, crescent in form, and composed of many thousand men. It was, in fact, a greater part of Longstreet's corps. The onset was thrilling in the extreme, as the men swept grandly forward, the little battle-flags with the Southern cross in the center fluttering saucily and jauntily aloft, while the setting sun made of each bayonet and musket-barrel a literal gleam of fire that ran along the chain of steel in a scintillating flame. As they swept over the plain they took up all the scattered fighting material, and nothing was left but the wounded which had sifted through, and the dead.

Then ensued the death struggle, a last fearful grappling in mortal combat. The enemy threw forward all their reserves to meet the shock, and for a space of fifteen minutes the commotion was terrible. Bursts of sound surpassed everything that was ever heard or could be conceived. The baleful flashes of the cannon, darting out against the dusky horizon, played on the surface of the evening clouds like sharp, vivid lightning. Long lines of musketry vomited through the plain their furious volleys of pestilential lead, sweeping scores of brave soldiers into the valley of the Shadow of Death.

And now while a hundred thousand men were battling for supremacy, men gathered from ocean to ocean; from Maine to San Francisco; from North to South, East to West; from every hamlet and town, from every mountain and plain; while Ate and her attendant Furies stalked over the field, their swords reddened with the slaughter, the sun, as if glad to put an end to such frightful carnage, himself blood-red, sank below the top of a wooded hill.

At last the enemy staggered, wavered, broke and fled in utter rout. Where Longstreet was dealing his heavy blows, they were throwing away their knapsacks and rushing madly for the rear. Only one final stand was made by a brigade in the woods close by; but as the long gray line closed in on each flank they threw down their arms and surrendered with but few exceptions; those few, as they ran, turned and fired.

On the hill, which had been occupied by the Washington Artillery of eighteen guns in the earlier part of the day, the eye took in a dim and fast-fading yet extended view of the whole surrounding country. A vast panorama stretched out on an open plain with patches of wood here and there on its surface, and with but two or three hills in the whole range of sight to break the expanded level. It was unutterably grand. Jackson could be seen swinging his left on his right as a pivot, and Longstreet with his entire corps in the reverse method. The whole Yankee army was in retreat, and certainly nothing but darkness prevented it from becoming *une affaire flambee*.

The battle was over, and night mercifully covered a scene of slaughter having no parallel in song or story of the New World. The carnage had been appalling. Over four thousand lay cold and rigid on the bosom of Mother Earth. Fourteen thousand men of a common race and a common ancestry, speaking one language, having but one tradition, lay under the light of the stars disfigured and maimed, torn and bleeding.

As the soldiers returned from the field, the day's work over, picking their way with care, the excitement died away and the reaction came. The cries and groans of this vast host of wounded were borne on the breeze from every side. And one who heard the tidal wave of agony as it swelled and surged toward heaven was fain to clasp his hands over his ears and shut out the torturing sound. Happy was he, among the writhing mass, whose agony was quenched in the Lethe of a mortal hurt.

Show a soldier, not utterly hardened, when the excitement of battle is over, his own handiwork; tell him that his own finger had sped the missile that laid yonder man low, and ten to one he would recall the fatal act if he could.

Some great thinker once wrote:

"Give me the money that has been spent in war, and I will purchase every foot of land upon the globe. I will clothe every man, woman and child in an attire of which kings and queens might be proud. I would build a school-house on every hillside and in every valley on the whole earth. I would erect an academy in every town and endow it; a college in every State and fill it. I would crown every hill with a place of worship, consecrated to the promulgation of the Gospel of Peace. I would support in every pulpit an able preacher, so that on every Sabbath morning the chimes on one hill would answer the chimes on another, until the melody of the sweet, sounding bells would girdle the globe with its music, an invocation to heaven."

This is a calculation of so much money; suppose the moralizer had carried the computation a little further, for paltry considerations in the expenditures of war of dollars and cents are as nothing in the general summing up.

Reckon up the killed, and you would have a mighty host. Collect the tears that have been shed over soldiers slain in battle, and you would have an ocean.

Mass the evil passions, the hate, the bitter, burning rancor and revenge that war has engendered, and you have a Gehenna.

Yet men are born warriors and fight from instinct. All forces wage an unending war. From Chaos until now, between beak and spear; claw and tearing tooth; heel and horn; sting and tightening coil, has the invisible war been waging.

In this battle the consumption of ammunition in the First Brigade was enormous. The soldiers literally fired away the last cartridge, making an average of sixty per man, or one hundred and eighty thousand ounces of lead sent Northward on its errand of deviltry. Many fired more; I used up all of my allowance and filled my cartridge-box twice from the profuse supplies scattered on the field, and at the end of the battle I had ten left, making one hundred and thirty rounds fired. No wonder that my shoulder was black and blue, and that my face was so scorched and blackened by the burnt powder that my identity was hidden and my own comrades did not know me until I spoke.

On this day our soldiers found out the worthlessness of the Minie musket, thousands of which lay abandoned on the field, because after a score or two of shots the barrel would foul and the bullet could not be driven home. The ramrod was so slender as to possess little weight and it would get so greasy from the cartridge as to slip through the hands. The Enfield musket was by far the best arm the infantry ever had.

CHAPTER XXVIII.

THE WRECKAGE AFTER THE STORM.

It was a pitch-dark night, with no light but that of the stars, and a few of us who were trying to find the Seventeenth became lost on the field. Every now and then we fell or stumbled over a dead body; or worse still, some poor wounded fellow would moan so that it made the blood in our veins run cold, and filled us with dismay. My own wound proved to be a slight one after my friend John Addison had attended to it. We attempted to choose a path by striking one match after another, but the supply was soon exhausted, and then we came to a standstill. Looking around we could discern nothing but torches waving at far intervals about the field, flickering in the faint breeze that had sprung up with the coming of night, and which was borne to us tainted with the smell of blood. Starting onward my companion stumbled, and a horrified exclamation burst from his lips; his hand had rested, he said, on only the half of a head, whose top had been carried away by a shell. So we wandered aimlessly about, tripping every few paces, until at last, to our great relief, we reached an elevation and saw a camp-fire burning not far away. Steering a straight course for its light we arrived upon the spot, and with a delight no words could express, found the Seventeenth, or rather what was left of it, for only sixteen men had kept to the colors throughout the day, as we afterwards learned, the balance having been scattered in every direction and swallowed up in other organizations. The remnant had lighted a fire with empty ammunition and cracker-boxes that were gathered on the field, and were making themselves as comfortable as circumstances would permit. No one knew the extent of the losses in the regiment; indeed it had been as much as each one could do to keep the run of his own individual self.

For the first time in a week we had a full and a good meal; coffee, sugar, beef, bacon and crackers. Ambulances and men of the improvised sanitary squads looking after the wounded passed and repassed our fire. Every minute some lost soldier would come up, attracted by the light, until there were in our vicinity several hundred belonging to a score or so of different commands. Each man had a captured haversack and blanket, for those we discarded that morning and left under guard we never expected to see again.

That we had won a great victory every soldier knew, and the probabilities of a forward movement were freely discussed; all agreeing that the blunders of the first Manassas would not be repeated now that Lee had supreme control of matters. Every man, too, with whom we talked spoke of the day's battle as the hardest and most stubbornly contested one that had ever taken place in Virginia. Not one but what had shot away his whole supply of cartridges, and so far as we could learn, every soldier in Longstreet's Corps had fired every cartridge in his box as well as those in his haversack, making, as I said before, sixty rounds per man. The faces of all were smutty with burnt powder. Two-thirds had their clothes torn with bullets, and many were slightly wounded who made no trouble or fuss about it.

The sky Sunday morning was one mass of gray, granite-like clouds, and it seemed as if Nature had clad herself in sad-colored robes to mourn for the slaughter of her sons, to end in the usual weeping that followed every battle. After a hurried breakfast the soldiers separated, looking for their several commands. For some hours the army was halted in the field to get the men together, reform the organizations and fill their scattered ranks.

Lieut.-Colonel Herbert, now in command of the Seventeenth, with the colors and a small party of the original regiment were not far away, and formed a nucleus around which the absentees were rapidly collecting.

Every soldier of the Seventeenth expressed deep-felt sorrow over the disaster that happened to our colonel. He was loved and admired by the men; but more than all, trusted implicitly.

We learned later that his leg was shattered above the knee and the limb amputated below the hip, thus ending forever his military career in the field. The Confederacy lost one of its most brilliant officers when he fell.

Colonel Marye was of a highly nervous temperament, but in action he was the coolest man I ever saw. Nature molded and fashioned him for a soldier, and I have always thought that had this highly cultured, brainy soldier gone through the war unwounded he would have surrendered his army corps and made a name second only to Lee and Jackson.

The battle-field presented a horribly sickening sight. The wounded had all been taken care of, but the dead were resting just as they fell. Here was one with both legs torn off by a solid

17

shot, the ground for many feet around sprinkled with the blood that jetted out in a stream from the severed arteries; another had fallen on his knees and clasped his hands over his head, which had been fractured by a piece of shell—he was a frightful object, with the tongue protruding and the teeth clenched tightly upon it. An infantryman shot in the neck had unstrapped his knapsack, unrolled his blanket, lain down and covered himself over and then had quietly breathed his last. What a methodical, systematic person he must have been; the ruling passion so strong in death, it spoke in so many words, "I did my life's work well, and now the summons comes, I wrap the drapery of my couch around me and lie down to pleasant dreams."

Could a knife in the hands of an Indian have scalped a poor fellow more scientifically than did that bursting shell? And see here a man who had his two arms broken as if they had been stems. There lay five or six of our men, torn and mangled almost beyond recognition by one single shell that had burst so close to them that it did its fiendish work only too successfully.

A group had gathered around one dead form, and were gazing down upon it with fixed interest, and yet sadly enough. We joined them and found it to be a lad scarcely more than fourteen years old, shot through the forehead. His uniform was new and most tastefully made, doubtless to suit his boyish fancy; the long hair seemed even then to be fresh from the toying touch and loving hands of mother or sister; he was no soldier, one could see that; most probably he lived in the neighborhood and had joined the line in the charge; he rested upon the earth as fair as the marble Hyacinth.

"How anxious they must be at home about him," remarked some one near, as we stood looking down upon the slender figure.

"I can imagine how they watch and wait for him, and what would they say if they could see him now!" And the strong, rugged speaker, who had borne the brunt of a battle unmoved, drew the back of a rough hand over his eyes and passed on.

The ground which we traversed was where the heaviest fighting had taken place in the earlier part of the action. The carnage had been fearful, and blue and gray lay closely mingled. Death had found these victims in various attitudes and stiffened them into stone, and his icy hands had frozen to marble his lips loved by households; one was in the act of raising his gun to fire; another was about to open his cartridge-box and died in the attempt; a

third was retreating, and when struck was unloosening his knapsack; and a fourth had sat down to tie his shoe, when the fatal
ball had killed him instantly.

The missiles had struck everywhere; this man was shot in the
mouth; on that face a bursting shell had not left a single feature;
worse still, here is a head as completely severed from the body as
if the guillotine had done it; and there, the living, beating heart
seemed to have been torn out all quivering and bleeding.
Already the blackness of corruption had disfigured many faces
and rendered immediate burial imperatively necessary. Here
and there and everywhere were pools of clotted blood, as if blood
were the cheapest and freest-flowing commodity on earth,
showing where wounded and dying soldiers had lain. Scattered
about on the ground, because the nerveless hands had no further
use for them, were rifles, knapsacks, accoutrements, empty ammunition boxes, blankets, coats, and even swords.

How soon the vain glory of war vanishes before the carnage of
the field! how much of its poetic unreality dissolves into the stern,
hard prose of the hospital! how many of its undraped horrors are
disclosed upon the after battle-ground!

Every dead body had been searched, every pocket was wrong
side out, proving that the camp followers and robbers of the dead
had completed their work. Every corpse, whether in blue or gray
uniform, had been divested of its shoes and hat, and many even
had their outer clothing removed. As several of our brigades
passed we heard the troops curse fiercely the miserable pillagers
who, like birds of prey, flocked to the battle-field after the action
to accomplish their foul purposes. A true soldier rarely conde-
scends to strip his fallen enemies; he will take a pair of shoes or
a hat if he needs them badly, but it must be from necessity and not
from desire of gain.

The brigade had a formal roll call by companies so as to report the losses to the Adjutant-General. A rather remarkable
personnel answered to their names, and presented as its chief
feature the charm of variety. Many of the men were slightly
wounded, and had arms in slings or heads bound up. Adornments in the way of fine hats, officers' long-tailed coats and cavalrymen's jack boots picked up on the field, were sported by their
fortunate possessors with an air of supreme satisfaction and
hardly concealed pride. This element was all the more noticeable, in that each man's next neighbor in the ranks was either
hatless, coatless or shoeless, as the case might be; but all had

blankets and full haversacks, confiscated on the battle-field with due honors of war.

Our regimental losses were about seventy-five killed and wounded; those of the brigade, between two and three hundred.

Now that the list had been made out, the brigade took up its march. The farther we advanced the more evident became the fact that the enemy's retreat the night before had been almost a panic; knapsacks, guns, and all sorts of miscellaneous articles belonging to the equipment of a soldier were scattered in the greatest confusion along the pike. Every soldier loaded himself down at first, but later on, as the contents of the knapsacks were ransacked, only the letters and daguerreotypes were taken out and handed around, the balance pitched away for the comfort and use of needy soldiers behind. Many a fair Northern girl could not have been otherwise than flattered at the praises her beauty elicited, albeit from Rebels, as her picture passed from hand to hand along the ranks.

Continuing on our way we passed a beef which had been freshly slaughtered and skinned by our obliging enemy, who had left it as a slight token of their esteem, surmising how long it had been since we had so partaken; to be sure, they had been in too great a hurry to eat it themselves, but that made not the slightest difference in the world, as our own men could stop just long enough to hack off a chunk before they hurried on.

On our way we passed a small house on the roadside, from which the yellow flag was flying. It had been taken by the Yankees as a hospital and their surgeons were even then busy in their work. Evidences of the nature of their labor appeared before us in a most ghastly, hideous form; on a table running the length of one room all the amputating had been done, and the floor was slippery with the vital blood that ran out and dripped from every crack and crevice in one dire percolation; as fast as the shattered limbs were severed from the trunk they were thrown out of the window, and there they lay in a heap five or six feet in height, a sickening collection of legs, arms and fingers of all sizes and lengths, Rebel and Yankee commingled. Never before was seen a more shocking and tangible evidence of the cruelty of this struggle—each amputated limb the exponent of a human being disabled and doomed to suffer so long as life might last.

All in and around the yard lay the wounded, almost an acre of them, both of the blue and gray, while the surgeons of the North and South, animated by a single noble purpose, moved among the crowd, with sleeves rolled up and arms covered with blood, doing all that human power could do to alleviate pain and to save life.

Following the Sudley road the brigade crossed Bull Run at the ford and came to a halt, and rations for one day were issued, consisting of two crackers and a quarter of a pound of fat bacon, the last we were going to get for many a long day.

Having halted, the order was read to the brigade congratulating them on the results of yesterday's battle. The old First had brought from the field five stands of captured colors. The brigade, consisting of the First, Seventeenth, Seventh, and Eleventh Virginia Regiments, eighteen hundred muskets strong, had captured a battery of four pieces, spiked by the enemy, who had been unable to carry it off because nearly all the horses had been killed.

Toward evening the rain, which had been pouring nearly all day, cleared up temporarily, and the brigade halted to pass the night. The soldiers smoked, read the captured letters, and talked and fought the battle over again until dark, when they turned in. It was so warm that but few fires were lighted. Preparations for sleep were made simply those nights; the rationale was merely spreading the blanket on the ground, lying on it and rolling up in it tightly. The head was next reclined on a cartridge-box, and a hat put over the face, then off into Dreamland.

To the student of military history Pope's campaign will be considered the most unique in the annals of war. Possessed as he was of an overwhelming belief in himself, boundless imagination and nervous aberration in action, he was the last man on earth to be intrusted with a supreme command. During the short two months as commanding general of the Army of the Potomac he issued more orders, gave more directions, and wrote more voluminous reports than did Grant in his four years of successful campaigning. It is difficult to conceive how he found time in that short period to write so much. His correspondence in the war records would make a respectable book. His orders to his subordinates were so profuse and contradictory that it is no wonder confusion prevailed, and in the great game of military chess he kept king, knight, bishop and pawn on the jump, without method, and played, as it were, from impulse. In the natural course of events his checkmate from such an adversary as Lee was certain to be quick and complete.

Pope, of course, had his scapegoat. For many years Fitz John Porter had to bear all the opprobrium of Pope's complete fiasco.

The story of Pope's campaign can be told in a few words by extracts from his own reports. Beginning at his Orlando Furioso proclamation in taking command of the army, his dispatches, in the light of cold reason, show his character to a dot.

He wrote to Halleck regarding the Battle of Cedar Mountain (Reb. Records, Vol. 12, p. 12 and 133): "On Thursday morning the enemy crossed the Rapidan at Barnett's Ford in a heavy force. Brigadier-General Bayard with his cavalry fell slowly back, delaying the enemy's advance. General Banks was ordered to take position at Cedar Mountain with orders to hold the enemy in check until Sigel's corps arrived and had a good rest after their forced march. General Roberts reported to me that he had conferred freely with General Banks, and urgently represented to him *my purposes,* but that General Banks, *contrary to my wishes,* had left the strong position which he had taken up and had advanced at least a mile to assault the enemy, believing that they were not in considerable force. His advance led him over the open ground that was everywhere swept by the fire of the enemy. The action lasted about an hour and a half and our forces suffered heavy loss and were gradually driven back."

On August 23, 1862, he wrote to Major-General Sigel: "The Rappahannock River has, owing to the rain, risen six feet and is entirely impassable at any ford, the enemy (Jackson's corps) therefore, on this side, is cut off from those of the other. You will accordingly march at once upon Sulphur Springs and thence to Waterloo Bridge, attacking and beating the enemy wherever you find him. You will have an effective force of 25,000 men."

To General Banks he sent the same instructions, and McDowell's corps was divided to support this movement. To all these corps commanders he ended by saying: "Be quick, for time is everything." On the same day (August 23, 1862) in his dispatch to Halleck he writes: "The river has risen six feet, the enemy's forces (Stonewall Jackson's) on this side which have crossed at Sulphur Springs are cut off from those of the south side. I march at once with my whole force on Sulphur Springs and Waterloo Bridge, and hope to destroy these forces before the river runs down." On the next day he telegraphed to Halleck: "No force of the enemy has been able to recross the river, and are enclosed by our forces and will undoubtedly be captured."

When the whole of Pope's army closed in at Waterloo Bridge it was literally a water haul; neither wagon, gun, nor Rebel was to be seen, and all this pother, these manoeuvres, these masterly concentrations of forces were false alarms. McDowell, who was in the advance, wrote to Pope under date of August 26: "General Milroy burned the bridge at Waterloo before he left. What is the enemy's purpose, it is not easy to discover. Some have thought he means to march around our right through Rector-town to Washington; others think that he intends going down the Shenandoah; others that it is his object to throw his trains around in the Valley to obtain supplies. It is also thought that a large portion of his army have retired to Culpeper army by the Sperryville road." General Mansfield wrote to Halleck about this time: "Stonewall Jackson has 125,000 men at least. He is fortifying between Louisa Court House and Gordonsville." (Reb. Records, Vol. 51, p. 742.)

Pope answered McDowell by writing: "I believe the whole force of the enemy has marched for the Shenandoah Valley by the way of Luray and Front Royal." (Reb. Records, Vol. 12, p. 67.)

Now at the very time Pope was closing in to capture Jackson at Sulphur Springs, that ubiquitous Rebel was twenty miles in Pope's rear at Manassas Junction, where a vast depot of supplies for Pope's army was concentrated, and where the ragged, dust-begrimed Rebels were drinking champagne from tin cups and eating canned fruit from the sutlers' stores, preparatory to applying the torch to Pope's reservoir of supplies.

On the 26th of August Pope sent a dispatch to McDowell in which he says: "Fitz John Porter, with Sykes's and Morrell's divisions, will be within two and one-half miles of Warrenton to-morrow night. I will use all of my efforts to have Sturges's and Cox's divisions within three miles of you to-morrow night, and have requested General Halleck to push forward Franklin's division at once. I think our *fight should be made at Warrenton,* and if you can postpone it for two days we will be all right." (Reb. Records, Vol. 10, p. 69.)

On the evening of the same day he telegraphed to Washington: "Our communications have been interrupted by the enemy's cavalry at Manassas."

On the next day, August 27th, he wrote to Major-General Kearny: "At the very earliest dawn move forward to Bristow Station with your whole command. Jackson, A. P. Hill and Ewell are in front of us. I want you to be here at day-dawn and we shall *bag the whole crowd.*"

At the same hour he wrote to McDowell: "March rapidly on

to Manassas Junction. Jackson is between Gainesville and Manassas Junction. If you march promptly we shall *bag the whole crowd.*" On the next day, August 28th, he wired McDowell: "You will move on to Gun Spring to intercept Jackson. I will push forward Reno and Heintzelman, unless there is a large force at Centerville, which I do not believe. Jackson has a large train which certainly should be captured."

At 10 P. M. of the same day he notified Heintzelman: "McDowell has intercepted the retreat of the enemy. Sigel is immediately on his right, and I *see no possibility of his escape.*"

On the next day, August 29th, he telegraphed to Banks: "Destroy the public property at Bristow, and fall back upon Centerville at once."

On the next day, or rather night of August 30, his dispatch to Halleck reads: "We had a terrific battle to-day. The enemy, largely reinforced, assaulted our position early to-day. We held our ground firmly until 6 P. M. when the enemy, massing with very heavy columns on our left, forced back that wing about a half a mile. At dark we held that position. The troops are of good heart and marched off the field without the least hurry or confusion. The enemy is badly crippled and we shall do well enough. Be easy, everything will go well."

On the next day he wires Halleck: "I should like to know whether you feel secure about Washington. Should this army be destroyed, I shall fight it as long as a man will stand up to the work."

After Pickett's disastrous charge at Gettysburg, Lee rode among his men, saying: "This failure is all my fault; nobody is to blame except myself." Now see what Pope says.

On the day after the battle his dispatch to Halleck reads: "One commander of a corps who was ordered to march from Manassas Junction to join me near Grovetown, although he was only five miles distant, failed to get up at all and worse still, fell back to Manassas without a fight. What makes matters worse there are officers in the Regular Army who hold back from either ignorance or fear. Their constant talk indulged in publicly is that the Army of the Potomac will not fight. When such example is set by officers of high rank, the influence must be very bad among those in subordinate stations. You have hardly an idea of the demoralization among officers of high rank in the Army of the Potomac, arising in all instances from personal feeling in relation to changes of commander-in-chief and others. These men are mere tools and parasites, but their example is producing very disastrous results. I am endeavoring to do all I can and will most assuredly put them where they shall fight or run away." (Reb. Records, Vol. 12, p. 83.)

If there is any greater insult offered the gallant men who bore aloft the standard of their country, by their commander-in-chief, it has never been recorded.

The part that the Seventeenth Virginia took in this battle is briefly told by Colonel Corse, who at the Battle of Manassas was temporarily commanding the brigade. He says:

"At 4.30 P. M. an aide brought me an order to move forward in support of Jenkins and Hunton; I promptly obeyed and over-took the two brigades advancing. I at once put my command about 250 yards in rear of the advancing brigades, keeping my distance when moving forward, and then the whole line became engaged. At this time discovering a battery on the left and rear of the Chinn House, I ordered a charge of the whole line. The order was gallantly responded to and brilliantly executed, the enemy being driven from their guns. The Seventeenth, led by the ardent Colonel Morton Marye, advanced in perfect line. Just before reaching the guns Colonel Marye fell severely wounded. The charge on the guns was a success. The enemy's support was routed.

"Samuel Coleman, of Company E, Seventeenth Virginia, in the hottest of the fight, wrested from the hands of the color-bearer of the Eleventh Pennsylvania Volunteers his regimental colors, and handed them to me. These colors I have already had the honor to forward to you. The loss to the Seventeenth Virginia is five officers wounded, four men killed and thirty-nine wounded." (Reb. Records, Vol. 12, p. 626.)

CHAPTER XXIX.

INTO MARYLAND.

On Monday the march was continued toward Fairfax Court House; the rain that had held up during the night now came down in streams. We had eaten the last mouthful in the morning; indeed, but for the contents of the captured haversacks there would have been nothing. Nearly all of that day we tramped in the mire of the roads, while a constant cannonading went on in our front.

Late in the evening we found ourselves again at Chantilly, that stately old residence over which some of us had stood guard in the lovely autumn nights of '61.

Had not the rain poured in torrents, we would have arrived at an earlier hour, in time to participate in the sharp action which our van had had with Kearny's division. However, it made no difference, for our ammunition was soaking and we had not a gun in the division that would have gone off.

Standing there in the summer rain we beheld the change that a few months had produced in the old place. The fences were levelled, the out-buildings had been torn down, the splendid forest of trees cut, every shade tree and even every fruit tree felled for fuel. As for the house, it was scarcely habitable; the furniture had been smashed for kindling wood, the windows dashed to pieces with the butt end of muskets, the plastering had been knocked from the walls and the rooms so defaced and defiled that they discounted a hog-pen. On what was formerly the lawn lay many wounded and dead; among others General Phil. Kearny, whose remains most of our soldiers viewed—the most brilliant, chivalrous, dashing officer in the Yankee Army. He was killed in a charge. He rode in the advance with his sword in the air and the bridle-rein held between his teeth, for he had lost his arm in the Mexican War. Had General Kearny lived he would probably have commanded the Federal Army. His body was sent by General Lee under a flag of truce to the enemy's lines.

The two forces were but a little distance apart; the one flushed with victory, the other sullen from defeat, and for the nonce equally limp, wet and miserable. But for the dash of the rain, the sharp "Halt!" and challenge of the enemy's pickets could readily have been heard.

It is said by fishermen who ought to know, that "eels at length not only get used to being skinned, but after a while take to it as a pleasure." On the same principle perhaps soldiers come to enjoy repose in a driving rain and being cradled in a mud-puddle; be that as it may, their sleep was as sweet and sound as if they had lain on beds of down, while their frames were so inured to hardships and seasoned by exposure, that what would have threatened illness and death a year ago, now had become a matter of the slightest moment.

The waking the next morning was a stiff affair, not a bit of fun anywhere about it; then it took so much time to straighten limbs and warm bodies that had been chilled through. To our great delight, though, the warm beams of the sun darted between the rifts in the clouds and dried the wet clothing; but even then the situation was deplorable. Some few had a ration left, which they ate quietly without attracting any attention, while haversacks of the majority were turned wrong side out and the very dust of defunct crackers scraped out and devoured. One man of an enterprising turn of mind carried his resources so far as to boil his greasy haversack for a soup, a soup purely of his own invention. He said "it filled him up, anyhow, and did away with the goneness in his stomach."

About noon the regimental sutler was on the spot, having followed the command with a steady persistence and faithful, untiring devotion worthy of a better cause. Animated by love of money, that "root of all evil," he had crossed battle-fields, forded runs and breasted storms to join us. A charge was made on his wagon by the starving soldiery; some straddling the horses for a place of vantage, others standing on the wheels and struggling to get a first grab at the viands. Jonah, that was our sutler's name, was equal to any emergency, and like his illustrious namesake, could not be kept down; he had no conscience, or if he had he stretched it to any required distance, which was in his case tantamount to many miles. Like Chester, also, he charged, and obtained his price too; having sold out his entire stock, which consisted entirely of edibles, Jonah, with an empty wagon, a full wallet (his was no credit business) and a light heart turned his horse's head rearward and disappeared through the shadows of the woods.

Just as the wheels of the wagon were rumbling away in the distance a member of the Seventeenth made a piteous com-

plaint to a body of his comrades. He said that notwithstanding
the high respect he entertained for every member of his valued
regiment, who were all honorable men, yet one of their body cor-
porate had so far forgotten his meums and tuums as to appropriate an oilcloth that had been most serenely and unsuspiciously
left drying on the bushes. He stated that he had gone through
the brigade on the strength of an extemporized search-warrant,
but without the faintest shadow of success; he assured us that
he was without a blanket and would be in a woeful fix, for the
ground was still damp and the nights cool; he implored us if any
of our number had seen his property walk away from the bush
in spite of the eighth commandment, to reveal its hidden quarters
and make him a friend for life.

It is needless to say that no sign of the lost property was ever
vouchsafed, so artfully were these constant thefts accomplished;
and so our soldier told us some time after that for a makeshift
he had begged a newspaper, a copy of the *New York World,* and
lain on that; and inasmuch as it had kept the dampened earth
from personal contact, it answered its purpose quite well. He asserted that for two weeks he had had nothing to lie upon but
that paper, which he would fold up as carefully every morning as a
lawyer did his parchment or the beauty her curl papers; but that
on one occasion it had rained, and he held nothing in his hand
but so much pulp. He told us with incipient tears in his eyes
that he would always cherish a tender feeling for the *New York
World* so long as the bullets might spare him.

But on the morning of the third of September all these triv-
ialities of the camp, all these little incidents which made up camp
life were merged into the interest of the march, when an army,
no longer a mass of individual interests, became a unit to be
thrown upon the foe; a force inspired by one aim, moved by the
will of one man, counted as so much man-power toward one end.
The head of the column was turned northward, passing by Frying Pan Church, which name was rather suggestive of some hot
Gospel and a place that hath no seasons, like the tropics.

Still no sign of our commissary wagons and not a mouthful of
food had the men that day. Some of our best soldiers were left
on account of sickness, and many began to straggle from ranks
to seek in farm-houses along the route something to allay their
gnawing hunger. Of course each one was a serious loss, for we
never saw any of them until after the campaign.

Keeping at a steady gait the column passed Guilford Station

on the Loudoun and Hampshire Railroad, and then, turning, headed up the pike for Leesburg. All along the route the citizens testified their delight at our advance and brought food to the road, all that had been left them to give, and offered it to the hungry troops; through this kindness most of us obtained one meal that day, though some were not so fortunate, and could only look longingly back and curse the wagons. That night we camped near Drainesville.

By six in the morning we were on the tramp again. Steadily, one by one, the strength of the army decreased as soldier after soldier, weak with hunger, dropped out of ranks and out of sight. The farm-houses all along the way we would find filled with sick and straggling men.

There was a direful and shameful blunder somewhere about this time; here was the great Army of Northern Virginia, which after four months' fearful fighting and constant action, with ranks decimated by the casualities of battle and sickness (on its way as an army of invasion), and instead of being reinforced and its losses repaired, instead of strict discipline being maintained, instead of being properly fed, they were allowed to march day after day with no rations, while each soldier was suffered to leave ranks and roam at will all over the country. Then thousands were barefooted and obliged to fall behind because of their stone-bruises. Again, not a single article of clothing had been issued, and the men had not changed their shirts for two weeks; the clothing left under guard on the battle-field of Bull Run was never returned. In fine, instead of having a thoroughly equipped army to invade the North, there were long lines of limping, starving soldiery, streaming wearily on, as disheartened and miserable in feeling as they looked; there was no elasticity or vim in the crowd.

Napoleon, that master in the art of war, uttered the maxim that "an army only moves on its belly," and if our general officers were blind to the fact, the privates felt it; every soldier in the ranks saw the wretchedness and mismanagement of the situation and it had a very bad effect; it looked as if his Government had even ceased to care about keeping him alive by feeding him, and so, many lost heart and became embittered toward the officers.

Two days of continued and steady tramping brought us to the little town of Leesburg, not far from the Potomac River. The commissary wagons had not arrived, and in those two days, as in the weeks passed, not a single ration had been issued. The most

the officers could do was to bivouac their commands alongside
the corn-fields on the route and let each one help himself. The
amount of provender which a hungry soldier could get outside of
under such circumstances would shame a dray horse and cause a
tow-path mule to blush with envy; some have been known to
stow away sixteen ears of corn at a single meal, and they were
not nubbins either.

It may seem incredible, but it is true, that owing to the failure
of the Commissary-General to get his supplies up in time, Lee's
army on the advance lived alone on green corn and apples—the
only instance of a like nature upon record. Of course this diet
was good for a change, *yet on a long run*, and this is not a figura-
tive expression by any means, it did not yield much sustenance;
the men became thinner and weaker and the food caused chronic
diarrhea and flux, which still further decimated the ranks and lost
us several thousand men; still with splendid bravery the army
pressed onward.

It was a goodly sight to watch the troops when they were
halted for their evening meal—an apple orchard or a corn-field;
in the latter instance a hundred fires would be lighted and blaze
up in the twinkling of an eye and soon the air was redolent with
the odor of roasting ears; then after thousands of jaws had been
set in motion like so much complex machinery without stop, the
ground around would be covered with cobs, a memento of the
Army of Northern Virginia. The Spanish troops, it is said, were
ever traced by the rank smell of garlic that flowed out from them on
all sides into the purer atmosphere like a river and poisoned it for
miles around. So any keen-scented Yankee might readily have
traced our winding way by snuffing in the breeze the palatable
aroma of the roasting corn.

Leaving Leesburg after a brief halt, long enough indeed to
bring around us every old man, woman and child in the place, for
a portion of the Seventeenth hailed from the town, the command
struck for the fords, bivouacking for the night ere we reached
them; but almost before the stars were out of the skies the march
was taken up again.

Every hundred yards or so some soldier would drop unquestioned from the ranks; indeed, such had become the condition of
their feet from walking over those rocky roads, that many who
had been barefooted all along were obliged to fall behind; and
this they did by dozens. To a casual observer the army seemed
to be going to pieces; to such an extent was straggling carried

on that it looked more like the retreat of a demoralized legion than a body of troops flushed with success and advancing to conquest.

In the middle of the day, September 6, 1862, as the blue waters of the Potomac, gleaming in the sunlight through intervening trees, met the eyes of the soldiery, a rolling cheer rang along the lines, was caught up by the brigades behind, and we could hear it faintly sounding in the rear and at last dying away in the distance.

The soft autumn sunshine danced on the rippling waters and lit up the emerald sheen of the banks beyond. Here at last was our Promised Land with its broad fields of waving grain, its barns full to bursting, its orchards bending low with fruit, and to our longing eyes looking as fair as the goodly land of Canaan to the prophet's wistful gaze; its farm-houses, settled into the landscape cozily, here and there dotted the scene with all the interest of home life, and gave it *soul* as it were. It was a lovely picture and the eyes of the famished soldiers lighted up as they gazed. A few fleecy clouds alone broke the limpid blue; a light breeze murmured among the leaves, while the birds, singing on the boughs, carolled their sweetest songs to the undertone of distant cannonading. To my mind the most exquisite verse ever inspired by the war was written by Randall, the Southern poet, in describing this advance into Maryland, and the gathering of the Union Hosts:

"From blue Patapsco's billowy dash
The Yankee war shout comes,
Along with cymbals' fitful clash
And the growl of his sullen drums."

Preparations were made for crossing at once. The river was about a hundred yards wide, but owing to the fine dry weather of the last few days the water had subsided to its lowest mark, rendering the stream easily fordable to the infantry. But if the tide was low, the current was strong and swift, as we found to our cost.

The men were not long in getting ready for their wade, each consulting his own individual conscience; some took off the last rag, and making bundles of their clothes stuck them on the top of bayonets and plunged into the eddying tide; others again were satisfied with denuding only their lower half, while the reckless, don't-care set crossed as they were, and then stretched themselves on the opposite bank to dry; but the majority waded, wearing their one abbreviated garment.

It was a genial, joyous, side-splitting evolution, that crossing over. The gravest man in America sitting on that shore watching the proceedings would have laughed until the tears rolled down his saturnine face; old Henry I, "who never smiled again," would have caught himself in a grin before he knew it; the very fishes opened their broad mouths, and the rooks cawed till they were hoarse, and the mules gave prolonged snorts of infinite satisfaction. The bottom of the river was one mass of rock, worn to the slipperiness and smoothness of polished ice or glass, upon which it was impossible to maintain a sure footing, no matter how carefully one might pick his way, consequently the soldiers were slipping and falling in every direction.

Here would be a great giant of a fellow whose ribs, through a long course of starvation, were as plain as the bars of a gridiron and as distinct in the sunlight as the rails of a plank fence, with his pack in shreds and tatters on the end of his gun, treading cautiously on a treacherous rock—down he goes head foremost, like a sportive dolphin, and disappears from sight; a few bubbles rise to the surface and dance down the stream, then he himself emerges, mad enough to kill somebody, the water pouring from his gun-barrel and the bundle containing all his worldly possessions gliding along on the surface of the river, bent on seeking unknown lands.

There goes a short, stumpy fellow, walking on his toes, the water up to his neck, his eyes looking volumes, while with hands high up above he holds his gun and clothes like an "Excelsior" banner and vanishes; then we see him strike valiantly for shore, his musket gone but his bundle safe. Here are a dozen soldiers who, as a precautionary measure, have joined hands and are making their way across carefully. One steps into a deep hole and clings tightly to his comrade, who holds with a dying clutch to the next man, and down they all go like a row of tottering ten-pins.

Once across, we are all on the *qui vive* to watch the camp darky who brings up the rear on his mule. Warily, watchfully, as if treading on so many eggs, he makes the endeavor to pass over, cheered or jibed, as the case might be, without stint or mercy. But that old darky was used to the soldier's ways and did not mind them; his mule was an ancient animal which, having been turned out to die by some wagon-master, had been caught by this Uncle Ebony, patched up and fed on stolen grain until strong enough to follow at a slow pace in the wake of the regiment with his master on his back; the mule was almost hidden from view by the pots and kettles which adorned him like the beads and medals on an Indian princess, and which disclosed his rank. Uncle Ebe spurred his steed to the river's edge, but "Israel," the mule, pointed his ears and stuck his feet down; then he opened his mouth and entered a protest in a voice that was heard a mile along the shore.

"Don't let that old 'Ancient Mariner' stop!" shouted a soldier. "Whip him across, old man!"

"Hurry up, Uncle," vouchsafed another on the opposite side, "we want our skillets over here; send him along."

"The old cuss always did need a baptizing," added a third. "Run him in the water and make a good Baptist out of him."

But Israel had an opinion of his own and cherished it; and not until the wagons came along and the drivers lashed their cruel whips into the flanks of the opposition, did he consent to change his mind. In they went, mule and rider, and of course the result was what every one expected.

Down they plunged, and we caught a glimpse of first a woolly head and then heels of mule and man inextricably mingled; the heads had it, there was a rattling of pans, and finally when they managed to come to the surface it was hard to tell which of the two was the more frightened; the eyes of the sable rider rolled around like milk-white moons in an inky sky, and his teeth chattered like castinets; amid a roar of laughter they made for the slope, our venerable servitor saying as he climbed the bank:

"Dis here nigger's nebber gwine to cross dat ribber any mo', you hear me? Let dem Yankees cotch me forst."

Then with a grunt of satisfaction, "Dis chile an' dis ole hoss an dis ole pan got a good washin' sho."

But there were many disgusted people other than Uncle Ebony, nearly all of whom had been deprived of property, hence the air was full of lamentation.

One soldier was heard to remark as he made his inventory, "Confound it all, I don't mind losing my gun nor my shoes, but I hate to lose that 'ere haversack chock-full of good bread and meat that I begged this morning from an old woman who lives over thar by the mill."

As soon as the soldiers had crossed, they immediately fired their muskets, fearing the charge had become wet, and for a few minutes it sounded like a heavy picket fight.

An order was issued that men without shoes could remain in

18

Virginia and not accompany the army in advance. This idiotic proclamation cost us ten thousand men. Of course many took advantage of this, and many threw away their shoes so as to remain behind, while hundreds of muskets were withdrawn from our already depleted brigade. From first one cause and then another, the regiments, brigades and divisions had dwindled into one-half of the strength which they carried to Manassas.

No sooner had our feet struck the loyal soil of Maryland than an order was read from General Lee, prohibiting any trespass upon public property; of course corn-fields and fruit trees were not included in this category.

CHAPTER XXX.

THE CAMPAIGN OUTLINED.

As soon as General Lee decided to invade the North he sent word to D. H. Hill and McLaws, who were in Richmond, to rejoin the army with their divisions without delay.

General Lee in his vast plan looking to an offensive campaign in the North, and with the avowed purpose of transferring the seat of war into a rich region where the army could get ample supplies, made brilliant tactical combinations, which had they been carried out would have materially changed the character of the contest. His plan of operations was to capture Harper's Ferry with its garrison of eleven thousand men; then mass his army and deliver battle to McClellan. With this view he directed Jackson to take his own two divisions, and those of Anderson and McLaws, and proceeded to carry out the first steps of this plan. Longstreet's two divisions under Jones and Hood, and D. H. Hill's division were to remain and hold the enemy in check while Jackson was performing his part.

"It was the custom," says Colonel Walter Taylor, General Lee's Adjutant-General, "for the Commander-in-Chief to send orders marked 'Confidential' to the commanders of separate corps or divisions only; and to place the addresses of such separate commander on the bottom left-hand corner of the sheet containing the order. General D. H. Hill was in command of a division, and a copy of army movements was of course sent to him. It seems that through the carelessness of some one, this order of Lee's divulging the plan of movements was negligently and heedlessly thrown aside and picked up by the enemy. The result was that Lee's combinations not only miscarried but the army came near being destroyed.*

Lee was caught in a bad trap, with his forces divided into two parts and separated by miles from each other. Of course the Federal general determined to strike at once.

Notwithstanding the unfortunate circumstance, the stubborn defense of Boonsboro or South Mountain Pass by Longstreet and

---

* "Upon learning the contents of this order, I at once gave orders for a vigorous pursuit."—General McClellan's testimony, Report on the Conduct of the War, Part I, page 440.

Hill, and especially by the wonderful celerity of Jackson in capturing Harper's Ferry, including the gallant resistance made by McLaws's division at Crampton's Gap against the whole of Franklin's corps, General Lee was enabled to unite his forces in time to give battle at Sharpsburg.

Longstreet and D. H. Hill in resisting the attacks of the bulk of McClellan's army had suffered very heavily; Jackson, too, having been compelled to hasten by forced marches from Harper's Ferry to Sharpsburg, his route was strewn with foot-sore, broken-down and disabled soldiers, so that when he reached the battle-field he had only skeleton regiments, which in many cases were not as large as a full company.

On the morning of the seventeenth of September both combatants, the Army of the Potomac and the Army of Northern Virginia, met face to face once more. Lee's entire force amounted to thirty-five thousand two hundred and fifty-five men. (Adjutant-General Taylor's book, "Four Years With General Lee," page 73.)

General McClellan in his Official Report states that he had at Sharpsburg eighty-seven thousand one hundred and sixty-four men all told. (Extract from General McClellan's report, "The Conflict," page 209.)

Those were fearful odds, *more than two to one!* but they were the flower of Lee's army who were to breast the fury of the onset—the bravest, the very staunchest of the whole South. It was the Army of Northern Virginia eliminated and purified of all the delicate and broken-down, the sick as well as the cowards and skulkers; it was an army of veterans, every soul of them undaunted and every musket true.

They were, as Colonel Taylor says, manoeuvred and shifted about from place to place, as first one point and then another was assailed with greatest impetuosity and force. The right was called to the rescue of the left; the center was reduced to a mere shell in responding to the demands for assistance from the right and left, while A. P. Hill's command, the last to arrive from the Ferry, reached the field just in time to restore the wavering right.

Just at this point was our danger, for Antietam Creek was held only by four hundred men all told, being the skeleton Georgian brigade of General Toombs, when confronted by General Burnside's corps, consisting of ten thousand seven hundred and four men. (Swinton's Campaign of the Army of the Potomac, page 220.)

Burnside's attacks, from some cause, did not take place until one o'clock, and having brushed aside the small force that stood in his way, he allowed over two hours of precious time to pass before he attacked the crest of the hill held by Kemper's small brigade of three hundred and twenty-five muskets. Had he promptly carried the hill, the Rebel right would have been turned and he could have struck the whole line on the flank and rear. As it was, it was not until three o'clock in the afternoon that he stormed the summit and literally rushed over the frail line opposed to him.

But success came too late; for the division of A. P. Hill, which Jackson had left behind to secure the surrender of Harper's Ferry, had reached the field from that place by way of Shepherdstown after a forced march of seventeen miles, and uniting his reinforcements with the two brigades of Kemper and Toombs that had been broken by the attack, he drove Burnside back over all the ground gained, to the shelter of the bluff bordering Antietam.*

When darkness put a stop to the conflict it found both armies utterly exhausted as well as suffering terribly from the loss of blood and of life. It had been the most stoutly contested action of the war, and was emphatically a drawn battle. Some successes had been gained on both sides during the day, but at night the Rebel and Yankee hosts occupied practically the same ground that they had held in the morning.

The casualties were exceedingly heavy on both sides; the Federal loss at Sharpsburg, killed and wounded, was twelve thousand five hundred men, the Rebel loss eight thousand. (Official returns from the Adjutant-General's Office, "United States Army Reports on the Conduct of the War," Part II, page 492.)

The morning of the eighteenth was passed in rest by both armies. McClellan determined to renew the battle on the nineteenth, when he expected reinforcements should have arrived from Washington. But during the night Lee withdrew across the Potomac and in the morning stood once again on the Virginia side.

A force of several thousand men, a part of Porter's corps, was thrown across on the nineteenth to follow up Lee and harass his rear-guard under A. P. Hill, who had but two thousand muskets. Hill says in his report: "A simultaneous and daring charge

---

* "The three brigades of my division did not number over two thousand men, and these, with the help of my splendid batteries, drove back Burnside's corps of ten thousand men."—Hill's report of the "Army of Northern Virginia," page 129.

was made and the enemy driven pell-mell into the river. Then commenced a more terrible slaughter than the war has yet witnessed. The broad Potomac was blue with the floating bodies of the foe. Few escaped. By their own account they lost three thousand men killed and drowned; from our brigade alone some two hundred prisoners were taken." (A. P. Hill's Report on the Campaign in Maryland.)

So ended the invasion of Maryland. Leaving several thousand men behind cold in death, our army returned to its old quarters. The moral effect was unquestionably on the side of the enemy, for with them rested the prestige of driving us back.

Returning to the army which had just crossed the Potomac, we find that in an hour's time it was continuing its march through the rich fields of Maryland; a fair, fruitful country, smiling in peace and plenty, which seemed to our eyes, so long resting upon deserted fields and briery meadows in Virginia, as being scenes of purely idyllic rustic life, where the injunction of the priest of Ceres's temple, "Marry the vine with the palm," had been obeyed.

The country people lined the roads, gazing in open-eyed wonder upon the long lines of infantry that filled the road for miles; as far as the eye could reach rose the glitter of the swaying points of the bayonets. These were the first Rebels those Marylanders had ever seen, and though our rags could not have been prepossessing, we were treated as neither friend nor foe; yet they gave liberally; every haversack was soon filled, for that day at least. No houses were entered by our soldiers and no damage was done, evidently to the great relief of the farmers in the vicinity, who soon found how perfectly safe their property could be in the very midst of an invading army.

On the tenth the Seventeenth defiled through the long streets of Frederick City, our reception being decidedly cool. Of course we were disappointed; it was not what we had expected. True, the streets were generally filled with citizens, as well as the balconies and porches; but there was no enthusiasm; we heard no cheers and saw no waving handkerchiefs; instead we were greeted with a deathlike silence that could be felt, while some houses were tightly closed as if some great public calamity had befallen the people. Friendly faces were at windows and doors, whose smiles would have been a little less covert had there not existed such evident fear of showing any manifestation of favor toward us.

The marching soldiery did not attempt to imitate the cautious silence of the Frederick civilians, but with full haversacks and light hearts they joked and appeared to have a good time. Witticisms and badinage flew from lip to lip, some even raising a song, the air being caught up by the brigade, and in such manner we passed through that most loyal city in Maryland.

Confederate currency suddenly rose in value. Orders had been issued that the store-keepers in the town should keep open their shops and sell goods for the "d—— Rebel issue," as one of them named our Confederate "Promise-to-pay." It would only take an hour or two to riddle a store completely; not a thing left behind but empty shelves and a supply of notes, enough to paper the walls. Some of the merchants put the money carefully away, to redeem it if by the chances of war it should eventually be of any value.

Another day's march brought us to Hagerstown, where the corn-fields and orchards furnished our meals. The situation of our army from a sanitary point of view could not have been worse. The ambulances were filled with the sick and footsore, and the country lined with stragglers.

The fastidious may skip the following:

Among the shadows of the soldier's life the twin evils of vermin and the camp itch were most serious and distressing; they followed Johnny Reb persistently, refused to leave him, resisted every effort of force, opposed every attempt at compromise, and waged war of extermination with him as fierce in its way, as resistless in its combined resources, as Johnny Reb's upon them, and that, too, until the gray uniform was doffed for the citizen's suit, when they disappeared with the garb they had loved so well, and vanished with it out of mind.

Those insects, which in camp parlance were termed "graybacks," first made their appearance in the winter of sixty-one. At first the soldier was mortified and almost felt disgraced when he discovered the van-guard of the coming crowd upon his person. Their crawling made his flesh creep; their attacks inflamed his blood and skin. He made energetic efforts to hide the secret and eliminate the cause; he would quietly and with an abstracted air most artfully withdraw from the company of his comrades, and then with considerable alacrity, but with as much secretiveness as though he were going to commit some fearful crime, steal out into the woods. Once hidden from the eyes of men he lost no time in pursuing and murdering with a vengeful pleasure the lively descendants of Egypt's third plague, flattering himself the while, poor soul, that he would then have peace and comfort of mind and body, and be able to hold his head up once more before his fellows. On his stealthy way back he would be sure to run in on a dozen solitary individuals, who did their best to look unconcerned, as if indeed they were in the habit of retiring into the dim recesses of the forest for meditation and self-communion.

The satisfaction so gained did not last long; in a day or two his body would be infested again; and then by this time rendered desperate he would try every expedient, but all to no purpose; it was simply impossible to exterminate them. The men would boil their clothes for hours in a hissing, bubbling cauldron, dry and put them on, and the next day the confounded things would be at work as actively and enthusiastically as ever. Even at Fort Warren, where underclothing had been so plentiful that each man had an entire change for every day in the week, it was found that these pests skirmished around as usual, though where they came from or how they arrived were mysteries we never solved.

The "salamander grayback" had more lives than a cat, and propagated its species more rapidly than a roe-herring; its progeny never died in infancy, and were sprightly from the incubation.

Once lodged in the seams of clothing, there they remained till time mouldered the garments. You might scald, scour, scrub, clean, rub, purify, or bury the raiment under ground, and you only had your trouble for your pains; they only seemed to enjoy it and multiplied under the process.

On the march particularly, when for weeks the troops had had no clean clothes, the soldiers were literally infested. Many would place their underclothing, during the night, on the bottom of some stream and put a large stone upon them to keep them down, hastily drying them in the morning for the day's wear. In such manner a temporary relief would be gained. Every evening in Maryland, when the army had halted and bivouacked for the night, hundreds of soldiers might be seen sitting half denuded on the road-side or in the fields, busily engaged in a relentless slaughter of the vermin. This daily expulsion and execution was a habit just as needful, and as regularly indulged in, as washing the face and hands; without the daily destruction of a hundred per man (and this was no unusual quota) life would have become a burden too heavy to bear.

In our march along the turnpike every ear of corn and every

green or ripe apple in the bordering fields fared no better than they did in Virginia; the soldiers made a specialty of cooking them as a variety, after a la raw; roasting, boiling or mixing them both together in a kind of soup, which was very nice and savory, but longing all the while for the old bread diet.

The conduct of the citizens of Hagerstown toward us contrasted strongly with that of Frederick City, for not only were the men and women outspoken in their sympathy for the Southern cause, but they threw wide their hospitable doors and filled their houses with soldiers, feeding the hungry and clothing the naked to the utmost extent of their ability. We saw a citizen of that place take the shoes off his feet in the streets and give them to a limping, barefooted soldier.

On the morrow, instead of advancing northward, the order came to right about face and march back on the same road upon which we had advanced the evening before; so the brigade retraced its steps, and about four o'clock that evening, on the fourteenth, took position in a corn-field on a sloping hill. A savage attack was made on our left to break the line, but was repulsed. Though the musketry firing and the cannonading was for a short time severe, no determined infantry charge was made upon our brigade; several batteries shelled us, and a feeble attack was undertaken, which was, however, easily checked, for the regiment was in place behind a fence; altogether our loss did not amount to more than half a dozen wounded, among them that gallant soldier Lieutenant Arthur Kell, of Company H, who was badly hurt in the head by a piece of shell.

In the early dawn of the fifteenth the brigade marched toward Sharpsburg. Squads from the different companies obtained permission to forage for themselves and comrades. Being the only private left in my company, I joined two expert foragers of Company H; leaving the road and striking across the fields we soon came to a handsome brick residence about three miles from Sharpsburg, standing in the center of well-kept grounds; we knocked at the door, but after waiting a while and getting no response we entered; to our great astonishment we found the place deserted, the inmates doubtless having been frightened away by the firing at Boonsboro a few hours before. Not an article had been carried off that we could see; the parlor door stood open, the piano lid was raised, the pictures were hanging upon the wall, and the curtains were looped gracefully, as if some dainty touch had just arranged them. We entered the dining-room ; there sat the cat on the window-sill ; indeed, the home-life had been so recent within the house that it was difficult to realize that our hostess's step would not at any moment sound upon the stairs and her voice be heard in greeting.

We had no time to linger, the warning notes of the cannon reverberating in our ears while we were in search of something to eat. The cupboard, like that of an ancient miser, was empty; so was the kitchen, hence we went to the spring and filled our canteens with ice-cold water, glad to get that if nothing more substantial. But a dairy nestled at the foot of the hill, and on repairing there we found that some agency had placed at the door several buckets and cans of milk, over which the rich, yellow cream had already risen. We of course substituted the milk for the water in the canteens; then we noticed there was a loft over the dairy, and climbing up to pursue investigations we found it a perfect store-room; several barrels, among other things, were upon stands, the contents of which on nearer acquaintance proving to be cider, at once the canteens were emptied of the milk and filled with the juice of the apple; then an exclamation from one of the party brought us in a group around a barrel of apple-brandy. Of course out went the cider and in gurgled the brandy; not to be changed for anything, no, not even Jupiter's nectar.

Here ensued an animated discussion ; the whole squad, excepting the sergeant, wanted to roll the barrel to camp and leave everything else behind; but then came the difficulty about obeying orders; the dispute waxed high, so to end the matter the sergeant stove in the head of the barrel with the butt of his musket, and the precious liquid, that would have made glad, for a time at least, the whole brigade, poured in a useless stream upon the floor.

In the room were a half dozen tubs of applebutter, which we confiscated for the use of our comrades; then we started in the direction of the burnished steel that flashed in the sunlight before eyes like beacon lights to the mariner. Marching on as hurriedly as we could, our squad soon overtook the brigade.

Long and lovingly were many lips glued to the mouths of those canteens, and honestly the owner's health was drunk, not asking or even caring whether he was friend or foe; only Colonel Corse blessed us as he took a long, lover-like kiss from the mouth of my canteen. I intended saving some in case I was wounded in the coming battle, but when the vessel was returned to me there was not a drop left.

CHAPTER XXXI.

THE BATTLE OF SHARPSBURG.

The order was given to "Fall in" and our skeleton brigade took up their position on top of a high hill behind a post-and-rail fence. The storm so long gathering was about to burst, but the men having become callous and indifferent from extreme hunger, thought only that in case of a victory they would find plenty of the enemy's haversacks to satisfy the cravings of their empty stomachs.

As the Virginians with drawn faces sat in ranks, with eyes blind to the beauty of the scene which looked its richest in its autumn robing, and its sweetest in the morning freshness, they, hungry souls, had no other meditations, no other sentiments save those over their empty haversacks, the banquet halls deserted, and their "aching void," which nothing earthly filled.

Just about this time a cow,—a foolish, innocent, confiding cow,—with a pathetic look in her big eyes and all unknowing of soldiers' ways, came grazing up to the line; a dozen bullets went crashing through her skull before she knew what hurt her, and a score of knives were soon at work; in an incredibly short time, more quickly than a rabbit could be skinned, the hide of the cow was taken off, and a ravenous pack of wolves could not sooner have laid bare the bones than did our hungry brigade. Everything was eaten, even the tail, which but a short hour ago had been calmly and quietly switching flies from her back.

There were no available cooking utensils in the whole regiment save those which the old darky carried for the benefit of the officers for whom he cooked; and those we had no more chance of using than if they had been the Queen's. Our kitchen apparatus consisted of a tin plate and a large tin cup holding about a quart, which cup was carried by each private, fastened to the left shoulder with a small strap sewed on the jacket for that purpose; by means of these we could accomplish most satisfactorily all the cooking we required in the way of boiling, frying and stewing, but neither plate nor cup answered as wherewithal to cook the beef, and, as has been stated, skillet or pot or frying-pans there were none.

The soldier is an inventive genius, or twin brother to it, inasmuch as Necessity is the mother of both; and at this important period of action he was not to be balked of his meal because there happened to be no double-acting, patented, warranted-never-to-wear-out, self-regulating, non-fuel-consuming range nor a French chef on hand. Perish the thought! No. He hunted around and found flat stones lying all about in profusion; these he heated hissing hot and broiled the beef upon them.

Now to give one more instance of the soldier's unfailing ingenuity, which by long practice and much thought had become a science.

There lived not far from Gordonsville a widow who was noted for her niggardliness and extreme parsimony; so stingy and mean was she that a placard was nailed on her gate, under her own direction, with the inscription:

"No soldier fed or housed here."

The best foragers of the brigade met their match in the old woman, and returned defeated from the field; at last she was left in undisturbed possession of the place, and no hungry soldiers were ever fed at her table.

But one day a famished-looking, lank, angular specimen of the genus Reb appeared at her farm-house and knocked at her door.

When the animated figure of War and Famine combined stalked into her yard, the old lady was speechless with wrath; she opened the door, prepared for immediate hostilities, but the sad-faced defender of the soil was asking in a humble voice and with a deprecatory manner:

"Please, marm, lend me your iron pot."

"Man, I have no iron pot for you!" This was snappily jerked out, while an evident determination was shown to shut the door in his face.

"Please, marm, I won't hurt it."

"You do not suppose," she began in angry tones, "you do not for one moment suppose I am going to lend you my pot to carry to camp, do you? If I were fool enough, I would never see it again, so don't think that you are going to get it. Go over there to Mrs. Hanger's, she will lend you hers; one thing is certain, *I won't!*"

"Marm," he still pleaded, "I will bring your pot back, hope I may die if I don't! If you don't believe me I won't take it out of the yard but will kindle a fire just here; please, marm."

"What do you want with it?" asked the old woman, who was beginning to feel that she would be none the worse in pocket by granting the request, but might, on the contrary, be gainer in some way.

"I want to bile some stone soup," answered the soldier, looking pitifully at his questioner.

"Stone soup! what's stone soup?" and the old lady's curiosity began to rise.

"How do you make it, and what for?"

"Marm," replied the mournful infantryman, "ever since the war began the rations have become scarcer and scarcer, until now they have stopped entirely and we-uns have to live on stone soup to keep from starving."

"Stone soup," mused the woman, "I never heard of it before, must be something new; one of these new-fangled things; cheap, too; well, how do you say you make it?"

"Please, marm, you get a pot with some water and I will show you; we biles the stone."

The ancient dame trotted off full of wonder and inquisitiveness to get the article. Yes, it was worth knowing the recipe; fully worth the use of the pot, besides she would make her dinner off that soup and save that much! So, very much mollified, she returned and found the soldier had already kindled his fire; placing the kettle over it he waited for the water to boil, in the meanwhile selecting a rock about the size of his head, which he washed clean and put in the pot; then he said to the old woman, who had been peering into the pot through her spectacles:

"Marm, please give me a leetle piece of bacon about the size of your hand to give the soup a relish."

The old lady trotted off and got it for him; another five minutes passed.

"Is it done?" she inquired.

"It's mos' done, but please, marm, give me half a head o' cabbage just to make it taste right."

Without a word the cabbage was brought; and ten minutes slipped away.

"Is it not done by this time?" again she asked.

"Mos' done," with a brightening look, and then as if a new idea had just occurred to him: "Please, marm, can't you give me a half a dozen potatoes just to give it a nice flavor like."

"All right," answered the widow, who by this time had become deeply absorbed in the operation. The potatoes followed the meat and cabbage, and another ten minutes followed that.

"Isn't it done yet? 'Pears to me that it's a long time cooking," she said, getting somewhat impatient.

"Mos' done, marm, mos' done," insinuatingly. "Jest get me a small handful of flour, a little pepper and some termartusses and it will be all right then."

The things were duly added from the widow's stores and bubbled in the pot a while; then the soup was pronounced done and lifted from the fire. The soldier pulled out his knife with spoon attachment and commenced to eat; he lost no time between mouthfuls; the economical widow hastened in, and returned with a plate, which she filled; on tasting the first spoonful she exclaimed, "Why, man, this is nothing but common meat and vegetable soup!"

"So it is, marm," responded the soldier after a while, for there was not a minute to spare for talking; "so it is, marm, but we call it stone soup."

The old lady carried the pot back into the house, but not before the man had emptied it, learning for the first time how a soldier's ingenuity could compass anything and outwit even herself. She said, "They have Old Nick on their side," and tradition adds, she even kept that stone and swore by it.

The enemy's guns had begun to play upon Sharpsburg as a small party of the Seventeenth entered the village on a tour of sight-seeing and touring generally. The many hills echoed and re-echoed the war music that for the last three months had been so familiar to our ears.

Yes, the place was indeed forsaken, not so much as a stray dog being seen upon the streets; but soon the shells began dropping on the housetops, making a fearful noise as they tore up the plank, split the rafters, and sent the shingles flying in the air. As the din was at its height a young girl of apparently sixteen years appeared on the street bareheaded, her long hair streaming wildly. The Sharpsburg maiden was mad, it seemed, not from love but with terror, and tore frantically along, screaming piercingly as a shell exploded over her head. Her presence at such a time gave rise to much conjecture which was never explained; there she was making her way out of town, indifferent to every feeling except the blind, overpowering instincts of dismay ; and we never knew or heard more.

Keeping on, our squad halted before a gate which opened into one of the most enticing-looking gardens; the grounds were beautifully laid out and were bright with flowers and rich in luscious fruits; the purple grapes hung in clusters, the trees bent beneath their burden of golden peaches, russet pears and ruddy-cheeked apples. The temptation to enter was too strong to resist; in the center of the garden nestled as pretty a vine-covered cottage as the most romantic maiden would wish to live in with her own love-crowned king; the front doors were locked, but on going to the rear we found on the back porch an old couple, as calm and composed as if war and carnage had been a thousand miles away. It would have been a sweet domestic picture at any time, one worthy of an artist's brush, that "Old John Anderson" and his wife, sitting placidly and lovingly hand in hand in the home that their joint labors had beautified and consecrated in their journey of life, so near the bottom of the hill where they would soon sleep together; but all the more striking was it when the boom of the cannon rattled the casements and shook the very foundation of the house beneath their feet.

I went up and remonstrated with them for remaining in the village. I told them that the battle would probably rage near that very spot, and that shells would fire the house even if they did not succeed in first splitting it into kindling wood, and urged them to leave the place while there was yet time.

The old man replied that they had no place to go, that this had been their home all their lives, they knew no other, and they would rather die here than leave it; he had not done the Rebels any harm, he said, that they should come and drive him out of his house; no, *they would not go;* they intended to stay; "do we not?" he added, appealing to his aged spouse, who only answered by an emphatic nod. Seeing that argument was useless, we left the house with a farewell word of warning; they vouchsafed no answer, but sat awaiting the result without fear.

The Yankees carried the village by a charge a few hours after; let us hope that the worthy couple had changed their minds in time.

Walking leisurely out of the garden and turning into the road which led to the Seventeenth, we were passing a group of soldiers who were lying behind a fence watching the flash of the enemy's artillery upon a hill about a mile off, when suddenly a twelve-pound shell from those very guns struck the ground in front of us, and then, as if cast by a child's hand, rolled gently in among the group and there rested with the fuse sputtering and blazing. The effect was ludicrous; every man jumped, hopped, ran or rolled from the harmless looking black ball as if it had the small-pox, nor drew up until a respectable distance had been put between them; then with bowed forms and faces to the ground they awaited its supreme pleasure; it came soon enough, and carried away a whole panel of the fence by the force of its discharge.

"What a mercy the fuse was so long!" we said as we returned and gathered up the fruit that we were carrying for future delectation.

The Yankees were preparing for the combat. On the heights some two thousand yards away fresh batteries took position and opened, ours replying, and so the forenoon wore away; the war clamor increased, and soon on our left the splashing of musketry and then the steady, rattling discharges showed the battle was fully joined.

We soon heard the old cry, "Fall in," and in line we advanced and took our places, waiting.

Our position was directly in front of the village of Sharpsburg on a high hill behind a new post-and-rail fence. The topography of the country consisted of a succession of undulating hills and corresponding valleys. The elevation upon which we stood sank rather abruptly to a deep bottom, and rising suddenly, like the waves of the sea, formed another crest about sixty yards on an air line from our position. Any attacking force would be invisible until it arrived on the top of the crest opposite, and in pistol-shot distance, or what we call point-blank musketry range.

In our front about a mile away was Antietam Creek, spanned by a bridge and guarded by Toombs's Georgian Brigade, which was only a skeleton command.

Our army surrounded Sharpsburg in a semi-circle, and we could lie there and hear the raging, frenzied battle on our left; reports of the cannon were incessant, at times it seemed as if a hundred guns had exploded simultaneously and then run off into splendid file-firing.

Then the fight commenced at Antietam Bridge, where Toombs waited with his Georgians. The Yankees had commenced to shell their front, which we all knew was a prelude to the deadlier charge of infantry.

The shells began to sail over us as we lay close behind the fence, shrieking their wild war-song, that canzonet of carnage and death. We cowered in the smallest possible space as the Hotchkiss, with the shriek of a demon, which made the bravest quail, burst far in the rear; it is not more destructive than others, this projectile, but there is a great deal in the terrific noise it makes to work on men's fears, caused by the jagged edge of lead which is left on the shell as it leaves the gun; for this reason alone the moral effect of the Hotchkiss shell is powerful. The Chinese apply this principle of warfare most successfully when they beat their gongs.

The enemy was silent for a while, but it was the calm that is but a preface to a hurricane. The musketry at the bridge broke out fiercely, rising and swelling into full compass. Sharp work was going on, and in about an hour's time we saw Toombs's small brigade rushing back, its line broken but its spirit and morale intact; it retreated to the village, was reformed and stood waiting as our reserve.

We made ready, and expected to see the victorious enemy follow hard upon the heels of the retreating Rebels, but to our astonishment an hour of absolute inactivity followed; no advance nor demonstrations was made in our front, while the battle on our left was raging as fiercely as ever.

At last, toward evening, the shelling was renewed. Brown's battery, supporting our brigade, replied, and soon came the singing overhead of the Minies; there is a peculiarly tuneful pitch to the flight of these little leaden balls, and a musical ear can study the difference in tone as they skim through the air. A member of the Seventeenth, an amateur musician of no mean order, speaking of them in this connection said:

"I caught the pitch of that Minie just now; it was a swell from E flat to F, and as it disappeared in the distance the note retrograded to D, a very pretty change."

It was now late in the evening, and the men, having become cramped from lying in the same position for such a length of time, were moving about and seeking relief from the long constraint in walking up and down, when the guarded, stern, nervous voice of our commanding officer sent every soldier back into line:

"Quick, men, back to your posts!"

There as we waited and each man looked along the ranks, the slight frail line, stretching out behind the fence to withstand the onset of solid ranks of blue, he felt his heart sink within him and grow faint.

Yet who could but be proud of such soldiers as those? They were the *fleur de mille* of the army; by unquenchable pride and indomitable will only had they been enabled to keep up at all in

19

this campaign; dirty, gaunt and tattered as they were, yet they showed their lineage.

Marshall Villais, as he witnessed the Scotch gentry fighting in the ranks under the Chevalier St. George in the battle of Malquapet, exclaimed:

"Pardi! gentilhomme est toujours gentilhomme."

Yes, this string of tattered men lying there with rifles clenched tightly in their hands, awaiting without a visible tremor almost certain destruction, had marched wearily on and on, although their gaunt frames seemed as if they might sink at every step; they had followed their colors through the long, hot, dusty way, while fatigue was relaxing their muscles, closing their eyes, and deadening all but their wills; they had dragged themselves to the field with stone-bruised feet and aching limbs; they had fought and won battles while hunger was gnawing at their vitals; they had never halted, though nearly naked, covered with dust, devoured by vermin and half famished at all times; through the smoke of battle, through the torrid heat of a summer's sun, through pain and incessant hardships they had never faltered.

Neither the Knights who followed Coeur de Leon to the Holy Land or those who swore fealty to the Holy Grail ever did their duty more nobly, more staunchly than did those dust-covered bronzed men.

The brigade was a mere remnant of its former strength, not a sixth remaining. The Seventeenth, that once carried into battle eight hundred men, now stood on the crest, ready to die in a forlorn hope, with but forty-six muskets. The old organization of the Riflemen, Company A, that often used to march on a grand review in two platoons of fifty men each, carried into Sharpsburg but one musket. For the Alexandria Riflemen, the crack company of Alexandria, was not at Sharpsburg; many had fallen dead and wounded in the battles; more were sick and in the hospitals, and the few that were left after the Manassas fight had dropped exhausted by the wayside, and I was the only one of the rank and file left, and Lieutenant Tom Perry the only officer. It is but little wonder that the thin, attenuated line of the brigade made up their minds that they were doomed to fall, knowing as they did that we had no reserves. Well, a man can die but once.

Suddenly an eight-gun battery tried to shell us out, preparatory to the infantry advance, and the air around us grew resonant with the bursting iron. Brown's battery of four guns took its place about twenty steps on our right, for our right flank was entirely undefended, and replied to the enemy. A shell burst not ten feet above the Seventeenth, where the men were lying prone on their faces; it literally tore to pieces poor Appich, of Company E, mangling his body terribly and spattering his blood over many who were lying around him; a quiver of the flesh and all was still.

Another Hotchkiss came shrieking where we were cowering, still the line not move nor utter a sound; the shells were splitting all around and whirling the dust up in such quantities as threatened to bury as well as wound and kill us.

Oh those long, long minutes! as we were waiting with closed eyes, waiting disfigurement or death, expecting a shock of the plunging iron with every breath we drew; would it never end?

For fifteen minutes the men had tightly clenched their jaws and never moved; a line of corpses might have been as motionless.

At last! At last! the firing entirely ceased; Brown's battery limbered up and moved away, because they said the ammunition was exhausted; but curses loud and deep came from the brigade and they were openly charging the battery with deserting them in the coming ordeal; and it was in truth a desertion, for instead of having thrown their shells at the enemy's eight-gun battery, thereby drawing their fire upon us, they should have lain low and waited until the infantry attack was made, and then every shot would have told; every shell, grape or canister-charge would have been a help.

But there was no use wasting further thought, the guns moved away and left us to our fate; and there was an end of it.

An ominous silence followed, premonitory of the deluge. The Seventeenth were lying, with the rest of the brigade, flat upon the earth behind the post-and-rail fence, their rifles resting on the lower rails. The men's faces were pale, their features set, their hearts throbbing, their muscles strung like steel.

We heard the low tones of the officer:

"Steady, men! Steady! They are coming! Ready!"

The warning click of each hammer as the guns were cocked ran down the lines; a monitory, solemn sound, chronicling for many the brief seconds before the awful plunge into Eternity was made; for when that click is heard the supreme moment has come.

The hill in front of us shut out all view, but the advancing Federals were close upon us; they were mounting the hill, the loud tones of their officers, the clanking of their equipments and the steady tramp of the approaching columns were easily distinguishable, and then Colonel Corse said quietly and calmly, but in a tone which all could hear:

"Steady, my men!   Seventeenth, don't fire until they get above the hill."

Each man lying flat upon his breast, his weapon resting, as I said before, on the lowest rail of the fence, sighted his rifle about two feet above the crest, and then, with his finger on the trigger, waited until an advancing form should interpose between the bead and the clear sky beyond.

The first object we saw was the gilt eagle which surmounted the flag staff, and after that the flutter of the flag itself; slowly it mounted, until the Stars and Stripes were flying all unfurled before us.   Then a line of hats came into sight, and still rising the faces beneath them emerged and a range of curious eyes were bent upon us; and then such a hurrah as only Yankee troops could give broke upon our ears and they were rapidly climbing the hill and surging toward us.

"Keep cool, men, don't fire yet!"   Colonel Corse shouted, and such was the perfect discipline that not a gun replied; but when the Yankee band flashed above the hill-top the forty-six muskets exploded at once and sent a leaden shower full into the breasts of the attacking force, who were not over sixty yards distant.   It was a murderous fire and many fell; most of them retreated over the hill; a few stopped to fire, and it sounded like the sputtering of a pack of firecrackers.   The men in frenzied haste reloaded their muskets and lay silent and expectant; we could easily hear the officers expostulating and urging the men to reform, and they made a rush the second time, but it was without heart, and when we poured in a close fire, they broke in a panic and disappeared, officers and men, over the brow of the hill.   We had no time to feel jubilant, for the rattling of drums in our front, the measured tread, the clanking of the accoutrements showed that the Yankee reserves were coming up.   We braced ourselves for the shock, and every man looked backward, hoping to see reinforcements, but not a soul could be seen between us and the village.

Our losses had been trifling up to that time, but in our front the ground was strewn with the dead and dying Federals; we noticed many walk, hobble and crawl over the crest; all undisturbed, for no one fired, and the order to remain in ranks was implicitly obeyed.

The Seventeenth was on the extreme right and in the air, and it was by the merest chance that the first attacking force had not overlapped us.

Had we known what the next fifteen minutes would bring forth, every officer and man would have fallen back to Toombs's Georgia Brigade, which had reformed on the edge of Sharpsburg; for the South Carolina Brigade, which was on our left, gave way; thus our small force had both flanks unsupported.

The enemy knew our position perfectly, and their line far overlapped ours.

We heard the commanding officer of the unseen foe give the order "Forward, march! Dress to the colors! Double-quick!" and in a shorter time than it takes to write this, they came over the rising ground with a ringing cheer; when they reached the eminence every man in the Rebel line who could sight a gun pulled trigger. The two hundred or so muskets of the brigade exploded like a bomb; the discharge tore gaps in the line of blue; it reeled, bent and doubled up, some of the soldiers breaking for shelter; but grit to the back bone, the rest stood their ground and raised their guns. I can never forget that moment; it was photographed indelibly on my mind; the sun glanced and gleamed on the leveled barrels, and the black tubes of the muzzles, not over twenty feet away, turned on us with deadly meaning. I crouched to the ground, and fortunately I was behind a post instead of a rail; I shut my eyes; a second of silence, then a stunning volley, the crash of the splintered wood, a purple smoke, a smell of sulphur, the spat and spud of the bullet, and the Seventeenth Virginia, or the remnant of it, was wiped out. The attacking force of the Eighth Connecticut and Ninth New York and their reserves, a Rhode Island regiment, mingled together, swept forward without stopping to load their guns, and went over the fence pell-mell and disappeared down the hill. I glanced back and saw the remainder of our brigade moving to the rear without order or formation, at a gait which proved they believed the race would be to the swift, just as the battle had been to the strong.

As after-events proved, it was a sensible retreat, for the men rallied on Toombs's brigade and drove back the Ninth New York and Rhode Island Regiment and the One Hundred and Third New York Regiment.

There had been some desperate fighting on the field of Sharpsburg that day, but no one on our side held such a forlorn hope, fought such odds at such a bloody sacrifice as did the Seventeenth Virginia. It was the only battle in which I ever engaged where the forms and faces of the foe were plainly visible.

There was but one of our regiment who was taken prisoner besides myself, Gunnell, of Co. F. We shook hands warmly; he was unhurt, but his clothing was perforated with balls. I had a bullet hole in my old slouch hat and my cartridge-box was smashed.

Two of our victors stopped and took us in tow, and kindly allowed us to walk up our line to see who was killed. It was a sad, sad sight; Colonel Corse lay at full length on his face, motionless and still; I thought at the time he was dead; I stepped across the dead body of our brave color-sergeant, and near him, with a bullet through his forehead, lay that gallant, handsome soldier, Lieut. Littleton, of the Loudoun Guards. I looked around for Tom Perry, but he was not there, nor was Lieut. Col. Herbert, nor about half a dozen privates I knew, so they must have skedaddled in the nick of time. Of the forty-six muskets, as I found out afterwards, that we carried into battle, the bearers of thirty-five lay on that ground dead or wounded. Every officer was shot down except two.*

The guards were impatient, so we crossed the fence, and not ten feet away was a surgeon and a group of men around a stricken officer; he was deadly pale and appeared to be mortally wounded. We inquired who he was and they answered that he was General Rodman, commanding a division, and that a bullet had penetrated his breast; afterwards I heard that Sam Coleman, of Co. G of the Seventeenth, fired the fatal shot.

Hurrying back a few hundred yards to the top of another hill out of reach of shot and shell, captured and captors turned to look upon the scene before them. Our forces seemed to be giving ground, and as line after line of Yankee reserves pushed

---

*In the summer of 1904, forty-two years later, I visited the scene of conflict and stood on that historic spot, and the scene is absolutely unaltered; a new post-and-rail fence occupies the same place where the Seventeenth lay; a few feet from the fence is a cannon planted mouth downward, marking the spot where Division General Isaac P. Rodman fell. A few feet away is a monument in honor of the 11th Connecticut Volunteers; on it is inscribed: "This regiment had 400 men engaged, and lost in killed and wounded 194 rank and file."

About ten paces distant is a lofty granite shaft in honor of the men of the Ninth New York Volunteers. The inscription reads: "The greatest mortality occurred on this position. The regiment contending with a *superior force* of infantry and artillery." On the reverse side is written: "Hawkins' N. Y. Zouaves. Carried into action 373. Killed 54, wounded 158, missing 28, in all 250 men."

forward it looked dark for the Rebels, as if the star of the Confederacy had neared its going down and Sharpsburg was to be our Waterloo.

A fearful struggle was now taking place in the woods half a mile or so to the left, and the concussion of the guns seemed to make the hills tremble and vibrate.

But a change took place in the situation, a marvelous change before our eyes; one moment the Federal lines were steadily advancing and sweeping everything before them, another, and all was altered. The disordered ranks, while so proudly conquering, were rushing back in disorder, while the Rebels rapidly pursued; their bullets fell around us, causing guards and prisoners to decamp.

"What does this mean?" we asked.

But its import no one could tell, although the reflux tide continued to bear us back. Finally a wounded prisoner, a Rebel officer, who was being supported to the rear, answered the question so eagerly put to him.

"Stonewall Jackson has just gotten back from Harper's Ferry and those troops engaging the Yankees now are A. P. Hills."

How the Southerner's face glowed as he told us this; what a light leaped into his eyes, wounded as he was. Well, we pass over the supreme, ineffable content of that moment, for we felt all would be right now. If Old Stonewall is up, not a man in our army need trouble himself about the result. Yes, we were safe!

Still receded the wave of blue; still forward rushed the wave of gray, heralded by the warning hiss of the bullets, the sparkling flashes of the rifles, the mingled hurrahs and wild yells to which the hoarse cannonading on our left served as a low bass accompaniment, the purplish vapor settling like a mist over the lines.

Still we receded, stopping on the top of every rise of ground to watch the battle. It was sunset upon the hills; again we paused to see the reddened rays strike upon the windows of the little town of Sharpsburg, more vivid now than ever the flames bursting from yonder house which an exploding shell had fired.

We were thinking of that line of motionless comrades lying on the crest of the hill low down beside the fence; and wondering if the sun was lighting up their pallid faces.

At last the bridge was reached, the stone bridge that crossed Antietam Creek, the key-point of the Federal position, the weak point in their line, the spot so anxiously watched by McClellan; he had sent repeated dispatches to Burnside late that evening as

A. P. Hill was pressing back the hitherto advancing tide; and their burden was:

"Hold on to the bridge at all hazards. If the bridge is lost all is lost."

And just here was the point where Toombs's Georgians had made such a gallant defense of the river early in the forenoon; and they were the dead of that intrepid command lying so thick upon the ground.

The battle in our front ceased suddenly, though on other parts of the field the firing was kept up. As we approached the bridge we were astonished to find so many troops, not a man under ten thousand it appeared, and they were all fresh. Certainly there seemed no danger of Burnside losing the bridge with all those splendid soldiers ready to defend it. Had those men advanced earlier in the day instead of being held back as they were, this would have been a black day for the South. We had no reserves and A. P. Hill in the morning was miles away.

The Yankees had established a field hospital at this point, where the desperately wounded in the immediate vicinity were carried. A group of four figures lay just as they had fallen, killed by the explosion of a single shell. One of Toombs's Georgians was killed just as he was taking aim, one eye open and the other closed; the figure was hideously life-like. The profound stillness was pierced at intervals by the booming of some vengeful gun that, like the fabled dragon, seemed never to sleep.

Let the sun sink beneath the boundary rim, let the shadows gloom the horrid scene and hide the Goddess of Slaughter as she moves over the stricken field gloating over the evils that the passion and ambition of politicians have wrought.

Oh death in life! what a piteous scene! shut both eye and ear if you can, still the blood-reeking forms will be plain before your view and you will hear sounds that seem as if a thousand accursed "Inquisitors" were torturing their despairing victims.

Night came on at last, putting a stop to the dreadful carnage of the day, and the tender, pitiful stars shone in the vast dome and looked down upon the scene of desolation and death. The firing had lulled itself to silence and only the groans of the dying were heard, borne on a murmuring breeze which swept across the hills, as refreshing and tender in its touch as a cool hand laid upon a fevered brow.

We prisoners were taken across the stream, where were gathered all of that unfortunate class, representing every command in the Southern Army, and numbering some five hundred, inclusive of about a dozen officers.

Colonel Corse, commanding the Seventeenth Virginia, in his official report says of this battle:

"About 4 P. M. the enemy was reported to be advancing. We moved forward to the top of a hill to a fence and immediately engaged the enemy at a distance of fifty or sixty yards, at the same time being under fire from their batteries on the hills beyond. My regiment being the extreme right of the line engaging the enemy, came directly opposite the colors of the regiment to which it was opposed, consequently being overlapped by them as far as I could judge by at least one hundred yards. Regardless of the great odds against them the men courageously stood their ground until, overwhelmed by superior numbers, they were forced to retire.

"I have to state here, General, that we put in the fight but forty-six enlisted men and nine officers; of this number seven officers and thirty-two men were killed and wounded and two taken prisoners.

"It was here that Captain J. T. Burke and Lieutenant Littleton were killed, two the bravest and most valuable officers of my command. Color Corporal Harper fell fighting heroically at his post. These brave men I think deserve particular mention.

"I received a wound in the foot which prevented me from retiring with our line and was left in the hands of the enemy, but was rescued by General Toombs's brigade, which drove the enemy back beyond the line we had occupied in the morning. In this charge Lieutenant W. W. Athey, of Co. C, 17th Virginia, captured the regimental colors of the One Hundred and Third New York Regiment, presented to them by the City Council of New York City, which I herewith forward to you. Those who deserve particular mention for their distinguished gallantry were Lieutenant Thomas Perry, Co. A, Lieutenant S. S. Turner, Co. B, Color Corporals Murphy and Harper and Lieutenant Athey of Co. C." (Reb. Records, Vol. 19, p. 905.)

Lieutenant-General Longstreet says of this battle:

"The name of every officer, non-commissioned officer and private who shared in the toils and privations of this campaign should be mentioned. In one month these troops had marched over two hundred miles upon little more than half rations and fought nine battles and skirmishes, killed, wounded and captured nearly as many men as we had in our ranks, besides taking arms and munitions of war in large quantities." (*Ibid*, p. 841.)

General D. H. Hill says in his official report: "It is true that hunger and exhaustion had nearly unfitted these brave men for battle, our wagons had been sent off across the river on Sunday and for three days the men had been sustaining life on green food. In charging through an apple orchard at the Yankees, with the immediate prospect of death before them, I noticed the men eagerly devouring apples." (*Ibid*, p. 1025.)

Further on General Hill says:

"The Battle of Sharpsburg was a success so far as the failure of the Yankees to carry the position they assailed was concerned. It would, however, have been a glorious victory but for three causes:

"1st. The separation of our forces. Had McLane and Anderson been there earlier in the morning, the battle would not have lasted two hours, and would have been signally disastrous to the Yankees.

"2nd. The bad handling of our artillery. This could not cope with the superior weight, calibre, range and number of the Yankee guns. Hence it ought only to have been used against masses of infantry; on the contrary our guns were made to reply to the Yankee guns, and were smashed up or withdrawn before they could be effectually turned against massive columns of attack. An artillery duel between the Washington Artillery of New Orleans and the Yankee batteries across the Antietam was the most melancholy farce of the war.

"3rd. The enormous straggling. This battle was fought with less than thirty thousand men. Had all our stragglers been up, McClellan's army would have been completely crushed or annihilated. Doubtless the want of shoes, the want of food and physical exhaustion had kept many brave men from being with the army, but thousands had kept away from sheer cowardice. The straggler, lost to all sense of shame, can only be kept in ranks by a strict and sanguinary discipline."

McClellan was in one respect at least wiser than Lee. At the beginning of this campaign he issued an order taking sternly repressive measures against straggling. In this order dated at Rockville, Maryland, September 9, 1862, he says in part:

"The safety of the country depends upon what this army shall now achieve; it cannot be successful if its soldiers are one-half skulking to the rear, while the brunt of the battle is borne by the other half, and its officers inattentive to lend every energy to the eradication military vice of the straggling." (Reb. Records, Vol. 14, p. 225.)

On the day after, he had a proclamation read to every regiment in the army, and it is safe to say he thereby saved himself from utter defeat. It runs: "The straggler must now be taught that he leaves the ranks without authority and skulks at the severest risks, even that of death.

"Every division shall have a rear-guard, behind which no straggler of whatever corps or regiment shall be permitted to remain. The bayonet must be used to enforce these orders. Resistance will be at the risk of death." (*Ibid*, page 229.)

In a dispatch to President Davis nine days after (September 13) General Lee says: "Our ranks are much diminished, I fear from a *third* to *one-half* of the original numbers by straggling, which it seems impossible to prevent with our present regimental officers." (*Ibid*, p. 606.)

On September 23, in his dispatch to the Secretary of War, General Lee reports:

"You will see by the field returns sent to General Cooper the woeful diminution of the present for duty of this army. The absent are scattered broadcast over this land." (Reb. Records, Vol. 19, p. 622.)

Enough is shown by these extracts to show that fully one-half of the Confederate army were absent—nearly every barefooted man left the ranks unquestioned, and thousands threw away their shoes and received permission from their officers to fall out. Now these men were not cowards, they each one argued that "my musket won't make any difference in deciding the fight."

General Lee's order to the chronic straggler was about as operative as a judge's admonition would be to a hardened criminal. He says in a general order issued September 4, 1862:

"Stragglers are usually those who desert their comrades in peril. Such characters are better absent from the army on such momentous occasions as those about to be entered upon. They will by bringing discredit upon our corps as useless members of the service and especially deserving odium come under the special attention of the provost marshal, and be considered unworthy members of an army which has immortalized itself, and will be brought before a military commission to receive the punishment due to their misconduct. The gallant soldiers who have so nobly sustained our cause by heroism in battle will assist the commanding general in securing success by aiding their officers in checking the desire for straggling among their comrades." (*Ibid,* p. 592.)

Colonel Beach, of the Eighth Connecticut Infantry, in describing his attack upon our regiment says:

"We advanced over the hill; the enemy lay behind a fence and it was impossible to see them, and our men were under fire for the first time and could not be held." (*Ibid,* p. 455.)

Colonel Fairchild, who commanded the Ninth New York (Hawkins's Zouaves), which captured our position, says:

"We charged across the corn-field, and arriving at a fence behind which the enemy were awaiting us, we received their fire, losing large numbers of our men. We charged over the fence, dislodging and driving them from their position, down the hill toward the village." (*Ibid,* p. 459.)

CHAPTER XXXII.

PAROLED.

In the morning a guard came and took the name of each prisoner, his regiment, brigade and division, age, height, and it is possible the color of his eyes; indeed, had he been an insurance agent his questions could not have been more searching.

All of the enemy who were brought into contact with us were much struck with our appearance; such a motley collection of shreds, patches, and tatters could not have been duplicated outside of a rag-picker's treasures; indeed our uniforms were as scrappy and torn as a Tipperary beggar's dress suit. Could Barnum have shown us around in iron cages, the bearded female, the fat woman, the learned pig would have sunk into insignificance beside us.

The truth is, a month had elapsed since any private had put on clean underclothing; and it is a solemnly sad fact that fully one-third of the prisoners there collected had neither shirt nor drawers, but wore a dilapidated uniform over the bare skin. Blankets or oilcloth not a man of us owned, our sole wealth consisting of a smutty haversack which contained for rations perhaps a few green apples.

Dirty? Well, we were! not clean dirt either, or a mild type of dirt, but dirt absolute and invincible, dirt which had accumulated, hardened and stuck fast, had almost become scales; dirt which cracked at intervals like varnish on furniture. No wonder the Northern papers described Lee's army as composed of the lowest type of humanity, certainly they had that appearance; and a well-dressed, comely Yankee soldier beside a Rebel prisoner made the latter seem a shabby, beggarly rascal, meaner looking than any Armenian or unspeakable Turk; and then most of the prisoners having fought the greater part of the day, displayed faces so darkened with powder smoke as to need only a woolly wig to convert them into first-class Congo Africans.

My own costume was on a par with that of the rest of my comrades. When I left Richmond in August I had a good suit of underclothing, but as time passed my uniform got dirty, then ragged, and remained so; my shirt and drawers were so infested with vermin that I had to sink them in running water in the night, and at last they became so shredded that I threw them away,

hence I was a fit mate for the most forlorn rag-picker that could
be found within the purlieus of Saint Giles or the Five Points.
An old slouch hat, so worn that the brim had to be pinned to the
crown, covered my head; a gray jacket with wooden buttons half
concealed my bony form, and the skin, encrusted with several
layers of dirt, showed through every slit of the jacket. I had
bathed many times in the streams, but having no soap the dirt
remained. A pair of old blue breeches I had picked up off the
battle-field completed the inventory, for I was barefooted these
two week agone.

"By the Lord, Johnny," said a blue-coat, "if you Rebs dress like
that and fight naked, I'm going home."

I could not help telling him that I was the most fashionably-
dressed man in the regiment, he just ought to see the others.
The Northern soldiers crowded around us in great exultation,
showing the Extra Press Edition that had just arrived from
Washington and Baltimore, in which their side had claimed a
great victory. By those accounts the Rebel army was utterly
broken and dispersed, and Lee surrounded, was wildly fleeing to
the Potomac; a portion of McClellan's army was in hot pursuit,
and not a single Rebel would cross the river.

A hot discussion followed:

"Do you believe that stuff?" asked a prisoner of an officer who
lounged up to the group.

"Of course I do; the paper would not have made the statement if it had not been so."

"The hell they wouldn't!" growled out one of Jackson's foot-
cavalry. "That paper says nothing about Harper's Ferry, where
Old Jack captured eleven thousand of you with forty pieces of
artillery. I saw them." And he spit the tobacco from his mouth
with an expression of intense disgust.

"Johnny Reb," said an offended Yankee, "if you say we lost
eleven thousand men, you are a damned liar."

"Well, I did say so, and it is no lie either; wasn't I there?
Didn't I see them with my own eyes? and all their artillery taken
too; ain't it so, boys?" he asked, appealing to his companions in
misfortune. A chorus of assents followed, and the Yankee
walked off, muttering something about "d—— Rebel lies."

Several of us were sent under guard to Sharpsburg to get
water for our compatriots, and so had a good opportunity to examine the damage done to the village by yesterday's shelling.
It was surprising how little destruction had been caused by such

severe pounding. A few holes and fissures and some shattered bricks were all. One house had been set on fire, but being isolated, burned quickly and did no further damage.

Our lines were drawn in about a mile from the village, so the cavalrymen told us; and to our intense relief they acknowledged that all accounts of an utter Rebel rout was bosh.

While yet at the pump, surrounded by soldiers and guards, all struggling to secure a well-filled canteen, one of the prisoners shoved a Union soldier aside. The action was resented with vigor; then the Yankee struck the Rebel and the Rebel knocked the canteen over the Yankee's head.

"Fight!" cried the crowd of soldiers, and despite the expostulations of the guard a ring was formed near the pump in the middle of the road, and both combatants placed therein. One big, broad, brawny Yankee, with a width of about three feet from shoulder to shoulder, patted the Reb on the back and said:

"Don't be afraid, Johnny, the boys will see fair play. I'm from West Virginia myself, so go in and win."

They were just about to commence, and the Rebel to get thrashed in the bargain, for he looked unsteady on his pins, when a mounted officer rode up and in loud, angry tones ordered the crowd to disperse and the prisoners to return to their places. This little incident shows the American love of fair play, and I have always been thankful that officer came along, for he saved my bones a severe rattling.

So the fight was stopped, though the men went off grumbling.

One fact which impressed the Confederate prisoners very strongly was the prime condition of the Federal soldiers—impressed them as strongly as our poverty-stricken appearance astonished them. Stout, hearty, their personnel showed that they were neither over-worked nor under-fed; rather the reverse, under-worked and over-fed. They were in a bad plight for marching, and could not compare with our men in endurance and speed; they had six days' rations in their haversacks, making a heavy load in itself, besides sixty rounds of ammunition, a musket, accoutrements, blanket, oilcloth, overcoat, knapsack well filled, and shelter tent; all together not weighing under sixty pounds. How could they be expected to make good time so weighted? As our preachers are ever wont to tell us of the "heavenly race," it's the riches of the wealthy that impede progress. We had no such excuse for not putting in an appearance either in the earthly race nor in the other. We were poor enough, Heaven knows! We were like the old woman who, after a not very religious life, sent for the minister to attend her dying bed; when the worthy man began to tell her "flesh and blood could not enter heaven," she stopped him with the remark, "I ain't flesh and blood, I'm just skin and bones, I'm all right." And so without a word more died comforted.

We carried our guns, it is true, perhaps a single blanket swung over our shoulders, but very often no blanket, a haversack whose normal condition was emptiness, and we owned not one superfluous pound of flesh.

It was like a two-horse sixteen-mile race; Johnny Reb, a blooded bay, very spare; flesh reduced, muscles well developed; thoroughly trained, welter weight. Billy Yank, black stallion; good stock; untrained; fat and pursy; rather short in wind; handicapped with forty pounds extra.

Jackson's men were especially noted for fleetness, hence their sobriquet of "Foot Cavalry;" they were often known to break down even the horses in a long forced march of days.

In his congratulatory report issued September 29th, 1862, General McClellan claimed everything; he says:

"Our loss was 2,010 killed, 9,416 wounded and 1,044 missing; total, 12,469. The Rebel loss in killed and wounded was 25,542. We have not lost a single gun or color on the battle-field of Sharpsburg." (Reb. Records, Vol. 19, p. 181.)

Surgeon-General Guild gives the Rebel loss in the battles of Boonsboro, Crampton's Gap and Sharpsburg as 1,567 killed and 8,724 wounded and 500 captured.

As regards the strength of the contestants, General McClellan placed his own army at 87,164 men, and our Rebel force as 100,000 men. (*Ibid.*)

The number of Confederates to a man who fought at Sharpsburg, as proven by the Reb. Records, was 35,255.

On the 18th of September every city, town, hamlet and village of the North made preparation to illuminate with fire, and celebrate with the crash of martial music and the cheers of the loyal people, the great victory won.

Then followed Lee's dispatch.

The world had learned to take the words of Robert E. Lee at their true value. The pyrotechnic proclamation, the boasting dispatches, the prevaricating reports of the generals on both sides found no favor with him, and the grandest compliment that man or woman ever received was paid him by his enemies, for the North always waited for his official report of a great battle before it exulted over a victory or mourned over a defeat. Claiming great victories was the invariable custom of every commander of the Army of the Potomac except Grant. The North had gone wild over McClellan's success at Sharpsburg until Lee's address was read, then the reaction came and McClellan, the organizer of the great Union army, speedily lost his official head. In that address Lee wrote for posterity, not to tickle the conceit of his people nor flatter their self-love or pander to their passion; every word, every sentence, every line addressd to his army was weighed in the scales of justice and truth, and his enemies accepted his version without one whisper of detraction—without one word of doubt. Here is his address:

"General Orders   Headquarters of Army of Northern Virginia,
    "No. 116.   October 2nd, 1862.
    "In reviewing the achievements of the army during the present campaign, the commanding General cannot withhold the expression of his admiration of the indomitable courage it has displayed in battle and its cheerful endurance of privation and hardship on the march. Since your great victories around Richmond, you have defeated the enemy at Cedar Mountain, expelled him from the Rappahannock, and after a conflict of three days, utterly repulsed him on the plains of Manassas and forced him to take shelter within the fortifications around the Capital. Without halting for repose, you crossed the Potomac, stormed the heights of Harper's Ferry, made prisoners of more than 11,000 men, and captured upward of seventy-five pieces of artillery, all their small-arms and other munitions of war. While one corps of the army was thus engaged the other insured its success by arresting at Boonsboro the combined armies of the enemy, advancing under their favorite general to the relief of the beleagured comrades. On the field of Sharpsburg, with less than one-third his numbers, you resisted from daylight until dark the whole army of the enemy, and repulsed every attack along his entire front more than 4 miles in extent. The whole of the following day you stood prepared to resume the conflict on the same ground, and retired next morning without molestation across the Potomac. Two attempts subsequently made by the enemy to follow you across the river have resulted in his complete discomfiture and being driven back with loss. Achievements such as these demanded much valor and patriotism. History records few

20

examples of greater fortitude and endurance than this army has exhibited." (Reb. Records, Vol. 19, pp. 644-645.)

The great soul of Robert E. Lee harbored no small feelings, and hate found no lodgment in his heart. In the hurly-burly of war he found time to perform a knightly act. He writes to the Secretary of War in Richmond:

"Sir:—Mrs. Phil. Kearny has applied for the horse and sword of Major-General Phil. Kearny, who was killed near Chantilly. I shall send them at once as an evidence of the sympathy felt for her bereavement and as a testimony of the appreciation of a gallant soldier."

After every battle the soldiers, no matter what uniforms they wore, were more eager to hear the enemy's account of the battle than their own officers' version. By steering betwixt and between, as it were, the average man could get pretty close to the truth. The opinion of the Federal officers on the battle of Sharpsburg made the Southern veterans who were in the engagement feel proud.

In Parker Snow's book, "The Southern Generals," page 77, he says:

"A Federal officer high in rank wrote to the *New York Tribune:* 'It is a wonder,' he said, 'how men such as the Rebel troops are can fight as they do. That these ragged wretches, sick, hungry and in all ways miserable, should prove such heroes in a fight, is past explanation.' "

We learned to our delight that all the prisoners were to be paroled and sent home instead of being forwarded North and confined in prisons. Full rations were given to us, and if our haversacks became empty there were soldiers among those who came up to talk to us, to fill them anew. So if Johnny Reb was still dirty he ceased to have the gnawing pain that hunger ever produces, and which green apples and corn are apt to induce in greater measure.

On the second day after the capture the whole battalion of prisoners, numbering five hundred and fifty officers and men, having been duly paroled, were marched under guard to the Potomac en route to the Confederate army. By the cartel the prisoners were to remain at their homes until notified by the proper Southern officials that they had been exchanged.

There is nothing so bad that it might not be worse; a fact too well assured for dispute.

Reaching the northern bank of the Potomac we found that side of the river heavily guarded by a strong force lining the shore. They had thrown up a hastily constructed breastwork and lay on the alert, both infantry and artillery, as if expecting an attack. A fierce contest on the opposite shore had taken place the evening before, they said, in which the Rebels had driven them back with fearful slaughter; and they were only wishing those same Rebs would advance that they might have a chance to retaliate.

"We can't go any farther," said our guards, "as your forces hold the other side. You are free men now; so pitch in and wade across."

It needed no second bidding and we went in just as we were.

"Good-by, Johnny Reb!" shouted the lines in blue.

"Good-by, Billy Yank!" halloed the gray as they picked their way carefully over the rocks.

The bank of the Potomac on the northern side was flat, on the south it rose almost perpendicular from the water's edge to a considerable height. Arriving on this shore we saw before us the evidence of a hot action and great loss of life. The Federal advance had literally been hurled over the rocks and hills by A. P. Hill's rear-guard; their dead lay on the beach, in the water, and on the side of the hills in scores; many had actually run over the steep bank in their terror and dashed themselves below. Hundreds of muskets were scattered about, as well as other munitions of war. None of our soldiers, nor ever the camp followers, could gather up the booty, for right across the Potomac any number of muskets would send their leaden messengers over at the first sign of a living thing. The enemy for the same reason could not cross, our sharpshooters being on the hill. To the dead it mattered not; neither "war nor rumors of war" could harm them further; but to the wounded it was fearful agony to lie there alone unattended and dying within sight of their friends. Several prisoners started to help some who seemed to be suffering terribly, when the warning voice of their own officer across the river was heard, ordering us to keep on our journey and not linger.

A ten minutes' walk took us away from the scene of panic and blood, where we found our advance-guard.

"In what condition is the army?" we inquired anxiously, afraid almost to hear the answer.

"Is it scattered, demoralized?"

"O, Uncle Robert and his boys are all right," they replied.

Then we were thankful. Though the bright dreams of Northern conquest, of marching in triumphant array through Washington, Baltimore and New York were not to be gratified this time, yet the "army all right" we could afford to be patient; and accepting the good, ceased to grieve over the bad.

We met Colonel W. H. F. Lee, commanding the cavalry, at that point, and by him were ordered to keep together and report at Winchester. We obeyed orders for some time, but the men began to drop out and wander wheresoever their wills led them.

Many of the houses along the route harbored wounded soldiers of both armies, who had been unable to stand the dangers of an ambulance journey to Winchester.

As the column journeyed on, it dwindled away at every step; some wanting to get furloughs and return home at once, started in a business-like way for Winchester; others took their liberty more leisurely and sauntered along as if they had a hundred years in which to make the trip; others, and by far the majority, went to some neighboring homestead to revive the inner man and to rest.

Our little squad of two, representing the Seventeenth, wandered a mile or two from the turnpike to get out of the immediate army trail, and stopped at a large mansion; on our approach the host, an old gentleman, came out and opened wide his doors "on hospitable thoughts intent."

After a good dinner he told us he had as guest a prisoner, a wounded Yankee, who had been left behind after undergoing a severe surgical operation; and he added, the man was the greatest original it had ever been his pleasure to meet. Then he took the party in and introduced us to the invalid.

A dark, thin-visaged man of about thirty lay smoking a pipe and reading a novel. He threw his book aside and apologized for not rising, as his leg had been cut off by the surgeon only ten days previously; and he was as nonchalant about the fearful maiming as if he had only lost the joint of his little finger.

He proved to be one of the most accomplished conversationalists that I had ever listened to, though he never spoke of himself save in a general manner. Of his life and its underlying mystery none could tell; but that his career had been checquered and eventful, none could doubt. A sailor, his tattooed arm showed that; a traveler in foreign climes, a soldier under Garibaldi with the mark of a sabre cut across his forehead;

a gentleman through all, as was evidenced by that indefinable air of good breeding which, when not innate, can never be acquired; altogether he proved as great an enigma as he was an attraction. The charm of his voice and manner were such that it deepened every hour, and of the garnered gleanings of his well-stored, cultured mind one could hardly tire. By what strange chance he had been influenced to join the Northern Army as private in the ranks we never learned.

After a leisurely saunter the squad reached Winchester, where thousands of the stragglers were assembled; they were then fitted out in new uniforms and (thanks to the gods!) new brogans, and returned to their regiments; and within a week Lee's army was stronger than when it marched into Maryland.

Of all the battles of the war, the privates of the ranks were proudest of that of Sharpsburg, for it had been essentially their fight; it had been a contest wherein the individual prowess of the rank and file saved the day; it had been a hard stand-up, face-to-face, hand-to-hand affair, a battle wherein skeleton regiments and brigades, half starved and foot-sore, had held their own against the finest, best equipped army ever formed in the New World, and under a leader who was the idol of his soldiery.

The failure at Sharpsburg can easily be traced to that vice which more than any other saps the vitality of an army and destroys its efficiency, the vice of straggling; it is almost as much to be deprecated as desertion, though in that instance the evil had been pardonable, for thousands of the men were barefooted, starving and sick.

It is no exaggeration to say that during the advance into Maryland forty out of every hundred wandered from their commands into the adjacent country; many of these were shirkers, cowards and skulkers, who took every opportunity to slip away and avoid danger, yet when obliged to go into action made good soldiers.

General McClellan had printed handbills distributed by thousands among his troops, before the Battle of Sharpsburg. They bore the date September 10th, 1862, and contained an order against straggling, and a stringent order too.

"No soldier," so ran the paper, "should under any circumstances leave his place in the line. If he be incapable from any cause of keeping up, the officer commanding his company should place him in the care of the ambulance corps. Should an able-bodied man leave ranks without orders and become a straggler, he will be tried by a drum-head court martial and shot. The

company and regimental officers are ordered to make returns
to the adjutant-general, and account satisfactorily for every missing soldier."

The following letter, printed in the *Savannah Republican,* was
written by the most famous of the Southern war correspondents,
Percy W. Alexander, and pictured in graphic language the deeds
and needs of the Army of Northern Virginia.

"Conditions of the Southern Army, 1862.

"Winchester, (Va.) Sept. 26th—My condition is such as to
render it impossible for me to rejoin the army for the present.
I was not prepared for the hardships, exposure and fastings the
army has encountered since it left the Rappahannock, and like
many a seasoned campaigner have had to 'fall out by the way.'
Indeed I can recall no parallel instance in history, except Napoleon's disastrous retreat from Moscow, where an army has
ever done more marching and fighting under such great disad-
vantages than General Lee's has done since it left the banks of
the James River.

"This army proceeded directly to the line of the Rappahannock,
and moving out from that river fought its way to the Potomac,
crossed the stream, and moved on to Frederick and Hagerstown;
and a heavy engagement at Boonsboro Gap and another at
Crampton's Gap below; fought the greatest pitched battle of
the war at Sharpsburg, and then recrossed the Potomac into Virginia. During all this time, covering the full space of a month,
the troops rested but four days. And let it be remembered to
their honor, that of the men who performed this wonderful feat
one-fifth of them were barefooted; one-half of them in rags, and
the whole of them half famished. The country from the Rappahannock to the Potomac had been visited by the enemy with fire
and sword and our transportation was insufficient to keep the
army supplied from so distant a base as Gordonsville; and when
provision trains would overtake the army, so pressing were the exigencies of their position, the men seldom had time to cook their
rations. Their difficulties were increased by the fact that cooking
utensils in many cases had been left behind, as well as everything
else which would impede their movements; it was not unusual to see
a company of starving men have a barrel of flour distributed to
them, which it was utterly impossible for them to convert into
bread with the means and the time allowed them; they could

not procure even a piece of plank or a corn or flower sack upon which to work the dough.

"Do you wonder then that there should have been stragglers, that brave and true men should have fallen out from sheer exhaustion in their efforts to obtain a mouthful to eat along the roadside?"

The *Richmond Whig,* in an editorial dated October 21, 1862, says:

"We again return to the subject of the condition of the Army of Northern Virginia, which we discussed at some length in our issue of yesterday. As we remarked in the conclusion of our last article, the Government has begun to move in the matter of furnishing supplies to the troops, and several wagons loaded with shoes and clothing had reached Winchester as early as the middle of last week. We understand that other shipments of clothes, shoes and perhaps blankets have been made to the same destination. These supplies will afford great relief as far as they go, and we only regret that they are not ample enough to meet the wants of the entire army. Much good will be accomplished, however, if even a portion of our ragged and barefooted defenders have shoes put upon their feet and clothing upon their backs. Many of them have not changed their clothing since they left Richmond; they have slept in it, fought in it, crossed the Potomac in it, marched over dusty roads and through storm and sunshine in it, yet they have not changed it or washed it because they had no other to put on when that was taken off. The reader will not be surprised to hear, therefore, that many of the troops are covered with vermin and their clothing rotten and dirty beyond anything they have ever seen. There is no negro in Virginia who is not better off in this respect than some of the best soldiers and first gentlemen in all the land."

Colonel Freemantle, of the English Army, on a tour of inspection, in speaking of this battle, writes to the *Edinburgh Review* and *Blackwood's Magazine* as follows:

"In the line of march, returning from Sharpsburg, were many rich landed proprietors marching contentedly along with an old tattered flannel shirt and a pair of ragged Yankee uniform trousers for their only clothing, while their feet bled at almost every step they took."

A short while and the Army of Northern Virginia was in its glory again; each soldier in the First Brigade was furnished from top to toe; and there was a grand review held on the plains near Winchester. Of this grand pageant Colonel Freemantle writes:

"I have seen many armies in my time file past in all the pomp of bright uniforms and well-protected accoutrements, but I never saw one composed of finer men or that looked more like work than that portion of General Lee's army which I was fortunate to see inspected."

General Lee was once asked by a lady of what battle he was most proud. He replied:

"Of Sharpsburg, for I fought against greater odds; and then, he added, stroking meditatively his long, thick beard, "to the rank and file all the credit of that day belongs."

CHAPTER XXXIII.

FREDERICKSBURG.

In a few weeks the paroled prisoners having been exchanged, were ordered back to their commands. By that time the army had retreated, all unmolested, through the valley of Piedmont, Virginia; had massed at Warrenton and then taken up the line of march to Fredericksburg. The rations were ample, the clothing warm and the morale of the army was excellent.

In those two months the two great armies had exactly reversed posts on the programme; the Rebels had ceased attacking and were acting on the defensive, and their foe, no longer anxious about the safety of their National Capital, but strong in numbers and flushed with the hope of putting a speedy end to the war, had become the assailants; were ready to try conclusions once more, and determined to force the fighting. The scene had changed from the green fields of Maryland to the heights along the Rappahannock; the summer breeze which had swept over the field of Sharpsburg was now the keen, searching blast which carried frost upon its wings; the leaves which had danced in the sunshine were strewing the ground thickly in their dying.

"Rustling to the eddying winds,
And to the rabbit's tread."

On November the seventh, McClellan, the organizer of the army (and its savior too), was relieved from command and Burnside appointed in his place.

General Burnside differed from all his predecessors in one important matter of opinion: McDowell, McClellan and Pope had all expressed their convictions that the rout of the Rebel army should be the great desideratum; Burnside, on the contrary, contended that the capture of Richmond was ever the great object to be desired, and with that idea fully ingrained in his mind he determined to march in a straight line from Washington to Richmond and capture the Rebel Capital.

Putting his columns in motion, he reached the banks of the Rappahannock opposite Fredericksburg on the seventeenth of November, but was delayed for two weeks by the failure of the pontoons to arrive; this delay was fatal, for at the end of that time Lee had taken up his position and stood directly in his path.

Fredericksburg is a quiet, sleepy little town, looking like New Amsterdam when the redoubtable Van Twiller was its Governor nearly two hundred years ago; it rests upon the branch of the river which, with a general course northeast to southeast, makes a sharp bend a mile above Fredericksburg and for some distance runs between the heights upon either side; those on the east fall steeply to the river bank; on the west the hills in the rear of the town rise about a mile from the river and then trend away until they sink into the valley of the Massaponax six miles below, leaving an irregular plain some two miles wide in its broadest part. Westward the hills rise by a succession of low, wooded ridges until they are lost in the wooded region known as the Wilderness.

On the crest of these ridges lay the half of Lee's army under Longstreet. D. H. Hill was posted at Port Royal twenty miles down the river; between them lay Jackson, ready to support either wing.

Burnside had determined to cross near or at Fredericksburg, and December the eleventh had been the time appointed for the attempt. His plan was to throw three bridges across at Fredericksburg and then move at a point three miles below.

The attempt to lay the upper bridges was savagely resisted by Barksdale's brigade of Mississippians, and for a time delayed, but they were brushed away at last, and the work finished. The whole day of the twelfth was spent in getting the men over, thus giving Lee time to bring up Jackson's corps. It was no part of Lee's plan to dispute the passage, as he wished to receive the attack on his strong position. The extreme Rebel left above Fredericksburg was protected by a mill-pond, sluiceway and canal, the bridge having been destroyed; and here the attack could only be made upon Marye's Hill, which rises steeply a little behind Fredericksburg.

On the thirteenth General Burnside had in line of battle over one hundred thousand men, besides a heavy reserve of some twenty thousand on the other side. Lee's strength was about seventy-five thousand. (Official Report of Major-General Burnside.)

The attack was made all along the line but early repulsed. Burnside tried to break the Rebel line by repeated and continuous charges upon Marye's Hill, but was driven back each time with fearful carnage.

Finding his efforts futile, he abandoned the attempt and the next night retreated, re-crossing his pontoons and leaving twelve thousand two hundred and fifty men behind him in killed and wounded and missing.   (Report of Adjutant-General of Army of Potomac.)

The Rebel loss was five thousand three hundred and nine.

Our brigade was not actively engaged during the day; indeed not a third part of the army was in the fight; we were held as a reserve, and witnessed the attack on our left.

We lay on our arms the night of the twelfth, listening to the noise made by the enemy in crossing. The Seventeenth was full in ranks again, and was looking very differently from the slim, weak line that was crouching behind the fence in the last battle.

The morning of Saturday, December thirteenth, broke with a heavy fog resting in the valley and hiding each army from the other; as the sun rose, the thick vapor slowly lifted from the ground, unfolding a splendid display, as in a group we stood on the crest of the hill on the right and in the rear of Marye's Hill, watching with absorbing interest the panorama.

Across the river on the lofty heights could be seen the Stars and Stripes floating in the wind; the earthworks with their huge guns were outlined against the sky; at our feet lay the ancient town of Fredericksburg, filled with the blue-coats, who seemed to swarm like bees in a hive, as in large bodies they marched out and took positions.

About ten in the morning the battle opened on our right, A. P. Hill's division receiving the attack and beating back the enemy, while all the time the Yankee batteries on the heights were keeping up a continuous fire.

Then came the charge on Marye's Hill. Had the enemy known against what he was running he would never have made such a hopeless effort, or one that involved such a sacrifice of life. Marye's Hill is about fifty yards high and slopes abruptly toward the city to a stone wall which forms a terrace on the side of the hill and the outer margin of a road which winds along its foot leading to Hamilton Crossing. The road is about twenty-five feet wide and is faced by a stone wall some four feet high on the side nearest the city. Standing on Marye's Hill such is the sudden slope that the road at its foot is not discernible; the house, a handsome old Virginia residence, is built on the top of the hill facing Fredericksburg, with a long, wide porch extending the length of the house in front; beneath the roof was born and reared the colonel of our regiment who had been so severely wounded in the Second Battle of Manassas. Once the scene of hospitality and that courtly elegance found in the old families of Virginia, it was now dismantled and awaited the fate which seemed in store. The once large family which had gathered within its walls was scattered, as were the residents of but too many Southern homes; the large lawn bounded by the stone wall and sunken road in front lay stripped of all the grand old trees which formerly contributed so much toward the beauty of the place; standing on the porch, one could trace the winding of the road from the town, rising till it passed at right angles the stone wall road and met on the left of the lawn the "Brompton Gate" (for that was the name by which the place had ever been known), from which a broad carriage-drive led to the entrance overlooking the town.

The crest of Marye's Hill was now crowned by two batteries of artillery, while about fifty guns were placed a half mile back to enfilade all the approaches, which must be made in an open plain over three hundred yards wide. The sunken road, like the ditch of a fortress, afforded complete protection and perfect security to the troops within. Kershaw's division occupied this cut, standing in double ranks, or four deep.

What chance had flesh and blood to carry by storm such a position, garrisoned too as it was with veteran soldiers? Not one chance in a million.

In company with Bob Willis, we straggled to the front and lay in the rear of the Washington Artillery of New Orleans, which hurled grape and canister at the attacking force. All that day we watched the fruitless charges, with their fearful slaughter, until we were sick at heart.

As I witnessed one line swept away by one fearful blast from Kershaw's men behind the stone wall, I forgot they were enemies and only remembered that they were men, and it is hard to see in cold blood brave men die.

Just before sunset, everything being quiet along the line, many of the reserve, without orders, crowded to the front and were spectators of that last forlorn hope led by the gallant Humphries. In front was Meagher's brigade of Irishmen, who marched to their death like men who knew no fear.

> "They cared little for shot or shell,
>   They laughed at death and dangers,
> And they'd storm the very gates of hell,
>   Would the gallant Irish rangers."

History records no more dauntless, valorous advance than the reckless charge of Meagher. Every soldier knew the Rebel position was impregnable; they had seen charge after charge repulsed, they had seen brigade after brigade rush forward with deadly determination, only to recoil before the hailstorm of iron and of lead; their very route lay over a field where the dead lay thick "as the leaves in Vallombrosa;" and yet not an Irishman in the brigade, as far as we could see, left his place in the ranks.

From the hill back of the heights the division of Pickett watched the advance, filled with wonder and a pitying admiration for men who could rush with such unflinching valor, such mad recklessness into the jaws of destruction.

"A brave man dies but once, a coward dies a thousand times." None of the bitterness of death was theirs, as with steady step and heads erect they came toward that bristling crest so ominously silent. Across the plain, with no martial music to thrill them, only a stillness that would strike terror into spirits less gallant—across the plain still onward sweeps the dauntless brigade with serried lines and gleaming steel.

It was superb!

Still closer they advanced, while twice one thousand veterans lay behind yon stone wall, with eyes ranged along the deadly barrel and fingers pressing the trigger.

Men held their breath.

There was no smoke or battle-fume to obstruct the view, nor wood to mask the movement; but as in a grand review, the whole advance could be seen in all its glory and in all its horror.

The brigade came on a run, and bent as it moved until it was the shape of a half moon with the concave toward the town. Batteries opened upon them; and then broke out the murderous musketry. Men staggered, reeled and fell, but the others pushed on. From the wall and road came a living sheet of fire, still the Irish rushed forward; but at every foot they dropped by scores; some almost reached the wall and then fell dead with their feet to the foe; human nature could stand no more, for the number of killed was fast counting up by thousands, and half of them were down; the ranks broke and each man sought safety in flight.

Another solid line emerged to support the first, but did not advance half the distance before it went to pieces under the fire; in fifteen minutes the battle was all over. The ground was covered with the fallen, three thousand, and the Battle of Fredericksburg was ended. ("Of the 1,200 I lead into action only 280 appeared at parade the next morning." Brigadier-General Meagher's Official Report.)

Never in the annals of grand exploits has this charge ever been surpassed. Tradition has thrown a halo of romance over Arthur and his Knights, poetry has enshrined in imperishable lustre the charge of the six hundred at Balaklava, but greater than this last was Meagher's advance; for a man's courage is in ratio with his motion. It is far easier to ride to the death with the shrill blare of the bugle ringing in the ears, rushing on in a wild excitement which keeps up with the mad gallop of the bounding horse; but to advance step by step with unloaded guns, to leave the world with the blood beating temperately in the veins, required courage indeed. Ireland may well have wept for her sons that day, but the Cypress was twined with Laurel.

The butchery over, and night came; another day and toward evening ammunition (forty rounds) was served out. There was little rest among the troops, for they were expecting to advance; the dawn found the men bewildered and dazed; why had they not gone forward and taken the Federals in the trap.

Ah, why indeed!

The Army of the Potomac was caught in a trap, caged as it were, within a narrow space from which there was no escape. There was the little town crowded and packed with men, a rapid river in their rear, across which was only a frail line of pontoons as useless in this hour of emergency as Mahomet's Bridge from Earth to Paradise. There lay the enemy with our artillery commanding every exit, and ready at a moment's notice to throw into the town, among the mass of soldiers, shell and shot from nearly a hundred guns.

Well might the Northern army have feared. What could they have done if this tempest had rained upon them? Advance was impossible; retreat equally so; all that would have remained for them wound have been to stand and die in their tracks or to surrender.

The nights of the thirteenth and fourteenth of December were indeed pregnant with the fate of the two contending people. Was there no voice in earth or sky to whisper into the ear of the sleeping Captain, the man with the gray beard and the eagle eye, and bid him wake and strike?

No, the minutes come and go. The wind sweeps over the bare plains, chilling the wounded and freezing his blood as it drips slowly from his veins; it brings no echo of the faintest

footfall of the fast flying army; the guns upon the hills that
might have uttered a protest with tongues of flame seemed to be
as deep in slumber as the men beside them.

Still the minutes come and go, when every second is precious
and only the stars see the hurrying ranks of blue, filing in almost
frenzied haste over the pontoons, with army blankets piled ten
deep to muffle the rapid tread of feet and the rumbling of the
artillery over the swaying bridge.

So the precious moments are accumulating into hours, while
the vanquished host steals noiselessly away man by man, company
by company, regiment by regiment, brigade by brigade, division
by division, corps by corps, all traversing the narrow way unmolested, winning safety by degrees.

At last, when the northern light heralded the dawn and roused
the quiet Rebel army, it saw the rear-guard of their foe file across
the bridge and the foe was safe.

Had General Lee opened all his guns in the night and charged
with his infantry—then—then!

Well, the privates around the camp-fire thought their hour of
victory had come at last; from that hour to this day they could
not understand why "Uncle Robert" let the chance slip and did
not allow them to end the war there with one bold rush.

Jackson, with the inspiration of genius, wanted to advance in
the night; he expected and made his preparations in event of
the repulse of Burnside. General Lindsay Walker, his Chief-of-
Artillery, told me that when he opened his guns and ordered his
horses to the rear, Jackson rode up and ordered him to let the
horses stay. "But, General," said the tall artilleryman, "half of
the horses will be killed." "No matter," curtly responded Stonewall, "keep them with the guns."

The horses were kept as directed, in all the terrible fire,
"Which," said General Walker, "showed me that Jackson intended
to advance that night."

Like Napoleon at Leipsic, Lee let a golden chance slip by. His
medical director, Doctor Hunter McGuire, states that Jackson
asked him on the night of the battle how many rolls of cotton
bandages and compresses he had in stock, and upon the doctor
replying that there was enough for the wounded, Jackson impa-
tiently replied that he supposed he had, but he wanted to know
if there was enough to tie around the arm of every soldier in his
command. Later on Jackson admitted to him that it was his

purpose to make a night attack with both his artillery and in- fantry.

In his official account of the battle General Kershaw, who with Cobb's Georgia and Ransom's North Carolina brigades repulsed during the day every attack of the enemy, and especially Meagher's great charge, says: "Marye's Hill, covered with our batteries, then occupied by the Washington Artillery, falls off abruptly toward Fredericksburg to a stone wall which forms a terrace on the side of the telegraph road which winds along the foot of the hill; this road is about twenty-five feet wide and is faced by a stone wall about four feet high on the city side; the road having been cut out of the side of the hill in many places, is not visible above the surface of the ground; the land falls off rapidly to almost a level surface which extends to about 150 yards, then with another abrupt fall of a few feet to another plain which extends some 200 yards, and then falls off abruptly to a wide ravine. I found on my arrival that Cobb's brigade occupied our entire front, and that my troops could only get into position by doubling on them; this was accordingly done, and the foundation along the line during the engagement was *four deep*. As an evidence of the coolness of the command I may mention here that notwithstanding their fire was the most rapid and continuous I ever witnessed, not a man was injured by the fire of his comrades. Under cover of his artillery fire a most formidable column of attack was formed, and emerging from the ravine impetuously assailed our whole front. The attack was continuous, some few officers and men got within 30 yards of our lines, but in every instance their column was shattered by the time they got within one hundred paces." (Reb. Records, Vol. 21, p. 590.)

It was just before this charge that General Lee, anxious about his center, rode up to Marye's Heights, and after a long examination with his field-glass turned to General Longstreet and said:

"Those people are throwing their whole weight on this point; do you think you can hold the position without reinforcement?"

"General," answered the corps commander, "every inch of the ground is so covered by guns and musketry that a chicken could not live to reach that sunken road." ("Battles and Leaders of the Civil War.")

Colonel Stephens, of the 13th N. H. Infantry, who acted as reserve and witnessed the successive charges on Marye's Heights, reports under date of December 22nd, 1862:

"As yet all the accounts that I have seen or read from Union or Rebel sources approach not in delineation the truthful and terrible panorama of that day. Twice during the day I rode up Caroline Street to the center of the city toward the point where our brave legions were struggling against the terrible concentration of the enemy's artillery and infantry, whose unremitting fire shook the earth and filled the plain in the rear of the city with the deadly missiles of war. I saw the struggling hosts of freedom stretched along the plain, their ranks ploughed by the merciless fire of the foe; I listened to the roar of battle and groans of the wounded and dying; I saw in the crowded hospitals the desolation of war, but I heard from our brave soldiers no note of triumph, no word of encouragement, no syllable of hope that for us a field was to be won. In the stubborn, unyielding resistance of the enemy I could see no point of pressure likely to yield to the repeated assaults of our brave soldiers. For three-quarters of an hour before we were ordered into action, I stood in front of my regiment on the brow of the hill and watched the fire of the Rebel batteries as they poured shot and shell from sixteen different points upon our devoted men on the plains below. It was a sight magnificently terrible. Every discharge of the enemy's artillery and every explosion of his shells was visible in the dusky twilight of that smoke-crowned hill. There his direct and enfilading batteries, with a vividness, intensity and almost the rapidity of lightning, hurled the messengers of death in the midst of our brave ranks vainly struggling through the murderous fire to gain the hills and the guns of the enemy. Nor was it a straggling or ill-directed fire; the arrangements of the enemy's guns were such that they could pour their concentrated and incessant fire upon any point occupied by our assailing troops, and all of them were fired with the greatest skill and precision. During all of this time the rattle of musketry was incessant. Then came an order for our brigade to fall in; silently but unflinchingly the men moved out from their cover, and when the line was formed, started in a run, and the pace was so rapid that many of the men relieved themselves of their blankets and haversacks. The words 'Forward! charge!' rang out, we crossed the railroad and low muddy swamp on the left, all the time the enemy concentrating their terrible fire by batteries and pouring it in on our advancing line. Suddenly the cannonading and musketry of the enemy ceased. The shouts of our men were also hushed, and nothing was heard along the line save the command. 'Forward, men! close up! steady!' In this manner we continued to advance in the direction of the enemy's batteries until we got within 20 yards of the celebrated stone wall. Behind that wall, and in rifle-pits on its flanks, were posted the enemy's infantry, according to their statement, four ranks deep, and on the hill a few yards above lay in ominous silence their death-dealing artillery. It was while we were moving steadily forward that with one startling crash, with one simultaneous sheet of fire and flame they hurled on our advancing lines the whole terrible force of their infantry and artillery fire. The powder from their musketry seemed to burn in our very faces, and the breath of their artillery was hot upon our cheeks; the leaden rain and iron hail in an instant forced back the advancing lines upon those who were close to them in the rear, and before the men could be rallied to renew the charge the lines had been hurled back by the irresistible fire of the enemy to the cover of the ravine or gully which they had just passed. The enemy swept the grounds with their guns, killing and wounding many. Of the three brigades participating in that charge, in the space of a few minutes the awful loss was 1,226 lying on the field." (Reb. Records, Vol. 21, pp. 341-342.)

Burnside, from his post of vantage in the belfry of the Court House, seemed to have gone mad in this carnival of death. When French's division withered away he sent his aide, Colonel Taylor to Hancock to "put everything in." In his frantic desire to carry the heights he sent in successively the divisions of French, Hancock, Howard, Sturgis, Birney, Griffin and Humphries—in all 20 brigades or 102 regiments. Of the thousands who rushed for that fatal stone wall with desperate determination, not one reached it alive. It will never be known how many times the Union troops made the attack. Their advance was like the billows breaking into atoms on a rock. The last charges were feeble, for the troops had to push their way over the prostrate lines of their comrades who were first sent in, and who, after being repulsed, had thrown themselves flat on the ground to escape the scathing, pitiless fire that swept the plain.

Many brigade official reports speak of these prostrate soldiers begging their advancing line to retreat, even going so far as to grasp the legs of the men of the moving column and prevent them obeying orders. From a thousand throats would come the cry, "Go back, go back! It's certain death to advance!" and the piles of dead gave fearful emphasis to the cry.

In a space of four hundred yards by about eight hundred yards lay the bodies of thousands. The Official Records show that these seven divisions lost in killed and wounded in their attack on Marye's Hill 8,789 men. (Reb. Records, Vol. 21, pp. 129-137.)

The regiment that went the farthest, dared the most and died with their feet touching the stone wall was the Sixty-ninth New York, of Meagher's Irish Brigade. The following is the report of Capt. James Saunders, Commanding the Regiment:

"Camp near Falmouth, Va., Dec. 22, 1862.

"In compliance with general orders I hereby certify that the Sixty-ninth New York Vols. entered the battle of Fredericksburg on Dec. 13, 1862, with 18 commissioned officers and 210 rank and file, in which they lost 16 commissioned officers and 160 rank and file, leaving me, Lieuts. Milliken and Brennen, to bring the remnant (52 men) off the battle-field." (Reb. Records, Vol. 21, p. 251.)

Ah! They were men! those lads of Sixty-ninth. In that olden and glorious time we Rebs would have taken off our hats and bowed low before the survivors of that gallant regiment, the bravest of the brave.

CHAPTER XXXIV.

THE CONFEDERATE STATES OF AMERICA.

"The Confederate States of America." That is how the soldiers of Lee's army headed their letters in the last days of the old year of 1862. Their cause seemed on the eve of triumph; everything was going their way; the army had learned to consider itself invincible; Bull Run, Williamsburg, Seven Pines, The Seven Days' Battles, Harper's Ferry, Crampton's Gap, Boonsboro, Antietam, and Fredericksburg they looked upon as victories. The Rebels could not bring themselves to think that any army could keep long at the game of hammering the uncracked, unbroken anvil. Encircled by the rim of fire, the Confederacy had held its own except that New Orleans and Norfolk had fallen, but their occupation by the enemy had nothing to do with the general result.

If the end of the year found the Southerners jubilant, it was anything but a time of happy portent to the Northerners. The war was proving a serious business to them. The novelty and excitement had worn off, "the old flag furore," as Mr. Seward expressed it, had died away. The cost of carrying on the conflict was enormous. Volunteering had ceased and a general conscription law was being forced through Congress; many weak-kneed patriots were lifting up their voices; their grand army was in a bad condition. Scott, McDowell, McClellan, Pope and Burnside,—five changes in a little more than one year, and each change was from bad to worse.

The feelings of the North were voiced by Quartermaster-General Meigs, a man closer to the Administration than any one else. In a personal letter to General Burnside shortly after the Battle of Fredericksburg, urging him imperatively to advance, he says:

"In my position as Quartermaster-General of the Army, much is to be seen that is seen from no other standpoint of the army. Every day's consumption of your army is an immense destruction of the natural and monetary resources. The country begins to feel the effect of this exhaustion and I begin to apprehend a catastrophe.

"General Halleck tells me that you believe your numbers greater than the enemy's and yet the army waits. So long as you con-

sult your principal officers together the result will be that pro-
verbially of councils of war.   Every day weakens your army.
Exhaustion steals over the country.   Confidence and hope are
dying.   While I have been always sure that ultimate success must
attend the cause of freedom, justice and government sustained by
18,000,000, against that of oppression, perjury and treason, supported by 5,000,000, I begin to doubt the possibility of maintaining the contest beyond this winter, unless the popular heart
is encouraged by a victory on the Rappahannock.

"What is needed is a great and overwhelming defeat of the
Rebel army.   Such a victory would be of incalculable value.   It
would place upon your head the wreath of immortal glory.   It
would place your name at the side of Washington's.

"If by a march such as Napoleon made at Jena, or as Lee made
his communications and interpose between him and Richmond,
if you are successful he has no retreat.   His army would be dispersed and a greater portion would throw down its arms.   The
gallantry of the attack at Fredericksburg made amends for its
ill success, and the soldiers were not discouraged by it.   The
people, when they understood, took heart again.   But the slumber of the army since is eating into the vitals of the Nation.   As
day after day has gone by my heart has sunk, and I see greater
peril to our nationality in the present condition of affairs than I
have seen at any time during the struggle.   Wash., D. C., Dec.
30, 1862."   (Reb. Records, Vol. 21, pp. 917-918.)

CHAPTER XXXV.

A LONG REST.

After the Battle of Fredericksburg the fine weather, clear, cold and bracing, which we had been having, changed into a real Virginia winter, with a good deal of the Northern thrown in. It snowed, froze, thawed and rained by turns, with here and there bright days. All military operations were brought to a sudden close and both armies went into winter quarters.

The First Brigade attached to Pickett's division was about two miles from Guiney's Station on the Richmond and Fredericksburg Railroad. The camp of the Seventeenth was pitched in a pine woods well sheltered from the wind and with a good stream of water running near. As soon as the place was allotted each mess went to work to build cabins. There was no attempt at laid-out streets or parallel right-angle squares, but the houses were arranged haphazard according to the inspiration of the moment, and thrown together in higgledy-piggledy style, which would have made it necessary for a stranger socially inclined to employ a guide or strike off a camp directory.

Every style of camp architecture was to be found, including hut, hovel, shack and shed, and every other plan of building that limited genius could devise. Officers and men messed together, therefore their style of tabernacle was no better than ours. Some energetic fellows worked like beavers and erected a good, substantial log-house, with fine-drawing chimney and canvas roof, snug, air-tight and rain-proof. These industrious bees had to submit to every kind of jibe and joke from the mocking drones for their pains. John Zimmerman and Mark Price took a week in constructing their hut; indeed if they had intended spending the rest of their lives in it they could not have taken more pains with the spare means at hand. At last they finished it and a crowd assembled to see them take possession.

"Look yonder," drawled a long, lazy Reb, with an air as if he had come from the good old State of North Carolina, as he sat in the sun with an axe in his hands which he was too lazy to use; "jes' look a yonder, them boys is a buildin' a pallis; ef they ain't I'll be doggoned."

"When are you going to send for the mason and plasterer?" asked another sitting near.

"The decorator will be driving up soon," yelled an old Reb.

"Don't forget the carpets and furniture," suggested the fourth. "Expect the President to come and see you, don't you?"

By this time the crowd was watching the finishing touches with much interest, each man having his say.

"The boss-plumber and his assistants have just come." And saluting, profoundly, the self-elected courier retired.

"The stove and kitchen range will be here presently," said one confidentially to the rest.

"I saw the piano coming with Uncle Robert's compliments as I left the depot," remarked another in a matter-of-fact tone.

"Lor! boys, stop yer fooling; hear me? He's going to have a pair of stone dogs on the porch, he is," exclaimed a bystander while his comrade made haste to chime in: "And a bay-window an' a observatory for flowers at each end, an' a fountain playin' before the door, and statues, and a brass knocker on that door, you bet."

"Found a fortune? I tell you what, fellows, those boys have discovered a gold mine digging around these woods." And this old Reb emphasized his remarks with a prolonged whistle express-ive of admiring awe.

"Say, mister, want a driver for your carriage? I'll milk your cow too and I'll feed your canary birds," volunteered one of the men, gravely touching his hat.

"Got any room in that hotel for boarders," inquired a man, run-ning up, "because General Lee has just sent word to know if he can board with you, him and his staff."

The builders took it all patiently enough, working steadily on. One voice generally answered back:

"All right; you're having you're laugh now; but wait till the snow comes, and you'll all be crowding in then."

Some lazy soldiers, "born tired," did not even attempt to build, they merely put up an old tent, run a trench around it and erected a rude fire-place at one end. Others dug deep holes in the ground and roofed them over, proposing to hibernate like ground-squirrels. Again there were real Indian wigwams to be seen, only they had hearths and cheering fires.

Some of the huts were large and roomy, holding a mess of a dozen comfortably; others were of a size capable of accommo-dating three or four, while here and there one would come across

a modern Diogenes in his tub, or Southern Thersites, who, retiring from human sympathy and companionship, dug some hole
or built some den in which he proposed to drag out the winter
by himself.

The latter part of December was fearful; a long rain followed
the battle, then a hard, bitter freeze came. So intense was the
cold that the men did nothing but cower over the fire piled high
with wood night and day, or keep snugged up under blankets,
which in such weather rose in value to a thousand dollars a square
inch. The earth was frozen as hard as granite; the streams
were solid; indeed Ice-King held all nature in a relentless grasp.

All drills, inspections and even guard-mountings were suspended during this freezing weather. A man hardly dared poke
his nose out of the tent, except when obliged to go for wood and
water and to draw his rations.

Then came on a thaw for three or four days, with really warm
weather, when everything melted; when the streams burst their
bonds; when the earth became soft until it seemed to have no
bottom and mud reigned supreme. It was everywhere; the roads
were almost impassable and it was difficult to haul the rations
to camp from the station. A detail of seventy-five was made from
the Seventeenth to assist the brigade wagons back to camp.

It was a cheerless task. The heavy army wagons came toiling
laboriously along; many became stalled in the mud, the wheels
sunken below the hubs, horses straining, the drivers cursing and
lashing the poor animals, while a dozen men pushed at each
wheel, all and everything covered with the liquid mire; such was
December in Virginia.

The Christmas of 1862 was cheerless indeed; the weather was
frightful and a heavy snow-storm covered everything a foot deep.
Each soldier attempted to get a dinner in honor of the day, and
those to whom boxes had been sent succeeded to a most respectable degree, but those unfortunates whose homes were outside the lines had nothing whatever delectable partaking of
the nature of Christmas. Well! it would have puzzled the
divine Soyer himself to furnish a holiday dinner out of a pound
of fat pork, six crackers and a quarter of a pound of dried apples.
We all had apple dumplings that day, which with sorghum molasses was not to be despised.

Some of the men became decidedly hilarious, and then again
some did not; not because they had recently joined the tem-
perance society nor because they were opposed to the use of in-

toxicating liquors, nor because they had promised their wives and sweethearts that they would not, but because Temptation did not assail them (though the assailing would have been on the other side if poor Temptation had had a drop), but because not a soul invited them to step up and partake. One mess in the Seventeenth did not get so much as a smell during the whole of the holidays; and a dry, dismal old time it proved.

We read in the Richmond papers of the thousands and thousands of boxes that had been passed en route to the army, sent by the ladies of Richmond and other cities, but few found their way to us. The greater part of them were for the troops from the far South who were too distant from their homes to receive anything from their own families. The Virginians were supposed to have been cared for by their own relatives and friends; but some of them were not, as we all know.

New Year came and there were but few calls made. Nobody kept open house; the observance being considered a Yankee fashion, the soldiers agreed to dispense with it; notwithstanding, had any one opened his doors and received according to custom, with wines, liquors and refreshments, he would have received sixty thousand callers before night.

Late in January a severe and continued snow-storm came on and covered the earth to a considerable depth, affording sleighing if we had only had the teams. One evening, while the snow was lying hard and crisp upon the ground and the air was cool and bracing with a frosty nip in it which sent the blood tingling in the veins, the First Brigade, sitting around the cabin fires, heard all at once the old Rebel yell ringing out with a will. Rushing out they saw Toombs's Georgia Brigade not a hundred yards away, sweeping toward them in a regular line of battle, their haversacks filled with snow-balls and all shouting like mad.

In an instant officers and men divined the situation.

"Fall back, men!" the former shouted. "Fall back and rally by the colors!" And back they ran to the woods not far distant, while the colonel dispatched his aides to General Pickett for reinforcements.

Through the camp came Toombs's men, capturing two or three hundred of the Seventeenth, whom they paroled on the spot and then kept on; in the meantime two companies of the Seventeenth had been thrown out as skirmishers, to keep the Georgians back long enough for Kemper's brigade to form. The skirmishers did their best and accomplished their object, but they were captured to a man. Then came the shock of war, and the two brigades closed in snowy combat. All of the three Virginia regiments were in front, while Colonel Corse, with the Seventeenth, made a circuit and attacked in the rear. The struggle was obstinate and the snow-balls rained, or rather snowed, upon each line. The contest was waxing warm and blood began to flow from noses. The cautious and timid began to steal toward the rear.

The Seventeenth, after making the circuit and getting behind the enemy, were just about to charge, when they discovered the startling fact that they had jumped from the frying-pan into the fire, for Wright's brigade of Georgians had now come up and caught them *flagrante delicto*. The Seventeenth, although between two forces, made a gallant stand, but soon surrendered; they could not stand the murderous snow. Colonel Corse, game to the last, shouted, "No surrender, boys! No surrender!" But he was pitched head foremost into a snow bank and two Georgians sat on him until he cried enough and yielded himself prisoner of war.

But the triumph of the Georgians is short. Listen to the yells over there! Here come in full tilt Armistead's and Hunton's brigades and Wright's command wheel to meet them, making a demi-curve right and left. Close fighting ensues; and the prisoners, being retaken, turn on their captors. It is nip and tuck! But now Toombs's brigade gives ground; their ammunition is exhausted, not a ball left in their haversacks, and they are too hard pressed to make more. The three brigades hem them in; Hunton overlaps their right wing and takes them in the flank and rear.

Kershaw's brigade advances and attacks. By this time the ranks of the Virginia Brigade are broken, owing to their rapid assault and the roughness of the ground, and before they can dress their line Kershaw bears down upon them.

No authentic return of the loss in this battle was ever made to the Adjutant-General; but considering the severity of the snow, it was surprisingly small.

In the great battle the colors of the Georgians consisted of an old red undershirt; the Virginia banner was a pair of old gray breeches carried aloft on a pole.

It is needless to say that all of the men covered themselves with glory and with snow.

Nothing occurred to break the monotony of camp in this, the

dreariest month of all the year, if we may except the regimental court martials, formed to try the soldiers for trivial offenses, principally for absence without leave.

All were convicted or discharged by impartial judgment, but all were not punishable by the same methods. A broad line was drawn between the better class of privates (gentlemen, in fact) and those of a lower rank socially. The one had their pay stopped and were deprived of their two weeks' furlough, which punishment was submitted to willingly. The latter class was condemned to the ignominy of wearing a barrel shirt and of walking two hours each day on a beat, with a fence rail on their shoulders; and these men, not being either thin-skinned or sensitive, carried their rail and drew their pay, well content to get off so easily.

At first the men would laugh uproariously at such unfortunates, ask for the pattern and beg to know who was the tailor, and whether they had dressed to go courting, but when the novelty had worn off, took no further notice of them. Half a dozen could be seen at any time walking up and down under guard with all the solemnity of important duty. The barrel shirt was not handsome by any means, fashionable as it afterwards came to be. It consisted of a flour barrel with the bottom knocked out and two armholes cut out on either side, after which the garment was ready for the wearer. Of course the presentation was comical enough as the genus were seen strolling up and down the beat, and at first sight utterly irresistible, but beyond being not very graceful in its outlines nor flowing in its drapery, it was found not so bad after all when one became accustomed to it, and then it was capable of a great deal of ornamentation, and suggestive of bread.

About the middle of February and at a time when the mud was deepest, the sky dullest, the weather gloomiest, there came one of the most inexplicable military orders that ever puzzled the soldiers' brains or induced profanity.

One bitter, bleak, cold day the long roll was beaten and the order given to pack haversacks and fall into ranks.

"Where are we going?" asked the soldiers, pouring out of the cabin huts, wigwams, holes and dens, with no very blissful expression upon their faces.

But the officers did not know and could not even guess.

"Shall we leave our cooking utensils and other property behind, for of course we are coming back?" we further asked of them.

The colonel said "No!" orders were positive to take everything as we were to change position and make a long march."

With a groan and a curse each man loaded himself down with
his goods to the extent of his ability, and looked with sadness
and unfeigned regret at the comfortable quarters which they were
obliged to leave and at all the articles of winter menage which
they could not carry away—to march in the depth of mid-winter,
no one knew where.

Early in the morning the brigade started up some road,
whether north, south, east or west no one seemed to care. It
began to snow and the large flakes beat straight in our faces.
None could guess the direction we were going, and no man
troubled himself to ask. The soldiers were silent; and as they
marched through the pine woods, already bending beneath their
pure white burden, looked like a funeral cortege following some
loved leader in grief too deep for words; or like a deaf mute college taking an airing, rather than a body of troops on the march.

All day steadily the tramp was kept up, and every hour the
snow grew deeper and the walking more difficult. At last when
it was dark we were halted and told to go into camp. Then came
murmurs, grumbles, growls, snarls, maledictions, imprecations,
fulminations, execrations, denunciations, anathemas and dam-
nations! all more thickly than the snow flakes.

Camp, indeed! Camping meant making ourselves comfortable
with such help as roaring fires, the aroma of boiling coffee, the
delicate odor of frying meat, and the solacing pipe. What was
camp but a mockery, in a bare pine woods with no axes and only
green pines and everything wet?

And yet some managed to start a fire, though most of us failed,
despite patience and perseverance. Scooping out a hole in the
snow the soldiers lay down and tried to sleep; but it was a cold
sleep, or rather a half unconsciousness between sleep and waking,
in which there were fleeting dreams of icebergs; of being shut
up in refrigerators to keep from spoiling; of being captured and
locked up for safe keep in an ice-house; of being spun around
in a mammoth ice cream freezer and of being impaled on the
North Pole—all heavenly visions on a hot August night; but
with the thermometer at zero such dreams were too much like
reality for comfort. At such a time one could understand the religious promptings of those Greenlanders to whom the missionary went with account of what a very warm place old Satan's
home is. "That," said they with one accord, "is the very place

for us; that is where we want to go, we want fire." And the astute missionary, changing his tactics, preached of Gehenna's bitter cold, how whale blubber froze in chunks and how there were whole icebergs of oil; then the Greenlanders repented.

The morning disclosed a scene which would have induced the thriftiest New England farmer to feel like banging his door, going back to his fire and letting the cattle starve for one day.

The snow lay fully a foot deep and the frosty air cut like a knife. Most of the men were without gloves and but few wore boots, consequently their sufferings were intense. They lay covered by their blankets, not daring to turn for fear the snow would come into their hollows. Some fires were started with infinite difficulty and coffee was boiled.

Then came the order to march.

"Where?"

"Why, right-face back to our quarters again." Of course the camp followers had cleared out our settlement; had helped themselves to axes, pots, kettles, superfluous clothing, chairs, tables, canvas roofs and everything which could be put to any use. Had a vote been taken then and there among the men (as they stood and surveyed the ruins and added up their losses), whether or not the war should end in a surrender, from sheer disgust and exasperation that knew no bounds, the brigade would in all likelihood have voted aye, to a man.

What military dunderhead we had to thank for this delectable manoeuvre we never found out, nor was its meaning ever explained.

After this we remained in camp until the great spring movement commenced.

CHAPTER XXXVI.

HOOD'S MEN VISIT THE THEATRE.

Early in March the long roll called the men out of their warm holes into the line, and orders were read them to prepare to abandon winter quarters and to make ready for a long march.

That evening saw Pickett's division on the tramp in the direction of Richmond. Expectation was rife as to our destination; maps were studied, predictions made, but none really guessed the truth. It was a toiling, tedious journey, for the roads were of course execrable at that season, and a more disagreeable march we never made.

Reaching Richmond and resting one day, the division began to file slowly through the streets, and then commenced straggling the soldiers dropping out of ranks in spite of the most stringent orders. Every confectionery store would be crammed by the men darting out like so many children, to buy a cake or stick of candy. The officers halloed themselves hoarse, but the men *would*, and there was an end of it. It was impossible to arrest them; when any of the sentinels, whose duty it was to patrol the streets, would come up to one of the veterans and demand his pass, he was met with such a storm of ridicule and curses as made him glad to give them a wide berth. Most of the men wanted to spend the night in the city, intending to overtake their commands the next morning.

It happened that Hood's brigade of Texans and Arkansans, as wild, daring, desperate a set as ever lived, were marching that night up Broad Street, passing the theatre just as the doors were opened to admit the rapidly gathering audience. The soldiers had been drinking, and were sauntering along to suit themselves, some in ranks and others keeping along the pavement. As the door swung backward and forward to admit the stream of people, revealing the brilliant lights, the temptation was too strong. A rush was made, and in a trice a company of soldiers were pouring in just as they were, in full marching order, camping accoutrements and muskets. Some bought tickets because they had the money, but many not feeling any Confederate Promises-to-Pay concealed in the linings of their pockets, went in anyhow.

What could the poor door-keeper do when the laughing, reckless, armed soldiery, who had stormed far more redoubtable defenses, pushed their way into the hall?

Simply nothing but hold up his hand in meek protest. In five minutes the whole pit was jammed with the Texans, the lights sparkling radiantly upon the polished barrels of their muskets and shining full upon their war-bronzed faces. They did not enter the galleries, dress circle, or boxes, which were soon filled with citizens, but were content to occupy only the place to which they had assigned themselves.

With open and undisguised wonder they stared at the surroundings, their naivete showing plainly to the amused observer that it was the first time they had ever been in a theatre.

It was a war play, full of stirring incidents and to the highest degree melodramatic. It was called "The Virginia Cavalier."

After a period of restless waiting the orchestra tuned up. The leader gave the signal and the music commenced. Slowly rose the curtain, disclosing to the enraptured gaze of the soldiers a lake upon whose rippling bosom floated a fairy-like craft. The moon was shining full upon the water, casting its mellow radiance upon a far lovelier maiden than tenderest dreams had ever pictured. Evidently she was keeping tryst, for she sat in the boat listening as intently as Ellen Douglas when she waited for the notes of Fitz James's bugle to break the sweet hour's stillness.

At last the lover comes, and as she steps on land to greet him is enfolded in his warm embrace. Here followed a love scene.

He is the Cavalier of the play and has come to bid her good-by before leaving for the war. Of course the parting was affecting; thrilling them to the depths of their hearts. Many a tear-drop glistened and rolled down upon the rough faces.

It was all real to these soldiers, and as the play unfolded itself they sat like fixed statues, hardly daring to breathe while they followed the fortunes of the Cavalier.

In the last scene of the last act the groupings and the surroundings were perfect; the effect admirable. In the background was a line of breastworks, or rather rifle-pits, which looked as natural as though they had just been thrown up. Behind these parapets could be seen the half-concealed Yankee troops, their bayonets bristling like a forest of spears. The Stars and Stripes (that banner which these veterans had only seen at intervals during the last two years, in the rifts of battle-smoke) drooped from its staff, breathing defiance in its every listless fold and recalling many a frightful scene.

In front of the works, pacing up and down upon his beat, was a Dutch soldier, evidently from Vaterland and just mustered in. He was apparently intensely proud of his brand new blue uniform with its bright buttons, and strutted loftily along with his head held high in the air, carrying his musket in a peculiarly awkward manner, and wishing in his heart that his dear Gretchen and his little brother Hans could be there to see how fine he was, and how splendidly he was doing it, and how all the people were admiring him.

Yes, he was doing his part well, being simply himself, the veritable Dutch recruit, with every detail of his dress and manner perfect, standing as we had often seen many of them stand the long hours through when as prisoners they had mounted guard over us.

In the distance the scenery represented the camp with its white tents and its troops drilling. On each side of the breastworks was pitched a small shelter-tent fronting the audience, within which were several soldiers, smoking, yawning and playing cards, their accoutrements hanging up, and the camp kettle actually boiling on the fire. Even the old theatre habitues applauded heartily the faithful rendition, and every soldier present recognized the marvelous exactness of the scene. What must then have been the effect upon those matter-of-fact, unsophisticated fellows, who had followed the plot with their hearts in their eyes and their souls in their ears.

When this familiar picture rose before them they sniffed the battle from afar, their nostrils dilating, their eyes gleaming with excitement, and each hand unconsciously clutching its musket with a firmer grip.

The play went on; the guards were retired and proceeded to cook their breakfast. From the camp kettle there rose the grateful odor of boiling coffee; the crackers were toasted by the coals, and the pieces of bacon stuck on the end of bayonets sizzled and fired in the flames. After they had all "squenched" their hunger, as the "Marchioness" expressed it, they lounged at ease, and filling their pipes commenced smoking while they discussed the war in stage whispers; the Dutchman narrating in his dialect, amid peals of laughter, his peculiar ideas of military affairs.

So the play advanced preparatory to its culmination in a grand *mise en scene*. Unexpectedly came the whip-like crack of a rifle; then another and another in rapid succession. The guards seized their guns and sprang to their feet. The officers in hoarse, quick tones ordered the men to come inside the works; and they scrambled in fast enough. Again was heard the skirmish fire; and next appeared three or four videttes, who vanished from sight within the fort.

The Arkansas troops and the Texans rose mechanically to their feet, and never took their gaze from the picture formed by the green baize.

They were on the battle-field once more. At Gaines' Mill, before Fort Reliance; they were waiting for Hood to give the word to the Forlorn Hope to advance; they were standing again in the hot summer evening at the foot of the hill by the Chinn House in the Second Manassas, gazing on the guns, which, loaded to the muzzle, were pointing at their hearts; they had forgotten that this was but mimic warfare, and they were standing again as they had stood before, waiting for the signal to storm the works.

In the distance could be seen on this immense, roomy stage the form of a Rebel scout, who crawled flat upon the ground to reconnoitre the place. Then he retired and came back with several sharp-shooters, who commenced to fire upon the fort.

Hood's men began to get restless; low murmurs were heard, and their eyes were beginning to blaze with unsuppressed excitement and passion.

Then came the Rebel storming column; they stopped, were dressed in a line and then fixed bayonets. The Southern Cross was flaunting proudly in the air, and the supreme moment had arrived.

From the fort no sign was made except the steady, watchful gleam of the row of eyes and the sullen menace of the grim black guns. Suddenly a report was heard and something like a shell burst over the works. It was so unexpected that a nervous scream or two issued from feminine lips. The faces of the soldiers in the pit became fixed.

The Rebel stormers were ordered to charge, and they sprang to their task. A rattling volley met them; some fell, but they reached the fort. The guns exploded every second, the line staggered, they reeled and fell back. Through the smoke could be seen the Union flag still floating.

The Rebels rallied; they reached the entrenchment and climbed the parapet. A hand-to-hand fight ensued; cold steel clashed with cold steel; the blue and the gray were mingled in a frenzied combat. The whole scene was made lurid by the sul-

22

phurous, ghastly glare of the burning chemicals, and the amber-colored smoke rolled in clouds to the roof.

The struggle continued, and according to the programme the Rebels were driven back for the second time.

Yes, they were beaten back, and many had fallen in the contest. The Texans could stand it no longer; the blood was rushing through their veins with the old war-fever, with all the savage instincts of battle aroused. There was the foe, shouting in exultation; there waved the flag which every man of them had charged over and over again; there they were, falling back, their comrades in gray.

"Up, men, and at them!" cried Wellington at Waterloo. "Drive 'em, boys!" sang out a tall, gaunt Arkansan.

The old wild yell burst from scores of lips. They charged the works!

Over benches, up the aisles toward the stage they surged like a raging torrent, carrying everything before them.

The orchestra dived through the subterranean doors, disappearing like so many rats. Women were shrieking and fainting, men grew pale and speechless as the Rebel soldiers, with their guns at a charge, began to climb the stage, yelling like so many demons.

It was a part of the performance not laid down in the bills.

Fortunately, very fortunately, there were stringent orders against carrying loaded guns in the streets of the city, or the play might have turned into a real tragedy. Just as the foremost had reached the stage the lights went out and Cimmerian darkness fell upon the lately brilliant house.

A calm, clear voice was heard begging the soldiers to take their seats. In a flash the gas jets were blazing out again.

The sudden reaction among the men was laughable. Crestfallen and ashamed, now that their enthusiasm had died away, they returned to their places.

The manager, D'Orsay Ogden, then appeared before the foot-lights, and in a neat little speech said that in the whole course of his theatrical experience he had never received so high a compliment; that he considered it a tribute to the mounting of the piece, unparalleled in the history of the stage.

The next night the division bivouacked at Chester, a place half way between Richmond and Petersburg. It had turned suddenly cold and by evening the thermometer was in the neighborhood of zero.

Worn out by the march, our men soon finished their supper and turned in for the night, sleeping in couples or in quartettes so as to obtain all the warmth from a partnership in cover. A soldier learns the art of sleeping comfortably on the ground on a cold night only by long practice; it is as much a matter of education as the manual of arms. He has to acquire the art of sleeping with his head under the blanket all the time; he has to be master of the craft of slumbering steadily on, spoon-fashion, with two or a dozen men, not moving unless they move, and turning when all turn. He must lie on his side, for under a blanket of limited dimensions four men, to obtain the benefit of its warmth, must occupy the smallest space possible. The middle men, like the pigs in the center, were always kept warm, for there was not the slightest danger in the world of their missing the covering by a slide, a hitch or a surreptitious pull, when there was a man to preserve the balance on either side, and fight for it if need be. Lots were drawn for those positions always.

That evening, because the weather was so intensely cold, the men generally doubled or stretched out into sets of spoons, and every stitch was made available. During the night a heavy snow-storm silently fell, and covered the sleeping host to a depth of fully eight inches with its light, fleecy mantle. Not a man had roused while gentle Nature, with a pitying love for her children, had placed blanket, sheet and robe over each recumbent figure, lightly and tenderly as a mother's hand would wrap her sleeping infant; flake by flake, noiselessly enfolding them from the biting cold, and letting them dream on.

In the morning Pickett's division was nowhere to be seen; naught was there to meet the eye of dawning day but a wide expanse of snow, rising and falling in regular hillocks like the billows of the sea or like snow-covered graves in the churchyard.

A hostile army might have defiled within pistol-shot of the place and never suspected but that those mounds of snow were the last resting places of the departed.

At last the oppressive and unusual heat awoke an officer; he shook loose the snow, sat up, rubbed his eyes, looked again and half rose. Where was he? Another look and another rub of the eyes and then he understood that each motionless wave was sentient with life, and in a trice, like the dragon teeth sown by Cadmus, would rise ready for the fray.

He stood up, prepared to enjoy the coming scene. Just then a head popped out with the suddenness of a Jack-in-the-box, and with a bewildered countenance looked around; another, another, and yet another; then by tens and by hundreds the "whited sepulchers" were burst asunder, and the sleepers arose, impetuously dashing the snow from eyes, face and body, and looking as wildly around as if their disembodied spirits had come to take up quarters once more in the same old tabernacles of flesh and blood.

Those who looked on said that they will never see such another sight till the dawning of the resurrection morn, the Dies Iraes when the trump shall sound and the graves shall give up their dead.

CHAPTER XXXVII.

THE BIVOUAC AT PETERSBURG.

About three miles from Petersburg the division halted in the midst of a huge pine forest, where the land was low, sobby and wet. Surely a worse situation could not have been found outside of the Dismal Swamp. The wood was green pine, and everybody knows what a trial that is to patience and a sweet temper. The bark burns, 'tis true, but says to the fire, "so far, and no farther shalt thou go." Our only way then to circumvent such obstinacy was to cut down a colossal monarch of the woods, whose circumference measured several feet, and keep a fire against it until the heart caught, and then, as with human beings, you might bask in its fervid glow; otherwise a green fire is worse than a balky horse, a scolding wife or a smoky chimney.

On the second day of our camp in the woods, without tents or shelter of any kind, there came such a snow-storm as rarely visited those latitudes; a steady snow, that without intermission for two days and nights covered the road two feet deep on a level. The sufferings of the men can hardly be imagined. Almost impossible to start a fire as it was (the cold intense from want of shelter), the men slept days and nights coiled up in their blankets. Rations, too, were far from sufficient; no coffee had been issued to the troops for a long time; but with a strange perversity, or rather mockery, large rations of sugar were given out. Not wishing to lose so much of the sweetness of life where we were in need of as much as we could get, we invented a new dish consisting of brown sugar and snow. Large quantities of this grub were consumed without the consciousness of any comfortable sense of fulness, but the heat of our bodies was more equably diffused thereby, the inside being kept about the same temperature as the outside.

For half a month we managed to exist; three-fourths of the time without fire, camping in a place which was literally under water during the thaw, our feet always wet. Cold and hungry, we passed as dismal days as were ever dragged out by a Siberian exile. Amid all this desolation of mud, what had we to fall back upon for consolation? Our very spiritual comfort was wanting, for any minister who might have been disposed to preach to such water rats would have been obliged to climb a tree.

But there was one gleam of sunshine that came to us amid all this shade, and left a smiling memory; one light spot amid so much which was cheerless, and that was a keg of Widow Malone's whiskey.

We called him "the Widow Malone" because he bore the same name as General Dashwood's aunt, who sang the famous song at the Embassador's ball. He was a private in Company A and hailed from the old North State; a bon comrade and a gallant soldier.

The widow was a jocund fellow; and shared generously with the company all he had. If the prayers of the ungodly availed anything, his father would have been saved without repentance. There were turkeys which looked so fair it was almost a sin to eat them; ducks from Currituck, so sweet that we would devour bones and all; chickens so tender that they had not come to years of discretion; pigs that would tempt a Jew to fall from grace; hams which had been cured by hickory smoke, and boiled in the same pot with Esau's porridge; a haunch of mutton so juicy that we squared all accounts with his fathers and forefathers for furnishing hides of which to make drum heads; the whitest of bread, the nicest of preserves and pickles, besides many other viands and delicacies prepared by loving care and willing hands, all calculated to make glad our waste places.

There they were all set before us; is it any wonder that Company A wished they had two stomachs each, like a camel?

The men were very hungry, remember, and as blue as indigo and as woe-be-gone as the wicked on a lone isle. It is not strange, therefore, that they charged that keg like a battery. The most abstemious were reckless and the old battered tin cups were replenished again and again; even John Zimmerman, the one good man in Zion, spliced the main-brace the first time for twenty years. Every drop was as precious to those wet, shivering soldiers as the ambrosia which the divine Ganymede handed to the immortal Jupiter.

We drank the widow's health in deep potations; then his illustrious father's, whose devotion to his son touched us deeply. In fact, we drank to the widow's whole family, past, present and forthcoming, yes, even unto the third and fourth generations.

In the midst of the revel the drum beat for dress parade.

"Fall in, boys!" cried Sergeant Saunders, and it was in truth a "fall in." Company A meandered to its stacked muskets and formed a zig-zag.

"Right dress!" said Corporal Stickly, spreading his legs far apart and sticking his bayonet in the ground, looking the while like a gigantic tripod. The men were holding on to each other and getting that strength and mutual support which a line of bricks have, propped up one against another.

"Forward, march!" cried Captain Billy Smith, running plumb against a tree.

"Steady, boys," and it was good advice but unheeded. Down he fell headlong, but being picked up by some who tumbled around him a few times before they succeeded, he walked off, trying to look preternaturally dignified.

Away they all staggered, rickety and uncertain in every limb, to take their places on the right of the regiment, which was drawn up in a line on a simple inspection of the dress parade.

The rest of the regiment gazed in wonder, for not a man of this festive company could stand steadily, and when the whole line went through the manual of arms, Company A's performance discounted a Georgia militia muster, or even the acrobatic feats of the clown in the circus. It must be confessed that every mother's son of them was tight as a brick and saw a dozen different objects at once. The colonel, standing some forty paces off, was magnified into several colonels; the earth and the sky were in a ceaseless spin, and the ground shook as with an earthquake. Who could have been expected to maintain a perpendicular with all nature behaving in this unseemly manner?

The regiment was in a broad grin; officers, with twitching features, vainly endeavored to silence the laughter. One glance to the right was enough to upset the gravity of the most solemn patriot there.

Why, just see that man raising his foot as if he were going up a pair of stairs and then coming down with a bang. Look how they lurch, as if they were at sea in a high storm with the vessel rocking from side to side. Watch that fellow pick himself up! What superhuman efforts they are making to impress the fact that they are as sober as judges. Evidently they are thinking every man of them is drunk but himself. What a variety of expressions their faces wear, from the simpering smile and broad expanse of grin, straight through to the funereal.

The climax was reached, however, in the last formula of the evolution, when all the company officers, in full dress, met in the center of the regiment directly in front of the colors, and marching to where the colonel stood, saluted him. The officers of Company A were in the same plight as the privates; but they felt they would be satisfied if they accomplished that walk without disgrace.

Summing up all their will, their pride, their strength, they essayed the regulation step with every eye of the command upon them. The sword belt of one of Company A's lieutenants had slipped below the waist, and with every step he took the sword was banging on the ground; it got entangled between his legs and tripped him up. He stumbled, recovered, lurched forward, then fell to the ground.

This was too much for discipline and a smothered roar burst from the men. Lieutenant Addison and the rest of the company's officers were sandwiched among the balance of the rank, and by their aid, one on each side, their tottering feet were guided right. Then the regiment broke and the men made their way back to camp.

"But for the number," said the colonel, "I would have put them under arrest; but it would have been an unheard of thing to clap a whole company in the guard-house, officers anl all."

Afterwards we came to the conclusion that of all the liquors in the world, of all brews ever distilled, that of pure, unadulterated North Carolina apple-jack was the strongest, most foot-tripping, head-turning, and most demoralizing generally, and the most insinuating.

The exposure, the constant dampness of feet and clothes, the continued eating of sugar and snow soon began to tell upon the health of the men. Colds, throat and lung diseases, inflammation of the stomach were very prevalent, and when later on in March the division fell into line of march to Suffolk, many of us had to be sent to the hospital in Petersburg.

Very sadly the sick beheld their comrades file down the road and disappear. Lonely and desolate enough we felt when the rough-looking ambulances started on their way to sick quarters.

As for myself, what with the racking pain, increased by the jolting of the ambulance until it became intolerable agony, I fainted and was taken out as one dead.

CHAPTER XXXVIII.

IN THE HOSPITAL.

The "Confederate Hospital," as it was called, was an immense tobacco warehouse in Petersburg, which had been temporarily assigned to the use of the wounded and sick. There were two wards, one on the ground floor and the other above; each consisted of a vast room with narrow beds ranged in long, parallel rows about two feet apart, and each ward about six rows, or several hundred cots. The beds were only coarse cotton bags filled with shucks, with the adjuncts of a small pillow and one blanket. Sheets, coverlets or bolsters there were none, our Government being in far too straitened circumstances to offer any but the barest necessities. The luxuries generally found in hospitals were for richer treasuries than ours.

Our medical staff was trained and of the finest material, composed of men whose hearts were in their work, and who performed their duty with a devotion that could not have been surpassed. They were fearfully hampered by the want of proper medicines and were obliged sometimes to fall back upon the simple herbs and whatever materia medica our own country might afford. Quinine was especially wanted and could always command fabulous prices when brought into our lines for sale by the regular blockade runners. The United States Government displayed the utmost vigilance in suppressing the traffic, even though their own soldiers suffered in our prisons for the want of it. The large percentage to be made by its importation proved too great a temptation to the money-loving and money-getting on both sides, hence it was apt to find its way over in greater or lesser quantities in a hundred different methods of which the Federal authorities never dreamed. Women brought it rolled up in their hair; it was sewed in the hems of their dresses; the trunks that came with regular passes by way of Fortress Monroe had false bottoms which the soldiers who tumbled out their contents never suspected; men carried it in the soles of their shoes. The need, however, was far above the supply, and its want was sadly felt.

Chloroform was also in great demand. Many ill-fated soldiers were obliged to undergo amputation without any narcotic whatever, sustaining in keenest nervous sensitiveness the tortures of the knife and the horrible agony of the saw.   Thus were the horrors of war doubly aggravated to the South, against which the ports of the world were closed even in so merciful a matter as that of medicines.   It would seem that when the unfortunates were brought to such extremity, when human nerves were put to such rack as this, for the sake of the humanity which we all shared, hatred and malice might have well afforded to lay down weapons of warfare.

John Randolph of Roanoke, a bitter, cynical man, one whose hand was against every man and every man's against him, was once heard to say of a stricken foe, "When God lays his hand upon a man then I take mine off."   So great a nation as the United States might well have extended a like generosity in this one instance of chloroform, without any fear that the great Rebellion would have lasted thereby one day longer.   The refusal of a few in authority to grant so slight a boon, not slight to the agonized dying, and the vigilance lest it should find its way to our hospitals would not have been endorsed by the Northern people at large.

The doctors made their rounds every morning and evening, the seriously ill and badly wounded of course receiving more attention; but as regularly as the day rolled around would come those two examinations by the assistant doctors, while the chief surgeon went through the hospital and inspected the graver cases.   His office was in the building, where he was ready day and night to attend with his advice and assistance all who might need either.   Among the hundreds of patients his time was fully employed.

The rations for the sick were but little better than the fare other soldiers were receiving—hardtack and fat pork, with rye coffee.   The want of delicacies in the hospitals was marked; but for the unremitting, kindly attention of the women in Petersburg, whose fervor never flagged during the whole war, whose hearts were "open as day for melting charity," the admittance would have been tantamount to an order on the sexton for a grave, or a civil request in behalf of the patient for a coffin from the obliging undertaker.   It was their fair hands which brought and administered the luxuries which the enfeebled patient demanded, and which the Confederate Government could not supply.

Nearly every lady in the city visited the hospital more or less frequently, always carrying radiant sunlight into the murky gloom of the place, dispelling the homesickness, the hopelessness—the despair to which the sick are but too prone to yield when helpless among strangers. They always chose the most dangerously ill to carry to their homes, where the delicacies so much needed, and constant attention, would tell in the close encounter between life and death. Thus hundreds who turned from the smell of fat bacon, whose appetites were all unequal to the hard biscuits, and who were daily growing weaker and more emaciated,—who were fast sinking into an apathy which death only would end,—were saved from being swept into untimely graves, and brought back to life from the very Valley of the Shadow of Death.

We had no Sanitary Commission in the South; no great and good organization to lighten the cares of the sick, to pour oil on the wounds, and bring comfort to the bedside of the distressed and dying. We were too poor; we had no line of rich and populous cities closely connected by rail, all combined in the good work of collecting and forwarding supplies and maintaining costly and thoroughly equipped charities. With us every house was a hospital; every latch hung outside the door, and the dirtiest gray-jacket was taken by the hand and the last crust shared with him.

We had sad enough scenes of suffering in these hospitals, for all were alike everywhere; an epic poem of sombre coloring in every wan, pallid face, in every wasted form; an unwritten sermon on the uncertainty of life in the covered figures that lay as motionless as if the ward were a mausoleum. Mental pain and physical agony mingled their groans; while the three terrible sisters whom De Quincy has shown to us in the weird, spectral light of his impassioned fancy sat by the bedside of each soldier.

The day could be spent pleasantly enough, for there was the doctor's call, and the visitors, which always had a brightening effect. Then there was the sunshine pouring through the window; the songs of birds in the cages near; the sound of the bustle of city life which fell pleasantly upon the ear; the reading of books and newspapers (if patients were convalescent), the chance dropping in of comrades bringing in all the gossip of the camp; and above all, letters from home. These all tended to lighten the weary hours and relieve the monotony of otherwise lagging time.

There were many sick who had no mental resources to fall back upon, who could read neither books nor papers, who had no friends to come to them, who, being obscure and illiterate, did not receive the same attention, although they were not altogether slighted. So they lay in their cots with staring eyes, brooding over their helpless condition, sinking without an effort to rally, and filling, as a class, a majority of the graves.

Then many, very many, of the sick died in the hospitals simply from nostolgia or homesickness. A soldier from the far South would be brought in with a wound or a long, lingering camp-fever, which seemed to require only time to insure certain restoration to health; but as the days passed with no familiar face by his cot, one might observe, if he were an habitue of the ward, that his features grew paler and thinner, his looks more weary and listless, until some morning one might stop by his side and notice that the pallor of death—one can never mistake it—was upon his brow, and his breath coming in gasps from his livid lips. Then you could watch him dying (as I have done a score of times), and if charitably inclined wipe the gathering dampness from his brow or fan him until all was over and the suffering soul released. The simple truth of the matter was, the poor soldier had grown hopeless and despairing. He had lost all control over himself and would cry like a child; and then, not having been roused from this fatal, nervous apathy and weakness, the downward path into the grave had been too sure, dying because he had not nervous force enough to hold on to the attenuated thread of life.

So passed the days, dragging their slow length along to all and bringing the end of all things to some. It was the long nights which came as a terror to every man that lay beneath the roof of the hospital; it was to me as a hideous dream. The vast room, with the narrow beds side by side, became like the dim caverns of the Catacombs, where, instead of the dead in their final rest, there were extended wasted figures burning with fever and raving from the agony of splintered bones, tossing restlessly from side to side, with every ill, it seemed, which human flesh was heir to.

From the rafters the flickering oil lamp swung mournfully, casting a ghastly light upon the scene beneath, but half-dispelling the darkness, bringing out dim shadows everywhere and rendering the gloom only more spectral. Up and down the aisles moved the nurses with muffled footfalls, looking to the eye of the fevered patient like the satellites of the Venetian Doges gliding through the torture chamber. The sickening odor of medicine, the nephritic air shut in by the closed windows, rendered the atmosphere heavy and unwholesome. The groans heard at intervals, the wanderings of delirium, the occasional querulous demands of the sick to the servitors, the shriek of agony as a broken limb would by a rough touch or careless movement be jarred, all combined and coming ceaselessly from so many lips among the hundreds lying there, made sleep or quiet rest impossible except to the strong or those under the influence of anodynes.

The first glimmer of dawn coming stealing through the windows, rendering more dim the hanging lamp, was welcomed with as much joy as that with which the Brahman hails the rising of the Sun God.

Early every morning the wards were inspected by the assistant surgeon, who passed rapidly along the rows of beds, giving a quick glance at each. He neither stopped nor listened at such a time to complaints or entreaties, while his black vassals kept at his heels. His mission is a mystery to a new patient, but if he watches he will see the doctor suddenly stop, approach a form lying in bed, feel his pulse, his brow, his heart, and then speak a few rapid words to the servants with him. They take in their strong arms the stiffened figure whose eyes shall no more watch longingly for the coming of the day, and bear him out, while the surgeon, going to the headboard, copies in his note-book from the card the name, company and regiment of the deceased.

In the morning paper, under the heading of "Died in the Hospital," there is a name and that is all; all of the life which surged out to the great ocean of Eternity. Alone in the darkness of the night, with no friend to catch the last fond, lingering look or close the dying eyes; the last of a life with all its hopes, its fears, its loves, its duties. Who stops to ask a question about him? Who seems to care? It makes as much stir, this death, as a pebble cast in the stream; a slight bubble on the surface and no more; in the meantime the servant has turned over the shuck mattress, given the blanket a shake, beaten the pillow, and taken down the card; then the bed is ready for another occupant, who may be placed thereon fifteen minutes after. This was a common occurrence. Is it any wonder that men grew callous and fearless, when death was all around them?

We read of the ravages of the plague in India, and through burning verse which thrills us we follow English soldiers in their banquet song. Breathing the tainted air, they know they must soon be stricken, so they fill high their brimming glasses, and with resonant voice chant the awful chorus:

"Stand to your glasses ready,
    Drink to your fair lady's eyes;
Here's to the dead already,
    Here's to the next man who dies!"

More unconcerned, more regardless of death is the hospital patient; for oft-times he sits up in his cot chewing contentedly his hardtack and drinking his coffee, while the soldier who rests next to him, and whom he has learned to know, is dragged off to his final resting place. It makes no impression on him; he eats not a mouthful less, nor drinks a spoonful more. The King of Terrors has appeared so often before him and lingered so long that he has lost that "majesty that doth hedge a king;" and so the soldier looks upon him without the twitching of a nerve or the hurried beating of the heart.

Southern hospitals during the two latter years of the war were quite different from what they were at first, when their proper organization had hardly been effected. First and last they would have borne the same comparison that the crude material of the militia does to the well-drilled and perfected army. Large and airy buildings were set apart and converted into permanent hospitals wherein the best arrangements were made for both sick and wounded. Systematized regulations and order reigned in every department from the kitchen up. Instead of the indiscriminate visiting and nursing of the charitably disposed, which, no matter how much needed at first and how helpful, was in some cases more injurious than otherwise, regular nurses were permanently appointed at stated salaries with certain defined duties. These appointments were made from the best and highest ladies in the land, the most refined and delicate, who with tenderness and Christian charity took the place of professional nurses, superintended the linen department and saw that the food was properly and nicely served. The gentleness, the patience, the loving sacrifice of those women no words can describe. They served with a self-abnegation which never faltered (for the pay was a mere pittance and never could enter as a motive) throughout the long days of summer, and the longer nights of winter found them unwearied watchers by the sick and dying.

And so the days passed, bringing in the sick and wounded in a steady stream.

The convalescent, without a smile for many weeks on their pale faces, were assisted out with a furlough in their pockets, into the waiting ambulances, which drove them gently to the depot.

There, though every seat be filled by the reckless soldiery, yet when the cry goes out, "Make way for sick soldiers," the words are as potent as the warning note of the Sultan's crier in Bagdad; for the crowd opens a passage and they are helped to the best seats in the car; and the mightiest soldier will sit beside him and do his will.

The statistics of the Confederate States show that many more died in the hospitals than were killed on the field of battle.

Through the unremitting care of Miss Fannie Bannister, of Petersburg, a veritable angel, and Mrs. Judge Joynes, of the same city, I rallied from an attack of inflammation of the stomach which dragged me to the very pit of the grave, and then, reduced in weight but happy at heart, was sent to Richmond among my friends, with an indefinite leave on a sick furlough.

CHAPTER XXXIX.

CHANCELLORSVILLE.

As long as the South remains a people and cherishes her traditions, the name of Chancellorsville will ever be a word of sorrow, a sound of woe; for it was there that she lost the soldier whose star never paled, the man of the times, the one who had always plucked the flower of success from the nettle of defeat.

Who but Jackson could have surprised the great Army of the Potomac in broad day; who but Jackson could have kept his troops together in that tangled wilderness?

Who but Jackson could have inspired the gray infantry with the firm belief that their general was invincible?

And there lives not a Southerner who does not believe that had Stonewall Jackson lived, Appomattox would have been a word with no bitter memories. America would doubtless have been one country, as destiny determined it should be—but the shame of defeat, the horrors of reconstruction would have been spared the South.

Before General Hooker had reorganized his army and matured his plans he had many a doubt about his ultimate success. In a report made April 21, '63, he says:

"You must be patient with me—I must play with these devils before I can spring. Remember that my army is at the bottom of the well and the enemy holds the top." (Reb. Records, Vol. 25, p. 241.)

But his mind changed and a wild elation took the place of despondency. One week after this dispatch he held a grand review of the Army of the Potomac and beheld that mighty host in all of its pride, strength and power; he felt as certain of success as a man could be in this world. The ranks were full, the men in perfect condition, and the officers brimful of enthusiasm. Victory was in the air. His disposition was to make a flank movement and cross the Rappahannock at United Mine Ford, and once over the river he felt the battle was won. Colonel Galbraith, of his staff, told me years later that on the evening before the advance, General Hooker and several general officers were examining a map of the Wilderness, and Hooker, placing his finger on the spot marked

Chancellorsville, said: "Gentlemen, if I can plant my army there, God Almighty can't drive me out."

So he issued this congratulatory order to his troops:

"Gen. Orders, No. 47.   H'd Q'r's Army of Potomac,
"Camp near Falmouth,
"April 30, 1863.

"It is with heartfelt satisfaction the commanding general announces to the army that the operations of the last three days have determined that the enemy must either ingloriously fly, or come out from behind his defenses and give us battle on our own ground, where *certain* destruction awaits *him*.

"By command of Major General Hooker." (Reb. Records, Vol. 25, p. 171.)

Three days later, after placing his army at Chancellorsville (in the tavern of that spot he was wounded), fighting the battle and recrossing the river, he issued this order:

"General Orders, No. 49.
"Camp near Falmouth, Va., May 6, 1863.

"The Major-General commanding tenders the army his congratulations on its achievements of the last seven days. If it has not accomplished all that was expected, the reasons were of a character not to be foreseen or prevented by human sagacity or resource.

"By our celerity and secrecy of movement our advance and passage of the river was undisputed, and on our withdrawal not a Rebel ventured to follow.

"The events of last week may swell with pride the heart of every officer and soldier in this army." (Reb. Records, Vol. 25, p. 171.)

If the hearts of the soldiers swelled with pride over their achievements it was more than the Northern people did. Instead their hearts were filled with sorrow, anger and bitterness. They had hoped for so very much and gotten so little. To cross a river and return cost him 13,000 men. Lee's congratulatory order was read in the North, and then General Hooker was forced to step down and out.

"General Orders, No. 59.
"Head Quarters Army of Northern Virginia,
"May 7, 1863.

"With heartfelt gratification the General commanding expresses
23

to the army his sense of the heroic conduct displayed by officers and men.

"Under trying vicissitudes of heat and storm you attacked the enemy strongly entrenched in the depths of a tangled wilderness, and by the valor that has triumphed in so many fields forced him once more to seek safety beyond the Rappahannock.

"We are especially called upon to return our grateful thanks to the only Giver of Victory for his signal deliverance.
                                        "R. E. LEE,
                              "Commanding General."

In the opening days of May, 1863, when the buds were bursting into blossoms and the daisies were sprinkling the green fields of Virginia with drops of white, the blue gamecock of the North and the red one of the South, gaffed, spurred and trimmed, stood defiantly eyeing each other, ready, willing and anxious to try conclusions once more.

To a "Looker on in Vienna" the chances were all in Hooker's favor. He justly described his command as the "finest army on the planet," the esprit de corps was high and one hundred and twenty thousand men stood ready to follow him to the death; and he, brave, dashing, impetuous, was a fit leader for such men.

Hooker had two important factors in his favor; first, his superiority in numbers; second, the absence of Lee's left arm, for Longstreet was with his division in North Carolina. And just here it may be said that such an error in grand strategy like to have cost the South dear, for it deprived Lee in a critical period of the game of his trusted lieutenant, when Sedgwick with 20,000 men came rushing on his flank at Salem Church, and forced Lee to change all carefully laid plans for the defeat of Hooker.

Hooker was undoubtedly a well-trained soldier and able tactician, and his plan to interpose his army between Lee and Richmond was a fascinating one; but he made the fatal mistake of not knowing the topography of the country. He chose for his battle-ground a section which neutralized the superiority of his artillery, for in weight, in numbers and in metal his guns overmatched those of his adversary. Lee was aware of the false move, for his scout service was the finest in the world; but he did nothing to check it, for he was only too glad to let Hooker lose himself in the tangled labyrinth of the Wilderness.

Federal General Warren, describing the Chancellorsville section, said:

"A proper understanding of the country will help to relieve the Americans from the charge so frequently made at home and abroad of want of generalship, of handling troops in battles, battles that have to be fought out hand-to-hand in forests where *artillery and cavalry* could play no part, where the troops could not be seen by the officers controlling their movements, where the echoes of the sound from tree to tree were enough to appall the strongest hearts engaged, and yet the noise would hardly be heard beyond the immediate scene of strife. Thus the generals on either side, shut out from sight and hearing, had to trust to the unyielding bravery of their own men.

"Who shall wonder that such battles often terminated from the mutual exhaustion of both contending forces? But rather that in all these struggles of Americans against Americans, no panic on either side gave the victory to the other like that which the French under Moreau gained over the Austrians in the Black Forest." (Reb. Records, Vol. 25, p. 193.)

The truest criticism of General Hooker's campaign was made by his second in command, Major-General Crouch. He says:

"In looking for the causes of the loss of Chancellorsville, the primary ones were that Hooker expected Lee to fall back without risking battle. Finding himself mistaken, he assumed the defensive and was outgeneraled, and he became demoralized by the superior tactical boldness of the enemy." ("Battles and Leaders," Vol. 3, p. 171.)

General Howard, commanding the ill-fated Eleventh Corps, said that the cause of disaster was, "though constantly threatened and apprised of the moving of the enemy, yet the woods were so dense that the foe was able to mass a large force, whose exact whereabouts neither my patrols, reconnaissance, nor scouts could ascertain." (Reb. Records, Vol. 25, p. 630.)

When the scouts brought General Lee the news that preparations were being made by Hooker to cross the Rappahannock the first step that Lee took was a peremptory order to Longstreet to rejoin him at once. Lee had only two courses to pursue: one was to make a hurried retreat, and choosing some strong defensive position, entrench, and delay the enemy until Longstreet reinforced him. This was the safest course, and no leader but a master in the art of war would have set at naught all the rules of military tactics and divided his army, numerically inferior to the enemy, leaving his center open and undefended save by a strong skirmish line. But Lee took the same chances that he did in the Manassas campaign.

General Gordon, in his book, states that it was Jackson's proposal to flank Hooker, and in the famous conference in the woods, when he and General Lee sat on a couple of cracker-boxes, and Jackson formulated his views, it is a historical fact that General Lee agreed to his lieutenant's plan of campaign then and there without a single modification.

In the attack Stonewall Jackson formed his men in three lines, Rodes in front, Trimble's division under General Colston in the second, and A. P. Hill in the third line. The orders were clear and explicit, each brigade commander received positive instructions which were well understood; the whole line was to push forward from the beginning, keeping the road for their guide. Under no circumstances was there to be any pause in the advance.

At 5.15 P. M. the word was given to move forward, the line of sharpshooters being 400 yards in the advance. "So complete," says Rodes, "was the success of the whole manoeuvre, and so great was the surprise of the enemy, that scarcely any organized resistance was met with after the first volley was fired. They fled in the wildest confusion, leaving the field strewn with arms, accoutrements, clothing, caissons and field pieces in every direction. The Rebel advance moved steadily; the front lines firing and loading as they marched, while the rear came to the front, fired and loaded as the march continued."

Colonel Lee, commanding the Fifth-fifth Ohio, says: "The attack by Jackson was evidently a surprise, and my battalion was held in a useless position under a murderous fire, and the immense mass of fugitives passing by and through it conspired to dishearten and scatter the men so as to prevent any further stand to be made."

General Carl Schurz gives his testimony to the same effect. "It was," he says, "an utter impossibility to establish a front; the whole line deployed on the old turnpike facing south was rolled up and swept away in a moment. The Rebels were formed in columns by divisions; his skirmishers throwing themselves into the intervals whenever their advance was checked. They had at least three lines deep, the intervals between the lines being very short, the whole presenting a heavy, solid mass."

Jackson struck the Eleventh Corps just exactly at 5.30 P. M. and no troops in the world could have stood the onslaught. General Schurz says: "My division has been made responsible for the defeat of the Eleventh Corps, and the Eleventh Corps for the failure of the campaign. We have been overwhelmed by the army and the press with abuse and insult beyond measure." "We have borne as much as human nature can endure," says Colonel Schimmelfennig. "It would seem as if a nest of vipers but waited an auspicious moment to spit out their poisonous slanders upon this hitherto honored corps. The fortunes of war stationed the Eleventh Corps on the right of the line, and had Hooker placed his oldest and staunchest corps in their place, the result would have been the same."

Every soldier of any experience knows that the bravest command will go all to pieces when surprised, and the lions turn for a time into sheep. Just consider the situation: A peaceful summer evening, the troops exultant over the rumor that the enemy were in full retreat to Richmond, the men building their fires and getting their suppers ready, when suddenly, without a moment's warning, the camp is filled with hundreds of rabbits, squirrels, foxes, and dozens of deer—to say nothing of whirring quail, hawks, owls; and as startled eyes look into each other, like the stroke of the thunderbolt comes a deadly sweep of bullets, and then the Rebel yell from thousands of throats—a long line of gray figures suddenly emerging from the thickets, and their rifle barrels glinting in the rays of the declining sun. Run! why the Knights of the Round Table would have sprinted, and Leonidas and his Spartans would have caught up and passed the rabbits. Remember, too, that there was no place for the Yankees to make a stand until they reached Chancellorsville two and a half miles distant. It was every man for himself and the Devil to take the hindmost. Every soldier knows that it is almost impossible to rally troops on the run. At Brandy Station, a little later on, my regiment, the Fourth Virginia Cavalry, the crack command of Stuart's cavalry, were surprised by Gregg, and ran like sheep, and had all the fight taken out of them for that day.

It is very easy to criticise the shamefulness of a panic, but not if you have been a participant in one yourself.

Some one asked a Dutchman of Schurz's division what he ran for, and his answer was the answer of all: "What I skedaddle for? I runs because hell broke loose all around."

Colonel Harting, of the Seventh Pennsylvania, says: "At about 5.30 P. M. the regiments on our right were suddenly attacked— and they broke through our command. The first we ever knew of the enemy was that our men, when sitting on their knapsacks, were shot in the rear and flank. A surprise in broad daylight, a case not heard of in the history of any war; it was so complete that the men had not time to take their arms before they were thrown into the wildest confusion. Some guns of Dieckman's battery in front, without firing a single shot, broke through the whole mixed crowd, and we could do nothing but retreat through the woods." (Reb. Records, Vol. 25, p. 655.)

Had it been an open country, where the Yankee batteries could have taken position, they could have stayed the rout, but it was only in open spots that the guns could be placed. Captain Martin, of the Sixth New York Artillery, says: "My guns were served with great difficulty owing to the way the cannoneers were interfered with in their duties. Carriages, wagons, horses without riders, and panic-stricken infantry came rushing through my battery, overturning guns and limbers, smashing my caissons, and tramping my horse-holders under them."

Another artilleryman says: "We would have to cut down the trees and clear away the underbrush before we could place the guns, and all this took precious time, and before we were ready the enemy would be before us."

On and still on; through the scrubby underbrush, matted with vines, with here and there deep gullies choked with tangled briers and fallen trees, where they had to slide down and climb up. On and still on; through bushy cedars and branching juniper, crisscrossed with wild runners as elastic as rubber and strong as wire, where the men had literally to force their way, tearing their clothes into ribbons. On, still on; till emerging breathless they reached some abandoned field growing up in their primeval wilds—here the lines would be re-aligned and in every clearing would be found some fresh regiment of the blue-coats with a battery or two just unlimbered, pouring shot and canister anywhere and everywhere; when the gray column would sweep forward, pause an instant, level their guns and a crackling noise of musketry would burst out; then, panting, gasping, they would plunge on again into the apparently impenetrable depths of the slashes. The skirmishers were soon mingled with the line of battle. None knew where they were going. Whole regiments became separated as they toiled and struggled through the twisted, tortuous undergrowth of bushes and saplings—the hustling of the shell, the song of the bullet flying over the hears made them forget their labors, and they headed intuitively to where the sound of the cannon was the heaviest. They had two and a half miles to go, and before half that distance had been traveled it grew dark in the bushes, but on, still on; wet with perspiration, scratched and in tatters, the gray line, as restless as fate, made their way toward the redoubts of Chancellorsville. What with forcing their way through the pathless wilderness, loading and firing, but never falling back, the commands had become all mixed up in inextricable confusion, but the genius of the men drove them onward. Jackson seemed inspired; he was galloping at full speed from one point to another, guided by the sounds of the battle. "Forward!" was his one command. His fiery ardor nerved his soldiers, exhausted as they were, to renewed efforts. In one instance a murderous fire from a battery swept through a briery meadow across which a North Carolina regiment was marching. The men cowered before the storm. Jackson rode forward and cried: "Follow me, your general will lead you." To one of Ransom's regiments, that stopped to breathe, he said: "Follow! No brave soldier will stop now."

I have heard scores of soldiers around their camp-fires tell of their last view of Jackson, of his stern, set mouth; his eyes, generally so calm and cold, now blazing with the light of victory. He issued his orders to his aides, short and sharp like pistol shots. A whole company of cavalry was attached to his staff as orderlies and he kept them all on the jump. One of them, Martin, told me that as he followed him in full tilt across a broom-sedge field he suddenly reined up before a group of three soldiers who were lying down, but busy loading and firing. Jackson asked them why they were not with their comrades in front. One raised himself up and said: "General, we can't, we are all three wounded." And he stuck his leg in the air, covered with blood. "Then," said Martin, "he told me to go back and get assistance, and he darted off and I never saw him again.

It was like madness for Jackson to go ahead of his picket line that night. He intended attacking Hooker at the earliest dawn, and was anxious to place A. P. Hill, who was in reserve, in front, and his own troops, mistaking him in the darkness, fired on him and that volley set the whole Yankee artillery to firing; and he received his death wound. It was one of the North Carolina regiments that fired the fatal volley.

Lieutenant-Colonel Oscar Heinrich, Chief Engineer of the Army, says: "The enemy soon opened with shot, shell, canister, grape and shrapnel. General Pender, who occupied a part of the front, became actively engaged. General Lane got scared, fired into our own men, and achieved the unenviable reputation of wounding severely Lieutenant-General Jackson and Major-General A. P. Hill.   If Jackson had lived, what would have been the result!"

The greatest praise came from his enemy, General Howard, who says:

"Stonewall Jackson was victorious.   Even his enemies praise him; but providentially for us, it was the last battle that he waged against the American Union.   For in bold planning, in energy of execution which he had the power to diffuse, in indefatigable activity and moral ascendency, Jackson stood head and shoulders above his confreres."

And Hancock, the superb, gives this tribute: "The Confederate Army could better have lost a corps of thirty thousand men, than Stonewall Jackson."

CHAPTER XL.

THE PILLAR OF THE CONFEDERACY FALLS.

Richmond was the Paradise of the convalescent. Several private hospitals were conducted by ladies, and if any soldier proved lucky enough to get into one of those, he considered himself the happiest man alive. He was nursed, petted, spoiled; he had the best books to read, the nicest fare, the softest of beds, and everything was done for his comfort; he breathed the sweet perfume of flowers, he saw the fairest of company and followed his own sweet will if well enough.

It was now early May, that dainty season of the year when Nature, bursting from the icy clasp of winter and the cold embrace of March, threw herself, beautiful with a thousand charms, into the arms of youthful summer. Richmond had never looked to greater advantage; the trees decked in the most vivid green, Capitol Square was in its brightest verdure.

One Sunday evening, May third, came glorious news to the Rebels, in a dispatch from General Lee, announcing that he had gained a great battle near Chancellorsville; and that he regretted the wounding of Jackson.

Of course the city was in a glow, but did not show its joy in demonstrations. There was no display, no triumphant strains of music, no burning bonfires or salvos of artillery; the people only drew a long sigh of relief, or flocked to their churches, whose bells tolled the summons.

On the street bright faces could be met at every step, and the people carried their hearts upon their sleeves. There was an unwritten language which helped from eye to eye of strangers even, as the ypassed each other, which told hom unrivaled was the exultation, and how the city had but one heart to throb out its deep rejoicing. The happy children appeared happier as they bounded along the streets; the birds seemed to sing more sweetly, the roses bloomed more richly, the air was purer and all nature smiled in glad accord.

Next day the ladies of Richmond, with their customary thoughtfulness, visited every merchant, seeking contributions of food, clothing, medicines and money for the wounded. A vast amount of stores was collected and sent off. The depot of Broad Street was filled at the coming of the trains, with long lines of ambulances ready to take the wounded to the several hospitals.

Thus a week passed, and when the sky was the color of iridescent opal, when the waters of the James rippled with music, while the flush of proud satisfaction still lingered on every face, while even the most timid and fearful were beginning to feel that final success was both assured and near, while the whole populace were ready to break out into the chant of praise, there came the startling news that fell upon the community like a thunderclap:

"Jackson is dead!"

From mouth to mouth passed the intelligence that calm, lovely Sunday afternoon; from street to street it spread until it wrapped the whole city in gloom. Men heard it and grew pale as they listened; shocked surprise was upon every face. He who told it and he who caught the import of the three short words gazed at each other in dumb amazement. Women were seen in the streets, all unmindful of the publicity, wringing their hands and weeping as bitterly as if one near and dear to their hearts had been taken. You see they loved him so!

"Jackson dead."

"No!" they said, fighting off the fact. "It could not be, it is a rumor brought by some alarmist. These mistakes often occur; half truths are so frequently exaggerated. No! Jackson could not be dead. He, the pride, the idol of the South, was not born to die until his mission had been accomplished. That which they had heard was folly! No one could be expected to believe it.

What? Stonewall! Our Stonewall dead! the man who had stood in the leaden hail at Manassas, and been therein baptized into his world-renowned name; who had moved unharmed where death had been thickest at Kernstown, at Port Republic, and Cross Keys; who had breasted the iron hail at Gaines' Mill; who had courted death at Sharpsburg and Bull Run. He dead? No, they could never believe it.

But still the wires brought but one answer. To the thousand inquiries which flashed back, the keys of the instrument returned only one reply; proclaimed but one sad, inflexible fact:

"Jackson is dead."

It was true.

Then it was given to us to see what passionate love this strangely reserved, retiring "Man of Destiny" had acquired over the thoughts of his people.

Grief, like a pall, settled over the city; men, women and little children, nay, the whole Confederacy bowed its head in deep tearful sorrow; a sorrow which came home to every heart in a throbbing pain, as if he had been one's dear flesh and blood. It was no use to reason over the matter, to ask why this should be so, why we thus grieved for a man whose face many had never seen, whose voice we had never heard. The pride and the love were there indisputably; and we could have given up all hope of our country's cause as easily as the life of Stonewall Jackson. Indeed, the two seemed identical, and the one was never after so bright when the other had passed away.

Next day, about three o'clock in the afternoon, every bell began to toll, and no one upon whose ears the mournful cadence fell but knew that all that was mortal of our loved leader had been brought to the city on the train. The day was at its sultriest; the rays of the sun had poured down remorselessly on the brick pavements all the morning, and the air was dry and hot. The heat was reflected from the walls of the houses, from the streets, from the tin roofs, from the shining surface of the river, and rose in quivering, spiral undulations. It was an hour when the thoroughfares were generally as deserted as a village church-yard; when window-shutters were tightly closed; when the city seemed to slumber until the going down of the sun; but this afternoon the effect of the tolling of those bells was marvelous. From every door poured the people, until dense crowds lined the streets. From the Broad Street depot down to Ninth Street, from thence to the Governor's house was a surging mass of humanity.

They took the coffin from the train and placed it in the hearse. At the sight the people who were gathered round broke into lamentations; men pulled their hats over their eyes; soldiers were not ashamed to wipe the fast-falling tears from their rough faces; women broke out in sobbing and the sorrow was universal. The hearse moved along slowly and with difficulty; the police tried to make way for the horses through the dense crowd which pressed so closely to the coffin. A poor woman running alongside wept all the way as she went; her dress betokened that she was of the lower ranks, and her long black hair had fallen about her, but she kept her place and would yield to none. Rich and poor, high and low, learned and ignorant, old and young, it made no difference then.

When the cortege arrived at the Governor's mansion the casket was borne sadly within the doors. Still the crowd lingered, and after a while his little child was brought out. Women gathered around it and touched its dress almost reverentially, and with streaming eyes remembered that this was all that was left to them of Stonewall Jackson.

The day of the funeral, when the procession was to pass through the streets, a quiet, saddened crowd gathered along the pavements on the route. No noisy demonstrations of any kind greeted the ear. The people had had time to realize their loss. A solemn stillness brooded upon the whole scene, and the city stood reverently in the presence of her dead. No one seemed to be talking; there was all the hush and the serenity of the Sabbath about the day, and more of sadness than any Sunday we ever saw.

The procession as it wended its way slowly through the streets was watched by thousands, but what they noticed most, that which they looked upon with streaming eyes after the flag-draped casket, was the riderless horse which two of Jackson's men were leading and which moved slowly behind the hearse.

To the slow wail of the dead march Jackson's old veterans who were in the city at the time followed the battle-steed as they had done so many times before; and as they walked they wept like children, strong men as they were. We watched them as they passed, wondering at the devotion, the indescribable enthusiasm with which this great soldier inspired his troops.

The body of General Jackson lay in state at the Capitol after the procession had finally wended its way there and then dispersed. Thousands were admitted to look their last upon his calm face; and many found it impossible to effect an entrance into the building, even at the expense of patient waiting in the great crush. Toward night, after the doors had closed to the public, a weather-beaten, war-worn, mutilated soldier demanded admittance, and requested to see the dead hero.

He was refused.

"It is too late," they said; "they are closing the coffin for the last time."

But still he pressed forward and would take no denial. When one of the marshals of the day was about to force him back, the old soldier, with the tears rolling down his bearded face, exclaimed, raising the stump of his right arm:

"By this arm which I lost for my country, I demand the privilege of seeing my general once more."

The appeal was all-powerful and the coffin lid was raised, and Jackson's old soldier gazed his last upon the face of his dead leader.

Of all the generals on the side of the South he, and he alone, had infused into the minds of the rank and file of the army unquestioning confidence and utter reliance. They believed in his star as the Imperial Guard believed in Napoleon; looked up to him with the same feelings with which the Russian soldiers regarded Suarroff; they marched to battle with him as blindly, as trustingly as the Legions followed Caesar. No other general could get from the soldiers what Stonewall secured without an effort. The privates of the army adored him; and no matter whether the ground was covered with snow, or rain poured in blinding torrents, or the sun beat with vivid force upon the heads and their feet sunk in the dust a foot deep, they would follow the old tattered uniform, that old faded gray hat, that kindly, rugged face, until nature itself would rebel.

He was kind to his soldiers and always considerate of their wants and comforts. While many generals, lower in rank than he, yet proud of their position and of the gold lace and silver stars, were overbearing and haughty in their demeanor toward the privates, Jackson was as their elder brother.

There was a young soldier of his division, a boy in years, who, stopping to fill his canteen from a branch on a forced march, became separated from his command, was taken suddenly sick and it was weeks before he rejoined his regiment. His colonel, disbelieving his tale of sudden illness, ordered him to the guardhouse. He appealed to the brigadier, who refused to take any action in the matter. That evening as Jackson sat in his tent, with several of his generals around him, listening intently to their reports of the condition and efficiency of the men, there appeared suddenly among them a boy who could not speak for his choking sobs. One of the brigadiers, indignant at the intrusion, started to eject the offending private who dared to interrupt a council of war; but Jackson interposed and drew the weeping boy to him, who, when he found voice, narrated his wrongs. Jackson listened to his story without a word of interruption. He perceived the truth which spoke in every tone and shone in the eyes of the boy; and with his own eyes humid, he arose and took the young soldier's hand in his and walked with him through the camp. Two strange figures; he with his cap pulled low over his face, the child-soldier with the marks of tears staining his cheeks. Together they proceeded until the colonel's tent was reached.

"Release this soldier from arrest," he said sternly to that officer; then turned and wended his way back to his tent.

There are numberless instances which are treasured and repeated by his people as a monk tells over his beads, incidents of small moment in themselves, but all combining to prove the infinite tenderness of the great, kindly heart, until we hardly know which to revere more, the genius of the warrior or the wonderful nobility of the man.

One dark, cold, rainy night an officer went with dispatches to Jackson's tent. The General after making him remove his dripping overcoat, insisted that he should remain all night and share his tent, as the weather was far too inclement to think of going any farther in the storm. They both retired, but about midnight the officer awoke, only to see Stonewall, heedless of the rest so much needed, kneeling by the fire and holding up to its warmth his companion's wet clothing, that he might have dry apparel to put on in the morning.

Dr. Moore, of Richmond, tells the following incident:

"The troops of Jackson, after a long forced march, when the order to halt having been given, had fallen on the ground utterly worn out and faint. The officer of the day went to the General and said:

" 'General, the men are so tired they are all asleep; shall I wake them and set the watch?'

" 'No,' he answered, 'let them sleep, and I will watch the camp to-night.'

"And all night he rode round that sleeping camp, which had no other guard through the silent hours than the one lone figure and the stars. Refreshed and strong the men awoke at morning light, and were never told who had kept vigil over their quiet slumbers?"

It was his fearlessness of which his men were proud, and for which they loved him most. A leader must be conspicuously brave to merit the admiration of his followers. At Gaines' Mill he sat on his horse in a terrific artillery fire, and as his division filed by him, they saw him composedly pouring some molasses from a canteen on a cracker and eating his frugal fare as if he were a thousand miles from danger. This was no matter of ostentation; what he did was as if no eyes were upon him. He never asked what men thought of him; never sought to win the enthusiasm of his men by "General Orders" of high-sounding words or by clap-trap deeds. He said nor wrote no word intended to enhance his own reputation. He was utterly incapable of making use of meretricious aid to spread abroad his own fame. He never tried to awe his soldiers or wrap himself in mystery so as to heighten the effect his daily presence would dispel; he never arrayed himself in gilt or bright insignia of rank to tell to the army "there goes General Jackson." If they did not recognize the old faded uniform discolored by storm and sunshine, if they did not know whose the eagle eye beneath the old gray cap, whose the clear-cut features, he might pass unknown for aught else there would be to inform them.

But listen and you may catch a faint sound as of the murmuring sea. It increases every second until it reaches you in the mad shouts of the troops, who are screaming and yelling with almost insane enthusiasm. You ask the reason and they point you to a horseman who is approaching at a rapid gallop.

"It can only be Jackson or a hare," they say, and General Jackson it is, shrinking, as was his wont, from demonstration of any kind. He dashes on more rapidly as the shouts increase in volume; but see! he has thrown down his hat and they are passing it along the lines, where it will reach him farther on. The yells are fairly deafening now, and men are throwing their hats wildly in the air. There is not a man of them who would not give his life for him freely.

It was Jackson's great bravery, his decision, his coolness in times of danger, his determination, his utter forgetfulness of self and indifference to his own comfort which combined to make him one of the greatest men the world has even known. His supreme devotion to duty and intense faith in the cause for which he was fighting enthused the men with something of his own inspiration.

How ceaseless, silent and deep must have been the influence which flowed from the example of his daily life into the lives and hearts around him.

He had a home which drew him with bands of tenderest love, and yet he never asked for a furlough or was absent from the army a single day; nor did he ever pass a night away from his command. As his soldiers fared, so did he; he desired nothing better.

He delighted in the simplest flower of the field, saw beauty in the world around him which escaped the eyes of most men; he loved the song of birds, the prattle of little children; and withal he was as tender, gentle and soft-hearted as a woman. The man who colored to the eyes when a young girl asked him for a button from his coat, the man whose life was one of kindly deeds and Christian charity, was yet the inspiring genius of our war.

His was the mind which never grew confused over the vast combinations of the field; he it was who knew just when to strike and where; who aimed his blows at unexpected points, who followed up his advantages and turned them into assured victories.

Like Cromwell, he could advance to bloody battle with a prayer upon his lips, and hurl the colermus on the foe with a hymn in his heart. No man dared scoff when he kneeled in prayer or when as his old darky expressed it:

> "De soldier was in de presence
> Ob his Hebbenly Brigadier."

There is no confounding the innate religion of the man, his great faith, with fatalism. His piety enhanced his lofty attributes and challenged for living warrior and dying Christian the respect of the world. There is nothing that civilization so venerates as a thoroughly consistent walk of one who lives with the "crown of life in view." Jackson's great, earnest piety gave us an example of power which comes from the union of all that is lofty and ennobling in character when joined with the faith of the Christian. The sincerity, purity and elevation of his character were only brought into clearer view by his prominence as a leader of armies, and with both characters blended into one we can detect no flaw.

It was the fateful day of Chancellorsville that Jackson, General Fitz Lee the cavalry commander, and the guide rode slowly up the old plank road, the orderly bringing up the rear. From the conversation of the two the soldiers knew that they were trying to find where the left flank of Hooker's army lay. He heard Fitz Lee tell Jackson that he could pilot him to the very spot. After riding several miles along that secluded, desolate road without hearing a sound or meeting a soul, for this unused track was little better than a blind path which had been a thoroughfare once but now had almost passed out of existence and was only known to the country people around, they met an old negro. Fitz Lee halted him and asked if he knew where the enemy was.

"Yes, go up on dat little hill," pointing to a small elevation a hundred yards away, "and you can see dem Yankees as thick as bees."

When the top of the elevation was reached a sight was before them so grand, so unexpected too, that the orderly had to bite his tongue to prevent a wild cheer from bursting from his lips.

The three sat on their horses and looked down. There lay the right wing of Hooker's army in perfect security. They felt so safe that they had not even thrown out pickets to guard the old plank road. In a large field, a half-mile away, thousands of blue-coats could be seen; most of them were getting ready for their meals, others were drilling in squads, and many were stretched out, resting from their fatigue. It was, as it afterwards proved, Blenker's Dutch Division. They were as unsuspecting as the chirping, clacking brood of chickens ruffling their feathers in the barn-yard in lazy content, utterly unmindful of the hawk in the sky which descended slowly in gyrating circles toward the earth, then pausing in mid-air measured the distance before his final swoop. Yes! there rested the right wing, with an almost impenetrable thicket in their front, a rapid river in their rear, all unmindful of ill, all unconscious of harm, little imagining the tempest which the grim Prospero who sat on horseback not far off was soon to raise about their ears; laughing in their beards like the doomed Tyrians in the Thracian games when Shotmanez's Assyrian guards stood ready with dagger and sword to butcher them as they stood.

What a spectacle! Twenty thousand men on the plain, one man on the hill with almost as potent power in his hand as Mercury had when he borrowed Jove's thunderbolts to launch them at the Titans. A terribly impressive tableau, that needed no calcium glare or blue lights to heighten the effect. Jackson, with his stern, composed face as if cut in marble, his eyes flashing as he gazed, knowing that at last the foe was in his power. The great, the mighty Army of the Potomac was in his power at last. Surely Napoleon had not more cause to shut up his telescope at Marengo with the assurance that General Melas was in his toils and the battle won, as he ordered Kellerman to charge the Austrian center.

Jackson spoke not a word, his iron self-control preventing him from giving any sign. Turning he rode back and said to the orderly:

"Tell A. P. Hill to move his column up the road."*

His mind, like Napoleon's, was with his comrades to the last.

"Tell A. P. Hill to prepare for action," he said, and died.

To General Lee and his soldiers his loss was irreparable; there was no man to take his place, while the vital blows his corps always struck were never made again.

---

*General Fitz Lee personally gave me these particulars. His last ride with Jackson is historic.

24

When the keystone of the arch gives way the strength of the structure is gone; though it may hold together for a time, in the end it is certain to crumble into a pile of ruins.

General Jackson was the keystone of the Confederacy; when he fell it was a question of time only how long the arch would withstand the pressure.

When King Harold went down before the onset of the son of Robert the Devil, at Hastings, the hopes for the people were buried with him, and the Norman William and his royal court reigned over all England.

When Gustavus Adolphus was shot at a bal masque in Stockholm the great Swedish-Russian-Prussian coalition, which he conceived and accomplished, was dissolved and Sweden sank from that hour.

When John the Fearless was assassinated on the bridge of Montereau the royal robes dropped from the House of Burgundy, never to be replaced.

When the Protector drew his last breath at Somerset House the great fabric whose cornerstone was civil and religious liberty went down with a crash and a dissolute king and a pampered nobility ruled over the realm. So with Jackson; when he fell the cause for which his great mind planned was doomed to ultimate defeat.

The *New York Times,* in its issue of May 5th, 1863, says of Jackson:

"The interest excited by this strange man is as curious as it is unprecedented. A class-mate of McClellan's at West Point, he was considered slow and heavy. He has exhibited qualities which were little supposed to dwell in his rugged and unsoldier-like frame. Like Hannibal he is accustomed to living among his men without distinction of dress or delicacy of fare, and it is hard for a stranger to recognize him.

"Every dispatch from his hand has its exordium: 'By the blessing of God.'

"Those who have heard him uplift his voice in prayer, and have witnessed his promptness and daring in battle, say that once more Cromwell is working on earth and leading his enraptured soldiers to assured victory."

On the 27th of June, 1862, in the battles around Richmond, when heroes were spent in fighting, Jackson sent to each division commander and his staff officers this sharp command:

"Tell them this affair must hang in suspense no longer. *Sweep the field with the bayonet.*"

At Cedar Run, when that born soldier, General Winder, received his mortal wound and his division was falling back in disorder, it was Jackson who threw himself at them, stopped the rout and shouted to the men:

"Rally! brave men, and press forward; your General will lead you! Jackson will lead you! Follow me!"

The appeal was not in vain; and the day was saved.

Jackson could never brook delay. His staff not rising early enough, he made the cook throw away the coffee, pack up and drive off in the wagon. It was a lesson they never forgot.

Jackson captured Harper's Ferry on Sept. 14th, 1862, by moving his troops and planting them in the night, and General Mills found every line of retreat blocked.

At his last battle, Chancellorsville, he appeared the very incarnation of the genius of war. He led his men, and his voice was heard crying continually:

"Forward! Press on!" And he would lean forward upon his horse and wave his hand as though to impel his men forward.

When his troops began to break and fall out of line, his last act was to ride along the line unattended, and he kept saying:

"Men, get into line. What regiment is this?"

"Colonel," he cried to an officer, "get your men instantly into line!" Turning to an aide, he said:

"Find General Rodes and tell him to occupy those works." He then added:

"This disorder must be corrected; as you go along the right, tell the troops from me, to get into line and preserve their order."

CHAPTER XLI.

AFTER CHANCELLORSVILLE.

A month of absolute rest followed the battle of Chancellorsville; General Hooker was engaged in his old business of reorganizing the army; Lee was maturing his plan to carry the war into Africa. Had the Confederate Government's foresight been as good as their hindsight it would have discouraged any movement of the Army of Northern Virginia. Certainly for once the policy of "masterly inactivity" had been the best.

It seemed as if the process of disintegration was in progress in the Army of the Potomac, and if left undisturbed would ruin its morale. Hooker's great host was fast losing confidence in itself, the people had lost faith in Hooker, while he was at daggers drawn with his most influential officers.

Dissensions, bickering and backbiting were the order of the day. Mutual mistrust between the officers high in command had gotten to that pitch when, as in the reign of terror, no shoulder-strap felt safe. Scores of officers, gallant fighters and true patriots, had been driven into retirement, or were eating their hearts out performing routine duties in the rear. Politics and jealousy were the bane of the army. McClellan, the idol of the Army of the Potomac and its preserver after Bull Run, was a private citizen in New Jersey; Fremont, the central figure at the beginning of the war, was laid on the shelf; McDowell, that accomplished soldier, turned down; Fitz John Porter disgraced; Pope cast from his pinnacle; Burnside sent out West; Franklin, a soldier every inch, retired to private life; Casey sent to Coventry and many others of lesser note cashiered. Over the head of the commanding general the sword of Damocles hung suspended. Hooker expected it to fall on him every day; Averell saw his doom, and Crouch, the next in command and an object of envy, hit back lustily; he said in a dispatch dated May 12, 1863:

"The higher officers of this army do nothing but read, talk politics, play cards and grumble."

Pleasanton, that dashing trooper whom the Southern cavalrymen regarded as the toughest fighter they ever met, was already marked for dismissal on account of his politics. Brooks, Sturgis, —all sent to the shades. Halleck, the commander-in-chief (whom

McClellan denounced in his book, page 137, as the most bare-faced villain in America), frowned upon many deserving officers, and his frown meant ruin. Stanton, the ablest Secretary since Carnot, was simply feared and hated by the army, but he kept them up to the mark, and his information on military affairs was marvelous and his industry untiring; still he made enemies of every man with whom he shook hands, and if he took a prejudice the object was sure to feel its effect.

Even Meade said that, "When he was awakened by a staff officer who bore him his commission as general-in-chief of the army, he thought at first that he was about to be dismissed."

The Navy took a hand also. Admiral Porter detested Butler and metaphorically kicked him every chance he had, and the redoubtable Ben, whom President Lincoln said "was like a kitchen knife sharpened on a brick bat," met him more than half way; and so they went at it tooth and nail, might and main. It was a regular Kilkenny-cat affair. All, from the spurred, booted general down to the drummer-boy, were drawn into the whirlpool—all except one, who towered like a lofty granite shaft above the head-stones. And just here it may be said that no fair-minded man can read through the official records of the war without seeing that Lincoln was the genius of the century.

His dispatches were all so true—so full of horse-sense; his acute mind was like a reflector piercing the fog; his judgment was wise, and his deductions almost infallible. Among the "ca-hierage," envy's hiss, hatred's shriek and folly's bray he stood, simple and serene, with malice toward none and charity for all.

The burdens resting on Lincoln's shoulders were so great that a man of common mold would have soon broken down. The Abolitionists on one side, the Peace party on the other, never ceased trying to disturb his equipoise. He was beset with politicians, besieged night and day by swarms of office-seekers and place-hunters. The strained relations with England and France caused him many sleepless nights, yet calm, cool and resolute he pursued the even tenor of his way. No man ever saw him hopeless or with his passions aroused, and through all he stood unswervingly true to his purpose of preserving the Union intact.

When, like fractious children, soldiers, statesmen, citizens grew faint of heart and weary of soul, it was to Lincoln they turned for consolation and comfort.

When the States of the North, mourning, and, like Niobe, "all tears," over their hecatomb of dead, to Abraham Lincoln they turned, and leaning their sorrow-bowed heads on that broad breast, gained hope and inspiration from the beating of that mighty heart.

PART II.

CHAPTER I.

IN THE CAVALRY.

Each infantryman had happy dreams of a transfer to the cavalry; but such transfer was harder to obtain, the soldiers used to say, than an invitation to dine with the commander-in-chief.

To be sure they had done little to distinguish themselves, these cavalrymen of the Confederacy, having been mostly on post duty, the monotony of which had been relieved here and there by an occasional skirmish; but then they never knew what hunger meant; they had camp darkies to do the stealing and cooking; and above all they had horses to ride. So it came to pass that many a time the infantry, which toiled on foot, worn and weary along the road, with shoulders chafed by the heavy guns, with waist rubbed bare of skin by the friction of forty rounds of ammunition, as they watched the dragoon cantering gaily along looking as if grim war was one vast holiday, felt their souls swell with envy unspeakable for this "something better than they had known." At last this envy took up its abode in their hearts like the devils of old, and became a chronic malady.

The cavalry! Why, it was to their imagination what the Scottish Cuirassier, the body guard of Louis the Thirteenth, with its royal rank and privilege, was to the common musketeers of the line.

It meant waving of plume, jingle of spur, dash of steed, and comfort generally. For all wild and reckless spirits who sighed for adventure, to whom hard toil, meagre fare and uneventful life were well-nigh unendurable, there was a glamour thrown over this branch of the service that was most fascinating, and they longed to enter the magic circle, and by the camp-fire plotted and planned and dreamed golden dreams of the time when they too would be horsemen and ride to the sound of the bugle.

Not only to these adventurous spirits, revelling in anticipation of dash, foray and hostile incursion, was the hope of the cavalry service so attractive, but particularly was it promising to the lazy and timid, who looked upon a transfer as a relief from all toil, all trouble, and especially from all danger. It was a common saying that no one ever saw a dead man with spurs on; and every one knew that four legs could get out of trouble more quickly than two.

As for myself, I was so sick of being an infantryman that I would have hailed a transfer to any branch of the service with delight, and night after night I sat brooding how to accomplish my wish. Nor was I alone in this; a squad of choice spirits aided me in the deliberation; Courteny Washington, Willie Spellman and Boyd Smith all had forwarded their applications, and they were sanguine of success, for they were backed by powerful friends; and no debutante every dreamed and talked more of her first ball than did they of what they would do in the "Black Horse Cavalry."

I knew General Lee well; his estate, "Arlington," joined the summer seat of my family, and the two were on intimate social terms; my father was one of the pall-bearers of Washington Parke Custis, who was buried with impressive ceremonies from Arlington House.

I dusted my jacket, borrowed a respectable cap, and went to General Lee's tent; a sentinel paced to and fro, but took no notice of me, and I soon found myself in the great commander's presence. He greeted me gravely by a wave of his hand, and when I told him my name he took me by the hand and asked me several questions about my family, which, embarrassed as I was, I stumbled through; then I mustered up courage to ask him to give me a transfer to the Black Horse Cavalry. He smiled, told me to write a personal application to him, and then dismissed me, the happiest soldier in the army. Thus I had the good fortune to be transferred to the cavalry, the paper bearing the date May 20th, 1863; and in the whole army there was no happier heart than mine. It is doubtful whether Nature is capable of yielding more intense pleasure than to find one's hopes unexpectedly gratified.

Instead of cleaning the mud from my heels and gnawing dry hardtack diversified with branch water, I would hereafter swing along "a la knight and warrior" of old, who in history, fiction and song bear themselves proudly in the saddle. For what poet, painter, novelist or historian would dare present his hero walking on his own legs? Well, so I dreamed, and if the anticipations, no wiser grown by two years' experience, were all *couleur de rose* once more, it made no difference then.

Yet it was with a sad heart that I bade adieu to the old brigade, endeared by so many ties, ties ever of the strongest when bound together by common toil, danger and hardship; a sad task enough to go from soldier to soldier, from comrade to comrade and take his hand in a farewell that might be eternal.

Good-by, old brigade! surely a stauncher, braver set of men was never collected in any country, in any clime, for good or for evil, for grand incentive or great enterprise. And an affectionate farewell to its commander, General M. D. Corse, who was a soldier among soldiers, and held the respect and confidence of every man who served under him.

Old brigade, a long good-by. Never again to be with you, ragged, rationless, tramping on the forced march five miles an hour, drilling beneath the hot sun or charging under rain of shot and shell; yet at this last hour only pleasant memories arise of the jovialness, the green woods of Fairfax, the old barracks in Alexandria—and then like the sailor who leaves his home with aching heart but to whose nostrils the salt air comes stealing along winning him to the waters, so I shake off my sadness and turn my face toward Richmond, there to report to the Department. It was the first of June. After having enjoyed the furlough (for blessings never come singly), en route I fell in with a kinsman on his way to join the Thirteenth Virginia Cavalry.

Orders were received to proceed to the Valley and thence to Maryland or Pennsylvania, or wherever our commands might be. How and in what manner this was to be accomplished the authorities did not inform me.

"Here's your passport, now go." That was all he said. He never asked if I had a horse or money wherewith to buy one, evidently thinking that it was none of his business. As many of the emancipated infantrymen, transferred like myself to the cavalry, had neither, the dilemma might have been a serious one, only that we all had become so used to trusting luck that we permitted nothing to disturb us. We set out on a wild-goose chase, that of catching up with moving cavalry three hundred miles away. We tasted the first sweets of our new life when we traveled to Staunton by rail; had we been infantrymen we would have been placed under charge of some officer ordered to collect scattered soldiers, consolidate them into one body and march them by easy stages to their destination. Several of these same bands were passed on the road, and I winked ecstatically to myself and grinned broadly in a self-abandon beautiful to behold.

There was a hilarious crowd on board, composed of officers and cavalrymen returning from furloughs, sick leave and details.

They were all fat and hearty and full of mischief. Woe to the unfortunate man under three score who chanced to come to the station in a citizen's suit. It would not be long before he would be called to the car window by some smooth-faced, harmless-looking soldier, whose eyes seemed "homes of silent prayer," benign, innocent and trusting. Hardly would conversation have begun before a comrade from the car window would suddenly blow a cornucopia filled with meal full in his face, completely blinding him, while the treacherous decoy would then snatch the hat from his head, and as the cars moved off the luckless citizen would be left hatless and furious, while the shouts of merriment from the troopers inside could be heard above the noise of the train.

"Why did you treat that man in such a fashion?" some officer would ask.

"O, he is only a confounded citizen!" would be the reply.

It was not strange that these rough, ragged soldiers should regard these able-bodied non-combatants with antipathy and contempt; their very presence was an insult to them. Indeed it required greater moral courage to keep out of the war than it did to volunteer, for women would show their scorn for cowards in every way. If hints and ridicule proved unavailing, he would receive from some fair unknown hands such anonymous gifts as a flannel petticoat, a cotton night-cap, a pair of pantalets, or some article of female gear, intimating that nature had made a great mistake when she molded him in the form of a man.

On reaching Staunton and placing ourselves at the service of the provost marshal, he ordered us to proceed to Winchester, ninety miles distant. Proud of our new dignity and not feeling in the humor to tramp all the way, we showed him our transfer to the cavalry, and that marvelous paper obtained for us a passport to travel by the regular stage which left every morning for the Valley City. Reaching there we started on a hunt for the cavalry, which was somewhere between the Potomac and the Susquehanna.

CHAPTER II.

GETTYSBURG.

I reached Winchester a day or two after its capture by Ewell. The place was crowded,—soldiers everywhere; not the ragged, starved, foot-sore fellows that had rendezvoused in the town after the Antietam campaign, but convalescents making their way northward to join their commands. All were hopeful, eager and buoyant. Detachments of infantry under some officers were leaving every hour striking northward with a swinging gait. I made many inquiries as to Stuart's whereabouts, but none could give me any reliable information. I bought a very pretty little mare for $1,000 Confederate currency, from a soldier, and I strongly suspected that she had been stolen, but it was no affair of mine. Mounting her I struck for the Potomac at Williamsport and crossed the river there. Shade of Pegasus, but I was radiantly happy! I felt as did Monte Cristo, "that the world was mine." How I exulted as I passed the groups of infantrymen plodding along the dusty roads whilst I was riding my own steed. It was with a heart so high that I sang one-half of the time and whistled the other half. The mare was a jewel, and her dog-trot, even and smooth, carried me over the ground at the rate of fully six miles an hour. That night I put up at a Dutch farmer's and had a glorious supper. The next morning they filled my haversack with cold bread, a huge hunk of beef, a jar of pickles, another of preserves and a whole chicken, and would not charge me a cent. In return I told the farmer to take his horses and convey them to some safe place. I certainly relieved his mind when I informed him that nothing else on his farm would be touched.

I interrogated every soldier I met as to whether he knew anything of the cavalry, but not a word could I obtain that was satisfactory. Stuart seemed to have disappeared from the face of the earth. Well, I did not bother much; the glorious summer weather, the fruitful country, the queer Dutch farmers filled every hour with a novel delight. I determined to make my way to the front and trust to chance.

On the morning of the 1st of July, 1863, as I was riding leisurely along the Emmitsburg pike, I heard the sound of musketry; but without stopping my horse I rode on until I saw in the distance the spires of the court-house rising above the trees. The firing still continued, but it was scattered shots, with here and there the loud boom of a gun, merely an affair of a small skirmish I thought. After fifteen minutes of hard riding I came to a sudden halt; there beside a creek was a line of battle, and one glance showed me the gray and butternut of our men. I was perfectly astounded, for I had been told all along the route that Lee and his whole army were on the banks of the Susquehanna.

I was halted, and requested to be carried to the commander.

He was a soldierly-looking man. I explained who I was, showed him my transfer to the cavalry signed by General Lee, and asked him where I would be likely to find my command.

He answered: "That is more than I know. This is Pettigrew's North Carolina Brigade. I have not seen a cavalryman since I have been in Pennsylvania."

I then asked him if I could be of any service on his staff. He said, "No, this is merely an affair of the out-post, and the enemy consists of only cavalry."

I then inquired, "What place is that over yonder?"

"Gettysburg," he replied.

Just as he finished, there came borne on the wind the far-off sound of cheering, and looking in the direction of the town I saw long lines of blue-coats defile from the place.

"There is going to be some fighting after all," he said; "you had better get to the rear."

And "get to the rear" I did, little thinking that it was to be my superlative good fortune to witness one of the greatest battles of modern times.

I will write of this struggle, not only what I saw, but what I learned afterwards.

Gettysburg is now cited as one of the seven decisive battles of the world. It certainly was the toughest stand-up, give-and-take fight in which Yank or Reb ever engaged, and it is the one battle above all others that America, North and South alike, will always take most pride in; for on those massive rocks the high tide of Rebellion beat with such frightful force as to cause those everlasting hills to tremble, to totter and almost to fall. On those granite heights the flower of the Saxon race wrestled three whole days, with courage so true, a heroism so intense, a determination so indomitable that the whole earth marveled and applauded and Columbia smiled through her blinding tears, her pride almost conquering her grief, stretching forth her arms and gathering her sons to her heart, uncaring whether they fell under the Northern Stars or the Southern Cross.

America in the course of time will, like all nations, fulfil her destiny; but in ages to come, no matter what befalls, there is one Mecca that will be forever sacred to the hearts of the people, and that is Gettysburg. The cause for which the blue and gray fought will be forgotten, but their splendid bravery never.

As one of Lee's soldiers I know that never was the *esprit de corps* of our army so high as when on that eventful June day in '63 they crossed the Potomac on their way northward. There was not a private in the ranks who did not feel positively certain of victory in the coming conflict, and the feeling among the soldiers, carefully fostered by their officers, was that by one supreme effort they could end the war and conquer a peace.

The vice of straggling, which came near being the destruction of the Confederate army in the Antietam Campaign the year before, was not seen on the Gettysburg advance. Lee took sternly repressive measures, and there were but few coffee-coolers seen along the line of march. Strict orders were also issued that the artillerymen should not ride on the guns or caissons.

It must be confessed, judging by the doctrine of chances to win the coming battle, the Confederates had ten to one in their favor. There was no danger of such an army as Lee's being routed; no matter whether they were driven back, repulsed, or surrounded, their superb mettle would stand the strain, and such a thing as a panic or a rout to these veterans of a score of battles was impossible. The soldiers were well-clothed and well-fed; their ranks were full, and Longstreet's return from Suffolk with a part of his corps which was absent at Chancellorsville, served only to make assurance doubly sure.

The Federal army, on the contrary, were disheartened by their failure in the previous campaign. The bad blood between their generals seriously affected the morale of the army; and the swapping of horses when crossing the stream, and the substitution of Meade, an unknown man outside of his corps, for the dashing, fighting Hooker, had a bad effect upon the Federal army.

Yet, as events proved, it was the wisest move that the Government could have made. The Federal army wanted a man in this campaign who would make no false manoeuvres—a safe, clearheaded, sagacious leader; a trained soldier, one who would throw no chance away; and they got him.

The Gettysburg Campaign was unique, and in some respects without a parallel in the annals of the world. In future ages military students will wonder how two armies moving in a thickly settled region, not a hundred miles apart, with no impassable mountains and no unfordable rivers, with regiments of light cavalry and detachments of mounted scouts, could manoeuvre for days without any clear idea of each other's whereabouts. And this wonder amounts almost to a miracle when such an event happens in a country bisected with railroads, and with the telegraph wires in every town.

Hooker knew Lee was north of the Potomac somewhere; but Lee did not even know where Hooker was until the 28th of June, so he states in his official dispatch.

Five days had elapsed and not a word from Stuart!

In this campaign Lee had lost his right arm in the death of Stonewall Jackson; and in Stuart's absence he lost his eyes, and he was like a blind man—sightless and with only one arm.

Now where was Stuart, whose paramount duty was to keep the commander-in-chief informed of the movements of the Federal army?

When Stuart, on June 23rd, requested Lee's consent to make a detour around Hooker's army, General Lee answered the evening of the same day:

"If General Hooker's army remains inactive, you can leave two brigades to watch him, but should he appear to be moving northward I think you had better withdraw this side of the mountain to-morrow night, cross the Potomac at Shepherdstown next day and move over to Frederick. You will, however, be able to judge whether you can pass around their army without hindrance, doing them all the damage you can, and *cross the river east of the mountains*. In either case, after crossing the river you must move on and feel the right of Ewell's troops.

"I think the *sooner you cross into Maryland after to-morrow the better*.

"Be watchful and circumspect in all your movements." (Reb. Records, Vol. 27, p. 923.)

Comte De Paris says:

"Stuart submitted his plan to Lee, and has stated in his report that the latter authorized him to execute it, even pointing out to him the contemplated movements of Ewell's corps, that he might join Early's division between Gettysburg and the Susquehanna. The official account of the general-in-chief, no less positive, is directly at variance with this statement. According to this account, Stuart did not propose the movement on the enemy's rear except as a means for delaying his passage over to the left bank of the Potomac. This consideration alone influenced Lee in allowing him to penetrate into Maryland east of the Blue Ridge, but upon the express condition that the cavalry should resume its natural place on the right flank of the army as soon as the enemy had started for the North. This, as it will be seen, was a concession made by Lee to the views of his lieutenant, and, as almost always happens in such cases, the somewhat vague terms used by the former were no doubt interpreted by the latter in a sense most suitable to his wishes. Hence a misunderstanding which raised a question of veracity between them, the consequences of which proved fatal to their cause." ("Battle of Gettysburg," p. 61.)

Now Stuart loved the pomp and pageantry of war; a skirmish to him was like a drink of champagne; but the delight of his soul was a wild foray around the enemy's army, fording streams, collecting unsuspecting convoys, burning bridges, capturing wagon-trains, and returning to camp with laughter and song, laden with plunder. It was a fine role for a partisan, but not for the leader of the cavalry corps of the army. It would have gone hard with the chiefs of cavalry of Napoleon, Frederick, or a Von Moltke to have disappeared from view on the eve of a campaign.

Stuart, on the receipt of General Lee's dispatch, lost not a moment. He left four thousand cavalry under the command of General Beverly Robertson at Winchester, Va., for the purpose of keeping General Lee advised of Hooker's movements.

General Robertson was a bon vivant and ornament of the boudoir, and a superb dancer; but not a success as a cavalry officer; and Lee never heard a word or received any aid whatever from him during the whole campaign.

Stuart took with him the brigades of Fitz Lee, W. H. F. Lee, and Hampton—in all thirteen regiments and three squadrons, together with Breathed's horse artillery of six guns.

On the night of June 24th Stuart started with six days' rations, and passed through the mountains near Thoroughfare Gap, thence on to Dranesville, where, if he had exercised his usual vigilance, he would have detected the march of Meade northward and would have turned back to join Lee, but instead he crossed the Potomac on the night of June 27th, thence to Rockville, and burned a long wagon-train. On the 28th, 29th,

25

and 30th he created havoc among the sutlers and teamsters, and on the afternoon of July 1st arrived at Carlisle, men and horses both utterly exhausted and broken down; and there ended the greatest fiasco ever committed by a veteran soldier.

The Federal army was no longer a free agent. Meade was forced by the inexorable logic of events to find the invading army and attack at all hazards, wherever it might be. The crisis was so urgent that instant action was necessary. To find Lee and to assail and drive him out of the loyal States was an absolute necessity. A failure to do so would give England just the chance she was waiting for to acknowledge the Confederacy; and then there was the Peace party at the North, that grew more and more defiant as the stay of Lee north of the Potomac was prolonged. That the Government at Washington grew desperate, was shown by the tenor of their dispatches. Adjutant-General Williams on July 1st telegraphed the corps commanders that in the event of defeat they should retreat at once to the defenses in Washington. (Reb. Records, Vol. 25, p. 463.)

Stanton showed that his nerves were wrought up to the highest tension, for he issued an order the like of which even the autocratic Czar or the iron-natured Frederick the First of Prussia would not countenance. Under date of June 30th, 1863, the Secretary of War promulgated this ukase:

"*Corps* and *other* commanders are authorized to order to ininstant death any soldier who fails in his duty at this hour." (Reb. Records, Vol. 27, p. 415.)

This order gave carte blanche to any officer to kill any soldier at will, if he thought he failed in his duty. The officer to be judge, sheriff and executioner; the condemned to have neither trial, voice, nor defense. If such a life-and-death order was ever issued in civilized warfare before, it was never recorded.

The North never understood the South. Even the educated men, graduates of West Point, who ought to have known better, declare that it was Lee's object to subjugate and force slavery on the Northern States; which piece of information would have been startling news to every private in the Rebel Army.

General Doubleday says in his book:

"This charge, which was to determine the fate of the campaign, and settle whether freedom or slavery was to rule in the Northern States." (Page 188.) And further on he says:

"It was not intended by Providence that the Northern States should pass under the iron rule of the slave power." (Page 192.)

Future historians, in writing of the Civil War in America, will be struck by one singular fact in reading the various letters and telegrams of prominent civilians and officers of the Northern States during the wild excitement of Lee's invasion into Pennsylvania. It is this: The real sense of personal injury, that a Rebel army should invade the soil of a free State. The Federal soldiers might stable their horses in the fairest mansions of the South, and send from that section congratulatory dispatches to the Government telling of the cotton, corn, and barns committed to the flames, and it was all right in the eyes of the Northerner; but if a well-conducted Rebel army invaded a loyal State, the burst of frenzied indignation was simply overwhelming. It was as if the hosts of Lucifer had invaded heaven.

Nearly all the great battles were fought on fields not dreamed of by the opposing commanders, and Gettysburg was no exception to the rule.

The Goddess of Fortune had smiled on the army of Northern Virginia for the past year, and success seemed beyond the shadow of a doubt; but the day Stuart started on his raid and got lost, the smile of the Goddess changed to a frown that only deepened as the campaign progressed. Every step that Lee took was a stumble, and every move that Meade made was lucky, until it seemed as if "the very stars in heaven fought for Sisera."

It was most unfortunate that Lee received the tidings of Hooker's whereabouts on the 28th of June, for that date was a most inopportune time; had the news reached him a day earlier it would have found him at Gettysburg with his whole army united on the morning of the 1st, and that would have insured him certain victory.

Had the news that Hooker had crossed the Potomac reached him a day later, he would have by that time been across the Susquehanna and investing Harrisburg.

On the night of the 30th Stuart was vainly looking for Lee in the vicinity of York, and he passed within seven miles of Ewell's column en route to Gettysburg. Had they effected a junction it would have saved Stuart's command from a long, fruitless, exhausting march, which impaired the *esprit de corps* of the troopers and broke down the horses.

Bates, in his book, says:

"It was one of those accidental circumstances which seemed to favor us in this campaign, while almost every incident at Chancellorsville was against us."

Then the untoward event of Pettigrew's men being barefoot caused Gettysburg to be the battle-field, and gave to Meade the strongest position in the region.

Who would have dreamed that a cavalry detachment would have made such a dogged, plucky struggle as Buford made.

For an hour General Heth, C. S. A., held the fate of the country in his hand; had he advanced with his division he could easily have swept Buford aside and occupied the hills around Gettysburg. Heth was a good soldier, but he was one of the safe, cautious kind, and Buford raising such a racket caused him to halt and send for reinforcements.

Napoleon would have bestowed upon Buford the baton of a grand marshal for such a magnificent fight.

Buford's soldierly eye appreciated Gettysburg as a defensive point, and his struggle to hold off Heth's division until the Union infantry came up was simply superb.

Then it was a most unlucky circumstance that placed Hill in the front on the first day's battle. Had Longstreet or Ewell been in his place, the history of Gettysburg would have been changed. Hill never before had an independent command; he had always served under Jackson. In the battle of the first of July he manoeuvred and acted as the veriest tyro. Instead of following Jackson's tactics pursued at Kernstown, Cross Keys, and Port Republic, Hill attacked in detachments. His corps was the very flower of Lee's army.

When Doubleday took command at 10.30 A. M. he formed Wadsworth's division, consisting of two brigades, in a most advantageous position—a stretch of woods that ran through an open field on top of a hill, about two hundred feet wide and about double that distance in length, known as McPherson's woods. In that grove was his *point d'appui*. He placed Meredith's Iron Brigade, consisting of the Nineteenth Indiana, Twenty-fourth Michigan, Second, Sixth and Seventh Wisconsin regiments, with Stone's and Battle's brigades on their right and left respectively. The brigades of Robinson's division, ten regiments in all, were placed in the rear and threw up hasty entrenchments.

Heth's soldiers were full of fight, and he gave Archer permission to advance and let that officer make one of his characteristic rushes without any supporting force.

Archer crossed Willoughby Run and aimed for the woods, and as a fearful artillery-storm of projectiles had swept through the place he doubtless thought the Yankees had retreated. He was soon undeceived, for Meredith's soldiers had clung to the spot, and received him with a furious discharge that broke his line, and the fine regiments of Meredith made a charge and drove him headlong across Willoughby Run, taking Archer and one thousand of his men prisoners.

In accordance with all military rules, Davis should have supported Archer, but he received no order until the remnant of Archer's brigade reached a place of safety, and then was told to go ahead, and he made a spirited charge and ran straight into Cutler's Union Brigade, consisting of the Ninety-fifth, Seventy-sixth, and One Hundred and Forty-seventh New York, Fourteenth Brooklyn and the Fifty-sixth Pennsylvania.

Their forces were about equal, and after a give-and-take fight Cutler retreated some three hundred yards.

Doubleday, who was watching the contest from a near-by hill, sent the Sixth Wisconsin, and the arrival of that crack command turned the scale, for Davis was attacked both in front and flank.

He struggled against these odds expecting every moment that assistance would arrive, but he was left to his fate and his fine brigade was knocked into smithereens, and two of his regiments surrendered. Heth was stunned for a time, and then sent for Pettigrew's and Brockenbrough's brigades, which should have supported Davis. Some time was wasted after those troops were drawn up. Heth waited until Hill arrived; and that officer deferred action, ordering his numerous batteries to open. Why he did not send his troops in, he does not state in his official report. While his soldiers were resting, Rowley's and Robinson's (Federal) divisions, fourteen regiments in all, reached Gettysburg, and coming in a run, those fresh troops were hastily but judiciously formed. Thus a golden opportunity had been frittered away.

Then, think of sending O'Neal's brigade against this force unsupported! The Confederates were simply torn to pieces, losing 503 killed and wounded, and 193 taken prisoners.

Next Iverson was pushed forward and attacked the two Federal brigades of Baxter and Paul. He made a gallant fight against these odds, when Cutler's brigade struck him on the flank and his force went to pieces; losing 320 in killed and wounded, and 508 captured.

Iverson says in his report:

"When I saw white handkerchiefs raised, and my line of battle still lying down in position, I characterized the surrender as disgraceful; but when I found afterwards that 500 of my men were left lying dead and wounded on a line as straight as if on dress parade, I exonerated, with one or two disgraceful individual exceptions, the survivors, and claim for the brigade that they nobly fought and died without a man running to the rear." (Reb. Records, Vol. 27, p. 579.)

It would have been an easy matter for Hill to flank the Federals and forced them to withdraw. He knew that Ewell was close behind him, and why he should have attacked the enemy in driblets will ever be a source of wonder.

Daniel's brigade, after Iverson's butchery, drove all alone against the same Federal force, and his command was wrecked. Ramseur came next and shared the same fate. Then Lane, Perrin, and Scales made the first concerted move during the day, and the Federal line was broken at last. But it is doubtful if they could have driven the Federal troops out of their barricade, thrown up at the edge of the town for just such an emergency, had not Early, of Ewell's corps, arrived with his fresh division, and forming in line, supported by a powerful artillery fire, advanced.

Thus it will be seen that Hill put in action Archer's, Davis's, Brockenbrough's, Pettigrew's, McGovern's, Ivison's, Scales's, Thomas's, Lanes's, Daniel's, Ramseur's, and O'Neal's brigades—ten in all.

These troops were veterans, trained under Jackson, and with as proud a record as Napoleon's Imperial Guards, and they believed themselves invincible; yet for the first time in all these years their faith was shaken, for they had been brought to a stand-still by a force inferior to their own. Now it must be understood that the *corps d'armee* of the opposing forces were not of the same size. The Confederate army had three, each one denoting one-third of its strength. The Federal army had seven, representing one-seventh of its strength. Thus the First Corps, numbering 11,200 men, had held its own all the morning of the 1st against double their number. They fought as gallantly as ever men did, and their official loss was 6,024; more than half their number. They lost but few prisoners except when crowded in the streets of Gettysburg.

Just here I may state that on the night of the 1st of July I fell in with the friend of my boyhood, Captain William Broun, Company F, Forty-seventh Virginia Infantry, of Brockenbrough's brigade, and he gave me a graphic account of the fight.

Captain Broun was a clear-headed, nervy officer, and a braver, stauncher soldier Virginia never gave to the Confederacy. He said:

"When near Willoughby Run, on the appearance of the enemy, Archer's brigade was thrown forward to clear the front of what was considered merely cavalry videttes, but which proved otherwise and resulted somewhat in a surprise, wherein General Archer and quite a number of his command were made prisoners by the Federals. At once the balance of the division was deployed in line, Davis's (Mississippi) brigade on the left of the road, Brockenbrough's (Virginia) brigade on the immediate right of the road, and Pettigrew's (North Carolina) brigade on the right of Brockenbrough's, with artillery (Purcell's battery) in position on the crown of the hill in rear of Brockenbrough's brigade and near the road. In the position thus described, the troops on the right of the road were subjected for some hours to artillery fire and witnessed the varying results of the fighting taking place on the left of the Cashtown road until the afternoon, when a general advance seems to have been made. This movement by the Confederates on the right of the road was observed at once by the enemy and measures taken to meet it on the open ground between the Cashtown road and the bluff of timber in which General Reynolds was killed. To do this, a Federal brigade, which had been previously either engaged or in support of its lines on the left of the road, changed front on its left regiment, and as Brockenbrough's brigade had crossed Willoughby Run and ascended the hillside nearest Gettysburg, met us face to face about fifty or sixty yards distant. Across this open field then took place one of the most stubbornly contested musketry fights in which I was ever engaged.

"Our (Brockenbrough's) brigade pushed steadily forward; step by step the enemy were pressed back, but contesting soldierly, steadily and stubbornly every inch of ground, and at no time exhibiting either unsteadiness of action or purpose, but a determination to resist to the utmost all efforts to force them backwards. Thus the contest waged on and on, beyond the old barn on the left of the brigade line to nearly the seminary buildings, when Pender's division relieved us, the fighting line, our ammunition exhausted, and continued the pursuit on to and through Gettysburg, I suppose.

"At the old barn referred to, which was occupied by the enemy, occurred an instance of their firing on the rear of the brigade, after it had passed some distance beyond and the barn was well within our lines. Major Lawson, of the Fifty-fifth Virginia, sent back a detail, which stopped this rather unusual mode of warfare, and the annoyance ceased.

"The loss of the brigade was severe both in officers and men, when considered from the standpoint of its effective strength, which was not over 1,000 or 1,100 muskets."

It seems incredible that A. P. Hill, who had learned the art of warfare under such a master as Stonewall Jackson, would not have asked himself what *he* would have done in this case. Had Hill followed Jackson's tactics at Port Republic and Cross Keys he never would have sent his brigades in singly to attack a strong, fortified position. McPherson's woods, the key of the battle-field, could easily have been turned by a flank attack on the right.

The Federal commander, General Doubleday, wrote a voluminous account of this battle, every phase of which he witnessed from his post of vantage, and it was but natural that he should claim all the glory and prestige for his men, yet in all fair-mindedness he felt constrained to say:

"There had been a great lack of co-ordination in these assaults, for they were independent movements, each repulsed in its turn." ("Chancellorsville and Gettysburg," p. 145.)

Had Hill handled his troops with only mediocre ability, he would have routed the First Corps, for the simple reason that he outnumbered them, and he had plenty of time to finish the work before Doubleday was reinforced.

Hill commenced the attack at 10 A. M., and Howard, with the Eleventh Corps, did not reach the field until 12.45 o'clock.

There was no excuse for this succession of military blunders; there were no deep ravines, thick coppices or swamps to hide an ambushed force or delay the advance; on the contrary, the whole country was open, and the men of the opposing force fought under the eyes of their respective generals.

Any one versed in military art, on viewing the scene of the first day's fight at Gettysburg and studying the topography of the battle-field, following intelligently the movements of the respective troops, must confess that Hill was out-manoeuvred and out-fought by Doubleday.

But little attention has been accorded the first day's battle at Gettysburg; but it was the day most pregnant for weal or woe for the South.

No soldier, no matter what uniform he wore, can deny that

Doubleday's fight for time was an heroic one. That his men, for the first time contending on their own soil, fought like Trojans, every Rebel who was on that historic field must admit.

"We have come to stay," chanted his men as they took position; and they did stay.

"Meredith's Iron Brigade lost 1,153, Cutler's brigade of six regiments lost 2,128, Paul's brigade lost 1,041, Rowley left 644 men on the battle-field, Biddle had 896 men killed and wounded, and Stone's loss was 853." (The losses of the Army of the Potomac. Reb. Records, Vol. 38, p. 219.)

When Ewell hurried to the assistance of Hill he rode to the crest of Oak Hill, and sweeping the field with his glass he took in the situation at a glance. He saw that the spot on which he stood dominated everything, and he ordered ten batteries to take position and enfilade Doubleday, while Early's division attacked Howard. Then Hill for the first time put his whole force in motion; and under the combined advance, the First and Eleventh corps collapsed.

Gordon on the left and Hill on the right burst like a tornado upon Howard and Doubleday, and although some regiments of the First Corps kept their alignment and organization intact until they reached the town, they were swallowed up among Howard's frenzied men, who rushed wildly through the streets of Gettysburg. Some of the Union batteries tried to get in position on the streets and defend the town, but the onrush of the demoralized Federals was too great, and all the batteries limbered up and went in a gallop to the rear of Gettysburg, where Steinwehr was rallying the fleeing troops on Cemetery Heights.

With a yell of victory on their lips, the men of Rodes and Gordon entered the town at two different points and poured a volley into the struggling mob. One of Gordon's men told me that after the first discharge nearly every Yankee soldier threw himself on his face and remained motionless until the Rebels were almost treading on them, and then the blue-coats cried out that they had surrendered.

Fighting in the streets of a town was of common occurrence in the Old World, but Gettysburg was the only place where such a thing happened in America. It was a glorious sight for a Rebel soldier to behold the fragments of two crack Federal corps surge in wild confusion through the highways and byways of Gettysburg.

There was one man who beheld the rout, knowing the weighty

import and the tremendous consequences involved, and that was
the Commander-in-Chief of the Confederate Army, who halted
his horse on the top of a hill overlooking the town.   The hour he
had dreamed of had come at last.

It was half past four o'clock; Hill's and Ewell's corps were on
the ground;   thirty thousand muskets and eighty guns were in
line;   thirty thousand veterans were vibrant, pulsating, mad to
advance;   men not brought in a line and fighting from a sense
of pride and duty, but soldiers whose hearts were thrilled with
victory—animated by an impulse that makes an army invincible.

The Federal army was scattered miles apart;   what a chance
that fortune had placed in Lee's hand, not merely to take the
Heights, but to cripple, if not to crush, the Army of the Potomac
in detail.

The Fates had spun their web, and on that eventful evening the
Goddess Opportunity offered Lee the Southern Confederacy on
a golden platter.

Lee had but to form his two corps in line—or even one—and
press onward.

The Federal detachments were thronging the highways;   and
to the unmilitary reader it is best to explain that when an army
is on the march it is stretched out for miles, with all the impedimenta of artillery, caissons, wagons, ambulances, &c.   An attack
is sure to throw all the vehicle drivers into confusion and jam
the road, and it takes much time to send them to the rear, the
infantry having to deploy on each side to let them pass.   No
fight can be made in column—a line has to be formed, and if the
enemy in line of battle strikes a body of soldiery strung out on a
turnpike it has every advantage of attacking from front and both
flanks.   When there are several roads, the attacking forces have
trebly the advantage.

Had Meade made a contract with Lee to deliver the Army of
the Potomac into his hands, he could not have disposed his forces
in a finer fashion for the accomplishment of that end.

The two strongest corps of Meade were, for the time, scattered to the winds, and the other five were not in supporting
distance of each other.

The largest, the Sixth corps, was at Hanover, twenty miles
away.

Comte de Paris, a Federal officer, says:

"The situation of the Federal army was critical in the extreme;   they had brought into action ten brigades of infantry,

two of cavalry, and ten batteries; about sixteen thousand five hundred men in all, against fourteen brigades of the enemy's infantry, and twenty batteries of artillery, aggregating more than twenty-two thousand men.

"The Federals had no more than five thousand men left in fighting condition.

"The First Corps was reduced to 2,450 men. Out of 11,000 men nearly 4,000 had been left on the field of battle, and about 5,000 were taken prisoners; the rest had been scattered.

"The fugitives crowded the roads leading out of Gettysburg; they hurried in the direction of Taneytown and Westminster, carrying confusion and discouragement into the ranks of the regiments that were coming to their assistance.

"Steinwehr had made good use of his two small brigades in constructing earthworks. Despite these wise precautions, there was still wanting sufficient troops to occupy the position thus prepared.

"It had taken them one hour thus to reform under the eyes of the Confederates; and the historian will now ask, as the Unionists themselves were then asking each other in astonishment, how is it that these adversaries, generally so prompt in striking blow after blow and to take advantage of success, have allowed them this precious respite, instead of gathering by a final effort the fruits of their victory? When Ewell entered Gettysburg in the midst of a mass of fugitives disarmed by fear, and was picking up prisoners by the thousand, the sun, which was still high in the heavens, promised him more than three hours of daylight; he had time, therefore, to deliver and to win a new battle. The two divisions of Early and Pender—that is to say, one-half of the Confederate forces—had not been in action more than one hour; two of their brigades had not been at all engaged; victory, moreover, imparted strength and confidence to the most exhausted. In short, more fortunate than their adversaries, the Confederates had in their midst the respected chieftain whose slightest wishes had hitherto been eagerly obeyed. Lee was on the ridge of Seminary Hill before half-past four, whence he surveyed the battle-field around him so stubbornly disputed by Hill—at his feet the town of Gettysburg, which Ewell had just entered, and in front of him the slopes of Cemetery Hill, which the Federals were scaling in great confusion. Hill and Longstreet were at his side, Ewell only two-thirds of a mile from his post of observation. Hill's corps, as we have stated, had not seriously harassed

Doubleday's retreat.   Lee did not order him to cross the wide and open valley which separates the heights of Seminary Hill from those of Cemetery Hill in order to attack the Federals in the position along which they were forming with so much difficulty.   This valley and the opposite slopes, which the next day were to be so thoroughly drenched in blood, did not, however, present any formidable obstacles.   It is true that the Southern General, on perceiving that Ewell was pressing the enemy closer, sent him an order by Colonel Taylor to attack the hill, if he could do so with any chance of success, as soon as he saw his troops in the town; but he had himself very serious doubts on the subject, Colonel Long, whom he had charged to make as thorough an examination of the enemy's positions as possible, having reported that they were very strong.   So that, while ordering Ewell to make the attack, he recommended him at the same time, according to the language of his report, to avoid a general engagement so long as the army had not arrived on the ground.   According to Colonel Taylor, who was the bearer of the dispatch, the order to attack the enemy was much more peremptory, and Johnson has since stated to the latter that he did not understand why it was not carried out.   Lee would seem to have been disposed to aim at a partial success dislodging the Federals from their last retreat, but in order to achieve this result he did not wish at this moment to risk a new battle with the only forces under his control.   It was for this reason that he had not pushed the Third Corps forward. This extreme caution may be condemned, but the motives can be easily understood."   (Comte de Paris's Battle of Gettysburg, pp. 123, 124, 125.)

"It has been said, and very justly, we think, that if Jackson had been alive and in command of his army corps on the 1st of July, he would not on that day have left Cemetery Hill in the hands of the Federals.   The fact is, that Lee, having the utmost confidence in his lieutenant, would not have hesitated to risk a great deal in order to afford him the means of striking a decisive blow."   (*Ibid.*)

Bates, another Federal general, who was present, says in his book (p. 80):

"The insignificant division of Steinwehr would alone have presented but a feeble barrier to a powerful and triumphant foe intent on pushing his advantage, and to the left where the country is all open and nature presents no impediment to an advance, it could have been flanked and Steinwehr easily turned out of his position."

It detracts nothing from Napoleon's reputation that a lack of decision caused him to forfeit a great victory at Borodino; nor from Frederick the Great, who fled in despair at the battle of Rosbach; nor from Wellington, when from inexcusable carelessness he came near losing his army at Torres Vedras. The failure of Gettysburg has been charged to Stuart, Longstreet, Ewell, and Johnson, but the truth is that Lee himself at the supreme hour failed to rise to the occasion.

Man of woman born, no matter how great, makes mistakes, and it is but natural that for years Lee's soldiers, who so loved, trusted and admired him, should have laid the blame on his subordinates for failing to carry out his orders. But on the evening of the 1st he was on the battle-field in person; there was no need for Jupiter to delegate to another the casting of the thunderbolt.

Colonel Walter Taylor, Lee's Chief of Staff, holds his commander blameless. He says:

"General Lee witnessed the flight of the Federals through Gettysburg and up to the hills beyond. He then directed me to go to *General Ewell* and say to him that from the position he then occupied he could see the enemy retreating over the hills without organization and in great confusion; that it was only necessary to 'press those people,' in order to secure possession of the heights beyond; and if possible, he wished him to do this. In obedience to these instructions I proceeded immediately to General Ewell and delivered the order of General Lee. No further steps were taken, as Ewell was probably overcome by physical fatigue and mental excitement."

General Lee's report does not back the account of his chief of staff; he says:

"It was ascertained from the prisoners that we had been engaged with two corps of the army formerly commanded by General Hooker, and that the remainder of that army, under General Meade, was approaching Gettysburg.

"Without information of its proximity, the strong position which the enemy had assumed could not be attacked without danger of exposing the four divisions present, already weakened and exhausted by a long and bloody struggle, to overwhelming numbers of fresh troops. General Ewell was therefore instructed to carry the hill occupied by the enemy, if he found it practicable, but to avoid a general engagement until the arrival of the other divisions of the army."

General Ewell says in his report:

"On entering the town I received a message from the commanding general to attack the hill if I could do so with advantage. I could not bring artillery to bear on it, and all the troops with me were jaded with twelve hours' marching and fighting."

It is clearly shown that Ewell received no peremptory order to advance. "You may fight if it pleases you," were his instructions.

Lee had so long relied upon Jackson, that in this supreme hour he did not rise to the occasion as Stonewall would. The Rev. J. William Jones, an intimate friend of General Lee, says:

"Prof. James J. White and myself were in his office in Lexington and we chanced to go in as he was reading a letter making some inquiry about Gettysburg. He said with an emphasis that I cannot forget, and bringing his hand down on the table with a force that made things rattle: 'If I had had Stonewall Jackson at Gettysburg I would have won that fight and a complete victory which would have given us Washington and Baltimore, if not Philadelphia, and would have established the independence of the Confederacy.' "

Napoleon likened a campaign to a game of chess; and on the evening of the 1st the Federal game was not worth a candle. The First and Eleventh Corps routed the Second (Sickles's) at Taneytown, the Third at Emmitsburg, the Fifth at Hanover, the Sixth at Manchester.

That was the time to bring everything to the charge; castles, knights, bishops, and pawns. Jackson would have done it! There was one in that hurly-burly who wanted to do that very thing; and that was Gordon, afterwards Lieutenant-General in the Army of Northern Virginia. He says in his book:

"The whole of that portion of the Union army in my front was in inextricable confusion and in flight. They were necessarily in flight, for my troops were upon the flank and rapidly sweeping down the lines. The firing upon my men had almost ceased. Large bodies of the Union troops were throwing down their arms and surrendering, because in disorganized and confused masses they were wholly powerless either to check the movement or return the fire. As far down the lines as my eye could reach, the Union troops were in retreat. Those at a distance were still resisting, but giving ground, and it was only necessary for me to press forward in order to insure the same results which invariably follow such flank movements. In less than one-half hour my troops would have swept up and over those hills, the possession of which was of such momentous consequence. It is not surprising, with a full realization of the consequences of a halt, that I shoud have refused at first to obey the order. *Not until the third or fourth order of the most peremptory character reached me, did I obey.* I think I should have risked the consequences of disobedience even then, but for the fact that the order to halt was accompanied with the explanation that General Lee, who was several miles away, did not wish to give battle at Gettysburg. It is stated on good authority that General Lee said, some time before his death, that if Jackson had been there, he would have won in this battle a great and possibly decisive victory. But no soldier in a great crisis ever wished more ardently for deliverer's hand than I wished for one hour of Jackson, when I was ordered to halt. Had he been there, his quick eye would have caught at a glance the entire situation, and instead of halting me, he would have urged me forward and have pressed the advantage to the utmost.

"From the situation plainly to be seen on the first afternoon, and from the facts that afterwards came to light as to the position of the different corps of General Meade's army, it seems certain that if the Confederates had simply moved forward, following up the advantages gained, and striking the separated Union commands in succession, the victory would have been Lee's instead of Meade's.

"I should state here that General Meade's army at that hour was stretched out along the line of his march for nearly thirty miles. General Lee's was much more concentrated. General Hancock's statement of the situation is true and pertinent: 'The rear of our troops were hurrying through the town, pursued by Confederates. There had been an attempt to reform some of the Eleventh Corps as they passed over Cemetery Hill, but it had not been very successful.' And yet I was halted!

"My thoughts were so harrowed and my heart so burdened by the fatal mistake of the afternoon that I was unable to sleep at night. Mounting my horse at two o'clock in the morning, I rode with one or two staff officers to the red barn in which General Ewell and General Early then had their headquarters. Much of my time after nightfall had been spent on the front picket line, listening to the busy strokes of Union picks and shovels on the hills, to the rumble of artillery wheels and the tramp of fresh troops as they were hurried forward by Union commanders and placed in position. There was, therefore, no difficulty in divining the scene that would break on our view with the coming dawn. I did not hesitate to say to both Ewell and Early that a line of heavy earthworks, with heavy guns and ranks of infantry behind them, would frown upon us at daylight. I expressed the opinion that, even at that hour, two o'clock, by a concentrated and vigorous night assault, we could carry those heights, and that if we waited till morning it would cost us 10,000 men to take them. There was a disposition to yield to my suggestions, but other counsels finally prevailed. Those works were never carried, but the cost of the assault upon them, the appalling carnage resulting from the effort to take them, far exceeded that which I had ventured to predict." ("Gordon's Reminiscences of the Civil War.")

General Gordon does not state who refused him permission to make this night attack, but Gov. William Smith, of Virginia, who commanded a brigade at the battle, told me that it was General Early who twice rejected his earnest appeal.

I have heard many Northern soldiers say that the South never had the remotest chance of succeeding, and that even if Meade's army had been defeated and scattered, the North would have risen to a man and have swept Lee's army off the face of the earth.

Had Lee advanced on the evening of the 1st, not even the combined efforts of every man in the North could have checked for a day the march of a veteran army of sixty thousand men. All the millions of warlike Persia could not retard the 30,000 Greeks, led by Alexander; nor could the savage horde of all Britain stop one legion of Caesar's. With the whole of Ireland raging against him, Cromwell marched at will through the island, burning, pillaging and killing. All the militia of Indiana and Ohio could not withstand John Morgan and his three regiments of cavalrymen. The occupation of Northern cities by the Confederates would have given both England and France the pretext they longed for, of acknowledging the South as belligerents. This would have opened her blockaded ports and given her army all the supplies they needed.

The night of the 1st of July was an anxious one to the commanding general of the Federal army. It seemed as if the wheel of Fortune had turned against him. His *corps d'armee*, no matter how they forced their march, would be too late to meet the attack which Lee ordered to be made at dawn of day.

The rank and file of the Confederate army felt now no doubt of the result. The news of the rout of the two Federal corps, magnified as it passed from lip to lip, had reached that point where it was believed that half of the Federal army was destroyed; and as the Southern soldiers sank to sleep that night they were morally certain that they would utterly defeat the foe on the morrow. Visions of marching through Baltimore and a triumphal parade up the avenue in Washington flitted through their minds.

The inner history of the Battle of Gettysburg can only be learned by patching up the scattered fragments of a manuscript torn in small pieces.

Meade was so wrought up as the time passed, that he called a council of war at noon. Neither he nor his corps commanders could fathom Lee's inaction; they dreaded the blow, but where was it to fall? This portentous silence meant something. Judging the future by the past, Lee was the last man on earth to dally when the opportunity offered. Witness his stroke against McClellan in the Seven Days' Battles around Richmond, when he assaulted at the dawn of day the works at Mechanicsville; and who at sunrise got Longstreet's corps through Thoroughfare Gap to aid Jackson. This inertia on the part of the Confederate commander was inexplicable to the Federal generals. But they decided to stay where they were and to attack Lee the next day.

There was not a private soldier in Lee's army who did not expect to be aroused at the earliest dawn and commence the fight. Instead, an absolute silence reigned; the men slept until they were awakened by the rising sun in their eyes, and hurried through their breakfast of fat pork and hardtack. The sun rose high in the heavens and still not a movement was made. It was incomprehensible, and every group of soldiers was discussing the matter and trying to find a solution of the delay.

Lee had distinctly and explicitly ordered Longstreet to attack as soon as it was light enough for forming his troops; and everything was ready.

Lee's plan was simple—it was to storm the heights and find a weak spot somewhere. The plan of battle as given out to the corps commanders for the battle of the second day was that Ewell and Hill were to assault, the artillery keeping pace with the infantry, and that Longstreet, with his corps several lines

26

deep, should carry by storm the left center of the enemy. Stuart was on our right with ten thousand horse, to strike if the attack was successful and convert the retreat into a rout.

Hill and Ewell were ready at sunrise, but Longstreet was riding about, so his orderly states, all the morning, placing his troops in position and changing frequently their dispositions.

General Gordon truly says: "Co-operation by every part of the army was expected and was essential."

As the sun rose higher in the heavens and lifted the mists, Lee chafed and fretted; he saw the golden hours slip by unmarked by a single movement. What raging thoughts must have filled his breast at Longstreet's delay!

When the fate of the country was hanging by a hair, he shrank from suspending Longstreet, just as he refrained from court-martialing Huger for disobedience of orders at Seven Pines and the Seven Days' fight, and later on from dismissing Whiting for getting helplessly drunk and ruining Beauregard's plan to defeat and capture Butler; and also from relieving Early from command in the Valley long after his army had lost confidence in him. It was Jackson who put A. P. Hill, second in command, under arrest just after the battle of Antietam, for disobedience of his orders in failing to make a forced march.

Think of the Commander-in-Chief waiting from 5 o'clock A. M. till 4 o'clock in the afternoon on the pleasure of his subordinate.

Longstreet was a magnificent fighter and a thorough soldier, but his heart was not in his work. He states that at the beginning of the campaign Lee promised him to fight an offensive-defensive battle and force the enemy to attack him in his own chosen position; now the situation was exactly the reverse, and he naturally felt sore at being ordered to assault the enemy in his stronghold. He put off, backed, filled, and dallied, doubtless thinking that Lee would, on second thought, countermand his orders to advance, and make a flank movement and force Meade out of the heights.

As after-events proved, he was perfectly right; but that does not exonerate him from the grave fault of disobedience of orders. Longstreet knew that implicit obedience is the first duty of every soldier, high and low.

If Lee was paralyzed by reluctant subordinates, Meade was in the same fix; and Sickles, commanding the Third Corps, a civilian general, by the way, came within an ace of destroying the army by taking position a mile in advance of the main line without orders and of his own volition. Meade only discovered the false—almost fatal—disposition of the Third Corps when too late to rectify it. Every precept of military science, nay, every principle of common sense should have taught Sickles that the proper place to station his corps was at the foot of Little Round Top, and with that crest crowned with artillery, Marye's Heights and Malvern Hill would have been in comparison an ant mound to a mountain.

When the assault was to be made by Longstreet, Lee's orders were for them to advance in the center, and for Ewell to charge as soon as he heard Hill's guns. It was impossible to secure uniformity. To send a message to the left wing of the Confederate army a staff officer or courier would have to make a long detour on the outside circumference of the half circle and ride fully four miles. Hill did not get this order to advance until an hour after Longstreet's notice, and when Hill advanced, Ewell did not hear his guns and did not move at all.

General Gordon in a magazine article says:

"Pressure—hard, general, and constant pressure—upon Meade's right would have called him to its defense and weakened his center. That pressure was only spasmodic and of short duration—Lee and his plan could only promise success on the proviso that the movement was both general and prompt. It was neither. Moments in battle are pregnant with the fate of armies. When the opportune moment to strike arrives, the blow must fall, for the next instant it may be futile. Not only moments but hours of delay occurred."

Doubleday, in his book on Chancellorsville, writes a page remarkable for its truth, force and power. He says (p. 52): "In the histories of lost empires, we almost invariably find that the cause of their final overthrow on the battle-field may be traced to the violation of one military principle which is that the attempt to *overpower a central force by converging columns is almost always fatal to the assailants;* for the force in the center is nearly double the strength of the one on the circumference, yet this is the first mistake made by every tyro in generalship. A strong blow can be given by a sledge hammer, but if we divide it into twenty small hammers, the blows will necessarily be scattering and uncertain. Let us suppose an army holds the junction of two roads; if all close in at once, the attacking force would probably confuse and overpower it. It seems easy, but practically it is nearly impossible; for no two routes are precisely alike. The columns never move simultaneously, and therefore never arrive at the same time. Some of this is due to the character of the commanders. One man is full of dash and goes forward at once; another is tired, or over-cautious; a third stops to recall some out-lying detachment. The result is, that the outer army has lost its strength and is always beaten in detail."

This was written before Gettysburg was fought, and yet how perfectly it fitted the bill.

Napoleon's favorite tactics were in defiance of this military rule, and his victory at Marengo and Ulm was in the advance of converging column; but he made his marshals set their watches by his, and at the exact time they were to be at a certain place. Yet he lost his empire from this very cause; and Grouchy's failure to converge at Waterloo caused his ruin.

Longstreet started to the attack on a hot summer afternoon, and his splendid corps struck at Sickles's Third Corps. Had Sickles placed his back to Little Round Top, he could have withstood the onslaught of Lee's whole army; for with the fire of his guns and musketry, he could have so swept the plain that not a fleeing rabbit could have made the crest safely. Sickles has always stubbornly avowed that the position he took was a correct one. Any person who has ever stood on the tower on the crest of Big Round Top, with the scene before him as a map, could see at a glance what a colossal blunder he made.

Had Longstreet moved, even two hours earlier, Sickles would not have had the support of General Sedgwick's corps, that at the beginning of the battle was at Westminster and did not reach Gettysburg until between 2 and 3 o'clock in the afternoon. There was a Titanic struggle for four hours when Longstreet struck Sickles. The shock was so terrific that the Federal army reeled, staggered, and all but fell.

In a battle, time is priceless! Had Longstreet moved even thirty minutes earlier, he would have taken that rock-crowned post of vantage, Little Round Top, without a struggle. As long as America shall last and tourists visit that historic battle-field, they will wonder at the turn of Fate that made *five minutes* the turning point of that battle; for had the Confederates seized it, they could have crowned the great hill with batteries and taken Meade on the flank; would have forced him to evacuate his position. Five minutes settled it; for Hood's men were scaling the slope, and the Union signal service men were furling their flags when a Maine regiment which was passing by was ordered to rush to the crest. The sides of Little Round Top are composed of boulders of rock from the size of a paving stone to that of a house. The advance of Hood's men was stayed for a fraction of time, and five brigades from Hancock's and Humphreys's divisions all sent in a double-quick to the summit. Hazlett's battery reached the top, and among the gorges, crags, and rocks a furious contest raged. One man behind those granite boulders was a match for five. The colonel of the Third Arkansas regiment, speaking of the herculean wrestle, said: "The hills were so steep, the rocks so sharp, that without scaling-ladders it was impossible to advance."

Every Federal general officer fell: Cross, Zook, Brooks, and Hazlett; but the Federal rank and file clung to the rocks of refuge with splendid courage. It was a fight at pistol-shot distance, and the soldiers of both sides went down by the hundreds. But the men of Hood's division, who had never suffered a defeat, met their match in that grim line of blue that stayed their impetuous rush and held them back.

As Longstreet pressed the left center, Meade threw every man, reserves and all, into the breach, and he committed, apparently, a monumental error in taking the last soldier from his extreme right (two brigades of the White Star Division), thus leaving Culp's Hill undefended. Stewart's (Confederate) brigade, of Johnson's division, walked quickly in and took possession. This was about 7 o'clock in the evening, and the Baltimore pike was a short distance away. Here was packed all of Meade's ammunition wagons and ordnance stores. If General Edward Johnson had but followed up his advance, he would have struck Meade in the rear when his left was denuded of troops. Such a blow as a fresh division striking at that critical moment, the Union rear, would have utterly routed their army. Johnson made no advance whatever that evening, but assaulted the next morning after Meade had learned of his error and heavily reinforced his right. Johnson was repulsed with great loss.

I asked a staff officer of General Johnson's why he did not advance when there was not even a skirmish line to oppose him? His reply was that Johnson said he was afraid the Yankees were leading him into a trap. This was certainly a case of a wrong man in the wrong place.

The crisis came in the second day's fight when Humphreys flanked Barksdale, and was in turn flanked by Wright's Georgians and Perry's Floridians. Under this flank assault Humphreys's line broke and crumbled; and just as the sun dropped below the horizon the scene was such as beggars description. Little Round Top was full of flashing fire from the artillery posted there; Death's Valley, at the base, showed dimly through the sulphurous smoke. Every gun on Cemetery Heights was bellowing; the clouds of dust and haze half obscured the scene; broken caissons, slain horses, overturned cannon, muskets by the thousands, knapsacks, canteens, boxes of ammunition covered the ground; the dead lay everywhere, the wounded cumbered the earth by the thousands, uncared for, forgotten in the maddening fight. Masses of soldiery half-hidden, moving standards half-seen, screams of defiance, the Yankee hurrah, the Rebel yell breaking out at intervals, officers on horseback galloping wildly, shrieking their commands which none heeded. It was as if pandemonium had broken loose in the wreck of matter and the crash of worlds.

More than half of Hancock's men were prone in the dust. Sykes's Regulars were torn to pieces and the Army of the Potomac almost a mob. Order and form was lost, and regiments, brigades, and divisions were mixed and mingled together in a mad, swaying mass. Sickles fell with a shattered thigh, and his men, those who were left, broke and rushed to the rear. If a general advance by Hill and Ewell had then been made, the most complete victory since Waterloo would have been the result. But it was not to be. The Confederate reserves stood stock-still in their tracks. The Rebel brigades of Hays and Hoke scaled the heights, and sixty pieces of artillery fell into their hands. As these veterans stood beside the smoking guns, they felt that they had the citadel within their grasp, and the wild Rebel yell echoed from the topmost crest of Cemetery Heights; but no reserves came to support them, and with despair and rage in their hearts, they retired down the hill.

Hays, in his official report, says:

"A little before 8 P. M. on July 2nd, I was ordered to advance. With my own and Hoke's brigade on my left, I immediately moved forward, and had gone but a short distance when my whole line became exposed to a most terrific fire from the enemy's batteries, from the entire range of hills in front, and to the right and to the left; still both brigades advanced steadily, up and over the first hill, when the canister opened upon us in point-blank distance, but owing to the darkness of the evening now verging into night, and the deep obscurity afforded by the smoke of the firing, our exact locality could not be discovered by the enemy's gunners and we thus escaped *what in the full light of day could have been nothing less than a horrible slaughter.*

"Taking advantage of this we continued forward until we reached the second line behind a stone wall; still advancing, we came to an abattis of fallen timber, and then a third line with rifle-pits where their reserves were; these we broke. Then with a rush we reached the summit and captured the artillery, and every piece of artillery had been silenced. After a silence of several minutes their lines of battle attacked us, and as I had no reserves, I retired." (Reb. Records, Vol. 27, pp. 480-481.)

Hay's Louisiana Brigade, which was claimed by the enemy to have been almost annihilated, lost but few; only 29 were killed, 159 wounded and 80 taken prisoners; in all 268 men.

In a letter to the Governor of North Carolina, Major Tate, under date of July 8th, 1863, gives a thrilling account of this charge of Hays. He says:

"Longstreet had charged on the south face and was repulsed. A. P. Hill charged on the west face and was repulsed. Our two brigades, late in the evening, were ordered to charge the north front, and after a struggle such as this war has furnished no parallel, 75 North Carolinians of the Sixth Regiment, and 12 Louisianians, and Hays's brigade scaled the heights and planted the colors of the Sixth North Carolina and Ninth Louisiana on the guns.

"The enemy stood with a tenacity never before displayed by them, with bayonets clubbed, musket, sword, and pistol and rocks, firm as a wall, yet we cleared the heights and silenced the guns. In vain did I send to the rear for support; the enemy hurried his troops on both flanks, got in my rear, and I had to retreat. On reaching our lines I demanded to know why I was not supported, and was coolly informed that it was not known we were on the works.

"To think of the monstrous injustice done us! I assure you that the fighting was no sensation or fancy picture; such a fight as the Yankees made inside of their works has never been equalled. Inside, the enemy were left lying in great heaps, most all with bayonet wounds, and many with their skulls broken by the stocks of our guns. We left not a living man on the hill."

Nearly a year later, when a prisoner of war, I discussed Gettysburg with Federal officers and soldiers; and later on, after escaping from prison in Ohio and making my way through the enemy's country in disguise, I talked with the Union soldiers who were in that battle, and every one, without a single exception, said: "The Rebs had us whipped once at Gettysburg, but they did not know it," and on asking which battle it was, the answer was invariably, "about sunset on the second day."

The third day at Gettysburg dawned clear and cloudless; it should, by all precedents, have been one of driving rain; for there was enough concussion of the atmosphere to have started every cloud that encircled the globe, into action.

Lee had one more chance; if he could attack at sun up, before the shattered regiments, brigades and divisions could reorganize, victory was certain.

To an ordinary foe, such a stunning blow as that which struck the Federal forces the night before would have taken all the fight out of the soldiers; but the Army of the Potomac was as thrice-tempered steel.

Man to man, I do not think the rank and file were equal to the privates of Lee's army for several reasons: one was, that nearly every Southern soldier was a native-born American, and until their Government was a fixed fact, they put all thoughts of promotion aside; and in the ranks were men often higher in the walks of life than their officers. It was a source of pride to the wealthy, well-educated youth to serve as a private soldier. It proved his patriotism, and the women showed their love and affection very plainly for the men who carried the guns.

In the Union Army it was different; to remain a private in the ranks was tantamount to confessing a willingness to be a day laborer instead of a boss. No rich, well-born, educated Northerner was content to carry a musket after the patriotic delirium which animated them for the first year had died out.

There were plenty of foreigners, mill hands, apprentices and human drift-wood to serve in the ranks, but he who had prestige, brains, or political influence was soon sporting chevrons, straps, or stars. The officers of the Army of the Potomac, educated, proud men, were every whit as brave as those of the Confederate Army; and give the American gentleman a few hours of daylight, and no matter what the history of yesterday, they will be found ready to meet, with steady front, any crisis to-day or to-morrow. The old Anglo-Saxon race never showed its undying tenacity and bravery more vividly than it did on that day of July 3rd, 1863, when at noon of the next day the disorganized mass that Humphreys acknowledged was beaten at sunset, proudly and fearlessly confronted the victor.

Lee yet had a good opportunity to win if he had assaulted Meade at daylight on the morning of the 3rd, and he so ordered.

Longstreet says: "I met General Lee very early on the morning of the 3rd, and anticipating any remark that the Commander-in-Chief might make, I said: 'General Lee, my scouts have returned with sufficient information to lead me to believe that there are excellent chances of inducing General Meade to attack us.' To which General Lee replied by pointing to Cemetery Hill and saying: 'The enemy is there, and I am going to strike him.' I said in return, 'General, I have seen men fight by companies, regiments, brigades, and divisions, but never anything like you propose.'" (*Baltimore Sun*, October 25, 1889.)

Longstreet again shirked duty, and let the whole forenoon pass; and it was not until 1 P. M. that the Confederate artillery of over 100 guns opened on Cemetery Hill to sweep the plateau so as to allow the infantry to assault, and Pickett's Virginians were to lead, supported by McLaws, and D. H. Hill's division of his own, and two divisions of A. P. Hill's corps; in all numbering some twenty-seven thousand men. Longstreet again disobeyed his chief's orders, and only 14,000 were formed for the charge.

It would have made little difference; the position, so strong by nature, had been rendered nearly impregnable by art, and defended as it was by one hundred and thirty-five cannon and forty thousand muskets, it seemed like madness to storm the works.

Lee thought that if two brigades could reach the summit, as Hays and Hoke did the evening before, a storming column of thirty thousand men could go to the same spot, especially if the heights were swept clear by heavy artillery fire. But he did not take into consideration that it was dark when the assault was made.

At 1 o'clock in the afternoon the Confederate batteries opened their fire; being on the rim of the circle, they had a great advantage in delivering a concentric fire; but Colonel Alexander, in command of the artillery, made a grave mistake in not concentrating his fire, first on one spot, and then on another. One discharge from his 100 guns on one battery would have annihilated it. Had he given orders to commence on the left center and then range along to the right, he would have not only silenced but crushed the enemy's batteries.

At 2 P. M. the artillery ceased and the vital moment had come.

Longstreet says in his report:

"I gave the order to General Pickett to advance to the assault; I then found that our supply of ammunition was so short that the batteries could not reopen. The order for this attack, which I could not favor under better auspices, *would have been reversed.*"

I have often talked with General Pickett, after the war, about this charge. He told me he felt supremely confident that his division could make an opening in the line, and felt proud to show the army what the Virginians could do; and that, of course, he felt assured that right behind his assaulting column were heavy reserves that would hold all he could take.

There is one point in this famous charge that historians make no mention of, yet it was a vitally important one; and that was, that it was always the custom when the infantry made a charge for the batteries to accompany them. Had this been done, Pickett could have held the heights until succor reached him. Instead of his eight batteries keeping step with him and pouring a furious fire in the teeth of Hancock, only a single one (Captain Miller's) followed him.

The madness of Pickett's charge! It was superb—like the charge of Balaklava; but it was not war. Let us see what Pickett and his reserves were going against, and put yourself in the place of one of his soldiers.

He started from the woods, and to reach his objective point on the heights he had to walk one and a half miles. Each man had his gun, bayonet, haversack, blanket, and heavy cartridge-box. The line had to move slowly so as to save their strength for the supreme effort. Eighty cannon commenced their practice on the advancing lines. There were two Yankee lines of battle on the Emmitsburg road behind a stone wall; enough alone to break the Rebel advance. These were driven back after a bloody contest. The line had to cross an open plain, and then those guns changed their solid shot for shell.

Imagine the scene of that line of devoted men, breasting, with heads thrust forward, the iron hail-storm. Had the whole valley been wreathed in smoke the long lines of gray could have swept up unperceived to the foot of the heights without losing many men, and might have stood some chance of splitting the Federal line, but the officer commanding the Union artillery, General Hunt, with the intuition of a born soldier, had ordered his artillery to cease firing, and the dense battle smoke that had accumulated during the hours of bombardment slowly drifted skyward, and in the bright glare of the July sun every Rebel soldier's figure was painfully distinct.

When a line of battle is on a charge the order is given before they start to "guide to the colors;" that is, if a man drops, the one next him closes up toward the flag, which is always in the center, and thus the line, which gaps continually when men are killed and wounded, is kept intact.   Of course the more men that drop out the shorter the line becomes.

Pickett had two lines in his division, but as the fire became severe his lines continued to shorten, and before he reached the crest became so short that his right was in the air, and over-reached by the attacking line.   This allowed a flank fire, which is the most deadly of all.

A man can kill with a shot-gun several swallows sitting on a telegraph wire, but suppose he climbs to the top of the pole and shoots down the wire with a raking shot, he can bag dozens.

It is impossible for any troops to keep a perfect alignment under such a fusilade; they must either break and run to the rear or rush desperately forward.

Armistead struck the center of the Union works, which was occupied by Webb's brigade.   This command having lost the pick of its men on the first day, had the nerve knocked out of them by the furious cannonading, and when Pickett's line came surging up the hill they broke despite the frenzied efforts of their officers, and abandoned their works, which was a hastily constructed barricade of fence rails, thrown up a few yards in advance of the regular stone wall that ran along the crest of Cemetery Ridge.

Into this gap dashed Armistead, with his hat on the point of his sword, cheering on his men.

Lieutenant Mason, one of the few of Armistead's men who got out safely, told me that night that not over sixty, or at the most one hundred soldiers, got over the stone wall that was abandoned by Webb's brigade; but there was one command that stood there and died there after the infantry had fled, and that was Cushing with his battery.   A more splendid exhibition of valor has never been witnessed; for he fought his guns after the infantry supports had left him, and disdaining to fly he fell at the feet of his Napoleons.

The rest of Pickett's men stopped at the stone wall, and lying down, poured an irregular fire on the confused squads, hurrying lines, and groups of blue-coats on the level plateau.

The fire of the Yankee artillery on the right and left was concentrated and swept the hill-side in the center, and every Rebel
was compelled to throw himself flat on his face to escape annihilation.   For a few minutes, at least, Armistead's men were out of
the rim of this fire, and looked back for the gray line of reserves
to push through the breach that Armistead had made; but the reserves had drifted back.

There has been a great deal of controversy in the South as
to why these troops retreated.   The truth of the whole matter
is this: the advance was a bungle; the officers of the various
commands received no explicit instructions.   They were to advance, that was all; and no orders were given where to rally in
case of defeat.   Had the point just above the Emmitsburg pike
been chosen, where there was a dip in the ground affording security from the fire—or even the Emmitsburg road, the retreat
of Pickett's division would have been a simple retirement instead
of a total rout.

Many brigades of the supporting line became bewildered and
marched at random over the smoking plain.   Many halted and
threw themselves on their faces and simply waited.   They were
ready and willing, if handled intelligently, but were confused and
disheartened.

Then Armistead's men stood victors for a brief moment on the
crest of the hill, the rest of the division were loading and firing.
Most of the soldiers were lying down waiting for the reserves, and they were ready to join with their comrades in the
rush, but when alone and unsupported, the Federal troops closing in on both flanks, the Rebel line went to pieces, and it was *sauve
qui peut*.   Many surrendered, and many, running awful risks,
raced back across the metal-swept plain.

Meade put in every available man; it was neck or nothing
with him.

When Pickett started, the cry went along the lines of blue,
"Here they come!   Here they come!" and Meade established a
cordon of slightly wounded men, who were ordered to lie on the
ground a few paces in the rear of the last reserve and shoot any
who attempted to run to the rear.

Longstreet says of this fight:

"The brigades of Trimble and Pettigrew, under the concentrated fire of artillery and musketry, after Pickett reached the
ravine, wavered and broke, and Anderson's division was ordered

to their support; he was halted, and the enemy threw their entire force upon Pickett and crushed his division into fragments."

Pettigrew cannot be blamed.   Heth's division had borne the brunt of the battle of the 1st of July, and his loss was enormous—far surpassing that of any division in the army.   Pickett's loss out of 5,500 men, in killed, wounded, and captured, was: Garnett's brigade, 941; Armistead's, 1,191; Kemper's, 731—in all, 2,710; but of these 1,599 were captured, leaving 1,101 killed and wounded.

The three brigades of Heth's division *did not lose a man by capture,* but in killed and wounded the First Brigade (Pettigrew's) lost 1,105 out of 1,700 men in line; about 70 per cent.

Out of 600 men in line, the Second Brigade (Lane's) lost 389 and the Fourth (Scales's) lost 535; in all 2,029.*

The losses of some of the North Carolina regiments were appalling.

Look at the famous Twenty-sixth North Carolina Regiment (of Pettigrew's brigade) raised by Gov. Vance, which went into battle with 900 men.   Fox in his book states that they came out of the charge leaving 800 men on the field killed and wounded; no prisoners were captured.   This heroic record does not cease here: Company F can duplicate the famous dispatch of Sam Houston: "Thermopylae has its messengers of defeat, but the Alamo has none;" for Company F, Twenty-sixth North Carolina, went into the fight with three officers and eighty men, and every man was killed or wounded.   So the report of General Longstreet that Pender's men wavered was most unjust; they fell and died; none surrendered; and if the history of the world can show more magnificent fighting, it has never been told in song or in story.

Cold statistics prove that while Pickett's charge was magnificent, the steady discipline and pluck of Pettigrew's men has never been matched but once, and that was when Ney's grenadiers of "The Old Guard" died in their tracks at Waterloo.

The histories of Gettysburg written before the publication of the Rebellion Records do Pettigrew's brigade great injustice. I know that around our camp-fires we laid the blame of Pickett's defeat to the failure of Pettigrew's North Carolinians to support him; and the Federal writers fall into the same gross error.

---

*Medical Surgeon L. Guild's report of the casualties of the Army of Northern Virginia, Reb. Rec., Vol. 27, p. 338.

Bates in his book, "Battle of Gettysburg," says (p. 160):

"For Pettigrew with his green and already decimated levies quailed before the terrific fire of Hay's men."

Comte de Paris in his book says (p. 216):

"Pettigrew on Pickett's left does his best to support him. His own brigade and that of Archer have reached Hay's line but have failed to effect a breach. Trimble, who is following them closely, sustains them vigorously. Lane's North Carolinians have already penetrated the first line of Federals drawn up as it is at the foot of the declivity, and beginning to scale it he draws near the wall. Archer's and Scales's North Carolinians have passed the same walls a few minutes before; but Pettigrew's two brigades on the left have remained in the rear and cannot, or will not, arrive in time to support him. After a contest at short range, very brief but exceedingly murderous, in which Trimble is seriously wounded, his troops and Pettigrew's retire even before the two brigades of Thomas and Perrin have reached their position, and while Pickett is still fighting on the right."

If Pickett's division had met the fire that Pettigrew's men had to contend against, not a man would have been left alive to reach the crest of the hill. The point where Pickett struck the Federal line was their weak spot. The point of Pettigrew's and Trimble's advance was directly in front of Cemetery Hill. Scales was on the right and in the rear of Archer, with Lane on the left and Wilcox in the rear; as they advanced Wilcox lost his way in the smoke of battle and Pettigrew and Trimble were the targets of fifty guns of Osborne's posted on Cemetery Ridge. When Pickett closed up the bridge, too close for the Federal guns to fire, the forty pieces of Hazard's turned on the reserves; thus ninety cannon were firing on an average three times a minute. These guns, loaded with grape and canister, swept the plain at point-blank distance with a continuing sheet of iron hail; added to this, the terrific infantry fire did not leave a space as large as a man's hand untouched by a leaden bullet. The supporting lines were leveled to the ground. Pettigrew was destroyed for the time, and the Federal reserves, consisting of the brigades of Hall's and Harman's, the Nineteenth Massachusetts, One Hundred and Fifty-first Pennsylvania, Twentieth New York, and Forty-second Regiment of the line, amounting to twelve regiments, stood four deep, ready to defend the ground if Pickett succeeded in holding the crest.

One man lying down behind a stone wall is a match for three men advancing across the open to attack him. Bates says in his book (p. 161):

"As an example of the futility, and at the same time the accuracy of the Rebel fire, it may be stated as an observation of the writer made soon after the battle, that the splashes of the leaden bullets upon the shelving rock and the low stone wall along its very edge and behind which were Hancock's men, for a distance of half a mile, were so thick, that one could scarcely lay his hand upon any part of either the wall or the rock without touching them. All this ammunition was of course thrown away, *not one bullet in a thousand reaching its intended victim.*"

The fragments of fourteen regiments of Pickett's division, panting, breathless, smoke-begrimed, reached their own lines. Every Rebel soldier who witnessed the scene knew that the great charge had failed; but there were no symptoms of panic; not a private in the ranks left his place, and they waited, expecting every moment to see the long lines of blue come surging toward them, and they all hoped they would.

There were many unthinking people in the North who blamed Meade for not attacking Lee after Pickett's repulse. Deluded mortals! the condition of the Federal army on that evening was desperate. Attack! Why! another day's battle would have disrupted it.

On the night of July 3rd, when Lee was making preparations to retreat, sending his staff officers in every direction to hurry up the movement, he was asked by General Pickett if he thought the Union army would make an active pursuit. General Lee's answer was striking, and showed how well he understood the situation. He said: "That army [meaning Meade's] will be as a brooding dove for the next twelve months."

We often read of battles in Europe where the villages and towns of the enemy are held, of the outrages upon the citizens, of every house having its billet to lodge and feed so many soldiers; of the private dwellings being seized and used for hospital purposes; and of worse things still: of insult, rapine and arson.

The conquered town of Gettysburg was held by the Rebel soldiery for three days, at a time when their blood was at fever heat, and later on when the soldiers were savage with disappointment at their defeat; yet there was not a single act of violence nor so much as a spoken word of insult in all that time. One of Archer's command, a captain in the Thirteenth Alabama, who remained in the town, wounded, told me that during the first day all the towns-people remained hidden away in their cellars; that on the second and third days, getting over their fright, many came out on the streets; he never saw one of the Rebs even address a woman without lifting his hat.

As Lee has said:

"Had Stonewall Jackson been at Gettysburg, I would have established the Southern Confederacy."

As Sweden without Charles XII; as the army of Parliament without Cromwell; as the troops of the Louvre without Napoleon; as the Revolutionary Patriots without Washington—so was the South without her Jackson, and impartial history will decide that he was the greatest master of the art of war that America ever produced.

It has often been said and written that the firm faith and fervent hopes of the patriotic people within the Union were nearer despondency and despair in those fateful July days than at any other time.

But these ideas are all false, as every American soldier who fought in the sixties knows, for the darkest hours of the American Union was in June, July and August, 1864, after the battles of the Wilderness, Todd's Tavern, Spottsylvania, South Anna, Yellow Farm, Cold Harbor and numberless skirmishes had been fought, and when the lowlands of Virginia were literally drenched with blood, and when Grant's appalling loss of five thousand officers and over sixty thousand men of all arms bathed the North in tears and made the stoutest heart despair.

Gettysburg has been called the high-tide of the Rebellion, and the spot where the gallant Cushing fell, the high-water mark.

'Tis not so. The tide reached its flood just after Cold Harbor, and it was one year after Gettysburg was fought that the star of the Confederacy shone with its brightest lustre; but as the summer waned, the splendor of that star which the world watched with breathless interest grew dimmer each hour until it was quenched forever at Appomattox.

A fitting wind-up of the Gettysburg Campaign is Lee's order to his troops on entering the enemy's territory:

"Order No. 73.   Chambersburg, Pa., June 27th, 1863.

"*It must be remembered that we make war only against armed men.* The Commanding General, therefore, earnestly exhorts the troops to abstain, with the most scrupulous care, from unnecessary or wanton injury to private property, and he enjoins upon all officers to arrest and bring to summary punishment any soldier disregarding this order."

From the dim traditions of the Assyrian Empire, from the pages of Herodotus, or the struggle of Rameses, we may search the records of hostile campaigns and crusades—we may study the histories of the Golden Age of Greece, or the annals of Imperial Rome, or the various dynasties of Europe, but we can find no record of a nobler utterance from the lips of a warrior than that from the pen of General Lee, which brought comfort and peace unto thousands of Northern hearts.

How many statues, monoliths and mausoleums of great conquerors which adorn the parks of both the Old and New World, on whose base, carved in letters of gold, can be found a loftier sentiment than this: "We make war only against armed men."

In the flush of success the tears of women, houseless, homeless and shelterless are lost sight of, but the South endorsed then, as she will forever, that immortal decretal penned by Lee: *"We make war only against armed men."*

CHAPTER III.

This renowned troop was organized before the war by Major John Scott, of Fauquier County, Virginia. Its members at the commencement of the conflict were the very pick of the county, both as regards men and mounts—a body of men chosen from the garden spot of the State, Fauquier being the largest and most fertile county in the rich Piedmont section. The Black Horse then had blood in the horses and blood in the men.

The organization was the result of a dinner given by William H. Payne to Mr. John Scott, near Warrenton, Virginia.

As the gentlemen sat over their wine, discussing "Uncle Tom's Cabin" and the impending conflict, Mr. Payne, a fire-eating young lawyer of Fauquier, asked Mr. Scott how he would like to command a squadron of cavalry. Mr. Scott, feeling assured that an internecine conflict was close at hand, replied that he was willing to accept any position.

It was Mr. Payne who spread among the young planters of the county his idea, and it was enthusiastically received at a meeting of the young men at the next court day in Warrenton.

The company was organized, and John Scott elected captain, Robert Randolph, a planter, first lieutenant; Charles H. Gordon, second lieutenant; and Alex. D. Payne, third lieutenant.

At the John Brown raid the Black Horse saw their first active service.

On April 26th, 1861, the troop was mustered into service.

Captain John Scott was summoned to Montgomery, Alabama, to assist in forming the new Confederate Government, and Private Billy Payne was accorded the unusual honor of being elected captain over the heads of his superiors.

It was a wise choice; it was under his splendid leadership that they imbibed from him the dash, the daring, the eclat, which made them the crack cavalry command of the Confederacy.

Captain Billy Payne, afterwards General, was a born soldier, a typical Virginian, whose bright mind, united to his soldierly abilities and great heart, made him the idol of his troops.

It was during the first and second years of the war that this company stood highest, when it numbered about seventy-five men, fifty of whom were as gallant fellows as ever swung themselves into the saddle. All young men, all dare-devils in the most literal sense of the term, they at once made up that material of which cavalry should be composed. Every men was a finished horseman and a dead shot; familiar with every blind path and hog-track in the section; thus forming the finest company of light cavalry and scouts ever raised in the South.

It is said that the Black Horse made a goodly showing on that morning when they filed through the little town of Warrenton, the county seat of Fauquier, on their way to Harper's Ferry during the John Brown trouble, mounted on their coal-black horses, with nodding plumes, burnished sabres and waving pennons, looking, as they were indeed, the very flower of the cavalry. The Austrian Hussars of the Royal Household never presented a more gallant or martial appearance or rode better. Such a troop Cardinal Richelieu, who had the warrior soul beneath the livery of Rome, would have loved to see by the side of the French King Louis.

In 1863 all this had been changed by two years of campaigning. Uniforms had long given way to the gray, ragged, discolored jacket and breeches such as those worn by the infantry. The jaunty plumed hat had been superseded by a black felt slouch, or forage-cap. The stylish Wellington top-boots, which used to shine like an ebony mirror, had degenerated to the coarse cowhide and jack-boots, or worse still, the regulation army brogan. The black Virginia racers had been succeeded by animals of all hues as well as all sizes and breeds.

Yet the same hearts beat under the tattered jackets as did under the buff facings of the once faultless uniform; and though rough to look upon, they were brave and gallant soldiers, true as steel, and withal gentlemen to the core. They were no longer holiday soldiers, delighting in their own warlike shadow, loving to hear the clank of the long sabres against the spurs; but were changed to veteran cavalrymen and accomplished scouts with each a record of daring deeds, of hand-to-hand encounters, of midnight forays, of dashing raids by the light of the stars, of solitary watches and sudden captures. They were the same men who in days of peace were leading lazy college lives or ornamenting the home circle in a gentle, easy-going existence, which ran on to its close like the smooth, broad, peaceful current of the river; men whose lines were cast in pleasant places; whose days were spent in riding after the hounds, looking over their broad ancestral acres, shooting over their dogs and practicing a profuse hospitality which they held as sacred as their creed. They took life with its sunshine as a kind of long holiday, brimful of pleasure, to be enjoyed with mirth, joviality and content; in the faces of whom could be traced that bonhomie which comes from taking things easily as they chance, without care or fret, fit descendants of those cavaliers who were

"The kindliest of the kindly band
    Who rarely hated ease,
Who rode with Smith around the land
    And Raleigh round the seas."

Scions of this old race, the old refinement and the old courtesy lingered in word and glance; and lazy looking as some of them were, they were as desperate a set as any men on earth, holding life so cheaply that after constant skirmishes and combats, danger only charmed and never repelled them.

In this company were over a dozen of the most celebrated scouts in the Army of Northern Virginia, whose experience had many times led them into the midst of hostile camps under every conceivable disguise; who had lived with their lives in their hands, their hands on the pistols, their pistols on the cock, until, like the Carlist guerrilla troopers, they found the keenest pleasure in life only when they were in danger of losing it.

In 1863 Captain Randolph had tried to swell the ranks of his company so as to form of it an independent battalion; but as one hundred and sixty only could be enrolled the effort failed. Even the attempt proved an unfortunate step, as it placed in this hitherto proud company about fifty of the most trifling, scary, no-account men that ever propagated a base-born race. They loved so much their worthless hides that they never placed them where they could possibly be perforated either by shot, shell or sabre. They would keep in ranks and march decently enough, but the sound of a cannon ten miles off would send them running to the rear. One would drop out to get a canteen of water, and that would be the last seen of him for a week. Another would clap his hand to his stomach in mute pantomime, and seek medical aid so far away that his comrades who did not understand the subterfuge might have mourned him dead. A third would stop to arrange a blanket on a sore-back horse, and take six weeks to do it. A fourth would slyly unbuckle his pack and let it fall. Of course he must dismount to rearrange it, and it is needless to say this would be the end of him, and so on until the last of these human rats had disappeared into some hiding-place. Hence by the time the Fourth Regiment drew up in a squad row to charge, only the cracks of the Black Horse would be there stripped for the fight.

In scouting it was still worse; these timid recruits avoided the vicinity of a blue-coat with as much precaution as the Arab would a leper—hiding in the thick pine bushes and there staying until hunger sent them begging to some farm-house near. Sometimes a good half dozen would valiantly rush upon a blood-thirsty Yankee all unarmed, who would be caught in the desperate act of carrying a half dozen canteens of milk purchased from some neighboring farm. Quietly making his way to camp he would suddenly find himself confronted by these Black Horsemen and ordered to surrender. Of course he would yield himself and all portable possessions, his boots, his hat, his watch, &c., not forgetting the milk; and thus despoiled he would be permitted to go. His captors would re-enter the thicket and proceed, like some other soldiers of whom we have read, "to cast lot for the raiment," and then they would present themselves before Captain Randolph and lie worse than old Ananias himself.

The men were in truth not worth their salt, always deserting their comrades in times of menace. The gallant members of the organization had such contempt for the cravens that they made no effort to conceal it and rarely took any notice of them. This made no difference to them—what shame had they? They merely followed as jackals follow the lion.

At this time the Black Horse was commanded by Captain Randolph; and if ever nature intended a man for a soldier, he was that man. The military profession suited his taste. His habits and bent of mind, his magnetism and cool courage made him an ideal cavalryman and one who would be certain to rise should this branch of the service have opportunities to make itself a .name.

Little discipline was to be found in the cavalry, for although regular drills had been kept up in the past in evolutions, the sabre exercise and infantry tactics, but owing to incessant movements during the last two years of the war there ceased to be any drilling whatever. Few of the cavalrymen knew the manual of the sabre, indeed the men as a general thing looked upon that weapon, so far as its use for purposes deadly were concerned, with the most sovereign contempt. Many wore them under protest, while others liked to have them at home or upon a furlough, imagining they imparted a suggestion of possibilities, a fierce and warlike appearance. A huge sabre hanging by the side was sure to bang and rattle against the boots, not to speak of the clanking on the floor when one sat down, scaring little children into fits, and then it was so ornamental.

In regular service and for pacific purposes troopers found them very serviceable, and so these cavalry sabres were used in a way that would have made the old Cuirassiers of Kellerman or the Black Hussars of Duke Charles open their eyes with wonder. They were as axes and toasting forks, "devil a bit else," as Mike Cleburne used to say; for at the end of every march, after tent poles had been hacked down, a fire made, the weapon would be drawn, and upon it the meat, whose juice was the only blood it ever tasted, suspended over the flames. No richer, ruddier human fluid stained black the points of cavalry sabres, and black you always found them.

Then again in summer and autumn, when fruit hung low and ripe on the boughs, sabres were found uncommonly useful.

But they had bloody scars. Often on the march, as we passed some farm-house, an incautious brood of spring chickens or an old goose would be spied contentedly waddling along the road like a buxom widow going to church. Then a circling sweep of steel flashing in the sun, and the blood of the fowls would crimson the road.

The sabre has seen its day and will rank hereafter in museums along with the bow and arrow, the lance and matchlock. A brace of six shooters and the breechloader render the sabre for military use more harmless and inoffensive than the club of the aborigines.

What is read in newspapers of desperate cavalry charges in which hundreds fall, cleft from chin to chin with deadly steel, is in this day the veriest bosh. A century ago fighting was carried on in just such style, because the old flintlock fire-arm, after some dozen rounds, refused to go off or the flint would be broken or lost; it was a weapon not safe to count upon all day. The bayonet never failed, and on it the soldier, placing his only confidence, was anxious to close with the foe. In the same manner the dragoon would fire off his holster bellmouth pistol, and then make a dernier resort of his sabre, in which case it became a terrible instrument of destruction. In this age, however, it would be folly. Suppose, by way of illustration, that in some great battle two hostile brigades of cavalry had met; one is drawn up in line awaiting the charge, with breech-loading carbines and a pair of Colt's pistols carrying six shots each. The impetus of the rush may bear down the opposing line, but in the melee which would follow the sabre would be but a poor match for the twelve shots of each trooper.

For deciding the fortunes of great battles the day of cavalry is numbered. For raids, cutting off communications and as mounted infantry, it is serviceable, but that is all.

In the Seven Years' War, Seyditz, Frederick's chief of cavalry, was the greatest leader which the world ever produced. By constant drilling he formed a body of horsemen which under him were simply incomparable. Firing and dismounting were thrown in the background, and riding was made the specialty; he laid down several rigid rules for the guidance of his officers. In a charge, he said:

"No firing shall be indulged in, and only cold steel used. No commander will allow his troops to fire a shot under penalty of infamous cashiering."

By these tactics Frederick the Great won, through his splendid cavalry, the battles of Zorndorf, Rosbach, Sturgan Leuthen and others, making Prussia the first country in Europe.

Cromwell also won by the fierce charges of his cavalry, under Fairfax, the battles of Naseby and Marsden Moor.

The introduction of breech-loading fire-arms has effected as great a revolution in this branch of service as the use of iron has rendered of solid granite fortifications, and stately line-of-battleships in maritime service things of the past.

Victories for ages have been won by cold steel. Typical of carnage, it held its own for centuries; but as human invention continued to perfect the art of destroying life, iron and lead have become, for the present, the all-potent factors.

Yet there are exceptions to all rules. Bob Martin, of the Black Horse, always used his sabre in a charge, but he was the only cavalryman I knew who did.

CHAPTER IV.

A DUSTY CAMP.

The Black Horse formed a part of the Fourth Regiment of Cavalry. The First, Second, Third and Fourth Virginia constituting Fitz Lee's brigade.

The camp was pitched on both sides of the old Fredericksburg road, and had our commander racked his brains for months he could not have succeeded in selecting a more confoundedly disagreeable location in the whole section. The old dirt road was a wide thoroughfare, and notoriously the muddiest, most bottomless, miriest highway in winter, and the dustiest in summer, in Virginia. When biting, chilling winds swept over the country, the murky water, lying in pools all along the route, would freeze, and in the thaw make a vast bed of mire, which destroyed the patience and moral sense as to the rightful use of words of all who waded through it. It roused every teamster and every artilleryman of both armies, as they whipped and spurred their caissons through the sticky mud, to a degree of profanity frightful to contemplate. When the parching heat of summer drew on, the ooze and slime were changed into fine dust. In sooth, our commanding general must have had a bad attack of cramp-colic, and felt at enmity with all the world, when he ordered the cavalry to camp along the unpleasant length of this road; for within a short distance fine and shady locations were to be had. The troopers were strung out upon this lane for half a mile. Very few had even shelter tents, and not even a bush near for protection against dew or the vertical rays of the midsummer sun. Fuel there was none, the few sticks necessary to boil the coffee and fry the meat having to be brought upon the men's backs from a forest nearly a mile away. It was the same way with the water, requiring a long tramp to fill the canteens from the distant branch.

Our situation was not a pleasant one, as may be imagined; but all during the month of August the cavalry remained in the same spot. During this time there was a great drouth, not a drop of rain having fallen. Everything was dry and scorched; the dust on the road seemed as deep as the sands of the deserts; while cavalrymen and supply-wagons were passing, and this was incessantly, there hung over that route a cloud of fine pulverized dust which filled every crevice, arrayed every object, animate and inanimate, with a light drab-colored covering of its own. This dust lined the inside of clothes, irritated the skin and inflamed the eyes; every mouthful of food was powdered with it as thickly as the epicure seasons with cayenne pepper his turtle soup. Each man ate his peck of dirt at this camp.

Fredericksburg was about three miles off, but it had but little attraction for the soldiery, even in its best days. Now it was enough to give the most cheerful temper in the world an attack of blues to ride through it. Twice had the old burg been shelled and sacked, once by Burnside in the December before and again by Sedgwick only three months back, when he defeated the Rebel force which defended it, and tried to advance and assist Hooker, who was tangled up in the Wilderness at Chancellorsville, himself soon after repulsed.

The streets were entirely forsaken, and the pavements almost hidden by the grass. Most of the houses were abandoned or occupied by the camp followers and human jackals that followed in the army's wake. The gardens attached to the dwellings were grown rank with weeds and thistles, from amid which here and there a rose would struggle into sight, as if to its fragrance and beauty were entrusted the keeping of a few sweet memories. Windows were broken in and the doors were hanging by one hinge; the plaster had been knocked from the walls, showing the rafters. In many roofs were jagged rents and holes, made by the shells or plunging round shot, through which the blue sky glimmered. Here and there were black, charred ruins, the remains of some happy homestead. The palings which once enclosed the dwellings were torn down, leaving only the posts. In many places the pavement was wholly obliterated and merged into the common road; and nearly all the shade trees had been cut down for fuel. Every house bore the imprint of war, either by bullet or shell, while some were completely honeycombed, threatening to topple over every moment.

On a hot summer evening Fredericksburg was the very incarnation of the "Deserted Village." No children enlivened the streets or pierced the warm air with their happy, gladsome voices; no women sauntered along the pavements or showed fair faces at casement or windows; no bustling merchant hurried about intent on business; no family groups sitting at ease in the shadowed porch watching the setting of the sun; from no open window came the happy laugh, the strains of a piano, the voice of song nor the murmur of low conversation; instead there brooded over the place an oppressive silence, broken only by the sound of the echoing hoof-strokes and the rattling of the sabre as a few cavalrymen passed along the street.

Some enterprising sutlers displayed meagre wares, but none ever appeared to invest in his stock. Here and there a vagrant cur would skulk through the streets with a fearful look as if expecting each moment to hear the crashing of a shell. A cat would slink by and disappear up some shattered steps and into some half-open door. Everywhere gloom and ruin reigned supreme.

A few days in camp and the condition of the troops improved. Immediately after breakfast most of the men struck off in squads, and reaching some spreading trees would be down under their shade, or spending the hours in the mysteries and delights of draw poker. There were no drills nor inspections, the whole day belonged to the trooper to dispose of as he might please. The camp was in fact abandoned. Our meals were the same as those issued to the infantry, simply hardtack and mess pork; but the cavalry fared infinitely better, as they were in the habit of foraging and helping themselves unscrupulously to whatever they might want. So by the time the infantry arrived the country was pretty well stripped.

No finer pastures in the world are to be seen than in the lowlands of Rappahannock; while the uplands were parched and browned by the long drouth, down in those damp bottoms the grass was up to the knees. A few weeks had wrought a marvelous change in the horses; from walking skeletons, scarcely capable of carrying their riders, they waxed strong, fat and lusty; hardly able to move after the long, exhausting marches of the campaign, they kicked up their heels in the grassy meadows in an abandon of lazy ease.

Every evening they were driven to camp, when each man selected his own horse and bestowed upon him a feed of oats and a good grooming; in the morning they were again fed and turned out to pasture. It was wonderful to see how soon the vast herd, numbering thousands, would in half an hour be secured and tied up. The horse himself knew the routine as well as his master, and recognized his call without fail, or better still would come of his own accord directly to his own appointed hitching post, there to get his food and enjoy the pleasure of the currycomb.

A horse guard was always detailed each morning, which,

mounted, took positions on the boundaries and kept the animals from wandering away.

So the month of August, 1863, passed swiftly by, with not even the sound of the distant cannon to remind the men that there was a war going on. Once a day would sound the cry of—

"Watermillions, here's yer fine watermillions!" ringing clear and resonant, piercing the ears of all. This cry acted like the beat of the long roll to the infantry, bringing officers and privates to their feet with a bound. Then ensued a mad rush for the cart; because the terms of the sale reminded one of the barber's placard:

"First come first served."

The vehicle was generally home-made, mounted on two ill-assorted wheels, and drawn by some old cavalry horse that had been turned out to die, but rallied enough to draw a cart slowly and with what seemed to be his last expiring effort. In this unique vehicle was a large pile of melons surmounted by an ancient African, grinning from ear to ear at the result of his call.

In a moment an eager crowd surrounded him, and the fruit was sold without loss of time. Two dollars apiece was the impartial price. Perfect fairness was observed by the soldiers, who, much to their credit, always acted with scrupulous nicety so long as justice was done them; but encountering one disposed to cheat or overcharge, the luckless trader was soon brought to understand that "honesty would be the best policy."

A farmer came into camp one day with a two-horse wagon full of this delicious fruit—and the finest melons in the State are grown in these sultry, moist lowlands on the Rappahannock River. Stopping his team in front of the company he announced his wares.

"What's the price?" inquired the crowd of soldiers.

"Five dollars apiece," was the reply.

"Now, old man, that's too much; we have never paid but two dollars for the finest, and that is all that we can afford; we don't get but eleven dollars a month, remember."

"I've got nothing to do with that," said this country skinflint. "Them melons is worth five dollars apiece, and if you don't buy 'em, there's plenty that will."

So, tying the canvas cover tightly over the pile he cracked his whip and essayed to move on. The horses started and so did the tongue, but never the wagon. He cursed and swore, while the soldiers only answered with jibes and sneers. He entreated;

they only laughed.   Undeniably at their mercy, he tried cajolery, all to no purpose as he found.   Time was passing, and there was a long way home, so at last he gave in and cried out in despair:

"Gentlemen, I'll give you half of these here blessed melons if you gives me back my linchpin."

The compact was made and the linchpin restored, and the soldiers had a glorious feast.

The happy inspiration of stealing the linchpin originated with the reckless dare-devil Dick Martin.

I thought the infantry were good foragers, but they could not hold a candle to the cavalry.   Dick Martin took me aside one morning and told me where an old Harpagon, about five miles from camp, had a good field of corn just in the roasting-ear state and asked me to go along with him.   Of course I went; I knew that that corn crop was doomed, so I might as well get the good of it as another.

Within an hour we had filled our long forage-bags and carried them out into the road, and were sitting on them taking a rest when the owner came riding up—a wizened old fellow, with the most hooked nose I ever saw on a human face.   He stopped, entered into conversation with us and began abusing the soldiers for stealing from him.   To my astonishment I heard Dick Martin out-Herod Herod and damn the thieves with a force and redundancy of language that so pleased the old fellow that he invited us to his house to fill our canteens with buttermilk.   We declined, however, and as he shook Martin's hand in adieu he said he wished all the soldiers in the army were as honest as he.   I remarked sotto voce, "If they were, the old man would not have stick nor stone left."   Well, I reached the camp, left the corn in my shelter-tent and went to turn my horse loose, and when I returned my corn was gone, stolen by some of my own comrades.

CHAPTER V.

ON PICKET.

It was in the latter part of August; orders were given to be prepared to go on picket early in the morning; and until a late hour the men were busy cooking rations and cleaning equipments.

Before the mists had been chased by the rising sun, the company in close column of fours marched down the road. Men and animals were in perfect condition, brimful of mettle and in buoyant spirits.

The route lay along the banks of the river, upon the winding course of which, after several hours' riding, the regiment reached its destination and relieved the various pickets. A sergeant and squad of men were left at each post, the company being spread out several miles on the river banks to act as videttes, whose duty it was to watch the enemy on the other side of the Rappahannock.

The next day our squad, Sergeant Joe Reid in command, sauntered down the bank, but seeing no one we lay at length under the spreading trees, smoking as solemnly and meditatively as the redoubtable Wilhelmus Keaft and all the Dutch Council, over the affairs of state.

The Rappahannock, which was at this place about two hundred yards wide, flowing slowly oceanward, its bosom reflecting the roseate-hued morn, was as lovely a body of water as the sun ever shone upon. The sound of the gentle ripple of its waves upon the sand was broken by a faint "halloo" which came from the other side.

"Johnny Reb; I say, J-o-h-n-n-y R-e-b, don't shoot!"

Joe Reid shouted back, "All right!"

"What command are you?"

The spoken words floated clear and distinct across the water, "The Black Horse Cavalry. Who are you?"

"The Second Michigan Cavalry."

"Come out on the bank," said our spokesman, "and show yourselves; we won't fire."

"On your honor, Johnny Reb?"

"On our honor, Billy Yank."

In a second a large squad of blue-coats across the way advanced to the water's brink. The Southerners did the same; then the former put the query.

"Have you any tobacco?"

"Plenty of it," went out our reply.

"Any sugar and coffee?" they questioned.

"Not a taste nor a smell."

"Let's trade," was shouted with eagerness.

"Very well," was the reply. "We have not much with us, but we will send to Fredericksburg for more, so meet us here this evening."

"All right," they answered; then added, "Say, Johnny, want some newspapers?"

"Y-e-s!"

"Then look out, we are going to send you some."

"How are you going to do it?"

"Wait and see."

The Rebs watched the group upon the other side curiously, wondering how even Yankee ingenuity could devise a way for sending a batch of papers across the river two hundred yards wide, and in the meantime each man had his own opinion.

"They will shoot arrows over," said Martin.

"Arrows, the devil!" replied the sergeant; "there never was a bow bent which could cast an arrow across this river."

"Maybe they will wrap them around a cannon ball and shoot them across; we'd better get away from here," hastily answered a tall, slim six-footer, who was rather afraid of big shots.

A roar of laughter followed this suggestion, but the originator was too intent on his own awakened fears to let the slightest movement of the enemy pass unscanned. Eagerly he watched while the others were having all the fun at his expense. Presently he shouted:

"Here they come!" and then in a tone of intense admiration, "I'll be doggoned if these Yanks are not the smartest people in the world."

On the other side were several miniature boats and ships—such as school-boys delight in—with sails set; the gentle breeze impelled the little crafts across the river, each freighted with a couple of newspapers. Slowly, but surely, they headed for the opposite bank as if some spirit Oberon or Puck sat at the tiller; and in a few minutes had accomplished their voyage and were drawn up to await a favorable wind to waft them back.

Drawing lots, Joe Boteler, who found luck against him, started to town, with a muttered curse, to buy tobacco, leaving his comrades to seek some shady spot, and with pipes in our mouths sink deep in the contents of the latest war news from the enemy's standpoint, always interesting reading.

It was a cloudless day,—a day to dream,—and with a lazy *sans souci* manner and half-shut eyes, enjoy to the soul the deep loveliness of the scene which lay around us like some fair creation of the fancy, listening the while to the trills of the blue-bird which sat on the top of a lofty tree industriously practicing his notes like a prima donna getting a new opera by heart.

Joe returned in the evening with a box of plug tobacco about a foot square; but how to get it across was the question. The miniature boats could not carry it, and we shouted over to the Yanks that we had about twenty pounds of cut plug, and asked them what we must do? They hallooed back to let one of us swim across, and declared that it was perfectly safe. We held a council of war, and it was found that none of the Black Horse could swim beyond a few rods. Then I volunteered. Having lived on the banks of the Potomac most of my life, I was necessarily a swimmer.

Sergeant Reid went to a house not far off and borrowed a bread trough, and placing it on a plank, the box of tobacco was shipped, and disrobing I started, pushing my queer craft in front of me. As I approached the shore the news of my coming had reached camp, and nearly all the Second Michigan were lined up along the bank.

I felt a little queer, but I had perfect faith in their promise and kept on without missing a stroke until my miniature scow grounded on the beach. The blue-coats crowded around me and gave me a hearty welcome, and relieving the trough of its load, heaped the craft with offerings of sugar, coffee, lemons, and even candy, till I cried out that they would sink my transport. I am sure they would have filled a rowboat to the gunwale had I brought one.

There was no chaffing or banter, only roistering welcomes.

Bidding my friends the enemy good-by, I swam back with the precious cargo, and we had a feast that night.

O, Johnny Reb and Billy Yank had great respect for each other in those days.

The vidette holding his post in the night on the banks of the river must be on the *qui vive* every moment. The truce of the day ceases as soon as the sun has set and the evening star is seen. A strict watch is kept; the pickets are doubled and the whole post is on the alert.

Then with the coming on and deepening of night the imagination is apt to play fantastic tricks and weaves shadows of its own. A floating tree is changed by magic moonbeams into a pontoon boat filled with armed men. The splash of a muskrat or otter is the low, hoarse tone of command; the leaping of a fish from the water that sends the spray brightened into silver drops, is the gleaming of some rifle-barrel. It is not strange then that ever and anon there should float the tone of stern command:

"Halt! Who comes there?"

The vidette watches through the night with his senses playing freaks, while the owl, fresh from his day's snooze, chills his blood with its maniacal laughter.

We stayed over a week on picket duty, and life the while was like that of the lotus eater: so calm, so dreamy, so full of perfect rest.

The opposing videttes did not fire upon one another, but bathed in the cool, clear waters of both shores without fear of the deadly rifle-ball. Just as the wind shifted, the little international fleet would make their voyages—always loaded with papers or notes. One of the little boats arrived freighted with fish-hooks; so the Black Horse squad had fresh fish in addition to pure coffee. There was no further intercourse, for the enemy had forbidden any such continued indulgences; but they could not prevent the boat business and the little vessels were on the go all the time.

It was with real regret that the videttes moved away, sending frail messengers on their final trip, laden with several courteous missives to the boys of the Second Michigan Cavalry, in appreciation of the *entente cordiale* which had reigned between us.

CHAPTER VI.

THE HON. JOHN MINOR BOTTS.

The cavalry had had several light, trifling skirmishes during the late summer, and it was evident that no offensive operations would be commenced until the next spring. It was getting late in the fall, and neither army, after the deadly wrestle at Gettysburg, felt like commencing the struggle anew.

The brigade went into cantonment near Brandy Station, a barren spot in all truth. It was the place where both armies had camped as they advanced, first one and then the other, until the vast plain had been packed smooth and beaten solid as a parade ground.

It had turned quite cold by this time, especially in the night, when the ground would be white with frost. Tents were rare and camp-fires a necessity, but fuel was scarce and hard to obtain. Rations of plain, simple hardtack and fat pork three times a day had been reduced to a minimum, with an insufficient supply at that. It was simply impossible to obtain any country produce, for there was none to be had.

Brandy Station, in Culpeper County, on the Virginia Midland Railroad, and indeed the vicinity for miles, was only a wild, barren waste, which showed the ravages of war to a greater extent than any section of battle-scarred Virginia. It was a contested point, which both sides claimed on account of its proximity to the railroad as a base of supplies; and because, too, its level lands were so well adapted to an armed camp, the Rapidan River near by constituting the line of defense; it was occupied alternately by both armies, and every fresh tenure rendered it, if possible, more bare and desolate, the trail of war more apparent. It had been the scene of several cavalry engagements in which shot and shell had swept over the wide plateau, compelling the relinquishment of most of the houses in that vicinity. Even if the owners had felt no fear for their families, from the missiles, which is not probable, they had been pillaged to a state of starvation by the thieving soldiery wearing both uniforms, and so had been forced to pull up stakes and leave for more promising lands. Fine houses had been torn down to supply material with which to build winter quarters. Shade trees of noble growth, as well as orchards of

28

choice fruit, had been cut down as fuel for camp-fires. As for wood, there was not even a stump. One could stand at the railroad station and let his eye wander over a radius of miles and see no sign of human habitation, no smoke ascending, no cattle grazing, nothing to arrest the eye as it wandered over the wide expanse.

There was one exception, one oasis in the desert, one gleam of light which shone amid all this poverty, to be hailed by the wearied scout, traveling through the surrounding wretchedness, with as much joy as the sailor catches his first sight of land from the masthead. Tired horses would prick their ears and increase their gait without the incentive of the spur, as if they had sniffed their oats from afar; for like the sanctuary founded by the Hospitallers in the fourteenth century, all footsteps, even in war, whether of friend or foe, turned that way and entered its wide gates.

It was a most remarkable thing to note in the midst of this ravaged land, this stately place, rich in all a country-seat needs to make up its adornment, well stocked, well pastured, well wooded,—fabled plenty, as it were, in the centre of famine,—the land of Goshen in famine-stricken Egypt.

This was the estate of the Honorable John Minor Botts, one of the most brilliant men whom Virginia ever produced, and at one time after the war considered a possible nominee for the Presidency. Brainy, a thorough scholar, a deep thinker, he was, withal, a bundle of contradictions. A more right-hearted, wrongheaded man never lived; but he was obstinate, head-strong by instinct as well as by practice. He was just the man who would take his place upon the judge's stand and watch a four-mile race, staking his money upon a favorite horse, who yet, when the horse was falling back to the rear, would not see what was patent to every one else: that his wager was a losing one, but with his natural, dogged disposition would only cry the more: "I double the bet that Planet wins!"

Once choosing his course, he kept it; neither threats, intimidation, persuasion or entreaties could move him one jot; he was of the stuff that martyrs are made, and he would die at the stake before he would recant. He, as an old-line Whig with all the strong characteristics and prejudices, served his party two years in Congress, and would have risen high in power but for his well-known peculiarities.

At the beginning of the war-fever he assumed the position that the secession of a State from the American Union was a heresy and a crime; and upon this dogma he planted himself and maintained his opinion with dogged resolution, defying the universal unpopularity and invective that either assailed him or let him severely alone. However, if it was his desire to be made a martyr of, he was disappointed; the tide of affairs was rushing on too wildly for men to give much thought to the opinion of any one man, and Mr. Botts was permitted to go his way unheeded. While the stars of Lee and Jackson were rising high above the horizon, he continued outspoken and bitter in his denunciations against the "Jeff Davis Government," and refused to be conciliated even by the offer of a Cabinet position.

At last the authorities, thinking patience had ceased to be a virtue, arrested him in Richmond and sent him to his country seat in Culpeper. He was told he might at any time go North, where his predilections seemed to center.

This did not suit him; he had the same repugnance to taking an active part in favor of the North that he had in the South; for once again he refused the Cabinet appointment which was tendered him, this time by Mr. Lincoln. He would accept, like Mr. Sampson, "nothing from nobody," and only asked to be let alone so that he might sit on his metaphorical and literal fence and hurl anathemas upon either side.

Mr. Botts's idea was to play the part of the great pacificator; and when the hour should arrive, as "arrive it must," he used to say, and the North and South, all exhausted by the protracted struggle, and weary of the war, should conclude to reunite, then would they find in him a most admirable person; the very man for the time, who with wonderful prescience had kept himself bottled up for just such an emergency. Of course he would be made President, and thus harmonize the conflicting elements of the Union. It was an original idea, ingenious, and not wanting in boldness, and might have succeeded, only it did not.

His property was scrupulously respected by both armies, though the Rebels would steal his potatoes sometimes, and burn a few fence rails.

So in this desolate region he passed his days, though far from quietly; there was too much excitement,—too much food for thought. He lived in the center of opposing armies and with keen interest watched the unfolding of history. No less than five pitched-battles between opposing cavalry took place within plain view of his house; but no matter what the result: whether the blue whipped the gray, or the gray thrashed the blue, it made no difference to him; nor did he lose a sheep or a cow in consequence; for even while the bursting shells filled the air, his cattle grazed on his broad fields as free from harm as if peace were smiling over the land.

In person Mr. Botts seemed about sixty-five years of age, was nearly six feet high, stout, and the very personification of health. His brow was low and broad, his jaw like a bulldog's; his eyes in repose were dull and glassy, but when animated by his theme they flashed with a hidden fire, and became luminous with intelligence. His voice was as clear as a bugle, every syllable falling with a perfect enunciation of its own.

Whatever his faults may have been, they were still undeniably great ones; for littleness of any kind was foreign to his nature. With him hospitality was a virtue; no Arab ever held the rights of a guest more sacred, his door was open to all and his roof offered as welcome a shelter to the blouse and jacket of the private as to the shoulder straps of the officer. He was popular with both armies; both admired that independence of thought as well as the courage which rendered him incapable of dissembling.

One day he would entertain general officers of the Yankee army at his table, and the next day the stars of the Rebel commander would be met there. His table was always loaded with the choicest and best in the season, and as a host he was unrivaled. The charm of his conversation was like hearing a rich tide of music, and in his presence one forgot place and circumstance, as vivid imagery, rich thought and sparkling humor issued from his lips.

He loved the blue as well as the gray; the gray as well as the blue, provided no horse thieves had been prowling recently around his premises, and provided you did not once pronounce the word "Democrat," which would inflame him as much as the matador's red flag did the bull in the arena. He was as jovial an old fellow as one could find from the Potomac to the Brazos.

After supper, seated beside the broad hearth, glowing with a large wood-fire, was the time to appreciate our host; his marvelous conversational talent would bloom and expand as at no other hour. On every subject he was at home, and invested it with the charm of his own mind; even with regard to the war, that threadbare topic, it would be a revelation to hear his views, so different from the old set formulas; it was like first hearing an air played by some camp musician, and then listening to its measures from the hands of the maestro as he draws his magic bow and gives you the melody of his artist soul.

Mr. Botts never believed that the South could succeed in establishing an independent Confederacy. Their one opportunity, he often told me, was before the blockade was established, when the Confederate Government had the chance to send all their cotton to England, and with the proceeds buy munitions of war and build ships.

Neither did he think the result of the war would be the reconstruction of the South; rather that there would be an amicable reunion with the simple abrogation of slavery.

No matter what his political opinions were or how strongly they might read, now that his future is past,—now that future events justified his prophecies, unpalatable as they then were,— well! there are hundreds of soldiers of both armies who have a pleasant thought and kindly remembrance for the man who took them in, fed them when they were half famished and asked no reward, who never turned man nor beast from his door, but welcomed all at a time when many estates in that section, and especially in Madison County, belonging to Southern men (to their shame be it said), had huge placards on the gates bearing the inscription: "No soldiers entertained here."

One evening, in the winter of 1863, I asked Mr. Botts to give me his calm, cool opinion of the two armies (Lee's and Meade's), and said that I believed he was the only man in America who was in a position to judge. He spoke freely and fully, and when in my room I jotted down the main points of his conversation in my diary before I retired that night.

"As far as personal bravery goes," he remarked, "I can perceive no difference; man to man, if equally well led, would be Greek meeting Greek. The Federal army is under stricter discipline, is numerically superior in men and munitions of war; and the natural question follows, why, with all of these advantages, they are invariably defeated in their advance to Richmond? The cause is easy to explain. If the Federal army has heavier artillery and stronger battalions, the Confederate army has more patriotism: I mean by that, the love of State is stronger in the average man, than love of the Union; just as to the mediocre man, his love for his earthly father is stronger than his love for his heavenly One. The one is tangible, the other intangible and founded on faith and sentiment. His State, to nine men out of ten, is dearer than the Union for the simple reason that his State holds all that he values on earth, while the Union is an abstract affair—a mere sentiment. Then every game-cock fights best on his own dung-hill, as was proven at Gettysburg. The South has one powerful advantage, and that is, her army is controlled by one man, and that man is unquestionably the greatest captain of the age. As for the Army of the Potomac, it is cursed and hampered with politics, and where you find politics you are bound to find corruption. At least half the officers in the Army of the Potomac owe their positions to influential politicians. Thus the *esprit de corps* of Lee's army is far higher than Meade's."

I asked him if the Union officers with whom he had conversed agreed with him in his views.

He answered, "No, they think the conflict is between a feudal aristocracy and democracy, and between a monarchical and a republican form of government."

I asked him what course ought the South to pursue.

He answered: "I have thought long over that matter, and I see but one way out of the hole that Jeff Davis, Bob Toombs, and the like kidney have dragged the South into. There is only one course of action which, in my opinion, will save Lee's army from certain destruction: Let Davis seek a truce from President Lincoln and march the Rebel armies to Mexico, and drive out Maximilian."

So during the last year of the war the voluntary hermit strolled upon his estate, listened calmly to the noise of the cannonading, busied in the little cares of a farmer's life; and the great mind which should have occupied itself in the graver question of policy fraught with the weal or woe of a country, the high intellect which was capable of vast combinations contented itself with studying out an improved stall for his blooded horses, or a new model yoke for his oxen.

After all, he was content, and no man can desire or ask to be more.

I write this freely of Mr. Botts, because he was a near relation of mine, and he was proud of his blood, even though, as he used to say:

"You are one of the damndest Rebels who ever acknowledged Jeff Davis as your master."

Still his house was my home, and his hand-clasp was always warm and reassuring.

CHAPTER VII.

HARD TIMES.

Time in camp was chiefly spent in collecting wood, and cooking all manner of things that might induce our meager rations to go as far and last as long as possible. But two crackers and a half pound of fat meat per day (the devil of a particle else!) offered no great range for experiment; neither did it satisfy the hunger of able-bodied men. They resorted, however, to the old expedient of chewing tobacco; while for the same reasons the horses began to nibble the bark from whatever tree they were fortunate enough to find.

The Black Horse embodied the glummest set of men ever seen. Some tried to forage, but would come back in the evening completely fagged out and in a savage humor, for there was nothing to be had. The lonesome farm-houses here and there had naught to give or sell; the inmates themselves owning scarce enough to keep body and soul together.

At last orders came to change camp; and it was with something of the old buoyant feeling that the troopers found themselves in the saddle again.

There is a true old saw to the effect that "it is neither wise nor desirable to jump from the frying-pan into the fire;" but these soldiers had successfully accomplished it; for if Brandy County was bad, Madison County was worse. One was negative unhappiness, the other, positive wretchedness.

It was a common saying among the cavalry, "that when a crow undertook to fly over Madison County, it must needs take a haversack to keep from starving."

Truly they were a sad people to camp among, for having been almost eaten out, they had but little left and hoarded that.

The cavalrymen found it an unlucky region for even a passing ride after dark, provided he carried no rations with him; he might travel for hours through the low, scrubby pine woods, and reach some house at last, only to be told there was absolutely nothing for either him or his horse. In vain would he try the old dodge of asking for a place by the fire and a handful of hay; they would tell him that their children had not enough to eat and that their cattle were starving. What could he answer? Nine times out of ten it was a woman who would tell this; the men were in the army, and sometimes it was only necessary to look into the wan, pinched faces of herself and children to know that every word which she uttered was true. There was nothing then to do but to mount his anatomy of a steed and keep moving; keep on with his stumbling over the rock-bound road as best he might, for to an impartial observer it seemed as though all the stones in the universe had been dumped into Madison County.

Although poor, Madison County gave to the South splendid soldiers; it furnished a company to the Fourth, and its commander, Captain Strother, we considered one of the most daring and skilful officers in the regiment. His men were worthy of him, for they always followed his lead unfalteringly.

The Fourth went into bivouac near Madison Court House, and then commenced a battle of endurance against starvation. Very often the men would get no meat at all, only two crackers a day, which would be eaten in two minutes, and then nothing else would pass their lips until the next day. They began to grow mutinous, and many saddled their horses and openly left the camp, to be absent for days on foraging expeditions in the neighboring county. The officers tried to check this but failed. Indeed they perceived that the men were weakening from famine, and that it was too much to expect from human nature to sit still and die by inches.

Worse was to come; the hard bread was to be changed to a pound of meal a day; meal it was called, but the God of Hungry Souls save the mark! Nothing more or less than a mixture of ground corn cobs, husks and saw dust; it was withal so sour that any decent dog would reject it. This was often every morsel they would have for their rations, and they dared not sift it, for there would not have been enough of pure meal to fill a cup. Full rations consisted of a pound of this acidulated dry bran and a quarter of a pound of fat pork, which served to grease the skillet.

It is a startling fact that long and continuous hunger brings out the animal in the face, and the likeness becomes so strong that the most careless glance is arrested by it. Little by little the intellect disappears from the countenance, divine reason from the eyes, and the face grows gaunt, lean and lank, while its expression becomes that of a lower order of creation, a brutish animal. One soldier resembles a fox, another a cat; there is a hyena; yonder with locked jaws and savage eyes is a bull-terrier; the one with that honest, open look is a mastiff, and so on from one to another, until you fancy the doctrine of the transmigration of souls an easy creed to believe. After all, Circe, changing by her magic potion the Grecian Argonauts into swine, is but an allegory representing hunger.

What a great leveler famine is; under its potent influence the courier forgets his craft, the king his kingly way, the Chesterfield his politeness, the gentleman his creed and all men become the same; for it strips away every mental attribute as the valet disrobes a form, leaving all molded after one image.

A soldier can stand sieges, breast battles, and bear hardships, and still, like a cork, dance buoyantly from wave to wave of adversity, but this slow perishing in blank inaction day after day— this long drawn out agony, is more than men can endure. Neither they nor their *amor patriae* can resist its assault.

If the troopers were famishing, so were their horses, for it was now December, and the pastures were brown and bare. Of course the animals had to depend upon the issued rations, which, to do them justice, were only enough to sustain life. It was sad to see the wistful, half-human gaze the poor brutes cast upon their owners, mutely imploring food. In their distress they would actually eat bushes, dried sticks and leaves. Fully one-half of them were incapable of getting up a gallop, a trembling trot being their fastest gait. The truth was, the cavalry looked like a hospital for all the broken-down street-car horses; or a glue factory where all antediluvian steeds awaited slaughter. A cavalryman in his saddle presented a far more dilapidated picture than ever did the lean knight, De la Mancha, mounted on his Rosinante.

What a deplorable, suicidal policy it turned out to be, that pursued by the Government in making the horse the personal property of the cavalryman, and permitting him to return home when anything happened to his cattle, even on such excuses as the animal's thinness. These "horse details," as they were called, kept, on an average, fully one-fourth of the men absent.

About this time a large squad of the Black Horse, much to their delight, obtained horse details, and not possessing a private corral of their own, prepared to go within the lines of the enemy and capture mounts from their friends the blue-coats. This was the general custom of the Fauquier men under such circumstances, and thanks to its success the cracks of the Fourth managed to keep in the saddle. As for the riff-raff of the company, few of them had horses, and so kept up with the wagon-train; or if there were any of them so unfortunate as to own one, something was always happening to the poor animal, and once off on a furlough it required strong faith to hope to see him again under six months.

Our party, composed of seven, saddled our lank animals and struck for the camp of the enemy, our caparisoned chargers so impaired by want of food that they could hardly get out of a walk; such spectres, in short, that the sun found it hard to cast a shadow with them.

The balance of the command cast envious glances upon us, for it was like being in Purgatory and seeing one's friends depart on a ticket-of-leave for Paradise. As for me, I was so starved that no thought entered my head except that connected with my stomach. I had dreamed, talked and thought of nothing but eating for the last two months, and my rapture was like Justice Greedy in Massinger's great play: "A new way to pay old debts," and I felt like exclaiming:

> "Oh here will be feasting for over a month,
> I am provided; guts croak no more,
> You shall be stuffed like bagpipes."

Yet in all of this trying period I heard no word of discouragement or distrust from the soldiers; not one among the rank and file had a doubt of success; and the country people lived literally from hand to mouth, raising no crops, stripped bare of all cattle, and managing to keep from dying by a thousand shifts.

The young boys and girls set their rabbit-gums as regularly as the day came, and the whole country flocked to a deserted Yankee camp, snatching the half-consumed rations which were liberally left behind, and laying in a stock of hardtack and pork, which did much toward keeping them alive.

Even among some of these unlettered country people, who could not understand what the fighting was about, there was no cry of submission; they would only ask us, with wan faces and sunken eyes, "For God's sake drive the Yankees out for good; and soon, too, for we cannot stand it much longer!"

CHAPTER VIII.

WITHIN THE ENEMY'S LINES.

The Federal army, now under command of General Meade, lay for the most part in Culpeper County, though one corps of infantry and a division of cavalry had gone into winter quarters in Fauquier.

Along the Orange and Alexandria Railroad, their line of communication and supply, strong garrisons were encamped at all of the various stations to protect the road from the attacks of Mosby, whose name had now become a household word.

The Rebel army was stretched between the Rapidan and Gordonsville, with General Lee's headquarters at Orange Court House; the Rapidan River being the dividing line between the hostile forces.

It was the design of our detail to get within the enemy's line on foot and lurk near their camp in Fauquier, so as to take prisoner any cavalrymen they might find, and by this simple process obtain good mounts.

With this intention we made an early start from camp so as to get through Madison County before dark, striking off in the direction of Little Washington, about twenty-five miles on the left, where we proposed crossing the Rappahannock by flanking the enemy's pickets, whom we did not think extended so far.

Our little junto, after a tiresome ride on our decrepit nags, camped for the night in the woods; an unlooked-for proceeding, as we had fully expected to reach the river before dark, but the road was so rocky, the horses so weak, that we could only go at a very slow gait. However, this we accomplished the following evening.

Situated upon the hill above the river was a large farm-house We rode up and were received most hospitably by the old farmer, who made us alight and took us in.

We determined to make an attempt to cross the river after midnight, for it was impossible to find out beforehand whether or not the ford near by was guarded by Yankee videttes; besides, it commenced to rain, and with every hour the down-pour increased until at last a storm was raging. This made us particularly anxious to cross before the rise of the river would render (it might be for days) all fording impossible.

Our kind entertainers promised to attend to the horses for a very moderate sum, so there was nothing to detain us.

That night was as dark as dark could be; one could not see his hand a few inches before his eyes. We marched in single file and with lock-step, each man's hand resting on the shoulder of his file leader, like so many convicts on the way to prison meals.

It was enough to try the nerves of any one to listen to the roar of the turbulent water, all unseen in the blackness, as it rushed, seethed and bubbled over the rocks.

"I am familiar with every foot of this ford," said Taylor, "and I know it to be safe. My only fear is that the enemy's pickets are on the other side, but that must be risked."

"Shall we take off our breeches?" asked one.

"If you wish; I do not propose to shed mine," answered Caynor, a slab-sided fellow, with features like a sheep.

"I will for one," said I, "for in case we should be swept down stream we will certainly drown with our clothes on."

"That's so," chimed in several.

Out of the six, five removed their lower garments and rolled them in a bundle. We strapped our pistols more firmly around our necks, having left our sabres and carbines behind; and then in the same order, single file, with Taylor in front, we made our way down the slippery bank. Slippery? perhaps it was! for the head file's feet flew from under him and he slid into the water, followed by the rest, whose hold one upon the other had never loosened.

Like a gigantic colony of bullfrogs we plumped squarely into that big pond. Whew! Ugh! How cold the water was, just as it came from the mountain rills. It started our teeth off in the castanet business, with sufficient vim to supply music for a whole ballet.

"Hold on to one another, boys!" shouted Taylor above the storm; "don't let go your hold, whatever you do!"

The water was up to our waists, and the current was nearly carrying us off our feet. In close order we were slowly making our way across, and had nearly reached the opposite bank, when plump! splash! the hind man, who happened to be my unfortunate self, stumbled headlong; and as I only clutched the more tightly, I pulled the next man down; he hung onto the third and carried him down, and so on until the whole crowd was scrambling at the bottom. Very fortunately, though the water was deep, a bend in the bank above kept off the current, or the consequences would have been more serious. As it was, all the denuded five lost their bundles, which swept downward and were never seen again. A few steps brought us to land, and then we listened with hearts in our mouths.

"All right," said the leader, "the Yankees are not here."

"It may be all right for you," replied one of the shivering soldiers, "but what are we going to do?"

"I'll be damned if those weren't the last pair of breeches I had!" said Doc. Butler, one of the sufferers. "I feel like I had been burned out of house and home, with those garments gone."

"Drowned out, you mean," suggested a friend, who could not enter as deeply into the sorrows of the occasion as he might have done, having kept his trousers on.

"I'll be blessed if I go to anybody's house in my bare legs!" exclaimed Lal. Ashton, a long, shambling-looking fellow.

"Not only my breeches, but my drawers and my boots too!" moaned I.

"If this is what you call scouting," remarked Ned Martin, "I have a contempt for it. I've enough of it; let me get back to the infantry as fast as I can."

"Come on, fellows," said the leader, "we can't stand talking here all night. We'll go to Marshall's, about a mile from here; maybe he has enough breeches for you all; we'll stop there tonight anyhow if the Yankees are not around."

In the same close ranks we started off. It was freezing; each man was shivering, while our limbs were purple with cold. We reached the house and a loud knock on the door caused a light suddenly to spring up within, and then the flames disappeared to be followed shortly after by the master at the open door. Shading his eyes from the flaring tallow dip, he peered intently into the darkness. He was very pale and evidently thought us to be some marauding party of the enemy, for after a few brief words of explanation he drew a long breath of relief and invited us to enter.

No sooner did his eyes rest upon the strange crowd, fully apparelled as to the upper half, the lower denuded, than he dropped into a chair and laughed until the tears rolled down his cheeks. If he made an effort to recover his voice and do the honors of the house, one sight of the lugubrious set would start him off again as if he had just began, until it seemed probable we would spend the night there.

The serious crowd, who, by the way, had been standing as solemn as owls, looking like so many pelicans arrayed with one feather, gently reminded him that they were cold.

"Gentlemen," said he, "I beg your pardon, but I have lived here as boy and man for fifty-eight years and never saw a sight like this; O Lord!" he exclaimed, going off in a fresh paroxysm, as with an effort he conducted us up-stairs to a room in which there were three beds.

"Can you manage to crowd in here together?" he asked.

We answered that we could, and we did.

In the morning we were awakened by our host, who informed us that breakfast was ready and that his "old woman" had over-hauled his wardrobe and found breeches for all. "And some of them are pretty dilapidated," he added as he left the room.

He was right; two pairs seemed to have done service for years in stuffing a broken window; two were comparatively good; but one pair had evidently been worn by the gentleman whose duty it was to scare the crows from the corn-field; they were simply fearful to look at.

But on they had to go; our host was a short, pot-bellied man, while we were all thin, very thin; and those breeches, which would have fit Mynheer Vanderdecker, could have held us all. It was that or nothing, so in we dropped, and cut each one as funny a figure as the "Artful Dodger" himself. Ashton, who was six feet tall and about as fat as a mullen stalk, saw his outfit refuse to come below the knee, leaving his shanks sticking out in a re-markable manner.

"I was never so dressed in my life before!" he exclaimed piteous-ly; and he was believed.

My share of this unique contribution was a pair of Yankee pants discarded as worthless by the owner.

It was a ludicrous procession which filed into breakfast. The old lady nearly went into fits, though she tried to be polite and con-dole with us, yet as she listened to our recital she wiped her eyes repeatedly.

Having finished our meal and made our adieus, we started on our journey, the sorriest-looking collection of humanity that ever greeted human eyes. Ashton stalked in front, an old slouch hat falling over his face, his jacket reaching only half way down his back and his pants gathered loosely around his waist by his pistol belt and hanging in ruffles around the bare, thin knees. The rest were equally grotesque.

Lal. was heard complaining of his stylish and novel suit: "Because it let the wind in," he said, as if a man could ever be satisfied this side of Eden.

It was still raining, and forsaking the road we made our way in as straight a line as the crow flies, through woods, fields and briers, meeting no soul on our journey. It was nearly night when we halted, and seeing a house, stopped for the night. The owner, an old gentleman bent double with age, informed us that the Yankee camps were but a short distance away.

On the following evening the party drew up in a woods near by and after a stormy discussion agreed to separate. Taylor only wished to rejoin his wife, who lived not far distant; the two Butlers wanted to go home and remain there; Ashton and Caynor had no fixed idea about anything; they did not covet a horse; the only object in life that the soul of the former craved was a pair of breeches. So they all scattered, leaving Ned Martin and myself to pursue the object of our journey.

After a little deliberation we struck out for Libertyville, a small village of one house not far from Bristow Station, around which the cavalry were camped. The pines were thick, and as we could have found no better place for an ambuscade, we lay in wait for three days. All in vain, the Yankees had learned caution by frequent lessons. Not a cavalryman stirred from camp alone nor even in squads. A courier sent from one brigade to another, not the distance of a half mile, must needs have a large escort of horsemen.

They seemed to think the dense piney woods concealed scores of bushwhackers and guerrillas ready to seize the first trooper who incautiously ventured out; consequently, stringent orders had been issued against any soldiers stepping outside the cordon of guards which encircled each cantonment.

During those three days we halted over a score of Yankee deserters who, without arms, were striking northward. These were not disturbed, but instead, all the information was given them that they needed with regard to roads and route. They were a hard-looking set, real gallows-birds and bounty-jumpers, of whom the Northern army was well rid. They, without a doubt, only bred dissatisfaction wherever they went.

Southern scouts in this section were taken care of, each household extending the warmest welcome without a thought of consequences if discovered. But it was not safe to linger in any house where negroes waited; it would have been worth hardly a cent's toss-up as to whether or not they would slip over to the Yankee camp and give information that Rebel scouts were in the dwelling. Consequently it was the custom to leave the premises immediately on obtaining food; making a lair in the deepest recesses of the woods, where scouts were safe enough. No enemy ever penetrated into the depths of the forest.

Finding how fruitless was our mission, and hearing that the Black Horse had been sent inside the lines for the winter, on scouting duty, and had established a rendezvous at Salem, a village in Fauquier, some seventeen miles away, Martin and myself proceeded thither, where we found the troop scattered in various farm-houses, engaged in recuperating themselves and horses, but ready at the shortest summons to mount and away on foray or raid.

The Christmas holidays passed like a dream. The mountain region of Fauquier County was comparatively untouched by the war; except an occasional raid no enemy camped on its hills. It was considered the most fruitful section of Mosby's Confederacy.

The inhabitants were, without a single exception, devoutly loyal to the State, and fed and sheltered the Black Horse troops and Mosby's partisans throughout the war.

Every winter the Black Horse were sent on detached service to Fauquier, not only to recuperate but to do all the damage they could to the enemy; and they aided Mosby materially in his raids, and several of his officers were taken from our ranks.

CHAPTER IX.

CAPTURED.

But few prisoners were taken that winter. The Yankees had learned caution and kept their men within the confines of camp. Still, by close watching a group would be darted upon and gobbled up and sent within our lines. It would seem at first sight almost impossible for one man to convey several prisoners alone through a dangerous country and by circuitous routes over fifty odd miles, making sundry stops on the way, and finally delivering them at their destination to the provost guard; yet it was done frequently, and but few escaped.

A cavalryman would receive the prisoners confided to his care, as a charge which he was to transfer to the proper authorities, receiving as voucher the receipt of the provost marshal at Orange Court House. Consequently he omitted no precaution, and never relaxed his vigilance. He would travel all day with the prisoners in advance, the halters of the horses tied together to prevent any scatter or break for liberty. Certainly there was a chance of running afoul of some Yankee scouting party, when of course the scout abandoned his prisoners and lost no time in saving himself. But if luck befriended him, and he met none other than a scout like himself, he would stop at some farm-house, where the whole party would get supper and sit chatting amicably by the fireside. Should the scout think that he could trust one of his men or all of them, he would place him or them on parole not to attempt escape on the route; but if he found them hard cases he kept a close watch at all times.

All this is very well, it may be said; but how can one soldier guard three all day and all night without relief; and not only for one day and night, but oftentimes for three days in succession?

The manner of it was simplicity itself. When the hour for retiring arrived, the prisoners were compelled to disrobe and assume the very same garb which Adam wore before Mrs. Eve came along to worry him about his tailor's bills. They were then placed two or three in a bed, which was always in the top room of the house, and in which they were tucked in by the trooper as carefully as a mother arranges the covering around the form of her sick child. This done, he would depart to his own rest, car-

29

rying with him every vestige of their clothes and even their shoes; then locking the door after him, he would lie on a pallet outside and sleep with his pistol in his hand.

Of course the prisoners might escape if it so pleased them; there was nothing to prevent them from tearing up the sheets, making a rope and sliding to the ground, for the slumbers of the guard were profound. But then they would have been obliged to wander all unclothed through a country unknown to them, traversed by Rebel scouts, and in the midst, too, of a bitterly hostile population, wherein the hand of not only every man, but every woman and child, would have turned against them.

Recapture could hardly have been avoided, and death by some cowardly bushwhacker was possible, so that the risk was very great. None but a man of coolest nerve and intrepidity would think of giving it a trial.

Among the thousands of prisoners sent by scouts to the provost marshal I never heard of but three or four who ever succeeded in escaping.

On the morning of the sixteenth of January, 1864, I mounted my horse and started on a scouting expedition all by myself.

My object was to lie by the Federal cavalry camp near Warrenton and capture a good horse at all hazards. I had a mount, but the steed was in a pitiable condition, and nothing but months of perfect rest and full feeding could bring him up again. I was riding along unsuspicious of danger, quietly pursuing a side road which led into the Warrenton Turnpike, about two miles from Fauquier Springs, when I saw through the scattered trees, not a hundred yards away, a scouting party of Union cavalry wending its way leisurely along the pike.

My only chance, I thought, was to dismount and slip off unperceived; and if I could reach that little stone church over yonder, I might hide and get away. They might not even chance to look that way.

So I slipped quietly down and started for the little edifice. The blue-coats were going slowly along the road, all unconscious of their foe. Had I been near thick pine woods I would have been perfectly secure, but it was an open oak grove, through which pursuing cavalry could speed at a gallop. The church was on my left and I was doing my best to reach it, darting stealthily from tree to tree as rapidly as possible.

Everything went well; the Federals had almost disappeared, and in a minute I would be safe. I neared the church door and was about to enter; a second and I would have been inside, when I dropped to the ground as if shot. A Federal cavalryman had left the ranks and was cantering toward the church. He stopped within fifty yards of me, where there was a stream flowing. He started to water his horse and I watched him with straining eyes; saw him give his steed the bridle, and taking a pipe from his saddle pocket, charge and proceed to light it. I watched the curling smoke float above his head. The horse finished drinking and he gathered the reins preparatory to riding off. I drew a long breath of relief, but it was too soon; for just then my confounded, infernal horse gave a long, loud neigh.

The suddenness of the shock upon that young blue-jacket almost made him drop from his saddle, but only for a moment. Looking earnestly in the direction from which the sound proceeded, he saw my horse fully accoutred. Giving a long halloo he advanced slowly.

He had passed beyond without discovering me, but his shout had been heard and a score of comrades came flying toward him.

In a second I rushed through the open door of the church. It was a small, common edifice, such as one often sees in the country; a plain square building with no attempt at adornment. It had been ravaged and nothing remained but the pulpit. There was no place which could serve for concealment; but in the corner was a ladder leading to the loft. Up this I went without a word, pulling it after me; and then I sat there in the dark with beating heart to wait developments.

I had not long to wait. In half a minute the church was thronged with the dismounted troopers.

"He's not here," said a number of voices.

"I tell you he is, for I saw him enter," replied a positive voice.

"Then where is he?" chorused several.

"There!" exclaimed one of the number excitedly, "up that hole yonder, look!"

Then was heard the clicking of many revolvers. By a kind of mesmeric instinct I felt that a score of eyes were gazing into that black cavity.

"Shoot up," suggested one.

"Let's burn the d—— old thing down," proposed another voice. "Smoke 'em out."

It was not a pleasant conversation to listen to; it might have been more soothing, to say the least, though I could not deny that it was both racy and edifying. I realized for the first time how a coon feels when a ramrod is inserted down the crevice and screwed into his hide; realized also the anguish of a rabbit's soul just on the eve of being smoked out of its hollow. I did not know what to do. It seemed Hobson's choice, whether to be burned or suffocated, and ended by cursing under my breath with might and main the wretched old brute who could find no other time for displaying his hideous music but when my fate was hanging trembling in the balance.

Oh, confound him! A thousand times confound him! Confound that infernal bellows of a throat, that locomotive steam-whistle of a voice, that anatomy of pent-up sounds, that staring-ribbed dynamite of pure cussedness!"

Meantime a babble of voices was going on below.

"Silence!" exclaimed an authoritative voice, whose tones came ringing out clear and loud above the din. Then followed:

"I say up there!"

No response.

"You had better answer; if you do not we will burn the place. We know you are there. Do you surrender?"

"Yes," came the reply.

"Then throw down your arms to me." And the pistols in response went tumbling through the hole.

"Now come down yourself."

In a minute I was standing in the midst of my new-found foes, about fifty of them, with an officer. All had their pistols out. My captors were Company F, First Pennsylvania Cavalry.

"Who are you?"

"Black Horse cavalryman," I hastily answered.

"What are you doing here?"

"On a scout; I ran into you unexpectedly, and as my horse was broken down I took to my heels and thought myself safe enough."

"No," spoke up a trooper, standing near with a broad grin upon his face, "I saw your spurs disappearing through the door."

"Bad luck to you!" was the reply. "Is this the way you stop good Christians going to church to say their prayers?"

"Mount him on his horse and bring him along," ordered the officer; and so the old, detestable animal was pulled forward and I was in the saddle once again. Then, with an escort, I made what looked like a triumphant entry into Warrenton.

The prisoners were conducted before the provost marshal, a very little man, with a big head filled so full of self-conceit as to leave no room for anything else. Of common sense he seemed to be deficient. He frowned as Mars was supposed to do; he strode up and down the tent like Achilles on hearing of the death of Patroclus, and interrogated his culprit in a voice he was doing his best to render solemn and stern. He assured me I was a guerrilla and deserved to be shot, and would be too if he had his way.

We reminded him that for every scout captured there were ten of his side; and there was such a thing known in war as retaliation.

He broke into a storm of invective, the purport of which was that every Rebel found with arms ought to be hanged as high as Haman.

He was told that Mrs. Leslie's receipt for cooking a hare would suit his case—"First catch your hare."

The little fellow, like the "little pot—soon hot," fairly frothed with rage, and too angry for speech motioned the sentry to take us to the guard-house. As we were hurried off the sentinel said:

"I am glad you treated the little cuss so; for our soldiers hate him worse than poison. He was nothing, nohow, but a bar-keeper before the war."

The next day the prisoners were put on the cars and sent to Brandy Station, where I was placed in what was known as the "Bull-Pen," an enclosure of about four acres of bare ground around which the tread of the sentry never ceased.

It was bitter cold; keen northwest winds rushed hurling across the wide, bare plains of Brandy, with no forests to break the force of the blast; it swept on with a dirge and a wail, chilling and congealing all within its path.

We had no blankets and were exposed to the rigor of the weather; no overcoats, no shelter, no fire, and the situation seemed desperate. Moreover, in this pen were confined all the riff-raff and criminals of the Union army. Deserters, soldiers confined for murder, waiting the court martial which was to try them; thieves, bounty-jumpers—in short, it was an assemblage of rascality which could have been found nowhere else outside of the State Prison, and hardly there, so untamed and defiant.

All during the first night we prisoners saved ourselves from freezing only by walking up and down incessantly; and but for the kindness of the soft-hearted guards, giving us at intervals cups of hot coffee, we could not have borne the suffering and exposure.

Such awful curses, profanity and thieves' Latin among the

prisoners were probably never heard before by untutored ears. The prisoners would have been fearfully maltreated had not Jack, a huge Irishman awaiting trial for stabbing and killing the sergeant of his company, proved a benefactor in our hour of need. By his prestige as a desperate, reckless fellow he had gained a great mastery over the lower, meaner ruffians; and though he might not restrain the full current of curses hurled at us,—an evil to which we soon became used and which we did not mind so long as we could remain unharmed,—the brutes were afraid to proceed to overt acts. Jack had the rations of the Rebels well cooked; he let them cower over his fire, and shared with them at night his little shelter-tent.

All around us were the great hosts in their thousand tents and cabins,—some decidedly tasteful,—which filled the immense plain as far as the eye could reach. On a bright, clear evening the outlook would have been exhilarating to any one but a wretched captive. The air was filled with the sound of martial music of the brass bands, and the inspiriting blare of the bugles, all sweet sounds. The full, well-groomed cavalry horses champed their bits, and the refrain of many camp songs came to the listening ear. Later on the lights appeared and the wall-tents of the officers were illumined by many candles, and from what the guards told me I knew the wine was flowing, cigars were burning, and the exciting game of draw-poker was in progress. The colonel, the major and captain were as comfortable and more contented than they would have been at home. I saw the interior of an officer's tent with plank flooring carpeted, a hot blazing stove, a thorough camp equipage, books and magazines scattered around in profusion. A box just opened, full of delicacies, showed that his friends had not forgotten him; and O Shades of Bacchus! a whole line of bottles, ranged around the corner of the room, stood like the sentinels around our slushy "bull-pen." The warriors of Sardanapalus never lived more luxuriously. The private soldiers too in their winter quarters were more than comfortable, they were well housed and comfortably clad. With warm underclothing and uniform, a thick overcoat with a capacious cape, and oilcloth poncho for wet weather, and two great woolly blankets, he could bid defiance to every north wind which blows. A patent stove warmed his tent or cabin, and novels and newspapers served to while away the tedium of camp, or as was generally the case, a well-worn pack of cards was on the table. His rations were so abundant he could not use them. Hardtack, flour, real coffee, sugar, rice, hominy, beans, pork and beef hung around in the mess tent, and ambulances were delivering boxes and parcels every hour, containing every luxury from friends, and presents from the "Sanitary Commission."

Billy Yank was comfortable in body and stuffed to the throat with the good things of life. Certainly fifty per cent. of the men were better clothed, better paid and better fed than they were at home.

Besides this, his duties were generally light, especially during six months of the year. He was elevated to the position of a hero: every daily paper gave him tribute and the illustrated pictorials flattered his self-love. Truly Mr. William Yank, the defender of the Union, the savior of his country, was a fortunate individual with a mind at rest, for he well knew that if he lived his future well-being would be the study of a rich and prosperous nation.

And Johnny Reb, his erring brother on the other side—let us visit his camp this biting weather and see how he is getting on. Enter at random any officer's hut. A flame in a rough fireplace lights up the rather dark interior; the officer's sword hanging from a nail offers the only decoration visible; an armful of pine needles serves for floor carpet; a rough pine bench to sit on, and a couch of pine poles on which is spread a thread-bare blanket serves for a resting place by night. Add to this a primitive table of a pile of cracker-boxes and—that is all. A dirty, greasy cotton bag, ycleped a haversack, is suspended over the fire-place, containing his daily rations, which consists of a piece of rancid fat meat and a double handful of half-ground meal.

As is his quarters, so are his soldiers', for all fare alike. Johnny's clothing is ragged despite the loving attempt at tailor's art to make tear and gap meet. Not half of them have an overcoat, and not one in five a whole pair of socks. His solitary blanket serves him as a coat by day, and covering by night, and as this nondescript figure paces his beat, his very bowels yearn for loving words from home, and above all for a good square meal.

Outside are the erstwhile war steeds, so thin and attenuated that they lean in their weakness against the trees, whose bark they have gnawed off in their hunger. A most unsoldier-like camp, with no music except the fife, drum, and bugle, the manipulator of the former having scarcely enough wind in his bony anatomy to fill his instrument; and as for the drummer, he could have used his fleshless fists to beat his sheep-skin with.

Stroll over this encampment on a day when the snow is two feet deep on a level, and see Johnny Reb in his poverty. A more cheerless, woe-begone, deplorable picture could not be found in the broad limits of the land.

Who can say that the men who bore these harrowing hardships uncomplainingly were not actuated by an ennobling principle.

Five or six of the Fourth Virginia Cavalry were brought into the pen and lodged with their comrades. Captured as they had been at their homes in Fauquier County, it was a bitter change from cheerful, happy firesides to those barren acres of desolate earth. Their friends, though (sad to relate), were glad to welcome them and Jack extended his wing over each. For one whole week, while we remained there, he saved us all from being frozen or kicked to death. He had a soft spot in his heart for poor humanity even though he had been handy with his knife. All that *we* knew or cared to know was, that he stood by those miserable, shivering, cowering prisoners to the last, and shook their hands with a hearty grasp as he told them good-by.

"Take care of yourselves, boys," were his parting words, "and may no harm come to you at all, at all."

The squad of prisoners, numbering some twenty, were placed on the cars and sent to Washington. Arriving there we were marched along the street, attracting much attention on the route, and followed by a crowd. Up Maryland Avenue, thence to Pennsylvania Avenue, from which we turned off toward the left, and approached a solid, square-looking building standing on the corner, and there we halted. Sentinels were pacing the pavement in front; the windows were barred with iron, through which there glowered and glared scores of faces; while from the open door a cry went up from the inmates:

"Fresh fish! Fresh fish!"

The building was the old Capitol Prison; its lodgers were Rebel prisoners, and the new arrivals were the individuals introduced to its walls as "Fish."

In a few moments we were ushered into the presence of Colonel Wood.

Our names, companies, and regiments were taken, we were then thoroughly searched, as if it were customary for private soldiers to carry their gold watches, diamonds, breastpins, and bonds into battle. It is needless to say that nothing worth having came of that inquiry; not a cent was found in those pockets.

We were next placed in our different quarters, and no sooner had the door closed than we were surrounded by a crowd of prisoners eagerly asking the latest news from Dixie.

For hours the new arrivals were engaged in answering inquiries of the interested, each of whom had a hundred questions to ask, and not until late that evening did we get a chance to retire and give our wearied jaws a rest.

CHAPTER X.

THE FIRST ESCAPE.

The old Capitol Prison was in ante-bellum days a fine, large, solid structure of granite, situated back of the new Capitol of the Nation. It was used as a rendezvous for the captured, who there remained until its apartments overflowed, when the garnered Rebel material was discharged into the various entrenched camps for prisoners, such as Point Lookout, Elmira and other forts.

The rooms were large, well ventilated, very comfortably heated by open grates at each end, and never seemed to want occupants. Around the sides of the room were bunks, each room accommodating as many as sixty prisoners. The dining-room was a large, low apartment, with a table running its entire length. The fare was ample and wholesome, much better indeed than Dixie could afford to give her troops. Those who had friends North lived luxuriously, for all boxes and bundles were promptly delivered to the ones whose names they bore; while visitors were allowed to see the inmates of the prison once a week in the colonel's office.

Each man was left to follow at will the devices of his fancy, provided of course his wishes did not include a saunter up the Avenue or a stroll into the park just across the way. So, barring the restraints of captivity, the prisoners had nothing of which to complain.

Yet it was not a hopeful outlook that the future gave. That all exchange of prisoners was ended was patent to all. The tone of the Northern papers showed that it would be the policy of their Government, as a war measure, not to exchange. It was a bitter thing to look forward to, that of being caged like so many wild beasts compelled to remain passive while the great struggle was going on around; neither to suffer with comrades the reverses of war nor enjoy the fruits of future triumphs; never more to feel the color tingling in the cheek at the sound of the bugle, nor know the mad enthusiasm of the charging line; to realize with a deep sinking of the heart that while the prisoner's name is not scratched from the rolls, his place is filled as is that of the dead comrade; to know that the hour of a Commonwealth's greatest peril is at hand, and that in her defense one arm is idle which fain would strike a blow. For Northerner or Southerner the dragging out of a prison life was grievous enough to bear. It is not hard to understand that, and many held death a preferable fate.

So communing, I determined to attempt an escape at all hazards, and at once set my brains to work to discover if possible the ways and means of accomplishing that purpose.

The prison was closely guarded, with a sentinel at each door. Every passage and the pavement outside was patrolled day and night. No one was allowed to be in the passage except the officer of the day. No prisoner was permitted to leave the room without being accompanied by a sentry. They were all marched to meals in line and rigorously guarded the while. Every evening they were sent to the open yard for exercise, but the enclosure was surrounded by a high wall, on the top of which sentinels paced with loaded muskets, watching everything that took place below.

There was absolutely no chance then to slip away by any of these avenues of escape, and so I finally determined that the only practical method was to file asunder the window bars and drop into the street, running the risk of being shot by the guard beneath.

I immediately commenced to work out my plan, the only one which presented the faintest chance of success; and yet it was full of difficulty. The bars were of forged iron at least an inch and a half in diameter; and as they were about six inches apart, it would be necessary to file two before space enough could be obtained to admit the egress of a body. There were no tools to begin with; then, too, the work would have to be performed unperceived by the sixty men who inhabited the room, for in every one of these apartments was placed a spy, generally some recreant, traitorous Southern soldier, whose business it was to watch and report attempts of the kind to the authorities. As a matter of course all concerned in such plots were severely punished. Then again, if those obstacles should have been successfully overcome, there still remained the need of escaping the observation of four sentries patrolling the pavement beneath, who had orders to shoot without halting any Rebel prisoner seen outside the building.

Yet my mind had become only more determined to accomplish the task. Jack Shepherd, I reasoned, had taken French leave of Newgate with fifty times these odds; and Baron Trenck had twice escaped from the iron prison at Gatz, when the whole

garrison had orders from the stern Frederick to watch him with
sleepless eyes. So taking heart I commenced by abstracting
from the supper table that night, despite the watchfulness of the
guards, two of the knives, which I hacked one against the other
so as to make respectable saws. Then I retired early and slept
until three o'clock in the morning, at which hour I rose and gazed
around. It was just the time when slumber most weighs down
the weary eye-lids and sleep resembles death. The whole room
was as silent as the graveyard; while from the open grates there
smouldered the coal fires like dull yet watchful eyes, which only
deepened the gloom of the surrounding shadows.

Cautiously the work was commenced; the knives were thickly
covered with grease, which deadened the sound. Below paced
the sentinel, all unconscious of the work going on so close to him.
The window was on the first floor, and when he walked in front
of it the sawing ceased; when he passed it recommenced. Two
hours' hard work and the iron bar was about a quarter through,
then the dawning of day brought the task to an end. Filling the
crevice with grease and soot to hide all traces, I betook myself to
my couch, or rather plank.

In a week's time, by hard and unremitting labor, and with many
narrow escapes from detection, the task was accomplished. The
two iron bars were ready to fall apart, held up as it were by a
thread, needing only a violent wrench to loosen them, and the
way was clear. I only waited a dark night to make the trial.

The morning of the day arrived at last which I determined
should either be my last in prison or my last on earth. A bitter
cold, dark day, with thick clouds sweeping over the sky and the
wind blowing a hurricane. Slowly enough the hours went, the
hours indeed of the final day in prison.

But not as I had planned. The commandant entered the room
and ordered all the prisoners to be ready to start immediately
after an early dinner for Point Lookout.

They say nothing is wasted in this world, but I felt that those
long hours of night work was an exception. My patient labors
useless. Well! the wild dream of liberty was over; and the first
impulse was to bow to an unrelenting destiny and struggle no
more.

Climbing into my bunk I thought over the situation. Upon
one thing I made up my mind, that death was preferable to a
long, unknown and lingering captivity at Point Lookout. I had
heard appalling tales of this prison, of the negro sentinels. Ah!

that was where it touched me, those negro guards. The humiliation and degradation of being under charge of those black men nerved me to a degree of resistance which was ready to brave a thousand deaths rather than submit.

I had a citizen suit sent me by friends in Alexandria, Virginia, and I determined to wear it over my uniform.

In the afternoon the crowd of prisoners, some four hundred in all, were formed into ranks on the street fronting the prison, the line extending a couple of squares. They were to walk four abreast with guards on either side at intervals of about eight feet apart. Orders were then read forbidding the men to move or slip out of place, under penalty of being bayoneted on the spot.

Everything being in readiness, the long column commenced its journey; not having any music to march by, the Rebels determined to improvise some for themselves. In a little while Dixie, that forbidden tune, was ringing out loud and clear on the loyal air, shouted lustily from four hundred throats. That unwonted strain filled the streets, causing many hearts to throb with wild excitement. Windows were lifted, doors thrown open, and in an instant the thoroughfares were thronged by curious citizens, who listened wonderingly to the air as dear to Rebel hearts as the dire refrain of "Ca Ira" to the Jacobins of Faubourg St. Antoine. The guards, however, soon stopped our music. I did not join in the strain, I was far too highly wrought up; none but the tenor of the grand opera sings when he is about to play a game of which annihilation is the forfeit.

My idea was to jump into the first open door and make my way through the house and out at the back door.

No poor, hunted fox, hard pressed by hounds, ever looked more eagerly for a hole or opening through which to dive.

But in vain my eyes searched every quarter; the doors were either closed or blocked by people watching the procession.

I was becoming desperate. Then the thought struck me to strike the guard and make a rush.

But that was impracticable; for even had I succeeded in escaping the guard, the people who lined the pavement as spectators would have stopped me and one bayonet thrust ended the matter.

By this time the column, moving steadily on, was nearing the wharf. If anything was to be done at all it must be done then. I was on the pavement; groups of people stood close to the houses to allow the line to pass. There were three citizens within two or three steps of me. Wheeling suddenly by the moving guard, who brought down his musket, I pulled myself together and exclaimed in a tone of assumed indignation:

"These d—— Rebels will run over me!"

The guard half halted, but my citizen's dress met his eyes; and besides the guard behind him was treading on his heels, so he kept on, and I was free, but not safe; the citizens saw the ruse; but very disloyal they must have been, for they did not betray me, they only grew pale and hurried away, leaving me alone on the sidewalk.

It was worse than having to stand a shelling from a battery of guns, to remain there watching the long line which passed, see the familiar faces of comrades, who, true as steel, uttered no exclamation of surprise, only the significant flash of the eye showing a full appreciation of the situation.

It was a strange experience for a Confederate soldier to be walking there unmolested amid the surging crowd of the Avenue, jostling against the blue-coats, who never deigned so much as a glance; and for an hour or two I sauntered up and down the street or lingered in the lobbies of the hotels, enjoying the novelty of the surroundings, and feeling as independent as a successful sutler.

As the evening wore away the necessity of making some plans for the future became more and more apparent. The first idea which came to me was to select a horse from the scores that were hitched along the Avenue, and make a bold rush for Virginia. But second thoughts showed the futility of such an attempt. The city was encircled by a cordon of guards, and without money or passport, detection and arrest would prove certain; so I concluded that the wisest and only possible way was to apply for money to a man whom I knew to be a Southern sympathizer, then go to Baltimore, and making a detour, cross the Potomac high up in Maryland.

A few squares and I stood before the entrance to the dwelling of this gentleman, Mr. William Selden, my uncle-in-law, who was Marshal of the District under Buchanan, and a strong Southern sympathizer, and whose eldest son, John Selden, was a famous soldier in Lee's army.

A hurried knock and I was admitted into the parlor. Both the master and mistress appeared; and my tale was no sooner told than I was taken in their arms and into their hearts.

A hot dinner was placed before me, a valise of clothing given me and a roll of greenbacks stuffed into my pockets; then, with a cigar in my mouth, I sat back in a hack with the most insouciant air it was possible to assume, and was driven to the Baltimore and Ohio Depot.

I could not help reflecting on the ups and downs of a soldier's life. This time yesterday I was eating from a tin plate a loaf of dry bread, drinking coffee from a battered tin cup, surrounded by a crew of ragged men, and those confounded guards watching every mouthful; and now— Well! I felt that life was amply worth the living.

Reaching the depot, I watched my chance, and as a sudden rush was made I managed to slip by the guard at the door, whose duty it was to demand passports. Soon the whistle sounded; the bell rang; the conductor shouted "All aboard!" the train gave a sudden jerk; then the telegraph poles danced by as if engaged in a mad, wild reel.

A couple of hours later found me seated at Barnum's Hotel table. I called for champagne, drank under breath a number of disloyal toasts, and paid the waiter with the air of a prince.

Later on I went to the theatre. "The Taming of the Shrew" was the attraction, with Seymour in the leading role. It was the first Shakespearian play I had seen for years. Then I went to a fashionable down-town restaurant and made the money fly. Nor is it needful to add I did not sleep on the hard planks of the bunks that night, though as I sank into the yielding, soft bed I had to pinch myself to be convinced that it was no dream.

It may have been the unaccustomed luxury of the feather bed, or excitement, or both combined—I could not sleep. I felt exactly as did Christopher Sly the tinker, when he went to sleep on the ale-house floor, and found himself when he awoke on a silken-curtained couch, and he exclaimed, "What! would you make me mad? Ask Marion Hackett, the fat ale-wife of Wincot, if she knows me not?"

And again and again I thought of Christopher Sly's words: "This is an excellent piece of work, would 'twere well ended."

A good breakfast, then I strolled down to the depot to make inquiries, determined to leave the next morning for Frederick City, and cross the Potomac near that point. I would have liked to remain longer, but the money was nearly gone; in truth, after paying hotel bills and my passage on the cars to Frederick City, not a ragged five-cent stamp would be left to recall the dismal story of boyish thoughtlessness.

The next morning I walked to the depot and found to my dismay that I was too late; the cars had left a half hour before, and there was no other train that day.

Here I was alone in a strange city, knowing no soul, and without money. My whole fortune consisted of one dollar and fifty cents. Count it as I would, it made no more. Turn my pockets inside out as I might, no vagrant note was found lurking in the folds. Call myself an addle-pated fool as often as I pleased, and repent as sorely as the prodigal son, it did no good; so I wandered up and down Baltimore Street all that day, spending the last of my little store for dinner. Then I felt like Jonah after he had been swallowed by the whale, that there was plenty of room to move about in, but that the future was confoundedly uncertain.

As the evening drew near I was at my wit's end. Stop the first citizen and tell him a piteous tale, trusting to luck in striking a Secessionist instead of a Unionist? The risk was too great and might lead to my being handed to the first convenient policeman, and then Fort McHenry was not very far off. But something had to be done. The night was drawing near; the wind was sweeping around the corners and up and down the thoroughfares with a chilling touch. The lamps were being lighted in one home after another, while the warm glow of the household fires shone with mocking brightness before my longing eyes. Intensely Southern as were the mass of Baltimoreans, how many doors would have opened by magic could they have known.

At last I reached the point where some risk had to be run, for it was impossible to wander through the streets all night. I determined to go where the largest mansions were found, ring the bell of the most imposing dwelling, ask to see the owner of the house, tell him who I was and what I wanted; and then if I perceived his sympathies were not forthcoming, to trust to my heels for safety and make another trial.

The first attempt daunted my hopes utterly. Going up a wide flight of marble steps I timidly rang the door-bell and waited the result. The door was opened by a stately old servant:

"Is the master in?"

"Yes'r, walk in the parlor."

"No, tell him I would like to speak to him at the door."

Away hied the man, and in a few seconds an elderly gentleman came and peered out distrustfully.

"What do you want?" he inquired through the half-opened door.

"Why, sir," stammered I, not knowing what to say, "I want to know whether your sympathies are on the side of the North or the South."

"That's none of your business!" was the curt rejoinder, and the door was slammed in my face, then locked and bolted; leaving me staring like a fool into space.

I relinquished this plan as a decidedly unsatisfactory one, and went wandering down the street disconsolately, when suddenly I sprang forward and accosted a gentleman who happened to be standing within a doorway.

"I think, sir, I have met you in Richmond."

He quickly replied, "You came by flag of truce, did you not?"

"I would like to have a few moments' conversation with you," I said.

"For what?"

"Just to ask if your sympathies are with the South."

"Undoubtedly; but what are your reasons for asking?"

"Simply because I am an escaped prisoner from the Old Capitol, who has no money nor friends, and know not where to turn or what to do. If you are a Unionist I ask you not to betray me."

The gentleman answered not a word, but beckoned me to follow him into the house, carefully shutting the door as he ushered me in to the parlor; then, motioning to a seat, he asked to be told the facts of the case, which soon convinced him of the truth of the appeal. He called in his wife and sisters, who listened breathlessly to the recital of my adventures, and gave me a warm and cordial reception. Not only this, but a notice was sent out to some friends and kindred spirits and soon the room was filled with disloyal ladies, who kept the new-found Rebel talking till long past midnight.

"It was worth all the suffering," I thought, "when such charming women smiled upon me; it was the dream of the soldier realized at last."

The host, Mr. McGee, was at one time in the Army of Northern Virginia, but his health utterly failing him he was discharged and returned home. It was a strange coincidence, our meeting; and I determined to hold full faith hereafter in my luck.

A purse sufficient to meet all exigencies was made up by the company.

30

That night as I sank to sleep on "downy feathers" it was with a happy belief that all hardships were over, and that soon enough my feet would tread the soil of Old Virginia. Could I have seen with prophetic eye through what I would be called upon to pass ere I should see comrades and home again, sleep would have been banished from my eyelids. Ignorance was indeed bliss that night.

After an early breakfast I was driven in a private carriage to the depot. I carried sixty-six dollars in greenbacks in my pockets. With no feigned gratitude I parted from the friend who had fed and sheltered me and sent me on my way rejoicing, and that, too, at his own great risk. Had he been deceived or betrayed he must have suffered for his charity by an extended incarceration in some military prison.

CHAPTER XI.

CROSSING THE POTOMAC ON A RAFT.

A short ride and I reached Washington Station, from which place I took horse-cars for Frederick City, five miles distant. When nearly there an infantryman entered, note-book in hand. At first I mistook him for a baggage agent; but instead of wanting to check my trunk, his object was to check me if he could. He noted the name of every passenger; who they were; how long they intended to stay; their destination; their business, etc. Now if I had told the truth I would have been marched off in the twinkling of an eye; even the embryo Father of his Country would have prevaricated in a case like this; so I assured him that I had been born in Frederick City, raised there, lived there all my life, and had never left there except in this instance, when I had run over to Baltimore to see the sights, and was just returning.

"Where is your pass?"

"O, I left it at home; everybody knows me here."

"Then report at the provost marshal's immediately on your arrival," was the curt rejoinder.

Now I had a constitutional and natural antipathy to that particular class of officers, and would rather charge a battery any day than be interrogated by them or be asked to grant the little request with which so many poor privates found it impossible to comply—

"Show your passports."

Hence I told him that if he would examine the provost's books he would discover my name already registered.

This seemed to satisfy him, for he answered "All right," took down my name and passed on to the next passenger.

A devilish close shave, I thought.

Reaching the town I proceeded to the hotel and registered a fictitious name, giving my residence as Hagerstown, Maryland; and after a hearty dinner went down the street to buy several little articles which I desired to carry back South. The most important purchase was a pair of spurs, for which I hoped to have pressing need before the night ended.

In the evening I called upon two Southern sympathizers whose names had been given me in Baltimore, and whose patriotism was cheap, resembling those very low-priced prints warranted fast, yet which never wash without fading. They were afraid to talk, declined even to give advice as to the best way to cross the Potomac, and actually refused to furnish any information with regard to the routes and roads to the fords. I unbosomed my mind, and used no measured terms or epithets either, then left, thinking an honest foe better than a cowardly sympathizer.

In the evening I walked the streets for hours, having concluded the safest thing would be to mount the first army horse I could find and strike for some upper ford in the river; but there were no such horses to be seen. The property of citizens I respected too much to touch, though a year later I would have been less conscientious in such an emergency.

In wretchedly low spirits I left town. It was about ten o'clock and very dark. I had intended crossing the river at Wright's Ford, which a negro had informed me was the nearest crossing place, but in the obscurity of the night I lost the way and wandered only God knows where. For hours, through swamps, woods, fields, and meadows I stumbled; falling into deep holes, scrambling out as best I could; feeling my way out of forests, and forcing a path through briers, until I was nearly dead from exhaustion. My clothes were torn, face scratched, hands bleeding. Finally, after having struggled and strayed nearly all night I struck a road, and following it up came to a small house, whose owner I roused by a sturdy knocking at the door.

He soon appeared, light in hand. I had my tale cut and dried and informed him I had an uncle on the other side of the Potomac who was expected to die, and it was of the utmost importance I should get across the river at once. He directed me to follow the road running near the house for about twelve miles farther on, to a large brick edifice called Greenleaf's Mill, the owner of which could put me in a way to cross. It was still dark and very hard to keep the road, but soon day broke; the sun rose and I pushed forward with vigor.

The owner of Greenleaf's Mill proved to be a good friend indeed to the cause. He gave its needy representative a good hot breakfast, and let me sleep undisturbed in the house all the long day until five o'clock in the evening. Then after a hearty supper his guest stood ready to follow out the enterprise.

The miller was afraid to give any advice, for he said if trouble should come he did not want to think it would be attributable to counsel of his. He declared he could not believe my story, since United States detectives had been lately roaming through that immediate section, passing themselves off as escaped Rebel prisoners, appealing to the sympathies of the people, and using every cunning device to make them commit themselves. If successful their beguiled victims were immediately arrested, and either forced to take the oath of allegiance or suffer a long imprisonment. Consequently all entreaties could only induce the cautious miller to give his departing guest the name of but one Secessionist who lived four miles farther on.

I commenced walking, and in an hour reached the designated house. The owner was absent but his wife civilly invited me in. She was evidently suspicious and thought her visitor exactly what he was not. Her husband, she said, had gone to a horse-race and would not be back for hours. They were honest, industrious people, she informed me, and "good Union folks, too," she took the trouble to add.

The worthy woman tried her best to carry out the role, and made her bright, interesting little daughter of some twelve summers sing for the edification of the supposed detective, "Just before the battle, mother," and the "Star Spangled Banner."

Finding the hostess and her husband were Irish, I revealed my secret, but the revelation had only the effect of adding "Hail Columbia" and "We'll hang Jeff Davis to a sour apple-tree" to the already loyal repertoire.

So the time passed listening to these patriotic ditties and other Union sentiments, when sure enough, about ten o'clock, the husband returned from the race, singing in the joy of his heart "The Sprig of Shamrock;" and if the truth must be told, as tight as a brick. His wife introduced the stranger as a Confederate soldier escaped from Washington, at the same time by sundry winks and signs trying to make him understand it were well to be on his guard. But a wink is no better than a nod to a blind horse. Whatever acumen the lord of her bosom was apt to evince in general, verily he had none then which liquor had not deadened, for all his natural feelings bubbled up. Grasping the hands of his guest with real Hibernian warmth, he bade me welcome, and more than welcome; nay, the whole house was mine. He loved the gray, bedad; he had a son in the Twelfth Virginia Cavalry, as fine a sprig of a boy as ever breathed the breath of life; and he did not care a darn who knew it.

This frank avowal thoroughly frightened the more politic wife, who began to make hurried and nervous excuses, declaring he was drunk and did not know what he was talking about. But her smaller half broke in impetuously upon this caution with the remark that the pride of his life was that his only boy was a Rebel and in the Southern Army, and he'd be there himself, bedad, if he wasn't so old. This assertion left the wife not a single plank to stand upon, and she did what a woman generally does under such circumstances, burst into tears.

We hastened to assure her that her alarm was groundless, that we would be as loath to meet a Yankee detective at this moment as we would his Satanic Majesty himself. I showed my gray jacket, and by a little reasoning convinced her that so far from being the loyal spy she thought, I was an honest Rebel soldier whose sole desire was to get over the river with all possible speed. The tears were dried, the songs renewed, but this time they were "Dixie" and the "Bonnie Blue Flag," sung too by the same innocent lips which but an hour ago caroled immaculate Union ones. This only proves, however, that circumstances alter cases; and that women are born actresses and can rise to the level of all emergencies.

The jovial host opened several bottles of home-made wine and insisted on drinking toasts illustrative of his feelings, and that, too, so continuously that midnight found me still passing what Mr. Swiveller would call the "rosy." On retiring to rest he brought me an ancient sword of the size, shape and general appearance of a scythe blade, which hung up over the bed, so in case of a morning foray the old war relic might prove handy.

It was a terrible weapon according to our host, and had committed great execution in the hands of his grandfather in the great Irish rebellion of '98. With it near no one would dare attack, and before harm could come to me it would be necessary to cross over his dead body; and then he bade me good-night, or rather good-morning, and retired.

After a few hours' sleep and a hearty meal I was ready for anything. A neighbor had dropped in, who heard the story and gave in return the benefit of his advice. There was a certain negro, living not far away on the banks, who would ferry me over the river for ten dollars, and it would be as well and safest to avail myself of his services.

Not content with showing so much kindness, the true-hearted entertainer insisted on going a part of the way and pointing out the different fords. We went first to the Aqueduct on the Monocacy Creek, but found it heavily guarded. No persons were allowed to pass save those with passports from the provost.

Nothing now remained but to wade across the run, so making a detour of a mile or so, I rolled up my pants to attempt it.

"So soon as you get across," said the Irish friend, "go to the village near by called Slicksville, and buy ten yards of rope and a hatchet, and if you can't find the darky with a squint in his eye, to row you over, build a raft and paddle across in that way."

Shaking him warmly by the hand I started to cross the creek, which emptied into the river at right angles. The water was at freezing point and about four feet deep; it was necessary to wade nearly a hundred yards to gain the opposite shore. I emerged blue and numbed with cold. As I turned to take a parting look, there stood the kind-hearted fellow waving his handkerchief in a last token of farewell. A noble heart beat in that man's bosom.

On my way to Slicksville I met a farmer, who informed me that he had just left the village and that there were two detectives in the place. Knowing that certain capture would ensue should I venture near, I branched off the road leading there, and striking the towpath of the canal, walked heedlessly along, not knowing what next to do or where to go. The canal was parallel with the river, in fact on its very brink; but it had been constructed on the crest of the hill, while the river rushed along at the bottom some seventy feet below. Keeping on, I came across an abandoned canal boat which lay in the dry bed of the stately old ditch, whose waters had been turned off since the beginning of the war. The craft had been deserted of course, and by a happy inspiration the idea flashed across my mind that out of the idle timbers a raft might be constructed upon which to cross the river.

Before starting to work I scouted around to find if there were any enemies near. I learned that the nearest picket was at Monocacy about a mile below, where there was a block-house, garrisoned by a command called Scott's Nine Hundred, who, if the citizens of the vicinity were to be believed, were as arrant a set of thieves as ever plundered a hen roost or stole linen from a hedge.

About five o'clock that cold evening, February the seventh, 1864, I commenced constructing the raft. The canal boat had been moored at the time it had been abandoned, and fastened to stakes driven down in either bank, by two large ropes, one at the bow and the other at the stern. The ropes were the very things that were needed, but then I had no knife with which to cut them. However, I was not to be deterred by such a trifle as that, even if I had been obliged to emulate the example of the rats and gnaw them in two—yes, though they had been cables three inches in diameter I was bound to have those ropes at all costs; so I hunted around and found a treasure in a piece of an old rusty iron hoop, which being broken in sections and sharpened on a stone made a knife that answered every purpose. With it both lines were cut, and with cold, stiffened fingers I set to work to unravel them. This consumed about an hour, and then I found myself in possession of six small inch ropes about fifteen feet long, or nearly thirty yards altogether, more than enough to bind the largest raft.

It was night when this work was done; it was stinging cold and I had neither overcoat nor blanket.

The next step was to construct a bridge from the boat to the tow-path, which was accomplished by placing in the bottom of the canal, about six feet apart, the two high stools or wooden horses (as they are called) on the boat, on which rested planks and beams. Thus was formed an easy transit from the craft to the path, obviating the necessity of jumping down to the bed of the canal and then climbing up the bank every time a move was made from one to the other.

The bridge having been finished, I concluded from very weariness to postpone further operations until morning. So descending into the deserted cabin, a little, close hole about the size of a big dry-goods box, and groping about in the dark to find some place in which to sleep, I finally climbed into a bunk.

There I encountered an old mattress about as soft and pliable as sheet iron, and a quantity of rags which might have been a quilt or coverlid before the flood. The smell of it! Pau! it took the breath away. I jumped out in a hurry and went on deck; there the bitter, icy wind was sweeping, and I had either to freeze or return to yon combination of foul odors which would have done credit to a patent phosphate fertilizing factory on a hot summer day. I chose the latter, went back and laid down on the mattress, and got under the filthy rags, and with hands clasped tightly over my face, thought of damask roses and the spices of Araby.

At the dawn of day I awoke, and going out on deck breathed the pure air once more. I commenced work with a will. Tearing the large wooden covers off the apertures in the deck, and carrying them across the improvised bridge to the bank, they were pitched down the steep slope to the river edge. A quantity of loose planks were lying around, as well as nails, so that by fore-noon there was a large pile of lumber collected. Several times during the morning I came within an ace of being caught. Once I was just about to hammer out some nails from a piece of timber on the shore, when by a sort of uncontrollable impulse I stopped and crept up the bank. On reaching the top I had hardly time to conceal myself before half a dozen blue-coats passed along the tow-path, so close indeed that I could have touched them with outstretched hand.

About ten o'clock the raft was finished which was to bear me across the water, fortune as dear to me as Caesar's to himself and country. I determined to start at once. Grasping the im-provised paddle I was about to mafle off, when several citizens riding by on the tow-path above saw me, and jumping from their horses pulled the raft back.

I indignantly asked what was meant.

One of the citizens replied that the canal boat belonged to him, and he wanted to know who I was, where I was going, and by what right I proposed helping myself to his lumber.

It was useless to attempt to deceive him, caught *flagrante delicto,* so I made a virtue of necessity, owned the truth and asked for help.

"No, sir!" he said, "I am a loyal man; I can not help you, but I won't betray you. My advice is that you go to the nearest gar-rison, give yourself up and take the oath of allegiance."

My only reply was a bitter curse, which could not have been mistaken as otherwise than a most emphatic denial.

"Well, anyhow," he resumed, "I can not let this raft go; there's fully twenty-five dollars' worth of timber here."

"Well," said I, "if you set the liberty and happiness of a fellow-man against the sum of twenty-five dollars there is nothing more to be said. I never overrated myself, but I hoped that I could bring more than that sum. Here is your twenty-five dollars, every cent I have in the world; take it; but I am going to cross the river to-night if I have to swim."

This seemed to touch his companions, who demurred against his accepting the money, so he refused the proffer, and said with further generosity:

"You may have the plank, but if you try to cross before dark you will be killed to a certainty; for as soon as you reach the middle of the stream you will be in musket-range of our soldiers and they will pick you off as they would a wild duck floating on the water."

This struck me as being a solemn fact, and fortunate indeed it was that he had come up on the moment of departure and prevented the maddest step that could have been taken.

"You can try it if you are bent upon it, but take my advice and don't make the attempt until dark," still urged the owner of the raft as the party remounted and rode off.

There were yet several hours of light, so after a mental consultation I thought I had better lie low even though I was fighting-hungry. I went within the cabin and fastened the door, intending to get some sleep, but in a short time was aroused by some one trying to effect an entrance. I was on my feet in a second and as quick as thought had squeezed through the stern window, about twelve inches square (but then I was thin, very thin), and climbed the bank. I then found the intruder was a young country fellow, a coarse-looking rustic, who being gifted with an inquiring mind was on a voyage of discovery. Leaving him to pursue his investigations undisturbed, I walked leisurely up the path, intending to return when his labors were ended and his departure taken. I had not proceeded far, when hearing a noise in the rear, I looked and beheld two Yankee cavalrymen riding down the path at a gallop.

"The game is up!" I thought.

But no, they approached with a rush, with no thought of drawing rein. We cheered them as they passed, for they were only trying their horses in a little private scrub-race.

"Surely," thought I, "after so many narrow escapes and providential interposition my efforts must be crowned with success." I fell to discussing the chances for and against my ultimate good fortune. I thought of the French philosopher who, being in a maze of doubt regarding the immortality of the soul, and wandering a labyrinth of speculation, determined to solve the question by a method altogether unique in ethics. He prepared to throw a stone at a tree; "If I strike, I believe; if I miss, I'm eternally a skeptic." So he fired away, struck, and had an easy conscience and a firm faith ever afterwards.

This determined me to try my fortune by the same novel yet decisive mode for consolation—my faith was below par then. The chances against success were heavy; the danger close. So I chose a tree and selected a stone.

"If I strike that tree, I will some day reach Virginia safe and sound; if I miss it, then either captivity or death will be my portion."

Taking off my jacket, and looking straight at the trunk of the lordly oak some twenty paces off, I drew back with every muscle braced and stood ready to cast the die. Surely little David, when he put the pebble in the sling to hurl at big Goliath, never felt more acutely or eagerly the momentous results depending upon the flight of the stone. The rock sailed through the air, and the tree was struck plumb in the center.

As apparently trivial, childish as this act was, it instilled in my mind a profound conviction of ultimate success; a confidence so firm that even in the darkest hour, and amid all scenes, surrounded by lines of steel, environed by massive walls of granite, my faith remained staunch and firm. By constant brooding upon the subject I felt as would the warriors of ancient Greece had they heard the decrees of fate pronounced by the Oracle itself.

Many, many times, when suffering the pangs of hunger and cold; when ill-treated and trodden on; when life itself became a thing of no value; when despair stood ready to counsel apathetic submission to an apparently irresistible destiny, did the memory of that tree-test come back, and nerve the almost helpless heart to stern endurance and greater efforts. It was superstition, yes, but a superstition whose faith was as strong as that of religion's; a superstition whose power was potent for all good.

At last the sun went down and the gray shades of evening fell upon the scene, dimming all views, merging all objects and colors into one dull, opaque mass.

Untying the raft I stepped in and shoved off. It was about ten feet square, and bore the burden well. It progressed swimmingly until it reached the current twenty yards from shore. The river, about two hundred yards wide at this point, was running like a mill race. The water foamed and bubbled, speeding down with a seething rush and roar. The current caught the broad, unwieldy craft and sported with it at its own wild pleasure; spun it around and round despite my frantic efforts to guide it. It shot suddenly forward, then became entangled in a whirlpool and twirled like a top. I battled wildly to guide its course, but it was no use; the waters were having their own way and were making a high old jest of it. The swift, tumultuous current tossed the raft as if it were the merest chip, dashed it here and there like a bubble on the surface. Wet with perspiration and with aching muscles I strove more and more to stem the tide and at least shape its course to the opposite shore.

All in vain; the utmost endeavors only caused it to revolve in a circle, while all the time the planks, borne on the bosom of the current, had been impelled swiftly down the fast-flowing river. In the meantime the violence of the eddying stream had commenced to dash the raft to pieces. Several large timbers becoming loosened and detached, floated away, and in a few minutes the whole thing would go to wreck. Not far off were the lights of the block-house at Monocacy, toward which the fast crumbling raft was hurrying with frightful velocity. In five minutes, if the boards could hold together so long, it would be caught under the arches of the bridge below. Such paddling was never witnessed on the Potomac, and it was only by intense physical exertion that I succeeded in returning to the shore which had just been left, and not one minute too soon; jumping on shore I gave the cursed old concern a spiteful kick, which caused it to shoot far out into the stream. It dashed down the river and disappeared in the gloom.

In far deeper gloom I walked back to the canal boat, too miserable to speak; and sat for some time incapable even of thinking. After all I had gone through, it was hard, very hard, to wind up at the same point from which I started, only worse off.

Tragedy and comedy are inseparably linked together, and as woe-begone as I was, I thought of a story I had heard, and burst into hysterical laughter. Dick Martin told it to me one night in camp and said it was frozen truth.

"It was down in the Northern Neck, in Virginia, the summer before the war. A neighbor had an old razorbacked sow, which used to raise a plentiful lot of pigs every year, and when these young porkers were large enough to follow her, she would break in his corn-field, despite fence or stone wall. If she could not squeeze through a panel of the fence she would root a hole in the wall, and once in, would play havoc with the growing crop. There was one particular spot in the stone wall through which she was accustomed to make her entrance and her exit. Often would the farmer fill up the aperture, only to find that the hog with her long snout had mined her way through on the very next day. He stood this until, as Mark Twain would say, 'it became monotonous;' so he sought a hollow log in the shape of a 'U,' with which he stopped the hole, both ends opening, of course, on the highway. It was a very warm day that I chanced to be traveling along the road, and rested for a moment under the shade of a large tree near by. In the few minutes I saw a tall, gaunt female swine, with a whole brood of pigs, making her way with divers grunts of satisfaction toward the corn-field, advancing, as if she had not a second to lose, to her special aperture. In she went as if it were an accustomed runway, her whole family at her heels. In the shortest space of time she emerged; but instead of finding herself among the succulent corn-stalks she had struck the dusty turnpike. If ever a hog was puzzled, she was. However, after giving her head a wise shake, she essayed the trip again and once more reappeared on the same side of the fence. The old sow was posed and staggered, for nice as her brains would have been in a frying-pan, they were not equal to the situation. Her little eyes blinked, her little rat-tail wiggled, and she grunted her perplexity to her noisy offspring. Making a detour, and taking the bearings so as to be sure she was right this time, she confidently made her third trial. She passed in at the hollow log and came out as she had entered. But no sooner had she emerged the third time with the same result than, casting a horrified look around, she gave a frightened squeal and set off down the road as if the Devil were after her."

And so I felt like the old sow. I had gone into the hole; yonder was the corn-field I had hoped to reach and I found myself just where I started.

Nearly frozen, half starved, wholly demoralized, I sat there on the tow-path wondering what in this world of sorrows I was to do next. I must go to some house, get something to eat, and some sleep, then pick the flint and try again.

"Homme propose, mais Dieu dispose."

It was a dim, misty night; a sudden wind had risen, filling the sky with floating clouds and chilling the blood of any half-clothed unfortunate who walked the earth. I kept on and had hardly gone two miles when suddenly there came the quick, sharp challenge:

"Halt!"

In the dim light a squad of men could be seen, and the glint of the musket barrel showed who they were. I felt like Samson when the Philistines got him the second time.

CHAPTER XII.

RECAPTURED.

There were five soldiers who demanded a surrender; and each had his musket leveled, the hammer drawn back, his finger upon the trigger.

Striking a match, the Federals surveyed their trophy, felt my pockets for arms and ordered me to come along.

According to a preconcerted plan, I tried the countryman's dodge, and told them that I only lived a mile through the woods; begged the soldiers to go home with me, promising them something to drink if they would come.

It would not work, the Yankees had evidently more than a suspicion who their captive was, and had no idea of giving me a chance to escape through the woods; so with two on each side and the fifth leading the way, the party kept down the tow-path toward the canal boat. On the way they informed me that they were a part of the garrison at the Point of Rocks; that a citizen had given information at the post to the effect that a large party was building a raft, intending to cross to the Virginia side, which they had been sent to apprehend.

Reaching the canal boat, the soldiers made a close examination, of course finding nobody; then, continuing their investigations, they went down the bank. At the very point where I had started with the raft was a skiff with two paddles. Oh, if I had only waited two hours! If—oh, the momentous weight of an "if!"

Some Virginians across the way had evidently seen the worker on the raft, and conjecturing at once who it was, had come in a boat to the rescue, and were probably looking for me then as the party pounced upon the skiff, the sides and bottom of which were soon stove in by the butt end of the muskets in the hands of the enemy. So in addition to the woes of prisoners, came the keen regret that friends would suffer in trying to give aid. But there was little time for either sorrow or regret. The sergeant gave the order to march, and in an hour the party arrived at its destination, Point of Rocks, a station on the Baltimore and Ohio Railroad.

Seeing there was no further use in concealment, I acknowledged to the sergeant my real identity. He took me to the adjutant, a fine, gentlemanly looking fellow, who merely asked if I had papers of any kind, and upon being answered in the negative, courteously declined the proffered offer to submit the contents of my pockets to inspection. He invited me to sit down, and for half an hour conversed very pleasantly upon the topics of the day; asking many questions about the South, the morale of the army, the state of the commissariat, in all of which he seemed much interested.

At last the guard returned and I was taken into one of the unoccupied rooms of the depot, where a half dozen meal sacks were given in lieu of blankets, and a sentinel placed in the room.

I fully intended trying to get away that night, and could easily have done so; for there was but one guard, who would probably fall asleep. Then escape to the woods could be effected before any alarm would be made. I went to sleep with the determination to waken somewhere about midnight, but was so broken down by hard work, exposure and excitement, that I did not open my eyes until late in the morning. Performing a hasty toilet, I went to breakfast with the guard, eating and chatting sociably together. The rations drawn by a private soldier in the Federal Army made one Reb open his eyes. How happy and contented our comrades across the way would be if they could live like the rank and file of this Yankee host. Breakfast consisted of loaf bread, hot biscuit, coffee with plenty of sugar, fried ham, cold beef, hardtack and molasses. This the guard averred was his regular breakfast rations; for dinner, he declared, beans, rice and hominy were issued; and that he had never bought a cent's worth of food since he had been in the garrison. When I told him how the soldiers of the South fared, officers and men, he said if his Government fed him so he would desert the first opportunity.

After breakfast I was taken before the commandant of the post, a big, brawny, red-faced fellow, who first tried to scare me into fits by his scowling face and bullying tones; then, seeing that a boy who had been trained in the school of danger was not apt to quake in his shoes and become frightened because a moon-faced officer put on a sour face and howled, he ordered his satellites to treat me as a spy instead of a regular soldier in the Confederate Army. He searched me, but I saved the money by slipping the rolls into my mouth, a suggestion for which I had to thank my friend the guard of the night before. He whispered the hint to me in parting, and so I was enabled to save ten dollars. It was ever thus, Billy Yank helping Johnny Reb. The examination was of the strictest kind; pockets were turned inside out, clothes shaken, boots removed, and stockings too, while the colonel stood by as if he expected to discover treasonable documents which would consign the youth before him to the gallows; and while putting an end to him, reflect undying credit on himself. Visions, no doubt, of the capture of Andre and appropriation by Congress from the United States Treasury to fill the pockets and swell the fame of the brave captor, flashed across his mind. And yet, as old Tony Weller said of matrimony, "it was a pity to go through so much to get so little;" for the most rigorous scrutiny failed to discover anything except an old Richmond passport, which only served to establish the identity of myself.

This puffed-up individual was the colonel of the First Maryland Union Regiment, but he could hardly have been a native of that proud old State. The lieutenant-colonel, who had lost his arm in battle, was a gallant and unmistakable gentleman, who treated his Southern prisoner with marked courtesy; so also was the adjutant. Save these two, all the officers of the First Regiment with whom I came in contact were rather a rough set of men.

After the search was ended I was subjected to a pumping process, which brought up one pint of information to a barrel of lies. I recounted truly my escape, but everything as regarded the strength and condition of the army, of course, as a soldier, I did not answer. I was then dismissed and sent back to the depot to await the first train to Harper's Ferry. At eleven in the morning the cars stopped; I was put on board and in an hour disembarked at the Ferry, and was immediately taken before the provost marshal and subjected to another examination, in which, despite all protest, pockets and boots underwent another severe scrutiny, it is needless to say with the same barren results.

Then I was placed in the garrison guard-house, a horrible place, worse by far than a jail. This prison was cold, dreary and filthy beyond belief. Originally it had been a part of the old Armory building, burnt during the first year of the war. Nothing but the walls had been left standing; these had been roofed over, and converted into a decent shelter so far as the rain was concerned, but afforded no protection against the biting blasts of winter. There were three large rooms connected by doorways which had no doors, but instead stood a sentinel with loaded musket to prevent going from one apartment to another, save those who had the authority to pass. The room upon the left was for the use of the officer of the day; that in the center was for Rebel prisoners, while in the one on the right were confined Yankees held in durance for a gamut of crimes, running from desertion to murder.

The newly arrived prisoner was placed by mistake in this den of lions; my citizen's suit covering the uniform was doubtless the cause of the error. In a few seconds, in fact as soon as the guard had disappeared from the door, I was attacked by the Yankees, and a lively fight ensued. Of course it was all one way, and would have ended seriously, but fortunately the officer of the day, hearing the racket and fearing that murder was being committed, rushed in, and striking right and left with his sword, soon quieted the tumult. I was but a boy in years, slight in form, and was carried out from my encounter with a roomful of savage roughs, with eyes bunged, nose bleeding and clothes torn; whereupon the officer declared that I myself had raised the row, in fact was dangerous and must be handcuffed, and handcuffed I was. Honor to the man who conceived the kindly thought! Due honor to his bravery! It had been the fable over again of the lamb muddying the stream; but all honor to the officer's charge, his keen perception of the situation, and his prompt measures to preserve the garrison.

I was then placed among my own people in the center room, only six all told, picked up here and there at different times.

For a couple of weeks I remained just about as happy as disembodied spirits confined in the chambers of Dante's "Inferno." The food was insufficient, our treatment cruel and inhuman in the extreme. The guards were accustomed to strike and kick the men in their charge on the slightest provocation. Of course they were not Americans. The true Anglo-Saxon race has but little of the tyrant or bully in it. They were Dutch, but few speaking any English at all, though the regiment was known as the Ninety-third Pennsylvania. There was not a prisoner there who did not bear, either upon his face or his person, some legible scar or wound made by those Dutchmen. Because I would not give one of the guards my brier-wood, I was knocked senseless and my head cut open by a brick which the Dutchman picked up and threw so quickly that I did not have time to dodge. I will carry the scar of that ignoble wound to my dying day.

Another was struck on the chest by the butt of a musket, which resulted in a hemorrhage; a third suffered from a bayonet thrust through his leg, while a fourth felt his nose grow almost to

31

the size of a turnip, rendered thus corpulent by the stroke of a fist. All this without the shadow of a cause. There was absolutely no authority to whom one could appeal, for the officer who had temporary charge of the prisoners was a captain in the Ninety-third, by whose orders four out of six captured soldiers were handcuffed. There could be no appeal to him.

It was hard to become accustomed to those iron bracelets; and it would be a long time before the wearer learned to use his hands. Both must be moved at the same time, the right must follow the left, or else a sharp jerk would further wound the lacerated flesh; even in deepest sleep, dreams were tinctured by iron fetters, and the wearer wakened twenty times a night.

But custom soon became a habit; and after the first week they could be worn as unconsciously as the maiden sports her golden bracelet.

The Yankee prisoners next door made day and night resonant with songs and howls. At least twenty fights in the twelve hours were averaged, only checked by the officers rushing in and hammering away with their swords at every head, while the sentinel stood and watched the fun with a grin of satisfaction on his dull, beery face.

How the Northern prisoners learned to hate the Dutchmen; they reviled them, they cursed them, they denounced them in all the choice terms drawn from a large and unique collection of Billingsgate, and they mimicked their broken English until the said Dutchmen were beside themselves with rage.

Those prisoners were a rough set; half of them were born in the gutter, reared in the streets, and had served a term in Bridewell or jail. They gravitated as naturally to prison as a sailor just landed from a long cruise goes to a gin shop. They passed their time in all sorts of cruel practical jokes. One circumstance will serve for illustration, happening as it did under the eye of the Rebels, who could attest its truth.

A guard was standing in the doorway dividing the center and west rooms, in which were confined the prisoners of both North and South. He was a big, savage Hessian, some forty years old, whose ponderous fist was ever ready to strike, whose mouth was always filled with tobacco juice, ready to squirt on the prisoners of either side—on their faces, their hands, their persons, it made no difference to the barbarian. He was very fond of smoking, and owned a real German pipe, the bowl of which was china, fully six inches in length, and held a handful of tobacco. It had a flexible gutta-percha tube, and when the amber mouth-piece was clasped between the teeth the top of the long bowl came to within a few inches of his eyes. One morning he was smoking at his usual post, when the officer of the day called him hastily into the guard-room. Leaning his musket across the doorway, he laid his pipe upon a cracker-box which stood near by, and hurried out. He was gone only a minute, but even in that time, as quick as thought, his pipe had been seized and manipulated in some mysterious manner, and hastily returned to the same place before he was ready to resume his smoke. He took it up. The prisoners on the Rebel side knew that something had been done, for they had seen the Yankee snatch the pipe and slyly slip it back; but the guard had brutally struck several of their number, so they considered it no business of theirs to give the word of warning. The pipe did not seem to draw, though the Dutchman worked at it until he grew purple in the face. Then he examined it; the fire had gone out. Drawing a match from his pocket he lit the tobacco and puffed away very contentedly. There were half a hundred pairs of eyes watching him with breathless eagerness, waiting some denouement. It came soon enough! A flash of fire darted from the bowl of the pipe and enveloped his face. The hair and beard were in a flame in a second, while the white smoke spread like a little cloud through the room and drifted upward toward the rafters. The strong man, one moment standing erect, the next was rolling over the floor in agony, lading the air with horrible shrieks and screams. Guards and officers rushed in. The odor of burned hair was filling the room with a nauseating stench. A surgeon was sent for; meanwhile the man was mad with pain, requiring a half dozen men to hold him in his frenzied struggles. The doctor arrived, and on examining the patient, disclosed to view a face the sight of which was sickening in the extreme. One side was blistered black; the left eye had been at the moment directly over the bowl of the pipe, and looked only like a black piece of cork. In his torture the soldier, in broken English, prayed to be killed; indeed his cries were so loud and fearful that they brought scores of soldiers around the building, who had heard the shrieks of the man half a mile away.

"Who did this?" sternly demanded the commandant, going into the room. Nobody knew anything about it; in fact there were no witnesses to point out even so much as a surmise, for the afflicted man was incoherent and could answer no questions. Only this much was known: some one had nearly filled the bowl with gunpowder, and a small quantity of tobacco on top. A few whiffs burnt the tobacco and ignited the powder with the result just related.

The catastrophe had a good effect upon the Dutch soldiers, who were a scary set at best. It made them more circumspect, while those on guard thereafter kept their eyes open and their hands to themselves.

At last one morning, to the joy of all, the prisoners learned that the Ninety-third Pennsylvania would leave the next day and another regiment take its place. The treatment meted out to them by these foreign ruffians had so embittered them that each Rebel hoped from the bottom of his heart they would leave their bones on some Virginia battle-field.

Sure enough, the next morning those bullying Hessians marched away, followed by the hisses and hootings of both Yankee and Rebel prisoners, who only wished that every parting curse could have been a good-sized brickbat.

Our men were overjoyed to find that the place of the Ninety-third was to be filled by the Fourteenth New Hampshire, who had guarded the Old Capitol Prison. The former charges of Lieutenant Webster renewed their acquaintance with him with pleasure, for he was as jovial and good-hearted a fellow as ever lived. He had all handcuffs off in an hour after his arrival. Glorious, sunny-tempered Webster! my heart warms at the recollection of his genial voice, warm glances and many kindnesses; he improved the situation in every way.

But all this time the subject of escape had never left the mind of at least one man who had once succeeded in eluding the vigilance of the Washington guards. I brooded, plotted and planned, but there was absolutely no chance at Harper's Ferry on which to build a hope. Even if I could succeed in getting out of the building, the river ran on one side, the precipitous mountain a few feet off hedged in the other, while on the right and left were two bridges guarded strongly by day and night. It was a cage within a cage; if one was forced the other would certainly hold. Yet I, who dreamed of liberty every moment, determined to make the attempt whenever and wherever an opportunity should occur, except at this one place.

Rebel prisoners were brought in nearly every day, singly and in twos and threes; mostly Mosby's men, captured on scouts.

On the twenty-second of February, 1864, a small squad arrived, all Marylanders, caught in trying to run the blockade to

Baltimore; and on the twenty-ninth, seventeen more, belonging to Mosby's battalion, were captured, and the one Rebel room of the prison was crowded in consequence. Of course the new acquisitions made it more pleasant for those already garnered.

But there were getting too many, evidently, for the comfort of the authorities; and on the principle that a man when his pockets overflow will carry his treasure to bank, orders were given to start on the morrow for Camp Chase in Ohio.

The Rebels filled one car and had a pleasant ride to Wheeling, West Virginia, where they were stopped for the night. The guard-room was in delightful contrast to the one just vacated, being immense in size, well heated, light, airy and scrupulously neat, with pillows and mattresses. The food was well cooked and very palatable.

But even amid these comforts the stern realities of war made themselves felt. On every side could be seen the Northern prisoners, fettered with ball and chain; and in such numbers that when they walked about over the floor dragging the iron balls, it sounded altogether like the mutterings of a thunder-storm. Many were the devices used by the unfortunates to lighten the burdens of the heavy ball, the most common consisting of a little wagon in which the heavy shot could be rolled about from place to place, just as a school-boy loves to trundle about mimic burdens in miniature carts.

Here was some tangible proof of the strict discipline of the Union Army, and the treatment accorded the Yankee private, of whom one had been wearing the ball and chain for six months with the prospect of six more, because of a personal difficulty with his sergeant, whom he had struck. Another lay in his bunk with his leg swollen to an enormous size, but the irons were not removed. Some were ill, but still wore the fetters. All this would not have been tolerated in our Army of Northern Virginia.

Each new arrival had to be initiated by being tossed in a blanket, just as the goatherds threw poor Sancho Panza in the inn yard. There was no use of resisting; a dozen willing hands seized the victim, placed him in a large, thick blanket, some twelve feet square; as many as could wedge in would grasp the edges, and then with united effort the body would be sent twenty feet into the air, only to fall and rise again. The fun of the thing consisted in the struggles and absurd gyrations of the tossed as he would fly through space—indeed it was irresistibly ludicrous.

Sometimes they would catch an old stager, who would be like

a lump and not move a muscle; who would rise like a log and fall like a stone; there would be no fun in tossing him, and his speedy release would be an assured thing. Indeed the game to him was rather pleasant than otherwise; the only inconvenience being the fear that the elastic cloth giving way, he might drop upon the hard floor. But this rarely happened, and the initiation having been gone through with, he might be sure of future peace.

CHAPTER XIII.

THE SECOND ESCAPE.

The prisoners spent the following day in the Wheeling prison, and had strong hopes that this would be their future home, for with the exception of Fort Warren, it was the most comfortable place of confinement in America. Some few prisoners would have been well content to spend the remainder of the war there. But no sooner had each man selected his bunk, chosen his comrade, and made those little arrangements looking to a protracted stay, than orders were received to leave in half an hour. There seemed no rest for the weary in that delectable region, so the men fell into line and marched to the depot. The cars were not forthcoming, however, consequently the prisoners were conducted back, with orders to be ready to start next morning before day.

"Where are we going?" asked one of the number of the officer in charge.

"Camp Chase," he answered curtly, as he turned away.

"Camp Chase!" the words sounded like a knell to all who heard them. We had listened recently to fearful accounts of this prison; tales of dreadful cold, insufficient rations, of the awful death-rate among the prisoners; all of which were much exaggerated doubtless in the telling, but which filled the mind with horror.

"Camp Chase!" the boding words chased sleep from the eyes that night, for neither the princely Clarence nor the noble Buckingham felt more aversion, or gloomy forebodings in going to the Tower, than did those doomed for that Ohio Hades.

Julian Robinson, of Mosby's battalion, and myself lay quietly in whispered consultation. We felt certain that the best and last chance was to escape en route, for once in that fortified place, we knew by hearsay that the opportunities of getting away were one in a million. Among the many thousands confined there, not more than a score had succeeded in the attempt to escape. No further exchange of prisoners could take place it was said, and who knew—the war might last for years yet. Better be killed at once than to linger out a life of torture and die a thousand deaths in lengthened imprisonment. So we made up our minds that in twenty-four hours we would be free in our physical bodies, if possible; in spirit, if fortune so willed it."

The best plan was to play the same game which I had played so successfully in Washington, only this time, instead of a citizen's suit, I determined to wear the Yankee uniform. Both of us had several changes of underclothing, and also a few dollars which we had held and concealed as a miser does his hoard. The money was destined to come into practical use, for before the journey commenced we traded the stock in hand for a blue overcoat and Yankee cap apiece. Of course the Federal prisoners knew what we wanted with them, but the little flame of patriotism which had once burned in their hearts had been utterly quenched by confinement, so they readily made the bargain; nay, they even gave the names of several Southern sympathizers living in Wheeling, to whom it might be well to apply in case we succeeded in taking French leave.

At three o'clock, before dawn, the prisoners were roused by the guards; a breakfast of hot coffee, bread and meat was ready for us. We were then formed into ranks of twos and marched down the street. In the confusion of starting, Robinson and myself became separated; the former being in the front and I in the rear of the column.

In all, there were about forty-five prisoners in the squad, and their route lay through the principal street. In fifteen minutes' walk the line had reached the suspension bridge, a magnificent iron structure thrown across the Ohio River, on the other side of which was the village called Bridgeport. There we were to take the cars to Columbus, where the prison was situated.

We slipped on our overcoats along the route. It was bitterly cold, the north wind sweeping in boisterous gusts down the river and whistling its wild refrain through the iron bars of the bridge, hanging so loftily in the air that it seemed to swing like a rope in the roaring blast. Beneath, two hundred feet, so distant that it made the head swim to watch it, ran the river; its bosom filled with huge blocks of floating ice, whose hard crackling and grinding sounded above the dash of the wind.

It was then light; the day had dawned but the sun had not yet risen. The bridge was several yards wide. After traveling the main roadway a short distance, the column deflected and took the part partitioned off for foot-passengers, which was about four feet wide. We had traversed about nine-tenths of the distance, and a dozen steps would bring us to the end of the bridge, where not fifty feet away was the depot. I was walking with Bob Ballenger, an Alexandrian of Mosby's Rangers, a tall, slab-sided fellow, who stumbled along as if half asleep, his chin sunk on his breast and his old slouch hat pulled over his eyes. Now was the time, and if Robinson's nerve had failed I would have to look out for myself. As I glanced forward I saw a blue-coated figure cross the line at the head of the column, and in a few paces more I saw my comrade leaning against the hand rail and heard him mock and jibe the prisoners as they passed. I pulled myself together; the head of the column was across the bridge. I threw my old slouch hat on the ground and replaced it with a neat Yankee cap, and stepped right by the guard, uttering the same exclamation I had used in my escape in Washington, with exactly the same result; the guard was bewildered, and half checked his pace forward and involuntarily brought his gun down from his shoulder, but he could not stop without having a scene; and he was not sure, and the natural attitude of the blue-coat decided the mental conflict in his mind, so he reshouldered his gun and stalked on.

Bob Ballenger, after the war was over, said he did not see me vanish, nor were either Robinson or myself missed until some minutes after, when the Rebel squad was turned over to the Ohio provost guard, who tolled off each name as the men stepped aside, and when we were missed a fine disturbance followed. Every one of our guards stoutly maintained that they brought the whole detachment over just as they were delivered to them. Thinking that we must have been left in the prison at Wheeling, two guards were sent back after us.

In a few seconds I was at Robinson's side; we uttered no words, but the pressure of our hands and the glance of our eyes told the tale though our lips were mute, for we were too happy to speak.

We were in a very tight place, and the first question was no idle one: what should we do?

It meant certain capture to stay on the bridge; we knew our absence would be noticed, for the roll was bound to be called at the cars, and if our absence was not discovered the guard would soon be returning to the prison. We could not go on to Bridgeport, for that would be like running into the foe; we could not jump off into the water, that would be certain death; and how could we return to Wheeling when on the other side of the bridge walked a sentinel who would arrest us on sight?

The truth was, the only possible course of action was to get back to Wheeling, guard or no guard, so after a little discussion

we decided upon a course of action; we would write a pass, and
if the sentinel refused to let us go on, we were to seize him and
throw him headlong into the river.   It was no time to stop then,
we were playing for high stakes.   If one enemy's life stood between us and liberty, it would have to go.

"I will offer him the pass," said Robinson; "you stand behind
him, and if he declines to recognize it, I will clap my hand over
his mouth, you grasp his legs and pitch him suddenly over the
parapet."

So I took a piece of paper and wrote with a lead pencil the
following:

> "Wheeling, West Virginia, February 24th, 1864.
"Privates Robert and James Smith, Co. H, Fourth Union West
Virginia Cavalry, have permission to cross over to Bridgeport,
Ohio, and return on the morning of the 25th.
> "JAMES ECHOLS.
> "Approved: J. C. BENTON,
>   "Col. Comdg."

With this document we walked toward the guard, hoping and
trusting that he was an ignorant gawk who would not have sense
enough to discover the imposition.

As we came within ten feet of him he halted us.   He was a
cavalryman, a tall, fine-looking fellow, with flashing black eyes.
He had his sabre drawn and was slowly pacing the bridge, whistling a lively stave.

"Halt!   You cannot go by without a pass."

"Here is one," answered Robinson, moving to one side and
leaning carelessly against the railing.   The trooper came up,
took the paper and was reading it, while I selected my position
behind him.

We could hear the beating of our own hearts, as with nerves
tensioned and muscles steeled we waited his decision.

Surely many men go through life little knowing the perils all
unseen which lurk so near; many a man stands unconsciously
even while the grim spectre Death opens wide his arms to enfold
the victim while he himself, it may be, never knows his hazard.

"Oh!" said the cavalryman; "this paper is not of any account."

I gave a quick look; there was no sign of a human being within
sight or call; only we three stood alone on the bridge, and the
dying cry would not be heard.

The sands of that soldier's life were nearly run; the threads of his woof nearly spun. Surely some good angel guarded him in that his moment of supreme danger. A second later and all would have been over, when he added:

"I know you boys have run the blockade over there, but you can slip by if you choose."

And then he resumed his march and his tune, which came near being left unfinished.

Once in Wheeling we called at the house of a Southern sympathizer and scared that worthy out of his senses; nor did we get a cent. However, he supplied us freely with advice to leave the city at once, which plan we immediately proceeded to put into execution. On our way through the streets we were recognized by some Yankees who had acted as guards in the prison, but who were fortunately unarmed. A lively race ensued; but as it was so early in the morning there were none on the streets to cry "stop thief!" and aid in the chase. There were only two pursuers; one, a short, fat little fellow, who dropped out of the race early in the game; but the other, a tall, long-legged Yankee, who could get over a square in a few strides of his seven-leagued boots, kept on to the outskirts of the city, and did not give over the run until his prey stopped and seized each a rock, when his patriotism, which had rendered his heels so lively, suddenly oozed out and we were left in peace. Then we made a spurt and did not rest until we had put several miles between us and the dirty, smoke-grimed city of Wheeling.

Our intention was to make a detour, strike the Baltimore and Ohio Railroad, down which we proposed to travel, trusting to fortune to steal rides and be helped along by our own and others' wits, and so make our way into Virginia. I had relations living in Cumberland, Maryland, who, if we could reach them safely, would certainly help us all in their power. In fact the railroad was the only route we could take, for the country was one succession of mountain ranges over which it was simply impossible to make one's way in the dead of winter.

Both of us thought we knew what good walking meant, having had practice as foot cavalry, and also imagined we had experience in roads; but those hills proved we were novices after all. It was only about fourteen miles to the point which we wished to strike, but it required eight hours of constant toil to make it. Up one mountain, down another, wading streams, forcing bushes and laurel brakes, until our strength was well-nigh gone.   Late in the evening we reached the railroad track, and did not stop until nearly ten o'clock, when we halted at a small cottage on the side of the road about a half mile from the depot, and applied for something to eat.

The owner, a young man, politely invited us in and supplied us with a most comfortable supper.   We repeated to him the varnished tale: that we belonged to the Union Army, had just returned from home in Preston County, West Virginia, and were en route to Washington, and had been left by the cars, having gone up the valley to obtain something to eat and had not returned in time.

He heard us so far without interruption, when a smile broke over his face and he replied courteously:

"Boys, you need not attempt to deceive me, you are escaped Southern prisoners.   I heard about you in Wheeling to-day, and knew you as soon as I set eyes upon you."

This knocked us flat and we confessed the truth and begged him not to betray us, telling him of all our sufferings and disappointments, until his sympathies became thoroughly enlisted.

He replied that he was a Union man but he would not divulge our secret to any one.

Thanking him, which was all that we could do, we retired to rest, utterly worn out with excitement and fatigue.

A good night's sleep and hearty meal made us feel as bright as a new dollar.   We were much surprised when our host told us that in the next room was a sick brother, a Federal soldier belonging to the First (Union) West Virginia Infantry, home on a furlough.

He had heard the conversation of the preceding night, but sent word that he would not abuse the rights of hospitality and have us arrested, as he could easily have done by sending a notice to the guard at the depot but a short distance up the track. He said further, that we had better make good use of the time, as the guards along the roads would be on the lookout for the two escaped prisoners.

We thanked him for his generous hospitality and showed our full appreciation of that high honor which forbade his taking advantage of a foe who had broken his bread and eaten his salt. We made a note of his name and regiment, asking that if the fortunes of war should ever throw him a prisoner into the hands of the Rebels, to write and let us know, and we would pledge ourselves to go to General Lee in person, in his behalf.   He complied, giving the name of John Rudkins, Company I, First W. Va. (Union) Infantry.

A cordial pressure of the hand and we took our departure.

Tramping steadily along all day we made very good time, passing several depots and stations on the route, some garrisoned. We were not molested, however, for we had traded off the blue overcoats and caps for suits of butternut in the most dilapidated condition, reminding one of the old fellow in the nursery tales: "Rags and tatters; tatters and rags."

En route we encountered many Irish laborers at work on the track, and in every instance found their sympathies were with the South.

There were three reasons for this: one was, that in their opinion the situation of the South was analogous to that of Ireland; another, that the Southern States were more Catholic than the North and had received the recognition and sympathy of the Pope; while above all, the feelings of the warm-hearted sons of Erin were always on the side of the under dog in the fight. Consequently, we Rebels soon learned that whenever we met an Irishman we had met a friend.

With the citizens we had, on the contrary, to be very cautious in act and guarded in conversation; generally representing ourselves as Rebel prisoners released from Camp Chase after taking the oath of allegiance, to which we were obliged to subscribe in order to save our lives. Fortunately our appearance, so gaunt, haggard and thin, corroborated our statements and no one doubted our words.

After a steady tramp all day along the track we stopped for the night at a small house near the railroad. The inmates, who were very ignorant, accepted all yarns as gospel. Upon inquiry we found that we had walked just twenty-four miles that day.

After a good breakfast, paid for in thanks, of which we had an inexhaustible supply, we continued our tramp. It was a bright, sunny day; the scenery along the route was superb; the mountains, rising grandly, hovered in their pride thousands of feet above the clear limpid streams at their base. Brooks came dancing here and there down the jagged steeps, tossing into the flowing river a shower of pearls. Looming up, like giant sentinels keeping unsleeping watch, were the beetling, overhanging crags of the Alleghanies. The white clouds floated over their topmost peaks, half concealing, half revealing them. On the height of the grade the view was entrancing and the eye could take in at one glance the whole effect: the sun touching the clouds and painting them in gorgeous tints beyond all earthly coloring, the background of peak on peak stretching in the distance.

Ever and anon came the great iron steed, toiling up the precipitous track with its long, winding burden, panting as it curved in and out upon its course, gaining as if with fiery throes the steep ascent. As it reached the crest it startled the echoes with its scream, and shaking its dusky head, plunged down the iron slope—spurning the dull earth with flying heels, and beating out in the twilight-air a stream of flaky fire.

The sun sank below the mountains, and we quickened our steps with the sudden reminder that we had eaten nothing since morning, and that it was time to drop sentiment and attend to fact. But mile after mile was traversed, and still no light gleamed through the window, no sound of civilized life broke upon our ears.

About midnight we were completely broken down, so choosing a secluded spot in the forest, and striking a match, soon had a glorious fire. Collecting an armful of leaves as a substitute for a bed, we were in a moment oblivious to all human woes.

An ample dinner given by a good Samaritan brought us up wonderfully next day; and we made good time, not stopping even to talk with the Irish section-hands working along the track.

No one took much notice of the two ragged individuals walking down the road. Who could have recognized the gay Cavalier or "Company Darling" of Mosby's battalion—Julian Robinson, the ladies' pet, the maidens' love—in that tatterdemalion limping along the railroad in the wild Cheat River region? I was in no better plight and so, collectively, we formed a tableau at which the children stared and the dogs barked.

To vary the monotony of the journey we were accustomed to stop and talk with every one we met, who, as characteristic of the people, were inordinately curious, and invariably asked three questions, viz:

"What are your names? Where do you come from? Where are you going?"

To each was improvised a different answer to suit the emergency; and certainly none could have traced us by the names, for the only ones we ever avoided taking were the ones our sponsors gave us.

The second interrogation was usually responded to by the information that we were paroled prisoners from Camp Chase.

"Look here, gentlemen," said Robinson, as a group of countrymen gathered around the stove in a little country store, after having listened to a frightful account of the horrors of Camp Chase, drawn from hearsay more than from imagination.

"Look at me; when I was first carried into that infernal prison I weighed fully two hundred pounds; and look at me now, why I would not tip the scales at ninety-seven."

"Dang my buttons!" exclaimed a listener, with open eyes looking at the slim body of the speaker, " 'pears as if you had died and come to life again."

"Good God! I'd as lief be killed at once as be sent there," remarked another with sincerity in his tones.

"If they are Rebels, they oughtn't to be treated as if they was dogs," growled an old rough-faced Unionist.

So they clubbed together, and we took up a collection amounting to one dollar and seventy-five cents, which sent us on our way rejoicing. We were in an enemy's country, and the first principle of military strategy teaches in that case to forage on the foe.

Several days' walking brought us to Farmington, a pretty place on the Baltimore and Ohio Railroad. Here we stopped at the house of Mr. Freeman, a devoted Southerner, who gave all the assistance in his power. At this point all of our plans, which had worked so well, were changed. It had been our intention to keep straight along the track of the railroad, and secure in our disguise, not leave it until we should be in Virginia. But Mr. Freeman explained that it would be impracticable to reach Cumberland even by walking, as there would be several bridges to pass which could not be flanked. To cross on foot would result in certain detection and capture; for all these bridges were garrisoned, and no one was permitted to pass without having first been subjected to a rigorous examination. Should a particle of suspicion attach to the words or actions of any one, he was at once arrested and sent to the provost marshal, to either clear or criminate himself.

"The only plan open for you," continued the host, " is to take the regular train to Cumberland, and from there make your way across the country south. Leave the track, by all means, if you do not wish to be discovered to a certainty."

"But we have no money," we urged.

"I will give you ten dollars, which will be sufficient to take you to Cumberland," replied our kind friend; "after that you will have no further trouble."

The next night we went on several miles, and took the train at Lymington Station for Cumberland. The whistle sounded and we were soon bowling along at the rate of forty miles an hour. We had frequent cause to congratulate ourselves that kindly fate had sent us to the house of Mr. Freeman, for at every bridge we passed were sentinels at both ends, besides squads of home-guards, who were constantly patrolling the road and arresting all suspicious persons. This was in consequence (so the conductor of the train told us) of several attempts lately made by Southern citizens to burn the railroad bridges, thus severing for a time communication between points on the Baltimore and Ohio Railroad.

At midnight the train stopped.

"Cumberland!" sang out the brakeman as the cars reached the platform. The weather during the last two or three hours had taken a sudden turn. A strong northwest wind had brought an icy blast which chilled everything and whirled the blinding snow-flakes in a wild dance through the air. It was as dark as pitch— yes, it was a wild night; the wind was increasing in fury every minute, sending the drifting, maddening snow flying through the streets.

The weather was fearful for us, who had not so much as a blanket or overcoat; nothing but those rags over our gray jackets, which seemed to give fluttering entrance to the cold, rather than to keep it out. The streets were choked by the flying mists that were whisked by the gale into every nook and cranny, and almost froze the marrow in our bones. The very lamps flared and flickered, and the congealing frost deadened their gleam and made them look like waning, waving torches.

A bitter night for the poor soldier on picket, who stands with his back to the blast; a cruel night for the sailor hanging to the shrouds as he reefs the sails; a cursed night indeed for all outcasts or unfortunates.

We had the name of a relation, a noted Southerner, who had supplied us with clothes and money at Harper's Ferry. After knocking up several housekeepers at different houses, for it was midnight, and alarming their families, we found the object of our search.

We were ushered into the parlor, ablaze with light and brightened by gleaming anthracite. The curtains were closely drawn; the red velvet of chairs and sofas offered enticing, bewildering welcome to our stiffened, all but frozen forms, which sank into the depths of their loving embrace. Pictures, mirrors and books formed a home scene which the eyes of the wanderers had not beheld for many a sad day. Over all gleamed the red flames of the fire-light, casting bright tintings into every corner, reflecting itself in the many polished surfaces and filling the air with a glowing heat which pervaded every sense.

A greater contrast to the howling tempest without could not be imagined.

The host entered. We told him the piteous story of our past hardships. He really seemed touched, for he was a warm-hearted man, whose every sympathy was with the cause of the struggling South. But just then his mother-in-law appeared upon the scene; across her face shone no tender light of compassion. She heard our story of suffering, without change of attitude or the blinking of an eyelid, and then we finished and waited. The vanquished warrior in the gladiatorial arena met with more pity watching for the uplifted finger of the Roman patricians. As well might one of the old Noblesse beg mercy at the hands of the Tribune of the Sections. It was the same old story: asking bread and receiving a stone. She informed us that her son-in-law had taken the oath of allegiance and to help us was to break his word, and he would be ruined.

Fortunately for us there was a noble, true heart in the house; an angel of mercy indeed; and as we were passing from the brightness to our death, all that sweet grace of tender womanhood found vent. As we reached the door the young wife came to us with tears raining down her fair cheeks, and pressed into my hand a roll of money, saying it was all she had. Then we stepped across the threshold into the darkness. The snow struck blindly in our faces; the storm was at its height, but the little act had put sunshine into our hearts and hope into our souls.

After a hurried consultation we decided to get into the country at once; for Cumberland was a dangerous place in which to linger.

Nothing but the severity of the storm kept the guards from patrolling the streets. We struck for the open without delay and at haphazard. It was so dark that we could not see each other, so hand in hand we followed a street which led out of town. At last we came to a high hill; we reached the top and stumbled on, not knowing where we were. Oh it was cold! Down that hill with the snow up to our knees, up, up a mountain, where we groped until the summit was reached, then down again until a

32

clearing was entered and the end, we felt, was not far off. Our limbs were inert, bodies numbed, while the stupor of death was upon us. At last we ran against a small house, and feeling carefully around discovered a door. We knocked and waited. No sound, no light flickered through the windows at the summons. We kicked harder, still no sign of life was vouchsafed. Getting desperate we tried the door; it yielded and we passed in. Striking a match and looking around we saw that the tenement was unfinished. The plasterer had just commenced his work upon the walls. With hardly enough life left to make exertion of any kind, by mere strength of will we collected planks and sticks and built a fire and sat cowering over the flames in fitful slumber until daybreak.

CHAPTER XIV.

CAPTURED AGAIN.

The next morning the storm had ceased; the sun shone coldly upon the white expanse. Looking cautiously out of the window we saw there no need to fear detection, for the shanty stood isolated in the middle of a big field. It was a wonderful stroke of luck which had turned our wandering steps to that spot, when for a mile around was a desolate waste.

"It is because you struck that tree," said Robinson, "I've never lost heart yet; if you had missed it when you tried your fortune on the canal boat, I would have despaired long before this."

But what was to be done now? I wished to heaven that men had been born without stomachs. We could get along very well if we did not have to run the risk of detection by hunting for food. I'll be hanged if a soldier's life isn't for all the world like that greedy boy in the "Tanglewood Tales:"

> "Victuals and drink, victuals and drink
> Were the only things of which he could think."

In truth the day was half done, we had burnt up all the loose timber in the house; a roaring fire went up the new chimney, and so it was warm enough; but there was no cupboard even for old Mother Hubbard to look for a bone.

Another council of war was held, in which it was decided that the idea of crossing the Alleghanies on foot was altogether out of the question, and then there was the Potomac to be gotten over before danger could be overcome. After my experience at Monocacy it was not probable that we would try a raft again. We had money and would take the night train to Duffield Station, in Virginia, or if that should prove impracticable, try Sir John's Run in West Virginia and strike for Winchester.

We sat patiently waiting for night. The wood had all given out. Next the carpenter's saw-horse fed the fire, then the flames devoured the window frames, and as the fiery element sank into a mass of glowing embers, we looked around for more fuel but there was none. We were not going to freeze as well as starve, so we jerked and pulled down the stair-steps, which furnished food enough for the fire. Soon the night came on; the sky had clouded, boding another snow-storm not far off. In the loyal city of Cumberland, some two miles away, began to twinkle lights one after another. The hours now dragged by with leaden heels, while we anxiously waited for midnight. Minutes seemed hours —days, as we sat there over the dying coals, for we were afraid to let the fire blaze at night lest it should serve as a beacon to guide inquisitive people in our direction. We presented a picture of absolute misery.

All things must come to an end at last; and even this comfortless, dreary day was numbered finally among the things that were. When the midnight stroke smote the air it found us safely hidden under the platform at the depot. The train was behind time, so creeping out like a couple of rats bent on obtaining refreshment, we hied away in the friendly darkness to a restaurant near by, and ate as if we were bent on committing suicide.

About one o'clock the rumble of the approaching train warned us to be ready. Getting on the off side of the track, we managed to elude the guard, whose attention was drawn by those entering from the platform in the regular way. In the short time it took us to duck in through the open door we saw that the snow had commenced, and the platform, but freshly swept, was covered an inch deep.

It had been so cold outside, and was so warm and comfortable within; the motion of the cars was so soothing, that in spite of all determination, in defiance of a most resolute will not to go to sleep, the drowsy god slowly wove his spell. The form of the passenger in front began to change shape, the swing lamps danced a jig; a thousand fancies flitted through the brain; the lulling sound of the rolling train became fainter and fainter, and sleep at last claimed us for his own.

Our dreams were rudely broken.

"Station!" sang out the conductor, putting his head in at the door, then out again, slamming the door after him, as conductors are wont to do to prevent puzzled passengers from asking questions.

Thus suddenly startled, we did not catch the name, but thought it sounded like that of our destination, so with brains in a whirl, and only half awake, we jumped from the train.

We were in the midst of a Yankee camp.

The sight woke us fully, and so startled us that every faculty was roused in a moment. We looked around; there were the cabins, in the dim light looking like marble in their pure covering of snow. But not a soul was to be seen; not a sentinel posted; not a lookout placed. Everything was buried in profound slumber.

It did not take long to get away from that place, and we soon reached the mountains and commenced our journey. Where we were or at what station we had gotten out we did not know. In dense ignorance we groped along, the driving sleet cutting our faces like the sting of whips. Blindly we moved on, for there were no roads nor paths; the night and the snow hid everything which could have served to guide. With the gait and the action of men without sight, we moved up an acclivity and down another, falling headlong, sometimes sliding off slippery rocks. At last we became lost in the compact laurel brakes, that were as dense as a swamp or morass of weeds, and as navigable as the Cretan labyrinth which puzzled Theseus with all the gods to aid him. We lost all idea of direction; plunging onward, gliding, slipping, pulling ourselves up the sides of perpendicular chasms by the branches of the laurel which covered them, then moving onward with involuntary velocity and falling at the imminent risk of breaking our necks; fording ice-cold streams, undergoing, in short, superhuman exertions, with aching heads and shortened breath, until we felt it was useless to struggle against an adverse fate, and that it would be better to lie down and let the snow cover us.

Our hands were bleeding, our rags were torn, and the snow rested upon the bare skin. It was intensely dark in those thickets; men had often been lost in their depths in broad daylight and never been found. In the night it was appalling, groping as it were in a dungeon or a vast coal mine. The snow had filled up and hidden all hollows, into which, blindly staggering, we would plunge at every other step, sometimes ankle deep only, and then again up to our waists. Not a sound broke the dead stillness but the crunch of our feet upon the snow.

The brains of both seemed at last to give way, and fancy played wild tricks. Imaginary lights gleamed amid the dense foliage; sweet music lulled the senses into perfect rest; voices shouted to us; then, as soon as we moved, the overtaxed muscles would bring a throb of physical pain, the illusions would vanish, and the same sullen silence reigned supreme.

We both felt that we were straining our powers to the utmost, and that the endurance of man had a limit.

"One more effort," said Robinson, "but one more; don't let's give up, for you know fate has told us that we are bound to escape. You struck the tree, remember that, old fellow! So cheer up and make one more trial!"

The trial was made in vain; the same toiling ascent, the same dangerous descent, and the same tangled, almost impenetrable thicket. Hope died out at last! The faith which had remained through all our days of hardship now folded her wings and left us. Desperation and despair usurped her place.

There was nothing now to hope for in life.

I managed to scratch a match on my knife blade and by its fitful light we looked into each other's faces; pale faces they were too.

"Let's make a fire and sleep here," proposed Robinson.

We tried to kindle one but could not. The frozen fingers would hardly hold a match, and there was no wood, only the green laurel sticks and leaves, which would not burn. The matches gave out, the last one glimmered on a look of despair in the eyes of each, and then darkness!

"I have seen the last of you, old comrade," said Robinson, as he laid himself down to die.

Death, at times, loses its terrors. The fearful unknown is not thought of, or if remembered, it is as Virraud, the leader of the Girondists recalled it: "In a few moments I shall know the great secret. All that has been shrouded from hidden eyes is to be made plain at last." So feel many men close within the Great Shadow; no more doubt, no more mystery; the profound secret which has filled mad-houses with ravings; which invoked the scholarly genius of Locke; which stopped from self-slaughter the hand of the thinker Hamlet; which occupied the mighty mind of Shakespeare; which filled the great intellect of Voltaire with wondering awe; which overthrew the reason of Swedenborg, and set at naught all human speculations, all human understanding—all will be as clear as the sun in heaven to those who have eyes, as distinct as the sound of the tempest to those who have ears.

To the soldier who loves danger and braves death, the King of Terrors has lost his sovereignty. Familiarity has bred contempt; and so when his majesty does approach in any guise, he is received as a matter of course, and taken by the hand with no fearful shrinking or dread. Azrael passes over the camp very often in his fatal flight, and his form is too well known to be greeted with dismay and outcry when he stops before the door of some tent and beckons the chosen one.

It is the most dreamy, contented feeling in the world to yield to the stupor of cold preceding death. No pain is felt, all that is past; and only a supreme, immeasurable repose overtakes the numbed nerves and quiets them like unto a narcotic. The great future of Eternity is thought of with wondering inquisitiveness, but no fear. It is like a little child going to sleep on a journey and wondering where it will wake on the morrow. Idle thoughts and speculations flit through the brain as to who will find the body, what they will say, how they will act, where the grave will be, if any one will grieve very much, who most will miss the absent form as the days go by; but withal there is no concern felt, nothing but lapsing peace, and finally unconsciousness.

So we, "comrades in death as in life," lay with dazed senses and let the time pass on, dying from exhaustion and cold.

Suddenly Robinson sprang up. "My God!" he exclaimed, "I hear a dog barking."

It was true, there was no hallucination nor delirium this time. Clear and distinct came the loud yelp of the house-dog not a quarter of a mile away. We were effectually roused, and got on our feet with difficulty, stumbling toward the sound. It never failed us and, more dead than alive, we reached the house, a small shanty standing on the side of the road. With barely strength enough to knock, Robinson fell in a dead faint on the threshold as the door was opened by its owner. Together we pulled him inside; in the warmth and comfort, Robinson opened his eyes and sat up.

The owner of the house was an Irishman, and as all of that nationality had invariably been our friends, we imagined that in this case it would be the same, and naturally told the truth. He did not seem surprised, and merely said that we were safe under his care.

He then called up his two daughters, who were sleeping in the next room, and told them to prepare a bed for the guests. In a short time they came in, fine-looking, winsome girls they were, and ushered us into a chamber. From the warmth of the couch we shrewdly suspected that it was the identical bed so lately vacated by the two young Irish lassies.

"Well!" exclaimed Robinson, nestling down into the soft depths, "this excels all the kindness we have yet received, getting out of their own warm bed to give to us. I hope the Lord will bless such generous hearts."

That morning was the 3rd of March, 1864, and the early hours had merged into high noon when we were awakened by a rapping upon the door and a voice bidding us get up. When we entered the adjoining room there was a nice breakfast smoking hot upon the table; and the manner in which those edibles were demolished made those girls stare.

"Where is your father?" we asked.

"O, he is only gone to a neighbors, and left word that you should not leave until his return," was the immediate rejoinder.

We sat by the fire and chatted, telling them of our own sunny home, when in walked the gallant Irishman, our noble host, accompanied by a stranger, and both were armed to the teeth.

"You are our prisoners!" curtly said the Irishman.

Two wearied, exhausted boys, more like the incarnation of famine than anything else; so weak that they could hardly walk; and with unhesitating trust and childlike confidence had told their woeful tale; who had thrown themselves upon the generosity of their host; who had rested beneath his roof, and were even then sitting upon that most sacred spot on earth, the family hearthstone, had been betrayed and given over to their enemies.

Prisoners again, and so near home too, it was cruel luck!

The house of this man was only two miles from Berkeley Springs, West Virginia.

"What is your name?" asked Robinson.

"What's that to you?" roughly rejoined the man.

"I only wanted to remember it in my prayers, that's all," was the answer. But the devoted patriot refused to give it.

"Get up!" he said, "and come on."

We rose, drew on our shoes and prepared to depart.

"Where are you going to take us?" I asked, addressing the Irishman, who was standing sullenly apart.

"To Sir John's Run and deliver you to the garrison there."

"One moment, sir!" cried Robinson, his wan, pallid face lighted by eyes which flashed in the intensity of his anger. "You are an Irishman! It seems incredible; for through all our long pilgrimage and wretched wanderings we have never met one who failed to give us words of kindly comfort, and cheered our hearts by sympathy, and we have met many. This was why we trusted you. Among all that noble-hearted race, North or South, I know of no man who would not die before he would do what you have done!"

The Irishman drew his hat over his eyes and slunk back. The two girls, during the tirade, had stood side by side on the hearth,

very pale and silent. As we turned to go, I faced them and said:
"I had thought that in the presence of a woman I could feel safe; and yet you have beguiled and betrayed us as basely as your father has done. One hint, one word from you and we could have put miles between us and that man. It would have been a greater kindness had you let us die last night outside your door."

The women looked at us with white, startled faces, but replied not a word; and as we left the house, I gave a last look backward; the door was wide open and I saw the younger girl with her head on the table, crying as if her heart would break.

CHAPTER XV.

SIR JOHN'S RUN.

With our hospitable host leading, and the tall mountaineer bringing up the rear, we started for the nearest Federal garrison, a station on the Baltimore and Ohio railroad, about three miles distant. It was a clear, frosty morning, and the whole landscape, clad in two feet of snow, gleamed like the iridescent opal, in the first blush of the rising sun.

We passed through a watering place know as Berkeley Springs, and the memory of the many mountain and other summer resorts I had often visited in the past stood out in sharp contrast to my first visit to this pleasure resort. No stage coaches with mettlesome horses and blaring horn, no welcoming landlord, no obsequious, grinning darkies to show the way; as Mr. Toots would say, "Quite the contrary." We passed through the place without meeting a soul, and inside of an hour reached the station and were delivered to the officer of the day. The Irishman told him the events which led to our capture, and that we were escaped Rebel prisoners. As he turned to go, Robinson made him a low bow, and said that if Harry Gilmor or Mosby ever heard of last night's proceedings they would hang him from the lintels of his door post. I ironically bade him good-by, and told him that I regretted having no money with me to pay him for his most kind entertainment. He scowled and went his way, and we were then placed in the guard-house; a habitation, by the way, with which we had become strangely familiar of late.

The station of Sir John's Run is of peculiar topography; it is situated on the Baltimore and Ohio Railroad, about twenty miles west of Martinsburg. The place is of contracted proportions, being sandwiched between the Potomac River and the Alleghany Mountains, which run parallel about forty yards apart. In the narrow plateau between the mountains and the river ran the railroad close under the beetling cliffs which rise abruptly.

On one side of the railroad, and scattered along the banks of the stream, were the huts and tents of the garrison, which having been detailed to guard the post had gone into winter quarters. The guard-house in which we were confined was situated directly on the steep bank of the river, which flowed swiftly by, some twenty feet below. The chimney was built close to the bank, while the entrance faced the railroad track. This structure consisted of old railroad ties placed upright in the form of a circle and roofed over with canvas. The door was merely a flap of the same material, which hung over the entrance in folds. The chimney was about ten feet high and very broad, and was constructed roughly of stones of all sizes cemented with dried mud.

The only occupant hitherto was an Englishman, who had been arrested on suspicion, but awaited a speedy release, as there had been nothing found to criminate him.

All day we remained in the guard-house, sitting by a blazing fire, and surrounded by officers and men, who asked questions without number.

This command of the Fifteenth Union West Virginia Infantry was the finest body of men we had ever seen in the Yankee Army; men of superb physique, with that neat, proud, self-reliant air which bespeaks the true soldier. They were veterans of many a hard-fought field, and were of course kind and friendly to fallen foes, as brave men ever are. We were neither searched nor subjected to any indignity; and all that day received many little tokens of good will from the boys in blue. We appreciated the day of rest and the ample meals; the over-wrought nerves grew quiet, the strained muscles relaxed, and the mind became alert, and hope, so lately dead, rose like a hardy plant that blooms all the brighter for having lain dormant.

That night as we sat smoking our last pipe before turning into the bunk, which was built for two but accommodated three by a tight squeeze, we made our plans, all indefinite though they were. As yet we were in profound ignorance as to our ultimate fate, but trusted that we might be unconditionally released. If not, then we would stand the hazard of the die again. At present what both needed was a long rest and plenty of food, both of which could be had for the taking; but unless something untoward should prevent, we resolved to strike for freedom again before another twenty-four hours should have rolled by. As we sat listening to the murmuring of the water, how we wished that the great partisan leader Mosby would swoop down like a hawk in a barnyard and liberate us, and—well, if the truth must be told, hang the damned Irishman from the lintels of his own door.

The next morning we felt refreshed and began to examine our surroundings, and see what were our chances of escape. One glance was enough to show that an attempt to leave that room would be almost like tempting death.

The guard-house was about the size of any small apartment, say eighteen feet across. It had no windows and only one entrance, in front of which, *on the inside,* stood a sentinel night and day, who watched every motion of the prisoners in his charge, and could hear every word spoken. Any attempt to force a way past him would be sheer madness, as a single out-cry would bring the sergeant and the entire guard to his assistance. The walls were of solid oak sleepers, the floor of plank, which precluded any idea of cutting or tunnelling a way out, even had it been possible to evade the guard. The chimney was wide enough to climb, provided of course no one would disturb us in the attempt, and provided also that the fire was out. But how in the name of mischief could we start on such an undertaking with that confounded guard staring at us? And then it was not altogether just such a death as a soldier would prefer—being shot or bayoneted while in a hole, like a possum, even supposing that the smoke would not suffocate the victims. O, if men only had wings and could fly! or were able to burrow under ground like a mole!

The guard informed us after breakfast that a Southern woman lived right across from the depot, about seventy-five yards away, and we decided after a few words to apply to her. It would impress the minds of the officers that we had no idea of escaping, and had settled down into a state of complete resignation. The short time of trial hardly warranted the demand upon her charity, but we addressed her a note, which the corporal of the guard kindly undertook to deliver. In a short time he returned with five thick, warm counterpanes and a message from Mrs. Sheppard asking if we wanted anything to eat. For the first time since the beginning of the war this question received a negative answer, for rations were superabundant. In the evening the kind, gentle lady came to see us, escorted by the colonel commanding, and it was then that we betrayed ourselves—gave ourselves completely away. It had been easy to keep up our assumed characters with the Yankees and play the buffoon before them, but in the presence of a lady it was a different matter. Habit was too strong; old manners came back; we bowed as we were wont to do, and did our best to entertain the honored visitor whose innate kindness had made her our welcome guest. Unlike the good little boy in the story book, we lost everything by being polite, for the colonel saw at once that we were not what we had represented ourselves to be, so he promptly, then and there, taxed us with the deception, and offered to let us go free if we would agree to take the oath of allegiance, a proposition we as promptly declined. Mrs. Sheppard informed us that she had a son in the Twelfth Virginia Cavalry of Rosser's Laurel Brigade, and asked us, in taking leave, to call upon her for anything we might wish.

Now that our true characters were known, it needed no prophet to foretell the result. We would be sent to Camp Chase on the morrow's train, and then if we did escape at some remote point, we would have all the fearful journey over again. Such a proceeding was not to be thought of; so whatever was to be done must be done at once. If successful the distance to the Southern lines was short, and safety sure. Should we fail we would fall doing our best.

Once more we rattled the dice; once more we paused before the cast was thrown.

CHAPTER XVI.

THE THIRD ESCAPE.

The sun sank below the mountain tops, the last time perhaps for us, who in silence watched it going down; but speculations were idle, so we reasoned, and proceeded to make ready.

Two plans were open, both desperate in their chances and almost hopeless in their risks.

One was to make a bold rush upon the guard, overpower, bind and gag him, then walk out unmolested; each thereafter to shift for himself. But this was almost certain death, for a single articulate cry, nay, the very movements of a subdued struggle with the guard would give the alarm and all would be over. Even supposing such an attack might in the one chance of a thousand succeed, in such a bright moonlight night how could we pass sentries and scale the mountains unperceived? It seemed only too sure that we would be shot down.

The other plan was to climb the chimney, drop down in the water, and either swim across the river or run along the bank, then cross the railroad and strike up the mountain side. This arrangement was almost as rash and hopeless as the other, for the sentinel inside would surely see the attempt, and either put his gun within the fire-place and pull the trigger, or else step outside and give warning, when sundry bullets would be ready to tap the first emerging head.

As it was with Tutchin when Jeffries, during the "Bloody Assize," gave him the choice of deaths, so it was with us. To rest supine, yield to fate—drag out a lingering life in prison, was to us only another form of slow, torturing death; hence we decided on the latter program as offering, not a surer means of escape, but one a little less certain of defeat.

When evening came on the sentinels placed on duty at six were relieved and others put in their places. It was a clear, cold night, with a northwest wind rendering the cold only more searching and bitter. The blast would often push its way down the low chimney, bringing with it clouds of smoke which filled the room, got into our eyes, and made indistinct for a while every object in the apartment. We coughed and wiped away the tears. The sentinel, more fortunate, could thrust his head outside the entrance to drink in a breath of fresh air and cool his smarting eyes. As he did this, mysterious notes, written stealthily, passed between us concerning the enterprise rapidly drawing near.

Ten o'clock! and again the guard was relieved. The tall, slab-sided fellow, who stood erect and vigilant inside the door, was replaced by a young soldier, apparently not over sixteen years of age. The fire was burning brightly, but Robinson had piled on an armful of green wood, which for a time effectually quenched the flames and sent a dense volume of smoke rolling up the chimney and half shrouding the room in darkness. A counter current of air blew down the chimney, and for some minutes the room was as dim as if lit by a torch which shone through a fog.

The Englishman, at a sign of entreaty, well disposed to help, approached the youthful guard and engaged him in conversation.

It had been settled that Robinson should take the first and better chance for life in the essay. I whispered eagerly, "Now! Now! Keep cool, don't lose presence of mind! Jump up! I will hide you!"

For one instant he sat motionless, as if turned to stone; then his massive jaw closed with sudden resolution. One quick glance; there stood the guard with his back to him, talking to the Englishman, who was facing the hearth, and then my comrade sprang up the chimney. I seized a blanket, and holding it before the fire as if warming it, effectually screened the movement from view. He mounted rapidly, coolly and deliberately. No awkward step of foot or touch of hand sent the stones rattling down, no hasty action betrayed his absence. As if to fix the fire, I knelt and looked up, perceiving only through the aperture the twinkling stars. His cast of the die had been thrown and he had won, why should the other fail?

Just then a heavy blow was struck against the outside of the house, so sharp and sudden that the young guard put his head out to see from whence the noise came. Years later, when we two old comrades in misfortune met, Robinson solved the mystery; he threw a heavy stone, that had fallen from the top of the chimney noiselessly upon the snow, to draw the attention of the guard and afford his fellow-prisoner a chance; a parting compliment, too, to give certain sign that he was free.

The time was at hand; to flinch was cowardice. Outside, the sound of voices growing louder, then retreating as if in pursuit, showed Robinson's flight had been detected. In less time than it takes to tell, for from first to last it had all seemed only the work of a few moments, while yet the guard was gazing into the night, eager in his youthful, unrestrained curiosity to learn the cause of the confusion, while yet the fire was bursting into flames, I jumped into the midst of the blaze and smoke and sought exit up the chimney.

I have been in some warm places in my life's experience, but that was the hottest of all. The flames set fire to my jacket, and my legs seemed as if they were in a fiery furnace; and but for the pair of corduroy trousers in which they were encased, trousers which shrivelled and cracked but did not ignite, the consequence might have been a first-class cremation.

There was now but one idea in my mind—to get out of the fast-climbing flames and the painful heat. All other dangers were for the time forgotten. Decorous climbing had become a hasty scramble, which sent the soot into my eyes and stones and mortar down the chimney. There was no effort at secrecy in the desperate struggle to reach the top, only a mad effort to escape burning—to draw into the lungs a breath of fresh air; then let come what might.

Luckily the chimney was built of large and small stones, so that the crevices between furnished good foothold. In a few seconds I was at the summit drawing in the sweet, pure air, the coldness of which was as refreshing as the drop of cold water would have been to the parched tongue of Dives. But only for a second did I linger; my clothes were on fire, and with one jump I sprang headlong into the river, knocking off in the act some of the large rocks which rimmed the top, and which went tumbling down, with no little noise, into the fire below. Altogether the novel ascent could not have consumed more than half a minute, but it seemed hours.

It was indeed a sudden change, from the blazing, contracted hollow of stones and soot into the wide, freezing river. Ugh! How congealing it was! I started to swim across, but was too numbed and the current too strong. This same strong current did me a good turn, however, when, inertly trusting to its guidance, it bore me on its bosom rapidly and noiselessly amid the floating ice some fifty yards down stream and out of reach of the immediate danger of being shot. I struggled then to the bank and climbed up. Life now depended upon my losing no second in putting space between me and my enemies, so I ran along the shore for about seventy yards, taking tremendous leaps as I went. I then sank down to gain breath. After a few deep respirations

I crawled on hands and knees across the railroad, and lying down flat, rested there another short while before attempting the steep mountain-side, which I climbed as I had never climbed before. Stinging cold as it was, the perspiration ran in streams down my face and body, but I neither paused nor looked around until nearly half way up, and then behind a large rock I rested again to take breath.

The scene below was plainly understood and proved most interesting. The whole garrison was evidently swarming around the guard-house like so many fire-flies upon a summer night. Many had lanterns and were trying to strike a trail, and it was quite apparent that the camp was fully roused and in earnest in its search. So secure did I feel in my elevation that I was tempted to give vent to a long, joyful shout, but prudently repressed it, remembering the old saw, "never whistle until you are out of the woods." I kept on, soon reaching the top of the mountain, which was only one of the range lying between the river and the coveted destination. But luck was all in my favor now, since it was a clear, cloudless night, and the blaze of the northern lights made the earth clear as day; a guide and beacon suspended so faithfully in the heavens that there need be no mistake about the route.

Since the world began has the faithful star hung out its pilot-signal for all wanderers on the earth's face; but no Arab on the pathless desert, no Indian on the trackless plain, no early voyager across the seas ever hailed it with more gratitude than I, for whom its steady rays meant safety and liberty. There was no danger of getting lost in the mountain wilds, when glittering above the tree tops, clear and bright, the north star pointed the way straight home. Turning my back upon it I kept on due south, looking neither to the right nor to the left, and though every mountain side which I descended was sure to have a stream of water at its foot, I would plunge in and make my way across. Issuing from the water chilled and numb, a few moments of violent exertion would restore circulation and bring back a comfortable glow. There were four of these creeks on the route, and in the valley a broad stream obstructed all progress, but I easily swam it, and at last, guided by the lone star, level country was reached.

The snow was about two feet deep on an average, but frozen so hard on top as to bear a man's weight, hence the intervening miles were skimmed over at a rapid rate, and after an hour's walk

33

a broad turnpike was reached which ran south, and this I henceforth kept. The cold was so intense, the wind so wintry that my clothes were as stiff as sheets of iron and I had need to keep on at a swinging trot to prevent freezing.

The measured motion calmed the nerves and cleared my brain; and speeding along in a dog-trot, I reflected coolly upon the incidents of the last few hours, marveling greatly that the guard had never turned his head to see, that he had not fired into the chimney after the first falling stone had betrayed the mode of exit. Surely the jump into the river must have been heard, and it would have been easy to have shot me. It must be presumed that they were all taken by surprise, and that some moments were consumed in calling out the guard, moments precious to a man speeding for his life. Then again the sentry inside doubtless lost all presence of mind, as some men are wont to do in emergencies, for he had only to step out, wait for his prisoner to come forth from the chimney, when he could have shot him. Perhaps the Englishman gave advice in keeping with his sympathies to the startled man, as inexperienced as his years were few, or in some manner baffled search for those who had enlisted his friendship. These conjectures and theories remain such to this day, for no light has ever been thrown upon the incident.

Not a soul did I encounter throughout the long tramp, though I traveled until the rising sun warned me of the necessity for concealment. Safety was far too near and dear to risk jeopardizing it by recklessness. Once, early in the night, I neared the sleeping camp of the enemy, upon whose beaten tramp a sentinel paced to and fro, his musket gleaming in the moonlight; but I stooped upon the snow, and with my knife hollowed out a place upon which I could place my feet without fear that the crunching of the snow under my tread would betray me, working laboriously and slowly until the danger was past and I could make up for the delay by greater speed.

On the left of the road, and some distance away, I came across an old deserted saw-mill half hidden by trees and bushes, affording a good refuge for the day. Burrowing down into the sawdust, which made a warm sort of lair, I slept till the sun went down, when again I proceeded in a trot all night, meeting no one on the route. I was terribly hungry, having fasted thirty-six hours, but I chewed away on a stick, resolved to run no more risk in asking for food unless I felt certain of the people.

Just as day was breaking I saw a large barn across a field, and

I determined to lie concealed in it for another day. On reaching the barn I climbed into the hay mow, and making a hole deep down, I covered myself carefully, and in an instant was sound asleep. I was awakened by some one standing directly upon me pitching the hay to the cattle.

It was impossible to sleep again, when hunger was so intense that a gnawing, acute pain made every other feeling subservient. At last, rendered desperate, I followed in the wake of the farm hand, to whose house a few steps brought us. I was kindly received and a breakfast prepared, which could hardly have come amiss after so long a fast. The family were Virginians, with every feeling enlisted in the Southern cause. They informed me, upon inquiry, that I had made thirty-five miles the first night and thirty-three the second, and that only a dozen miles were between me and Winchester. Sleeping all day, I continued my journey, flanking the town, and in two more nights' traveling, not going further into particulars, reached Confederate pickets at Woodstock and was safe at last.

The stone thrown upon the banks of the Potomac was guided by the hand of Destiny, and the prediction, though born of superstition, did not betray the faith that cherished it.

I will close this chapter by narrating an anecdote of General Lee, which shows his tact and kindness of heart and tells plainly why the rank and file of the Army of Northern Virginia idolized him.

While I was a prisoner at Harper's Ferry I met two men, dressed in citizens' clothes, who had been taken up by the blue-coats near the Ferry, and charged with being spies. They were handcuffed, and had been in prison some months. They said that they belonged to White's battalion of cavalry and gave their names, and made me promise, if I escaped, I would see General Jeb Stuart, state their condition, and get him to demand that they should be treated as prisoners of war. As soon as I reached the cavalry camp I went to headquarters to fulfil my pledge.

Stuart was seated in a large wall tent, surrounded by his staff and some military visitors high in rank. They were having a jovial time, and twice I essayed to get past the guard who stood at the entrance of the marquee, but was repulsed each time. Stuart's eye fell upon me, and I saw that he did not like it. The third time, my patience being exhausted, I made a final effort, pushed by the sentinel, and stood in General Stuart's presence. He was narrating an anecdote, and became furious at being interrupted by such a looking fellow as I, for there had been no time to change my unmilitary attire for a respectable uniform, and in thundering tones he ordered the guard to take me outside the camp. The sentinel obeyed, and I was ignominiously escorted beyond its boundaries. After all I had undergone, such treatment infuriated me; and to be arrested like a camp follower was too much. The next day I made a bee line for the commanding general's quarters near Orange Court House. A few tents on a hill, with the battle-flag, the staff of which stuck in the ground, showed where the leader of our army rested.

An infantry guard walked lazily along his beat, but said nothing as I passed him. An orderly stood near, and I asked him if General Lee was in. He said that he was, and I requested him to tell the General that one of his private soldiers wanted to see him. He returned instantly with the summons to come in.

I found General Lee sitting by a table covered with papers. He saluted me gravely, but did not recognize me until I mentioned my name and explained the cause of my ragged condition. I then told him of my visit to General Stuart and its object, and how bitter and unjust my treatment had been. Then I broke down. The General heard me through, and then assured me that General Stuart would never knowingly have treated any of his old soldiers in that manner. Then he told me to say to my colonel that I must have thirty days' furlough to recover from the effect of my long wanderings.

General Lee was always accessible. The humblest private found in him a kind and gentle friend; and it is no wonder they followed him with absolute confidence and unbounded love.

It is needless to add that I soon found my way to the camp of the Black Horse. I told Colonel Randolph of General Lee's request and the next day I was in Richmond.

CHAPTER XVII

A LITTLE REPOSE.

No greater pleasure is known to the soldier than the warm welcome extended him after a long absence, by his comrades. Men in the army learn to cultivate feelings of *esprit de corps* beyond the understanding of a civilian. Neither the temptations of business, the struggles of life which make men selfish and false, nor the rivalry of politics find lodgment in a soldier's breast. Cut off as he is from all the allurements of the world, the charm of social life, the fascination of money-making, all the endearing joys of home, he has to look for happiness in the kindness and good will of his comrades. Their joys and sorrows are his; he learns to look upon them as brothers; there is no sacrifice that he will not make for them; no trouble that he will not cheerfully take. Fellowship becomes almost a religion, none the less strong, perhaps, because it is the only one that some of them know.

I speak of a fact well known at this time; the freemasonry and camaraderie was much stronger among the privates than among the officers of Lee's army. The wealth and intelligence was, as a general thing, in the ranks. To the thoroughbred blood infused into the line was due the staunchness and bottom of Lee's men.

Great suffering in a common cause endear men to one another. The officers above the rank of captain knew but little of the hardships of war from personal experience. They had their black cooks, who were out foraging all the time, and they filled their masters' bellies if there was fish or fowl to be had. The regimental wagons carried the officers' clothes, and they were never half-naked, lousy, or dirty. They never had to sleep upon the bare ground nor carry forty rounds of cartridges strapped around their galled hips; the officers were never unshod nor felt the torture of stone-bruise. But the private of "Lee's Miserables!" will history ever do him justice? Mad with hunger, faint with thirst, shivering in the cold blasts of winter, or suffering on a mid-summer forced march such anguish that it would have driven a dog mad. Yes! he endured and suffered in a way that in olden times would have made him a canonized saint. Is it any wonder then that the soldiery had the strongest affection for one another?

There was no command in the army where this feeling of friendship was more ardent than among the gentlemen of the Black Horse Cavalry. Their pride in their organization, the perils they had incurred together, the varied experiences of good times had bound them together with links stronger than steel.

Several changes had taken place in the Black Horse during the past three months, that, so far as the company was concerned, were very unfortunate. The principal change was that they lost their loved, their trusted captain, who had been promoted to the colonelcy of the regiment.

As was remarked before, Captain Randolph was a born soldier. A braver man never lived. He seemed absolutely fearless, and in times of danger was as cool as an iceberg. He was a fair sample of the "beau sabre" that Stuart reared and inflamed with his own fiery ardor. Like Ashby, he was no strict disciplinarian, but ruled his men through kindness; at the same time his military traits made him just such a leader as daring men love to follow through thick and thin. It was with unmeasured sorrow that his troopers parted from him, while he felt most genuine regret on leaving the company which, under his leadership, had acquired world-wide renown.

He was succeeded by Lieutenant Alexander Payne, who before the war was a village attorney. Utterly deficient in military qualifications, under his leadership the morale of the Black Horse steadily declined.

The rations of the soldiers were now more adequate. The commissariat seemed to be supplied by fits and starts; and as the winter ended and the opening spring gave promise of an early campaign, the army received abundant supplies, on the same principle, perhaps, that hogs and chickens are fattened before they are killed. A pound of flour and a pound of meat, with occasional rations of rice, sugar, and beans were sufficient to make the soldier both plump and happy.

At no time during the war was the army in such superb condition as in the spring of sixty-four. They had become veterans, who had learned to have perfect confidence in themselves, at the same time they clung with firm faith to full assurance of ultimate success. There was not a private soldier in the Army of Northern Virginia who did not believe that the coming year would find the South victorious. Each man stood ready and determined, so far as his own endeavors were concerned, to make one grand effort toward ending the matter at once. The depleted ranks were filled with conscripts, who soon caught the ways of their comrades and felt animated by the same bright hopes and fears. Never since the beginning of the war had the soldiers in the ranks ever, for a moment, despaired of the final triumph of their cause, regarding the Confederacy as a fact which only needed blood and time; but this spring they were unusually jubilant. Only one more grand campaign, they thought, said, and wrote; only one more great, united struggle—and then a glorious peace. So they laughed lightly around the camp-fires over old stories, and spoke assuredly of the future which held in store a grand reward for all they had suffered.

What bright visions they had of the coming time of which they dreamed, when the loved Confederacy should reach from the Susquehanna to the Gulf of Mexico—from the Atlantic to the Pacific.

And the South! What a wonderful country it was destined to be! fruitful as the exuberant and teeming Egypt and as fair to the sight as the Eden of old. The planter would find that the vast fields of cotton, rice, sugar, and tobacco shipped in free trade to the marts of the commercial nations would pour the luxuries of the Old World at his feet. The seaboard State of Florida, with the finest ship-timber on earth, would build for the navies of Europe. Mines now slumbering, undeveloped, would open up to the light vast stores of wealth of which its people had no conception. Virginia, where runs her chain of glorious mountains, could supply a world with her buried iron. In Kentucky and Missouri, the gardens of the Confederacy, the waving fields of grain, ripening beneath a generous southern sun, would alone fill the nation's storehouses. Though the North and South would stand as separate and divided as if invisible walls of adamant intervened, separate in peace as in war, separate in tradition and council, there yet would flow the mighty Mississippi the length of the two domains, bearing on her bosom freighted ships which, sailing to and fro like messengers of peace, would heal the scars of war and carry wealth and prosperity in their wake. Manufactories would spring up, calling for skilled artisans from abroad. Emigrants would gather from all regions of the earth, and in the unnumbered, unclaimed acres of Southern States and Territories, find free homes and full protection. Slaves would be gradually emancipated, until the last one, in the course of time, would stand in the land of his adoption a free man.

And the Rebel soldiers who had come unscathed from the fiery baptism of a country's liberty, what reward and honor might not be theirs? Their places would be in the midst of happy homes, held in grateful esteem by proud and admiring countrymen. And what would the South do for Lee? A king, perhaps.

In this wise the soldier built his castles in the air and dreamed of a future of boundless comfort and glorious ease.

In Richmond the confidence was almost as high as when Lee's army started upon the Pennsylvania Campaign. Even the doubting ones, who had begun to despair after the reverses of July, plucked up fresh courage as they witnessed the spirit and confidence of the men of the Army of Northern Virginia, and saw how calmly they stood, prepared for the tremendous assault. Accustomed to the horrors of war, no longer shuddering at the suffering in the hospitals or the constant presence of hearses in her streets, having grown as familiar with the sound of the Dead March as of Dixie, Richmond had, during the winter, doffed her sombre garb of woe and come out in all the glad witchery of her beauty and charm. The city was filled with furloughed officers and soldiers, and starvation parties, water soirees and dry-bread balls followed one another in bewildering succession. There was but little effort of "style" at these entertainments; officers wore their uniforms, with the addition of paper collars, while the ladies spent a world of energy and expediency in renovating a wardrobe of several years' standing. An old silk which had been turned and washed, and washed and turned, was considered a bonanza still to its fortunate possessor, and with varied adornments of bright ribbons and crisp muslin bodies, they did good service. Occasionally a lucky member of this gay throng would receive an underground supply of raiment, all in newest Northern cut and fashion, which caused as much excitement in the female community as a wedding, and raked up lively envy in the heart of every woman not too old to peer at them through spectacles. A great demand for finery sprang up, and offered inducements to blockade runners without number.

It would amuse a modern belle to run over a list comprising the wardrobe of girls of that period, who yet managed to look fair and bewitching. They were generous, too, in the urgency of the times. One bridal veil trailed up the church aisle on the brow of many a bride. One pair of satin slippers went the round of intimate friends. A pair of kid gloves were nursed as tenderly as an infant, and—but it is needless to pursue the subject further.

With ten dollars about the value of ten cents in currency, it will readily be seen that new clothes were not drugs in the market, and whereas it would take an armful of notes to buy even a calico dress, new calicoes were not plentiful. Hoarded gold pieces and silver specie found their way out steadily, to meet the demands, and after these were gone, there remained but woman's wit and ingenuity. They made their own shoes, they wove their own hats; in the country they spun their own dresses, knit their own stockings, drank rye coffee, ate sorghum and corn bread, and made use of every device under the sun to feed and clothe themselves, the while praying for the Confederacy.

In Richmond the dancing went on for all that, six nights in the week, and sometimes as many as three parties a night. No matter if one of yesterday's festive crowd was a corpse next door, the insatiate dancers had no time to pause or think—or care! Death had been far too common in Richmond for such mock sentiment! Why! could you not look from your windows and see hearses passing every hour? Oftener with no carriage following the hearse, proclaiming that the dead man was a soldier for whom nobody cared. What mattered it? Time was fleeting and youth comes but once! Men and women were not heartless, only hardened.

Such old croakers as the *Richmond Examiner,* which found fault with the world in general, would lift up voices against it and say that merriment at such a time reminded one of the dancing of maniacs on board a doomed and sinking ship. But who cared to read such mutterings of coming storm?

General Jeb Stuart once said to a roomful of ardent dancers who had held high carnival all night:

"Dance away, young ladies; half of these young men will be dead or wounded next week."

April, that month of fickle temper, had come; the grass was green, the buds beginning to burst into flower and leaves, and the air was laden with the perfume born of the season.

The skies were blackening with heavy war-clouds rising from the horizon, and none could tell exactly at what spot the tempest would burst. All furloughs were revoked and orders issued for soldiers to join their commands at once. So with many a tender parting, the boys in gray started for the tented field, ready for the issue again.

Many a Troilus looked into his Cressida's eyes for the last time. Many a Penelope was doomed to spin her web in silence, waiting for the absent Argonaut.

Grant's guns were soon to be heard booming, and then—God! what a mustering of gray-jackets there would be.

CHAPTER XVIII

ON THE FISHING SHORE

Under orders, a squad of the Black Horse, which had been enjoying the attractions of the Rebel Capital, returned to camp. We reached our destination one raw, blustering evening, when the scene was not calculated to enliven the spirits of those fresh from the charms and comforts of the winter city—its anthracite fires, its blockade cigars, and its fairest daughters.

The Black Horse were camped in open woods in Culpeper County. There was not a tent in the whole command. The men sat round their poor fires, for a cold, piercing wind had sprung up, and with whirling smoke nearly blinding them, tried to keep warm.

The horses, tied to stakes and limbs of trees, stood shivering, with drooping heads and hair turned the wrong way as the keen blast whistled over them, whinnying plaintively whenever they perceived their masters sauntering by, or caught sight of them around the fire. A cavalry horse soon acquires a keenness of smell and vision not excelled by a dog, and can pick out his owner from among a thousand.

The nights were as bad as the days. Two weeks of luxury will spoil the hardiest soldier for a short time. Curling ourselves in blankets, with a protruding root of a tree for a pillow, it was cnly broken rest which came to us—only a kind of doze, which is often more disagreeable than utter wakefulness.

A bright idea struck General Wickham, brigade commander of the cavalry, and when a military idea got into his head without a surgical operation it was generally a very good one indeed. It was to eke out rations by supplies of fresh fish from the Rappahannock River. Owing to the absence of all nets for two years, its waters were full of fish, from the savory shad, the catfish with a mouth like a prima donna, the eel as slippery as a lawyer, down to the little sunfish.

Anything savoring of novelty or adventure was eagerly hailed by the men, so there were plenty of volunteers. It was a joyous crowd that found themselves on the fishing detail, and they set out without delay for the shore near Port Royal. The Commissary, long life to him, fearing that exposure to the air and water would ruin the health, issued a plentiful allowance of North Carolina whiskey to the happy few, which, it is needless to say, was not wasted.

Three weeks were spent on the shore. There was an old seine full of holes, or rather full of rents and fissures, with which the fishers cast, with faith like Peter's, for the denizens of the deep; but whether it was because the men were unskilled, or whether the fish had not sense enough to stay quiet after they had been caught, will never be satisfactorily explained; certes, the catches would have made no man rich in the plenteous, piping days of peace. Our detail got enough to fill their own stomachs, which was about all. It was a glorious life; plenty to eat, we attended to that you may be sure, and the work was not severe.

The visions of shad-bakes and fish-frys indulged in by the whole cavalry division must have been ecstatic, for in three days after the fishing had begun there came rumbling down the road a train of empty wagons half a mile long, intended for the loading of the fish which were supposed to be waiting to be carried back.

The wagon-master rode up to Sergeant Reid, who commanded the party, and the following colloquy ensued:

"Well, Sergeant, what luck?"

"Tolerable," was the careless answer.

"How did the seine work?"

"Tolerably."

"Well, Sergeant," said the impatient wagon-master, "I reckon we had better load up now, for I've got to get back to camp before morning. By the way, where's the fish?"

"In the river."

"Look here," said the irate master, "I'm tired of this fooling. I came after the fish, and I am bound to have them."

"All right," said the sergeant, "you shall. I say! one of you boys go down the bank and bring the barrel here! Make haste, for the wagon-master is in a hurry."

The barrel was brought and found to contain six herrings, one snapping-turtle, two shad, and one eel.

"Here," said the sergeant, "are all the fish on hand; you are welcome to them."

"Is this all?" asked the wagon-master in blank dismay; for he had been cherishing certain piscatorial hopes of his own, and was at that moment, as he leaned over the barrel, undergoing a few personal disappointments. "Are those all?"

"Every one," responded the sergeant.

"Well! if these are all, I'll be d—— if it is not a lazy and a greedy set you have here! After this, the quartermaster had better send a wheelbarrow instead of a division train. That's all!"

"You needn't get mad about it!" soothingly put in one of the detail.

"Mad! it's enough to make a saint swear."

"It isn't our fault, we can't catch fish if there are none in the river," said Bolivar Ward.

"It *is* your fault," said the master, in a towering rage. "I'm going to let General Fitz Lee know it's the laziest crowd that ever lived. I could get more fish in a minute, with a pail, than the whole confounded tribe of you have, with a half-mile seine."

Our whiskey rations were stopped after this, but it needed no stimulant to increase the appetite of any man there. The consumption of fish would have astonished an alderman. It was no uncommon thing for a soldier to eat two shad at one meal, while one of the Black Horse, Bolivar Ward, who loved the good things of life, could get outside of a dozen shad a day. These gastronomic feats were kept up as long as the party remained upon the shore, and no ill effects from the immense consumption were ever recorded.

After the first week our detail moved several miles farther down the river and found a fine landing. Near by was an old mansion, deserted by its owner, which we took possession of, and located our camp permanently. We made about three hauls a day and then rested from our labors until the morrow. Sometimes we effected a big haul, but oftener we didn't. However, that was the fault of the fish, not ours. Our consciences were clear and our stomachs full. Occasionally we sent a wagon-load of shad and perch to camp, which probably graced the officers' messes, while the catfish, suckers, and eels were doled out to the privates.

Some of the musically inclined succeeded in obtaining a violin and a banjo, and any belated wayfarer passing that way at night and peeping in through the cracks of that old building would doubtless have been as much surprised as Tam O'Shanter when he beheld the revel of the warlocks and witches at Allen Kirk. The blazing firelight generally fell upon a group of soldiers dancing like mad and shouting at the top of their lungs. The fantastic shadows from the firelight made as weird a scene as one would care to see.

As the weather became warmer, the fish were more plentiful

and the nets grew heavier. It was not such very hard work either; all that we had to do was to sit upon the bank and watch the proceedings, for the ubiquitous African made his appearance. They came in all stages, anywhere from the hoary-headed patriarch to the bow-legged darky of ten summers, and would do all the work for the privilege of filling their baskets. It was a stirring spectacle at night—the flashing of the torches, the singing darkies, as they pulled in the net hand over hand. The scene was like a Rembrandt, half in shade and half in light.

It is no wonder that the men forgot about war and its dreadful realities, that they kept along the peaceful pursuit without a thought of what the future might hold in store. Everything seemed so calm on the banks of the lower Rappahannock. The carol of birds filled the air, the river rose and fell as placidly and regularly as the breath of a sleeping child; not a vessel of any kind shadowed or rippled its surface; not even the crack of a random picket-shot was heard, and even the bugle was silent; those halcyon days were as a short time in paradise to the veteran Rebels.

Our Sybaritic life was broken only too soon. One sweet evening, the first of May, just as the men were preparing the usual supper of stewed terrapin and baked shad, a courier dashed up to the house and delivered a dispatch to the sergeant. It was an order from Brigadier-General Wickham, commanding us to break up the party immediately and return to camp. Futhermore, we were to conceal the seine in some safe place.

"Get your horses, boys, as soon as possible," said Reid; "the dance has begun."

A plaintive sigh and murmured words, plain to·the ears of all; they came from Bolivar Ward. Quoth he: "Oh! hard it is to give up my dozen shad a day, not to mention stewed terrapin and fried perch, for two crackers and a piece of rancid meat."

"Don't fret, man," answered Dick Martin; "you could not possibly have left more than six in the river, and these knew all about you and left for foreign parts this morning."

There was little time for regrets; the seine had to be carried to the house of a citizen a mile away, the horses groomed and fed, arms and accoutrements to be put in order, so that it was near midnight when the troopers started for camp, which was not reached until the next day. Then it was found to be deserted, the brigade having just marched to the front. The men .followed, and as they came in sight, stopped to shake hands all round. Strong were the friendships which the past three weeks had cemented, and sadder still would have been the farewells could they have looked into the future; for of the eighteen cavalrymen constituting the fishing detail, eleven were killed before three months were over; only one of the eighteen got through the fearful campaign of sixty-four, unhurt.

The game's afoot! A jovial day, my masters! only it was not Henry Quatre who made the cry to his plumed, steel-clad noblemen; but men afoot, and men booted and spurred, whose incentive was conscience, whose love was their land, whose stake was freedom.

The eyes of all Christendom were turned upon this feast of swords—the gathering of the eagles to their prey.

CHAPTER XIX.

THE BATTLE OF THE WILDERNESS.

Again, in the spring of 1864, the two great hosts confronted each other. The Northern army was led by a man whose name had ever been synonymous with victory; wherever his banner had been spread to the breeze, the eagle had perched upon it. Thus, Grant held the faith of the soldiers and the people. The Rebel army was commanded by the same great captain who had been at its head since the battle of Seven Pines, and whom the men adored. Both armies had unquestioning faith in the justice of their cause and both felt certain of success.

The United States Government had made unparalleled preparations for the contest with a view to overwhelming, by enormous weight, the proportionately small force opposed. General Grant then commenced his operations on the second of May, 1864, by what is known as the overland campaign.

The Army of the Potomac might well hope to end the struggle in one campaign; for never had it been in such splendid condition as regards efficiency, morale and numbers. Hooker had declared a year before that he commanded the finest army on the planet; but even his magnificent hosts could not compare with the legions of Grant.

The official returns of the Army of the Potomac on the first of May, 1864, show present for duty 120,380 men of all arms, not counting the Ninth Corps, which joined Grant in May, and which numbered 20,780, nor Butler with 18,680 more, in all 149,340 with which to capture Richmond.*

The Rebel army was brimful of fight, and though out-numbered by three to one almost, stood in their tracks awaiting the shock with no misgivings as to the result. General Lee's total infantry force at the beginning of the campaign was 50,403, to which add the cavalry force, 8,727, and the artillery corps, 4,854, as given in the same returns, and we have a total present, of all arms, of 63,984; in round numbers 64,000 men.†

Besides the grand Army of the Potomac, Butler, with the corps

---

*These figures were taken from the report of the Secretary of War, Stanton, to the first session of the Thirty-ninth Congress. Vol. L, 1865, 1866, p. 3, 5, 55.
†Adjutant-General Taylor's "Four years with General Lee," page 125.

of Gilmore and W. T. Smith, were to establish themselves in an entrenched position near City Point and operate against Richmond, or invest the city from the south side, or be in a position to effect a junction with Grant coming down from the north. Richmond was to be threatened westward also, by General Sigel, who was to form his forces into two columns: the one of ten thousand strong, under General Crook, to move for the Kanawha and operate against the Virginia and Tennessee Railroad; the other, seven thousand, under Sigel in person, to menace Lee from the direction of the Shenandoah Valley. And lastly, Sheridan with ten thousand cavalry was to get in Lee's rear and take Richmond by a dash.*

Grant's plans were carefully matured and every contingency provided for. The Northern Government realized that if this great aggregation of forces failed to win, then the doctrine of an indivisible Union was a failure.

General Grant believed that the Army of the Potomac had not been fought for all it was worth, and he determined to move straight against his adversary, and by virtue of his superior numbers, fight him day by day until he simply wore him out. His watchword was, advance, attack, and overwhelm the enemy whenever and wherever found. He announced that he intended fighting it out on this line if it took all summer.

There was no science—no strategy attempted; Grant evidently realized that to try out-manoeuvring such a consummate soldier as Lee, on his own ground, would be absurd.

Although one of the greatest generals of the times, Grant will never be considered a master of the art of warfare. He came perilously near an irretrievable defeat at Shiloh, and his first campaign against Vicksburg was a failure. But Grant never lost his head, and his tenacity of purpose was phenomenal. His metal was soon to be severely tried, for his work was cut out for him when he entered the Wilderness.

Lee adopted the same tactics that won him the victory over Hooker. He threw Longstreet's corps full upon the enemy, hoping to overwhelm their left wing, and but for the wounding of Longstreet, might have succeeded. Three days of fighting ensued, and Grant, finding that he could make nothing by a front attack, started a series of flank movements, and then it was that

---

* Swinton's "Army of the Potomac," page 409.

34

Lee, who stood strictly on the defensive, followed Johnston's tactics in his defense of Atlanta.

Lee's army was in the very pink of condition. It was probably as fine a fighting machine as the world ever saw, and the men had implicit confidence in their leader as well as in themselves. They had learned how to rush, how to retreat and how to hang on to an important point by their eyelids. No sooner would a line be formed when the enemy was near, than every man was busy throwing up a little mound for protection. "I ain't grudged nary a cupful of earth I done throwed on this here pile," said a piney-woods Georgian during a pause in a fire so severe that it had leveled a forest oak.

Give Johnny Reb his bayonet and a tin cup, and he would do his work quicker than a professional sapper and miner could with pick and spade.

It was these improvised defenses that Grant stormed in the slashes of Spottsylvania; and the withering fire that came from the depths of the woods was bewildering to the Federal officers. Often they would sweep the front with musket and grape before an attack, until it seemed as if the ground had been scraped by a patent harrow and no living creature was left. Then the columns would plunge confidently forward into the green depths, only to be met with a storm of lead that caused many a gallant soldier to take the measure of an unmade grave.

Behind these foot-high mounds the Rebel infantry felt safe, and they could shoot accurately, for when a man is lying down he aims his best, for his gun barrel naturally follows the conformation of the ground. A soldier firing, when erect, invariably shoots too high, and every veteran infantryman knows how loath he was to charge when he knew the enemy was lying prone on the earth.

By a wise foresight Lee ordered the musket cartridges to contain three buckshot in addition to the ball, and the hail of buckshot through the tangled bushes was like driving, leaden rain.

Grant, perceiving that he could not force his way in a direct line, now tried a manoeuvre, and swung his army to the left, aiming to seize Spottsylvania Court House, and thus interpose his forces between Lee and Richmond. This step was foiled by Fitz Lee's cavalry, which held their ground for two days of desperate fighting, enabling Lee to hurry up his infantry and plant his army across Grant's line of march. By this movement Lee was able to hold the Army of the Potomac in check for twelve days, causing them within that time a loss of forty thousand men. (Meade's Report, Rapidan Campaigns.)   The Rebel loss was not one-third so great, for they fought generally on the defensive, behind rifle-pits.

On the evening of the 5th of May Grant's line of battle, from some misconception of orders, was fatally defective.   Burnside, who was designated to support the Federal right wing, remained several miles in the rear, and the Federal flank was in the air. General Gordon, on the extreme left flank of the Rebel army, discovered this fact through his scouts, and verified it by a personal examination.   He instantly formed a plan to roll up Grant's army as Jackson did at Chancellorsville.   General Gordon in his book declared that he could have wrecked Grant's army, but when he laid the providential opening for a decisive stroke before General Early, that Confederate mar-plot refused his sanction.

General Gordon, in his book ("Reminiscences of the Civil War") says:

"General Early, in his book, states that General Ewell agreed with him as to the impolicy of making the morning flank attack which I so earnestly urged.   Alas! he did; and in the light of revelations subsequently made by Union officers, no intelligent military critic, I think, will fail to sympathize with my lament, which was even more bitter than at Gettysburg, over the irreparable loss of Jackson.   But for my firm faith in God's Providence, and in His control of the destinies of this Republic, I should be tempted to imitate the confident exclamation made to the Master by   Mary and Martha when they met Him after the death of Lazarus: 'Hadst thou been here, our brother had not died.' Calmly reviewing the indisputable facts which made the situation at Gettysburg and in the Wilderness strikingly similar, and considering them from a purely military and wordly standpoint, I should utter my profoundest convictions were I to say: 'Had Jackson been there, the Confederacy had not died.'   Had he been at Gettysburg when a part of that Second Corps which his genius had made famous had already broken through the protecting forces and was squarely on the Union right, which was melting away like a sandbank struck by a mountain torrent; when the whole Union battle line that was in view was breaking to the rear; when those flanking Confederates in their unobstructed rush were embarrassed only by the number of prisoners —had Jackson been there then, instead of commanding a halt, his only order would have been, 'Forward, men, forward!' as he majestically rode in their midst, intensifying their flaming enthusiasm at every step of the advance.

"Or had he been in the Wilderness on that fateful 6th of May, when that same right flank of the Union army was so strangely exposed and was inviting the assault of that same portion of his old corps, words descriptive of the situation and of the plan of attack could not have been uttered fast enough for his impatient spirit. Jackson's genius was keener-scented in its hunt for an enemy's flank than the most royally bred setter's nose in search of the hiding covey. The fleetest tongue could not have narrated the facts connected with Sedgwick's position, before Jackson's unerring judgment would have grasped the whole situation. His dilating eye would have flashed, and his laconic order, 'Move at once, sir,' would have been given with an emphasis prophetic of the energy with which he would have seized upon every advantage offered by the situation. But Providence had willed otherwise. Jackson was dead, and Gettysburg was lost. He was not now in the Wilderness, and the greatest opportunity ever presented to Lee's army was permitted to pass."

General Lee in person was on the extreme right wing, and with Longstreet's full corps he determined to attack and try to roll up their left flank and get in their rear. The Orange plank road was the only thoroughfare in the vicinity; there were blind roads and cattle tracks that wound in and out in bewildering confusion, through scrub pine, wild plum, and black-jack sapling, the undergrowth so dense that one could not see ten feet ahead. Many of the officers advanced by the aid of the compass, for all sense of direction was lost when once in the jungle.

The line under Longstreet made its way slowly and ran plum upon Grant's left wing, and swept everything before it. General Humphreys, of the Federal Army, states in his book that the onslaught was so sudden and fierce that the Federal lines and reserves were in inextricable confusion, but that the Rebel attack unexpectedly and inexplicably halted. The cause of this fatal halt was the wounding of Longstreet, who fell from his horse at the moment of victory, and as was the case of Gen. Albert Sidney Johnston at Shiloh, stopped the impetus of the charge and lost the fruits of the well-planned advance.

The cavalry of the North outnumbered that of the South by two to one. It was better mounted—better armed, for it had the Spencer and Henry repeating rifles, and army muzzle-loading carbines. Its horses had abundant feed and were in good condition, while the poor Rebel animals were forced to rely half the time upon what little pasture they could get on the halts, and

most of them, before the campaign was half over, were wretchedly emaciated. But these same horses were blooded, and would
run until they fell, and the riders were like their horses; so in the
sweet evenings of May, when the vivid green of the young leaves
almost hid the white and red of the blossoms, there in the dim
recesses of the Virginia forests the war squadrons mustered, and
the steeds literally sniffed the battle from afar, standing with
dilated eye and erect ear as the blare of the bugle sounded
through the woods and the monitory voice of the cannon was
borne in the distant mutterings.

Our detail from the regiment found the Fourth Virginia Cavalry
in position near Spottsylvania Court House. Everything evidenced
to the experienced eye that a battle was imminent. In the road near
by, ordnance wagons were pushed to the front. Ambulance horses
were hitched ready to rush to the scene of action as soon as the
first gun should sound. Orderlies and couriers, as well as staff
officers, were going at a gallop. The stragglers, thinking it full
time to disappear, were using every ruse to drop out of column;
dismounting, and busily examining their horses' feet, feigning
that the girth of the saddle was broken, and lining the road on
the way to the rear. The colonel's black cook was spurring by
on his mule, more intent on getting a safe place than his master's
dinner.

During a halt, while the men were wiping the perspiration from
their faces, a sudden ripple ran down the line.

"Give way," came the cry, "here comes Major Breathed, of
Stuart's horse artillery!" and soon the rapid hoof-strokes of the
horses and jingling of the equipments were heard; and as the
artillery passed along the road with the boy-major at its head,
the sunburnt troopers arose to a man and saluted him with the wild
Rebel yell. It was a tribute that the oldest general in the army
would have been proud to receive, and I see again the gallant
boy's face flush to a deeper red as he lifted his cap and rode with
bared head through the lines.

The mantle of the lamented Pelham, the greatest light artillerist of America, had fallen on Jim Breathed, the young Marylander.
He was about twenty-three years old, but like a boy of eighteen;
he was muscular and athletic, with a fine head well set on his
square shoulders; he was not what the ladies would term "a
handsome fellow," but his character was shown in his dark gray
eyes, which flashed and gleamed in a very striking way when he

was roused. His voice was rich and rare, being low and deep.
General Munford,who knew him best, wrote of him:

"A more dashing, gallant, generous-hearted Confederate soldier never drew a sabre or fired a cannon. He was recklessly
brave himself, and ever ready to lead his batteries where few
artillery officers would be willing to risk their guns, and then
he would turn over his guns to the next officer under him and
dash and lead the cavalry in a charge. While he would take
these personal risks and would stand by his guns or his wounded
men to the last extremity, he would never give up a man dead or
alive if there was any possible way of carrying his body out of the
reach of the enemy. He loved to hear the roar of artillery and
to witness the flashing of the guns; he was a splendid artillerist
and would frequently run to a gun and adjust it and sight it himself when it was not doing the work he expected of it, but while
he 'slashed and dashed' in and out of a battle he was as generous
as he was brave, and having been a doctor before the war he
often ministered to the men who a short time before had stood
up before his guns and fallen in the fight he had led against
them."

The Black Horse Cavalry was dismounted in a strip of woods
a short distance from Todd's Tavern, and lay flat upon the
ground behind a fence awaiting an attack. Between them and
the wood half a mile away intervened a large field. Across this
broad stretch the bullets of the Yankee skirmishers came sailing,
giving warning of their errand by a little puff of smoke issuing
from the woods and floating upwards until lost in air. The situation had its charm, for the missiles did not come in profusion, but
yet often and close enough to make the position exciting and
string the nerves to a tight tension. As the little rift of smoke
would rise across the way, a dozen carbines would reply and ring
out their stirring chorus. This was returned, and the firing increased, but it was all excitement and little danger. Few were
hit, and as the sun declined bringing out all those fresh, pure
airs and sweet odors which seemed to have been dormant all day
in the forest, every soldier saw that there would be no real work
at that time.

It was amusing to watch some of the new soldiers as the
bullets came singing over their heads; they changed color and
flattened themselves to the earth, not daring to look up. Others
became hysterical, danger affecting them like a strong stimulant.
They would laugh wildly, idiotically, or give a half-smothered

scream as a bullet split the top rail of the fence behind which they were cowering. Their relief must have been great when at dusk the enemy ceased firing and stopped damaging the trees. During the fusilade the regiment lost only ten men wounded, and judging from the rapid firing of the enemy, much lead must have been wasted in placing those ten Rebels *hors de combat*. Well, they were rich enough not to grudge it, neither did the safe and sound body of any Rebel there; so in that respect things were equal.

The campaign was all planned that night by the privates around the camp-fire, and really some shrewd guesses were made with regard to unfolding events. The troopers were disposed to grumble and curse the luck which compelled them to fight dismounted.

It was an innovation which had crept in lately upon their old custom, and one which they did not like. This fighting on foot was making infantrymen of them, they said, and furthermore, it was dangerous; much more deadly, in fact, than a rattling charge or dashing rush. Those who had gotten transfers from the infantry to the cavalry in the belief that this latter branch of the service was comparatively safe, now discovered what a sad mistake they had made. They found that the cavalry was called upon to do double service. It was no longer to be used only as eyes for the army, but as the mailed hand, also, which was to strike. They were to fight upon horseback when they met horsemen, and on foot when they met infantrymen, consequently the disgust of those timid foot-soldiers who had joined the cavalry because a dead man with spurs on could not be found, was laughable in the extreme. Instead of being ensconced in a safe place, with plenty of booty and plunder, the cavalry, during the fourth year of the war, had become the most exposed branch of the service, whose ratio of loss was higher than that of any other. It was to be hard riding, brushes, skirmishes, combats and battles all the time during the campaign, with a constant dropping of names from the rolls, which went to make up a fearful aggregate. The cavalryman could soon hold up his head proudly as he pointed to a list of the dead, and continued to listen to the eloquent silence which answered the roll call of the sergeant; a silence which told the tale but too well.

The sixth of May was an unusually hot day for that time of year. The men were soon in the saddle, and then began a series of manoeuvres which puzzled the brain of every soldier there.

They rode like the drunken sailor, "up and down and all round," and raised a dust in which it was almost impossible to breathe.

"Where are we going?" was on the lips of every trooper; but none could answer. Each one thought there would be tough fighting on the morrow, for the Yankees were on hand and evidently it was not the intention of Fitz Lee to retreat. But there they were, riding about the country like a darky delivering invitations to a rustic blow-out.

The Fourth did not halt until about noon, and then the troopers, opening their dusty haversacks, ate their rations of fat raw meat and crackers. Soon the bugle rang and the column was put in motion. From the right came the angry boom of the guns; but as yet the small-arms were silent. Crossing a field in that direction, the Black Horse dismounted and were placed as support to a section of Stuart's horse artillery that was replying to a Yankee battery about six hundred yards distant, and who were hurling their iron missiles with wonderful accuracy right into what seemed to an onlooker the midst of the Rebel battery.

For the cavalrymen, securely placed in a ravine, it was a grand sight to watch the evolutions. It was Breathed's light battery, the crack guns of the Army of Northern Virginia; and the way they were handled by the men was a spectacle calculated to stir the most sluggish blood and make it run like quicksilver through the veins.

The cannoneers were stripped to the waist, displaying their brawny arms and hairy chests. They swung the guns around as if steel and brass had lost their weight and were the playthings of the hour. In loading, the men would throw themselves unconsciously into attitudes and magnificent poses which, could a sculptor have caught, would have made his fame. The swelling muscles came out like whip-cords, denoting the hidden force of the frame; every position was an exponent of the strength of manhood in its rich youth, while each figure was thrown into bold relief against the flashes of fire which darted from the muzzles of the guns.

The shells of the enemy burst all around, but by a wonderful chance did not explode in the midst of the battery, which formed, as it were, the hub of the wheel, rimmed round with fire. The rim was a cordon of danger to cross, yet when once crossed there was safety to be found within. Many soldiers, especially old artillerymen, often observed this strange fact, a torrent of hail falling through the air, ploughing and tearing the earth to the right and left, in front and in rear, filling the air at a distance either way with bursting fragments, yet not hurting a man.

In this instance no one was wounded nor was any injury done, except the killing of a horse and the shattering of a caisson in the rear. The batteries moved off and the smoke soon drifted away.

Back to the horses and a quick remounting of cavalrymen was but the work of a moment. The walk was increased to a trot, and in half an hour we drew rein in the vicinity of Todd's Tavern, near the position held in the morning. A long halt followed. The dust was stifling. The troopers sat in their saddles with one leg thrown across the pommel, fanning themselves with their hats, wiping their faces, and draining their canteens of the last drop. There was no sound of fighting, only couriers sweeping by on foam-flecked horses showed that movements of moment were on the eve of execution.

Of course every man had his opinion of what was going to happen just there and then, but no two agreed on anything, except that it was a confoundedly hot afternoon, and that they would give a year of existence for a huge gourd of pure, cold water drawn fresh from the well.

The horses stood with drooping heads, as if they were like the tall grass in the fields, wilting beneath the rays of the sun.

About two o'clock the voice of Colonel Randolph sounded in the stillness:

"Fourth, attention! Prepare to dismount! Number four, hold horses! Dismount!"

Every three out of the file of four sprang to the ground, committing to the lucky fourth man the charge of the horses of his file. Sabres were unbuckled, revolvers unstrapped and hung upon the pommels of the saddles, leaving each trooper armed with his carbine; for this dismounting meant fighting on foot as infantry.

Drawing off from the road the line was dressed and the order given, and slowly the line started through the woods.

The cavalry was comparatively new to this work and did not take to it naturally. Out of the saddle was out of its element; but animated with a desire to do and dare everything, the men made the best of the unfamiliar situation when the time for action arrived. They moved timidly along at first, and evidently felt insecure. This was but natural, for three years of their lives had been spent in the saddle. They had learned confidence in handling revolvers, and would charge any odds upon horseback, but on foot, with weapons unfamiliar, it was too much to expect the stolidity and steadiness of veteran infantrymen.

The line of advance was like Hogarth's line of beauty: all curves. Neither did the officers understand any better than their soldiers how to align the ranks; still it was a superb body of men, who meant mischief, and they kept along pretty well.

On our way we passed a regiment of dismounted men, who seemed utterly demoralized and ready to strike for their horses at the slightest provocation. A bursting shell had made them as nervous as old women.

When the end of the field was reached, the ball opened and a rattling volley poured into the Confederate line. A battery on the left also paid it its respectful attention.

This was quite too much for some of the troopers, who broke and retreated to the rear; but the majority answered with a ringing cheer and increased the pace to a run, loading and firing carbines as they went. As they were in the woods, there was but little damage done to either side. The noise of the attack and the cheering induced the foe to retreat, when the men, overcome by excitement, lay like dogs on a trail and all organization of the Fourth ceased for a time.

The Black Horse, having in its ranks many old infantrymen, managed better, keeping the company intact and in line. Breaking through the woods they struck a blind road, which they followed through a meadow. Here a battery sighted them and sent off a few solid shot by way of greeting, but the men were moving too rapidly to stop, pushing steadily on to a covert of woods in their front.

"If I can not ride a horse," said one of the dismounted troopers as he skimmed over the ground, "I can at least hide behind a tree, and in one way or another see this fight." So he kept up with the line.

It was a line which would have made Hardie or Upton want to commit suicide; and it surged along like an irregular, long-league roller which comes thundering and tossing upon the reef. The patter of bullets was now heard as they struck the trunks and branches of the trees, cutting off tiny twigs, scattering the bark or imbedding themselves in the wood.

A short rest was here given to enable the men to recover breath. In five minutes the advance was resumed for about a half mile, the few skirmishers in the front retreating. At last a road running through the woods was reached, when a fierce volley came pouring into the face of the troop. Then each man, selecting a tree for himself, used it as a breastwork and returned the discharge by a hot scattering fire, the combatants being less than fifty yards apart.

For about fifteen minutes in the depths of the woods this close combat was carried on with small loss, as both parties were fighting under cover, the trees intercepting the missiles.

Each side was armed with breech-loading and repeating rifles, and every man pulled trigger as rapidly as he was able; consequently there was a shower of lead coming and going. A Federal officer upon a horse, imprudently exposing himself, went down, horse and all, under a volley.

In the very midst of this contest there occurred an act of superb bravery, or rather madness, which quickens the blood in remembrance; one of those reckless, daring deeds which soldiers love most to dilate upon around the camp-fire, but which few if any would care to emulate. In a road, Rebel-lined, there dashed a Yankee officer, splendidly mounted and wearing the shoulder-straps of a captain. He evidently had mistaken the enemy for his own men, and was as much startled on discovering his error as they in whose presence he found himself. To them the apparition was so unexpected that for a second none thought of firing. In that time he had jerked his horse savagely around. A score of rifles were covering him at half pistol-shot distance, and as many voices shouted out to him to surrender.

Well! did he surrender? There was hardly one chance in a million that he could run that gauntlet and escape. The men who had drawn the bead were all crack marksmen, whose aim at ten yards, where he was riding, was certain death. Not to surrender seemed madness. Did he? No! he risked the odds. He drove his spurs deep in the flanks of his steed. A violent spring of the animal and he was clearing the ground in mighty bounds. The man bent low in his saddle.

"Shoot him! Shoot him!" cried the troopers, and at every leap of the horse the rifle-crack was heard. I happened to be standing in the road and I was always counted a fair shot among the Black Horsemen, and as I saw his *ruse de guerre* I sprang into the middle of the road, and with the muzzle of my carbine bearing upon the officer's head, fired. The rifle snapped. The horse, evidently struck by one of the many bullets, flinched and quivered for a second but kept well to his work. The wonderful promptitude and suddenness of the movement must have disconcerted the aim of the marksman, for only the soldier's arm was seen to hang supine by his side, and then, like a flash, horse and rider were out of sight.

Is it strange that men are fatalists? Witnessing such immunity from death, is it any wonder that the veteran comes to believe that he cannot die before his time, and shares the faith of Madame de Sevigne when she declared that the cannon ball which killed the great Turenne was charged from all eternity to do that particular work?

" 'Every bullet has its billet,' " solemnly avers the soldier.

"But," replies the unbeliever, "what induces you to get behind a tree in a fight, if you are a fatalist?"

"O, that's a matter of habit," answers the tattered gray-back; "a matter of habit to prevent getting hit. Fate takes no account of wounds, that's small work—only of death. If we protect ourselves against the bullet, it's because we might be riddled through and through and Fate wouldn't let us die before our time.

"Why, there's—" and off the long-winded Reb will start to give proof of his theory; tell you how such a comrade died from a shot in the finger, how another recovered with a bullet hole clear through his chest, and so on ad infinitum, until he convinces himself that his creed is correct and the only one that a soldier should entertain.

CHAPTER XX.

THE BATTLE CONTINUED.

The men had by this time warmed up to the work before them, and when Lieutenant James sprang out and ordered a charge they answered with a will. The opposing force, evidently under the impression that we had received heavy reinforcements, gave ground and were pushed back across a swamp, fighting at every step and inflicting upon us quite a severe loss. Through the wood into a miry, boggy, swampy piece of land the line advanced in skirmish order.

Just then Dick Martin and I crossed the road, and as we spied the dead horse of the officer who went down by our first volley, we both rushed to it. I to secure a handsome leather haversack suspended from the pommel, and Dick to get the saddle, which was an unusually fine one, and which Dick was green enough to think he could bear safe and undisturbed to the rear. The rider lay near; he was a captain of cavalry, and a ghastly hole in his throat showed where he got his death wound. I unstrapped the haversack, which was full of something, and slung it around my neck. I never did a better day's work than I did then, for without that haversack I would have fared badly.

We two were about seventy-five yards in advance of the company, and noticing a Virginia snake fence near, which separated the forest from a field, both Martin and I crawled up to it and looked through the rails. One glance was enough; the field was literally full of Yankees, and a line of battle a half mile long was just in motion in our direction. Dick ceased to covet the saddle. He threw it off his shoulders and we fled back to the company just as a rattling volley came from our left, killing two men and wounding three. I rushed to Captain Payne and told him that there were thousands of Yankees in our front, and that we had better make tracks—and make them long and fast. Captain Payne was so nervous with this new species of warfare that he could not see how to get his command out. Martin also told what he had seen to Lieutenant James, and that astute officer had a soldier's instinct. He gave command to the company to right about face and retreat.

There was no panic; the men shouted and joked with one another as they sought the rear, stopping every few seconds to turn and fire in the direction of the wild hurrahs, which sounded so strangely in the woods.

I remember watching Harold Alston, a young English lad of some eighteen years, who had come, no one knew how or why, from his far-off home and joined the Black Horse as a private in the ranks. He was standing beside a hickory sapling capping his carbine, when a bullet passed through his sleeve and split the sapling in two parts. It was a close call, but the young Englishman, who was in his first battle, never flinched for a moment; and Ker Sowers, who witnessed the incident, called to Alston to lie down, and remarked to me: "If all Englishmen fight like that boy, no wonder that they have never been conquered."

Just then a line of battle appeared on the rim of the woods opposite and advanced across the field. They wore the yellow-seamed jackets of the cavalry. Our rifles began to ring out, and many of them dropped, but our scattering volley only served to spur them up. With a loud hurrah they poured a volley in our direction.

"Good-by, Black Horse!" yelled Joe Boeteller as he struck for the rear.

"O, that I had wings!" said Dick Martin.

Thrice happy were the long-legged ones. Every Black Horseman discounted his record that day as a runner. Through the woods, across swamps, into briers we tore, with the Yankees close behind, yelling like mad and sending pattering bullets after us. At last we reached a large field fully half a mile across, with a large farm-house in the center, and now it was neck or nothing, with the blue-coats not a hundred yards behind. A squad of us aimed for the house, and nearly crazed with thirst, struck for the spring. I filled my cap with water, and taking a few gulps kept on at a two-forty gait. Alston, the Englishman, was not so fortunate; he lay down at full length to lap up the water, and by the time he regained his feet the foe were upon him. I saw him, as I cast a backward glance over my shoulder, throw up his hands in token of submission. That was the last glimpse I had of Alston.

Disregarding the cries of surrender, I zigzagged as I ran, and when about to sink upon the ground breathless, I heard the rattling of small-arms on the farther end of the field and saw the blue smoke curling from behind the fence. This showed where our line of battle was stationed; so making a final spurt I reached the fence and dropped on the ground like a log. I could not have run ten yards more if all the Yankee army, with Ben Butler at the head, had been marching up the hill.

The whole brigade lay in position behind the fence which bounded the field. The rails had been pulled down and piled one upon another, forming a kind of breastwork. Silence of a few minutes followed, and then on came the Yankees in two serried lines. A fierce struggle ensued; the bullets struck everywhere, and now and then, searching out some crevice in the rails, would bury themselves in living flesh. Men began to drift to the rear. The commands of officers were heard above the din, urging the line to stand firm.

All at once a heavy volley was heard on the left, and that portion of the line surged backward.

"We are flanked! The Yankees are in our rear!" resounded through the ranks, and the whole brigade gave way and in great confusion retired over a mile. The cavalrymen discounted their horses in that race. But again they were striking for reserves as before, not panic-stricken. They did not understand rallying on foot and fighting back inch by inch for hours, they were used to more dashing encounters; with the charge and countercharge they were familiar, but the dogged, face-to-face fight they had yet to learn.

An interval of half an hour followed, in which the brigade was reformed. The men had fired so often that their faces were grimed with powder, and they stood like a long line of coal-heavers waiting to unload the next barge. About a fourth of their number were armed with the Sharpe's rifle, manufactured in Richmond, and a more unreliable arm was never forced into the hands of unwilling soldiers; they spit fire at the breech in every discharge, and scorched and blackened the flesh with the half-burnt powder, so that in firing the man so unfortunate as to possess it involuntarily turned aside his head when he pulled the trigger, having the while not the faintest idea whom or where the bullet might strike. And how they did recoil! Shades of an army mule!

The reserves to which the Rebels had retreated were about a half mile back, supported by a section of Breathed's horse artillery, the guns being in position in a field just back of the troopers, who were forming in the strip of woods. Squads of men were every moment arriving and taking position in the line. It was nearly dark in the woods at this time, and no further attack was apprehended. No pickets were thrown out in front, and not a thought of danger possessed our long ranks, which stood discussing the events of the day and giving in experiences. Colonel Randolph sat on his horse, his aids also mounted, the right leg of each thrown comfortably over the pommel of the saddle, as the group laughed and talked with the abandon of comrades in arms for whom danger had passed, when presto! as by the wave of Merlin's wand the whole scene changed.

By Mars the God of War! What a volley!

About five thousand rifles discharged through the falling twigs and leaves without premonition, bursting upon the unsuspecting troopers, scattering the mould on the ground, striking musket stocks and barrels, ripping through canteens, and piercing with fearful force the yielding flesh, the balls laid many a gallant form low.

Glorious, gallant Cuthbert Sowers, the pet of the Black Horse, fell at this volley. The shock was so sudden that for a second it seemed to paralyze the whole brigade and cause the men to run helter-skelter back a hundred yards or so; but the officers quickly rallied them into a steady, compact line, and they stood to their work like bulldogs.

It was a stubborn contest and a deadly one. Men were struck every second and a perfect torrent of lead seemed to pour from the muzzles of the repeating rifles. Inch by inch, step by step, was our line borne back by sheer force of weight. There was no running away; nothing but a dogged, stubborn determination to give ground as slowly as possible and exact a heavy penalty. For a half hour there was one of the hottest fights between the opposing brigades of dismounted cavalry that occurred during the war. Every tree, every sapling was marked by the flying lead, and a steady stream of wounded were going back.

At last the work became too warm even to hurrah or cheer; the men needed all the breath they had. It was hard, silent, deadly fighting. The combatants were in full view of each other whenever the purple smoke would drift away for a few moments. The advance was irresistible through the woods to where our small reserve was stationed and breastworks thrown up for protection, and better than all, a section of Breathed's battery.

As soon as we were ensconced behind this shelter, the two guns sent the solid shot ploughing and crashing through the trees and right into their teeth. This stopped the advance, but did not cause their retreat at first, but in a few minutes the combined fire caused them to recede, and then our men advanced and ran against a fresh line and were broken to pieces.

Nothing saved the regiment from a rout but those two guns of Breathed's battery. We drifted back. On each side of the section there was a small field to the left, and I found myself alone in it. Casting my eyes around I saw at a distance a long line of cavalry hastening toward the field. I could not tell the color of the uniforms on account of the dust, but I thought they were the enemy, so I ran to the battery and told the lieutenant that the Yankees were in our rear and he had better save his guns.

His reply was laconic and to the point:

"Not by a damn sight!"

Nothing more was to be said, so I turned back to the field, where the rifles were spitting fire at each other. Suddenly from out of the woods came two dismounted Yankees, not forty yards distant. I took aim at one and pulled the trigger before they caught sight of me. Thanks to the miserable home-made rifle the bullet shattered the soldier's arm. He dropped his gun, and holding his wounded limb went back to the woods. His comrade, instead of running away, fired hastily at me and sent a bullet through my slouch hat. I banged away at him and the confounded cap snapped; then I saw the blue-coat drop on his knee and take as cool aim at me as if he was firing at a mark. I was standing sidewise to him, trying to force a shell into the breech. I saw the flash and felt a jar, then dropped to the ground. Again he fired; this bullet struck my boot sole and slit the upper and lower leather wide apart.

I thought, "That bloodthirsty Yank will kill me yet, so I'll play possum," and I stretched myself out like one lifeless. Just then one of our scattered men, seeing me fall, ran across the field to help me. The Yankee fired at him just as the soldier stooped to pick me up. I saw the dust fly from his jacket just above the collar-bone, and the Reb gave a howl and put back to the rear.

Now, thought I, that Yank ought to be satisfied, he has crippled two men; so I watched him out of the corner of my eye. He rose, looked around and blazed away at somebody, and then to my great relief disappeared into the woods. I remembered that the hero Wolfe at Quebec, when he was dying of his wound, thanked God that the enemy was retreating, and said that he could die happy. I am bound to confess that I lost every bit of my patriotism when that bullet struck me. I had nothing of the hero in me. It was a matter of indifference to me who won the

35

fight. I did not care a Confederate dollar whether "Cassio killed Roderigo or Roderigo killed Cassio," I was too much concerned about myself. Was I done for? Was I mortally wounded? Where did that ball hit, anyway? I unbuttoned my jacket, drew a long breath. Lungs all right, arm ditto, head level and unperforated. I rose on my legs, or rather attempted to do so, and then I found where I was hit. Two round holes in my breeches legs above the knee showed where the bullet had gone through, and a warm thrill down my left leg indicated that the blood was running freely.

The surgeons had impressed one fact upon the men. They said, "As soon as you are struck, take your handkerchief and make a tourniquet by tying the ligature above the wound as tight as it can be made; this may save your life." It saved mine. I was not versed in surgery enough to know whether the bones were shattered or not. My leg was a dead weight; I could wriggle my toes, there was plenty of room for them after that Yankee had ruined my boot by that last shot, and even then I remembered with a pang that I had given two hundred and fifty dollars for those boots.

It was now dark and the chilling vapor of the near-by swamp stole over the fields. It was perfectly still; the evening star burned like a lamp in the sky. I raised myself and glanced around hoping to see some friendly light of a relief party moving over the field, but nothing could be seen or heard. I essayed to shout, but what with yelling all the evening there was not much voice left. I shivered from the cold; my leg, now swollen to double its natural size, pained me badly, and worse than all a consuming thirst possessed me, and in the passing of the long hours it grew worse, until the longing became torture. I would doze off and dream of rivers and fountains, and waken with my teeth chattering, mouth dry, and tongue like a piece of shingle. My wound had bled much and formed a sickening, glue-like puddle, that I could only wallow in, for I had not the strength to pull myself out. If I had only possessed an overcoat or a blanket it would have been less uncomfortable. Lying helpless on the bare ground in a light marching costume is an experience that any soldier who has ever tried it will never forget.

I wondered in a dim way where the Black Horse were? Whether or not I was lying inside the enemy's lines—if I had been missed and if I were supposed to have been killed? My thirst was such that had a Yankee come to me with a canteen I would have looked upon him as an angel. But the night passed away, and by the time the dawn came I was envying the rigid forms that I knew were lying around on the battle-field, for they could not suffer.

I was insensible when a searching party of our men found me. One of my comrades, Sym Green, of the Black Horse, who was hunting for me, came up, and seeing my condition, at first thought I was dead; I was reported killed in the battle. He went back for his horse, on which he managed to mount me, and walking by my side and supporting the useless limb, conveyed me to the road a half mile away, where our ambulances were waiting for the freight. I was placed within, and with cheering words my comrade rode off.

"This is the last load that I am going to take to-day," remarked the driver as he started his team. I asked him how many he had run. He said he had not counted them, but that he had driven from the battle-field to the improvised hospital at Spottsylvania Court House several times and had full loads each time. That many badly wounded passengers had been in that vehicle could easily be seen, for the bottom of the ambulance, being water-tight, was covered with the horrible crimson exudation to the depth of an inch or more, and the jolting over the stones had dashed the blood about like a miniature fountain, saturating me from head to foot, until I was actually bathed in the ensanguined fluid. Even under such circumstances one may derive consolation, and "it might be worse" has made many a man content and formed philosophers. How many hundreds, or even thousands, were that night lying dead, or mutilated beyond hope. Any reasonable man ought to be thankful, although every jolt was agony.

The Court House, distant about four miles from Todd's Tavern, was reached at last, and the driver, taking me in his arms to the court-house green, placed his burden on the grass. The rooms of the building were already filled to their utmost capacity, but he said he would bring the surgeon.

All around in the spacious yard lay the maimed of two days' battle, stricken in every possible way.

The day passed, but I lay in the court-house yard with hundreds of others, unnoticed and unattended. The night was glorious, soft and warm, and never had the stars looked so bright and radiant. The hours came and went and those nearest to death died in peace.

If one must die, how grand and appropriate seemed the place, with the earth receiving the resting form back to her bosom and the ethereal, boundless space opening to freed spirits. In the dread, majestic presence of Death, what are earthly ties, tearful voices or loving words? The golden bowl breaks just the same, the severed cord is loosened none the less surely. There can be no more glorious, no happier death than the martyr's and the soldier's. Both suffer, both endure, and death squares all.

About midnight I was wakened out of a dozing slumber by an exclamation, and opening my eyes saw by the mystic light a figure bare to the waist, with clotted blood so thick that only here and there, in little spots, could the white skin be seen beneath. I thought it some hideous dream.

"Hunter, is that you?" said the nightmare.

"Yes," I answered, rubbing my eyes, "but who in the mischief are you?"

"Shepherd, of the Black Horse."

I knew him well. He hailed from Louisiana, was an educated scholar, jovial comrade, and one of the handsomest men in the Army; about thirty-seven years old, six feet high in his stockings and erect as a pine.

"Where were you hit?"

"Right through my shoulder," he replied; "bad wound, but not very painful now."

"Is there no chance of seeing a surgeon," I asked.

"No, I was brought here before sundown; I saw thousands of wounded and they have been coming in ever since. There are but two surgeons here, and they can't begin to look over all these men, but I hope some of our friends will find me out soon. I am going to lie down, for I am faint."

So side by side we rested, and soon fell into a troubled doze.

It was some time in the night when the pain of the wound caused me to wake and struggle into a sitting posture. I looked around. Shepherd lay close beside me, his white face turned skyward; only his regular breathing showed that he was alive. The heavens blazed with millions of stars, but the beauty of the coming morn was lost upon those unfortunates who rested upon the sward of the court-house green. I struggled to rise, but everything spun around and phantom shapes came and went. The torturing pains grew less and I felt myself sinking, as it were, out of sight, then unconsciousness followed. A shooting pain, a thrill of acute feeling, and a voice sounding in my ears:

"Is he alive?"

"Yes, the whiskey has brought him to."

I then became conscious that a liquid was passing down my throat, and opening my eyes I saw the chaplain of the regiment, and the surgeon kneeling, with his finger on my pulse.

"I'm all right, doctor, but for God's sake give me water, and look after Shepherd there!"

The flask was put to his lips and he also sat up.

"I'm going to put you two in a room by yourselves," said the chaplain, "in the top of the court-house, and I think we can manage to carry you up.

Taking Shepherd first, they returned, and placing their arms around me, carefully steered their way over the prostrate forms, which lay almost touching one another.

Reaching the room above, they spread a blanket upon the floor and laid us upon it, and the doctor, assisted by the chaplain, made a hasty examination of our wounds. Shepherd's shoulder-blade was shattered by the bullet, and the surgeon told him that it was not mortal but that in all probability he would never have the full use of his arm again. My own was a flesh wound; the bullet only knocking off the end of the bone, and changing direction, passed upward and out, making a wide orifice and tearing the flesh and tendons dreadfully.

I drew a long breath of thankfulness. In the parlance of our camp, I had a "million-dollar wound," which meant a long furlough with no danger to life or limb.

CHAPTER XXI.

THE REAR-GUARD OF THE GRAND ARMY.

Both my comrade and myself felt better the next morning, especially as the surgeon, who though he had been constantly at work all night, yet found time to dress our wounds, and pronounced them improving as rapidly as could be expected. His only prescription being cold water to bathe the hurt.

The homeopathic plan, after a battle, was the only one our doctors followed, whether they all believed in it or not. Cold water was plentiful, and no other restoring agent being at hand, they all became advocates of the cold-water cure. In fact, the medical stores were very scant. We possessed none of those large, roomy ambulances which the Yankees had, filled with all the adjuncts of the medical profession; no "Old Sanitary" for us.

Our field surgeon's outfit consisted of a bag, in the depths of which were rolls of bandages, a case of amputating instruments, which some newly fledged doctors used on the slightest pretext, if they were in doubt, just to keep their hands in, as it were.

All the wounded were treated alike—the slightly, the badly, and the severely. Their wounds were bandaged with a handful of lint, over which was a bandage of cotton; then a canteen of water was placed in the patient's free hand, that he might keep the cloth always wet. In the other hand was a branch with which to wave the flies away.

After all, the simple treatment was possibly the safer and better. Mother Nature is a kind old dame, and will heal her children's wounds unless indeed they be mortal. The simpler the remedies the surer the cure; and the continual dripping of cool, clear water on the affected parts prevented erysipelas and fever.

Many of our most eminent surgeons freely confessed, in conversation and in print, that in hot weather clear water possessed greater curative powers than all the lotions in the world. Others of the fraternity would deny this of course, for when did doctors ever agree? Be that as it may, the stricken soldier had by far greater confidence in the efficacy of the pure element than in the drugs and nostrums of the laboratory. Then for suppurating wounds our surgeons used a porous bag filled with fresh earth; it was found to be an excellent absorbent.

After the doctor had taken up the severed arteries and bandaged my hurt, I was soon out of pain, and as I sank restfully back the last thing that I recollected was the doctors of medicine and divinity carrying out the body of a soldier who had died in the corner of the room.

Poor fellow, his personal effects were few: a rifle left on the field, a pair of shoes, and maybe a bag of tobacco and an old pipe, which were appropriated by the burial squad. A blood-stained blanket which he probably got of some dead enemy, and which, falling to our share, would, if we "shuffled off our mortal coil," be taken by the next chance soldier. No need of executors for the privates in the ranks—the first hand stretched out obtained the personal property, and retained it without fear of administrators or heirs.

A cup of hot coffee was brought us, and hardly had we finished ere the boom of a cannon broke the stillness of the soft, spring air. It was the signal gun, and then the battle opened. We could not move from our pallets, only stay and listen, wishing with a listless kind of hope for rescue.

For a half or three-quarters of an hour the firing continued, advancing nearer and nearer, showing that our forces were retreating. Then there was a lessening of reports, and while we wondered what it could mean, steps were heard outside ascending the stairway, and several of our comrades of the Black Horse entered the room, having been sent by the ever-kind and thoughtful Colonel Randolph to bring our blankets and clothes, which had been strapped behind our saddles.

They told us the news: In the morning our forces were struck by solid lines of infantry, who had driven them back until they had been ordered to retreat to their horses and retire beyond the village. They said, furthermore, in a short time the court-house would be occupied by Yankees.

This was anything but cheering news to two already down-hearted patients, and our spirits sank to zero, especially as, after a most fashionable visit as regards time, our comrades left us.

Soon after the fight was renewed; this time only about two miles away. A stand must have been made by our people, for not only the artillery, but the musketry as well, could be heard. It was a short conflict, for it ended as abruptly as it commenced and then came another interval of perfect silence.

Through the window poured a mellow flood of sunlight, the green baby leaves, but yesterday burst from the bud, taking a greener tint from the vivid-hued rays. A blackbird sang on a bough just outside, and the sweet odor of springtime came through the open window. One could close his eyes and imagine himself in some peaceful country home.

In a perfect agony of expectation we awaited the sounds we knew must soon follow, and in a few minutes several sudden reports blazed forth and then a shrapnel bursted over the court-house. The carol of the bird was hushed. Again the cannon voice and explosion of shell was heard farther down the village.

Shepherd got up.

"Good God! I can't stand this!" and he tottered from the room.

Another and still another report, and maddened by uncertainty I dragged myself, despite the burning pain, to the window and looked out. I forgot wounds, hurts—I was thrilled to the heart by the bravest, most daring scene my eyes ever gazed upon before or since. This was what I saw:

In front of the court-house, in the direction in which I was looking, was a large common or pasture of about one hundred acres, destitute of trees or shrubbery with the exception of an old dead apple tree standing in the middle. The common was bounded on the opposite side by a dense forest. In front of the woods, about half a mile distant, was planted a Yankee battery of four guns, and it was their shells which were exploding over the village. In the middle of the field were two figures; one lay behind the tree, seemingly nerveless with fear, for he made neither sign nor motion.

Standing out in bold relief was a soldier in gray, with neither brake, bank, nor cover protecting him. He stood there alone, fighting that four-gun battery. Evidently annoyed by his fire, a gun was turned on him; a solid shot went shrieking over his head but it did not daunt him. Upright, he used his repeating-rifle with wonderful rapidity, though with what effect I could not see. The gun of the battery was aimed better next time, for a long furrow was ploughed in the ground near where he stood; even that did not cause him to move nor retreat; instead, his rifle went up to his eye, a little puff of smoke, a faint crack, and the bullet sped on its errand; then the rifle was lowered, a shot from the magazine slipped into the barrel and fired in rapid succession. Another cannon-shot passed through the branches of the old apple tree, yet he did not even turn his head. He seemed not to know or care whether there was an enemy in the rear, and fought like a Titan against a host.

I was lost in amazement. Who was this man who alone was tackling with superb madness a whole battery of artillery? Shot and shell seemed no more to him than the clouds of Saracen arrows did to the lion-hearted Richard. Horatius at the bridge, D'Auvergne at the pass holding back unnumbered foes, never surpassed in splendid recklessness such an act as this. No gladiator's exhibitions to excite the huzzas of the populace. For less than this has history made men famous. The Athenians would have carried him into the senate chamber and recited an ode in his honor. How grim old Ney would have taken him by the hand and into his heart, and later on Lord Raglan would have given him the Victoria cross, and England voted him a pension.

Ah! bravery is a glorious virtue wherever it be found; the gods respect, men admire and women adore it. Under all conditions, at all times it is grand and noble, but grander and nobler is the courage which plans, which dares, which executes without hope and without reward.

The sole witness of this exploit now enacting on the heath ended his observations, for a shell from the battery exploded near the window with fearful force; a limb of the sycamore which shaded the court-house was cut in two, and one of the fragments of iron shattered the window glass above my head. This was a little too hot, so dropping to the floor I wiggled to the staircase and halloed for assistance. A soldier heard the call and carried me down the long steps into the court-room, and then, by the direction of the surgeon, laid me upon a bench on the raised dais where in peaceful times the learned man of law was wont to preside and dispense justice to all without regard to age, color or previous condition of servitude.

Listen! there is the rumble of wheels, and a faint cheer follows. The Yankees are closing in on the place. I wonder where the rear-guard is now. Killed, captured, wounded or beating a retreat?

Hardly had these thoughts flashed through my mind when the crack of a rifle was heard outside; through the open door I saw that man in gray retreating in a swinging gait; then through the window I caught a last glimpse of him; he seemed to be of middle age, tall and thin. Behind him, not a hundred yards away, came the battery in a gallop, and then vanished in a huge cloud of dust.

Once more! only once more, the report of his piece sounded, so faintly, Shepherd said, as to be barely audible, yet it was a deadly shot, for in a minute a squad of blue-coats came in, carefully bearing one of their number, shot through the groin, almost in front of the court-house door. He was laid beside me on the platform, and then his comrades left without saying a word. They were evidently in a desperate hurry. Shepherd interrogated the man, but he was too far gone to answer; his wound was mortal and his life was ebbing away with every breath.

Who was the hero or fanatic who killed him? I never could learn. Whether rendered savage, desperate, dangerous, by the death of some loved friend killed on the battle-field, or by the ill treatment of a member of his family by marauders, or a veritable madman at large, or having been a prisoner and made nearly insane by brutal treatment of his captors; or perchance born like Nelson, without fear, and loving, as Charles of Sweden did, the music of whistling bullets above everything else, none may ever know. Whatever feeling inspired him, the action was as brilliant as ever jeweled the chronicles of the Crusades. Whether he was killed in the battle which followed, or escaped to tell the tale, his was the proud title of the "REAR-GUARD OF THE A. N. V." A veritable stormy petrel of tempestuous war.

CHAPTER XXII.

OFF DUTY.

In a short time a young Yankee officer entered the room; he was as martial a looking fellow as ever eye rested upon; the true type of a dashing cavalryman. There was something of the holiday soldier about him, for though covered with dust, the perspiration running in streaks down his face, his bearing, his glittering equipments showed the care he took of them; two ivory-handled revolvers peeped from the holsters, his spurs were jingling, and his get-up foppish, yet he was the dandy of the battlefield and not the boudoir.

Following him were several troopers. He stopped and looked around; there lay those who were shot, in every attitude and form of misery; the floor itself where he stood was red and even stained his boots. He appeared shocked by what he saw, and turning to Dr. Randolph said he would send some stores from the hospital chest to alleviate in some measure the suffering of the wounded.

"I wish to God," he added, "that the authors of this war could witness such scenes as this!" Then saluting the doctor he left.

True to his promise, his men soon returned, bringing many necessaries and luxuries from their ambulance; among other things several buckets of ice water. We drank this precious liquid, bathed our hurts and wet the bandages, and many sank into refreshing slumber. The last thing before the eyes closed we saw the blue-coats on their errands of mercy, giving drink to the thirsty, food to the hungry, and playing the good Samaritan to their erstwhile deadly foes. In the time of our suffering there were no jibes nor taunts from them; instead, had we been the nearest and dearest, their courtesy and kindness could not have been more marked. Yes! though "Johnny Reb" and "Billy Yank" could fight each other in deadly combat, yet in times such as these the best in their natures shone out, and their virtues gleamed more brightly when displayed in the dark background of "war's horrid front."

"General Lee's right flank is turned and the game is up," I thought.

A rough shake aroused me; it was Shepherd, in a great state of excitement. .

"Look, Hunter! Look!" he exclaimed.

I thought I was still dreaming, for my last gaze had rested upon armed men in blue, and by some trick of fancy the color was changed into gray. There were a dozen or so in the room; old Rebs to perfection, and if imagination did conjure up this apparition, she did it with a marvelous attention to detail. The ancient slouch hat, the ragged jacket, the battered canteen, the discolored breeches, the brogans and stockings outside of pants, even the bright muskets, all convinced me that I was either mad or dreaming.

"What does all this mean, Shepherd; who are these men?"

"It means that Longstreet has just arrived and occupies the place without having fired a shot."

To the wounded, who had made up their minds to a long confinement in a foreign hospital with no exchange, it meant a lingering out of long days in a strange place with no familiar face at the bedside; the transition was sudden, but filled us with intense joy and devout thankfulness. No felon who had become resigned to his doom received the reprieve with more full-hearted gratitude than did those despairing Rebs, for convalescence would be spent in the bosom of their families, amid all those sweet, tender surroundings which make home a veritable paradise to the soldier.

Those old familiar forms, they gladdened our eyes, for to every patient not already dying, they showed their sympathy in a way that spoke louder than words could ever do; they shared their three days' rations with the hungry; it was not much, one or two half-cooked ash-cakes and a slice of fat meat, that was all, and though it meant starving one day, yet they never hesitated.

Uncle Peter, as Longstreet was called, had made a forced march and broken down half of his corps to reach Spottsylvania. He had taken position about half a mile outside, where he was engaged in throwing up breastworks.

My informant, one of Anderson's men, said:

"There's going to be some tall fighting hereabouts soon."

The hours seemed laden with death. From my high position on the platform I had a view of the whole court-room, and the picture that met my gaze was infinitely sad. Beside me on the dais was one of my own regiment, shot in the side, and from the nature of his wound he was not able to lie down; his suffering was intense.

On the floor, lying on a spread blanket, were five soldiers, all past hope, for the surgeon after a brief examination pronounced them mortally wounded.

There is a horrible fascination in watching dying men; turn your eyes which way you will, they invariably return to those whose sands of life are nearly run out. You can count the gasping breath, behold the spasmodic clutching at the air, the respiration getting fainter and taken at longer intervals, the glazing eye, the blackening lips, the ashy pallor of the face, and at last the rattling of the throat and convulsive shuddering of their limbs as the immortal spirit leaves its tenement of clay.

There were more than a hundred cavalrymen lying in the room, and the odor, the blood and the gathering flies made the place seem like a charnel-house. Nothing was done nor could be done. Utterly unprepared for the emergency, the dead and wounded lay side by side unattended.

This was not our surgeon's fault, all that man could do was done. For forty-eight hours he had been upon his feet without an hour's continuous rest. But what could one doctor and his assistant accomplish among all these maimed and mangled men? Only witness their agony, in despair that they could not respond to a tenth part of the piteous appeals for aid.

The lint, bandages and stimulants which our foes had supplied during their brief stay did incalculable good, and was one of those graceful acts which touched the heart.

One cup of coffee was given to each of the badly wounded who could drink, and a stimulant to those who imperatively needed it; real good Yankee liquor it was, pure and strong medicinal brandy, such as we had not tasted for years; but the demijohn was soon emptied.

In the evening several surgeons arrived and set to work. Limbs were taken off, and in the adjoining room the frightful noise of the saw severing the bones was plainly audible. The dead were removed and the living had their hurts dressed with lint and bathed in water, then the patients were made as comfortable as circumstances would permit.

During the night fifteen men died and their bodies were carried out in the morning; a melancholy procession, as one after another disappeared through the door.

Preparations were made to transport us to Gordonsville, where several post hospitals were stationed.

My companions in misery were Kelly, a little game-cock Irishman of the Fourth Virginia Cavalry, who was shot through the shoulder; Shepherd and a soldier of Company H, of the same regiment.

Together we lay in the vehicle, not a roomy ambulance with easy springs, but one of those huge, unwieldy affairs used for cavalry supplies, and in the parlance of the camp denominated "arks."

Just before starting, General Stuart rode up and cheered us by his kind words; he looked as if dressed for a holiday review. His last words were characteristic:

"You have done splendidly, boys! You have well earned your furlough; the Virginia girls will nurse you well and soon have you ready to follow me through Maryland."

He saluted and rode away and we never again beheld our cavalry leader.

The teamster cracked his whip, the mules started and our journey commenced. We lay on blankets spread upon the bare boards. The jolting was terrible, the torment simply excruciating. The cavalryman lying next to me was shot in the hip, and the shaking of the ark started his wound bleeding afresh, flooding the blankets. By continued shouting we made the driver, who sat on a saddle on the left rear horse, understand that we wanted the wagon stopped; he pulled up and asked me what the matter was.

"I'll drive to that house," he said, pointing to a place a mile away, "and leave him there."

The motion of the wagon recommenced, and still the red stream continued to flow; we were helpless and could do nothing to aid him. His face grew pale and more wan, until at last, when the driver came to a halt and the bleeding man was taken out, he was gasping his last.

"No sort of use to put him in the house," the driver remarked coolly; "he will be dead in a few minutes."

"Oh! don't leave him in the road," said Kelly; "carry him in anyhow."

"Well, I reckon they kin bury him."

The inanimate clay was left at the farm-house and our passage recommenced. The jar and shock was almost unendurable and we begged the man to leave us on the roadside and not to kill us in this manner; but he said, "No, I have orders to carry you to Beaver Dam Station and I am going to do it."

We tried prayers, threats and promises, for we had nothing with which to bribe him, but he was inexorable; so in sullen despair we lay, undergoing torture. The wagon rumbled along so slowly that yards seemed miles, and it appeared as if time itself stood still.

But we were doomed to bear other pain than physical, for about noon a cavalryman dashed up at a rattling pace, shouting out that Sheridan had just occupied Beaver Dam, burnt the depot and destroyed the railroad track for a long distance, and it was probable that he would take the very road which we were traveling.

Without waiting to find out the truth the teamster, panic-stricken, stopped the wagon, unhitched the horses, and mounting rode away to the woods in hot haste, followed by the other drivers of the train, leaving the wounded to take care of themselves. We listened for the hoof strokes of the approaching foe, but the sun declined and not a sound broke the stillness. At last, when darkness was near, the teamsters reappeared, looking very sheepish and making many excuses. Drawing the wagon to one side, they lighted a fire, cooked their rations, gave us some rye coffee, which, added to the hardtack and roast beef in my captured haversack, made a good supper.

We continued our journey the next day, the wagons heading for Bumpas Station on the C. C. R. R., where we arrived late in the evening, after a drive which left little life in any of us.

The wounded were distributed around. Shepherd, Kelly and I were placed on the floor of the station-house, a canteen of water and a cracker given us, and we were then left for the night.

The rumor that the track at Beaver Dam had been destroyed was only too true; Sheridan and his troopers had made thorough work in their raid and had left only a blackened, smoking waste of the station.

The hope, fondly cherished, that we would be sent to Richmond was doomed to disappointment, so we were forwarded to Gordonsville to remain until the road was repaired and the cars could carry the wounded to the Capital City.

On reaching Gordonsville we found the hospitals crowded with the wounded from the fierce battle of the Wilderness, but they were under excellent management; everything was neat and clean and very comfortable. The various wards were cool and airy, while a full corps of nurses gave patient and watchful attendance. In addition to this the ladies in the vicinity had organized a sanitary relief club, and every day they filled their allotted tasks, bringing sunshine with their sweet, bright faces, and doing more good by their very presence than all the herbs that Galen ever dreamed of. All those little luxuries which to the veteran of the camps brought back the memory of ante-bellum days, as well as tempted his palate, were offered him by fair hands. The rations too were wholesome and plentiful, and under these influences most of the patients improved rapidly. The color returned to wan cheeks and contentment was marked in the face of every convalescent. It was pleasant to many of those war-worn Rebs to lie at length on a clean, soft bed, with the cool air sweeping through the open door and windows, with no care on their minds, and a consciousness of duty well performed; and where their gaze could rest upon graceful, flitting forms, while the sweetest voices would charm away the weary hours, and willing hands anticipate every wish, and their pains and aches were lightened by the touch of tender hands.

Then would come glorious news of our comrades in the field, and the distant guns bore on the tidings of great conflicts, where the gray legions, standing at bay, met face to face and front to front the surging lines of blue.

At this time the privates of the rank and file had not much belief in Grant's generalship. His mad charges in which he lost thousands, his repeated attacks and repulses, until the vicinity of Spottsylvania resembled a great abattoir, where, instead of cattle being slaughtered, precious humanity gave up their lives, was not their idea of a master of the art of war.

In about ten days the damage done by Sheridan's raiders at Beaver Dam was repaired, and those of the wounded who could be moved were put on flats and started for Richmond. Many trains were loaded with the wounded.

It was an unpleasant ride for some, the track being rough and uneven, and the cars were those used for transporting timber, ties, pig iron and other third-class rate. But it was easy enough to gain patience and philosophy now, for thoughts of furlough and a gradual convalescence in the home circle lingered in the minds of the majority.

No thieving commissary to rob him of his daily meals, no guards, no work of any kind, but a glorious idleness, with care and trouble banished. So the antiquated cars racketed and rumbled along as best they could, and each revolution of the driving wheel brought us nearer home.

About twilight the train stopped at the depot, and the wounded, of which there were several thousands, were taken off and sent to the different hospitals. For hours the ambulances carried their loads, and then returned for more. Those in the front cars disembarked first, and were of course chosen in turn.

When our flat was reached the surgeon told us that the hospitals were jammed, and we would have to be carried to a temporary one. We learned what that meant later on.

It seemed that the Government at Richmond had failed, as it always did, to be ready for an emergency, even such a necessary one as the taking care of its own wounded. It had made no provision for the army which came pouring in, in a steady stream, from the different battle-fields, and with criminal carelessness had, in a time when wonders could have been accomplished, calmly folded its hands and waited for a miracle to occur.

When north, east, south, and west the air was filled with the sound of the raging conflict and Richmond was girt with flame, it found the officials helplessly wringing their hands and gazing appalled at the host of maimed from the battle-fields. Every bed in the hospital was occupied, and still the long procession came steadily onward. It was at this crisis that the women of Virginia arose in their grandeur and came out in colors that shone in spotless lustre. They cast aside the natural timidity of their sex, conquering those finer feelings which make women shrink from all that is abhorrent to the sight, and met the emergency by flocking to the city from all sections, and each carried back as many patients as her household could accommodate.

A half-dozen creaky ambulances emptied our flat, and soon dumped us into the shades of Chimborazo Hospital. There is no descriptive power on earth which could convey the abomination of this dreadful place. It had been erected in the distraction of the bloody crisis, by the authorities, who lay all the winter inert, and only at the eleventh hour provided long buildings like those seen in the marble yards to protect the workmen.

I quote from my diary:

"May 28th, 1864.

"Arrived in hell last night, and now am reclining on a bag half stuffed with sawdust, which is red and sticky. Haven't seen a doctor. This place of the spirits damned is a shed of rough planks about 150 feet long, I should judge, by about 50 feet wide.

36

The coffins in which we lie are about six by three feet. Shrouds, called bed-clothes, of coarse sacking. The mattresses are stuffed with shucks, straw, sawdust—anything that comes handy. There are only two brute attendants, both black (they call them nurses, God save the mark!) to take care of us. The odor is fearful, the heat unbearable. It is sweet to die for one's country."

All that day there was only one visit from a sorely harassed surgeon, accompanied by a brutal negro, who I saw take a dead soldier, preparatory to burial, and place the stiffened limbs in all kinds of fantastic attitudes, enjoying his diabolical exhibition with as keen zest as a child playing with a doll.

The beds were so close together that a patient could touch his right and left neighbor by simply stretching his arms. A narrow window placed at intervals half lighted the room, but wholly failed in any purpose of ventilation. Not a mouthful was given us for supper or for breakfast next morning, and it was not until noon that some hardtack and rye coffee was handed around by the callous Caliban. The condition of affairs in that close-cribbed Gehenna was shocking.

On my right a young soldier had passed away peacefully during the night; I tried to attract the attention of the hospital nurse, but failed, so pulled the blanket over the dead face. On my left was a stalwart soldier who raved in delirium, with none to notice or care for him. The water given us was lukewarm and unpalatable, and the all-pervading gloom depressed the spirits. The jolting of the train had started many wounds bleeding afresh, and there should have been at least a staff of surgeons to those hundred and odd patients, every one of them wounded seriously.

The second day was but a repetition of the first. Many begged to be taken outside to lie in the sun—anywhere to get out of that dark, foul-smelling place. I wrote an urgent letter to my sister, who occupied a Government position in the city, and begged her for God's sake to get me away.

On the third day several Sisters of Charity and a robed priest entered, bringing hope and comfort with them.

Just here I desire to give a willing tribute to the devotees of that denomination. The heart of the Roman Catholic Church South was profoundly interested in the cause of Secession. Their devotion was intense, their deeds the theme of all praise. In the very smoke of the battle the priests could be seen succoring the wounded or making content the last hours of the dying.

Neither hardships nor danger could daunt those faithful men, who worked from motives holy and pure. In the hospitals the garb of the sisters was ever seen, and the woe that they alleviated the Omnipotent only knows. These divine women would "go into the highways and byways," leaving others to attend the patients in the regular hospitals, and would sally out and hunt up the unfortunate in just such festering holes as we were stewing in. Blessings upon the sisterhood with its white caps, saintly presence, meek, soft eyes and tender touch; every veteran of the Army of Northern Virginia will always hold them in a most sweet remembrance.

The three days I spent in that hospital were the most terrible of my life; with nothing to do but to fight away the bloated flies which clung to the wounded spots until they were mashed. I am convinced that a month in that Hades would either have killed or maddened any patient. Like many, I sank into a listless melancholy and cared for nothing on this mundane sphere.

On the third day my sister, accompanied by the surgeon of the post, found me, and within an hour I was transferred to a private hospital in Franklin Street.

This home was the result of the efforts of a devoted woman who, without money, collected enough by persistent endeavor from the Richmond people to found a hospital, which was supported entirely by voluntary contributions. The most seriously wounded soldiers were treated there.

Miss Sallie Tompkins was the heroine and she threw her whole soul into her work; her hospital, "The Robertson," was incomparably the best in Richmond, and lucky the soldier whose form rested upon the snowy sheets of this retreat.

Miss Sallie as a quartermaster would have been worth her weight in gold; she was a born forager, and no matter how scarce vegetables might be in the beleagured city, she always managed to secure enough for her patients; indeed, fed them so well that some of them actually grew fat and refused to go home on a wounded furlough because they had such a royal time at The Robertson, which, by the way, was situated in the most fashionable part of the city.

If the sanitary side of the house was complete, the medical department was no less so under the management of one of the most eminent surgeons in the Confederate States, and his skill was only equalled by his kindness and great heart.

Doctor A. Y. P. Garnett was probably the most popular man

among the soldiers in the South.   He effected wonderful cures
at The Robertson, and would stay by the seriously wounded day
and night, fighting death step by step.

Surely if all the wounded that Dr. Garnett pulled through and
made whole would join ranks, there would be a very strong brigade of staunch, lusty fellows, who but for him would have made
rich the soil.

To have been born a gentleman and reared as such, to prove
worthy of one's birth and training, is to have reached the summit
of every man's high ambition.   Coming from a race whose blood
was pure for generations, Dr. Garnett inherited also the bright
brain of his ancestors, and by his talents made a name which has
ever been famous in Virginia.

He was the family physician of Mr. Jefferson Davis and of
General Robert E. Lee, and an intimate social friend of the leaders of the Confederacy.   Indeed his influence over Mr. Davis
was second to none, and he was often chosen by officers high in
rank to broach schemes to the President which conspired for the
benefit of the country.

Miss Sallie made a set of rules and expected obedience from
her soldier pets, who loved her, every man of them.   At eight
A. M. breakfast was served; at ten the lady visitors came, bringing
food, wine and flowers, and many remained all day, reading to
or writing for the disabled, or assisting Miss Sallie about the
house.   At two dinner was served in the patients' rooms and in
the dining-room; at seven supper, and until nine those patients
who were able were allowed to leave the hospital for recreation
or visiting; but they were to be back punctually at the stated
hour or the door was locked; but repeated summons always
brought Miss Sallie in person.   She would not say much, but
before those rebuking eyes the bravest soldier in the Confederacy would quake.

Miss Sallie trusted to the honor of her patients, and it was
laughable to see some half-tight six-footer blush and stammer
his excuses before the reproving four feet ten inches of femi-
ninity.

There were hundreds of the wounded sent home daily from
the various hospitals, and nearly every farm-house in southside
Virginia had one or more patients to attend to.

A party of ladies from the country came to The Robertson to
choose convalescents to take back with them.   I was drawn by

a Colonel Ashlin, and was to leave the next morning, Miss Sallie promising to have my ticket and passport ready.

Now I wanted my comrade, Will Edelin, to go along, Dr. Garnett having good-naturedly said that a little rusticating would not hurt him; but he looked too rotund and rosy to pass off for a patient under treatment. I told Edelin that he should go, but he said that without his furlough and medical passport it was impossible.

He helped me into the canal boat the next morning, and when the lines were being cast off, the mules touched up and the guard was driving everybody ashore whose papers were not *en regle,* I was taken with a succession of fainting spells, and hung on to Edelin so tightly and implored the guards so piteously not to take him from me, that despite his orders he weakened, and my friend was soon sitting on deck under the awning, as blithe as a cricket.

After an all-night journey we disembarked at Columbia, in Fluvanna County, where a carriage awaited our coming, and after a drive of about ten miles, reached our destination.

Our host was a genial, whole-souled man; his household consisted of two charming daughters. His estate lay on the Rivanna River, directly at the Falls. Two great mills, the property of Colonel Ashlin, supplied the whole country with flour.

This region of Virginia was rich, the famous valley never having been trod by a hostile foot. The Rivanna River turned the great wheels, the grist was ground as regularly and as well as if the "dogs of war" were chained, and the canal boat glided undisturbed on its way; and the driver's tin horn, instead of the bugle, echoed along the vales.

It was a soft place for a wounded soldier; such abundance of food I never dreamed existed in the Confederacy. Four kinds of bread for breakfast, and great racks of ice-cream, frozen solid, every day for dinner, and of course substantials *ad lib*.

Every dwelling in the surrounding country had its inmates, who received as much devoted care as if they had been the best beloved of the household.

Every girl in Virginia had her share of nursing to do, and it was too common to excite remark to see some wounded soldier. who had been carried into the farmer's house dirty, unkempt, and literally in rags, emerge therefrom spick, span and clean, with underclothing made from the garments of the girls, who had sacrificed their own comfort for the man who could pull a trigger.

The privates despised the drivelling and infirm Government at Richmond, and they had no affection for Mr. Jefferson Davis, who was never *en rapport* with the soldiery.

The President loved to be surrounded by a brilliant staff, and pomp and parade was dear to his soul. A private soldier was to him a thing of shreds and tatters, a being to be avoided, and I question if a ragged, powder-grimed Reb would have been admitted to an audience with the Chief Magistrate.

In searching the pages of my note-book I find only one sentiment of the soldiery, freely expressed at their camp-fires, and that was a deep hostility to President Davis, his Cabinet and his whole Administration.

This unfriendliness began in the summer of 1861, when Mr. Davis insisted on retaining Commissary-General Northrup in office, notwithstanding the protest of General Beauregard.

Northrup's administration was simply idiotic, and in the very midst of plenty the army was put on short rations. The appointment and retention of General John H. Winder as provost marshal was a most unfortunate step, as was also the forced resignation of Mr. Randolph as Secretary of War and the appointment of Judah P. Benjamin in his place.

Mr. Benjamin was a brilliant lawyer, but he knew as much about war as an Arab knows of the Sermon on the Mount. The pages of Vattel and of Grotius were more familiar to him than Upton tactics or Jomini's precepts.

Then Mr. Davis's constant interference in military affairs made him most unpopular with the Army. This dissatisfaction steadily increased, and had General Lee at any time desired to play the role of despot, a simple hint would have been sufficient. His trusty bayonets would have placed him, as the Ironsides of Monk and Fairfax exalted Cromwell, at the head of a Republic.

The truth of this is proven by a well-known fact: after the return of Lee from the unfortunate Gettysburg Campaign, while at Orange Court House, he placed his resignation in Mr. Davis's hands to be accepted or rejected. This leaked out and created thrilling excitement among his veterans. Had Mr. Davis accepted General Lee's abdication, there would have been an uprising which would have swept away the Confederate Government within twenty-four hours after the truth was known. I do not believe that General Lee in person could have held the soldiery in check; some would have grasped his horse's reins and have cried out as they did in the Wilderness, "General Lee to the

rear!" Then with steady tramp, sixty thousand Rebels, the survivors of scores of battles, would have marched into Richmond
calmly, coolly, deliberately, and there would have been such an
upheaval of Government as was never seen since the crumble of
the Bourbon race when Louis the Eighteenth was King. I
state but a simple fact; there would have been no meeting, but
simply a movement that generals, colonels, officers and privates
would have indulged in. Nobody, who did not live in those days,
can accurately estimate the white heat of passion that would have
pervaded the Army of Northern Virginia had the news gone from
lip to lip that President Davis had accepted the resignation of Rob-.
ert E. Lee.

CHAPTER XXII.

PRIVATE LAMBERT'S SHOT.

Just at this time another wounded soldier received his billet at the Ashlin's. He was a tall, athletic young fellow, and report said, a dauntless soldier; his name was Hardy; a native of Norfolk, Virginia, and a member of the Richmond Howitzers. He was as fine a raconteur as I ever listened to; and one of his stories so interested us all that I jotted it down as it fell from his lips.

"Talking of shots," said Hardy, meditatively stroking his moustache, "puts me in mind of the greatest artillery discharge made during the war."

"Is it true," queried Colonel Ashlin, "or is it a story like Will Edelin is hatching in his head now?"

"What is it, Will?" inquired one of Colonel Ashlin's daughters.

"What is what?" answered the little infantryman.

"That story that father said you were hatching in your head."

"O," he answered, "I was only thinking of Captain Flynn's shot. But go on, Hardy, and tell us your story."

"No," said the artilleryman, "peace before war; after you have finished your yarn, I'll begin mine."

"Out with it, Will," said Colonel Ashlin. "I know it's worth hearing."

"Well, when Hardy there spoke of a great shot I was reminded of a pretty tall one that did considerable damage down on the Eastern Shore of Maryland. It happened long before I was born, but the story has been handed down from father to son.

"There was an old Irishman named Captain Flynn who owned a small schooner which plied along the Potomac River and its estuaries, buying fowls, fruits and garden truck from the country people and selling them in the Baltimore markets.

"It happened that the Captain, a week before Christmas, dropped anchor off Cutler's Creek, and there came an unexpected freeze, and for four days he was held hard and fast. All his meat gave out, so he traveled over the ice to the home of one of his best customers, a spinster named Miss Tilda Jenks, who made her living by raising poultry.

"Miss Tilly was cited among her neighbors as being the sharpest and the shrewdest bargainer in the whole country round; indeed some of the old hands said that she could even beat a preacher in a horse trade.

"When Captain Flynn went to purchase a dozen fowls the ancient spinster promptly doubled her price. This made the old Captain so mad that he went back to his sloop, swearing he would starve before he would pay it. Then ensued a struggle between his stomach and his pride, which resulted in his going back the next day and paying the spinster her price. As he saw the great number of fowls in the enclosure he said:

" 'Miss Tilly, how much will you charge me to let me shoot in the thick of them, an' let me have all I kill?'

"The woman studied for a while and then answered:

" 'Captain, if you let me load your gun you kin have all you kill for one dollar.'

" 'Bedad! an' it's a bargain, an' here's your dollar,' answered the Irishman, 'an' now I'll go fer me gun.'

"He hurried back to his boat, got out an ancient bell-mouthed blunderbuss that had belonged to his grandfather, put in a handful of powder, rammed in a bunch of tow; next a double handful of shot was dropped down the barrel and held tight with another bunch of tow; then Captain Flynn sawed off about four fingers of the ramrod, picked the flint, called his crew, which consisted of an antiquated darky, and proceeded inland.

"Miss Tilly first carefully measured the gun with the ramrod, then, despite the protest of the Captain, she loaded the gun with only a thimbleful of powder and one of shot.

" 'A bargain is a bargain, Captain,' she said tauntingly, 'and here's your gun; now you can have all you kill.'

"Captain Flynn asked for an ear of corn; this he shelled along for about a hundred yards from the woodpile, then lying behind a log, he signified to Miss Tilly that he was ready.

"The gate was opened and the fowls of all sizes, sexes and condition came running, flying and fluttering out, and there was a confused mass of heads, wings and feathers mixed up as far as the eye could reach. The Captain sighted along the line, and uttered a prayer; the darky got behind a tree and clapped his hands over his ears; the spinster stood with her horn spectacles on her forehead, serene and confident; then the Captain, having finished his orisons, pulled the trigger. There was a thundering report that reverberated clean to the Virginia shore and back, then the smoke covered everything; when it lifted, there was the Captain, sitting up, rubbing his shoulder; Miss Tilly had her arms raised to heaven, crying, 'I'm ruined and undone!'

"The darky was dancing a jig.

"The spoils were counted: sixteen chickens, twelve guinea keets, five hen turkeys, one gobbler, two geese, two pigeons, four ducks and the old lady's pet pig."

"Well, well," said Colonel Ashlin, "you know I am strictly temperate, but Mary shall make you a julep for that story; now go on, Mr. Hardy, with your narrative."

"Well, my story is very much like Will Edelin's—it shows the power of a range shot, and it is the solemn truth, although it sounds incredible. I saw the shot with my own eyes, for I was Number 4 of the gun, and know the incident has been the theme of almost every camp-fire in the Army.

"You all know when Grant made his sudden onset on Lee at Spottsylvania, so as to split his army in two, he used every artifice to conceal his movements and then relied for success upon his heavy attacks and sudden charges. He was successful, for he broke through our lines like a tempest, shivering to pieces everything in his path, and capturing General Edward Johnson and his entire division. The line was re-established with great loss. In consequence of this, extraordinary efforts were made to prevent any more surprises, and the troops were cautioned to be on the alert, and be ready on the instant to repel any attack the wily, determined enemy might make.

"Of course you all know the Richmond Howitzers by reputation. There is not a soldier in the Army of Northern Virginia who has not heard them spoken of again and again in the bivouac. Probably no finer batteries ever served in the world; every battle was but another record of their triumph.

"During the series of savage assaults of Grant at Spottsylvania the position of the First Company of Howitzers was on the left of the center. The whole army had thrown up hasty breastworks protecting their front.

"The position which the Howitzers occupied was intended for a battery breastwork; there were embrasures for the guns, with the earth shovelled high on each side. Connecting, there were the rifle-pits of the infantry on the right. Just here came in a peculiarity of construction which every one noticed. It could not have been through design, but on this singularity hangs the whole action.

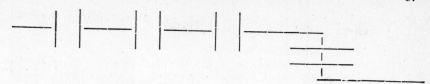

"This line of works was built directly across a large field which was bounded in front, about a quarter of a mile away, by a thick covert.

"The Howitzers were but a section, and had but two guns, which were on the left and adjoining the infantry, and the two guns of a North Carolina battery were immediately upon the left.

"Now bear in mind, the breastworks for the artillery were in length about twenty yards, the guns being about fifteen feet apart, a distance which gave us ample room to work them. Our breastworks were not immediately joined to the infantry entrenchments, but were fully twelve feet in front; thus the rifle-pits extended through the entire length of the field to an impassable swamp on the right, which was commanded by two batteries of artillery on a hill beyond. The field was nearly level along the line, except where it dipped gently in the center, close to the rifle-pits.

"It was a warm, sultry May morning and absolute silence reigned along the whole front. The artillerymen, wearied by their hard work of the past week, lay among their guns, almost to a man sound asleep, leaving the task of keeping watch to the infantry. All were not asleep, though, for another soldier besides myself sat on top of the breastworks. We were smoking our pipes and looking with a good deal of curiosity at the Texans and the Eighth Georgia, for it was the famous 'Hood's brigade' which held this part of the line. The command had joined in a score of conflicts and its battle-flags bearing the names of the engagements almost hid the stars and bars—that glorious brigade whose coming to the front in a double-quick had often brought hope to many a sorely-pressed regiment.

"Neither officers nor men expected any trouble that morning. The brigade was stretched on the ground in an aspect of contented rest. The soldiers, with that knowledge which the veterans have of making themselves comfortable, had by means of their guns and bayonets formed a rough shelter, on the top of which were stretched their blankets and oilcloths; even the sentries had grown tired of pacing their beat, and with the *sang froid* which prevails in our army, were sitting down with their muskets across their laps, half asleep.

"All at once a singular sound was borne upon the air; a curious, muffled noise like the tread of many feet. The lookout heard it, got up, yawned, stretched himself and gave a careless look in the direction from which it came. One glance was sufficient; with a blood-curdling yell he fired his musket. Instantly every man jumped to his feet; the embryo tents disappeared, the line formed in a second, the artillerymen sprang to their guns, cool, collected, ready for the fray.

"There in front was a sight to cause a warrior's blood to thrill. A gallant, glorious sight, with all the panoply of warfare.

"Issuing from the dark woods in splendid array were three lines of battle, with an interval of about seventy-five yards between them. They were coming in a double-quick and were now fully half way across the meadow, evidently intending to carry the works by a *coup de main*. The lines of blue advanced solidly, quietly and portentously in their silence, awful in their power.

"The loud tones of our officers came quick and decisive. Each soldier in the infantry grasped his rifle, the gunner in the battery sighted his piece. The foe, seeing that they were discovered, broke into a hurrah and increased their speed.

"In an instant the four guns bellowed, dense blue-black smoke hiding everything for a moment from view. The discharge made wide gaps in the mass but did not check them in the slightest. Those were veteran troops fighting under the eye of the splendid Hancock, and were doing well the work that was cut out for them. Their line was not extended nor did it overlap the artillery; the sole attack seemed to be squarely against the infantry, and they did not seem to care about the artillery at all.

"Again the guns, double shotted, poured death and destruction into their ranks. They staggered, the long line vibrated, but stiffened and advanced—always advanced. But when that ominous deadly musketry volley was heard, then was seen the result. They wavered, turned and fled, leaving many of their number lying on the field.

"The second line came on a run, the officers well in front, waving their swords and leading straight on to the works. The guns opened their storm of iron. The Texans hurled the murderous lead and the foes fell in scores, but still these grim warriors of the Army of the Potomac breasted the tempest and kept up their resistless advance. They neared the works and then for the first time pulled triggers at a few paces. A line of fire ran down their line, followed by the purple smoke, then forward they dashed until they reached the rifle-pits.

"Their right did not extend far enough to encircle or overlap the guns; they were within a few feet of them as they halted for a second. They were now safe from the artillery, which turned its attention to the third line of battle, now about a hundred yards away and just pulling for the breastworks.

"It was a moment of furious excitement, and the day seemed lost to the Rebels. The Texans had just given ground and their line had been forced back some paces in the rear of the works, when they seemed determined to make a stand, but it would have been in vain. The third line, once up, would rush like a tidal-wave and overwhelm the already staggering brigade before re-inforcements could come.

"The Yankees were strung out all along the ground at the foot of the works, calling upon their comrades to follow. The end seemed near; one rush and all would have been over. Their triumphant cheer rose, heralding victory.

"The battery was served as it could only be worked by men who knew that moments were precious. How those dogs of war barked in one successive roar, sending grape and canister into the mass of men.

"The second line reached the works and the guns were now rapidly served on the advancing third line of battle. The artillery had work to perform in its front. The artillerymen's blood-shot eyes gazed out of the clouds of dim smoke at the last line of blue, against whom they were hurling their iron bolts. All were looking—all save one, who in that time of awful peril and appalling commotion kept his head clear, his senses cool, his nerve steady. Amid all those scenes of dire disaster, screams of the wounded, yells of combatants, the hurly-burly of the death-dealing missiles hurling through space, there Private Lambert, of the Richmond Howitzers, turned and gazed around, taking in the whole situation. He was attached to the right-hand gun.

"I had just rammed the charge home, the other had primed the piece and the gunner had hastily sighted at the line of blue, which was not seventy yards distant. The cannon was charged to the muzzle.

"'All right!' cried the sergeant.

"The detail scattered to right and left, the lanyard was just about to be pulled, when up spoke Private Lambert:

" 'Hold up, men.' His military intuition had caught a great idea. The arm nerved to pull the string relaxed; he sprang to the trail of the gun, and calling upon me to help him up, he seized the handspike and slung it around in a semicircle until the muzzle projected over the right angle so as to rake the breastwork. The mouth of the gun was only a few feet from the right of the enemy's line which stood pouring its volley into the Texans. The man who held the lanyard, instantly divining Lambert's wishes, gave the line a jerk. The charge exploded with a thundering report and the cannon, full from the belly to the throat, raked the whole line.

"For a few moments the smoke which poured forth hid the scene, but it soon lifted, and there were the ranks motionless, dazed, turned into statues. Even the Yankee soldiers, who held their muskets leveled, with fingers upon the triggers, seemed to have forgotten to fire, and turned their terror-stricken countenances and looked in the direction from whence came that stunning report—that fatal shot. It was as mortal as the dart hurled at Phaeton.

"Then the whole force, demoralized for the time, hesitated. The delay was fatal. The yells of the Rebel reserves were heard as they hurried to the front, and put new life into the defenders. The Texans hearing this, sent forth a burst of fire and charged over the breastwork into the foe.

"Broken and shattered by that terrible flanking discharge, and feeling that the assault was a failure, they ran into and stampeded the third line of supports, and all retreated to the friendly shelter of the woods.

"It was a glorious victory, plucked from out the very jaws of defeat. The artillerymen were at first utterly dumfounded at the magic power of one shot, and the inexplicable rout of the foe at the very moment when the cheer of triumph was lingering upon their lips. An examination of the ground along the breastworks revealed the mystery.

"Heavens, what a shot! Private Lambert, with that quickness of perception which makes military genius of the highest kind, whether found in the general or the rank and file, perceived that it would be more fatal to enfilade the line than to fire across the field at the supports. He had the nerve, in that moment of supreme danger, to carry out the plan. When he whirled the gun sharply around, the muzzle covered a long line of some four hundred yards, which, owing to the breastwork of the battery being some twelve feet in advance of the rifle-pits, had the effect of raking the entire line, just as boys climb the telegraph poles by nailing foot pieces, so as to fire along the wire when the swallows sit close together.

"But that cannon shot! The effect was awful! Such a deadly discharge was never fired before in America. Eleven lay killed. Those close to the gun were so mangled as to be past recognition of anything like humanity. Twenty-seven wounded, nearly all fatally, most of the poor fellows dying soon after being carried into the field hospital.

"The Texans crowded up, and in their hearty soldier fashion congratulated the Howitzers in extravagant terms, sincere and honest, however, and the artillerymen felt that a compliment from them, as far as fighting was concerned, was the highest praise they could ever receive.

"General Pendleton, Chief of Artillery, visited the field that evening and said that it could not be equaled in the annals of war; yet Private Lambert is 'Private Lambert' still. He was honored by having his name read at dress parade, but that was all. Napoleon would have made him colonel of artillery on the spot. He had shown that he had the born intuition of a soldier, without which all military training is lost; yet 'Private Lambert' will remain 'Private Lambert.' "

It must have been this incident that Major Robert Stiles, a member of the Howitzers, speaks of in his book, "Four Years under Marse Robert" (p. 254):

"The troops supporting the two Napoleon guns of the Howitzers were, as I remember, the Seventh (or Eighth) Georgia and the First Texas. Toward the close of the day everything seemed to have quieted down, in a sort of implied truce. There was absolutely no firing, either of musketry or cannon. Our weary, hungry infantry stacked arms and were cooking their mean and meagre little rations. Some one rose up, and looking over the works—it was shading down a little toward the dark—cried out: 'Hello! What's this? Why, here come our men on a run, from—no, by Heavens! it's the Yankees!' and before anyone could realize the situation or even start toward the stacked muskets, the Federal column broke over the little work, between our troops and their arms, bayoneted or shot two or three who were asleep, and dashed upon the men crouched over their low fires

—with cooking utensils instead of weapons in their hands. Of course they ran. What else could they do?

"The Howitzers—only the left, or Napoleon section, was there —sprang to their guns, swinging them around to bear inside our lines, double-shotted them with canister and fairly spouted it into the Federals, whose formation had been broken in the rush and the plunge over the works, and who seemed to be somewhat massed and huddled and hesitating, but only a few rods away. Quicker almost than I can tell it, our infantry supports, than whom there were not two better regiments in the Army, had rallied and gotten to their arms, and then they opened out into a V-shape, and fairly tore the head of the Federal column to pieces. In an incredibly short time those who were able to do so turned to fly and our infantry were following them over the entrenchments; but it is doubtful whether this would have been the result had it not been for the prompt and gallant action of the artillery."

Take another instance, this time from my own command. Let the following tell the tale:

"Hdqrs. Cav. Corps, Army of Northern Virginia.
"April 14th, 1864.

"Colonel:

"I have the honor to report the following affair (*petite guerre*) which occurred near Catlett's Station on the 11th instant:

"Privates Richard Lewis and A. A. Marstella, both of Black Horse Cavalry, met with a party of four officers of the regular army, U. S. Army (a captain and three lieutenants). These two gallant scouts attacked the party, Lewis confronting the leading two, while Marstella presented his pistol at the two in the rear. One of these, Captain (Samuel) McKee, of the Second U. S. Infantry, offered resistance but was eventually killed. Not, however, until he had fired twice at his assailant. The Captain's comrade took advantage of this rencounter and escaped. Marstella having despatched McKee, reinforced Lewis, when the two remaining officers surrendered. They are First Lieutenants (James) Butler and (Thomas) Burns (Byrne?) of the Second U. S. Infantry, evidently veterans promoted for meritorious conduct from the ranks. They have been brought safely to my headquarters. This all took place within a short distance of the camp of a portion of the Fifth Federal Corps.

"The commanding general's attention is respectfully invited to these instances of the exhibition of extraordinary bravery and individual prowess. The officers were all armed and mounted, were veterans of the Regular Army—one says twenty years in the service.

"Would it be improper to send this report to His Excellency the President?

"Most respectfully, your obedient servant,

"J. E. B. STUART,
"*Major-General.*

"To COL. W. H. TAYLOR,
"*A. A. General.*

"(Indorsement No. 1.)
"Headquarters Army Northern Virginia.
"April 15th, 1864.

"Respectfully forwarded for the information of the Department in connection with this report on the same subject transmitted yesterday.   R. E. LEE,
"*General.*

"(Indorsement No. 2.)
"April 28th, 1864.

"Respectfully submitted to the President in compliance with a suggestion of General Stuart. As a bold deed it may instruct and please.   J. A. SEDDEN,
"*Secretary of War.*"

"May instruct and please!" As if the war was conducted for that purpose. Both of these scouts were educated gentlemen, well qualified to command a regiment, yet they remained privates in the ranks.

What an army could have been made, had valor and skill been the sole prerequisite to promotion. The efficiency of the Army of Northern Virginia would have been greatly increased. But Mr. Davis opposed such proceedings, and the privates made no protest. "When we are an established nation," I have heard hundreds say, and have said the same myself, "then I will join the Regular Army and claim that rank which rightfully belongs to me."

37

CHAPTER XXIV.

A TYPICAL VIRGINIA PLANTATION.

I remained nearly six weeks in this charming retreat. Edelin had left days before, so fat that he had hard work to cram himself into his uniform. By the aid of crutches I could amble my way readily, and so I determined to spend the rest of my furlough at the old family estate in south-side Virginia.

Two days of travel, broken by many delays, brought me to ancient Tower Hill, a grand old estate of a couple of thousand acres, situated on the Nottoway River, some twenty-five miles south of Petersburg, and which for two hundred years had been known by no other name.

The mansion was the kind often seen on the Hudson River a century ago; wide and roomy, with steep Dutch roof and dormer windows. On the left, about twenty yards distant, was ranged the double kitchen, the work-rooms, a meat-house, chicken coops, and store-rooms. In front of this, diagonally, were two large cottages used by members of the family and guests; one, especially, being given over to the bachelors, of whom there was always a relay on hand.

Shadowing the ladies' cottage was an immense English oak, which was the pride of the place. Upon the left was the cotton-house, peanut rooms and granaries. A large barn stood near, flanked by a long row of corn-houses.

Down in a hollow, about a hundred yards from the mansion, were the quarters of the slaves, scattered without order and generally built under the projecting arms of some big tree. A neat white-washed paling enclosed each house and garden, for these were the slaves' perquisites, their mistress buying up all their produce, which often ran up to a large sum. Everything about their cabins was neat and clean, and they were compelled to obey the sanitary orders of my aunt, who was the queen of that commune.

Down the road, next the vast orchards, was the still-house and the various buildings attached; here was stilled every year hundreds of gallons of apple brandy, the neighbors sending their carts loaded with apples to the still as regularly as they sent their grain for grinding to the mill.

Tower Hill worked over two hundred slaves, and looked like a thriving, industrious village. It was self-supporting. The sheep furnished the wool, and there were regular carders and spinners as well as dressmakers and tailors. My cousins were all becomingly dressed from the looms, and my uncle had a tasty Confederate uniform made entirely upon the place. Everybody was proud of that costume, from the little darky who picked the wool, to my aunt who furnished the Hungarian knot on the sleeve.

Superabundance of everything was here; chickens by the thousands, hogs by the hundreds in the woods, while droves of cattle fattened on the island, a portion of the estate about three miles from the house. The cellar was stored with barrels of old apple and peach brandy, while the store-room was a sight to behold, crammed with pickles and preserves.

The house and cottages were filled with guests and members of the family, refugees who had abandoned their homes in the enemy's lines and had flocked to the old roof tree, there to await the issue of arms. Over twenty-five of the kinsmen sat at the table every day, and the usual peaceful routine was kept up.

The elder sisters kept school for the younger, the matrons sewed for the soldiers, the mistress took her husband's place in the supervision of the estate, and the slaves worked along contentedly, though freedom could be had for the asking. A request to leave was granted by the master through necessity, for if refused, the slave had only to walk off into the Yankee camps, which almost surrounded this section.

Suffolk, about twenty miles north, and Reams' Station east, were both occupied by the Union forces, who welcomed all contrabands; yet during the whole four years of the war only four slaves left Tower Hill, showing that the mild, paternal government to which they were subject was not hateful to them, and that they were willing to wait for freedom, but would never have lifted their fingers to strike off their fetters.

They worked easily and were not driven. They had their hogs and poultry, and some had milch cows, and all took pride in their gardens. Every one was comfortably clothed, and as it was a famous game country, their larders were well stocked, not only with hogs and hominy, but with a menu that few citizens sat down to.

If they wanted to go to freedom and were kept back by fear, they had a good opportunity a few days before my arrival, for

Cavalryman Wilson and his blue-jackets made the first raid of the war in that section, and over-ran Tower Hill for a couple of hours. Every darky took to the woods, and did not emerge until after "dem Yankees done gone."

I must tell of this Yankee foray, for it stirred up the people who, though free from a direct invasion, could yet hear the boom of the cannonading at Petersburg.

General Wilson started out with several thousand troopers to cut the Petersburg and Welden Railroad and play the mischief generally. He was headed off by Mahone, Fitz Lee, and W. H. F. Lee, and utterly routed. He burned all of his wagons, spiked his guns and made his way as best he could to his own lines. His command was scattered all over the country, trying to put the Nottaway between them and the cavalry of the two Lees.

It was a cloudless hot day at old Tower Hill, on the 29th of June, 1864. A locust which made its home in the ancient oak followed the birds' matin song with his harsh treble throughout the heated hours.

It was near the noon hour; old Colonel Blow, the owner of the estate, sat dozing in his armchair in the shade of the oak, the children were in the school-room and the pack of hounds lay scattered around, some asleep and some snapping at the droning blue-bottle flies which cluster about a hound in preference to any other animal.

Captain Blow, of the Thirteenth Virginia Cavalry, and a finer soldier never followed the Southern cause, was home on a short furlough and had strolled down the road in the direction of Peter's Bridge. Feeling tired and dusty, he stopped at the foot of a branching cedar, and lighting his pipe, reclined in the angle of the snake fence. He was dreamily puffing away when he heard the beat of hoofs coming toward him. With the instinct of a true cavalryman he loosened his Colt's in the holster, and not dreaming of any danger, kept quiet until three blue-coats reined up directly in front of him. Both parties were amazed, but the Captain pulled himself together first and got the initial shot, which shattered the right arm of one of them. The other two shot several times, but were too excited and fired wild. Captain Blow's third shot struck the second blue-coat in the stomach, and he put spurs to his horse and rode off, followed by the others.

It was over a mile to the house, and the thermometer was in the neighborhood of a hundred in the shade. Captain Blow weighed two hundred and ten pounds and had the lumbago badly, but he went across the fallow and field, through the thickets, over ploughed ground until at last, almost spent, he reached his dwelling.

Seizing the huge tin horn on the kitchen shelf he blew a sturdy blast, then another and yet another. It was a signal for the hands to come to the mansion, and they dropped the hoe in the cornfield, left the plough in the furrow, and all, big and little, young and old, ran for the house.

"Fore God, Marse William, what's de matter?" was the cry.

"Bring my horse; the Yankees are coming!"

The announcement set the entire plantation in a fine commotion. The old negro-women threw their aprons over their heads and went into camp-meeting lamentations; the women of the household fled to their rooms to hide their valuables; the dusky maidens hied themselves like so many Dianas to the dim forests; the dogs barked, the guineas cackled and the dusky children broke into howls.

In the meantime the Captain was not losing a moment. The wagons were hitched by his orders, and came lumbering into the yard like a battery taking position.

The liquor was loaded the very first thing; next the trunks and personal effects, then the meat-house was stripped bare. Another gang of hands was driving all the horses, cattle, swine and sheep back into the woods, and every one worked with snap that did wonders. In half an hour the place was swept bare; then the Captain upon his thoroughbred swept down the road on a scout, and came flying back with the startling intelligence that a battalion of Yankees was not a half mile distant. He cautioned the females of the family to be polite; he warned his father, whose eighty years did not dim his fiery patriotism nor blunt the edge of his tongue, to keep strict guard over himself and give no provocation for violence. Then the captain galloped off to the woods, leaving half a dozen Niobes behind him.

With a clatter, a couple of hundred Yankee cavalrymen rode into the yard. They were not in rank and were evidently badly disorganized and almost faint with hunger and fatigue; some were so tired that they went to sleep in their saddles the moment the horse stopped.

Three officers were at their head, their uniforms torn, faces covered with dust and streaked with perspiration. They dismounted in the yard, from their panting, heavy horses, as did many of the men, who scattered around the lawn on a voyage of discovery.

"Hello, there!" they shouted, "anybody at home?"

The door of the house opened and a delegation met them. Old Colonel Blow, with his head in the air and his snow-white hair falling beneath his Panama hat, reaching his shoulders; my aunt, with compressed lips and her diminutive form drawn up to its utmost height; Mammy Hettie, the ruler of the female department of the plantation, a tall, stately negress, who wore a white turban which made her dignified presence doubly imposing; several little negroes of the female sex, from three to five years of age, acting as aides, clung to her gown.

The officers saluted, my aunt bowed, the old Colonel took off his hat, while Mammy Hettie's turban bobbed up and down.

"We must search the house," said an officer. "Two of our men have been shot, and the bushwhacker was seen to ride in this direction. Here, sergeant, take a file of men and see if there are any damn Rebels hid away."

"Sir!" roared the Colonel, "this is my private house. I give you my word of honor there is no one here except my daughters and their children."

"Oh, of course not!" sarcastically said the first speaker. "Go ahead, sergeant."

"I hope," said my aunt, her cheeks crimson and her eyes sparkling with anger, "that you will not rob the house of anything."

"If plunder is your object," hotly spoke up the Colonel, "your thieves better be quick, or you will be caught in the act."

The captain grew angry and uttered a taunt, when the second officer stepped forward and urged him not to search the house, that he had no time and that it was a harsh proceeding anyway; that a house was the very last place in the world in which a bushwhacker would hide. So the sergeant was recalled.

"Have you anything to drink?" asked number 1.

"No," said Colonel Blow, "the cellar is empty; but send one of your men down, he may be able to discover something."

"How far is it to Petersburg?" asked number 2; "and can the Nottoway be forded elsewhere?"

"About one mile down that road," answered the Colonel. "The river has only a few private fords. But may I ask how came you in such condition?"

"Some of Wilson's damn ignorance," responded the officer. "He ought to be shot by drumhead court martial. Three days ago he started on a wild-goose expedition against Lee's communications, and ran into a whole Rebel cavalry brigade, supported by heavy infantry force, which surrounded us, and a perfect trap he walked into—half of us killed, all our guns lost, and a few squadrons like ours escaped, and for three days we have been in the saddle and are utterly played out."

The old Colonel listened eagerly, and his slow pulse beat with the fire of youth. He was a bitter secessionist, none more so in the land, but he was a gentleman, and the laws of hospitality were as sacred as his religion; so he said with his courtly bow, "Gentlemen, if you will walk up to my sideboard I can offer you some very fair brandy, and my daughter will provide you with a lunch."

So the party proceeded to the dining-room, and my aunt put up food for them to take away. The men were helping themselves, as they soon had proof. One of "Mammy Hettie's" aides rushed in, her eyes bulging out, and screamed: "O Mammy Hettie! dem Yankees dun ketched ole Chantyclear an' am wringin' his hed off!"

Hettie sniffed, "I lubbed dat rooster; he done wake me in de mornin' for years; dunno how I'se goin' to do now."

Another bare-legged aide, her black skin a shade paler from fright, came dashing in. "O Marm Hettie an' Miss Livie, de Yankees dun busted in de co'n-house do' an' stealin' all de co'n!"

Mammy Hettie groaned, threw up her eyes and shook her turban dismally.

Still a third aide, a little kinky-haired African, fairly rolled into the room. "O Marm Hettie, dem Yankees is in de kitchen an' dun took de dinner off'n de fire!"

"I will go and stop that," said the second officer, who was evidently a gentleman. "You need not be afraid, madam, of any private property being disturbed."

In a few moments the party was assembled upon the porch. Old Tower Hill never beheld another such scene during its whole existence. There sat a score or so of cavalrymen, their heads upon their horses' necks, sound asleep; others were stretched out under the oak in the shade, some were emptying the corn-house and feeding their horses, others were searching the stables, but it is needless to add, found nothing but empty stalls; some were chasing the turkeys and geese over the lawn, and such a clattering, clucking and flapping of wings was never heard before.

All at once there came a sound which struck upon every ear.
Boom!

"The Rebels are coming!" cried the first officer. "Here, bugler, sound 'boots and saddles.' Fall in, men, fall in!"

A dozen cannon shots, not five miles away, heard in quick succession, quickened their motions, and soon every man was mounted.

"Here, old woman, don't you want to go with us and be free?" cried a trooper to Hettie; "here's a led-horse."

Mammy Hettie absolutely swelled with indignation.

"Go long! I b'longs to de quality an' don't 'sociate wid such as you."

"I've a great mind to blow your head off, you black imp you!" shouted the trooper, whose temper was not improved by the laughter of his comrades.

"I ain't no imp. You jes' better look out, our sogers jes' gobble you all up; see ef de' don't!"

"Shut up, old kink-head," shouted back the trooper.

"You better be gwine off here. Ef our sogers done see you dar will be some tall runnin'; dun run yourself near to def now. Ho, ho, ho!" and Mammy Hettie danced a war dance on the lawn.

Another peal from the cannon hastened their departure and the irregular body soon disappeared down the road. So ended the first and last raid on old Tower Hill, whose secluded position was its best safeguard.

By night all the wagons had returned with their stores, the cattle were driven back into the farmyard, and the irruption left nothing but a memory which is talked of to this day.

The soldier who was shot by Captain Blow died in a short time and was buried not far from where he fell—one of the thousand Northerners who fell in single combat and whose name was marked "missing" on the roster, and whose fate could only be conjectured by his comrades and kinsmen.

Many of those missing were ascribed to bushwhackers, but there was little of that in Virginia. Those Federal troopers owed their taking off to regularly enrolled partisan rangers, or soldiers on furlough, who rarely used severe measures unless cornered.

Those rangers conducted war on the same plan exactly as Morgan, and Marion, the Swamp Fox, did in the dark days of the Revolution, and history has ennobled the men of Seventy-six in high honor, not degraded them.

Speaking of Marion, the "Swamp Fox," as the British called

him, reminds me of a steel engraving that hung over the mantel in my home. It portrayed the dinner given by Marion to some captured officers of Tarleton's command, and was nothing more nor less than some roasted sweet potatoes.

I would gaze upon the picture in boyish wonder, and think if it was really true that men could live on such diet?

In war times, when nearly famished, I often recalled that picture, and would think, "O, how happy I could be if I only had some of General Marion's potatoes!"

CHAPTER XXV.

A couple of months at Tower Hill made me one of the army of convalescents, and discarding crutches I pushed my way to Richmond, determined to rejoin the Black Horse as soon as practicable.

August was a succession of blazing, scorching weather; in the daytime the rays of the sun beat down with blinding heat. The torrid waves seemed to hang palpable and lurid in the thoroughfares. Every one fled to the shade, and with the exception of the always-toiling ambulance, Richmond seemed as a deserted town. But after the sun set the city awoke; shutters and doors were thrown open and the streets were gay with mingled colors. On every porch sat white-robed ladies, their snowy dresses contrasting with the inevitable gray uniforms; wounded and convalescent soldiers would be seen in all directions, with every variety of hurt; some with faces bandaged, others with their bodies swathed, arms and legs in splints, or worse still, recently amputated, they walked, hobbled or rode, enjoying the night wind which cooled the torrid atmosphere.

At this time soldiers and people were radiant with hope, and all thought the war would soon end.

Indeed, to such a pitch had their confidence reached, that the young men and maidens, when they entered into an engagement to marry, agreed that it should take place as soon as the treaty of peace between the two sections was signed.

It is true that the people had often been buoyed up with proud hopes, only to have them dashed to the earth again, but their belief had rarely been so firm before. Their faith, like a river that ebbed and flowed, was now at high-water mark, and well it might have been; a glance at the military situation showed that the gigantic plans of the foe were in every case foiled.

The splendid Army of the Potomac, one hundred and fifty thousand strong, which left the Rapidan on the second of May, en route to Richmond, after some ten weeks of constant fighting, in which it met check after check, still advanced until shocked and paralyzed by the fearful slaughter of Cold Harbor. It then gave up the cherished plan of a straight overland march to Richmond, and transferred the scene of operations to the south side, going into an entrenched camp.

Butler, who with over twenty thousand men was to storm and capture Richmond in the rear, was himself assailed with resistless fury by Beauregard, and driven back in disorder, lay inert under shelter of his guns, amusing himself in the meantime by digging the Dutch Gap Canal, and shooting mortar shells in the night; a species of pyrotechnics that amused and amazed all the negroes who lived along the banks of the classic James, and caused them to wonder "what dem Yankees was doin', bustin' fire in de air dat away."

General David Hunter, who started with boasting words on his lips as he headed a column up the wide, fertile Valley, with some fifteen thousand men, whose task it was to capture Lexington, destroy the canal, which was one of the main arteries supplying the Rebel Capital with sustenance, and to burn Lynchburg, demolish the railroad and thus isolate Richmond, was met on his way as he was ravaging the fair country with fire and sword, by Early, and forced to a rapid flight, and barely succeeded in saving his demoralized command from annihilation.

Sigel, the ever-trying but unfortunate Sigel, who advanced to capture Staunton, was met at New Market by Breckenridge and the infant battalion of the Virginia Military Institute, and driven in headlong haste across the Shenandoah.

The great cavalry raids by Wilson and Kautz, which aimed to destroy the Petersburg & Weldon Railroad, and even hoped to seize and ravage Petersburg, were defeated and shorn of half their force by capture and death. The raiders, totally disorganized, made their way in groups and singly to their own lines.

General Sheridan, the greatest cavalry leader the North produced, at the head of a superb array of horsemen, well mounted, thoroughly equipped, whose ultimate destination was Charlottesville, started for Gordonsville to burn the depot with all its supplies and munitions of war. He was met at Trevillian Station by Hampton, and the hardest, most deadly cavalry combat ever fought on the American continent took place, and Sheridan was hurled back with great loss.

Now there was for a short time a breathing spell, and as the people looked back upon the past two months and witnessed all these victories and the unconquerable temper of our armies, is it strange that they thought the end near—an end full of proud exultation and triumph, not tears and woe?

Nor was this all. The Army of Northern Virginia, notwithstanding the terrible ordeal it had just undergone, was in the best of health and defiant in spirit. There was not a private in the ranks who did not feel assured of success.

On the Northern side all was gloom and despair. This loved Army of the Potomac had sustained its magnificent prestige in scores of battles but at dreadful cost. Six thousand officers, the very flower of the North and West, were killed or wounded in the brief space of two months, while the privates of the rank and file had fallen by the thousands. The advance of the army was but a succession of storming parties, and men fell like leaves in the roaring tempest. Grant's loss was greater than the whole army of his adversary.

The North resounded with the moans of the widow and orphan, and as the President of the United States witnessed the rapid decimation of Grant's ranks he might well have exclaimed passionately, as did Augustus to his unfortunate general, "Varus, Varus, what hast thou done with my legions?"

Cold Harbor was the climax to the score of battles fought north of the James, and the result, that five thousand officers and forty-seven thousand of the rank and file of Grant's army were killed and wounded; one-half of the best and bravest, leaving the other half badly shaken and with no stomach for further fighting. The sun of the Union seemed, in June and July, to be slowly sinking in a sea of blood.

Major Robert Stiles, in his deeply interesting book (page 287) says:

"So much for the amount, the disproportion, and the cause of the slaughter. A word now as to the effect of it upon others than the immediate contestants. Is it too much to say that even Grant's iron nerve was for the time shattered? Not that he would not have fought again if his men would, but they would not. Is it not true that he so informed President Lincoln; that he asked for another army; that, not getting it, or not getting it at once, he changed his plan of campaign from a fighting to a digging one? Is it reasonable to suppose that when he attacked at the Bloody Angle or at Cold Harbor, he really contemplated the siege of Petersburg and regarded those operations as merely preparatory? Is it not true that, years later, Grant said—looking back over his long career of bloody fights—that Cold Harbor was the only battle he ever fought that he would not fight over again under the same circumstances? Is it not true that when first urged, as President, to remove a certain Democratic office-holder in California, and later, when urged to give a reason for his refusal, he replied that the man had been a standard-bearer in the Army of the Potomac, and that he would allow something very unpleasant to happen to him before he would remove the only man in his army who even attempted to obey his order to attack a second time at Cold Harbor? Is it not true that General Meade said the Confederacy came nearer to winning recognition at Cold Harbor than at any other period during the war? Is it not true that, after Grant's telegram, the Federal Cabinet resolved at least upon an armistice, and that Mr. Seward was selected to draft the necessary papers, and Mr. Swinton to prepare the public mind for the change? And finally, even if none of these things be true, exactly as propounded—yet is it not true, that Cold Harbor shocked and depressed the Federal Government and the Northern public more than any other single battle of the war?"

A brief epitome of some of the salient features and results of the campaign of 1864, from the Wilderness to Cold Harbor, inclusive, may not be devoid of interest.

The campaign covered, say sixty miles of space and thirty days of time. General Lee had a little under 64,000 men of all arms present for duty at the outset, and he put *hors de combat* of Grant's army an equal number man for man. Mr. Swinton, p. 482 of his "Army of the Potomac," puts Grant's loss at "above sixty thousand men;" so that Grant lost in killed and wounded and prisoners more than a thousand men per mile and more than two thousand men per day during the campaign.

Again, Lee had, as stated, at the start, present for duty, less than 64,000 men, and the reinforcements he received numbered 14,400 men; so that, from first to last, he had under his command in this campaign, say 78,400 men; while Grant's had at the start, present for duty, 141,160 men, and the reinforcements he received numbered 51,000 men; so that from first to last he had under his command in this campaign, say 192,160 men.

Grant took nine days to recover from the effects of Cold Harbor, and Lee was preparing to strike. Early, in his "Memoirs," says: "Notwithstanding the disparity which existed, he was anxious, as I know, to avail himself of every opportunity to strike an offensive blow; and just as Grant was preparing to move across James River, with his defeated and dispirited army, General Lee was maturing his plans for taking the offensive; and in stating his desire for me to take the initiative with the corps I then commanded, he said: 'We must destroy this army of Grant's before he gets to the James River. If he gets there it will become a siege, and then it will be a mere question of time.' "

All Grant's strategic campaign had failed. Sheridan's grand swoop with ten thousand horsemen to seize Richmond, and Hunter's advance to the southwest to capture Lynchburg, were utter failures. The Federal march up the Valley to take Staunton was foiled and the hammer of Thor stopped for a time, for the arm was too weak to wield the weapon.

If a pitched battle in the open had occurred any time between the 15th of June and the 1st of August the Federal army would have gone to pieces. A true statement of the facts of Grant's overland campaign will be sufficient to show this.

The Northern people were not informed of the true state of affairs in the front. Correspondents of the independent type were sternly repressed.

It was Mr. Stanton the astute Secretary of War, who hit upon the novel plan of selecting a well-known correspondent and journalist and placing him at the Commander-in-Chief's headquarters, where he could obtain all the inside information, and thus write the unadulterated truth. It was a great scheme, and it worked well until the people "caught on," and then it was abandoned.

The journalist in this case was Mr. Charles A. Dana, acting at the time as Assistant Secretary of War.

If Mr. Dana, with all his facilities for gathering news, wrote truthfully of the events of the day, he must have been very dense. If he did not write as he thought, then he was guilty of gulling the public, and of running a kind of confidence game.

The Presidential election was in full swing, and bad news from the front emboldened the Peace faction and strengthened the Democratic party under the leadership of General McClellan, the former idol of the Army of the Potomac.

Mr. Dana's letters from the front were all *coleur de rose*. Every Rebel charge was repulsed with awful slaughter. All the Union advances were successful when well supported.

Under date of May 26th, 1864, he wrote:

"One of the most important results of the campaign thus far is the entire change which has taken place in the feelings of the armies.

"The Rebels have lost all confidence, and are already morally defeated. This army has ceased to believe that it is sure of victory. Even our officers have ceased to regard Lee as an invincible military genius. On the part of the Rebels this change is evinced, not only by their not attacking, even when circumstances invite it, but by the unanimous statement of prisoners taken from them.

"You may rely upon it, *the end is near as well as sure.*"

"The servant of a South Carolina officer who escaped, reports that he heard his master say that their losses were forty thousand men." (Reb. Records, Vol. 36, p. 78-79.)

Of the great Battle of Cold Harbor he describes it as a recognizance in force. He says:

"At noon we had developed the Rebel lines. As General Warren did not think an attack feasible, General Grant ordered the attack suspended."

It was, as usual, Lee's official report that awakened the North to the horrors hid in the woods of Spottsylvania; and the very people who cheered to the echo Grant's famous dispatch, that he proposed to fight it out on the overland line if it took all the summer, were now assailing him with the bitterest vituperation. Like a nervy gambler, he stood pat on his hand, and backed his boast, but at last he flinched when fifty-four thousand nine hundred and twenty of his best and bravest men fell by bullet and shell.*

After Cold Harbor he crossed the south bank of the James and found himself where McClellan had placed his army with the loss of but a few hundred.

The overland campaign will go down in history as the bloodiest and most fruitless ever fought.

General Warren wrote to General Meade under date of June 23rd, 1864.

"All of our efforts are attended with such great difficulties that I believe no one can regard any future operations with anything but the deepest anxiety and solicitude, and I venture to say that officers and men are getting very weary and nervous.

"I don't think the country appreciates our very trying position, with our unparalleled losses and exhausting efforts. We can scarcely say we are much nearer destroying Lee's army than when we were on the Rapidan.

---

*Grant's loss from May 5th to June 15th, 1864, was, by the official returns, 54,926. "Battles and Leaders," Vol. 4, p. 182.

"*I most fear Lee attacking our weakened lines,* than anything else." (Reb. Records, Vol. 40, p. 346.)

The officers might plan and order, but the rank and file had gotten to that state where they positively refused to make an assault on an entrenched position; as at Cold Harbor, the division generals issued the order to the brigadiers; they passed it to the colonels, who formed their lines and the order to advance was given, but not a man moved; they stood still and immovable.

In all the desperate battles fought in the Wilderness, Grant had no show. Once, and once only, did fortune smile upon him, and that was when with a dashing, brilliant coup, Hancock broke through Lee's center and captured General Johnson and his division. Had Hancock been supported as he should have been, the utter defeat of Lee would have been certain; for his line would have been taken in the rear and rolled up without order or formation.

That attack of Hancock's at daybreak was the only well-conceived plan of the campaign. It was a critical time for the Army of Northern Virginia, and Lee, for the first and last time, put himself at the head of the troops to lead the charge, and it was then that the troops took up the cry, "Lee to the rear!"

Major General Francis Barlow, in his official report, dated June 17th, 1864, says:

"But I have not the slightest idea that the Second and Third Brigades of my Division can accomplish anything in the way of assault. There are scarcely any officers in the brigades." (Reb. Records, Vol. 40, p. 123.)

General Gibbon, who commanded the crack division in the Army of the Potomac, in his report, dated July 30th, 1864, says:

"My division left camp on May 3rd, 1864, with 11,062 men. My losses up to July 30th are 5,075 in killed and wounded alone. Of course it is the bravest and most efficient men that fell. It is always so. These facts seem to demonstrate that my troops which at the commencement of the campaign were equal to almost any undertaking, have become by this time almost unfit for any." (*Ibid,* Vol. 36, p. 434.)

It seems that the very next day Mahone made one of his energetic, fiery attacks, and sent Gibbon's division to the rear in wild disorder. General Gibbon then issued the following order, which was read at dress parade:

"No. 51.

"The result of the enemy's attack upon our position is a source of great mortification to the General Commanding, as it is the first occasion where this division has failed to sustain its deservedly high reputation. The disgraceful conduct of the Second Brigade and portions of the Third, lost McKnight's battery."

And now comes Hancock, the Stonewall Jackson of the Army of the Potomac; the sightly, shapely Hancock, whose soldiers never yet failed to do all that men could do when under his eye, who must have been stirred to the depths of his warrior-soul when he issued his proclamation to the veterans who had followed him so long.

"General orders, No. 22.   June 27th, 1864.

"Major-General Hancock resumes command of the Second Corps. In so doing he desires to express his regret that during his absence from the command it suffered a disaster from the hands of the enemy which seriously tarnishes its fame. The abandonment of the line by regiments and brigades without firing a shot, and the surrender to the enemy of entire regiments by their commanders without resistance, was disgraceful and admits of no defense.

"This order will be read at the head of every regiment and battalion." (*Ibid,* Vol. 40, p. 468.)

One month after, Mahone won another victory, and the following circular was issued by the commander of the First Army Corps:

"Headquarters 1st Army Corps,
"Circular: Aug. 26th, 1864.

"General Hancock sends me word that he has been withdrawing during the night from Ream's Station. His men are very much demoralized and cannot be relied upon this morning. Lost heavily in killed and wounded, and nine pieces of artillery." (*Ibid,* Vol. 42, p. 123.)

To show the efforts made by Federal rank and file to get away from the Moloch that was claiming its thousand victims daily, the report of the Medical Director of the Army of the Potomac will prove interesting, and shows that conscripts, substitutes and the

38

like had but little patriotism. He reports under date of May 17th, 1864:

"A large number of sick and wounded, many of the latter self-mutilated, did not go to the field hospitals, nor accompany the regular trains, but straggled to Fredericksburg. About five thousand of these men were in that town at different times.

"About 600 malingerers have been turned over to the provost marshal; they got to Washington by the boat, and succeeded in getting off by the aid of bloody bandages and judicious limping." (*Ibid,* Vol. 36, p. 235.)

General Orlando Wilcox, commanding a Federal division, says in his report:

"At 5 o'clock Hill opened with his artillery, both shot and shell, but did little actual damage other than demoralizing the men, of whom there were many, even in the old regiments, who never had come to fight, but to run at the first chance, or get in the hospitals, then Ho! for a pension afterwards." ("Battles and Leaders," Vol. 36, p. 573.)

Some of the officers could not speak a word of English, says Hancock in his report, and had nothing in common with their men but panic.

Gibbon's division was ordered to retake the works, but they responded feebly, and fell back to their own works when they were ordered to charge; despite the expostulations and orders of the officers they could not be gotten to get up.

General Francis Walker, commanding a division in the Second Federal Corps, says in his book:

"On more than one occasion in July and August, 1864, the troops, after a march which placed them in a position advantageous to attack, failed to show a trace of elation which characterized their earlier days of the campaign. The fire had burnt out."

After the Battle of Cold Harbor the Army of Northern Virginia never felt so proud and jubilant. It is true the soldiers were more enthusiastic on the march to Gettysburg a year before, but they did not possess then that implicit confidence in themselves. These troops had fought five engagements on May 6th, five on May 12th, and over a score since Grant crossed the Rapidan, and with one exception had held their ground in every one of them.

The whole army would have hailed with shouts of gladness the order to close in and settle the contest by a give and take until one or the other was destroyed.

The day after Cold Harbor Lee's army was stronger than at the beginning of the campaign. It is true his losses were heavy, but reinforcements had come freely from the South, and the field returns on July 1st, 1864, show that there were in ranks, fit for duty, 62,497 men. (Reb. Records, Vol. 51, p. 1001.)

Of all men, Lee knew that the propitious hour had come to throw every available man into a general attack, but he was on a sick bed, utterly incapable of either planning or executing. There was no one he could trust for such a movement; Longstreet, his old war horse, had been badly wounded at the beginning of the campaign, as was A. P. Hill; Ewell was incapacitated by the loss of his leg, from taking an active part in a battle.

Colonel Venable, Lee's aide-de-camp, said he hoped to deal a severe blow to Grant, and felt keenly his failure to carry out his designs. "He exclaimed, 'I am too old to command this army!' and he repeated the phrase as he lay sick, excited, and restless on his bed. He said again and again, 'We should never permit these people to get away.' Some of us who were standing beside him felt that in his heart he was sighing for that great right arm which he threw around Hooker at Chancellorsville."

There was no one whom Lee could entrust his army with. The troops stood ready but the man was absent.

When Grant passed his legions to the south side of the James River all hope of a favorable attack was gone, for Grant set his whole army to work entrenching, and every able-bodied contraband was armed with a spade and pick. General Ord alone had three thousand negroes erecting breastworks, the most elaborate system of defensive works ever devised by man; they consisted of fortifications, protected by fosses, moats, ditches, with strong *chevaux-de-frise,* while outside were miles of entrenchments.

By the field returns of the Army of the Potomac the Chief Engineer reported as finished 68 forts for 605 guns. Nor was this all—the system of defense was so arranged that if one fort was captured, a concentric fire from a score of redoubts could be poured in, making the place untenable.

General Lee wrote to Jeff. Davis on June 15th, 1864:

"To attack the enemy here I must assault with a very strong line

of entrenchment and run a great risk to the safety of the army."
(Reb. Records, Vol. 51, p. 1003.)

Many and odd are the chances of war. Even the god Homer
nodded sometimes, and for once Lee was caught napping, for
General Ord crossed to the south side of the James and united
with Butler, and had Petersburg in his grasp before Lee dreamed
of his danger.

But Ord's men had no stomach for charging the breastworks,
which were manned only by the citizens of the city, and after
one or two feeble attempts, he postponed the attack until the
next day, and by that time reinforcements were rushed forward,
and Butler's attempt failed.

It was a case of a "Roland for an Oliver" a few days later,
when Beauregard planned a campaign of consummate daring and
skill to capture Butler's army.

Pickett was to strike his front, and when fully engaged, General Whiting, with his division, which was stationed at Chester,
midway between Richmond and Petersburg, was to slip in his
rear.

Pickett performed his share of the work and made a stunning
attack, but Whiting did not move all day; in fact he was helplessly drunk, and the brilliant movement, which promised so much,
ended in a fiasco.

Whiting was relieved of his command and sent to Fort Fisher.
He was a regretful, sorrowful man ever afterward; but the damage was done, the chance the Rebels had for a brilliant victory
was lost, and a dread disaster to the Army of the Potomac was
averted by what some of their officers said was a miracle, but in
reality was a bottle of whiskey.

In the sunny horizon which bounded the Southerners' hopes
there was only one slight cloud which dimmed the clearness and
occasioned fear. That cloud was not near home, though the city
was hemmed with battle-smoke and the windows of every house
shook and rattled with the concussion of the heavy siege-guns
of the foe; yet they frightened no one—not even the timid girls
nor old women, who always were predicting some fearful event.
No! our cloud was away off in the West, and the man we feared
was named Sherman, not Grant.

Still our papers brought good news, and the columns of
the *Richmond Examiner* caused the soldiers to shout and
dance for joy. Extracts from the Northern papers showed that
gloomy forebodings were indulged in; mutterings against the

war, which formerly were uttered with bated breath, were now openly discussed in public mass-meetings. The whole North was well-nigh speechless, and utterly sick at heart as they witnessed this rain of blood which soaked the earth from the Rapidan to the James. Murmurs against the war and the Government began to grow from an inarticulate growl into a voice of thunder.

The Irish in New York City had risen and threatened to end the war by an international conflict. The Copperhead Society of the great Northwest were arming and drilling. There were no volunteers now, for a place in the Army of the Potomac meant a place in the hospital or an unknown grave.

Substitutes for the draughted were only to be had by the payment of thousands of dollars, and were unreliable as soldiers. Bounty-jumpers swarmed like the lice of Egypt. Corruption reigned in high places, and patriotism was forgotten by many in the mad rush for wealth. Shoddy reigned supreme, and flaunted its diamonds and trailed its velvets in the blood-laden air. The patriots of the North, who loved the Union better than their fortunes or their lives, began to look into one another's eyes to find comfort in this carnival of death.

Gold, that unfailing barometer of public opinion, had risen to a premium of three hundred per cent. and the most thoughtful capitalists of the North were beginning to think that arbitration could conquer more than the sword.

The sole hope of the Union seemed to be centered in the superb army of Sherman.

As for us, such confidence was felt in our Army of the West, under Johnston, that we all felt that "Old Joe" would pull through all right.

CHAPTER XXVI.

THE SOLDIERS' HOME.

I was again an inmate of the Robertson Hospital as a guest, and attended many starvation parties, and the spasmodic gaieties of the Rebel Capital. I was unable to dance, but at least could look on those who did, and I was in for a real "Claude Melnott" campaign, when the boudoir and the parlor were exchanged for a military prison in the most sudden and unforeseen manner.

The dreamy stillness of the hot summer was broken by the loud alarm bell which hung high in a tower in Capitol Square, where its tones pealed forth like the chimes in a Turkish mosque. It called the faithful, not to prayers, but to battle. Then ensued scenes of wild excitement amongst the bombproofs. There were hurryings to and fro of my countrymen; Government clerks, who loved their flesh-pots better than any country on earth; auctioneers, actors, cooks, hospital nurses, all details, city exempts, vagabonds and riff-raff, all were obliged to obey that tocsin of war and seize the rifle with their soft hands. Pale were the cheeks, hollow the eyes, trembling the lips and fluttering the hearts of the citizens' battalion, as in the dead of night, by the lantern's glare, they looked in each other's white, ghostly faces and muttered in accents hoarse:

"The foe! they come! they come!"

Orders were issued for all furloughed officers and soldiers to report to the provost marshal; for it seems that one of the chief forts of the defenses around Richmond, called Battery Harrison, was taken by a sudden charge, and it was feared that Richmond would be stormed by the whole Northern army. Every musket that could be fired—every finger that could press a trigger was at a fancy price just then.

There was a wide gulf between the regulars and the home guards. If there was one thing an old veteran hated, it was being placed, hit or miss, promiscuously in the ranks amongst a mongrel crowd, and marched to the trenches as militia, and they hid and lay perdu, despite old General Winder's order, he being, by the way, the last person on earth to act in that stern martial capacity; a superannuated patriot, by the Grace of God and Jefferson Davis, sole ruler over the safety and liberty of the citizens of the Capital City for the first three years of the war. The rank and file of the grand army did not like General Winder and were not slow in expressing their opinions.

· It happened that a comrade and I had a pass from General Lee, countersigned by his Adjutant-General, to proceed within the enemy's lines in Fauquier County, our object being to capture a re-mount. Of course we felt secure, and boldly walked the streets and watched with keen relish the hunting down of those Things, or Its (for they were not men), who were dressed in citizen's attire. Our laugh soon changed into scowls, for about midnight we were stopped by a large squad of guards, and requested to show our passports. Our hands went into our pockets and produced the magic paper.

"This pass ain't no 'count," said the officer.

"No 'count?" repeated my comrade mechanically, forgetting his grammar in his amazement.

"No!"

"Don't you know that pass is from General Lee, Commander-in-Chief of the Army?"

"I know that, but I must obey orders."

"Orders! orders! what the dickens are your orders?"

"We have received commands from the provost marshal to take up all officers and soldiers in the city of Richmond unless they have a passport signed by himself."

"Provost marshal be damned!" was my comrade's irreverent reply. "Set out and leg it!" he shouted, making a dart down the street. I followed suit, but it was no go; two enfeebled convalescents could not use their legs, and in a few minutes we were in the midst of guards, objects of their especial care and tenderest solicitude.

"You had better let us go, Melish," we said. "If you don't respect this pass there will be the Old Scratch to pay in the army."

"I must obey my instructions," he replied; "I am only a lieutenant and whatever my captain says I've got to do. My orders are to arrest every soldier and every citizen unless he has a pass from the provost marshal."

"O for a squadron of Black Horse Cavalry," I sighed, "just to run this riff-raff provost guard out of the city!"

"O for a company of the old First Maryland, to scatter old

Winder's gang and to hang the old provost from the first tree," swore my companion.

"Come along; I can't wait here all night," said the leader.

"Where are you going to take us?"

"To the Soldiers' Home."

"To the Soldiers' Home? Good Heavens, lieutenant, we are not deserters or jail-birds."

"Can't help it, I obey orders. Forward, march!" said the officer.

So, joining the crowd of unfortunates, we were taken into the gloomy depths of the forbidding building known as the Soldiers' Home and nick-named Castle Thunder; truly a misnomer, and the very irony of the word could go no farther. It was used as a place of rest and detention for all those furloughed soldiers who had neither friends to stop with nor money to pay for their lodgings. It occupied the same relation to the veteran as the station-house does in peaceful times to the outcasts and friendless of a great city. As for it being a home—well, if there were any soft memories which could be coffined up in those sombre walls, they could only be the result of a morbid imagination.

All soldiers suspected of crime and waiting trial, all absentees, deserters and camp followers convicted of light crimes were placed in that house, around which was stationed a strong cordon of sentinels with relief and details. Into the guard-room we were marched.

We found the prison flavor so strong that it was not surprising that nothing but the direst necessity from hunger or cold ever tempted the veteran to voluntarily seek shelter there. It was a horribly filthy place, and when a Reb was seen unusually squalid and dirty the boys in the street would yell at him, "There goes one of the Castle Thunder fish!"

We were turned loose in a large room on the first floor, a wide, lofty apartment which traversed the length of the whole building.

What a sight was there! The room was lighted by gas jets which revealed, without a shadow of disguise, the nasty uncleanliness of the place. It was crowded with about as conglomerate a mixture of humanity as could be found anywhere on earth; the summons to arrest all without passes, but newly issued, had caught very many without the coveted document, for as the papers were only written that day, but few had the time or thought the necessity so urgent as to inconvenience themselves to the extent of obtaining them. They paid dearly for their neglect. Old gentlemen returning from their places of business were unceremoniously hustled into the prison; actors coming from the theater, hospital stewards carrying messages, wounded soldiers from the hospitals hobbling along the streets, gay and festive blockaderunners, teamsters strolling in from Camp Lee to see the sights, saw them in a way they little dreamed; farmers from the country,—all were caged together, looking as disconsolate as a collection of street dogs that have been gathered to the pound by the dog-catchers.

In this vast apartment, filled with all these people, there was not a single bed, trunk, bench or chair. A more ingenious mode of torture could not be invented. Many of the unfortunates were delicate citizens, wounded soldiers or sick convalescents, and by order of the provost marshal were compelled to stand the long night through. One, a wounded, white, ghostly-looking shadow, who had been scooped up by the drag-net, died before morning.

Some few who had blankets spread them close to the walls, and with the philosophy that would have done honor to the Stoics grumbled not nor cursed, but went quietly to sleep. Those who were less fortunate could not persuade themselves to lie on that floor. The grease, the accumulation of years, covered the planks with a crust of black half an inch thick, and was as sticky as tar. On top of this, scattered thickly, were the remains of rations, parings of loud-smelling bacon and cheese, ashes from pipes, stumps of cigars, shallow pools of tobacco juice, blood which had dropped from neglected wounds, vomit from weak stomachs, all welded by the trampling feet into a horrible repulsive mire.

To the soldiers who were well and strong a tramp all night was no great matter, but to the weak it was a fearful strain, and hour by hour they walked or staggered through the room, taking good care not to step upon the recumbent forms, for every touch was resented by a volley of oaths from the irate, half-wakened soldier.

The gamblers, auctioneers and gentry of that ilk had the worst time of all. Clad in duck, linen, and broadcloth, their stylish garments formed a striking contrast to the worn gray; they were objects of marked attention of no very favorable kind. The Rebs, on the *qui vive* to find something on which to vent their ill nature, and delighted to have the means of diversion during the long hours, found these gentlemen out, and taunts, jibes and the roughest jokes were shot off at them singly and in volleys. They could do nothing and dared not reply; and at last, drawn together in common suffering by the merciless raillery, they cowered in one corner like a pack of trembling sheep when they see the marauding dog jump the fence into the field.

The "Soldiers' Home" was that night under the charge of Lieutenant Bates, a Regular and not a Melish; he was incapacitated by his wounds for serving in the field and was given light duty. We made during the night an energetic appeal to him to be liberated, and showed our pass; but he was powerless to help us and told us to wait until morning, when all would be well.

"It's easy enough to preach patience," said Edelin, "but it's hard to practice it, especially in a hog-pen."

Back into the room we wandered, and it would have been a subject for Hogarth to fix by his magic pencil; the sorrowful, disgusted faces and the tired forms which stood under the glare of the gas; some of them, rich auctioneers, would have given thousands of dollars for a door mat to sit upon, and as for the gamblers, they would have pawned their outfits for a good couch. One of these votaries of fortune, more enterprising than the rest, came up to a group of soldiers and made the proposition that if they would let up on him and stand by him he would start an impromptu faro bank and share his gains fairly among his soldier backers. A count of noses showed eight who told him to drive ahead, the guard being one of them. Going out, he returned with an empty barrel and keg and a piece of plank. The barrel was then turned upside down, the board laid across and the cards fastened down by pins. Getting another pack he laid them on the table, dispensing, from necessity, with the nickel dealing box. Next, turning the keg behind the barrel, the gambler took his seat, and displaying a roll of new issue as the capital of the bank, declared the game was ready.

It took like wild-fire; in a minute the table was surrounded by an excited, struggling mass. Arms were frantically stretched over shoulders to place on the cards the bets. There were no chips; the body-guard would count the money laid down, and return or replace it according to the fall of the card. If five dollars, the lowest limit by the way, were bet, five dollars was returned, and so on; there was no limit. Next to the dealer, sitting on a drygoods box, with a huge camp kettle, like a drum with the cover bursted in, between his legs, filled with notes of different denominations, was the soldier partner. It was his duty to pay off all debts that were lost. When the bank won the dealer swept them with one wave of his hand into the brass receptacle. In half an hour the betting became high. The soldiers soon lost their stray dollars, and would have broken the bank in another way from that laid down in sporting annals, but the ring, including the armed guard, drawn into strong fellowship by what Macaulay terms the "cohesive power of public plunder," stood staunchly by the banker, and perfect order reigned. The citizens now were around the table, and as the fever took them the play ran high and deep. The big stakes silenced all noises, and every one watched with breathless eagerness the cards' slow slip from the dealer's hands. Many good and pious men gambled that night for the first time, for oblivion from the woes was worth playing for and paying for. As the day approached the betters thinned out, dead broke. Some walked off, others stood wearily by, watching the game. The few who backed against the bank were playing to either win or lose heavily. Thousands of dollars were thrown down on a single coup. None could have imagined that so much money, albeit it was Confederate currency, worth about four cents on the dollar, could have been discovered in a chance crowd. So the gaming went on. When the betters went straight they laid on the cards; when they coppered they used a small wooden button that came from off a soldier's jacket. In about three hours there were only about a half-dozen men around the board.

At the beginning of the play a middle-aged man, with clean-shaven face, stood leaning against a pillar trying to get a nap under these unwonted circumstances. Nobody knew him and nobody cared to ask. As he had on citizen's clothes, with a flat cap around which was a narrow piece of gold lace, every one thought him a recruiting agent or military conscript officer, or most probably a blockade-runner, and he had just enough military flavor to be exempt from the soldiers' ridicule.

As the excitement of the play increased he roused himself and approached the board as closely as he could; then he folded up half-way a thousand-dollar bill, coppered it on the deuce and won. The magnitude of the stake caused the betters to instinctively make way for him until he stood close to the barrel; then his high play became apparent and the ring grew anxious as they watched him. I have seen streaks of luck around the green cloth, but never such a run as that man had. He had lost nearly all his pile, and had but one note left; he bet on the ace, the deuce and tray, between which he left his bets stand intact; the ace split once and they all won twelve consecutive times, and by letting his small bet of fifty dollars lay, it had doubled until it had reached the grand total of one hundred and two thousand four hundred dollars. It was marvelous—incredible, but true.

"The bank's broke!" said the gambler, with a savage oath. "The crowd's broke, and damn me if I don't wish the bottom would fall out of all creation!"

The lucky man gave a soldier a thousand-dollar bill for his oilcloth and rolled most of his money up tightly; then, distributing some among the soldiers, he made a handsome gift to the guard and asked to be conducted to Lieutenant Bates, for it was a risk to wander in any crowd with a bundle under one's arm containing a hundred thousand dollars, even though it was Confederate scrip. So the blockade-runner told the lieutenant of the circumstances and placed the money in his charge. The owner recovered his liberty during the day and promptly reclaimed his package, and in a generous mood presented Bates with a beautiful gold chain.

There may be some of the citizens and sick soldiers who look back upon the weary vigil of that night with feelings the reverse of pleasant, but the soldiers, with the exceptions, of course, of the unfortunates who banded themselves into a syndicate to divide the spoils, not one of them ever regretted being taken up and being obliged to spend the night in Castle Thunder, for it had given them the opportunity to witness the biggest game of faro that in all probability ever took place in Richmond.

CHAPTER XXVII.

ENACTING THE ROLE OF JACK SHEPHERD.

My comrade, Will Edelin, of Leonardtown, Maryland, was a gallant, reckless veteran of the Maryland line.

His body was small but his ambition was boundless; and though diminutive in stature, he had more mischief to the square inch than any other soldier in the army. He was always getting into scrapes, but being one of the kind who are born lucky, he escaped the consequences of many a thoughtless act. He was rash to a fault and never stopped to consider what the result of some proposed escapade might be.

It was Edelin who was the chief of the ring, and his losses through the blockade runner did not improve his temper. He was in no less than three difficulties before an hour passed, then he said he felt better.

The sun streamed through the window and the aversion to the dirty place was stronger than ever. Certainly had the "Prisoner of Chillon" felt the ardent desire for freedom that possessed our party, he would have made a break for liberty anyhow.

To all who had watched and gambled the night through, a sickening reaction came. Heads ached to such an extent that it seemed as though they were loaded shells and a lighted fuse was only needed to blow them to pieces. Eyes burned and the bodies felt as though they were paralyzed. A consuming thirst kept the tin cup busily passing from hand to hand and every one longed for delivery from this dirt-begrimed place.

Edelin grew impatient. He was hungry and I was not far behind him. But I have written so much of hunger in these pages that I ought really to apologize for it as a very disagreeable habit,—a morbid desire of always wanting to eat, which accompanied our soldiers wherever they went; yet the stomach is the store-house, kitchen, pantry, cupboard, and chemical laboratory all in one.

An indignation meeting of the most violent kind was held; but beyond each man expressing his opinion and giving a piece of his mind in language exceedingly strong, nothing was done. A proposition to escape by making a break for the outside was at once negatived. They said: "Better wait a few hours and walk out on your own free account than to be carried out upon a stretcher with a hole through you," so the assembly resolved, after invoking anathemas on everything and everybody connected with the "Home."

My comrade and I strolled out into the prison yard, a piece of ground of about an eighth of an acre, surrounded by a thick wall about seven feet high. Close to this and inside the enclosure was a guard, the only one, who paced around the four squares.

The same thought struck us both, and when the sentinel was on the far side with his back turned, Edelin whispered, "Let's risk it."

"All right," was the response, and as two soldiers came up we asked them to give us a leg.

"Are you ready?"

A backward glance showed the sentry some fifteen paces away, near the end of his beat, his face turned toward the prison, his musket on his shoulder.

"Yes."

"Then over you go!" and the impetus of their swing sent us up the wall. A short struggle and we were on the top. A great shout from the prisoners greeted our success, and as the guard swung round he saw us. We dropped on the other side, which happened to be the backyard of a private residence, and we had certainly jumped from the frying-pan into the fire, for a savage-looking bulldog made a dash at us.

"Run! Run!" cried Edelin. A warning that was superfluous. One bound brought us to a plank fence, and how we got over we could never tell, but we found ourselves in a narrow alley which we skimmed through and only stopped when we had reached the open street. Assuming the leisurely gait of an ordinary pedestrian, we struck for the Robertson Hospital, where we knew that old Winder's crew couldn't take us, for Miss Sallie would have died in her tracks ere she would have suffered one of her patients to be disturbed. We found her a second Pythoness; several of her convalescents having been taken up, she had already been down to the provost marshal and had routed the whole establishment. An order had been issued for our release and if we had been patient for an hour longer we would have come out of the front door instead of rushing through the back alley.

A huge breakfast and a nap of a couple of hours made us all right and primed for anything. Edelin, who was much given to practical jokes, proposed his plan and of course I agreed.

Finding that Miss Sallie was out of the way, we got muskets and equipments and walked boldly out on the streets, demanding the passports of every man we met, and playing the part of Winder's pets to perfection. Our first place was the wide and spacious lobby of the "Spottswood," where a large crowd was collected. Upon our appearance with the demand for passes, the crowd scattered and broke as they do in a gambling haunt when the police are thundering at the doors. How pitiful was their talk—how fertile their excuses. It ended by an apparent reluctance on our part to let them go, until we were invited to the bar to take something. It was glorious fun that day, and the invitations to drink would have sufficed for a regiment. We felt then the unutterable sweetness and charm of power.

Honor was at low ebb, for some of the captives pledged themselves to be back within half an hour, only being desirous of dropping into their homes a moment to notify their families. Of course we never laid eyes upon them again.

Yes, power was sweet and we paid off some old scores that day. Whenever a general or colonel was met, we threw all the superciliousness and imperativeness we could command into our manners and demanded their passes or credentials. We held our weather eye open and whenever we saw the bona fide creature of the provost marshal's coming we dived down the first alley or into the first store we came to. This fun lasted until late into the afternoon, and then tired out and with a slightly rolling gait, we returned to our hospital well content. The last words Edelin said that night were:

"Say, haven't we had a bully time?"

CHAPTER XXVIII

EN ROUTE.

Two days later I started upon my trip northward alone, Edelin having given up the idea of a scout.

Taking the train for Gordonsville in company with many soldiers on their way to join their commands in the Valley, we arrived at the junction. The main train kept on to Staunton, while a locomotive carried me to Orange Court House, where it stopped, being the northern terminus of the road, for all communication was blocked farther north by the Rapidan bridge having been destroyed.

This ancient village seemed deserted. No dashing officers cantered up its streets, no streams of soldiery on the sidewalks gave it life, and hardly a human form was visible; only the open windows and the smoke curling from the chimneys showed signs of life within doors.

The first house at which we chanced to stop was our home, the latch-string standing ready to be pulled.

At sunrise I left for Culpeper Court House on foot, and in the twenty miles which I traversed I beheld no living being. The region between the Rapidan and Culpeper showed in a fearful degree the devastation of the contest. Not a single house was visible and a profound silence brooded over what was but two years ago a veritable garden spot.

A couple of hours' walking brought me to Brandy Station, which existed only in name. A blackened piece of ground showed where the depot once stood. In the distance, like an island in this waste, stood the fine mansion of John Minor Botts; thither I bent my steps and received a kind greeting.

About noon I reached the Rappahannock River and found that the bridge as well as the railroad had been destroyed. With a few beams which had floated blackened and charred to the bank, I soon constructed a raft which bore me across.

I began to be cautious now, for I was in the "Debatable Land," and at any moment some Yankee scouting party might be passing along and gobble me up. Keeping my eyes open, slinking along for several miles, I made my way to a comrade's house.

Taylor was not at home, but his wife welcomed me and gave minute information as to the state of affairs in general.

While on the way to Fayettesville the next day, a horseman cantered up. I cocked my Colt, hid it beneath my overcoat and awaited his coming. It proved to be Billy Thorne, of the Black Horse, a scout for General Wickham, who, hearing of my arrival from Mrs. Taylor, hastened to overtake me and join in any proposed raid. I was very glad to welcome him, for he knew every hog path and blind road in Mosby's Confederacy.

Thorne struck for Morrisville, an exceedingly small village in the lower part of Fauquier County, and close to the Stafford line. A few miles farther on was Thorne's home, which he proposed to make our base of operations. In the two days' travel we did not meet a single person.

We knew that every house was open to us, and the temper and devotion of the people can be imagined when it is known that the following order was scattered over the region, and the citizens warned not to entertain any Rebel soldiers:

"Headquarters Cavalry Corps.
"Col. B. F. Davis, Commanding Brigade.
"(Through Brig.-Gen. A. Pleasonton, Comdg. First Cav. Div.)
"Colonel:

"The Major-General commanding directs me to say to you that there are certain people, either bushwhackers or men detached from what is known as the Black Horse Cavalry, who operate on the right of and within our lines. All of whom he wishes you to put out of the way—no matter how, so they are gotten rid of. Communicate with General Gregg, near Bealeton, and he will, if possible, co-operate with you.

"Very respectfully, your obedient servant,
"J. H. TAYLOR,
"Chief of Staff."

There was also an order sent from Kilpatrick, the commander of the cavalry, to General Merritt, commanding a brigade of cavalry in Fauquier County, to burn all houses that sheltered any Rebel scouts.

On the evening of September twentieth, 1864, we unbuckled our belts and rested from our tramp.

The loving welcome from a pretty wife which my comrade received made matrimony appear a double blessing, and set me thinking that a benedict was no fool after all.

39

The next day our warlike intentions were knocked sky-high; we forgot our object, we forgave our enemies. We were only brought face to face with the fact that the sweetest, truest Southern women were there, and wanted us to stay and forego our hopes of spoil for a time. They procured a couple of fiddlers, and for a week we danced and danced, sleeping in the day, and tripping the light fantastic from sundown to sunup. It was the first chance for over a year that the maidens, who had been cooped up in their houses, surrounded by their foes, had a chance to be with soldiers of their own faith, and so,

> "When youth and pleasure meet,
> They chase the golden hours with flying feet."

CHAPTER XXIX.

ON A HORSE RAID.

The Black Horse had scattered, most of them having returned to their commands.

A good scout and guide, like a poet, is born, not made. A thorough knowledge of woodcraft, a forest-lore which includes everything worth knowing, the wonderful instinct of an Indian for treading the pathless woods, and a perfect perception of every blind path, road and stream in the whole section, must be had before a trooper is fit to send out upon a scout, whether to pick up information or to effect a capture. Not only this, he must be a man of keen observation, one always suspicious, ever watchful and who cannot be decoyed into any trap by any wiles whatever. A scout might be captured by the sudden appearance of a raiding party, and it was held as the fortunes of war, but to be caught by any lure would be held as unpardonable.

There was one man in the Black Horse who had been a sportsman in the ante-bellum days. As a successful turkey hunter and a county surveyor he had been known far and wide; the green woods had been his home since boyhood and his woodcraft was simply astonishing. Through the thickest, densest forest he could direct his way as straight as an arrow. Carry him blindfolded into the thickest timber that ever grew, and after circling around a little, taking his bearings, as he called it, he would get out as quickly as if he traveled by a compass. He was as fine a guide in a complex country as ever lived, and Billy Thorne was about as fine a specimen of a guide as the cavalry could boast. He could travel as straight as the crow flies from one point to another in the Piedmont section.

Thorne had been prowling around inside of the enemy's lines for the last week and he saw a good chance for a couple on foot to capture a mount from a cavalry brigade which lay encamped around Burke's Station, about twelve miles from Alexandria.

He proposed the trip to me and of course I gladly consented. Our preparations were quickly made, and then starting leisurely on foot, three days' easy walking brought us to Jack Arrington's in Fairfax County; a fine, roomy house situated at a cross-roads, and a celebrated rendezvous for the Rebel scouts.

Here we found Clarke, of the Black Horse, and Courtenay, an infantryman on sick furlough, both of whom signified their intention of accompanying us on the raid. Clarke and Courtenay being mounted it was thought best that they should return home and leave their horses where they would be safe from any Yankee raiding party which might traverse the country. Billy Thorne accompanied them and he came back alone, pretty badly used up by his hard ride.

"Where's the rest of the boys?" asked the host.

"Captured! not two hours ago."

"How?" interrogated Arrington.

"Well, it happened this way," aswered Thorne. "About four miles from here we stopped at a house on the road to get dinner. We tied our horses by the halters inside the fence, taking off the bridles but leaving the saddles, and then fed the horses with corn. Returning to the house we had hardly sat down to the table before the lady of the mansion rushed in crying that the Yankees had surrounded the place. Of course we hurried out, and there was a Yankee squadron in the road, yard, and all around the house. As soon as they caught sight of us they leveled their carbines and ordered us to surrender; instead of obeying we struck for our horses. Courtenay tried to slip the bridle, which hung on the fence near, over the head of his mare, but he was in such furious, blind haste that he defeated his own object. Leaving the horse he jumped over the fence and took to his heels, hoping to reach the shelter of the woods about a hundred yards away. Clarke put back; ran in and concealed himself beneath a bed mattress. I loosened the halter of my horse, and without waiting to bridle him, charged him at the fence; he cleared it beautifully and kept on, and," said Thorne, "if there was one, there were fifty Yankees firing their pistols after me, but nary a bullet touched. I didn't stop until I reached here."

"What became of Clarke and Courtenay?" inquired one of the Misses Arrington, who was sweet on the former.

"Indeed I don't know, I couldn't stop to inquire," answered Thorne.

After consultation, Thorne and I determined to take a position where the enemy would have to pass on the way to their camp, and see if we could help our comrades.

The place selected was on the top of a rough, rocky hill, beneath which was the very narrow road; our elevation was almost perpendicular and rose abruptly from the ground. We had hardly taken our station, when the battalion of cavalry appeared, riding in twos, with the field officer in front, and passed along the contracted road not thirty paces from the boulder behind which we were hidden.

It was a perfectly secure position, and we could fire down upon them without any danger to ourselves; nor could they have chased us, for the hill was too steep. On the impulse of the moment we drew a bead on the unconscious officer; but it was too cowardly. It would have been bushwhacking pure and simple and a Black Horseman would have been disgraced for life by such an act.

As the long line passed we saw Courtenay and Clarke riding along in the midst of their captors. Had we pulled trigger both of them doubtless would have been shot by the infuriated escort, in retaliation. As the rear-guard passed we shouted a farewell to our comrades, which they acknowledged by lifting their hats, and the Yankees by a few scattering shots, which we did not return. We then rode back to the house where our comrades had been captured, and found the old lady in tears; not particularly on account of the misfortune of our friends, but because the last one of her chickens had been confiscated by the troopers.

We learned that Clarke had soon been found, and then a score of Yankees dismounted, and in close skirmish order beat the swamp as school boys flush old hares, and they discovered Courtenay hidden behind a log. With many good-natured jeers they made him get up and return with them. This command, the old lady informed us, was four companies of the famous Eighth Illinois, the crack cavalry regiment of the Federal Army. They had been on a scout through the "Debatable Land," and had met nothing except on their return to camp, when they unexpectedly ran in upon our party and bagged two out of the three.

Where was our proposed foray now—what could two do? After considering the matter we decided to raise a squad of home guards, or "chinquapin rangers," as the soldiers called those skulking, thieving bandits who lived in the bush and prowled about, robbing and bushwhacking when they could do so with perfect safety. They were cowards, every one of them, though we did not know it then.

A small party of this gentry was soon found and they met at Arrington's, all splendidly armed. A garrulous, boasting set, the greatest vaunters it had ever been our lot to encounter; every man was a hero and had a private graveyard of his own.

Such pyrotechnic lying would cause the most ancient Gasconader of Lee's army to drop his head in shame. They were, by their own account, the most blood-thirsty set; they killed a dozen or so Yankees every month just to keep their hands in.

"Will you follow us into the enemy's lines?" we asked.

"Yes," they replied, "to Hades and back!" They only wanted to get close to the Yankees, that was all.

The next morning we set off on foot, and as we approached the railroad and the challenge of the Yankee pickets was heard, our doughty warriors changed color, and one by one dropped to the rear with the declaration that they would soon catch up. Of course that was the last seen of the blatherskites, and so for the second time our party was broken up.

We hated to tramp back bootless; even the "chinquapin rangers" would laugh at us. There was no telling what two men could do if they only tried. Thorne was inclined to run no desperate risks, for he loved his wife and children; but I persuaded him to try it, and so we determined to take a shy at the bluecoats.

A walk of a quarter of an hour brought us close to the railroad, and from a high hill close to the track we looked down. Below us was a company of infantry, and all along the railroad as far as our eyes could reach were sentinels about forty paces apart, who paced their beats regularly.

Our ardor fell several degrees as we beheld this sight. It would be a difficult feat to cross the railroad, heavily guarded as it was, and a still more difficult undertaking to get out, more especially if burdened with prisoners. We could not get in without crossing the line, which was the cordon of the camp.

But we had gone too far to retreat, so we quietly backed out of our proximity to the foe and went to the house of a farmer living near. To him we confided our intentions and asked his advice. He was a cautious old fellow and urged us to abandon our enterprise, saying it was mad and hopeless; but finding we were bent on making the attempt, he gave us full directions and drew a rough map of the country.

Our best policy, he said, was to pass over the railroad some eight miles below, where the road was not so heavily guarded, and cross Accotink Creek by a bridge made by a fallen tree, and to flank the Yankees on the other side when we returned.

These indefinite instructions were all that Thorne wanted, and he expressed his ability to find the place even in the night, though he had never been in that particular part of the country.

It was as dark as pitch when we started, and none but a number-one scout could have found his way; yet with his marvelous instinct Thorne pursued the course unerringly through the woods, in the inky blackness of the night, and struck the improvised bridge.

It was near midnight and the sullen patter of fugitive raindrops at intervals betokened bad weather. The stream was narrow and very deep and ran like a mill-race. It was a delicate task getting over that tree, but we both succeeded without paying the penalty of a ducking.

Not a hundred yards distant was the railroad, and the sound of the sentinel's tread on his rocky beat came faintly to the ear. The woods all around had been hewn down by the Yankees to prevent Mosby slipping across. The trees were cut so as to fall one upon another, thereby furnishing an impediment to cavalry, for they never knew at what point that dashing partisan would strike.

As we neared the track we had to move with extraordinary care—the snapping of a twig, the breaking of a limb, the rattling of our accoutrements would alarm the vigilant guard. Slowly, inch by inch, with infinite circumspection we passed on, putting each foot gently down, leaning with all our weight upon our guns, for at least seventy-five yards. At last we reached the railroad, which was on a level with the ground. Lying flat upon our faces on the track, we could see the unconscious sentinels' figures on the right and the left dimly outlined against the sky. We reclined for a few seconds inert, watching them breathlessly. They were stationary, and well it was, for had we been discovered we would have been obliged to fire, and as we were armed with double-barreled guns with twenty-five buckshot in each barrel, the issue could not have been doubtful. We were after horses, not bent on slaying. We had no deadly animosity to avenge, no wrongs to requite, and were most anxious to avoid anything like bloodshed—there was always time enough for that, God knows, in the constant battles and skirmishes, when it was our duty to do all the harm we could. One of the videttes was sitting on the rail smoking, the other leaning upon his gun, little recking of the proximity of their foemen. Once the guard on Thorne's side rose from his recumbent attitude and stood up; had he advanced one step it would have been his last, for Thorne covered him. The step was not taken; he filled his pipe and lighted it, and as the momentary flame cast a little halo of light around his head we could see every feature, and in that brief second tell the color of his eyes. He was fair-haired, with beardless face, and evidently a fresh recruit; his equipment showed that he was an infantryman.

With nerves strung like steel we glided noiselessly across and crawled for some distance, then resuming our natural attitude, we walked quietly and easily **away.**

Reaching a dense pine thicket we spread our oilcloth upon the ground, for we had no blankets, and lying close together, ignoring the rain, which had now commenced in earnest, slept as soundly as if we were in a soft bed of feathers, and covered with eiderdown, with an embroidered counterpane on top. A scout can sleep anywhere, even as Bolivar Ward used to say, he could slumber in the bed of a stream, enwrapped in a sheet of water.

CHAPTER XXX.

ON THE WATCH.

The beating of the drums aroused us from our dreams and showed that we were in the very midst of the Yankee camp. Our position was between Burke's and Springfield Stations, not over seven miles from Alexandria.

Opening our haversacks we ate our simple breakfast of bread and meat, and found that in our hurry we had not laid in a full supply and that our rations would not last over a day. This discovery alarmed us terribly. We reproached ourselves bitterly for such carelessness, but it was a stubborn fact that in another day we would be without food, and it was risking much to apply to the people in the neighborhood, who had been in the enemy's lines ever since the war commenced, and many of whom were Northern settlers who hated a Rebel scout as the watch-dog does the prowling fox; but when one is in a dilemma something must be done to get out, so we resolved to try the first house we came to and abide the consequences.

Skulking along the outskirts of the woods we reached a small cabin surrounded by the remains of a poor, sickly little corn patch, the bare stalks standing like naked soldiers in rows waiting for roll call. Going up, Thorne knocked at the door. A voice bade us come in.

Pulling the latch-string, the door opened and we entered. The only occupant was an ancient dame of about three-quarters of a century. On her head, covering her grizzled hair, was an antique mob cap, such as our great-grandmothers used to wear. A pair of immense silver-rimmed spectacles rested on her nose and she was in appearance for all the world like the old lady of Berkeley who had prayers said three nights over her. A coffee pot sat upon the hearth, the odorous steam puffing from the spout; a spoon was in the dame's hand, with which she had just been stirring the boiling fluid. She turned carelessly to look, evidently supposing we were Yankee soldiers, but she stopped and gave one brief, startled glance at our gray uniforms, and if old Satan had entered the door, his wife hanging on his arm, she would not have been more terrified. The spoon dropped from her nerveless hand, the silver spectacles followed and fell to the floor unnoticed.   She screamed and covered her face with her apron.

This reception certainly puzzled us.

"Madam," said Thorne, "we mean no harm, we are merely soldiers asking the way."

"For the love of God!" she cried "ain't you Southern soldiers?"

"Yes, madam, we are."

"O Lord! O Lord! you will be killed! You will be murdered!" she cried, sitting down in a chair and rocking to and fro, while the tears ran down her withered cheeks.

We comforted the poor creature and told her there was no immediate danger; that we were perfectly capable of taking care of ourselves, and by degrees she grew composed and entered into conversation with us.   She said she had not seen a Confederate soldier for three years, that her only son was a captain in our army, and that our uniforms, which she loved so much, startled her and almost made her faint.   Then she moved with alacrity to get a hot breakfast for us.   She also filled our haversacks with food, and gave us most important information.

She told us that the bivouacs in the vicinity were all infantry, the cavalry being encamped upon the turnpike about two miles higher up, and that the whole country was alive with soldiers visiting the farm-houses, and we had better be careful and keep in the woods.

We bade the old lady good-by and left a two-dollar greenback in her hand, which she did not want to take, but we insisted. She gave us a sweet, old-fashioned blessing, resting her shriveled hand upon our heads.

We concluded to strike at once for the cavalry camps.   Fortunately for us there was a fine, drizzling rain and the whole country was wrapped in heavy fog, which made objects indistinct.

Under cover of this friendly mist we reached the road and took position in the thicket which bordered the branch only a few paces distant, then carefully keeping our weapons dry under our oilcloths, we stood like Claude Duval and Sixteen Strong Jack, ready to challenge and cry, "Stand and deliver!" to any man on the King's highway.   Had either Thorne or myself been in the "profession" we could have sung the solo of Captain Macheath with fine effect, and certainly much feeling:

"Let us take to the wood,
    Hark I hear the sound of coaches,
    The hour of attack approaches.
    To your arms, brave boys, and load;
    See the ball I hold.
    Let the chemists toil like asses,
    Our fire their fire surpasses
    And turns our lead to gold."

There was no moral difference, in truth, between these noted footpads and ourselves, for both were after plunder, both hid in a covert ready to spring out upon the unwary passer-by; but war makes everything right and it was our duty to plunder society in the shape of anything that wore a blue coat. If Claude were caught it was but a step to Tyburn Gallows; should we be captured it only meant imprisonment.

The first wayfarer was an old countryman, jogging along to market with his produce; his ancient steed was a condemned army horse. The elderly tiller of the soil was buried in profound meditation, evidently working out perplexing financial problems connected with the sale of garden truck. He neither stirred nor spoke, and soon disappeared over the brow of the hill.

But hush! There comes the sound of a horse's tread. We made ready, but smiled in spite of ourselves, at the cause: a little darky as black as midnight came riding by on a mule; he too quickly disappeared.

A long interval followed; the fine, mist-like rain made our faces and hands cold and blue, but by cowering closely to the ground and shrouding ourselves in the oilcloths, we managed to keep dry.

There we were on the *qui vive* in a second, as a rumbling sound broke upon our ears; we hoped it was a sutler, but it proved to be a long wagon-train heavily guarded by a strong detachment of cavalry.

It gave us a curious sensation to see those blue-coats pursuing their course within a few paces of us, and yet feel free. The train was fully a quarter of an hour in passing. Of course an attack was out of the question, and it made our hearts sink to see the great number of troopers acting as escort. Our sole reason for coming right into their camp—into the lion's mouth, as it were—was that in their perfect security they would make no attempt to guard their convoys and it would be an easy matter to capture a couple of horses, and being well mounted, show a clean pair of heels and trust to luck to reach the open. But it seemed as if, in superabundant caution, the Yankees would send a whole cavalry company to guard an army mule which belonged to the regimental cook.

Our plan was to capture a small squad of cavalry, then mount and away before pursuit could begin. If we could not get cavalry, then a wagon was to be stopped and horses unhitched, and without saddles, we would make the essay; we would take anything but mules—we would rather have a running fight and certain capture than to ride a bare-backed mule in a scrub race, such as we were sure to have should we succeed in bagging anything.

Soon there came a solitary figure, dressed in citizen's clothes, on horseback. Either he was a sutler or a citizen visiting friends in the camps. If he were the former with a big wallet, on his way to the city to deposit his money in bank, we would take him anyway; if he was not, there would be but one horse, and the whole country notified of his absence, that the Rebel scouts were about, and the cavalry would be on the keen lookout for us everywhere, so, much against our wills, we kept quiet and let Mr. Citizen pass.

An hour slipped by, nothing was heard or seen. The bare branches of the trees gathering the moisture in great globules, dropped them with mathematical regularity upon our oilcloths. It was long after noon, so we crouched down and ate our dinner, blessing that kind old lady between every mouthful for her goodness. Then we lighted our pipes and watched; still no sign. We got up and stretched, and stepping boldly into the road walked up and down the highway. As far as the eye could reach it was utterly deserted. The dull air became heavier, the mist more dense, and the gleam of fires in camp could hardly be seen. It was a gloomy, dispiriting, lowering evening; just the kind to make the blazing fire a great attraction. With us, everything was damp, the leaves were wet, the trees exuded moisture, the fine rain found its way through holes and crevices and chilled the body by its touch. So the afternoon wore away and the gathering gloom warned us that night was fast approaching, and as far as this day was concerned, we had failed lamentably.

Wandering back, looking for some place to sleep, we ran across a hay stack standing in a field. Burrowing a hole clear to the center and creeping in, we were more than satisfied, for it was warm and dry. We wasted no time in preliminaries, but went to sleep at once; and so ended the twenty-four hours we had built such high hopes upon.

The next morning on poking our heads out of the hole we did not find the view inviting; it was raining hard and the vapor arose from the ground in streams. Our lair seemed so comfortable by contrast that after a discussion we agreed that nothing could be done on such a day, so we crept back and slept until dark; then being at a loss as to how to kill time, we resolved to pay our old dame another visit, for we longed for a good cup of hot coffee.

She was glad to see us, but her terror was pitiable lest some wandering squad of Yankees should drop in and see a couple of gray-jackets sitting by her fireside; her fears were more on our account than her own, however.

We again asked the old lady for advice, which she gave freely and sensibly. Our best chance, she said, was to go about six miles farther up and take a stand on the turnpike leading from Falls Church to Fairfax Court House. Both of these points were heavily garrisoned by cavalry troops in quarters, and they were continually passing from one point to another, for she had seen small squads.

Thanking her for the information we bade her a final farewell and plunged into the darkness.

It was raining a steady downpour, which seemed to soak everything, and was so dark that I could not imagine for a moment that Thorne could find his way to the haystack; but find it he did, making a bee-line for it, I holding close to his oilcloth.

Notwithstanding we had slept all day, we repeated the performance and only awoke late in the morning; we found the pitiless rain as lively and abundant as ever. With cramped limbs and feeling as blue as indigo, we pursued our way.

Keeping a sharp lookout and making many detours to avoid the camps which lay thickly strewn about, we struck the turnpike and chose a spot that had the double advantage of concealment and a good post of observation, for we could see from the hilltop, a mile or so down the road. About six hundred yards below us, on the side of the turnpike, which was as straight as an arrow at this point, was a cavalry brigade in quarters, and our spirits rose as we looked, for among so many it seemed likely that small detached parties must be traveling up and down the road. From our position we could watch them easily and hear the bugle sounding the different calls.

We lay there conversing in subdued tones, trying to predict the upshot of this affair. Thorne declared that if captured our bodies would be swinging from some tree ten minutes after. But of course he exaggerated the danger, for we were in full uniform; there was nothing of the spy about us, but it was safer not to try the experiment, and we resolved not to be taken so long as we had a bullet left, and not to yield until every chance was gone.

Several times different parties of dismounted cavalrymen passed within five feet of us, for we were lying in a thick bunch of tangled briers, directly on the side of the road, and no old hare ever hugged his bed closer when the hounds were drawing covert than did we. So near indeed did one fellow come to us that we hardly dared breathe. He sat down upon a stone within reach of our hands and took a pebble from his boot; his back was turned toward us, yet where was his sixth sense that it did not warn him? With many a curse he found the little piece of flint, threw it viciously away, then rising kept on his way.

For hours we stayed there; our feet were soaked; and still no mounted men except in large bodies passed us; so we could do nothing but shiver, and a feeling of utter desolation and hopelessness came over us. We could hardly hope to escape without a fight on foot; but when we thought of our determination to succeed—had come all this distance—dared all—to get horses, and yet the chance seemed almost impossible, it incensed us and we swore to ourselves that we would make a trial even though we had to steal into the camp in the night.

The rain seemed determined to drive us out. The place where we stood had become a puddle, so we placed one oilcloth on the ground and crouched together under the other. How terribly tantalizing it was to see hundreds of horses so near and yet as unattainable as if separated from us by an impassable gulf.

Another leaden-heeled hour limped by. It was about three o'clock; we were getting consolation out of our pipes, those old friends that never failed us, when suddenly Thorne uttered an exclamation:

"Lord! here they come at last!"

Down the road, about a hundred yards distant, was a light wagon escorted by two cavalrymen; it was leisurely advancing toward us. In a second our pipes were out of our mouths and in our pockets. With hasty motions we put fresh caps on the nipples of our double barrels, drew our pistols out of the holsters and were ready.

"I'll take the driver," said Thorne in a hoarse whisper. "You attend to the cavalrymen. Don't fire unless they show fight, but mount as soon as you can. I will lead, you follow me. Take the prisoners along with us if they don't resist, so they can't give the alarm."

"What if they make fight, though?"

"Kill them and run for it."

The wagon, drawn by a pair of sleek mules, was within a few yards of us, and the driver, a cavalryman, was whistling for want of thought. Great Scott! how he would have whipped up those mules had he only known that two Rebs were in that thicket.

CHAPTER XXXI.

A DASHING RIDE.

We both sprang out, each to his post, and with cocked guns and fingers upon the triggers, called out in tones not to be mistaken: "Surrender! Drop your arms!"

Language cannot convey the stupefaction of those men. They seemed petrified with astonishment—dumb with wonder, and to have lost all control of their limbs. They simply gazed down the barrels of the guns inert and speechless. But the final command to surrender or die brought them to their senses. One of the men dropped his hand to his holster as if to draw his pistol, and his action nearly cost him his life, for the cruel bore of my weapon was turned toward his forehead; one more movement and he would have been headless. He saw it and in the nick of time threw his hand up and yielded as his companions had done. He hated to surrender in full view of his camp, but a double-barreled shot gun, a firm hand on the trigger and the muzzle sighted prone at one's head is a great persuader.

It is said that Spain is the most charitable country on the globe; the rich never refuse to give alms to the poor, for frequently when on a journey, in passing through some dark defile, they hear a noise, and there are some half-score bell-mouth blunder-busses bearing full upon them while voices are heard crying in supplicating tones: "Alms, gentle stranger! for the love of God, alms."

Our process of reasoning succeeded as well as the Spanish brigands'. The driver after pulling himself together proved a real philosopher, who took things quite coolly; he unhooked his pistol-belt and handed it over with the politest bow imaginable. Each man's belt contained two revolvers and a sabre; the latter we threw away, and then we buckled the revolvers around our waists. So far everything was lovely and the attack had succeeded charmingly, but danger was near. A large party of cavalrymen were seen coming up the pike toward us, not half a mile away. Time was precious and we made the most of it. Ordering the three troopers to unhitch the mules, and threatening them with instant death if they hesitated or tried to delay us, they set to work with a vim, while we mounted the cavalry horses.

In an incredibly short time they had the mules free. Judging from the frenzied earnestness and wonderful celerity with which they accomplished the task, they seemed to be the anxious ones.

Bidding the prisoners each to mount a mule, and choosing the youngest, a mere boy, slight and delicate looking, for my companion, I swung into the saddle and ordered him to scramble up behind me.

"See here, Billy Yank," I said in a warning tone, "put your arms around me on the outside of my waterproof, mind, and hold on tight; if I feel your arms loosen for a minute, I will fire."

"All right, sir," he answered; "I'll hold on and not let go until you tell me to."

"And you men," I shouted, "stick to your mules. It's death if you don't; lead on, Thorne!"

Then we plunged into the woods; and not a moment too soon, for the head of the column of the detachment was not two hundred yards away. In an instant we were tearing through the pines like mad.

Thorne, mounted on the finest cavalry horse, led the way. Behind, in single file, bestriding the mules, barebacked, were the two cavalrymen, while the third, as I said, was behind me. Thorne rode straight on, looking neither to the right nor left. His task was to get out of those surroundings as soon as possible, and to strike for cover where we could rest secure. My duty was to keep the prisoners safe and close behind him, as well as to watch for the pursuing force.

The run was commenced right through a swamp, where the tangled vines crossed each other from limb to limb, forming an almost impenetrable barrier. Thorne, with bent head, went straight at it. There was a ripping sound, and through the obstruction he tore with the two mules and cavalry horse close at his heels; into the meadows and across, with the horses sinking over their fetlocks in the spongy ground.

But listen! From the rear came the faint halloa, the hurrah which is unmistakable. The Yankees were hard upon our track and running us down—the abandoned wagon, the discarded sabres and the trampled ground having told the story as plainly as tongue or pencil.

On, on we spurred; Thorne in the advance riding as straight as an arrow, save when he saw a little stretch of woods, a ravine or hollow which favored concealment, then he would deflect and rein up to give the horses a little breathing spell; now that he

40

knew the enemy was near, he saved the horses for the last heat, which he felt certain must come. On the level and where the earth was hard we pushed to the very utmost, but in muddy ground we pulled up.

We were hurrying along through belts of wood, which showered rain-drops in a stream upon us; over fields, dashing across in a wild gallop, scrambling over ditches we could not jump, forcing our way through jungles with the tenacious briers tearing our clothes and scratching our flesh until the blood began to trickle; plunging headlong into brooks and throwing up the spray, which soaked us through, but none minded it now. The Yankees were gaining upon us. The deep mud retained the imprint of our hoof-marks in plain relief, signs which they could follow at a gallop, only here and there striking a piece of flinty ground which for a moment baffled them and threw them into a little confusion. It was now that Thorne brought into play all his magnificent woodcraft, and his keen eye searched out every spot of hard earth which would retain no impression.

The cries of the pursuers waxed louder and stronger, for they were following hard behind us.

Spur onward! Captivity and imprisonment behind, glorious life and liberty in front!

Over a wide field we coursed. A frightened hare started out of his bed and scudded away. The rapid beating of the horses' feet, the hurried, labored breathing of the animals when stretched out in their speed, the cry of the enemy floating onward, were the only sounds we heard. Up a hill, where we paused to get breath, then down, in our mad progress. A fence barred the way; Thorne threw his horse bodily against it and the rails were scattered. Through this gap we rushed, and kept on into a dark belt of woods, then into a wide pasture, which rose gradually until it formed a lofty hill. Up the ridge we cantered, then, when the top was reached, looked back; there a sight met our gaze which caused our bridle-reins to shake and the spurs to be driven home.

About three-quarters of a mile distant was a detachment of blue-coats trailing us, while they raised exultant shouts, showing that they felt certain of our capture.

Turning sharply to the right, Thorne struck for a fringe of pine not far distant. Gallantly the horses skimmed along, with ears laid back and nostrils distended. The mules, goaded to their utmost speed, bounded in quick, hurried springs, which kept them well up to their places. We reached the wood and ran along its edge, next across a brown heather, thence over a corn-field with the tall, brown stalks breast high. Another hill and we flanked it, then in a line for a mile or more, when suddenly Thorne wheeled and headed for a farm-house lying upon the left and far away in the distance.

It was about four o'clock or a little after, and darkness, thank Heaven, was not far off. It we could hold out for another hour we would be safe; but could we do it and keep up these tremendous bursts of speed that made the horses' flanks like a mighty bellows at full blast?

The mules seemed to stand it better and did not show their distress so obviously.

Off again after stopping half a minute to let the horses drink at a branch. In this short interval Thorne turned and asked a prisoner, "Well, Billy Yank, how do you like it?"

"Damn bad; I never expected to take such a ride as this."

"To what regiment do you boys belong?"

"Eighth Illinois; what's yourn?"

"Black Horse Cavalry."

"Is that so! O, I say, Mister, how much further have we got to go?"

"Why, are you sore?"

"No, not yet, but I'm getting so."

We held the horses in a little, as we made our way across the open. Our ruse of turning to the right and left and riding through the pines, where the horses' tracks were very faint, had thrown the pursuing party into confusion and enabled us to gain a mile or so on them.

It is a great mistake to pity the fox when the hounds are trailing him close. Reynard is happier and enjoying himself more than they can understand, for the stakes are everything to him and comparatively nothing to the dogs, besides he has full confidence and perfect faith in his own sagacity, resources, fleetness, and a corresponding contempt for his foes. There may be a savage pleasure in running breast-high to the scent he leaves behind, but the keen delight, the vivid pleasure, the esctasy of hope and fear by turns predominating, are all his.

The house for which we were aiming was fully two miles distant and over a rocky and uneven country. Turning neither to the right nor left, it was in truth rough riding.

Up one hill and down another at moderate speed, dragging our horses through miry lowlands, urging them by voice and spur up steep declivities, rushing forward in a swinging gait on the level, we at last reached the house.

The farm-house nestled in a cosy little hollow at the foot of a hill; we drew up at the door and shouted for the owner. After some delay an old man with staring eyes and white face appeared. Either he wouldn't or couldn't answer Thorne's interrogations about the route and bearings of the country; so that irate scout pressed the cold muzzle of his revolver against the gray head and reiterated his questions. He found his voice at once, for a magical wand is a cocked weapon, which may go off, like Sir Lucius O'Trigger's pistol, of its own accord. He gave Thorne a clear description of where we were, the roads and the points of the compass.

"I am all right now, I know where I am; come along," said Thorne.

Our steeds answered the spur by a bound, and turning left oblique, Thorne headed his course through the yard. Over garden and field at a slapping pace, then down a branch to find an easy crossing, and still at full speed passed through a narrow fringe of trees, then up a steep hill to the main road; a fence hemmed us in and we drew up and looked around.

The whole road was filled with Yankees. A large wagon-train was toiling its slow way along the muddy turnpike, and on each side of the wagons rode the cavalry escort.

"By God!" said Thorne between his teeth, "they've got us sure."

It seemed so indeed. The fence that divided us was not directly upon the road which the Yankees were traveling; it had been originally, but the ancient road was so full of holes that a new one was marked by the wagons, which spread out in a side compass to avoid the bottomless holes and mire of the old route. As it was, the long line was not over fifty yards away.

By a happy chance we had our oilcloths over our shoulders, effectually concealing our gray jackets, and the gloom of approaching night as well as the rain made objects indistinct, and the soldiers, thinking of course that we were their own men, took no notice of us.

I cocked my double barrel and declared to the prisoners that I would kill the first one who moved or spoke.

We stood irresolute. Could we have traded our prisoners and mules for safety we would gladly have made the bargain then and there, but we were all in the same boat and must sink or swim together.

Thorne also, in a low tone, warned the captives that he would kill them if they betrayed us, if he had to die the next minute for it. They were deathly pale, had lost their presence of mind and seemed utterly speechless, and only stared hopelessly at us, for they knew a revolver was pointed at them, concealed by an oilcloth.

We were all side by side and not three feet apart. It was one of the moments that try men's calibre and test their daring. Had either of those men been of iron nerve and determination, he would have made the attempt and stood the risk and might probably have had us killed; but fortunately they were not of that cool and desperate stamp. They were all young, the eldest not being over twenty-three or twenty-four years, and this their first emergency and moment of peril found them all unnerved and panic-stricken.

For nearly half a minute we were en tableaux and at a loss what to do; then suddenly Thorne made a sign that was well understood by me, and wheeled his horse around as quick as lightning. The mules from force of habit whirled about, facing their file leader, and the whole party shot like an arrow down the slope. We had nearly reached the bottom before the Yankees recovered from their astonishment, then we heard them cry:

"They are Rebels! They are Johnnies! Catch them!"

But that was easier said than done. They poured down behind us in a tumultuous stream, shouting and yelling like mad. Not two hundred yards away an answering cheer met and mingled with theirs, and there were two parties in hot pursuit instead of one.

Strike out, good steeds, on your heels our safety lies! Now is the hour of sorest need; one grand burst and all will be well.

Fearful was the tax on their speed, but gallantly indeed the cattle answered it. Down the hill into a farmyard, with a clatter and rush, through gardens, smashing hotbeds and coal pits in our onset. Close behind like a tempest came the pursuers, their exultant yells and frenzied whoops sounding above the din of the charge and the jingling of their accoutrements.

If either of us ever breathed a prayer it would have been like the cavalryman in the "Bucktown Races," when Stuart led the run. A score of blue-coats chased one poor Reb, and kept up a rattling fire upon him; the pistols cracked at every jump but he got away at last. The next day he narrated his experience and declared at the most dangerous moment he commenced to pray, but he was so scared he could think of but one line of the annex to the Lord's Prayer, and repeated that line all the time, "Now I lay me down to sleep."

We flew like the wind. The trees plunged by in a kind of drunken reel; at every leap we drove our cruel spurs, already bloody, into the heaving sides of our horses and kept them up to the work; up another hill without drawing rein, then in a breakneck speed down again; a false step, a stumble would have been fatal, but none was made. As the bottom was reached we saw opening before us a large field spreading far to the right and left. The situation was desperate; before we could cross the Yankees would be upon us; they were already within a hundred and fifty yards; the game seemed up, the dance almost finished; the huntsman might have sounded the view halloo in his horn, for the quarry was earthed at last. The gray lost, the blue won.

But did the blue win?

Going at a pace that almost equalled "Tam O'Shanter's," we passed into the field. In the center stood a little thicket of hazel bushes, vines and creepers, a narrow covert which jutted out into the meadow; it looked dark within. With a sudden inspiration Thorne whirled his horse into the copse, and in a second we were dismounted, the prisoners made to lie flat on their faces, with a double barrel at their motionless forms. They had their instructions not to move a finger nor wink an eyelid. Hardly were we in position when the tramping of horses, the cries of foes, showed us the decisive moment had come.

Closer, and still closer, until we distinguished the shouting crowd in a dark mass, bearing directly upon us. We instinctively cowered and closed our eyes, for it looked as though they would charge over us bodily.

They reached the head of the ravine, then separated and rode at full speed on each side of us; the current of air made by their rapid passage could be felt on our hot cheeks. They kept on without drawing bridle-rein, and the sound of their hoof strokes grew fainter and fainter until they died away in the distance.

We drew a long breath.

"A damn close shave!" said Thorne, uncocking his gun.

"A sharp trick, I swear," remarked one of the prisoners as he arose from his recumbent posture. "If I hadn't felt certain of being released I would have tried to get away, you bet."

"Why didn't you try it when we ran into them on the road?"

"Why I calculated our boys would be bound to capture you, that's why."

CHAPTER XXXII.

AN ALL-NIGHT JOURNEY.

In a short time we ventured to get up and stretch ourselves; it was twilight and we had no fear of further pursuit. Thorne, leaving me in charge of the prisoners and horses, went on foot to a farm-house whose light we could see in the distance, to get his bearings.

He soon returned; we then mounted, rode through the field and entered the gloomy woods. We rode close to the prisoners, our cocked revolvers in our hands and with every sense alert, prepared to shoot on the slightest movement they made to escape. That they did not attempt a dash for liberty surprised us. A man with nerve would certainly have gotten off, for the gloom was almost opaque and it would have been chance shooting had any taken French leave.

A ride of a mile or so brought us to a house where, on making our wishes known, a huge fire was built, a plentiful supper speedily prepared, and Reb and Yank tried to see which could eat the most. It was nip and tuck. The two girls of the house refused payment, saying the sight of three prisoners squared the bill.

Once more on the road, we put our cattle in a dog trot and rode miles and miles in the darkness, each one absorbed in his own thoughts. Once in a while the barking of a cur came through the distance. A fitful gleam from each pipe showed that all were seeking comfort from their brier-roots, so on we went, and made our way without drawing rein until the northern light had climbed to its zenith and pointed still to the polar star.

Through stretches of woods where carpets of pine needles deadened the sound of footsteps, through wide ranges of field which loomed vast and obscure all around, by houses whose outlines cut the sky, up hills, into valleys, until the horses, with bowed heads and weary limbs, dragged into a walk and had to be spurred to increase their slow gait. Through the long hours of travel and the many confusing cross-roads Thorne did not hesitate once, but sped along with the instinct of a Bedouin of the trackless desert. The figures of the prisoners swayed on their animals as their senses were dulled by sleep, and a sharp order now and then was necessary to bring them back to consciousness.

Still onward the darkness increased, till Venus blazed resplend-ent on the earth.

Just as the day broke we reined up at Mr. Marshall's door—that sterling old patriot whose house was every soldier's home. Now we knew that we were safe among true friends and could afford to take that rest which we were so much in need of.

Giving the over-burdened, over-ridden horses a generous feed, both prisoners and guards threw themselves on hastily constructed pallets in the parlor and were soon in deep sleep.

The two daughters of our host took our pistols and kept guard over the three cavalrymen. Poor fellows! It was a use-less precaution, for they were too utterly broken down to need watching.

Four or five hours' rest, a drink of pure peach brandy, a hearty breakfast, and we remounted, and by keeping half way around the arc of a circle we reached Thorne's house after traveling all day, and his anxious wife met him, rejoiced to see him safe and well. She had heard the report that we had been captured and shot. There were tears and warm kisses too, for in those stormy times, "in Mosby's Confederacy," wives seemed to love their husbands better than in the piping times of peace; their hearts were in their mouths, so to speak, for when they bade their liege lords farewell it was even chances that it would be final.

A night's sleep made the whole party hale and hearty again; only the prisoners still felt sore from riding bare-back, which they showed by many facial contortions when they chanced to move. It was such practice as they had never dreamed of when they left home, and would be a fruitful theme in times yet to come.

Thorne and I now made a division of the loot. We each took one horse and a mule and the arms and equipments in equal pro-portions; we then separated, he going to Fredericksburg, sev-enteen miles distant, with two prisoners to deliver to the pro-vost guard there, while I, wishing to visit Orange Court House, determined to take the remaining prisoner along with me and place him in the care of the provost marshal. So shaking hands all around, we parted company, and each went his own way.

I found my companion a sensible fellow of some twenty-three years, and while not a man of education or refinement, he had a good share of shrewdness and common sense, and had knocked about the world a good deal in his time. He had learned by ex-perience that wise lesson which surpasseth the lore of books, "philosophy," without which life is not worth living to the average man. He took existence as he found it, and did not seem to cry over his mishap. He was a private in Company L, Eighth Illinois Cavalry, and was from Cleveland, Ohio, and his name was McCaughery.

We jogged along cosily together, he telling me of his many adventures both by sea and land, and he was either of a wonderfully roving temperament or else he was an accomplished liar. Either way, he was entertaining, and could sing a good song, so nobody under the circumstances would be disposed to be critical; I certainly was not, and the twenty miles was soon gotten over. Just as the sun took a farewell peep over the crags of the lofty Blue Ridge we came to a halt at the house of Mr. John Minor Botts.

Now I was rather uncertain, whether with all of his hospitality the great Virginia Unionist would take in a Rebel with a Yankee prisoner, even though the former was a kinsman. The old gentleman had a violent temper and I must confess I quavered a little as I heard his heavy tread advancing.

"How are you, my boy?" he said in his hearty, off-hand way.

"O, I am as the old darky said, 'poorly, thank God.' "

"Get off your horses and come in. Here, Bob," addressing a servant near, "come and get the gentlemen's horses. Come in, but first introduce your comrade to me.

"He's a prisoner, sir," I meekly said.

"A what?" he thundered.

"A prisoner, sir. I captured him near Falls Church."

"Why, damn my soul!" he yelled, his face growing crimson, "do you think I keep a prison pen?"

"No, sir; but I thought you entertained both sides."

"I do, but my house is not a resort for bushwhackers; a hell of a fix you would get me into."

"Well, Mr. Botts, what must I do—ride on to Culpeper?"

"No, my house is open to you. Why don't you discharge your prisoner and come in? One man would not make or break your infernal Confederacy anyway."

"No, I cannot do that, but I will parole him and he can get a place in the overseer's cottage."

"You don't suppose he will be fool enough to keep it?" asked the great Virginian, as he looked askance at the Illinois soldier, who sat unconcernedly on his mule.

"Of course he will, for if he should try to make his way across the open country some of our scouts would capture him, and thinking him a spy, kill him off-hand." The cavalryman pricked up his ears at this.

"I guess I'll stay," he said. "I'm safe now, and I don't want to run any risk, and my pay is going on all the time."

"Just as you damn please," said Mr. Botts. "There is the overseer's house across there. Tell him to make you comfortable."

"Good-by, Billy, until morning," I said. "For your own good, I hope you won't try to get away. You don't know the country, and ten chances to one some citizen, rendered savage by ill treatment, will bushwhack you, that's all."

"I tell you again, I ain't going to run no risk, and you'll find me at the house early to-morrow." So saying he dismounted, and limped in the direction of the overseer's house not a hundred yards away.

I cautioned my host to look well to the safety of his stables or he might find one of his thoroughbreds missing in the morning. He caught the hint and gave orders accordingly. I took my horse and mule to a secluded spot in a thicket near the house and fed them with my own hands.

Mr. Botts came out, and linking his arm sociably within mine, led me toward the open door.

"I have," said he, "already two guests."

"Who are they?"

"One is a Federal surgeon, captured by Mosby. He was carried to Culpeper and released unconditionally. The other is a lieutenant of Mosby's who was detached to pilot him to the Federal lines. Both are very bright, sociable fellows and I anticipate a pleasant evening. But walk in, here we are."

A step carried us from the chilly air into a warm, cosy, cheerful room; a hickory fire roared up the chimney, for there was a touch of frost in the air, and sparkled and gleamed on the cut glass and burnished silver which decked the sideboard.

"Walk up, gentlemen, and help yourselves," said Mr. Botts. "You will find a good choice there; if there is anything I pride myself on, it is my taste for good whiskey. I honestly believe I imbibed it with my mother's milk. Here," he continued with a comprehensive wave of his hand, "is a bottle of old rye left, sent me last fall by General Meade. There is some Cognac which ran the blockade from Washington, and here is old peach brandy, which, according to my thinking, is the best liquor ever brewed by the hand of man."

The North chose the rye, but the South stood by the peach,

and tipping glasses, the healths were drunk and the glasses drained.

A bountiful supper followed, and then when cigars were lighted the whole party made themselves comfortable in Mr. Botts's library, and under the benign influence of that "great tranquilizer" tobacco, the conversation grew friendly and unrestrained. What was said will prove good reading in another chapter, for though but a straw, it shows and reflects the feelings of the opposite side in the last year of the war and was taken down in my note-book almost verbatim.

Mr. Botts proved himself a better prophet in National politics than he ever did when betting on a horse-race in the good old times when Eclipse and Flying Childers were kings of the turf, for he invariably lost, and always had a good reason why, so good indeed, to his own satisfaction, that he would scrape together another pile and bet and lose it on the same horse with the same serene belief that only accident had destroyed his astute calculations.

DATE DUE	
APR 14 2001	
SEP 8 2014	